Collection folio junior

dirigée par
Jean-Olivier Héron
et Pierre Marchand

Roald Dahl, d'origine norvégienne, est né au pays de Galles en 1916. Avide d'aventures, il part pour l'Afrique à l'âge de dix-huit ans et travaille dans une compagnie pétrolière, avant de devenir pilote de chasse dans la Royal Air Force pendant la Seconde Guerre mondiale. Il échappe de peu à la mort, son appareil s'étant écrasé au sol ! A la suite de cet accident, Roald Dahl se met à écrire... mais c'est seulement en 1960, après avoir publié pendant quinze ans des livres pour les adultes, que Roald Dahl débute dans la littérature pour la jeunesse avec *James et la grosse pêche*, bientôt suivi, avec un succès toujours croissant, de *Charlie et la chocolaterie*, puis d'une série de best-sellers parmi lesquels *Le Bon Gros Géant, Charlie et le grand ascenseur de verre, Matilda...* Dans la seule Grande-Bretagne, plus de onze millions de ses ouvrages pour la jeunesse se sont vendus entre 1980 et 1990 !

Roald Dahl, ce géant qui parfois choquait les adultes, mais comprenait les enfants et les aimait, est mort le 23 novembre 1990, à l'âge de soixante-quatorze ans.

Quentin Blake est né dans la banlieue de Londres en 1932. Il a publié son premier dessin à l'âge de seize ans dans le magazine humoristique *Punch*. Depuis son premier album, édité en 1960, il a créé environ deux cents livres – un rythme moyen de six titres par an ! – devenant l'un des illustrateurs les plus célèbres en Grande-Bretagne, en France et dans le monde entier. Ses dessins, débordant de joie de vivre et de malice, ont influencé de nombreux jeunes illustrateurs. Il a fondé le département « illustration » du Royal College of Art. Il vit à Londres mais fait de longs séjours dans sa maison de l'ouest de la France.

Pour Roald Dahl, il a imaginé les dessins de *Matilda, Charlie et la chocolaterie, La Potion magique de Georges Bouillon, Les Deux gredins, Sacrées Sorcières, Le Bon Gros Géant...* tous publiés dans la collection Folio Junior.

Roald Dahl

La potion magique de Georges Bouillon

*Traduit de l'anglais
par Marie-Raymond Farré*

Illustrations de Quentin Blake

Gallimard

Titre original :
George's Marvellous Medecine

ISBN 2-07-051340-8
Loi n°49-956 du 16 juillet 1949
sur les publications destinées à la jeunesse

© Roald Dahl Nominee Ltd, 1981, pour le texte
© Editions Gallimard, 1982, pour la traduction française
© Quentin Blake, 1981, pour les illustrations
© Editions Gallimard, 1988, pour le supplément
© Editions Gallimard Jeunesse, 1997, pour la présente édition
Dépôt légal : février 1998
1er dépôt légal dans la même collection : janvier 1988
N° d'édition : 85849 - N° d'impression : 41559
Imprimé en France sur les presses de l'imprimerie Hérissey

*Ce livre est dédié à
tous les médecins.*

Grandma

Un samedi matin, la mère de Georges Bouillon dit à son fils :

— Je vais faire des courses au village. Sois sage et ne fais pas de bêtises.

Voilà exactement ce qu'il ne faut pas dire à un petit garçon, car cela lui donne aussitôt l'idée d'en faire !

— Et à onze heures, n'oublie pas de donner sa potion à Grandma, poursuivit la mère.

Puis elle sortit en refermant la porte.

Grandma, qui sommeillait dans son fauteuil, près de la fenêtre, ouvrit un petit œil méchant.

— Tu as entendu ce qu'a dit ta mère, Georges, aboya-t-elle. N'oublie pas ma potion.

— Non, Grandma, dit Georges.

— Et pour une fois, sois sage tant qu'elle n'est pas là.

— Oui, Grandma, dit Georges.

Georges s'ennuyait à mourir. Il n'avait ni frère ni sœur. Son père était fermier et, comme la ferme était loin de tout, Georges n'avait pas d'amis avec qui jouer. Il en avait assez de contempler les cochons, les poules, les vaches et les moutons. Et surtout, il en avait par-dessus la tête de vivre dans la même maison que cette vieille ourse mal léchée de Grandma. Passer son samedi matin à s'occuper d'elle ne le réjouissait guère.

— Prépare-moi une petite tasse de thé, dit Grandma à Georges. Ça t'empêchera de faire des bêtises pendant un moment.

— Oui, Grandma, répondit Georges.

Georges n'y pouvait rien, il détestait Grandma. C'était une vieille femme grincheuse et égoïste qui avait des dents jaunâtres et une petite bouche toute ridée comme le derrière d'un chien.

— Combien de cuillerées de sucre dans ton thé, aujourd'hui, Grandma ? demanda Georges.

— Une, répondit-elle sèchement. Et n'ajoute pas de lait.

La plupart des grand-mères sont d'adorables vieilles dames, gentilles et serviables, mais pas celle-la. Elle passait sa journée, toutes ses journées, assise dans son fauteuil, près de la fenêtre et elle était tout le temps en train de se plaindre, de bougonner, de ronchonner, de râler et de pester sur tout et sur rien. Jamais, même dans ses bons jours, elle n'avait souri à Georges, jamais elle ne lui avait dit : « Bonjour, Georges, comment ça va ? » ni : « Et si on jouait au jeu de l'oie ? » ni : « Comment ça s'est passé à l'école aujourd'hui ? » Elle ne s'intéressait qu'à elle. C'était une affreuse vieille mégère.

Georges alla à la cuisine et prépara une tasse de thé avec un sachet. Il mit une cuillerée de sucre en poudre, remua et apporta la tasse dans la salle de séjour.

Grandma but une petite gorgée de thé.

— Il n'est pas assez sucré, dit-elle. Ajoute un peu de sucre.

Georges ramena la tasse dans la cuisine et ajouta une autre cuillerée de sucre. Puis il remua et rapporta la tasse à Grandma.

— Où est la soucoupe ? demanda-t-elle. Je veux une soucoupe avec ma tasse.

Georges partit chercher une soucoupe.

— Et la cuillère, s'il te plaît ?

— J'ai remué pour toi, Grandma. J'ai bien remué.

— Merci bien, je remue mon thé, moi-même, dit-elle. Va me chercher une cuillère.

Georges alla chercher la cuillère.

Quand les parents de Georges étaient à la maison, Grandma ne se montrait jamais aussi capricieuse. Mais quand elle restait seule avec lui, elle le rudoyait sans cesse.

— Tu sais ce qui ne va pas, chez toi ? dit la vieille femme, en regardant Georges de ses petits yeux brillant de méchanceté. Tu grandis trop vite. Les garçons qui grandissent trop vite deviennent stupides et paresseux.

— Mais je n'y peux rien, Grandma, répliqua Georges.

— Si, tu peux, coupa-t-elle. Grandir est une sale manie des enfants.

— Mais on doit grandir, Grandma. Si on ne grandit pas, on ne devient jamais une grande personne.

— C'est idiot, mon garçon, dit-elle. Idiot. Regarde-moi. Est-ce que je grandis, moi ? Sûrement pas.

— Mais tu as grandi autrefois, Grandma.

— Un petit peu seulement, dit la vieille femme. J'ai cessé de grandir quand j'étais toute petite. Et je me suis débarrassée ainsi de tous les vilains défauts des gosses : la paresse, la désobéissance, la gourmandise, la saleté, le désordre et la stupidité. En as-tu fait autant, toi ?

— Je ne suis encore qu'un petit garçon, Grandma.

— Tu as huit ans, dit-elle en reniflant. Tu es assez vieux pour savoir ça. Si tu n'arrêtes pas de grandir, ce sera trop tard.

— Trop tard pour quoi, Grandma ?

— Question ridicule, répondit-elle. Tu es déjà presque aussi grand que moi.

Georges regarda attentivement Grandma. Elle était véritablement minuscule. Ses jambes étaient si courtes qu'il lui fallait un tabouret pour poser ses pieds, et sa tête n'arrivait qu'à la moitié du dossier de son fauteuil.

— Papa m'a dit que c'était bien pour un homme d'être grand, dit Georges.

— N'écoute pas ton papa, dit Grandma. Ecoute-moi.

— Mais, comment faire pour ne plus grandir ? demanda Georges.

— Mange moins de chocolat, répondit Grandma.

— Le chocolat fait grandir ?

— Il fait grandir dans la mauvaise direction, aboya-t-elle. Vers le haut et non vers le bas !

Grandma but quelques gorgées de son thé, sans quitter des yeux le petit garçon.

— *Jamais vers le haut, toujours vers le bas !* répéta-t-elle.

— Oui, Grandma.

— Et ne mange plus du chocolat. Mange plutôt du chou.

— Du chou ? Oh, non ! protesta Georges. Je n'aime pas le chou.

— Que tu aimes ou pas, peu importe, coupa Grandma. Ce qui compte, c'est ce qui est bon pour toi. A partir de maintenant, tu mangeras du chou trois fois par jour. Des montagnes de choux. Et tant mieux s'il y a des chenilles !

— Beurk ! fit Georges.

— Les chenilles rendent intelligent, dit la vieille femme.

— Maman lave soigneusement les feuilles de chou, répliqua Georges.

— Maman est aussi idiote que toi, affirma Grandma. Le chou n'a aucun goût sans quelques chenilles bouillies, ni sans limaces.

— Des limaces, non ! s'écria Georges. Jamais je n'en mangerai !

— Moi, dit Grandma, quand je vois une limace vivante sur une feuille de salade, je l'avale aussitôt, avant qu'elle ne s'enfuie. C'est délicieux.

Elle pinça les lèvres et sa bouche devint une petite fente plissée.

— Mmm, délicieux, reprit-elle. Les vers, les limaces, les punaises, les insectes... Tu ne sais pas ce qui est bon !

— Tu plaisantes, Grandma ?

— Je ne plaisante jamais, dit-elle. Les scarabées sont peut-être encore meilleurs. Ils croustillent sous la dent.

— Grandma, c'est dégoûtant !

La vieille mégère sourit en montrant ses dents jaunâtres.

— Quelquefois, poursuivit-elle, avec un peu de chance, on découvre un hanneton entre deux feuilles de céleri. C'est ainsi que je les aime !

— Grandma ! comment peux-tu... ?

— On découvre toutes sortes de bonnes choses dans le céleri-rave, continua la vieille femme. Parfois des perce-oreilles !

— Je ne veux plus écouter ces horreurs ! cria Georges.

— Un gros et gras perce-oreille, c'est vraiment un mets succulent, dit Grandma en se léchant les babines. Mais il faut aller vite, mon petit, quand on en introduit un dans sa bouche. Il porte deux pinces pointues à l'extrémité de son abdomen, et s'il t'attrape la langue, il ne la lâche plus. Alors, il faut le mordre, *crac crac*, avant que lui ne te morde.

Georges se mit à filer vers la porte. Il voulait fuir loin de cette écœurante vieille femme.

— Tu essaies de t'enfuir, n'est-ce pas ? dit-elle en pointant son doigt vers lui. Tu veux abandonner ta Grandma.

Près de la porte, le petit Georges fixait la vieille mégère. Elle le fixait, elle aussi.

« C'est peut-être... une *sorcière* ! » se dit Georges. Il avait toujours pensé que les sorcières n'existaient que dans les contes de fées mais, à présent, il n'en était pas sûr.

— Approche-toi, petit, dit-elle, lui faisant signe de son doigt crochu. Approche-toi, et je te confierai des secrets...

Georges ne bougea pas.

Grandma non plus.

— Je connais de nombreux secrets, reprit-elle en souriant. (C'était un petit sourire glacial, le sourire d'un serpent qui va mordre.) Approche-toi de Grandma. Elle te chuchotera des secrets.

Georges recula d'un pas, se rapprochant un peu plus de la porte.

— Tu ne dois pas avoir peur de ta vieille Grandma, dit-elle, avec un sourire sinistre.

Georges fit un autre pas en arrière.

— Certains d'entre nous..., dit-elle. (Tout à coup, elle se pencha en avant et se mit à chuchoter d'une voix gutturale que Georges n'avait jamais entendue.) Certains d'entre nous ont des pouvoirs magiques, qui peuvent transformer les créatures humaines...

Un picotement électrique parcourut la colonne vertébrale de Georges. Il commençait à avoir peur.

— Certains d'entre nous, continua la vieille sorcière, ont du feu au bout de la langue, des étincelles dans le ventre et des éclairs au bout des doigts... Certains connaissent des secrets qui te feraient dresser les cheveux sur la tête et jaillir les yeux hors des orbites...

Georges voulait fuir, mais ses pieds semblaient collés au sol.

— Nous savons comment faire tomber les ongles et faire pousser des dents au bout des doigts...

Georges tremblait. Ce qui l'effrayait le plus, c'était le visage de Grandma, son sourire figé et ses yeux brillants qui ne cillaient pas.

— Nous savons ce qu'il faut faire pour que tu te réveilles un beau matin avec une longue queue par-derrière.

— Grandma, arrête ! s'écria-t-il.

— Nous connaissons des endroits lugubres où grouillent, rampent et se tortillent de sinistres bêtes molles...

Georges fonça vers la porte.

— Tu peux toujours courir, dit-elle, tu ne nous échapperas pas...

Georges claqua la porte derrière lui et se réfugia dans la cuisine.

Un plan diabolique

Georges s'assit à la table de la cuisine. Il tremblait encore. Oh ! comme il détestait Grandma ! Il haïssait vraiment cette horrible vieille sorcière. Et tout à coup, il eut terriblement envie de faire quelque chose. Une chose énorme. Une chose absolument terrifiante. Une chose abominable. Une véritable bombe. Il voulait chasser cette odeur de sorcellerie qui flottait autour de la mégère. Il n'avait que huit ans, certes, mais c'était un courageux petit garçon. Il était prêt à défier la sorcière !

« Je ne vais pas me laisser terroriser », se dit-il.

Mais il était bel et bien terrorisé. C'est pourquoi il voulait se débarrasser d'elle sur-le-champ.

Enfin... pas tout à fait. Il voulait la secouer un peu.

Exactement, la *secouer*. Mais qu'inventer d'énorme, de terrifiant, d'explosif ?

Il aurait bien mis un pétard sous le fauteuil, mais il n'avait pas de pétard.

Il aurait bien aimé lui glisser un long serpent vert dans le cou, mais il n'avait pas de long serpent vert.

Il aurait bien aimé lâcher six gros rats noirs dans la pièce où elle se trouvait, mais il n'avait pas six gros rats noirs.

Georges réfléchissait à ce passionnant problème, lorsque son regard tomba sur la potion brunâtre de Grandma, posée sur le buffet. Encore un sale truc. On glissait dans la bouche de Grandma une cuillerée de ce médicament quatre fois par jour, mais il ne lui faisait aucun bien. Elle restait toujours aussi épouvantable. En principe, un médicament doit améliorer la santé des gens. S'il n'y réussit pas, il ne sert à rien.

« Oh ! oh ! pensa soudain Georges. Ah ! ah ! Eh ! eh ! je sais exactement ce que je vais faire. Je vais lui préparer une nouvelle potion, une potion si forte, si violente et si fantastique qu'elle la guérira complètement

ou lui fera sauter la cervelle ! Je fabriquerai une potion magique, un médicament qu'aucun médecin n'a inventé jusqu'à présent. »

Georges regarda l'horloge de la cuisine. Il était dix heures cinq. Il avait presque une heure devant lui, puisque Grandma devait prendre son médicament à onze heures.

— Allons-y ! s'écria Georges en se levant d'un bond. Vive la potion magique !

Une puce, un pou, une punaise des bois,
Deux gros escargots et trois lézards gras,
Un serpent de mer tortillant gluant,
Du jujubier le jus du fruit,
La poudre d'os d'un marsupilami,
Et puis mille et un autres produits.
Sentez-vous ? Vraiment répugnant.
Je remue, fais bouillir longtemps.
Belle mixture, en vérité !
C'est prêt !
Bouchez-vous le nez !
Et une cuillerée pour Grandma !
Allons, avale-moi ça !
C'est bon, n'est-ce pas ?
Va-t-elle éclater ? Exploser ?
S'envoler par-dessus les toits ?
S'évanouir dans la fumée ?
Pétiller comme du Coca ?
Qui sait ? En tout cas, pas moi !
Ma chère, chère Grand-maman,
Si tu savais ce qui t'attend...

Premiers ingrédients

Georges prit un énorme chaudron dans le placard de la cuisine et le posa sur la table.

— Georges ! Que fais-tu ? cria la voix aiguë de Grandma dans la pièce voisine.

— Rien, Grandma, répondit-il.

— Tu crois que je n'entends pas parce que tu as fermé la porte ? Et ce bruit de casserole ?

— Je range la cuisine, Grandma.

Puis ce fut le silence.

Georges savait bien ce qu'il allait faire pour préparer sa fameuse potion. Inutile de se casser la tête. C'était simple, il mettrait *tout* ce qui lui tomberait sous la main. Pas d'hésitation, pas de question, pas d'embrouillamini pour savoir si un produit secouerait ou non la vieille. *Tout* ce qu'il verrait de coulant, gluant ou poudreux, il le jetterait dans le chaudron.

Ce serait la plus géniale potion du monde. Si elle ne guérissait pas vraiment Grandma, elle produirait de toute façon un effet extraordinaire. Quel beau spectacle en perspective !

Georges décida de fouiller toutes les pièces de la maison, une à une.

Il irait d'abord dans la salle de bains : on y trouve toujours des produits amusants. Il monta l'escalier en portant l'énorme chaudron.

Dans la salle de bains, il regarda d'un air de convoitise la fameuse et redoutable armoire à pharmacie. C'était le seul meuble de toute la maison que ses parents lui avaient interdit de toucher. Il en avait fait la promesse solennelle, et il ne manquerait pas à sa parole. « Certains médicaments peuvent tuer un bonhomme », lui avaient-ils dit. Malgré son envie de donner un sacré remontant à Grandma, Georges ne voulait pas rester avec un cadavre sur les bras. Il posa le chaudron par terre et se mit à l'ouvrage.

Tout d'abord, il trouva un flacon de *shampooing cheveux gras*. Il le vida dans le chaudron.

« Ça lui nettoiera gentiment l'estomac », dit-il.

Il prit un tube de *dentifrice* et le pressa entièrement, faisant jaillir un long vermisseau.

« Ça fera peut-être briller ses horribles dents jaunâtres », dit-il.

Il y avait une bombe de *supermousse à raser* appartenant à son père. Georges adorait jouer avec les bombes. Il appuya sur le bouton et la vida. Une magnifique montagne de mousse blanche s'éleva dans le chaudron.

Avec les doigts, il vida le contenu d'un pot de *crème de jour vitalisée*.

Suivit un flacon de *vernis à ongles* écarlate.

« Si le dentifrice ne nettoie pas ses dents, dit-il, ceci les vernira en rose. »

Il découvrit ensuite un pot de *crème dépilatoire*. Sur l'étiquette, on lisait : « *Etendez la crème sur vos jambes. Laissez agir cinq minutes...* » Georges mit toute la crème dans le chaudron.

Ensuite un flacon rempli de liquide jaune : *lotion miracle antipelliculaire*. Dans le chaudron !

Brilladentine pour l'hygiène des dentiers.

De la poudre blanche. Dans le chaudron, elle aussi !

Une deuxième bombe : *déodorant corporel, garanti pour éliminer toutes les odeurs pendant 24 heures.*

« Elle devrait en utiliser beaucoup », se dit Georges en vidant la bombe dans le chaudron.

Puis un grand flacon de *paraffine liquide*. Il n'avait pas la moindre idée de ce que c'était mais il le vida quand même.

« J'en ai fini avec la salle de bains », pensa-t-il en jetant un dernier coup d'œil autour de lui.

Dans la chambre de ses parents, sur la coiffeuse de sa mère, il découvrit avec joie une troisième bombe. *Laque* : « *Vaporisez doucement à trente centimètres de vos cheveux.* » Il vaporisa toute la bombe dans le chaudron. Il adorait jouer avec les aérosols !

Un flacon de parfum, *Fleur de navet*, qui sentait le vieux fromage. Au chaudron, le parfum !

Au chaudron également, une grosse boîte ronde, *poudre peau rose*. Il y avait une houppette. Plouf, la houppette ! Elle porterait bonheur !

Deux tubes de *rouge à lèvres*. Il retira les deux bâtonnets rouges et graisseux et les ajouta à la mixture.

La chambre à coucher ne présentant plus d'intérêt, Georges redescendit au rez-de-chaussée avec son énorme chaudron. Il trottina vers la buanderie où étaient rangés les produits de nettoyage.

Le premier qu'il trouva fut un grand paquet de *superblanc pour machines à laver automatiques* : « *La saleté s'en va comme par magie.* » Grandma était-elle ou non automatique ? En tout cas, c'était sûrement une vieille femme sale.

« Il faut y mettre tout le paquet », dit-il en versant la lessive.

Ensuite, une grande boîte d'*encaustique parquet* : « *Enlève les saletés, les souillures et les taches de votre sol et le rend brillant*

comme un miroir.» Georges plongea la
main dans la cire orange et vida la boîte.

Puis un petit paquet rond en carton de
poudre insecticide pour chiens : «Atten-
tion : à éloigner de toute nourriture. Si le
chien avale cette poudre, il risque d'explo-
ser. »

« Parfait ! » dit Georges en renversant la poudre dans le chaudron.

Sur l'étagère, un autre paquet : *nourriture pour canaris*.

« Ça fera chanter la vieille perruche », dit-il en vidant le paquet.

Ensuite, Georges fouina dans une boîte qui contenait des brosses, des chiffons et du cirage. « La potion de Grandma est brunâtre, pensa-t-il. Il faut que ma potion le soit également, sinon Grandma saura qu'il y a anguille sous roche. » Il décida donc, pour colorer sa potion, d'ajouter du cirage, *brun foncé*. Splendide, une grosse boîte ! Il la racla à l'aide d'une vieille cuillère.

Dans le couloir qui menait à la cuisine, Georges aperçut une bouteille de *gin* sur un buffet. Grandma adorait le gin. On lui en

donnait un petit doigt chaque soir. Aujour-
d'hui, elle aurait un extra. Toute la bouteille ! Georges posa l'énorme chaudron sur
la table de la cuisine, puis il se dirigea vers
l'armoire qui servait de garde-manger. Les
étagères débordaient de bouteilles et de pots
de toutes sortes. Voici les ingrédients qu'il
choisit et versa un à un :
— *une boîte de curry,*
— *un verre de moutarde,*
— *une bouteille de sauce chilli extraforte,*
— *une boîte de poivre noir,*
— *une bouteille de sauce au raifort.*
— Ouf ! Ça y est ! s'écria-t-il.
— Georges ! cria la voix perçante de
Grandma dans la pièce voisine. A qui par-
les-tu ? Que mijotes-tu ?
— Rien, Grandma, absolument rien, répondit-il.
— N'est-il pas l'heure de prendre ma potion ?
— Non, Grandma, ce sera dans une de-
mi-heure.
— Bon, surtout ne l'oublie pas.
— Oh, non, Grandma, répliqua Georges.
Je ne pense qu'à ça !

Remèdes
pour animaux

C'est à ce moment-là que Georges eut une inspiration géniale. Les médicaments de l'armoire à pharmacie de la maison lui étaient interdits, certes, mais les médicaments que son père gardait dans un hangar près du poulailler... les remèdes pour animaux... étaient-ils interdits, eux ?

Personne ne lui avait interdit d'y toucher.

« Reprenons le problème, se dit Georges. De la laque, de la mousse à raser et du cirage, très bien. Ça fera tourner la vieille toupie. Mais il faut de vrais médicaments dans la potion magique, de vraies pilules, de vrais remontants, pour lui donner du muscle et du tonus. »

Georges prit le lourd chaudron déjà rempli aux trois quarts et se dirigea vers la porte qui donnait sur la cour. Il fonça vers le hangar. Son père ne s'y trouvait pas car il faisait les foins dans un pré.

Georges entra dans le vieux hangar poussiéreux et posa le chaudron sur un banc. Puis il regarda l'étagère des médicaments. Il y avait cinq grandes bouteilles. Deux remplies de pilules et de dragées, deux de liquides et une de poudre.

« Je les utiliserai toutes, dit Georges. Grandma en a besoin. Rudement besoin même. »

La première bouteille contenait une poudre orange. Sur l'étiquette, on lisait : *« Pour vos poules. Contre les parasites, les coliques, les becs irrités, les pattes estropiées, la coquerilite aiguë, la mauvaise ponte, la couvée difficile ou la perte de plumes. Posologie : une cuillerée par seau de graines. »*

« Ça alors ! se dit Georges en jetant toute la poudre orange dans le chaudron. La vieille perruche ne perdra plus ses plumes. »

La seconde bouteille contenait cinq cents dragées violettes. *« Remède de cheval contre les langues blanches : Le cheval doit sucer une dragée deux fois par jour. »*

« Grandma n'a pas la langue blanche, dit Georges, mais elle a une langue de vipère. Ceci la guérira sans doute. »

Au chaudron, les cinq cents dragées.

La troisième bouteille contenait un liquide épais et jaunâtre. *« Pour vaches, bœufs et taureaux. Contre la variole, la gale, les cornes recroquevillées, les naseaux écumants, les maux d'oreilles, de dents, de tête, de sabots, de queue et de pis. »*

« La vieille vache renfrognée souffre de tous ces maux, dit Georges. C'est le médicament qu'il lui faut. »

Le liquide glouglouta et gargouilla dans le chaudron.

La quatrième bouteille contenait un liquide rouge vif : *« Lotion insecticide pour moutons. Soigne les toisons malades, débarrasse des tiques et des puces. Mélanger une cuillerée dans cinq litres d'eau, et en arroser la toison. Attention ! ne pas dépasser la dose prescrite, sinon le mouton se retrouvera tout nu. »*

— Sapristi ! s'écria Georges. Comme j'aimerais verser cette lotion sur la tête de Grandma et regarder les tiques et les puces s'enfuir. Mais je ne peux pas, je ne dois pas. Donc, elle la boira.

Il versa le liquide rouge vif dans le chaudron.

La dernière bouteille de l'étagère était remplie de pilules vert pâle : « *Pour cochons. Contre les démangeaisons, les pieds trop sensibles, les queues sans tire-bouchon et autres cochonneries. Une pilule par jour. Dans les cas graves, on peut en donner deux. Attention ! ne jamais dépasser cette dose, sinon le cochon sautera au pla-fond !* »

« Exactement ce qu'il faut pour cette vieille truie, dit Georges. Donnons-lui la dose maxi ! »

Il jeta les pilules vertes par centaines dans le chaudron.

Sur le banc, il y avait un bout de bois qui servait à mélanger des peintures. Georges le prit pour remuer sa potion magique. Elle était épaisse comme de la crème, et, au fur et à mesure qu'il agitait, de magnifiques couleurs apparaissaient à la surface et se mêlaient. Des roses, des bleus, des verts, des jaunes et des bruns.

Georges remua longtemps pour tout mélanger. Mais il restait encore au fond du chaudron des centaines de pilules qui n'avaient pas fondu. En outre, surnageait la belle houppette à poudre de sa mère.

« Un gros bouillon et tout sera dissous », se dit Georges.

Sur ces mots, il reprit le chemin de la

maison, en titubant sous le poids de l'énorme chaudron.

Il passa devant la porte du garage et entra pour voir s'il trouvait d'autres ingrédients intéressants. Voici ce qu'il ajouta :

— un quart de litre d'*huile pour machine*, pour huiler le moteur de Grandma,

— un peu d'*antigel*, pour que son radiateur ne gèle pas en hiver,

— et une poignée de *graisse*, pour graisser ses vieux rouages.

Enfin, il retourna dans la cuisine.

A gros bouillons

Dans la cuisine, Georges posa le chaudron sur le fourneau et alluma le gaz à feu vif.

— Georges ! cria l'affreuse voix de Grandma dans la pièce voisine. C'est l'heure de prendre ma potion !

— Pas encore, Grandma, répondit Georges. Il n'est que onze heures moins vingt.

— Qu'est-ce que tu mijotes ? cria la grand-mère. J'entends des bruits.

Georges estima qu'il valait mieux ne pas répondre. Il trouva une longue cuillère en bois dans un tiroir et se mit à tourner vivement la potion. Cela commençait à chauffer.

Bientôt, la potion magique se mit à

mousser et à écumer. Une épaisse fumée bleue, couleur plume de paon, s'éleva et une odeur épouvantable envahit la cuisine. Georges étouffait, suffoquait et toussait. Jamais il n'avait senti une odeur aussi brutale et fatale, aussi poivrée et fumée, aussi tenace et pugnace, sorcière et mégère à la fois. Dès qu'il en respirait une bouffée, des feux d'artifice éclataient dans sa tête et des frissons électriques couraient le long de ses jambes. Quelle merveille de remuer cette fantastique potion et de la voir bouillonner, mousser, écumer et fumer comme si elle était vivante ! A un moment, Georges vit même surgir des étincelles dans un tourbillon de fumée. Il aurait pu le jurer.

Et soudain, Georges dansa près du chaudron qui bouillait à gros bouillons, et se mit à chanter cette étrange chanson qui lui passa par la tête :

Hourra ! Cornes à la sorcière,
Vive la chaudière !
Hourra ! Cornes à la potion,
Vive le chaudron !
Pétille, clapote, barbouille,
Siffle, crachote, gargouille !
Fais tes prières, Grand-mère !

La peinture marron

Georges arrêta le gaz sous le chaudron. Il fallait laisser refroidir la potion un bon moment.

Quand la fumée et l'écume se calmèrent, il jeta un coup d'œil dans le chaudron pour voir la couleur de sa potion. Elle était bleu vif.

« Ajoutons du marron, dit Georges. Si ma potion n'est pas brunâtre, Grandma aura des soupçons. »

Georges se précipita dans l'atelier où son père rangeait les peintures. Sur les étagères, il y avait des pots de toutes les couleurs, noir, vert, rose, rouge, blanc et marron. Il s'empara du pot marron : *peinture marron chocolat. Un litre.* Il enleva le couvercle à l'aide d'un tournevis. Le pot était plein aux trois quarts. Il revint en courant dans la cuisine, et versa la peinture dans le chaudron. Maintenant, il était rempli à ras bord. Très doucement, Georges mélangea la peinture à la potion avec la longue cuillère de bois. Ah ! ah ! elle devenait marron ! Un magnifique marron foncé.

— Et alors, ma potion ? cria la voix de Grandma dans la salle de séjour. Tu m'as oubliée ! Tu l'as fait exprès ! Je le dirai à ta mère !

— Je ne t'ai pas oubliée, Grandma, cria Georges. J'ai pensé à toi tout le temps. Mais il reste encore dix minutes.

— Méchant asticot ! aboya la voix. Vermisseau fainéant et désobéissant ! Tu grandis trop vite !

Georges prit le vrai flacon de potion sur le buffet. Il le déboucha et vida le contenu dans l'évier. Puis il plongea un cruchon

dans le chaudron et s'en servit pour remplir le flacon de potion magique. Il remit le bouchon.

Etait-elle suffisamment froide ? Pas tout à fait.

Il plaça le flacon sous le robinet d'eau froide pendant deux minutes. L'étiquette se détacha, mais aucune importance. Il sécha le flacon avec un torchon.

Maintenant, tout était prêt !

Oui, prêt !

Le grand moment était arrivé !

— C'est l'heure de prendre ta potion, Grandma, cria-t-il.

— Enfin, il me semblait bien ! grogna-t-elle.

La cuillère en argent qu'on utilisait pour la potion de Grandma était posée sur le buffet. Il s'en saisit.

Et c'est la cuillère d'une main et le flacon de l'autre qu'il entra dans la salle de séjour...

Grandma
boit la potion

Grandma était recroquevillée dans son fauteuil près de la fenêtre. Ses petits yeux méchants scrutèrent Georges quand il traversa la pièce.

— Tu es en retard ! cria-t-elle.

— Pas du tout, Grandma.

— Ne me coupe pas au milieu d'une phrase ! hurla-t-elle.

— Mais tu avais fini ta phrase, Grandma.

— Tu recommences ! aboya-t-elle. Quel exaspérant petit garnement ! Toujours en train de m'interrompre et de chercher midi à quatorze heures. Quelle heure est-il, au fait ?

— Il est exactement onze heures, Grandma.

48

— Tu mens comme d'habitude. Arrête de jacasser et donne-moi mon médicament. Agite le flacon d'abord, puis verse la potion dans la cuillère. Une pleine cuillerée, fais bien attention.

— Vas-tu l'avaler d'un seul coup ? lui demanda Georges. Ou à petits coups ?

— Ça ne te regarde pas, répondit la vieille femme. Remplis la cuillère.

Il déboucha le flacon et versa lentement l'épais liquide dans la cuillère. Il ne pouvait pas s'empêcher de penser aux incroyables et merveilleux ingrédients de la potion magique : la mousse à raser, la crème dépilatoire, la lotion antipelliculaire, le détergent pour machines à laver automatiques, la poudre insecticide pour chiens, le cirage, le poivre noir, la sauce au raifort et le reste, sans oublier les pilules, les liquides et les poudres pour les animaux... ni la peinture marron.

— Ouvre grand la bouche, Grandma, dit-il, et j'y verserai la potion.

La vieille sorcière ouvrit sa petite bouche ridée en découvrant ses dents jaunâtres et dégoûtantes.

— Allons-y ! cria Georges. Avale vite !

Il introduisit la cuillère dans la bouche de Grandma et fit couler la potion. Puis, il recula d'un pas pour regarder le résultat.

Quel spectacle !

— *Ouiche !* cria Grandma.

Et hop ! son corps bondit en l'air, comme si son fauteuil avait été une chaise électrique ! Oui, elle bondit comme un diable de sa boîte et... elle ne retombait pas... elle restait là... suspendue entre ciel et terre... à environ un demi-mètre au-dessus du fauteuil... toujours assise... raide... glacée... tremblante... les yeux exorbités... les cheveux dressés sur la tête.

— Tu ne te sens pas bien ? lui demanda poliment Georges. Qu'est-ce qui ne va pas ?

Suspendue entre le sol et le plafond, la vieille femme n'arrivait pas à articuler un mot.

Le choc devait être terrible.

On aurait dit qu'elle avait avalé un tisonnier brûlant.

Puis, *plop* ! elle retomba sur son siège.

— Appelle les pompiers ! cria-t-elle soudain. J'ai l'estomac en feu !

— Ce n'est que le médicament, Grandma, dit Georges. C'est un bon remontant.

— Au feu ! s'égosillait la vieille. Il y a le feu dans ma cave ! Un seau d'eau ! Une lance à incendie ! Vite, dépêche-toi !

— Calme-toi, Grandma, dit Georges.

Mais il fut un peu impressionné quand il vit qu'elle crachait de la fumée par la bouche et par les narines. Oui, d'épais nuages de fumée noire sortaient de son nez et se répandaient dans la pièce.

— Diable, tu flambes, dit Georges.

— Bien sûr que je flambe ! hurla-t-elle. Je flambe comme une crêpe au rhum. Je fris comme un lardon. Je bous comme un bouillon.

Georges courut dans la cuisine chercher une cruche d'eau.

— Ouvre la bouche, Grandma ! cria-t-il.

A travers la fumée, il ne voyait pas bien

la bouche de la grand-mère, mais il réussit à vider le quart de la cruche dans le gosier de Grandma. L'estomac de la vieille femme grésilla comme lorsqu'on fait couler de l'eau froide dans une poêle brûlante. La sorcière hennit et piaffa comme un cheval. Elle haleta, gloussa et cracha des trombes d'eau. Puis la fumée disparut.

— J'ai maté l'incendie ! annonça Georges fièrement. Tu vas très bien maintenant, Grandma ?

— Très bien ? vociféra-t-elle. Qu'est-ce qui va très bien ? J'ai de la dynamite dans le bide ! Une grenade dans la bedaine ! Une bombe dans les boyaux !

Elle bondissait sur son fauteuil. Visiblement, elle n'était pas très à l'aise.

— Cette potion te fera beaucoup de bien, tu verras, Grandma, dit Georges.

— Du bien ! hurla-t-elle. Du bien ! elle est en train de me tuer !

Puis son ventre commença à ballonner.

Elle gonflait !

Elle gonflait de partout !

Comme un ballon !

Allait-elle exploser ?

Son visage violacé devenait verdâtre.

Mais attendez ! Elle eut une crevaison. Georges entendit le sifflement d'une fuite. Lentement, elle se dégonflait, elle rapetis-

52

sait, reprenant peu à peu son vieil aspect ra-
tatiné.

— Tout va bien, Grandma ? demanda
Georges.

Elle ne répondit pas.

Advint alors une chose amusante. Grandma se tortilla puis se dégagea d'un coup
sec de son fauteuil et atterrit des deux pieds
sur le tapis.

— Extraordinaire, Grandma ! s'exclama
Georges. Ça fait des années que tu n'as pas
été debout ! Regarde ! Tu tiens sur tes
jambes sans canne !

Grandma ne l'entendait même pas. Elle était à nouveau figée, les yeux exorbités. Loin, très loin dans un autre monde.

« Fantastique potion ! se dit Georges, fasciné par le spectacle. Qu'arrivera-t-il maintenant à cette vieille sorcière ? »

Il obtint vite une réponse.
Soudain, elle se mit à grandir.
Très lentement au début... quelques millimètres... quelques centimètres... puis de plus en plus vite, quelques décimètres, à la vitesse de trois centimètres à la seconde. Au début, Georges n'y prêta pas attention, mais quand elle eut dépassé un mètre soixante-dix, quand elle eut atteint un mètre quatre-vingts, Georges sursauta en s'écriant :

— Eh, Grandma ! Tu grandis ! Tu grandis ! Attention, Grandma ! Attention au plafond !

Mais Grandma ne s'arrêtait pas.

C'était vraiment un spectacle fantastique de voir cette ancêtre décharnée devenir de plus en plus grande, de plus en plus longue et fine, comme un élastique étiré par des mains invisibles.

Quand sa tête atteignit le plafond, Georges pensa qu'elle serait obligée de s'arrêter.

Mais non ! Il y eut un crissement, et des morceaux de plâtre et de ciment tombèrent par terre.

— Arrête-toi de grandir, Grandma, dit Georges. Papa vient juste de repeindre cette pièce.

Mais elle ne pouvait pas s'arrêter.

Bientôt, sa tête et ses épaules disparurent complètement à travers le plafond. Et elle grandissait toujours.

Georges monta vite dans sa chambre. La tête de Grandma surgissait du parquet comme un champignon.

— Youpi ! fit-elle. Alléluia, me voilà !
— Tout doux, Grandma ! dit Georges.
— Nenni, petit ! Moi, je grandis !
— Mais c'est ma chambre, dit Georges. Regarde plutôt le gâchis !

— Quelle merveilleuse potion ! cria-t-elle. Donne-m'en un peu plus.

« Elle radote comme un rat d'hôtel », pensa Georges.

— Allons, mon garçon ! reprit-elle. Un peu plus de potion. Une autre cuillerée ! Je sens que je m'arrête en pleine croissance.

Georges tenait toujours le flacon et la cuillère. « Eh bien, pourquoi pas ? » songea-t-il. Il versa une seconde dose de potion et la donna à Grandma.

— *Ouiche !* cria-t-elle.

Et elle grandit de plus belle. Ses pieds étaient toujours sur le parquet du rez-de-chaussée, mais sa tête se dirigeait rapidement vers le plafond de la chambre.

— Je suis en bonne voie, mon garçon ! hurla-t-elle à Georges. Admire un peu !

— Il y a le grenier au-dessus, Grandma ! cria Georges. C'est plein de fantômes et de gnomes !

Crac, boum ! la tête de la vieille traversa le plafond comme si c'était du beurre.

Georges regarda la pagaille dans sa chambre. Il y avait un grand trou dans le sol et un autre au plafond et, entre les deux, droit comme un poteau, le tronc de Grandma. Ses pieds étaient au rez-de-chaussée et sa tête au grenier !

— Je continue ! cria la voix perçante de

Grandma depuis le grenier. Donne-moi une troisième dose, mon garçon. Il faut que je perce le toit !

— Non, Grandma, non ! répliqua Georges. Tu casses la baraque !

— Au diable, la baraque ! s'écria-t-elle. J'ai envie de respirer un peu d'air pur. Ça fait vingt ans que je ne suis pas sortie.

« Fichtre, elle va percer le toit ! » se dit Georges. Il redescendit les escaliers et se précipita dans la cour de la ferme. Si Grandma défonçait la toiture, ce serait abominable. Son père serait furieux. Et lui,

Georges, serait puni. C'était lui qui avait fabriqué la potion, lui qui avait donné les deux cuillerées...

— Ne défonce pas le toit, Grandma ! suppliait-il. S'il te plaît, surtout ne fais pas ça !

La poule brune

Dans la cour, Georges observait le toit de
la ferme, un joli toit de tuiles roses avec de
hautes cheminées.

On ne voyait pas la tête de Grandma.
Seule, une grive chantait, perchée sur l'une
des cheminées. « La vieille plante est restée
coincée dans le grenier, pensa Georges.
Dieu soit loué ! »

Soudain, une tuile se détacha du toit et
dégringola dans la cour. La grive s'envola
aussitôt.

Puis une autre tuile tomba.

Suivie d'une demi-douzaine.

Et alors, très lentement, comme une créa-
ture monstrueuse sortant d'un gouffre, la
tête de Grandma surgit du toit...

Puis un cou décharné...

Et ses épaules...

60

— Diable, j'ai réussi ! cria-t-elle. J'ai défoncé le toit !

— Tu ne crois pas que tu devrais arrêter maintenant, Grandma ? demanda Georges.
— Ça y est, j'arrête ! répondit-elle. Je me sens en pleine forme ! Je t'avais bien averti que j'avais des pouvoirs magiques ! Je

61

t'avais bien dit que j'étais sorcière jusqu'au bout des ongles ! Mais tu ne voulais pas me croire, n'est-ce pas ? Tu ne voulais pas écouter ta vieille Grandma !

— Ce n'est pas toi qui as fait ça, Grandma ! s'écria Georges. C'est moi ! J'ai fabriqué une potion magique !

— Une potion magique ? Toi ? aboya-t-elle. Balivernes !

— Oui, c'est moi ! C'est moi ! répéta Georges.

— Tu mens, comme d'habitude ! hurla Grandma. Tu racontes toujours des bobards.

— Je ne mens pas, Grandma. Je te le jure.

Là-haut, au-dessus du toit, le visage ridé de Grandma se tourna vers Georges d'un air méfiant

— Veux-tu vraiment dire que tu as fabriqué une potion magique, tout seul ? demanda-t-elle.

— Oui, Grandma, tout seul.

— Je n'en crois rien, dit-elle. En tout cas, je me sens très bien là-haut. Apporte-moi une tasse de thé.

Une poule brune picorait dans la cour, près de Georges. Cela lui donna une bonne idée. Vite, il déboucha le flacon et versa une dose de potion dans la cuillère.

— Regarde-moi ça, Grandma ! cria-t-il.

Il s'accroupit et tendit la cuillère vers la poule.

— Petit, petit, petit, dit-il. Viens picorer ici.

Les poules sont des volatiles gloutons et stupides. Elles croient que tout est bon à manger. Celle-ci s'imaginait que la cuillère était pleine de graines. Elle sautilla vers Georges, pencha sa tête de côté et fixa la cuillère.

— Petit, petit, petit, répéta Georges. Allons, petite poule.

La poule brune tendit le cou et becqueta la potion. Une pleine becquée de potion.

L'effet fut électrique.

— *Ouiche !* caqueta la poule, en bondissant droit dans le ciel comme une fusée.

La poule atteignit la hauteur du toit puis

s'écroula dans la cour. Elle restait assise sur le croupion, toutes plumes hérissées, hébétée, ridicule. Georges continuait à l'observer. Et Grandma aussi, depuis le toit.

La poule se remit sur ses pattes. Elle tremblait et *gloussaillait* d'une drôle de façon ! Elle ouvrait, fermait le bec, sans raison. Elle semblait vraiment mal en point.

— Regarde ce que tu as fait, imbécile ! s'exclama Grandma. La poule est en train de mourir ! Tu vas entendre ton père ! Il va te flanquer une bonne raclée ! Et tu ne l'auras pas volée !

Tout à coup, un nuage de fumée noire s'échappa du bec de la poule.

— Elle flambe ! hurla Grandma. La poule est en feu !

Georges courut remplir un seau d'eau à l'abreuvoir.

— La poule est rôtie ! Le dîner est servi ! criait Grandma.

Georges jeta l'eau du seau sur la poule. Il y eut un grésillement et la fumée disparut.

— Elle a pondu son dernier œuf ! hurlait Grandma. Les poules rôties ne pondent plus que des œufs durs !

Le feu éteint, la poule paraissait en meilleure forme. Ses pattes ne flageolaient plus. Elle agitait même ses ailes. Puis, elle s'accroupit comme pour le départ d'un cent mètres. Mais elle sauta en *hauteur*, fit un saut périlleux et retomba allègrement sur ses pattes.

— C'est une poule de cirque ! criait Grandma du sommet du toit. Un volatile acrobate !

Et maintenant, la poule grandissait.

Enfin ! C'était ce qu'attendait Georges.

— Elle grandit ! hurla-t-il. Elle grandit, Grandma ! Regarde, elle grandit !

De plus en plus grande, de plus en plus haute. Elle fut bientôt quatre ou cinq fois plus grande qu'au début.

— Tu vois, Grandma ? criait Georges.

— Diable, je vois ! répondit la vieille. Je ne vois que ça !

Georges, tout excité, sautillait d'un pied sur l'autre, en montrant l'énorme poule.

— Elle a bu ma potion magique, Grandma, répétait-il, et elle a grandi comme toi !

Mais il y avait une différence. Grandma avait grandi en s'étirant comme un élastique. Pas la poule, qui était restée joliment dodue.

Bientôt, elle fut plus grande que Georges. Elle ne s'arrêta que lorsqu'elle atteignit la taille d'un cheval.

— N'est-ce pas fantastique, Grandma ? cria Georges.

— Elle n'est pas aussi grande que moi !

chantonnait Grandma. Par rapport à moi, la poule est poulette ! Moi, je suis la plus grande !

Le cochon, les bœufs, les moutons, le poney et la chèvre

A ce moment-là, la mère de Georges revint du village où elle avait fait des courses. Elle gara la voiture dans la cour, puis sortit en tenant un sac de provisions et une bouteille de lait.

La première chose qu'elle vit fut la poule brune, gigantesque à côté du petit Georges. Elle lâcha la bouteille de lait.

Puis elle entendit crier sur le toit. Elle leva les yeux, vit que la tête de Grandma avait défoncé les tuiles, et lâcha son sac à provisions.

— Alors, Marie, qu'est-ce que tu en penses ? cria Grandma. Je parie que tu n'as jamais vu de poule aussi énorme. C'est la poule géante de Georges !

— Mais... mais... mais... bredouilla la mère de Georges.

— C'est la potion magique de Georges ! poursuivit Grandma. Nous en avons bu une ration, la poule et moi !

— Mais comment diable as-tu fait pour monter sur le toit ? demanda la mère.

— Je ne suis pas montée sur le toit, caqueta la vieille femme. J'ai les pieds sur le parquet de la salle de séjour !

C'en était trop pour la mère de Georges : elle resta bouche bée, les yeux en boules de loto comme si elle allait s'évanouir.

Un instant plus tard, surgit le père de Georges. Il s'appelait le père Gros Bouillon. M. Bouillon était un petit homme à grosse tête et aux jambes arquées. C'était un bon père, mais il était difficile à vivre car il était soupe au lait et s'énervait pour de petits riens. La grosse poule qui se tenait dans la cour, elle, n'était pas un petit rien ! Dès qu'il l'aperçut, M. Bouillon entra en ébullition.

— Vingt dieux ! s'écria-t-il en agitant les bras. Qu'est-ce que c'est ? Qu'est-il arrivé ? D'où vient cette poule géante ? Qui a fait ça ?

— C'est moi, répondit Georges.

— Regarde-moi, moi ! cria Grandma du sommet du toit. Ne t'occupe pas de la poule ! Ce n'est qu'une poulette à côté de moi !

M. Bouillon regarda le toit et aperçut Grandma.

— Tais-toi, Grandma ! fit-il.

Il ne s'étonna pas que la vieille ait défoncé le toit. La poule, seule, l'excitait. Il n'avait jamais vu un tel spectacle, mettez-vous à sa place !

— Fantastique ! brailla M. Bouillon en dansant sur place. Colossal ! Gigantesque ! Enormissime ! Miraculeux ! Comment as-tu fait ça, Georges ?

Georges raconta toute l'histoire à son père. Pendant ce temps, la grosse poule brune s'assit au milieu de la cour et commença *cot-cot-cot* à caqueter et à glousser.

Tous les quatre s'arrêtèrent pour la regarder.

Quand elle se releva, elle avait pondu un gros œuf brun, de la dimension d'un ballon de rugby.

— Avec cet œuf on pourrait faire des œufs brouillés pour une vingtaine d'invités ! s'écria Mme Bouillon.

— Georges ! s'exclama M. Bouillon. Combien de litres de cette potion magique as-tu préparés ?

— Des tas, répondit Georges. Un gros

chaudron, dans la cuisine, et ce flacon qui est presque plein.

— Viens avec moi ! hurla le père Gros Bouillon. Apporte ta potion. Depuis des années et des années que je m'échine à engraisser les animaux. De gros bœufs pour des steaks. De gros cochons pour des jambons. De gros moutons pour des gigots...

Ils allèrent d'abord à la porcherie.
Georges donna une cuillerée au cochon.
Le groin du cochon cracha de la fumée.
Il se mit à cabrioler, puis à grandir.

A la fin, voici à quoi il ressemblait :

Puis ils se dirigèrent vers l'enclos des bœufs noirs, que M. Bouillon engraissait pour vendre au marché.

Georges leur donna une dose de la potion, et voici ce qui arriva :

Ensuite, ce fut le tour des moutons :

Georges donna une ration de potion à son poney gris, *Vive-le-vent* :

Et enfin, juste pour s'amuser, il en donna
à *Alma*, la chèvre :

Une grue
pour Grandma

Au sommet du toit, Grandma assistait à tout ce qui se passait, et la tournure que prenaient les événements ne lui plaisait guère. Elle voulait être le centre d'attraction, mais personne ne s'intéressait à elle. Georges et M. Bouillon couraient par-ci par-là, excités par les animaux gigantesques. Mme Bouillon faisait la vaisselle dans la cuisine, et Grandma restait plantée là, la tête dépassant du toit.

— Eh, Georges ! cria-t-elle. Apporte-moi une tasse de thé, immédiatement, petit paresseux !

— N'écoute pas cette vieille chèvre, dit M. Bouillon. Elle est coincée, tant mieux !

— Mais on ne peut pas la laisser tomber, papa, dit Georges. Et s'il pleut ?

— Georges ! hurla Grandma. Sale gosse, sale vermisseau ! Donne-moi tout de suite une tasse de thé et une tranche de gâteau aux groseilles.

— Il faut la tirer de là, papa, dit Georges. Sinon, elle nous embêtera sans arrêt.

Mme Bouillon surgit dans la cour.

— Georges a raison, dit-elle. Après tout, c'est ma mère.

— C'est une enquiquineuse, dit M. Bouillon.

— Qu'importe, dit Mme Bouillon. Je ne vais pas laisser ma mère coincée là-haut pour le restant de ses jours.

Finalement, M. Bouillon téléphona à une société de dépannage.

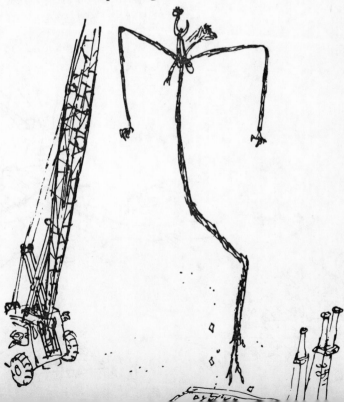

— Envoyez-moi aussitôt votre plus grande grue, dit-il.

Le camion-grue n'arriva qu'une heure plus tard, avec un chauffeur et un grutier. Le grutier grimpa sur le toit et attacha des cordes aux bras de Grandma. Puis, il la hissa à travers le toit...

D'une certaine façon, la potion avait amélioré Grandma. Elle n'avait pas perdu son mauvais caractère, elle n'était pas moins renfrognée, mais elle semblait guérie de toutes ses maladies. Elle était aussi fringante qu'un coursier ! Dès que la grue l'eut ramenée à terre, elle se précipita sur le gigantesque poney *Vive-le-vent*, et l'enfourcha. La vieille sorcière, haute comme la maison, galopait sur le coursier géant qui bondissait au-dessus des arbres et des hangars.

— Branle-bas ! criait-elle. Là où je passe, l'herbe trépasse ! Hors de mon chemin,

misérables crapoussins ! Sinon, je vous écrabouille !

Et autres imbécillités...

Comme Grandma était beaucoup trop grande pour rentrer dans sa chambre, elle dut passer la nuit dans la grange, au milieu des souris et des rats.

Le père
Gros Bouillon
a une idée géniale

Le lendemain, le père Gros Bouillon des-
cendit prendre son petit déjeuner, plus
bouillonnant que jamais.

— Je n'ai pas fermé l'œil de la nuit !
s'écria-t-il. Je ne pensais qu'à ça !

— A quoi ? lui demanda Georges.

— A cette potion magique, bien sûr ! Il ne
faut pas s'arrêter là, fiston ! Nous devons en
fabriquer *davantage* ! Des litres et des
litres !

Georges avait tellement donné de potion
aux moutons, aux cochons, aux vaches et
aux bœufs, que l'énorme chaudron était
complètement vide.

— Pourquoi *davantage*, papa ? demanda
Georges. Tous nos animaux sont devenus
gigantesques ! Grandma est aussi fringante
qu'un coursier, si bien qu'elle a dormi dans
le foin !

— Cher fiston ! s'exclama le père Gros Bouillon. Il nous en faut des tonneaux et des tonneaux ! Des tonnes et des tonnes ! Nous en vendrons aux agriculteurs du monde entier afin qu'ils élèvent des animaux géants ! Nous allons créer une usine de potion magique, et nous vendrons chaque bouteille cinquante francs. Nous deviendrons riches, et toi, tu seras célèbre.

— Attends, papa... dit Georges.

— Il n'y a pas une seconde à perdre ! s'écria M. Bouillon, si déchaîné qu'il mettait le beurre dans son café et le lait sur ses tartines. Tu ne comprends pas que ton invention géniale va faire le tour du monde ! Plus personne ne mourra de faim !

— Pourquoi ? demanda Georges.

— Parce qu'une vache géante donnera cinquante seaux de lait par jour ! répondit M. Bouillon en agitant les bras. Parce qu'un

poulet géant donnera une centaine de repas, et un cochon mille côtelettes ! Génial, fiston ! Fantastique ! Cela va changer le monde !

— Mais attends, papa... répéta Georges.

— Attendre ? Arrête de radoter ! cria M. Bouillon. Il n'y a pas une seconde à perdre. Il faut se grouiller !

— Calme-toi, mon chéri, dit Mme Bouillon à l'autre bout de la table. Et arrête de tartiner de confiture les *cornflakes*.

— Au diable, les *cornflakes* ! s'exclama M. Bouillon en bondissant de sa chaise. Allons-y, Georges ! Allons-y, fiston ! D'abord, préparons un plein chaudron pour faire un essai.

— Mais, papa... dit le petit Georges, l'ennui, c'est que...

— Il n'y aura aucun ennui, fiston ! coupa M. Bouillon. C'est impossible. Il suffit de mettre les mêmes ingrédients. Au fur et à mesure que tu les mettras dans le chaudron, je les noterai sur une feuille. C'est ainsi que nous aurons la recette magique !

— Mais, papa... insista Georges, écoute-moi, s'il te plaît.

— Ecoute-le, intervint Mme Bouillon. Notre fils veut te dire quelque chose d'important.

Mais le père Gros Bouillon était trop excité pour écouter les autres.

— Et ensuite, continua-t-il, quand le mélange sera prêt, nous le testerons sur une vieille poule, juste pour savoir si tout va bien ! Hourra ! Ça marchera ! Et nous construirons une usine géante !

— Mais, papa...

— Alors, que veux-tu ajouter ?

— Je ne pourrai jamais me rappeler la centaine d'ingrédients que j'ai jetés dans le chaudron pour fabriquer ma potion.

— Mais si, cher fiston ! cria M. Bouillon. Je t'aiderai ! Je te rafraîchirai la mémoire ! Et tu la retrouveras, va ! Alors, quel est le premier ingrédient que tu as mis dans le chaudron ?

— D'abord, je suis monté dans la salle de bains, répondit Georges. J'ai utilisé des tas de trucs, puis je suis allé fouiner dans la coiffeuse de maman...

— Allons-y donc ! cria le père Gros Bouillon. Montons dans la salle de bains.

Une fois là-haut, ils trouvèrent bien sûr des tas de tubes, de bombes et de flacons vides.

— Magnifique ! fit M. Bouillon. Voilà ce que tu as utilisé. Nous sommes sur la bonne piste. Il suffit de noter tout ce qui est vide.

M. Bouillon se mit à noter la liste des flacons, des bombes et des tubes de la salle de bains, puis celle des produits sur la coiffeuse.

— De la poudre peau rose, de la laque, du parfum *Fleur de navet...* Terrible ! C'est facile. Et ensuite où es-tu allé ?

— A la buanderie, répondit Georges. Mais es-tu sûr que tu n'as rien oublié, papa ?

— Si tu n'as rien oublié, moi non plus, dit M. Bouillon.

— Je l'espère, dit Georges.

Ils descendirent à la buanderie, et M. Bouillon nota le nom de tous les paquets et de toutes les boîtes vides.

— Vingt dieux ! s'écria le père. Tu en as mis, des trucs ! Pas étonnant qu'elle soit magique, ta potion ! Est-ce tout ?

— Non, papa, ce n'est pas tout.

Georges conduisit son père dans le hangar où il rangeait les médicaments pour les animaux. Il lui montra les cinq bouteilles vides sur l'étagère. M. Bouillon en prit bonne note.

— Et quoi d'autre ? demanda M. Bouillon.

Le petit Georges se creusa la cervelle. Il avait beau réfléchir, il ne se rappelait plus ce qu'il avait ajouté d'autre.

Le père Gros Bouillon sauta dans son auto, et courut acheter de nouvelles bombes, de nouveaux tubes, de nouveaux flacons, de nouveaux paquets, de nouvelles boîtes. Puis, il se rendit chez le vétérinaire et acheta les médicaments pour animaux.

— Maintenant, dit-il à son retour, montre-moi comment tu as fait, Georges. Montre-moi exactement comment tu les as mélangés.

La potion magique numéro deux

Georges et son père étaient dans la cuisine, et le chaudron trônait sur le fourneau. M. Bouillon avait rangé tous les produits qu'il avait achetés près de l'évier.

— Allons, fiston ! commença le père Gros Bouillon. Quel est le premier ingrédient que tu as mis dans le chaudron ?

— Celui-ci, répondit Georges en vidant le flacon de shampooing pour cheveux gras. Ensuite, le dentifrice... puis, la mousse à raser... puis, la crème de jour... puis, le vernis à ongles...

— Continue, fiston ! exultait M. Bouillon en dansant dans la pièce. Vas-y ! Ne t'arrête pas ! N'hésite pas ! Quel plaisir de te voir à l'ouvrage, fiston !

Un à un, Georges vida les flacons, les paquets, les boîtes; il vaporisa les bombes.

Comme tout était à portée de main, il acheva la besogne en moins de dix minutes. Mais, à la fin, le chaudron lui sembla moins plein que la première fois.

— Et après qu'as-tu fait ? demanda M. Bouillon. As-tu remué ?

— J'ai porté à gros bouillons, répondit Georges. Pas longtemps, mais en remuant bien.

Le père Bouillon alluma le gaz sous le chaudron, et Georges remua le mélange avec la longue cuillère de bois qu'il avait déjà utilisée.

— La potion n'est pas assez brune, dit Georges. Attends ! Je sais ce que j'ai oublié.

— Quoi ? s'écria M. Bouillon. Vite, dis-moi quoi ? Si nous avons oublié le moindre ingrédient, la potion ne marchera pas ! En tout cas, pas de la même façon !

— J'ai besoin de peinture marron, dit Georges. Voilà ce que j'ai oublié.

Le père Gros Bouillon se précipita dans la cour, fonça vers sa voiture, courut au village acheter la peinture et revint immédiatement à la maison. Il ouvrit le pot, le tendit à son fils, et Georges vida la peinture dans le chaudron.

— Ah, ah ! fit Georges. C'est beaucoup mieux. Ça se rapproche de la bonne couleur.

— Elle bouillonne, elle bouillonne, la

potion ! bouillonna M. Bouillon. Est-ce que c'est prêt ?

— Elle est prête, dit Georges. Du moins, je l'espère.

— Bon ! brailla M. Bouillon en sautillant de-ci de-là. Faisons un essai ! Donnons-en à un poulet !

— Ciel ! Calme-toi ! dit Mme Bouillon, en entrant dans la cuisine.

— Me calmer ! hurla M. Bouillon au comble de l'excitation. Tu veux que je sois calme, alors que nous venons de préparer le plus grand médicament de toute l'histoire de l'humanité ? Viens donc, Georges ! Remplis une tasse de potion ! Et donne une cuillerée à un poulet ! Il faut être absolument sûrs que nous ne nous sommes pas trompés.

Dans la cour, il y avait quelques poulets qui n'avaient pas eu droit à la potion magique numéro un. Ils picoraient dans la saleté comme le font ces imbéciles de poulets !

Georges s'accroupit en tendant sa cuillère remplie de la nouvelle potion.

— Petit, petit, petit, fit-il.

Un poulet blanc tacheté de noir leva son œil sur Georges. Il s'avança vers la cuillère et commença à picorer.

L'effet de la potion numéro deux se révéla fort différent, mais il ne manquait pas d'intérêt.

— *Ouache !* caqueta le poulet et il bondit à deux mètres du sol, puis retomba sur ses pattes. Son bec cracha des étincelles, comme si quelqu'un affûtait un couteau dans son ventre. Son corps ne changeait pas mais ses deux pattes jaunes s'allongeaient, s'allongeaient...

— Mais, que lui arrive-t-il ? cria le père Gros Bouillon.

— Ça ne marche pas, dit Georges.

Plus les pattes s'allongeaient, plus le poulet s'élevait. Quand les pattes atteignirent la hauteur de cinq mètres, elles arrêtèrent de grandir. Le poulet avait l'air particulièrement ridicule avec ses pattes longues, longues et son petit corps perché là-haut. On aurait dit qu'il était monté sur des échasses.

— Vingt dieux ! s'écria le père Gros Bouillon. Nous nous sommes trompés ! Ce poulet ne sert à rien ! Il est tout en pattes ! Personne ne mange des pattes de poulet !

— J'ai sans doute oublié un ingrédient, dit
Georges.

— Je le vois bien ! cria M. Bouillon.
Réfléchis, fiston, réfléchis. Qu'as-tu oublié ?

95

— Ça y est, j'ai trouvé ! s'exclama Georges.

— Vite, qu'est-ce que c'est ?

— La poudre insecticide pour chiens, répondit Georges.

— Tu es sûr que tu en as ajouté, la première fois ?

— Oui, papa, j'en suis sûr. Un plein paquet.

— Voilà qui résout le problème !

— Attends un peu, dit Georges. Avais-tu marqué du cirage brun dans ta liste ?

— Non, répondit M. Bouillon.

— J'en ai utilisé, dit Georges.

— Eh bien ! s'écria M. Bouillon. Pas étonnant que ta potion n'agisse pas.

Déjà, il courait vers la voiture, et fonçait vers le village pour acheter l'insecticide et le cirage.

La potion magique
numéro trois

— Ça y est ! s'écria le père Gros Bouillon
en surgissant dans la cuisine. Un paquet de
poudre insecticide pour chiens, et une boîte
de cirage brun foncé.

Georges vida entièrement le paquet et la
boîte dans le chaudron.

— Il faut bien mélanger, Georges ! hurla
M. Bouillon. Et porter à ébullition. Ça va
marcher cette fois ! Je parie que ça
marchera.

Après mélange et gros bouillons,
Georges remplit la tasse de la potion
magique numéro trois, puis sortit dans la
cour pour tester le produit sur un autre poulet. M. Bouillon courait derrière lui, tout

excité, en agitant les bras et en sautillant.

— Viens regarder ! dit-il à son épouse. Viens voir comment on transforme une poule ordinaire en une merveilleuse poule gigantesque, qui pondra des œufs gros comme des ballons de rugby !

— J'espère que ce sera mieux que la dernière fois, dit Mme Bouillon en les rejoignant.

— Petit, petit, petit, fit Georges en tendant la cuillère. Viens goûter cette bonne potion.

Un jeune coq noir magnifique à la crête écarlate s'arrêta près de Georges. Il regarda la cuillère puis se mit à picorer.

— *Cocoricouac !* coqueriqua le coq en bondissant dans le ciel, puis en retombant sur ses pattes.

— Regardez bien maintenant ! hurla le père Gros Bouillon. Il va bientôt devenir un géant !

Tous les trois fixaient attentivement le jeune coq noir. Ce dernier ne bougeait pas. Il semblait simplement avoir la migraine.

— Vous avez vu son cou ? demanda Mme Bouillon.

— Il s'allonge, répondit Georges.

— Pour s'allonger, il s'allonge, renchérit Mme Bouillon.

M. Bouillon, lui, pour une fois, ne disait rien.

— La dernière fois, poursuivit Mme Bouillon, c'étaient les pattes ! Cette fois, c'est le cou. Qui achèterait un poulet tout en cou ? On ne se nourrit pas de cou de poulet !

Le spectacle était extraordinaire. Le corps du jeune coq ne s'était pas du tout remplumé, mais son cou mesurait déjà deux mètres.

— Eh bien, Georges, fit M. Bouillon dépité. Qu'as-tu oublié d'autre ?

— Je ne sais pas, répondit Georges.

— Si, tu le sais, riposta M. Bouillon.
Réfléchis, fiston. Tu as sans doute oublié
l'ingrédient le plus important.

— J'avais pris de l'huile au garage, dit
Georges. Est-ce que tu l'as noté sur ta liste ?

— Eurêka ! s'écria M. Bouillon. Voilà la
solution ! Combien en as-tu mis ?

— Un quart de litre, répondit Georges.

M. Bouillon se précipita vers le garage.

— Et un peu d'antigel ! lui cria Georges.

La potion magique
numéro quatre

De retour dans la cuisine, M. Bouillon, très inquiet, regarda son fils vider le quart d'huile et un peu d'antigel dans l'énorme chaudron.

— Il faut remuer ! cria M. Bouillon. Bouillir et remuer !

Georges obéit.

— Tu n'y arriveras pas, Georges, dit Mme Bouillon. Tu as mis les mêmes ingrédients que la première fois, mais peut-être pas dans les mêmes proportions. Et comment y arriver ?

— Ne t'occupe pas de ça ! cria M. Bouillon. Ça marchera cette fois, tu verras.

Après quelques gros bouillons, la potion magique numéro quatre était prête. Georges en remplit une pleine tasse et courut dans la cour. Suivi par son père, puis par sa mère qui disait :

— Si tu continues ainsi, Georges, nous allons avoir un cirque au lieu d'un basse-cour !

— Mais dépêche-toi, Georges ! s'époumonait M. Bouillon. Une dose pour cette poule brune !

Georges s'agenouilla et tendit une cuillerée de sa nouvelle potion.

— Petit, petit, petit, fit-il. Goûte un peu...

La poule brune s'approcha, regarda la cuillère et picora.

— *Ouèche !* caqueta-t-elle.

Puis son bec se mit à siffler d'une drôle de façon.

— Regardez, elle grandit ! cria M. Bouillon.

— Tu es trop sûr de toi, dit Mme Bouillon. Pourquoi siffle-t-elle ainsi ?

— Tais-toi ! dit M. Bouillon. Attends un peu !

Tous les trois observèrent attentivement la poule brune.

— Elle rapetisse, dit Georges. Regarde, papa. Elle se ratatine !

En effet. En moins d'une minute, la poule s'était tellement ratatinée qu'elle était devenue à peine plus grosse qu'un poussin. Elle était ridicule.

Adieu Grandma !

— Tu as encore oublié quelque chose !
s'écria M. Bouillon.

— Je ne vois pas, dit Georges.

— Abandonne, mon fils, dit Mme Bouillon. Arrête ! Tu n'y arriveras jamais.

M. Bouillon était complètement déconfit.

Georges, lui, en avait assez. Il était toujours agenouillé avec sa cuillère d'une main
et sa tasse de l'autre. La ridicule et minuscule poule brune s'éloignait lentement.

A ce moment-là, Grandma traversa la
cour à grands pas. De toute sa hauteur, elle
lança un regard furibond aux trois petits
êtres au-dessous d'elle.

— Que se passe-t-il ? tonna-t-elle. Pourquoi ne m'a-t-on pas apporté mon petit
déjeuner ? C'est déjà malheureux de dormir
dans une grange au milieu de rats et de souris. En plus, si je dois mourir de faim, que le
diable m'emporte ! Pas de thé ! Pas d'œuf !
Pas de bacon ! Pas de tartine beurrée !

— Je suis désolée, mère, dit Mme Bouillon. Nous avons été très occupés. Je vais te préparer ton petit déjeuner.

— Non, c'est le travail de Georges, cet affreux petit paresseux ! cria Grandma.

A l'intant même, la vieille femme aperçut la tasse que tenait Georges. Elle se courba et y jeta un coup d'œil. Elle vit que la tasse était pleine d'un liquide brun, qui ressemblait à du thé.

— Oh ! oh ! Ah ! ah ! fit-elle. Voilà à quoi

tu joues ? Tu ne t'intéresses qu'à toi ! Toi, tu es sûr d'avoir ton petit déjeuner ! Mais tu ne penses même pas à ta pauvre vieille Grandma ! Tu n'es qu'un sale petit égoïste. je le savais bien.

— Non, Grandma, protesta Georges. Ce n'est pas...

— Pas de bobards, petit ! vociféra la vieille sorcière géante. Donne-moi cette tasse immédiatement.

— Non ! cria Mme Bouillon. Non, mère, ne la bois pas ! Ce n'est pas pour toi !

— Toi aussi, tu es contre moi ! hurla Grandma. Ma propre fille, qui veut m'empêcher de prendre mon petit déjeuner et souhaite que je meure de faim !

M. Bouillon leva les yeux vers l'horrible mégère.

— Bien sûr qu'elle est pour toi, Grandma, dit-il d'un air doucereux. Bois ton thé tant qu'il est bien chaud !

— Sûr que je vais le boire ! dit Grandma en tendant son énorme main calleuse. Va, donne, Georges.

— Non, non, Grandma ! cria Georges en éloignant la tasse de potion. Il ne faut pas ! Tu ne dois pas goûter ça !

— Donne-moi cette tasse, que diable ! hurla Grandma.

— Non ! cria Mme Bouillon. C'est la potion de Georges...

— On dirait que tout appartient à Georges depuis hier, brailla Grandma. Georges a ceci, Georges a cela ! J'en ai ras le bol de Georges !

Elle arracha la tasse des mains de Georges.

— Bois, Grandma, dit M. Bouillon avec un large sourire. C'est du bon thé, ça !

— Non, non, nooon ! hurlèrent Georges et sa mère.

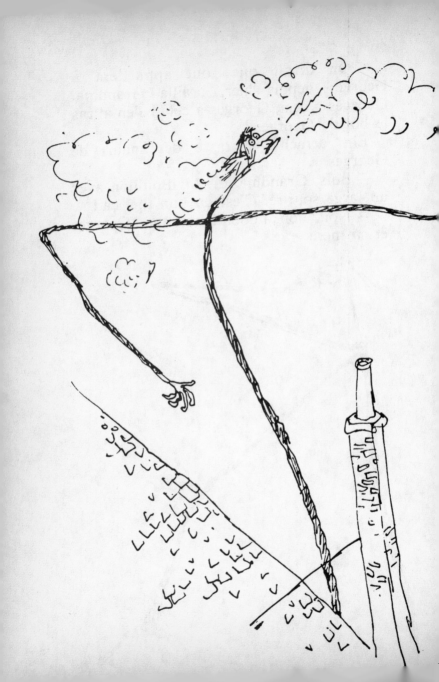

Trop tard, la vieille grande perche avait déjà porté la tasse à ses lèvres et avalé une gorgée.

— Mère ! gémit Mme Bouillon. Tu viens d'avaler cinquante doses de la potion magique numéro quatre. Regarde ce qu'une seule dose a fait à cette petite poule brune !

Mais Grandma n'entendait rien. Sa bouche crachait d'épais nuages de vapeur. Puis elle commença à siffler.

— Ça devient intéressant ! dit M. Bouillon, souriant de plus belle.

— Tu n'aurais jamais dû faire ça ! cria

Mme Bouillon, furieuse. Tu as réglé son compte à ma mère !

— Moi ? Je n'ai rien fait ! protesta M. Bouillon.

— Oh, si ! Tu lui as dit de boire la tasse !

Un abominable sifflement retentit au-dessus de leurs têtes. Grandma crachait de la vapeur par la bouche, par le nez et par les oreilles.

— Elle se sentira mieux quand elle aura craché son venin, dit M. Bouillon.

— Elle va exploser ! gémit Mme Bouillon. Comme une Cocotte-Minute !

— Calme-toi ! dit M. Bouillon.

Georges, lui, était affolé. Il se leva et

recula de quelques pas. Les jets de vapeur blanche jaillissaient de la tête décharnée de la vieille sorcière, et le sifflement strident crevait les tympans.

— Police secours ! Pompiers ! criait Mme Bouillon. Vite, une lance à incendie !

— Trop tard, dit M. Bouillon ravi.

— Grandma, s'écria Mme Bouillon. Mère, cours à l'abreuvoir et plonge la tête sous l'eau !

Mais le sifflement s'était arrêté. Le jet de vapeur, aussi. Alors, Grandma commença à se ratatiner. Sa tête, qui avait atteint la hauteur du toit de la ferme, descendait...

— Une bonne leçon pour toi, Georges ! s'écria le père Gros Bouillon tout agité. Regarde ce qui arrive lorsqu'on prend cinquante doses au lieu d'une !

Très rapidement, Grandma reprit sa taille normale.

— Arrête, mère ! suppliait Mme Bouillon.
C'est bon, maintenant.

Mais Grandma ne s'arrêtait pas. Elle
devenait de plus en plus petite. Bientôt, elle
ne fut pas plus haute qu'une bouteille de
limonade.

— Comment vas-tu, mère ? demanda
Mme Bouillon, inquiète.

Le minuscule visage de Grandma gardait
toujours son expression de fureur et de

méchanceté. Ses yeux, gros comme des
trous de serrure, jetaient des éclairs de rage.

— Comment je me sens ? piailla-t-elle.
Qu'est-ce que tu imagines ? Comment te
sentirais-tu, à ma place ? Il y a une minute,
j'étais une magnifique géante et maintenant
je ne suis plus qu'une misérable naine !

— Elle continue ! s'écria allégrement
M. Bouillon. Elle se ratatine encore !

Et diable, c'était la vérité.

Quand Grandma atteignit la hauteur
d'une cigarette, Mme Bouillon la prit dans
sa main.

— Que faire pour l'empêcher de rapetisser ? criait-elle.

— Il n'y a rien à faire, dit M. Bouillon.
Elle a pris cinquante doses.

— Il faut que je fasse quelque chose !

gémit Mme Bouillon. Elle est si petite que je
ne la vois presque pas !

— Tire-lui les pieds et la tête ! dit M.
Bouillon.

Mais déjà, Grandma avait la taille d'une épingle...

Puis, celle d'une graine de citrouille.

Puis...

Puis...

— Où est-elle passée ? demanda Mme Bouillon. Je l'ai perdue !

— Hourra ! s'écria M. Bouillon.
— Elle est partie, elle a disparu complètement ! cria Mme Bouillon.

— C'est ce qui arrive aux gens qui ont
mauvais caractère et ronchonnent tout le
temps, dit M. Bouillon. Sacrée potion,
Georges !

Georges, lui, ne savait pas quoi penser.
Pendant quelques minutes, Mme Bouillon se mit à errer dans la cour, le visage
défait, en répétant :

— Mère, où es-tu ? Où es-tu passée ? Où
es-tu allée ? Comment te retrouver ?

Mais elle se calma vite. A midi, elle répé-
tait :

— Au fond, c'est peut-être mieux ainsi.
Elle nous dérangeait un peu dans la maison.

— Tu l'as dit ! renchérit M. Bouillon. C'était une enquiquineuse !

Georges, lui, se taisait. Il frissonnait encore. Ce matin-là, un événement extraordinaire s'était produit. Pendant quelques brefs instants, Georges avait touché du bout des doigts la frontière d'un monde magique.

table

Roald Dahl

La potion magique de Georges Bouillon

**Supplément réalisé par
Christian Biet,
Jean-Paul Brighelli,
Daniel Laumesfeld
et Jean-Luc Rispail**

Illustrations de Serge Bloch

SOMMAIRE

ÊTES-VOUS SORCIER ?

ÊTES-VOUS SORCIER ?

Entre une grand-mère qui se dit sorcière, un jeune garçon apprenti sorcier, un père converti à la sorcellerie et une mère horrifiée par les potions, où vous situez-vous ? Répondez à ce questionnaire en comptant le nombre de △, □, ○ obtenus et reportez-vous à la page des solutions pour savoir qui vous êtes.

1. *Quel personnage seriez-vous ?*
A. La mère ○
B. Grandma △
C. Le père Gros Bouillon □

2. *A la place de Georges, vous auriez :*
A. Utilisé les médicaments interdits △
B. Laissé de côté les remèdes pour animaux □
C. Renoncé à l'idée de la potion △

3. *Vous auriez utilisé la potion numéro un pour :*
A. Vous faire grandir ○
B. Faire grandir les autres △
C. Engraisser le bétail □

4. *Lorsque Grandma veut boire la dernière potion, vous l'auriez :*
A. Avertie du danger □
B. Forcée avant même qu'elle en demande △
C. Incitée à boire ○

5. *A la place de Georges, auriez-vous :*
A. Noté la recette dès la première fois □
B. Noté les ingrédients de la potion numéro deux △
C. Rien noté du tout ○

6. *Vous auriez préféré :*
A. Guérir Grandma □
B. Vous en débarrasser △
C. La secouer ○

7. *Vous préférez que la potion produise :*
A. Des effets explosifs △
B. Des modifications de la taille ○
C. Une amélioration de la santé □

8. *Auriez-vous :*
A. Dégagé Grandma avec la grue ○
B. Laissé Grandma coincée △
C. Apporté une tasse de thé à Grandma □

9. *Quel animal seriez-vous ?*
A. Une limace △
B. Une poule ○
C. Un cochon □

10. *Quel personnage secondaire ?*
A. La chèvre Alma ○
B. Le poney Vive-le-Vent △
C. Le grutier □

11. *Quelle potion magique préférez-vous ?*
A. La numéro un △
B. La numéro deux □
C. La numéro quatre ○

Solutions page 145

1
AU FIL DU TEXTE
Quinze questions pour commencer
(p. 11-47)

Avez-vous bien lu les premiers chapitres ? Répondez à ce questionnaire sans consulter votre livre et reportez-vous à la page des solutions pour savoir si votre mémoire est vraiment fiable.

1. *A quel moment Grandma doit-elle prendre sa potion ?*
A. Le samedi matin à onze heures
B. Le soir au repas
C. Le dimanche à minuit

2. *Quel est le métier du père de Georges ?*
A. Médecin
B. Fermier
C. Boucher

3. *Que boit Grandma avant sa potion ?*
A. Du thé
B. Du café noir
C. De l'alcool fort

4. *Georges pense que Grandma est :*
A. Ensorcelée
B. Une sorcière
C. Un monstre

5. *Quelle est la taille normale de Grandma ?*
A. Elle est très grande
B. Elle est énorme
C. Elle est minuscule

6. *Georges commence à chercher un moyen pour :*
A. Tuer sa grand-mère
B. La rajeunir
C. La secouer

7. *Grandma prétend qu'elle adore manger :*
A. Des limaces et des insectes
B. Du verre
C. Des médicaments pour animaux

8. *Le médicament de Grandma est :*
A. Violacé
B. Brunâtre
C. Jaunâtre

9. *Dans la chambre de ses parents, Georges découvre :*
A. Du rouge à lèvres
B. Des somnifères
C. Une bouteille de gin

10. *Pour se venger de Grandma, le héros imagine :*
A. De l'attacher sur un cheval
B. De lâcher des rats
C. De la jeter dans le puits

11. *Pour préparer sa potion magique Georges se sert :*
A. D'un tonneau
B. D'un chaudron
C. D'une casserole

12. *Pour trouver les premiers ingrédients, Georges se rend d'abord :*
A. Dans la salle de bains
B. Dans la cuisine
C. A l'étable

13. *Ces premiers ingrédients sont :*
A. Des médicaments
B. Du shampooing
C. Des insecticides

14. *Quel est le reproche majeur que Grandma adresse à Georges ?*
A. Il est trop sale
B. Il est ignorant
C. Il grandit trop vite

15. *Pour brunir sa potion, le héros se sert d'abord :*
A. De cirage brun
B. De peinture marron
C. Du médicament de Grandma

Solutions page 145

Portrait de Grandma
(p 11-21)

Au début du livre, les deux personnages principaux sont dépeints, physiquement mais surtout psychologiquement.

1. Faites la liste des adjectifs qui se rapportent au personnage de la grand-mère (p. 11 à 15), vous en aurez ainsi le portrait. Puis choisissez l'un de ces adjectifs pour résumer le caractère de Grandma.

2. L'auteur laisse face à face les représentants de deux générations : l'enfance et la vieillesse. Les relations entre la grand-mère et le petit-fils ne sont guère paisibles. Pourtant, comme le signale l'auteur, « la plupart des grand-mères sont d'adorables vieilles dames... » (p. 13)
Réécrivez le début de l'histoire à partir de : « Grandma, qui sommeillait... » (p. 11) jusqu'à : « ... et n'ajoute pas de lait » (p. 12), en imaginant Grandma en « adorable vieille dame ». Remplacez le moins de mots possible du texte original.
- A votre avis, Grandma est-elle vraiment une sorcière ? Peut-on en être sûr ? Argumentez votre réponse.

La potion de Grandma

Inventez, à partir du texte, le genre de potion magique dont Grandma pourrait détenir le secret. Pour ce faire, associez à chaque nom de partie du corps cité p. 20-21 un nom d'animal cité p. 17-18. Par exemple : « *langue de limace* ».

1. A l'aide des ingrédients obtenus par ce moyen, rédigez une belle recette de potion de sorcière... (inspirez-vous au besoin d'un livre de cuisine !).

2. En vous aidant de la recette magique que vous avez mijotée, imaginez et écrivez la suite de l'histoire sous forme abrégée. Pour cela, vous partirez de l'hypothèse que Grandma est effectivement une sorcière et qu'elle va employer votre potion dans l'espoir de rapetisser le pauvre Georges...

Georges a une idée
(p. 22-26)

1. Agressé par Grandma, dont il a peur, Georges devient à son tour agresseur. Mais, au fait, quelles sont ses intentions ? Cherchez toutes les phrases (p. 22-26) qui donnent des indications sur les desseins du héros et classez-les selon l'importance que vous leur attribuez.
Ces intentions sont-elles cohérentes ? Laquelle, à votre avis, prédomine ?

2. Et vous, quelles transformations rêvez-vous secrètement de faire subir à votre entourage ? Imaginez que vous ayez le pouvoir de rendre les maigres obèses, de faire grandir les petits, de changer les bruns en roux...
- Dessinez ou décrivez par écrit l'allure de plusieurs personnes de votre choix, après transformation.
- Dans quelle mesure l'idée que l'on se fait d'une personne dépend-elle de son apparence physique ?
- Pensez-vous que la manière de voir le monde d'une personne puisse changer si son apparence physique est brusquement modifiée ?
- Imaginez l'état d'esprit d'un géant soudainement devenu nain.

Premiers ingrédients
(p. 27-35)

1. Les chapitres précédents laissaient présager que notre apprenti sorcier utiliserait, pour sa potion, des ingrédients à base de limaces ou de scarabées... Or il n'en est rien. Quelle est la différence fondamentale entre les ingrédients que Georges trouve dans la salle de bains et ceux suggérés dans l'incantation diabolique (p. 26) ou par les menaces de Grandma aux chapitres précédents ?

2. Pour mieux percevoir cette différence, insérez les deux séries distinctes d'ingrédients dont il vient d'être question à leur bonne place dans ce texte traitant d'alimentation « macrobiotique » :

« Qu'est-ce que la macrobiotique ?
C'est se conformer aux lois de la nature, en évitant tout particulièrement :
a) Les produits artificiels de la civilisation moderne : sucre raffiné, colorants et parfums chimiques, conservateurs, émulsifiants, produits exotiques, conserves, levure chimique, produits hors saison...
b) Les aliments d'origine animale : viandes, poissons, œufs, laitages... »

Remèdes pour animaux
(p. 36-41)

Il est beaucoup question, depuis le début de cette histoire, d'animaux en tout genre.
Les mots désignant des animaux peuvent être répartis en trois catégories :

a) ceux qui désignent des animaux réels, concrets, du récit ;

b) ceux qui désignent des animaux en général (par exemple lorsqu'il est question de remèdes pour animaux) ;

c) ceux qui désignent, par image, Grandma ou Georges.

Relevez tous ces mots en trois colonnes. Puis reliez par des flèches ceux qui apparaissent dans plusieurs colonnes.

A gros bouillons
(p. 42-44)

Cuisiner, c'est avant tout transformer des ingrédients en une matière comestible nouvelle : un plat. Il en est de même pour la préparation d'un médicament et, ici, d'une potion magique.

L'ébullition est l'une des phases essentielles de cette transformation. A propos, vous rappelez-vous le nom de famille de Georges... ?

Venant du verbe latin *bullire*, bouillir signifie tout simplement « faire des bulles ». Ouvrez votre dictionnaire et notez tous les mots commençant par le radical « bouill », de même sens que dans « bouillir ». Ensuite, relevez tous les verbes du texte (p. 42-43) qui indiquent les modifications de la mixture.

La peinture marron
(p. 45-47)

Après avoir imaginé le mélange le plus invraisemblable, voici Georges brusquement soucieux de vraisemblance : il faut que la potion soit brunâtre sinon « Grandma aura des soupçons ». (p. 45)

1. Pourquoi cette préoccupation de Georges quant à la couleur de la potion est-elle comique ?

2. Retrouvez les couleurs qui interviennent dans ces expressions :

A. Avoir une peur...
B. Etre... comme un linge
C. Etre... de peur
D. Devenir... de colère
(ou de honte)
E. Rire...
F. Une rue... de monde
G. Faire... mine
H. Rentrer à la tombée
de la nuit, c'est rentrer...

Grandma boit la potion
(p. 48-59)

Les modifications corporelles que subit Grandma sont visualisées avec art dans les quatre premiers dessins du chapitre « Grandma boit la potion ». Mais l'un des effets de la potion magique a été omis par le dessinateur : le feu lui sort de la bouche et des oreilles. (p. 51)

1. Dessinez à votre tour l'illustration de cet effet brûlant.

2. Que pensez-vous de l'effet principal produit par la potion magique : répond-il aux attentes de Georges ? Et qu'en pense la victime ? Cette dernière déclarait au premier chapitre : « Tu grandis trop vite. » Commentez ce reproche sous l'éclairage nouveau de ce qu'il advient.

3. Essayez de récapituler l'ensemble des dégâts causés par la croissance fulgurante de Grandma ; décrivez en quelques lignes l'état de la chambre de Georges après la soudaine « percée » de sa grand-mère.

La poule cobaye
(p. 60-68)

A la place de Georges, auriez-vous testé la potion sur une poule avant de l'administrer à Grandma ?
Organisez un vote à main levée sur cette question dans votre classe. Ensuite, regroupez-vous en partisans de la solution de Georges, partisans du « test de la poule », et abstentionnistes s'il y a lieu. Engagez alors le débat ; chacun des camps exprimera ses arguments en faveur de l'une ou l'autre thèse.

Dix questions pour continuer
(p. 69-90)

Les expériences se poursuivent sur les autres animaux de la ferme, on vient dégager Grandma de sa mauvaise posture, enfin le père de Georges a une idée de génie : autant d'événements dont vous avez sans doute retenu l'essentiel, mais les détails piquants ? Les avez-vous négligés ? Répondez à ces questions et reportez-vous à la page des solutions pour savoir ce que vous devez penser de votre lecture.

1. *D'où revient la mère de Georges ?*
A. Des champs de la ferme voisine
B. Du village où elle a fait des courses
C. De vacances

2. *Comment s'appelle le père de Georges ?*
A. Monsieur Bouillon
B. Le père Gros Bouillon
C. Court-Bouillon

3. *Pour tester la potion sur d'autres animaux, Georges et son père se rendent d'abord :*
A. A la porcherie
B. A l'étable
C. Au poulailler

4. *Lorsque le cochon avale une cuillerée de potion :*
A. Il meurt sur le coup
B. Il se met à hurler
C. Son groin crache de la fumée

5. *La chèvre s'appelle :*
A. Brisquette
B. Cornette
C. Alma

6. *La Grand-mère est dégagée de sa mauvaise posture par :*
A. Une grue
B. Un tracteur
C. Des chevaux

7. *Quels sont les effets de la potion sur Grandma ?*
A. Elle a perdu son mauvais caractère
B. Elle est guérie de toutes ses maladies
C. Elle est paralysée

8. *Grandma a passé la nuit :*
A. Au grenier
B. Dans la chambre de Georges
C. Dans la grange

9. *Une fois dégagée du toit, Grandma :*
A. Va se coucher
B. Dévore la poule géante
C. Chevauche le poney

10. *Le père demande à Georges :*
A. De jeter la potion magique
B. D'en fabriquer davantage
C. De la boire lui-même

Solutions page 146

Qu'en pensent les bêtes ?
(p. 69-79)

Soumis à l'épreuve de la potion magique, les animaux de la ferme deviennent gigantesques ou énormes.

1. Imaginez la venue des animaux de la ferme voisine : devant ce spectacle insolite et troublant, quelles pourraient être leurs réactions ? Ce spectacle les inciterait-il à rire ou à se moquer ? Auraient-ils quelque raison de redouter le même sort ?

2. Donnez la parole à l'un des animaux transformés par la potion afin qu'il explique à ses voisins ce qui vient d'arriver et ce qu'il pense de son nouvel état.

3. Un journaliste arrive sur les lieux. La vision de ces animaux géants lui suggère le récit :
- d'un fait divers pittoresque
- d'une catastrophe menaçant de s'étendre à la région.
Décrivez l'événement sous les deux points de vue.

Une grue pour Grandma

1. Pourquoi la « tournure que prenaient les événements » ne plaisait-elle guère à Grandma ? Quel est l'effet inattendu de la potion sur Grandma ? Etait-ce dans les intentions initiales de Georges ?

2. D'une façon tout à fait comique, Grandma réclame, du haut de son toit, une tasse de thé ! Imaginez que Georges se soit mis en tête de répondre à cette demande et racontez le trajet plein d'embûches qui l'aurait conduit jusqu'au toit.

3. Obligée de passer la nuit dans la grange, Grandma s'endort au milieu des rats : imaginez qu'elle ait fait un rêve épouvantable et racontez ce cauchemar.

Une idée comme une autre

L'usine de potion magique vous semble-t-elle une bonne idée ?

Comme Perrette dans la fable de La Fontaine *La Laitière et le Pot au lait*, le père de Georges se voit déjà enrichi par son invention destinée à éviter que personne ne meure plus de faim ! (p. 86) Pensez-vous que cette attitude soit condamnable ? Pensez-vous au contraire qu'elle se justifie ?

Organisez un débat dans la classe sur la question : si l'idée du père Gros Bouillon se réalisait, serait-ce enfin la solution du problème de la faim dans le monde ?

Grand choix de potions
(p. 91-103)

Les potions se succèdent à un rythme accéléré mais les résultats ne sont guère convaincants. Avez-vous une préférence pour l'une ou l'autre de ces potions ?

1. Répartissez-vous en quatre groupes, selon vos préférences pour l'une ou l'autre des potions.
Les quatre groupes s'affrontent en défendant les pouvoirs et vertus de leur potion favorite. Argumentez en imaginant tous les usages que vous pourriez faire de votre potion.
Ensuite, chaque groupe rédigera une annonce publicitaire d'une page destinée à la presse écrite et vantant les qualités de la potion magique du groupe. N'oubliez pas de prévoir slogan, dessin, photo, etc.

2. Puisque l'imagination autorise les inventions les plus étranges, parcourez le monde (par l'imagination) et dressez la liste des ingrédients qu'auraient pu trouver :
- une petite Esquimaude dans son igloo
- un petit Touareg dans une oasis du Sahara
- un petit Indien sous sa tente

Tel fils, tel père ?

Ce récit humoristique n'est certes pas un roman psychologique, et pourtant les relations familiales sont au cœur des événements et le conflit entre Georges et sa grand-mère est bel et bien le point de départ de cette expérience culinaire insolite.

1. Mais que diriez-vous du père ? de la mère ? A partir des éléments fournis par le texte, brossez le portrait des parents.

2. Que pensez-vous des relations entre le père et le fils ? La réaction du père devant le « forfait » de son fils vous a-t-elle surprise ? Quelle aurait été la réaction d'un père plus traditionnel ?

Plus de Grandma !
(p. 104-116)

Finalement, l'un des désirs exprimés par Georges dès le début du récit se réalise : se débarrasser de Grandma.

1. Voici un résumé de la fin de l'histoire qui comporte des erreurs. A vous de les retrouver et de rétablir la... triste vérité !

Entouré de son père et de sa mère, Georges se tenait dans la cour, la tasse de potion magique dans la main. M. Bouillon était déconfit. Soudain, la grand-mère immense s'approcha d'eux. Le père Gros Bouillon lui offrit alors de boire son thé, montrant la tasse que tenait son fils. Ce dernier, comprenant l'intention de son père, insista auprès de Grandma pour qu'elle avale la potion qui fait rapetisser, tandis que la mère criait : « non ! ». Grandma en but une petite gorgée et, à la déception de Georges et de son père, retrouva sa taille normale. Mais, bientôt, tous se réjouirent de voir la vieille grand-mère reprendre sa place au sein de la famille.

2. Rapetisser, grandir, grossir ne sont pas les seules possibilités offertes par une potion magique : imaginez qu'une potion (la numéro cinq !) ait eu pour effet non pas de faire disparaître totalement Grandma, mais de la rendre transparente. A quels incidents comiques donnerait lieu une présence aussi discrète dans la maison ? Racontez la journée d'une grand-mère transparente au sein d'une famille « en chair et en os ».

Quelle conclusion ?

Relisez la conclusion apportée par l'auteur après la disparition de Grandma (p. 116) :

1. Que signifie pour vous « toucher du bout des doigts la frontière d'un monde magique » ?
- En quoi est-ce seulement du bout des doigts et non pas à pleines mains ?
- En quoi est-ce seulement la frontière de ce monde et non pas à pieds joints dans ce monde, au cœur de ce monde ?
- En quoi est-ce un monde magique et non pas un monde extravagant, insensé, délirant ?

2. A votre avis, ce livre s'apparente-t-il plutôt à un récit d'aventures, à une histoire abracadabrante ou à un conte de fées ? Et si c'était une fable, quelle morale en tireriez-vous ?

Vingt questions pour conclure

Avez-vous bien lu cette histoire ? Répondez à ces vingt questions et reportez-vous à la page des solutions pour savoir ce que vous devez penser de votre lecture : votre attention a-t-elle été également soutenue tout au long de l'histoire ?

1. *L'histoire commence :*
A. Un samedi après-midi
B. Un mercredi matin
C. Un samedi matin

2. *Elle prétend que grandir est :*
A. Une sale affaire
B. Une sale manie
C. Une sale déveine

3. *Il manque à la deuxième potion :*
A. De la peinture marron
B. Du parfum et du dentifrice
C. De l'insecticide et du cirage

4. *L'intention de Georges est de :*
A. Terroriser sa grand-mère
B. La secouer
C. La faire exploser

5. *Georges se rend partout dans la ferme sauf :*
A. A la cuisine
B. Au grenier
C. Au garage

6. *Georges ne veut pas abandonner sa grand-mère sur le toit et sa mère :*
A. Lui donne tort
B. Lui donne raison
C. Lui donne une gifle

7. *Sa grand-mère lui demande sans arrêt :*
A. Que prépares-tu ?
B. Que fabriques-tu ?
C. Que mijotes-tu ?

8. *Avant de devenir marron la potion est :*
A. Gris-vert
B. Jaunâtre
C. Bleu vif

9. *Ayant bu la potion, la grand-mère crie :*
A. Au secours !
B. Au feu !
C. Au voleur !

10. *Ayant « gonflé de partout », elle finit par :*
A. Exploser
B. Avoir une crevaison
C. Se dégonfler lentement

11. *Dans le céleri-rave, elle trouve :*
A. Des perce-oreilles
B. Des pince-sans-rire
C. Des perce-neige

12. *Les poules rôties ne pondent plus que :*
A. Des œufs carbonisés
B. Des œufs brouillés
C. Des œufs durs

13. *M. Bouillon a :*
A. Les jambes arquées
B. Une petite tête
C. Une grande taille

14. *Ayant bu une cuillerée de potion, le cochon :*
A. Cabriole
B. Batifole
C. Carillonne

15. *Du toit, la grand-mère réclame du thé et :*
A. Une part de gâteau aux groseilles
B. Un nuage de potion
C. Son fauteuil

16. *La grand-mère passe la nuit au milieu :*
A. Des fourmis
B. Des souris
C. Des foins pourris

17. *La deuxième potion est testée :*
A. Sur un poulet
B. Sur un coq
C. Sur un dindon

18. *Georges n'avait jamais senti une odeur aussi :*
A. Brutale et fatale
B. Fatale et totale
C. Totale et brutale

19. *Devant son dernier échec, M. Bouillon est :*
A. Déconfit
B. Dépité
C. Dégoûté

20. *L'histoire se termine sur l'évocation :*
A. D'un monde fantastique
B. D'un monde aberrant
C. D'un monde magique

Solutions page 147

2
JEUX ET APPLICATIONS
Le parcours de Georges

Souvenez-vous que, pour trouver tous ses ingrédients, le héros a traversé diverses pièces et dépendances de la ferme. Ce parcours et les endroits où il a déniché divers produits ont été représentés dans le dessin ci-contre. Cependant, cinq erreurs s'y sont glissées : retrouvez-les. Retrouvez ensuite le parcours de Georges à travers la maison lorsqu'il rassemble les ingrédients de sa potion numéro un.

Solutions page 147

Un peu de cuisine

Cherchez la définition d'une « mixture » dans le dictionnaire, puis celle d'une « recette ». Quelle vous semble être la différence essentielle entre ces deux termes ?

1. La potion magique de Georges est-elle une mixture ou une recette ?
Pourquoi, et quelle en est la meilleure preuve ?

2. Que manque-t-il au père Gros Bouillon pour connaître la recette de la potion n° 1, autrement dit : pour faire de la mixture de son fils une vraie recette ? Cherchons ensemble la réponse, en plusieurs étapes :
- la première étape vous est indiquée par le père Gros Bouillon lui-même (p. 87)
- mais cela est insuffisant pour pouvoir parler, déjà, de recette. Pour savoir ce qu'il manque, voyez ce qu'en dit cette fois la mère de Georges. (p. 101) Si vous n'êtes pas convaincu, comparez le résumé des ingrédients (p. 49) ou encore les six premiers vers du premier chant de Georges

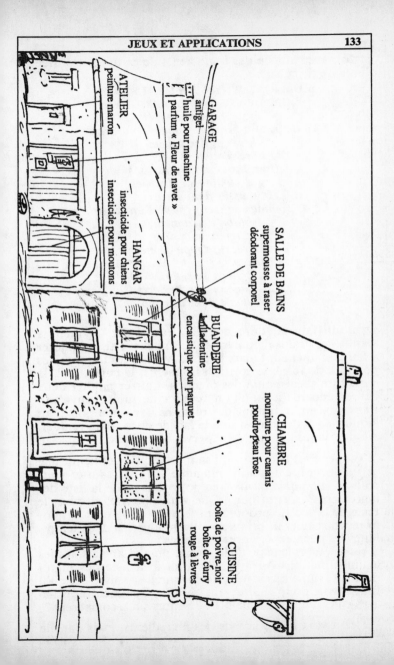

ATELIER
peinture marron

GARAGE
antigel
huile pour machine
parfum « Fleur de navet »

HANGAR
insecticide pour chiens
insecticide pour moutons

SALLE DE BAINS
supermousse à raser
déodorant corporel

BUANDERIE
Eau de Javel
encaustique pour parquet

CHAMBRE
nourriture pour canaris
poudre pour peau fine

CUISINE
boîte de poivre noir
boîte de curry
rouge à lèvres

(p. 26), avec la liste des ingrédients de cette recette tirée d'un livre de cuisine :

MULLIGATAWNY WITH MEAT STOCK
SOUPE DE VIANDE AUX LÉGUMES
pour 8 personnes
1 kg de bœuf à braiser coupé en morceaux
2 litres et demi d'eau
1 livre d'oignons hachés
20 grains de poivre écrasés
1 kg de tomates épluchées
10 gousses d'ail écrasées
1 kg de pommes de terre coupées en rondelles
1 bâton de cannelle
2 piments piquants
2 cuillerées à soupe de curry
50 g de coriandre fraîche hachée menu
2 pieds de céleri
jus de deux citrons verts
lait d'une noix de coco
sel

Dans un faitout, faire bouillir l'eau. Saler. Ajouter la viande, les grains de poivre et la cannelle. Laisser mijoter à feu doux pendant deux heures. Ajouter les tomates, les pommes de terre, le céleri, les piments, le curry, l'ail, la coriandre et la moitié des oignons. Laisser mijoter deux heures encore (le bouillon réduira de moitié environ). Faire revenir le restant des oignons dans une poêle, les ajouter au faitout ainsi que le lait de coco. Bien remuer. Ajouter le jus des citrons et servir bien chaud.

3. Tout ceci est encore insuffisant pour qu'on obtienne une véritable recette de potion magique. En effet, sauriez-vous réaliser le *mulligatawny* avec pour seul guide la liste des ingrédients ? Certes non ! Que vous apporte, en plus, le texte de la recette proprement dite ?
Pour vous aider à formuler votre réponse en deux temps, faites les deux expériences suivantes :
- barrez, dans le texte de la recette du plat anglais, toutes les informations que vous livre déjà la liste des ingrédients. Ce qui vous reste, c'est la marche à suivre : ce qu'il faut savoir pour réaliser une recette. Comment appelle-t-on, en grammaire, la majorité des mots qui la composent ?
- lisez à voix haute la liste des ingrédients, mais dans le

désorde. Cela gêne-t-il la compréhension de cette partie
du texte... et la réalisation concrète du plat ?
Maintenant, procédez de même avec la deuxième partie
du texte : lisez les phrases de la recette au hasard, dans le
désordre. Quel serait le résultat... dans votre assiette ?

4. Enfin, s'il est des recettes connues d'un seul individu, le
propre de la recette est de pouvoir appartenir à tous. Si
la communication est uniquement orale, la mémoire peut
suffire, mais aussi, comme dans le livre de Roald Dahl,
faire défaut. Que manque-t-il, en fin de compte, à la
potion de Georges pour devenir une véritable recette
qu'on puisse transmettre ? (Voyez aussi ce qu'en dit le
père Gros Bouillon, pages 87, 88 et 100.)

La cuisine des mots

1. Dans votre classe, écrivez chacun, sur un morceau de
papier, un chiffre suivi du mot gramme, ou pincée, ou
cuillerée, etc. Rassemblez tous les billets de la classe dans
un chapeau.

2. Inscrivez ensuite sur d'autres billets le nom d'une partie
ou d'un produit du corps humain ou animal (yeux, cornes, larme, ongle...) et regroupez tous les billets dans un
second chapeau.

3. Procédez de la même façon, en faisant suivre la préposi-
tion « de » d'un nom d'être vivant (humain, animal ou
surnaturel), puis d'un adjectif.

4. Ensuite, notez sur le tableau une liste de verbes de
cuisine inspirés de la recette du *mulligatawny* ou pris dans
le dictionnaire.
- Vous pouvez faire à présent la liste des ingrédients :
pour cela, tirez un billet du premier chapeau, puis du deuxième et du troisième, et placez-les sur une même ligne,
dans l'ordre, formant une phrase. Répétez l'opération jusqu'à épuisement des billets.
- Ensuite, écrivez le texte de la recette magique proprement dite. Pour cela, construisez des phrases infinitives en
remplaçant les quantités (« 200 grammes », etc.) de la liste
des ingrédients, par les verbes notés au tableau. Agrémen-
tez votre recette d'une ponctuation, de verbes sans com-
plément (saler, etc.), d'une ou deux indications de temps
de cuisson ou de récipients : votre recette est prête !

Pour tous les goûts

Les expressions ayant trait à la cuisine ou à la nourriture sont innombrables. En voici quelques-unes dont vous allez préciser le sens :

1. Mettre partout son grain de sel
2. Une dispute qui tourne au vinaigre
3. Sentir la moutarde vous monter au nez
4. Tomber comme un cheveu sur la soupe
5. Mettre quelque chose à toutes les sauces
6. Laisser quelqu'un mijoter
7. Jeter de l'huile sur le feu
8. Bouillir d'impatience
9. Boire du petit-lait
10. S'occuper de ses oignons

Ecrivez à présent le récit d'une dispute entre Georges et sa grand-mère, sous forme de dialogue, dans lequel vous glisserez adroitement ces expressions.

Sans œufs, sans « e », sans eux

Une fois devenue minuscule, la pauvre poule, victime de la potion, ne pondra plus d'œufs...
Croyez-vous que l'on puisse écrire un texte dans lequel il n'y aurait plus d'« e » ? C'est un jeu auquel s'est livré un écrivain français, Georges Perrec : il a écrit *La Disparition,* un livre entier sans jamais employer la lettre « e », ce qui est un exploit si l'on sait que cette voyelle est la lettre la plus employée dans notre langue..

1. Voici donc un texte qui résume le début de *La Potion magique* et qui ne comporte plus d'« e » mais... des blancs que vous allez remplir en vous conformant à la règle : plus d'« e ».

Sa Grandma lui avait fait ..... trop d'affronts. Il porta sa .... à son front, ... il dit : « j'ai un .... » ! Aussitôt, il fit .... cinq, six, ... ou plutôt vingt .... dans un gros .... Il touilla, mixa, ... du marron, transvasa la ...... dans un ......, qu'il ...... à Grandma. Aussitôt Grandma brûla, ..., flamba, ... si haut, si haut qu'à la ... on la ... sortir du ....

2. Si vous êtes en classe, continuez chacun votre résumé, avec des blancs, puis échangez vos feuilles. Attention : les « e » sont des « objets » diaboliques qui chercheront à se glisser dans votre texte à votre insu, surtout si vous ne voulez ... plus d'eux !

Solutions page 147

Potion ou lotion ?

Vous connaissez déjà les synonymes (mots qui ont à peu près le même sens) et les homonymes (mots qui se prononcent de la même façon comme vin, vain, vingt, vint).
Mais connaissez-vous les paronymes ? Ce sont des mots qui sont presque homonymes comme potion, lotion, notion, motion. Le français est très riche en paronymes qui peuvent donner lieu à de plaisantes méprises.

Ainsi, sauriez-vous retrouver, dans la liste suivante, les ingrédients des diverses potions ?

1. Un *flocon* de parfum
2. Une boîte de *mirage*
3. Un *bedon* d'huile
4. De la peinture *larron*
5. Un *caquet* de lessive

Et ceux-ci, dont les deux termes sont paronymes :

6. Un *cube* de rouge à *livres*
7. Une *tombe* de mousse à *caser*
8. Un *lot* de *crêpes*
9. Un *mot* de *moucharde*
10. De la *foudre* contre les *infectes*

A vous maintenant de trouver pour les ingrédients suivants les meilleurs paronymes :

11. Un litre d'huile
12. De la nourriture pour canaris
13. De la poudre blanche
14. Du vernis à ongle
15. Divers liquides

Solutions page 148

Cherchez l'intrus

Finalement, tous les animaux de la ferme seront victimes des diverses potions magiques. Heureusement que le père Gros Bouillon n'avait pas sous la main la ménagerie suivante :

Ce sont des listes de six noms ; dans chacune, cinq noms constituent une suite logique mais l'un d'eux n'a rien à voir avec la série : c'est l'intrus à trouver.

1. Agneau, lionceau, louveteau, corbeau, dindonneau, chevreau
2. Lion, lionne, paon, paonne, papillon, papillonne
3. Belette, chouette, alouette, fauvette, mouette, bergeronnette
4. Canard, cafard, blafard, guépard, lézard, renard
5. Héron, pinson, mouton, ourson, faucon, bison

3
LES GRANDS-MÈRES
DANS LA LITTÉRATURE

Enfance

Le jeune Alexis est élevé par ses grands-parents. Autant le grand-père est d'une sévérité qui confine parfois à la cruauté (il fouette pour un oui ou pour un non), autant la grand-mère est un personnage hors du commun qui fut pour l'enfant un refuge permanent. Habituellement, elle le protège, mais ici les rôles sont inversés...

« Ma grand-mère, qui ne craignait personne, ni grand-père, ni même les démons et autres forces impures, était terrorisée par les cafards. Elle devinait leur présence même de loin. Il lui arrivait de me réveiller la nuit et de me chuchoter :

– Alexis, mon petit, il y a un cafard qui court, écrase-le, pour l'amour du Christ !

Encore tout endormi, j'allumais la chandelle et je me traînais sur le plancher à la recherche de l'ennemi. Je restais parfois longtemps sans le trouver.

– Je ne vois rien, disais-je.

Immobile, la tête sous la couverture, grand-mère murmurait d'une voix imperceptible :

– Oh ! Il y en a un ! Cherche-le encore un peu, je t'en prie ! Il est là, j'en suis sûre...

Elle ne se trompait jamais, je finissais par découvrir le cafard dans quelque coin de la chambre, très loin du lit.

– Tu l'as tué ? Eh bien ! Dieu soit béni ! Je te remercie...

Rejetant la couverture, elle poussait un soupir de soulagement et souriait. Tant que je n'avais pas découvert l'insecte, elle ne pouvait pas se rendormir. Elle sursautait au moindre frôlement dans le silence profond de la nuit. Je l'entendais chuchoter, retenant son souffle :

– Il est près de la porte, il s'est glissé sous le coffre...

– Pourquoi as-tu peur des cafards ?

Elle répondait gravement :

– Je ne comprends pas à quoi ils peuvent servir. Ils sont tout noirs et ils courent, ils courent. Le Seigneur a donné une tâche à chacun, même au moindre puceron ; le cloporte montre que la maison est humide, la punaise que les murs sont sales, le pou annonce une maladie... Tout a un sens. Mais ceux-là, peut-on savoir quelle force les habite, à quoi ils sont destinés ?

Toute la journée, je tournoyais autour d'elle dans le verger ou dans la cour. J'allais avec elle chez les voisines où elle passait des heures à boire du thé et à raconter d'interminables histoires. J'avais poussé sur elle comme un greffon et dans mes souvenirs de cette époque, je ne revois que cette vieille femme remuante, à la bonté inépuisable.

De temps à autre, ma mère faisait une courte apparition. Elle posait sur tout le regard fier et sévère de ses yeux gris, froids comme le soleil d'hiver. Puis elle disparaissait rapidement sans que son passage me laissât le moindre souvenir.

Un jour, je demandai à grand-mère :

– Tu es sorcière ?

– Eh bien ! tu en as des idées ! s'exclama-t-elle en riant.

Elle ajouta aussitôt, pensive :

– Comment pourrais-je l'être ? La sorcellerie, c'est un art difficile. Et moi, je ne sais pas lire, pas une seule lettre. Ton grand-père, lui, c'est un homme vraiment instruit. Mais moi, la Sainte Vierge ne m'a pas donné cette sagesse. »

Maxime Gorki,
Enfance,
Traduction de G. Davydoff et P. Pauliat,
© Les Editeurs français réunis

Vipère au poing

Avant de connaître sa mère – la fameuse Folcoche – le jeune Jean Rezeau vivait chez sa grand-mère. Il retrace avec émotion les derniers moments de la vieille dame, dont la mort met un terme à la période heureuse de la vie de « Brasse-Bouillon ».

« Le protonotaire, la gouvernante, les vieux domestiques, la Belle Angerie, l'hiver à Angers, le chignon de grand-mère, les vingt-quatre prières diverses de la journée, les visites solennelles de l'académicien, les bérets des enfants des écoles respectueusement dépouillés à notre approche, les visites du curé venant toucher le denier du culte et le denier de Saint-Pierre et la cotisation pour la propagation de la foi, la robe grise de grand-mère, les tartes aux prunes, les chansons de Botrel sur le vieux piano désaccordé, la pluie, les haies, les nids dans les haies, la Fête-Dieu, la première communion privée, la première communion solennelle de Frédie avec, en main, le livre qu'avait porté notre père, et, avant lui, notre grand-père Ferdinand, et, avant lui, notre arrière-grand-père également Ferdinand, les marronniers en fleur...

Puis, soudain, grand-mère mourut.

L'urémie, mal de la famille, mal d'intellectuels (comme si la nature se vengeait de ceux qui n'éliminent pas l'urée par la sueur), lui pourrit le sang en trois jours. Mais cette grande dame – cette bonne dame aussi, mon cœur ne l'a pas oubliée – sut faire une fin digne d'elle. Écartant délibérément certains sondages et autres soins répugnants qui l'eussent prolongée quelques jours, elle réclama son fils l'abbé, sa fille la comtesse Bartolomi, qui habitait Segré, et leur déclara :

– Je veux mourir proprement. Taisez-vous. Je sais que c'est fini. Dites à la femme de chambre qu'elle prenne une paire de draps brodés sur le quatrième rayon de la grande armoire, dans l'antichambre. Quand mon lit sera refait, vous ferez entrer mes petits-enfants.

Ainsi fut fait. Devant nous, grand-mère se tint assise, le dos calé entre deux oreillers. Elle ne paraissait pas souffrir, alors que, je l'ai su depuis, cette fin est l'une des plus douloureuses. Aucun hoquet. Pas un gémissement. On ne donne pas ce spectacle à des enfants qui doivent emporter de vous dans la vie le souvenir ineffaçable d'une agonie en forme d'image d'Épinal. Elle nous fit mettre à genoux, se donna beaucoup de peine pour soulever la main droite et, à tour de rôle, nous la posa sur le front, en commençant par mon frère, l'aîné.

– Que Dieu vous garde, mes enfants !

Ce fut tout. Il ne fallait pas trop présumer de ses forces. Nous nous retirâmes à reculons, comme devant un roi. Et, aujourd'hui, à plus de vingt ans de distance, encore remué jusqu'au fond du cœur, je persiste à croire que cet hommage lui était dû. Grand-mère !... Ah ! certes, elle n'avait pas le profil populaire de l'emploi, ni le baiser facile, ni le bonbon à la main. Mais jamais je n'ai entendu sonner de toux plus sincère, quand son émotion se grattait la gorge pour ne pas faiblir devant nos effusions. Jamais je n'ai revu ce port de tête inflexible, mais tout de suite cassé à l'annonce d'un 37° 5. Grand-mère, avec son chignon blanc mordu d'écaille, elle aura été pour nous l'inconnue dont on ne parlait point, bien qu'on priât officiellement pour elle deux fois par jour, elle aura été et restera la *précédente*, l'ennemie parfaite comme une légende, à qui l'on ne peut rien reprocher ni rien soustraire, même pas, et surtout pas, sa mort. »

Hervé Bazin,
Vipère au poing,
© Grasset

Enfance

L'enfance de Nathalie Sarraute se partage entre son père qui vit à Paris et sa mère qui vit à l'étranger : les parents sont divorcés et les rares séjours en France de cette grand-mère lointaine ont laissé des souvenirs indélébiles dans la mémoire de l'enfant.

« Depuis quelque temps en sortant de classe, à quatre heures, je renonce à lambiner dans la rue, à bavarder, à jouer à la marelle, j'ai envie de rentrer tout de suite, je sais qu'elle a entendu sonner la cloche de l'école et qu'elle m'attend... je ne file plus droit dans ma chambre en passant par le couloir, je vais d'abord dans sa chambre à elle, qui donne sur le vestibule, je cours vers elle, je l'embrasse, je la serre dans mes bras, je l'appelle "babouchka" en russe, et en français je l'appelle "grand-mère", c'est elle qui l'a voulu, bien qu'elle soit la mère de Véra.

Mais il ne peut pas exister de vraie grand-mère qui me convienne, qui me plaise davantage. Elle n'a pourtant pas grand-chose dans son aspect de ce qui rend exquises les grand-mères décrites dans les livres...

Je pose mon cartable et je vais me laver les mains dans le cabinet de toilette qui sépare nos chambres et puis nous goûtons, elle fait du thé sur un petit réchaud et elle sort de son armoire un pot de confiture de carottes qu'elle a préparée suivant sa recette et que nous sommes seules, elle et moi, à apprécier... je lui raconte tout ce qui s'est passé à l'école et elle le rend intéressant, amusant, par sa façon de l'écouter... C'est avec elle que j'apprends les leçons les plus rebutantes... avec elle, même celles de géographie ont du charme, je n'ai plus besoin de mes cocottes en papier. Je ne les ai montrées qu'à elle, et une fois je leur ai fait la classe devant elle, je l'ai fait rire...

Nous rions beaucoup toutes les deux, surtout quand elle me lit des comédies... *Le Malade imaginaire*...ou *Le Revizor*... elle lit très bien, elle rit parfois tellement qu'elle est forcée de s'arrêter, et moi je me tords littéralement, couchée à ses pieds sur le tapis. »

Nathalie Sarraute,
Enfance,
© Gallimard

Oma

Oma, la grand-mère de Kalle, n'est pas n'importe qui ; lorsque son petit-fils viendra s'installer chez elle, elle saura le prendre en main. Mais elle l'emmènera aussi en voyage et commencera, grâce à lui, à s'intéresser au football.

« A soixante-sept ans, prétendent les gens, on est vraiment très âgé. Oma n'était pas d'accord. Comme beaucoup de vieilles gens, elle disait que l'âge n'est pas une question d'années. On peut être vieux et se sentir jeune. Oma se sentait plutôt jeune. Elle disait aussi : "Physiquement, je suis une vieille dame, mais j'ai le cœur d'une jeune fille." Et ceux qui la connaissaient bien savaient que c'était vrai. Oma n'avait pas beaucoup d'argent. Parfois, elle se plaignait de la modique retraite que lui avait laissée son mari, qui n'avait jamais été très riche non plus. Mais elle préférait rire plutôt que se plaindre. Elle savait d'ailleurs très bien s'arranger. Son appartement, à Munich, était tout petit et presque aussi vieux qu'elle. (...) D'une façon générale, elle aimait parler toute seule ou s'adresser aux objets qui l'entouraient. Les gens qui ne la connaissaient pas devaient s'y habituer. En plein milieu d'une conversation, elle se mettait parfois à parler toute seule. Quand les gens la regardaient, étonnés, elle secouait simplement la tête, comme s'il ne s'était rien passé.

Tout le monde l'appelait Oma, même les voisins, le boulanger du coin et les gosses de la cour, qui la taquinaient souvent mais, au fond, l'aimaient bien et l'aidaient à monter son sac à provisions au cinquième étage. Dans l'immeuble où vivait Oma, il n'y avait pas d'ascenseur. "Nous ne sommes pas des princes, nous", avait-elle coutume de dire quand elle s'arrêtait au troisième étage, tout essoufflée. Sur sa porte, il y avait un carton sur lequel elle avait écrit en lettres calligraphiées : "Madame Erna Bittel." Son fils lui avait demandé une fois pourquoi elle mettait "Madame".

– Que tu es bête ! lui avait-elle répondu. Moi, je veux qu'on me dise madame. Depuis qu'Otto est mort, les gens pourraient croire que je suis une vieille fille. Et ça n'est pas vrai. »

Peter Härtling
Oma,
traduction d'Antoine Berman,
© Bordas

Les Enfants Tillerman

A la recherche d'un foyer, quatre enfants décident de se rendre chez leur grand-mère, qui ignore leur existence. Mais le charme des enfants la décidera à les garder.

« Les enfants la suivirent dans la boutique. Sammy affirma qu'il était assez grand pour porter un sac, mais il réussit à peine à le soulever, aussi Millie fractionna-t-elle son contenu en deux sacs, un pour Maybeth et un pour lui. Elle mourait de curiosité.

– Au fait, Millie, dit enfin leur grand-mère, je ne crois pas que tu connaisses mes petits-enfants. (Elle les présenta l'un après l'autre.) C'est la nichée de Liza. Ils sont chez moi pour une quinzaine.

Et elle les poussa dehors sans laisser à Millie le temps de poser d'autres questions. Ils descendirent vers le quai le long de la rue écrasée de soleil. Dicey monta dans le bateau la première, et James lui tendit les sacs.

Sammy avait l'air soucieux.

– Si tu es notre grand-mère..., se lança-t-il enfin. Je veux dire, si tu dis que tu l'es... Parce qu'on le savait tous, d'accord, seulement tu ne l'as jamais dit... Comment on va t'appeler, maintenant ? (...)

– Tu peux m'appeler Gram, si tu veux, répondit la vieille femme.

– Gram, répéta Sammy, comme pour juger de l'effet produit.

Il s'éloigna de quelques mètres en courant, fit volte-face et lança plus fort :

– Ohé, Gram ? (Déjà il revenait.) Comment ça va, Gram ?

– Ça va, Sammy, dit-elle simplement. »

Cynthia Voigt
Les Enfants Tillerman,
traduction de Rose-Marie Vassalo,
© Flammarion

4
SOLUTIONS DES JEUX

Êtes-vous sorcier ?
(p. 119)

Si vous obtenez une majorité de △ **:** vous avez indéniablement un penchant pour la sorcellerie, mais plutôt par goût des transformations spectaculaires que par réelle croyance en votre pouvoir sur les autres.

Si vous obtenez une majorité de □ **:** le métier de sorcier ne vous déplairait pas mais vous l'exerceriez plutôt dans le sens de la médecine. Pour vous, détenir des pouvoirs surnaturels ne se conçoit que s'ils ont des effets bénéfiques.

Si vous obtenez une majorité de ○ **:** votre attirance pour la sorcellerie est quelque peu mêlée de crainte. Vous seriez même parfois tenté de condamner ces pratiques mystérieuses dont vous redoutez les dangers.

Quinze questions pour commencer
(p. 120)

1 : A (p. 11) - 2 : B (p. 12) - 3 : A (p. 12) - 4 : B (p. 19) - 5 : C (p. 15) - 6 : C (p. 23) - 7 : A (p. 17) - 8 : B (p. 25) - 9 : A (p. 32) - 10 : B (p. 24) - 11 : B (p. 27) - 12 : A (p. 28) - 13 : B (p. 30) - 14 : C (p. 14) - 15 : B (p. 45)

Si vous obtenez de 11 à 15 bonnes réponses : votre mémoire est telle que l'on pourrait sans doute vous demander de faire les courses pour la semaine sans vous donner de liste. Vous êtes quelqu'un de précieux.

Si vous obtenez de 6 à 10 bonnes réponses : vous avez retenu l'essentiel pour pouvoir vite lire la suite et savoir la fin au plus tôt. Vous péchez plus par impatience que par réel manque de mémoire.

Si vous obtenez moins de 6 bonnes réponses : vous avez bien retenu l'idée de Georges, vous vous souvenez qu'il a une grand-mère, mais de quoi sera faite la potion, de quoi se régale Grandma, c'est déjà trop vous demander et c'est dommage pour vous : si vous aviez fait plus attention, vous auriez bien ri.

La peinture marron
(p. 124)

A : une peur bleue - B : blanc comme un linge - C : vert de peur - D : rouge de colère - E : rire jaune - F : noire de monde - G : grise mine - H : à la brune

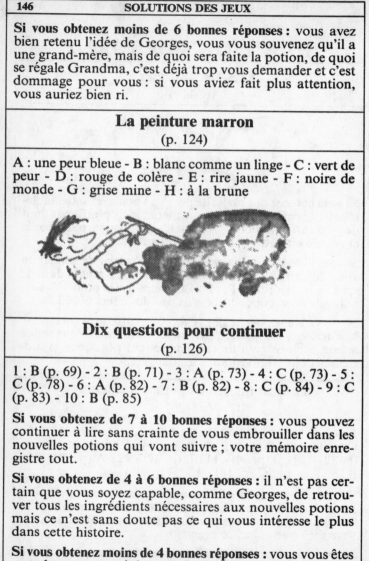

Dix questions pour continuer
(p. 126)

1 : B (p. 69) - 2 : B (p. 71) - 3 : A (p. 73) - 4 : C (p. 73) - 5 : C (p. 78) - 6 : A (p. 82) - 7 : B (p. 82) - 8 : C (p. 84) - 9 : C (p. 83) - 10 : B (p. 85)

Si vous obtenez de 7 à 10 bonnes réponses : vous pouvez continuer à lire sans crainte de vous embrouiller dans les nouvelles potions qui vont suivre ; votre mémoire enregistre tout.

Si vous obtenez de 4 à 6 bonnes réponses : il n'est pas certain que vous soyez capable, comme Georges, de retrouver tous les ingrédients nécessaires aux nouvelles potions mais ce n'est sans doute pas ce qui vous intéresse le plus dans cette histoire.

Si vous obtenez moins de 4 bonnes réponses : vous vous êtes sans doute contenté de regarder les illustrations. Pourtant vous avez sûrement passé l'âge où l'on ne s'arrête qu'aux images.

Vingt questions pour conclure
(p. 130)

1 : C (p. 11) - 2 : B (p. 15) - 3 : C (p. 96) - 4 : B (p. 23) - 5 :
B - 6 : B (p. 81) - 7 : C (p. 35) - 8 : C (p. 45) - 9 : B (p. 51) -
10 : B (p. 52) - 11 : A (p. 18) - 12 : C (p. 65) - 13 : A
(p. 71) - 14 : A (p. 73) - 15 : A (p. 80) - 16 : B (p. 84) - 17 :
A (p. 94) - 18 : A (p. 43) - 19 : A (p. 104) - 20 : C (p. 116)

Si vous obtenez de 15 à 20 bonnes réponses : vous avez bien
lu l'histoire de Georges Bouillon et vous connaissez la
recette de la potion magique presque par cœur. Bravo !

Si vous obtenez de 10 à 14 bonnes réponses : vous avez cor-
rectement retenu l'histoire et vous pourriez la raconter
mais en omettant quelques détails. Il vous suffit de revenir
sur quelques pages pour réparer vos erreurs.

Si vous obtenez de 5 à 9 bonnes réponses : vous n'avez pas
beaucoup apprécié ce conte ou alors votre mémoire vous
a trahi. Relisez les passages qui vous ont échappé et
revoyez le plan général en vous reportant aux titres des
chapitres.

Si vous obtenez moins de 5 bonnes réponses : par manque
d'attention ou par manque d'intérêt, vous n'avez pas bien
lu ce livre. Vous y prendrez peut-être goût une autre fois,
plus tard ou jamais. Quelle importance ? L'essentiel est de
vous plonger au plus vite dans un autre livre.

Le parcours de Georges
(p. 132)

1. Nourriture pour canaris : buanderie - 2. Parfum « Fleur
de navet » : chambre à coucher - 3. Rouge à lèvres : chambre à coucher - 4. Brilladentine : salle de bains - 5. Insecticide pour chiens : buanderie

Sans œufs, sans « e », sans eux
(p. 136)

Dans l'ordre : subir - main - puis - plan - bouillir - dix -
produits - chaudron - ajouta - potion - flacon - offrit -
toussa - grandit - fin - vit - toit

Potion ou lotion ?

(p. 137)

1 : flacon - 2 : cirage - 3 : bidon - 4 : marron - 5 : paquet -
6 : tube de rouge à lèvres - 7 : bombe de mousse à raser -
8 : pot de crème - 9 : pot de moutarde - 10 : poudre contre
les insectes - 11 : un pitre - 12 : pourriture pour panaris -
13 : moudre planche - 14 : ternis à oncles - 15 : divers
lipides.

Cherchez l'intrus

(p. 138)

1. *Corbeau* n'est pas le nom d'un petit d'animal
2. *Papillonne* n'est pas la femelle du papillon
3. *Belette* n'est pas un oiseau
4. *Blafard* n'est pas un animal
5. *Ourson* est le seul de la série qui désigne un petit
d'animal

Retrouvez les chefs-d'œuvre de **Roald Dahl**

dans la collection FOLIO **JUNIOR**

28/6/23

Finding Cassie

ANNA JACOBS

Allison & Busby Limited
11 Wardour Mews
London W1F 8AN
allisonandbusby.com

First published in Great Britain by Allison & Busby in 2020.
This paperback edition published by Allison & Busby in 2020.

A CIP catalogue record for this book is available from
the British Library.

10 9 8 7 6 5 4 3 2 1

ISBN 978-0-7490-2390-4

Typeset in 11/16 pt Sabon LT Pro by
Allison & Busby Ltd

The paper used for this Allison & Busby publication
has been produced from trees that have been legally sourced
from well-managed and credibly certified forests.

Printed and bound by
CPI Group (UK) Ltd, Croydon, CR0 4YY

Chapter One

Cassandra Bennington held out the mic so that the woman she was interviewing could give her answer. Then a deafening noise tore the world apart and everything went into slow motion as darkness swallowed her.

When she recovered consciousness, she was in an ambulance that was moving fast with its siren blaring.

A man said, 'She's coming to.' A blurry figure leant closer. 'You've been hurt but not badly, and you're on your way to hospital.'

She tried to understand how she'd got hurt but couldn't make sense of it. 'What happened? Was it – heart attack?'

When he didn't answer, she made a huge effort to bring him into focus. 'Please. Tell me.'

'Someone planted a bomb in the building you were

in. It went off and wreaked havoc. You were lucky you weren't closer to it.'

She stared up at him in shock. 'Why would anyone do that? It was only a block of flats.'

'Who knows why, love? We just pick up the pieces as best we can.'

The ambulance turned sharply to the left and came to a halt.

'We're at the hospital now. Let's get you to a doctor and make sure you're all right. Worry about other things later. You're alive and in one piece. That's what matters.' He patted her hand and started to move away.

'Wait!'

He half turned.

'What about the woman I was interviewing?'

'They were getting someone else out from nearby as we left. I'm not sure who, but if you survived, she probably did too.'

The woman had been so young – and very pregnant.

As they slid her out of the ambulance and jolted her into the brightly lit building, Cassie heard the paramedic say something in a low voice, then she heard the vehicle drive away, siren blaring again. She was wheeled into a cubicle in the casualty department and someone drew flimsy curtains on a hostile world.

She felt lethargic, utterly boneless, let them do what they wanted. She tried to answer their questions, not sure she was making much sense. She didn't want to talk, wanted to hide in some deep, dark cave and lie quietly, but they kept prodding her and moving her about.

After they'd made sure no bones were broken, they tended to a gash on her shoulder that needed holding together with butterfly strips, then dealt with a few minor scratches and scrapes.

'We're going to need all our beds for the serious cases, so you can go home in an hour's time – well, you can if someone comes to fetch you and promises to keep an eye on you tonight. Give the attendant your details when she comes round and tell her who to call.'

'Can I ask about the woman I was with?'

'Look, love—'

'She was pregnant. I can't bear to think of her being killed.' Cassie gave the woman's name and added, 'Please.'

'I'll have a quick look, see if she's been brought in.'

A couple of minutes later, the nurse returned. 'She's all right, just minor injuries. Is she a friend of yours?'

'No. I was interviewing her.'

He stared at her and said, 'Oh my goodness! You're Cassandra Benn, aren't you?'

'Yes. But please can you use my full surname on your records. I try to keep my private life out of the limelight as much as possible.'

'I won't tell anyone else here who you are, if that's what you want, but some of them will probably recognise you. I've seen you on TV. You do brilliant interviews, really incisive.'

'Thank you. Did they bring my backpack in with me?

It's dark blue, only a small one. It's got a big white P painted on the back.'

'There's a pile of possessions been brought in with the injured and dumped in reception. I'll go and have a quick check.'

To her shuddering relief, someone had brought her backpack to the hospital, though she had to identify its contents before the nurse would give it to her. She sighed in relief as he stood it beside the bed because she'd have been lost without it. It was dusty but when she looked inside, the contents seemed untouched.

'Now you've got your own phone, can you call a friend to pick you up, Ms Bennington, and can you—' Yet another ambulance siren sounded outside. 'Sorry. I have to go. Please try to rest.' The nurse hurried away.

How many people had been hurt, for heaven's sake? she wondered. The ambulances seemed to be coming in one after the other.

Someone outside the entrance shouted for a crash team to come at once and she shuddered. She'd never been quite so close to being killed before, and mentally blessed whatever fate or blind chance had saved her. She should be out there reporting the incident, but couldn't summon up the strength, just couldn't do it. Not this time.

For a while, not wanting to take the nurses away from people whose injuries were worse than hers, she tried to obey orders and rest, she really did. But she couldn't manage it lying on such an uncomfortable, shelf-like bed with all that bustle and noise just the other side of a flimsy curtain.

At least she was recovering, could feel her mind slowly coming back into clearer focus. Only, that was a double-edged sword because she had nothing to do with her thoughts except worry.

She noticed her watch on a stand next to the bed and put it on. It had a big, clear dial and seemed to be working still. It ought to be. It had been expensive, not bought to be pretty but because the brand was famed for the accuracy and toughness of its watches.

A quarter of an hour crawled slowly past, only two or three minutes gone by each time she looked. By then she felt so frustrated she swung round on the narrow bed and sat upright on the edge, swinging her feet.

That soon palled and she stood up tentatively, relieved not to feel dizzy. Staying here was silly. She was all right now, should get out of their way.

She winced as a man screamed hoarsely nearby.

A woman stumbled past her cubicle, weeping. Cassie could only see her feet, but she could hear the anguish in the tears all too clearly.

She couldn't do this any longer. Dragging off the gown, she put her outer clothes on again, grimacing at the mess they were in. It felt better to be fully covered on this chilly summer day, as if she'd taken control of herself again.

She sat down and waited, but ten more minutes crawled past and no one came to see her. 'Oh, to hell with it!' She stood up and grabbed the backpack, pushing aside the curtain at the front of her cubicle.

As she was moving through the reception area the same nurse spotted her and hurried across. 'You haven't been discharged yet, Ms Bennington. Please go and lie down again. Doctor will come back to you as soon as she can. She needs to check that you're fit to leave.'

'I feel a lot better, honestly. I'd rather go home now. I can't rest here.'

'Have you asked a friend to pick you up?'

'No. I'll catch a taxi.' It was how she mostly got about in London.

'You should—Oh, just a minute. Stay there.' He turned away to help with a woman who had walked into the busy area cradling her arm as if it hurt, followed by a man carrying a small child with a bloody leg.

Cassie took the opportunity to hurry towards the exit. She was in luck. A taxi was just dropping someone off and the driver was happy to take another fare.

She felt guilty for treating the hospital staff like that, but she had to get home, simply had to. She needed peace and quiet to recover.

She had never expected to be personally involved in a serious accident, let alone a terrorist incident even though she'd faced all sorts of risky interview situations. Did anyone expect such lunatic behaviour to touch their lives? Not unless they were in a combat zone.

As she sat in the taxi, it upset her that she hadn't known who to call for help. She had plenty of acquaintances but who could she consider a close enough friend to come to her aid? No one these days. And that upset her.

Since she and Brett had split up, she seemed to have lost contact with so many people. Or they'd lost contact with her. She'd been working hard, burying her upset about him leaving her by concentrating on other people's stories.

The taxi driver opened the rear door and it was a few moments before she realised they'd arrived.

'You all right, love?'

'Yes. Thanks.' She got out her credit card and paid him.

Once inside the house, she closed the front door and leant against it, whimpering because she hadn't realised that she wouldn't feel safe even here.

Another thing she hadn't expected.

It took her a few minutes to decide to go to bed. They'd told her to rest, hadn't they? She'd feel better if she did that – surely she would?

It took her a while to get to sleep but she welcomed the drowsiness.

She jerked awake a few hours later as someone rang her doorbell, then hammered on the front door. It was dark outside now and the street light shining into her bedroom made everything look surreal. By the time she'd remembered why she was feeling so groggy, the front door had opened and the person had come in.

She tensed and looked for something to protect herself with, then heard Brett call her name and relaxed.

The last person she wanted to see her like this was her ex.

He came upstairs calling her name again and stopped in the doorway of her bedroom, switching on the light.

She shaded her eyes against the glare and wished he'd stop staring.

'Thank goodness you're safe, Cassie!'

She wasn't ready to forgive him. 'Who told you to come barging in?'

'It was on the news.'

'What was?'

'The bombing. They said you were amongst the injured.'

'Oh.' Her stomach lurched at the memory of how helpless and bewildered she'd felt lying in the hospital – how out of touch, too.

'I wouldn't have walked in like that, Cassie, but I was worried sick about you. The nurse at the hospital said you'd discharged yourself, so I rang round our friends but no one had heard from you. And they hadn't heard from you for a while.'

'No. I've been . . . busy.' She felt at a disadvantage sitting on the edge of the bed, so got up, wincing as her bruised and battered body protested.

He came across to steady her and she let him, which wasn't like her.

He walked down the stairs in front of her, and to make matters worse she was glad when he did that, because she felt distinctly wobbly.

'Why don't you sit in your recliner chair with your feet up while I make you some coffee?'

'Good idea. Thanks.' She should have kicked him out and got her key back from him but she felt – fragile. And she'd kill for a coffee.

The hot drink was soothing and after she'd had a few mouthfuls, she managed to pull herself together enough to ask him what they'd said on the news. 'Do they know who did this cruel, stupid thing?'

'They didn't on the one I saw. Why don't I switch on the TV now? They've got regular updates on the news channel. Half the block of flats was destroyed apparently and several people were killed. You're lucky to be alive.'

She hesitated, suddenly reluctant to see the incident, for some weird reason.

He looked at her, frowning. 'You're in shock, I think, Cassie. I've never seen you so pale.' He placed his fingers lightly on her forehead before adding, 'And your skin's clammy.'

She considered this, feeling distant from everything, as if she were looking down at herself from the ceiling, then realised he was waiting for an answer so she nodded. 'I guess I am. Bound to be, I suppose.'

'I'd better stay with you for the rest of the night.'

'You're not getting back into my bed. We're not together in any way now.'

He gave one of his wry smiles. 'No. You made that plain when you chucked my things out of the door. When was that? Just over a year ago.'

'I can't think why you came. Does your new partner know?'

'Yes. And approves. I still care about you, Cassie. We were together for four years, after all. You'd come to help me if I'd been caught up in a terrorist incident.'

She was unable to deny that so just shrugged, then winced as her shoulder hurt.

His voice was suddenly sharp. 'What's wrong?'

'Something sliced into my shoulder. It hurt me when I moved it.' She didn't know what to say, didn't want to admit that she'd welcome his presence tonight. 'Um, thanks for coming. That was – kind.'

'Look, I can sleep down here on the sofa unless you've got a spare bed.'

She shook her head. She'd been frenetically busy lately, hadn't bothered to buy spare furniture after they broke up. She only did the most essential shopping these days, ate out mostly. Lots going on in the big, wide world. *Cassandra Benn Reporting* was getting high ratings. Her career had always been important.

Oh dear, he'd said something else and was waiting for her to answer. 'Sorry. Run that past me again.'

'You really shouldn't be alone tonight, Cassie. You should see how pale and bruised your face is. In fact, whatever you say, I am *not* leaving you on your own here. Surely we can meet as friends now?'

She could have stood up and looked at herself in the mirror over the fireplace only she didn't want to move. 'All right, stay. Um, I am grateful.'

He brought a cup of coffee for himself and sat down on the nearby sofa. 'Want to talk about it?'

She considered this, her thoughts still wheeling round in slow motion. 'Nothing to talk about. Loud noise, an explosion threw me across the room and knocked me out.' She rubbed the sore spot on the back of her head. 'Next thing I knew I was in an ambulance. I've got those – what do you call 'em? – butterfly plasters on my shoulder. They think something with a sharp edge hit me, or I hit it, and I got a bit of a cut. And . . . there's a lot of bruising. Nothing serious, let alone life-threatening. End of story.'

'Shall I switch on the TV, then, see what's happening?'

'Yes.' She turned towards the screen, forcing herself to watch as the story rolled out, wincing at the images of the block of flats half destroyed, cars scattered like a careless child's toys, people clustering together, hugging one another, weeping. 'I ought to be there, reporting on it.'

'Hell no. This time you should definitely leave that to someone else.'

'Mmm. I am a bit – tired.' She looked down at her empty mug. 'Any more coffee?'

'When did you last eat? Shall I make you a sandwich or something as well?'

'OK.'

He vanished round the corner into the kitchen area. 'You've certainly let things go here. The bread's mouldy and there's nothing I'd dare eat in the fridge, not much in the freezer, either. I'll nip to the deli.'

'Don't bother. There's cereal and milk. That'll do.'

'Your favourite standby. I'm sure I can find them. It's not the biggest of kitchens.'

But when he gave her the bowl of cereal, she took one spoonful, had trouble forcing it down her throat and pushed the rest away.

'I think I'll go back to bed.'

He insisted on coming up with her to make sure she didn't fall because she was still dizzy. She hated having to depend on other people.

'I'll be downstairs if you need me.'

'Are you sure Tina won't mind?'

'I've rung her. She agrees with me that you shouldn't be left alone.'

She waved one hand. 'Make yourself at home, then, why don't you? But you're wasting your time. I don't need a nanny.'

'I'm still staying.'

She could hear the old, familiar stubborn tone in his voice, so didn't even try to answer.

She'd missed him. They'd been good friends once, until she'd become too obsessed with her job. It was no wonder he'd turned elsewhere for company. He was the sort of person who needed the company of other people.

It was a long time before she got to sleep again but she didn't leave her bedroom, didn't want Brett to see how disorientated she was. Her thoughts were still skittering to and fro, one minute back to the scenes on TV, then reliving the wild ambulance ride, and even focusing on Brett sometimes.

He was just as attractive as ever, damn him. She missed him. He'd been a better partner than she had, was still being kind to her.

Eventually everything began to go blurry and she gave in to the urge to let go.

In the morning Cassie woke with a start as something banged downstairs, setting her heart pounding. Then she realised it was only a cupboard door. Brett must have got up. She stayed in bed, hearing him go out and come back a few minutes later. Probably been to buy supplies from the nearby deli. He was a hearty breakfast eater.

Reluctantly she got out of bed. If she didn't, he might call a doctor.

Her bare feet made no sound on the stairs and he jumped when she said, 'Good morning.'

He swung round, studying her face. 'You still look pale.'

She shrugged, then wished she hadn't because that hurt her shoulder.

'Come and have some breakfast.'

She still didn't care about food, but if she didn't eat something he'd make a fuss and it seemed easier to do what he said. She accepted a pot of yoghurt, ate half a spoonful, then another and suddenly discovered she was hungry after all.

'That's better,' he said quietly. 'Piece of toast? I got your favourite black cherry jam.'

'Yes, please.'

When he was sitting opposite her, also eating toast, she asked, 'How are your kids?'

'They've both flown the nest now. Kind of you to ask, considering they always treated you as an interloper.'

She shrugged. 'Teenagers can be like that. What about your parents? I did get on with them OK.'

He looked sad. 'They're showing their age, I'm afraid. Dad's got dementia and it's come on so quickly they've had to move him into a care home.'

'Oh no! I'm so sorry. Give your mother my best wishes next time you see her. She was always kind to me.'

They ate in silence till the toast was finished.

'Want anything else?' he asked.

She saw him looking at the clock. 'No, thanks. I'll be all right now, Brett, honest I will. You need to get to work.'

'You'll rest today?'

'Yes. And um, thanks for coming.'

'I'll pop in after work and bring you some groceries and takeaway.'

'You don't need to. I can go out and get some myself.'

'I'm doing it and Tina will agree. Surely you don't want to go out shopping and have the press following you around? There are a couple of journos hovering outside now. They tried to stop me and ask about you.'

She didn't reply, just flung her hands up in an 'I give in' gesture. 'Tell Tina thanks for lending you to me, then.'

When he'd gone the silence seemed threatening, and she found herself listening for footsteps outside the house. It was semi-detached, in an area full of commuters and the street was mostly deserted in the daytime. People could approach it without anyone noticing.

Suddenly worried that the outer doors might be unlocked, she rushed to check the front door then the back, leaning against the latter in shuddering relief when she found that it was locked and all the downstairs windows were, too.

Only, she still didn't feel safe.

She put the telly on and wished she hadn't, but couldn't bring herself to turn it off again in case she missed something important. Eleven people had been killed in that explosion – eleven! – and several more had been seriously injured, with over twenty suffering minor injuries, herself included, she supposed. The block of flats was half its former size with ragged edges and shattered windows even where the walls were still standing. The remaining occupants had been evacuated and relocated.

She'd definitely been lucky.

Why didn't she feel lucky, then?

Why didn't she feel anything much at all? Except fear.

Chapter Two

Hal Kennedy opened the letter informing him officially that his new house in the Penny Lake Leisure Village – what a mouthful for an address! – was finished and ready for his inspection. Which was no surprise because Molly Santiago had rung him yesterday to let him know unofficially. She had been very good throughout the build at keeping in touch about how the house was progressing.

He read the letter carefully then looked at his schedule for this coming week because he needed to make an appointment to go over the house with her for the snagging. He'd already researched snagging surveys online and drawn up a checklist, but didn't see the need to hire a professional surveyor. Not only did he trust his own ability to see clearly, but he trusted the Santiagos, whose development it was.

To them, this leisure village was clearly more than just a way to earn money – well, Hal had researched Euan's background before he even signed up for a house. He'd found that Euan was a multi-millionaire and that this was a semi-retirement project. The couple believed that this sort of housing development for older people filled a gap in the market, offering somewhere with a sense of community as well as a high standard of housing.

So many retirement developments featured nothing but tiny flats and he certainly didn't want to live in one of those. It'd be like living in a cupboard and he'd have to get rid of most of his possessions. But he did want, no, make that he would *need* to meet people, make friends, develop new networks.

He'd popped in to see his new house last week on the way back from Bristol, just casually, and Molly had been most welcoming, even though she needn't have let him into it yet. He'd been delighted with how his house was looking. He'd found a few minor details that needed dealing with and pointed them out to her, but mainly the interior had been nicely done and properly finished.

He was looking forward to moving out of this flat, luxurious though it was, because it was on a busy London street and he craved more peaceful surroundings. He'd have wound up his few remaining projects at work by the end of the following week. That'd be a relief, stage two of his big retirement plan completed, leading to stage three, the final one, actually moving into his new house.

He looked round and grimaced. 'Shabby' was the kindest thing you could say about his furnishings. He'd have to buy some new pieces for his house. Debbie had taken most of the good stuff with her when she moved out of here. Well, she'd brought them with her when she moved in, some lovely antiques, so fair enough for her to keep them.

How long ago was it since she'd left? Three, four years? It seemed like another life, given what had happened to him in the meantime.

He wasn't wasting his energy on vain regrets about the break-up, though he'd realised afterwards that they'd both been at fault, too focused on work. It wasn't his primary focus now. Cancer certainly put everything into perspective.

Hal paused, head on one side, surprised when he realised how long ago it had happened. He began pacing up and down again as he worked it out more exactly. Seven years ago they'd started living together and three and a half years ago they'd split up.

They'd managed the separation amicably, thank goodness, more amicably than it had been with his wife, all those years ago. Debbie was younger than him and was still an eager beaver public defence lawyer and he was . . . what? A jaded corporate lawyer of fifty-six, just recovering from a serious cancer scare and thankful these days for every breath he took.

They'd both seen the mess some couples got into when they parted company and how much it could cost both financially and emotionally to make the necessary arrangements if they quarrelled about details, so they'd agreed on the terms of their own break-up. Debbie had been fair, he had to give her that. He hoped he'd been fair too. Probably had because he'd never cared as much as she had about mere objects. He was more into books.

He passed a mirror and stopped to stare at himself in it, wincing. It wasn't the first time he'd been surprised at how old he was starting to look. Hair receding but still covering most of his skull, thank goodness, and all steel-grey now.

Distinguished, he told himself firmly. Inevitable to be starting to show your age, though fifty-six wasn't all that old. Body a little overweight, not much, but he really should get fitter.

The main trouble was he didn't feel old inside his head. Did you ever? So he had to find a new path in life, maybe volunteering with some charity or other. Once he'd stopped work and moved house, he intended to do some of the things he'd planned when he was younger, before he'd climbed aboard the legal treadmill and found out just how demanding it was.

When was the last time he'd done any sketching or painting? He might not be Michelangelo, but he'd enjoyed it. He hadn't gone for long walks in the countryside, either. As for learning to play golf, he hadn't even got as far as buying any clubs.

How quickly the years passed!

He'd had a health warning, so as far as he was concerned, he wasn't putting off anything from now on. *Carpe diem*. Seize the day. He'd seize every single moment he had left.

If he had to sum up his life since he left university and entered what people laughingly called 'the real world', what would he say? Continuously employed, one failed marriage and simultaneously failed attempt at gracious living in the suburbs, a grown-up son he hardly ever saw, one failed long-term relationship, an extremely successful career financially – and one serious health scare.

Who would miss him if he dropped dead tomorrow, though? He'd turned into rather a loner since Debbie left. Oh hell! He was getting into stupid territory. If he went on at this rate, he'd be seeing a shrink next and letting some stranger into his head to guide him into retirement as the human resources officer at work had suggested.

No way was he doing that! Self-help for coping with the coming changes was more acceptable to him, so he'd made a start by going online and researching 'mid-life crisis'. And had found that for most of the articles, he was getting a bit past the preparations stage and hadn't done any of the specified during-your-fifties planning until recently.

One sentence from his online research had stayed with him: 'Accept that you're no longer young and that no one is immortal. Get on with living.' That was a bit depressing but accurate. One of his colleagues had dropped dead last year and Hal suspected the shock of that had played a big part in his decision to retire, though not as big a part as the cancer.

But he also found 'Sixty is the new forty' repeated here and there online. Yes, that was a better motto, even if it did sound utterly corny. People generally did live longer these days. It wasn't like his parents' world. He could have another thirty years of active life left to him.

He grew impatient with himself. Why was he still worrying about that? He'd got it mostly covered, was financially secure and taking positive steps. Until he moved physically to Wiltshire and his new home he couldn't really see anything to do that he wasn't already doing.

'So just get on with it,' he muttered.

The next thing on his list was to chuck things out and pack what he wanted to take. Half the furniture was going for a start. That job was scheduled for next week.

He checked his diary and phoned Molly Santiago at the leisure village, arranging to go round his new home on the following Thursday afternoon. He was really looking forward to it.

When he switched on the news channel, he was shocked to hear of a terrorist bombing attack on a block of flats only a couple of miles away.

He changed channels after a few moments. He was sorry for the poor sods who'd been murdered, but it was nothing to do with him.

Hopefully there wouldn't be as much likelihood of an attack on a place out in the middle of the countryside.

Chapter Three

Mid-morning on the day after the explosion, the phone rang. Cassie checked who it was. Her boss. She hesitated, then answered. After all, Terry couldn't see her hand trembling, could he?

'Cassie, I heard about your narrow escape. Are you all right?'

'Um, a bit shaken up.'

'Good, good.'

What was good about that? she wondered.

'Steve's doing well with taking over your next programme. He's got it almost ready to go to air. How about you come into the studio this morning – just briefly, we don't want to stress you too much – and let him interview you about what it was like to be caught in a terrorist attack? If anyone can bring it to life for the viewers, you can.'

She couldn't speak, had begun to shake from head to toe at the mere thought of doing that.

'Cassie?'

'No. I – can't.'

'You're not all right, are you? Are you injured?' He sounded almost eager.

She fought for control of her voice. 'Only s-superficially. I need a few days' R&R to, um, put things into perspective. I'll be in touch next week.'

She put the phone down, then disconnected the whole system. Couldn't face any more calls, no matter who it was.

The trouble was, after that she couldn't think what to do with herself. She was so used to being non-stop busy. In the end she sat in front of the TV and watched it – well, she watched it now and then. The rest of the time her thoughts drifted and fluttered like falling leaves in autumn. She couldn't seem to focus on anything.

She snapped to attention, however, when her own programme came on mid-afternoon, not surprised to see that they'd found someone else for Steve to interview about the terrorist incident. He pushed too hard, he always did, and the poor woman fell to pieces on screen.

Cassie knew she'd have fallen to pieces too if she'd been stupid enough to let herself be interviewed.

She suddenly realised how she'd pushed other trauma survivors in interviews – not as hard as Steve had done but still too hard if they'd felt half as fragile as she did now. *Cassandra Benn always gets the story.* Guilt ran through her.

They turned the cameras away from the weeping woman, presumably to remove her, and brought in a psychologist to talk to Steve about the impact on survivors and what they should do to cope.

She listened carefully to the man's neat little list of the main effects. What he said made sense. She was feeling exactly as he'd said. But she could have told him a few more details about the impact on a person as well, details which mattered to an individual, not dry academic facts.

Oh damn, now he was talking about the deeper impacts on your whole life and its choices that might become evident later. Tears came into her eyes as she listened carefully.

That was never going to happen, not to her, no way. She'd always prided herself on not giving in to adversity.

Annoyed with herself for such a weakness and suddenly furious all over again at the evil sods who'd done this to her, she nonetheless watched the whole segment, then she went into the kitchen and cleared it up thoroughly. And about time too. She was getting her act together, doing something useful. Starting small.

What she needed was a few days' rest and she'd be OK. Definitely. She wasn't going to see any shrinks, thank you very much, or take more than a few days off work.

When someone knocked on her front door, she crept round to peep through the living-room window and didn't answer, because she could see that it was a complete stranger.

She had to move quickly out of sight because the person came round the house tramping right through her front garden to peer through the living-room window. The cheek of it!

When the stranger went away, she caught sight of herself in a mirror and was horrified at how haggard she looked. She'd definitely do something about her hair tomorrow, take more care with what she wore.

No one was going to see her today, though.

Wrong. Just before six o'clock a key turned in the lock and Brett came in again. As he was closing the door she saw two people outside trying to peer past him.

She jerked quickly to one side and her voice came out more sharply than she'd intended. 'Shut that damned door! Quickly!'

He did that and studied her. 'You still don't look well, Cassie. How are you feeling? Really.'

'So-so. It's not just me being weak, mind. It takes time to recover, some expert was talking about it on the telly.'

'Of course it takes time. You're not Teflon-coated. Horrors like that don't bounce off anyone, however well they hide it. And don't worry, no person worth their salt would ever accuse you of being weak, Cassie, believe me.'

He went into the kitchen, dumped two shopping bags on the surface and began to unpack various types of food. 'There, that should hold you for a while.'

'Thanks. How much do I owe you?'

'Nothing.' He hesitated, folding the shopping bags up

again and stuffing them in his pocket then fiddling with one of the packages.

'What is it?'

'Can you manage on your own for a few days? Only, it's Tina's birthday and we'd planned to go away this weekend, booked the hotel and everything.'

'You seem happy together.'

'Yes. I'm sorry about how you and I broke up, though. Very sorry. I couldn't think how to tell you about her. Actually, I reckon you and I make better friends than lovers.'

She didn't agree. He'd been a splendid lover. But she wasn't going to tell him that. 'Water under the bridge now.'

He started to leave then turned back again. 'Cassie, love, I know you're very independent but don't push other people away if they offer to help. I tried your personal phone and it's switched off. What's with that? How will your friends get in touch?'

'I don't want them to. What I need is peace and quiet. You can contact me by my private email if it's desperate. I haven't changed that.' She hadn't looked at it today, either. Why not? She usually checked it several times a day. 'Thanks for the food. Now, go away and enjoy your weekend. Give my best to Tina.'

She showed him to the door, locked it quickly behind him and went into the kitchen. After putting away the food, she again sat in front of the TV, but didn't switch it on. She was unable to think what to do next until something the psychologist had said came back to her.

Find something important that you really want to do, something that's been left undone for a while, and focus on that.

It sounded like a good idea. In other words, find a serious distraction. What did she really want to do, though? She'd been living a very full life. Couldn't have fitted another thing into it. Well, a full working life anyway. She'd had some marvellous experiences and met some wonderful people, as well as some not so wonderful ones.

It took her until later in the evening to admit to herself that there was one rather important thing she'd tried to do a couple of years ago but had failed to make progress on. Perhaps she should try it again?

No, why bother? It had upset her greatly last time. She didn't need any more upsets at the moment.

Decision made.

Later on there was a programme on TV about finding people you'd lost touch with or never met, often members of your own family. People who really mattered to these participants.

She was picking up the remote to switch it off just as they showed an old photo of a woman holding a baby. She let the gadget fall from her hand as she covered her mouth to hold in the tears she *never* normally let herself shed.

Only this time she couldn't hold them back and they overflowed down her cheeks. It was all the fault of the damned programme.

It was the fault of her parents, too. She'd never forgiven them for what they'd done, or for blaming her for being raped. Fortunately they now lived permanently in a remote part of Northumberland and were very involved in village affairs. That made it easier to avoid them. It wasn't as if they bothered to keep in touch with her, after all, except for a card at Christmas and on her birthday.

She'd seen them last year at a family gathering, which she'd gone to at the urging of her much younger sister. She'd regretted doing that, regretted it bitterly because it had stirred up feelings she'd thought she'd put to rest. They still disapproved of her, still considered the sun rose and set over her younger brother and sister, whom Cassie didn't see much of, either.

Her younger brother had been at the gathering too, but he'd managed to avoid her completely. Deliberately. Michael was so like their father, avoiding any emotions or troublesome situations, keeping a stiff upper lip – yes, and a pillar of the local church, too.

To her surprise she'd got on quite well with her younger sister that day, but the fifteen years between them and the fact that they'd never actually spent a lot of time together when Zoe was younger had left a gap that was hard to cross in adulthood.

Only, Zoe had got in touch and they'd started meeting for coffee whenever she was down in London. And that was – nice. Really nice.

The words from the TV psychologist came back

to her abruptly: *Find something important that you really want to do.*

Cassie's stomach clenched as the image she'd just seen of the baby slipped back into her mind. Her own daughter had been born a long time ago, over forty years, and yet it still upset her that her parents had taken her baby away from her shortly after it was born and forced her to give it up for adoption.

She wouldn't even have had a photo to remember her baby by if it hadn't been for a sympathetic hospital cleaner who disagreed with the nuns' punitive policies and took a camera to work for that exact purpose. Cassie still had the photo and had made a digital copy, but she didn't need to look at it to remember every detail of the baby's appearance.

She'd had a hard birth and been ill, had felt utterly helpless and been too young at fifteen even to leave school and get a job. She hadn't seen any way out of the situation, not with no close relatives except parents who'd threatened never to see or speak to her again if she didn't do exactly as they wished.

Could she do something about that loss now? Would finding her daughter help fill the aching hole that had never gone away? It might take her mind off her present stress to try. Maybe.

It took her a few minutes to decide she would try again.

Getting slowly to her feet, she went upstairs to unearth the paperwork she'd hidden away from Brett for the whole of their relationship. It had taken a bomb to shake the information out again, she thought sadly.

Dumping the tattered folder on the bed, she pushed the box of oddments back into the wardrobe, after which she sat staring at the folder for who knew how long. She was still hesitant even to open it – because that would also reopen old wounds.

Could she face making another attempt to find her daughter? Nothing had come of her first and only attempt so far. She'd done it carefully, gone through all the right channels. And oh, it had hurt so much when there had been no response!

Someone knocked on her front door and that jerked her out of her unhappy thoughts and into the present. She peeped out of her bedroom window. Her boss. She definitely didn't want to see Terry until she'd pulled herself together.

So she didn't answer the door.

Not until she saw him drive away did she go downstairs again and switch on her laptop. When she went to the online family finder site she'd used last time, nothing much had changed, except for a bright new illustration at the top. They still only took hard copy applications – in this day and age – and they didn't answer individual questions online. You had to phone up or write in for that.

Why force grieving people to jump through all these artificial hoops? That said something about the organisation that ran the home where she'd had her daughter.

They had been distant and unsupportive the first time

and though they'd passed on her letter to the daughter she'd given up for adoption, nothing had come of it.

Even though her research suggested they might still be the best organisation to help her to contact her daughter, she didn't have good memories of them. The church they represented was one which her parents were still members of. She didn't have good memories of that, either.

She hesitated for a long time, staring blindly at the screen. Did she really want to pursue this? It would hurt, she knew it would.

In the end she knew she had to. It was unfinished business and if anyone could find a better way to do it, her public persona Cassandra Benn could. She usually enjoyed a challenge, had faced and overcome many in her working life.

Her private self, Cassie Bennington, was more hesitant.

Which side of her was in charge today?

Oh, what the hell! *Just do it*, she told herself. It was taking her mind off the attack already, wasn't it?

Sort of. Frying pan and fire came to mind.

This time she tried to think laterally and searched online for other ways of doing this. It took her until the following afternoon to find a way round the cold formalities of government and various charity organisations. Eventually she made a different sort of application to a less obvious agency.

Good thing she wasn't short of money, though. They charged like a wounded bull for their 'special confidential services'.

She still didn't want to leave the house. She knew it was cowardly, but there you were. One thing at a time.

She phoned the agency and had a discussion with a cool but tactful woman who took her through what they could do to help her.

And she found hope creeping in. She closed her eyes. *Please let this not be a con.*

'I'd like to use your services to do that, then,' she said at last.

The woman's voice softened. 'We won't let you down, Cassie. I know we charge a lot but we give good value for it and we always act ethically, even if our methods are a little different from those of other organisations. I promise you can trust us. Now, my name's Mary and I'll be the coordinator for your case. If you need anything from now on, ask for me.'

'Oh, thank goodness.'

'Do you want me to visit you in person to discuss it? That's part of the service we offer.'

'Um, no.' She explained about the incident.

'Then we can do it via our special app, which guarantees secure communication.'

When she eventually got off the phone, Cassie did the other thing they'd asked for. She found the letter she'd written to her daughter last time, rewrote it slightly and used the app to email it directly to Mary.

She got an email back almost immediately, promising to have the letter delivered.

'But it'll have to go to her by post,' Mary said. 'And

remember, I can't give you any details about her and where she is unless she gives permission.'

'You can give her any of my details she might need, though,' Cassie said. 'My address, phone number, anything.'

'You're sure you want to do that?'

'Oh yes. Very sure.'

She wasn't actually that sure, wasn't sure of anything today. But at least she was doing something. And it had kept her occupied for several hours.

Maybe the psychiatrist she'd seen on the TV had known something after all.

She wasn't consulting anyone of his tribe about her personal situation, though. Not in a million years.

On the Monday Cassie still couldn't face going to work. She booked an emergency medical appointment but it took a bit of effort for her to leave the house.

She saw a doctor at the local medical centre and asked to get signed off officially from work for a while. She didn't have a specific doctor, had hardly ever needed medical help.

She refused this man's suggestion of counselling, spurned the mere idea of tranquilisers, keeping her cool only with difficulty when he tried to persuade her to try them. 'I do not do drugs, whether legal or otherwise.' No way was she going to stuff her body full of chemicals that doped your brain, forget it. She'd seen where that could lead, knew her mother had been on them for years.

In the end she pacified the doctor by saying she was

considering going away for a holiday and asking his advice about whether that was a good idea.

He approved of that but looked at her shrewdly. 'You do realise it'll take you a while to get over this? I'd like to sign you off for at least two months.'

She hadn't expected that. 'Two months away from work? Phew! I can't remember the last time I took even a week off.'

'Then perhaps your batteries have run down from more than just the recent incident.'

She stared at him as the idea sank in. She hadn't considered that possibility. But she had been feeling – well, a bit drained of energy lately. Even before the incident.

'I'm right, aren't I?'

She shrugged. 'Could be.'

'Give yourself time to recover completely, Cassie. Take a proper rest. I've only just met you yet it stands out to me. I truly believe you need it.'

She gave in, because she knew she couldn't do good work feeling as she did. 'All right. Two months it is.'

As she walked out of the surgery she wondered how she would cope with spending that long away from work. What did people who were out of work or retired do to fill their time? She had no idea. When she went back to work she might research it as a programme idea.

If she went back to work.

No, no. She wasn't retiring. She wasn't sure she ever would. And she hadn't lost her job – they wouldn't dare sack her. She was just *regrouping, pausing for breath*, so to speak.

* * *

When she got home, a journalist she knew was waiting outside her home so she slid down in her seat, telling the taxi driver to go past the front of the house and round to the rear laneway. She could get in through the garage at the end of her tiny garden.

Looking at her little-used car as she edged past it made her wonder if she really should go away for a holiday. She could slip out this way without anyone seeing her – and go where?

The idea stayed with her as she found something to eat. She put half of the cheese toastie back in the fridge uneaten, along with half the apple. She had to stop making too much. It was wrong to be wasteful. Then she told herself not to pretend: she just wasn't hungry at the moment.

As the day passed the idea of taking a holiday just wouldn't go away. Should she really take one? But where could she go that someone wouldn't recognise her?

She started pacing up and down, then caught sight of herself in a mirror and stopped dead, horrified by what she saw. Her hair was a mess, with the white roots showing all too clearly. Why did so many redheads lose their hair colour so young? It drove her mad keeping up with the colour and root treatments. Trouble was, her alter ego Cassandra Benn was famous for her bright-red locks, a 'fiery redhead' her PR blurbs sometimes claimed.

She stared into the mirror thoughtfully. She'd kept colouring her hair because she didn't feel old and wasn't giving in to anything that suggested her real age. But now, well, it'd be a brilliant disguise and would save her a load of trouble as well.

She rang her hairdresser and begged for help.

'But I'm closing shortly. It's Monday. I close early today.'

So she played the pity card and told Michelle, 'Please. I need to get away for a while. I'll pay you double if you'll take the colour out of my hair today. I know it's a big ask, but I'm being *hounded* by the press.'

'Oh, all right. You've been a good customer and it's been a quiet week, so I could use the extra money. I'll stay open if you come here straight away.'

'I can't thank you enough. I'm on my way.'

She drove herself there and had trouble finding a parking spot. Before she got out of the car she wrapped a big scarf round her head and since rain was threatening, she wasn't the only one doing that. No one seemed to recognise her, thank goodness.

When she got to the salon it was a relief to find only Michelle there. The hairdresser was about the same age as she was and chatting to her didn't feel threatening at all, even today. Indeed, she'd been going to her for so long she sometimes seemed more like a cousin or long-time friend.

'I could only face coming to you,' she admitted.

Michelle studied her and nodded.

'Tell me exactly what you want to do with your hair.'

Michelle listened without interrupting and entered into the need for disguise with enthusiasm, suggesting

Cassie let her hair grow while she was at it. After all, she'd had it short for the whole time she'd been a public figure. Why not go for a complete change?

Then she snapped her fingers. 'You could even wear a hairpiece on an Alice band to make it seem longer straight away. That'd really fool people.'

She went to a cupboard and took out a box, rummaging through the packages it contained. 'We sell quite a few of these.' She flourished a silvery white hairpiece at Cassie. 'This is probably a good match for the colour of your roots. Now, let me get at that head of yours and soon you won't recognise yourself. Close your eyes and relax.'

It felt good to do something non-threatening, especially good to let Michelle take control of her body for a while – do this, move here, keep your eyes closed.

She was sure a different appearance would help her make a new life for herself. She froze as she sat there having her hair rinsed. *New life?* She was only taking sick leave . . . wasn't she?

Then she relaxed a little. Perhaps she should take a serious look at what she wanted to do in future. She'd been a voyeur into one human trauma after another for years and had seen some of the worst sides of human nature as well as the best – but all of it vicariously. Now she'd reacted so badly to terrorism she wished she'd been less ruthless about exposing other people's reactions to life crises.

To her amazement, she was indeed feeling that she'd had enough of it. A new life might be good.

How had that idea crept up on her?

Michelle continued to fiddle around in her usual quiet way and Cassie stayed tuned out.

Then suddenly it was done.

'Open your eyes, Cassie.'

She stared at a woman with a head of silvery hair. And she didn't look old, at least she thought she didn't, just . . . different.

'You're lucky,' Michelle said. 'Some people's hair turns a coarse white, but yours looks lovely, all soft and silvery. Why have you fought it for so long? Some younger people are now dyeing their hair to get that colour.'

Cassie stared at the stranger in the mirror, turning her head from side to side. 'You've done brilliantly, Michelle.'

'Close your eyes again and let's try the Alice band.'

She obeyed, letting Michelle fiddle around.

'See what you think of this.'

Cassie stared at the woman in the mirror, who looked so much like an aunt of hers she was shocked rigid. But it was what she'd wanted, wasn't it? To look different, be unrecognisable. 'Brilliant. Show me how to put that thing on.'

She had a lesson in doing that and happily paid Michelle more than double her asking price. 'Thank you. You've helped me at a bad time. I really needed this and I can't tell you how grateful I am.'

But when Michelle broke their tradition by hugging her, she stiffened, couldn't help it, didn't want to be touched.

Michelle kept hold, shaking her gently. 'I know you don't like being hugged, love, but I'm doing it anyway. You need it. You need people, Cassie. We all do. Don't push them away. Learn to touch the rest of humanity, not just talk at it.'

That was the second person to say something similar to her.

She knew they meant well and she respected both Michelle's and Brett's opinions, but she had never been a touchy-feely sort of person. And come to think of it, her parents hadn't been, either.

What about her sister and brother? Was Zoe out of the same mould? She knew Michael didn't do 'that soppy, girly stuff'.

When things had settled down, she must catch up with Zoe. She wasn't sure Michael wanted to bother. But she and Zoe had got on quite well the last few times they'd met. She pulled a wry face – well, they'd been rather like two amiable strangers getting to know one another and liking what they found.

Could their relationship go further? Did she want it to?

She didn't know. Probably. Possibly. Oh hell, she wasn't sure of anything at the moment.

Cassie couldn't avoid continuing to think about it all as she drove home. If she did change her life, if that was going to be the best solution to her present – well, chaos of mind would be a good way of describing it – how would she make a living? She had some money saved but not enough to retire on completely.

There had to be a way, though. There was nearly always a way if you looked for it hard enough.

She didn't need to see a shrink, though. She'd always been independent and she was staying independent. What she needed now was to take action herself, find her own way to recovery. Surely that would make her feel normal again?

She would give the agency's search for her daughter a few days. Mary had told her they usually came up with results pretty quickly.

She hadn't asked them about the methods they used to find people – didn't care, just wanted results. After paying so much for their services, she expected a quick response, that was sure.

She needed to know one way or another.

Chapter Four

In Lancashire, Evie Milner stared at her mother in horror. 'You're going to *marry* him?'

'Yes, and then we are *both* moving into Keith's house.'

The girl's voice was flat. 'You should wait to marry him. You've only known him a few months.'

'Why? He loves me, fell in love with me at first sight. He wants us to marry so that we can be together properly.'

'He's a creep. I can't stand him, and I *won't* go to live with him.'

'How can you say that? He's always been so nice to you. Don't you dare speak about him like that!'

She couldn't tell her mother why, because she had no proof that Keith fancied her, and her mother would hit the roof and accuse her of trying to drive him away. But Evie knew the way he looked at her when they were alone together, and it made her flesh crawl. A grown man shouldn't look at a child that way, even a child of fifteen, which was nearly adult. It was illegal as well as disgusting.

All she could do was repeat, 'I will *not* live with him.'

'You don't get the choice. I'm your mother. Until you're old enough to leave home, I say where you live and what you do.'

'I'll run away first.'

'It's not happening instantly. Just let me finish explaining our future arrangements before you fire off threats. I want to try living with Keith before I make any permanent changes, so I've arranged for you to stay with Cousin Amelia for a few weeks while he and I settle in together.'

Evie couldn't see what good that would do. It'd only postpone the time her mother tried to get her to live with him as well.

'Keith doesn't want to move from where he's living, so he's going to do an attic conversion on his present house and that's where you'll be sleeping once it's finished. He's paying extra for them to do a rush job on it. That shows he does care about you and my relationship with you. You're so ungrateful.'

Evie felt helpless against her mother's blind rush into what she was sure would be another disastrous relationship, only this time she'd be tied to the guy by marriage. She dashed away a tear. She didn't know what to say or do to stop her mother or at least slow her down.

'Bear with me, Evie. It's a long time since your father left me.' After another pause, Fran added with false brightness, 'And just think of the lovely new bedroom and en suite you'll have all to yourself when the attic conversion is finished.'

And think of how I'll be kept upstairs and out of the way for most of the time, Evie thought. Children should be seen and not heard, even more so when they were fifteen years old and knew what certain noises in other people's bedrooms meant.

But when a creepy older man kept brushing against you on the stairs and staring at your chest, well, you couldn't help knowing what he was thinking. She shuddered at the memory of that, but she might have been mistaken. Or there again, she might not. Stupid she wasn't.

And her mother would be legally tied to him! It didn't bear thinking of.

Normally Evie would have protested at the thought of going to live with her mother's cousin, who was a flaky art teacher and lived way out on the other side of town. Amelia didn't know which way was up half the time when she was just starting a new painting. But anything would be better than living with Keith Burgess so Evie would put up with their cousin, with her vegan food and arty weirdos coming in and out of the house.

Though none of Amelia's weirdos had made her feel uncomfortable in the way Keith did. She'd better make sure she didn't do anything to upset their cousin and get sent home again.

Home! She didn't have a home like other kids did, never had done because they'd moved often as her mother struggled to make ends meet.

But staying with Amelia would only be a temporary fix for the latest disastrous relationship. She had to work out a way to avoid living with him long term. She didn't intend to visit for a weekend, even, simply didn't dare.

She went to stay at Amelia's for half term to see how things went, and to her surprise she found her cousin so controlling it felt like a different lifestyle from last time. Amelia made sure of what Evie was doing every minute of the day and night, and set out some rules she'd have to observe when she came to live here for longer.

She found out why, of course. She always found things out. She'd had years of practice at eavesdropping on conversations and phone calls, and at second-guessing her mother. It seemed Cousin Amelia was being paid to watch her carefully.

That sucked big time. What did they think she was going to do? Sell her body on the streets? Give it to any man who fancied her? As if.

She tackled Amelia about it one evening, choosing her time carefully, when her aunt was on her second glass of wine.

'Why do they think I need watching so carefully?'

Amelia choked on her mouthful then frowned at her.

'I don't misbehave, I do well at school, mostly get As. Why don't they trust me?'

'They haven't told you anything?'

Evie shook her head.

'Hmm. Well, you're old enough to know *all* the facts and I've told Fran that, so don't blame me. It's because your mother is adopted.'

'I know that already.'

'Did you know that *her* mother had her when she was only fifteen?'

This was news. 'Oh? Is that why she put her up for adoption?'

'Probably. But it's also why your mother wants you to be watched carefully.'

Evie was baffled. 'What's that got to do with me?'

'Your mother nearly went down the same path. She got pregnant at fifteen to someone she fell madly in love with, but luckily she miscarried before it could ruin her life. She didn't want you to know about that, so don't let on I told you. As a result, she and Keith are worried that you've inherited the family tendency to, um, start getting interested in men early.'

'That's ridiculous. I haven't even had a steady boyfriend yet.' *He* must have put that idea into her mother's head. Why?

Amelia shrugged. 'Well, me taking care of you oh-so-carefully is not only going to set their minds at rest, but help pay for a painting holiday in Greece this summer for me. And actually, kid, I enjoy your company.'

'I enjoy yours too.' That had surprised her, but Amelia had started to talk more openly to her about all sorts of things now that she was older, which was more than her mother did since she'd met *him*.

Evie lay awake for a long time trying to work out what she'd done to make her mother and Keith think she'd be so stupid and irresponsible. Or that she was man crazy. Even if she did meet a boy she fancied, she knew about birth control, for heaven's sake. This was the twenty-first not the nineteenth century.

Only she didn't fancy any of the boys she'd met at school, so it wasn't going to happen. She knew she was classified as 'gifted', for what that was worth, and she found most of the males in her year either immature, sports mad or else geeks with no interests beyond their computers.

But dull and restricted as her life was at Amelia's, she infinitely preferred it to living with her mother in *his* house. She was dreading the move, hadn't yet worked out how to get out of it.

And openly as her cousin talked, Evie didn't dare voice her fears about Keith to her either, not without proof of what she suspected. No, more than suspected. Was sure of.

When Amelia drove her home after the trial visit, Evie found her mother in a glow of happiness and Keith beside her looking smug.

Her cousin nudged her as they got her luggage out of the car. 'It's lovely to see how happy Fran is. Don't do anything to spoil it for your mother, love.'

Evie tried to smile, but it seemed Keith was staying over, so she'd have no time alone with her mother that night.

He seemed to stay over most of the time these days, so keeping out of his way was easier said than done. Worst of all, he continued to look at her in a way that made her feel as if she had no clothes on. And when he bumped into her, as he still did occasionally, he didn't move away quickly, which made her feel literally sick.

All she could do was try to avoid him and stay in her room as much as she could, pleading homework. Which didn't please her mother.

She didn't dare talk about the problem to her friends at school in case it got back to the guidance officer. That might get her into trouble for telling malicious lies, as had happened to one girl last year.

Or worse still, get her reported to social services, who might take her away while the whole situation was investigated. One of her classmates was in care and her tales of a series of placements wouldn't encourage anyone to go down that path except in utter desperation.

About a week after she got back from her cousin's, Evie stayed home from school for an agreed study day. This was supposed to teach them to work on their own. Duh! She already did that because the homework didn't keep her fully occupied and she liked to investigate topics which interested her in more detail.

The post was delivered early and when she picked it up from the hall floor, she found a letter for her mother, who had just come back from a long dental appointment and was going into work late as a consequence. 'This is for you.'

The sight of its contents made her mother scowl and she shoved the letter into her pocket.

'Bad news?' Evie asked casually.

'Never you mind.'

It must have been really bad news because her mother slammed around the house, snapping at her daughter for nothing. It was a relief when she went back to work in the afternoon.

When it came time to clear up the kitchen after tea, her mother's phone rang and she took it in the living room, calling, 'Take that bag of rubbish out to the bin, Evie, and don't open it up again. It stinks and it's full. Hurry up. Make yourself useful, for once.'

She took it out, hesitated and crept back to see if her mother was still on the phone.

She was and it must be to *him* judging by the soppy expression on her face. If he wasn't there with them, he often rang and she had started to wonder whether he was checking on her mother.

Evie gave in to temptation, went back outside and untied the rubbish bag. She had to fumble through some yucky scraps of food but it was worth it because she found the letter that had upset her mother so greatly, torn in half and screwed up.

Still keeping an eye on the house, she wiped it as best she could on the grass and slipped it inside the top of her knickers, for lack of any other place to conceal it. It always helped to keep track of what was going on and this had upset her mother big time.

She went back into the house and up to the bathroom, where she pulled the letter out with a grimace, wiped the smears of vegetable debris off her skin, then hid the slightly soggy pieces of paper in her bedroom. No use trying to read the letter now. Her mother's latest trick was to creep in on her suddenly and check what she was doing.

Evie sighed. She was finding this very wearing and still hadn't the faintest idea what to do about it. Her mother hadn't been like this before she met *him*.

She wished, as she had many times before, that she'd been born into a normal family, with two parents, a couple of siblings and maybe a pet dog.

She had never wished it as strongly as this, though.

It wasn't till the house was quiet and her mother fast asleep that she dared take out the letter. Thank goodness *he* wasn't spending the night.

What she read shocked her rigid.

Dear Ms Milner,
Your birth mother is very eager to make contact with you and has employed our agency to facilitate this.

You may have previously received a letter from her similar to the one enclosed and if so, she begs you to reconsider your decision not to respond at that time and give her a chance.

Your mother didn't give you up for adoption willingly. She was only fifteen when you were born and was forced to do this by her parents. She has always been deeply sad about that and would very much like to get to know you.

She would be happy to meet you anywhere and at a time of your choice.

Our company can provide sympathetic professional counsellors to make the meeting and its impact easier on you both, if that would help.

We have not disclosed your address and personal information to her in case you still do not wish to have a meeting, because we do respect people's privacy. However she has asked us to give you her own details to show good faith.

These have been added to the end of this letter.

Please don't rush into doing anything you may regret later. This is important and deserves careful thought.

If you wish to ask any questions or discuss the matter with our counsellors, that can be arranged by phoning the number at the top of this page and mentioning the reference number of your case, which is beneath it. The sessions will be paid for by your birth mother, of course.

*We look forward to hearing from you and
helping you both.*
Yours sincerely,
JSD Services

Evie stared at the letter in shock and read it through
again, more slowly this time. She knew that her mother
had been adopted because her grandparents had made
no secret of doing it. Her mother, however, had always
refused to discuss it, let alone speculate about her birth
parents. And now this letter had turned up out of the blue.

She looked at the end of it and immediately memorised
this unknown grandmother's details, just in case, then hid
the torn halves of the letter amongst her art materials,
hoping that a few more scruffy pieces of paper wouldn't
look out of place when her mother next went through
her things, another thing she'd started doing since she
hooked up with *him*.

When she lay down again, she had trouble getting to
sleep. She'd learnt more about her mother's past during
the previous two weeks than ever before, what with
Cousin Amelia's explanation and this letter. Though it
was still not a lot to go on. It was as if her mother wanted
to wipe away any traces of her birth mother.

But what if there was some medical emergency that
needed genetic information about the family? Evie had
read about such cases, because she was considering trying
to become a doctor. What would they do then? She or
her mother could die for lack of the correct information.

Her mother's first husband, Evie's father, had gone travelling the world to 'find himself' when she was five. He hadn't been heard of since. She didn't remember him very clearly. Her mother had got a divorce from him after a certain length of time and changed her surname to Milner, doing the same name change for Evie.

Her mother's adoptive parents, her Gran and Pop Milner, would probably have been upset if a birth mother had turned up while they were still alive. She missed them dreadfully. Drunken drivers should be stood against a wall and shot for the harm they did to innocent people and their families when they caused accidents.

Evie didn't get on with her father's parents, and was glad she hadn't had much to do with them. She had never been able to figure out why they were so cold to their daughter-in-law. Did they consider themselves so perfect they could scorn anyone who made a mistake? She felt sure if she tried to seek shelter with them, they'd bring her straight back.

But she did still have this other grandmother, it seemed, a mother who wanted desperately to meet the daughter who'd been adopted soon after birth, even if that desire wasn't reciprocated. Surely she'd want to meet her granddaughter too?

Evie didn't know whether she'd dare get in touch with this woman, though. If she did, it'd have to be done very carefully so that her mother didn't find out.

What was her grandmother like? How stupid it was that her mother wouldn't even meet her and find out.

What a tangle some so-called adults could get their lives into! Evie hoped she'd do better when she grew up. Apart from being a doctor, all she wanted was to meet a stable, normal guy who wanted to settle down, have a family and live a quiet, happy life doing something worthwhile.

Was that too much to ask?

First, however, she had to solve the problem of Keith and her own immediate future. She would not go and live with him. Didn't dare.

Thank goodness she would soon be going back to stay with Amelia again, and for a few weeks this time. It made for a long trip to and from school each day, but it was worth it. And after that, who knew?

She might even be forced to run away to escape him, but she'd only do that as a final, desperate resort.

She could only hope he'd prove to be more difficult to live with than her mother expected.

Chapter Five

On the Thursday morning, Hal set off for Wiltshire, looking forward to seeing his new home in all its finished glory. He had lunch in the hotel, something he hadn't done before. The meal was good, not haute cuisine, but who wanted that except on special occasions? He got too hungry for the prettily arranged but bird-sized portions he'd paid a fortune for when fine dining.

He'd definitely eat here regularly once he moved in.

Afterwards he strolled down to the site office and found Molly waiting for him, with a young man standing to one side, ready to take over the selling side of things.

They walked down to the detached house that Hal would soon be moving into and he paused in front to study it and nod approval. It was an elegant, classical house shape, with nice large windows and he didn't regret choosing that style. He'd never liked weird modern buildings with odd-shaped roofs and protrusions that looked as if a child had plonked the parts together.

Inside they moved slowly from room to room, going through a list of things to check that Molly had brought, after which she left him to go round again on his own.

'Come and join me when you've finished and we'll go up to the main company office in the hotel and discuss any further concerns you may have. Take your time. There's no rush.'

'Thanks. I would appreciate going round again on my own.'

He stood by the living-room window of his house for a while and realised suddenly that he was smiling. That was because from here he had a view of the lake for which the leisure village was named: Penny Lake. It was glinting in the sun, tempting him to walk round it. *Not today*, he told it mentally, *but soon.*

Then he walked round the house again, continuing to feel happy, as if he really had come home to stay. He'd tried to make other homes for himself and succeeded only temporarily. This time he was going to make sure things worked out on a permanent, long-term basis.

He needed it.

Apart from any other considerations, there was a lot of boring, fiddling detail involved in changing houses and he wanted to make this the last time he ever went through all that. He had better things to do with his life. Well, in theory, anyway.

He didn't know exactly *what* he was going to do

from now on, but he'd recovered from cancer and been given the chance to live a normal life again, so he felt he should do something worthwhile. He wasn't going to waste that precious time.

First he had to learn to relax and live at a gentler pace.

No, wrong. First he had to go and see Molly, sign anything else necessary and make the final arrangements to move here.

He chuckled softly. Which meant he'd have to buy some new furniture. He'd never done that on his own before, had always done it with a woman. Did men choose differently when it was for themselves? Who knew? He intended to take his time, moving in with his present bits and pieces and only buying more when he needed or loved something.

Home, he thought happily. Not a house to show off with, but one to snuggle into and relax. This place sure beat the stark modernist flat he was currently inhabiting in London. The sooner he got the final signing off over and done with, the happier he'd be.

Molly Santiago had been great to deal with, and her husband was just as nice.

Oh, he was so looking forward to starting his new life! He felt rejuvenated every time he thought of that.

Since her change of hair colour, Cassie found she could go to the shops or for walks without being recognised and it occurred to her that this was the first time in years she'd been able to do that.

It made her wonder whether she'd been more trapped in a celebrity bubble than she'd realised, cushioned against ordinary life, far less free than the average person in the street, for all her success.

Her boss threw a fit when she sent in a medical certificate covering two months' sick leave. Typically, Terry phoned her, was rude about her stamina and broke the call abruptly when she refused to change her plans.

After that, he sent his assistant to persuade her to come back sooner. Cassie hastily covered her hair with a towel before letting Roger in, not wanting him to see her new persona, for some reason.

She greeted him with, 'I've just washed my hair so I can only give you a few minutes.'

He talked rapidly and persuasively but she refused even to consider shortening the period of leave. 'I'm not making anything up. I really feel I need time to get over such a traumatic experience.' What the doctor had pointed out only backed up her decision.

Besides, she was suffering from PTSD, she had to admit that to herself, though she wasn't telling her boss. The mere thought of going out on interviews made her shudder and she kept jerking awake at night thinking she was in that ambulance again or could hear sirens wailing. Worst of all, the scenes from the TV footage kept replaying in her mind.

As a result of the insomnia she felt tired all day long and kept dropping off into a doze in her armchair.

What she had seen on TV made her feel sick, because

she had been so close to being killed like those other poor souls. And never, not for one nano-second, did she feel safe, even though she knew logically that she was.

She jerked to attention at the realisation that Roger had said something else. 'Sorry. Run that past me again.'

'Terry won't like your refusal to honour your contract. He may even cancel the show.'

'And I don't like how the incident has affected me,' she said quietly. 'Tell him I'm doing the best I can. I'll see you out now.' She patted the makeshift turban. 'I need to attend to my hair.'

He gave her a puzzled look. She was sure he'd go back and tell Terry that she had changed, lost her edge.

She had.

And she didn't miss that sharp, almost bullying interaction with the world.

Only, as a consequence she didn't feel like she knew herself properly any longer and that was unsettling. She had to find herself again, had to – whoever she now was – but hadn't quite worked out how to do it.

Once she knew the coast was clear she went out for a walk to pick up a newspaper, relishing her anonymity. She didn't discover till she got home that it was the newspaper's day for the big display of property for sale, something she never normally looked at.

She tossed that part aside automatically, but couldn't resist picking it up again and glancing at it once she'd finished reading the main section of the newspaper. Maybe 'reading' was the wrong word. 'Skimming through' was a better description. She couldn't seem to concentrate on anything for long.

Her eyes were caught by an advert in the supplement showing houses for sale in her suburb. When she followed the online link it gave and looked through the various photos, she saw a house nearby that was very like her own and couldn't resist studying the details.

She was astounded at how much hers was now worth. She'd known it had increased in value, of course she had, but hadn't realised by how much. Well, she'd certainly taken her eye off the ball there. She'd been too busy watching over her 'brilliant career' – which didn't seem important any longer, or even all that brilliant when viewed from the inside.

In the middle of the night, as she was tossing and turning yet again, she had a sudden idea. She got up, padding downstairs to switch on her computer and check out property prices outside London and the big cities, trying Lancashire and Wiltshire as examples of places she knew a little after doing projects there fairly recently.

She sat for a long time staring at the screen, amazed at how much lower the prices were in both places. Was this her key to freedom, taking money out of her house?

It could be. It really could.

But did she want to quit London and her public life completely and become simply Cassie?

What would she do with herself all day?

No, she couldn't possibly retire . . . Could she? . . . Should she?

She rubbed her aching forehead which seemed full of tangled thoughts, then switched off the computer and walked slowly back upstairs to bed, yawning. Lots to think about tomorrow. Lots to research.

Who'd have thought she'd suffer from PTSD? She would never in a million years have expected that to happen, had thought herself an exceptionally strong person. But no one was made of steel. She was flesh and blood, just like the rest of humanity and just as fallible.

She'd never have believed, either, that she'd recoil from the mere idea of grilling the poor innocent victims of similar crimes. She couldn't do it any longer. Just – could – not.

So, she had to find her way towards a new style of living, tread a gentler path through life. It was more than time to stop this breakneck rush from tragedy to comedy, violence and other extremes of human experience.

The following day Cassie decided to go for a drive in the country to take her mind off her problems. She'd not heard from the agency she'd contracted to help her and in her gloomier moments, felt as if she'd never find her daughter. But she was totally fed up of sitting around the house and could at least do something about that.

When the phone rang early that morning, she checked the caller ID and saw that it was her sister. 'Zoe. How nice to hear from you.'

'How are you?'

'Fine, thank you.'

'I doubt that. I worked with someone who was

involved in a violent incident and it upset him big time. Took him ages to get over it.'

'Oh. Well, I don't think I'm that bad.'

'Don't lie to me, Cassie.'

She didn't know what to say to that, so said nothing and waited to find out what Zoe wanted.

'Look, I'm in London and about to go down to Wiltshire to drop off a piece of furniture for a friend. She'd intended to come with me and we were going to visit an antiques centre we'd heard of afterwards, make a day of it. Unfortunately, she fractured her arm yesterday in a fall, so she doesn't feel like jolting about in a car. It suddenly occurred to me that you might like to come with me instead. It'd make a nice outing.'

'Thanks, but—' She broke off. Why was she refusing? 'Are you sure?'

'Very. I'd welcome the company and—' There was a distinct pause, then, 'Well, I don't think you and I see each other often enough, considering we're sisters. How about I pick you up at nine, and hopefully we can avoid the rush hour on the M4?'

'All right. Lunch is on me, though.'

'OK. And Cassie, I'm really looking forward to our outing.'

So was she, Cassie found to her surprise.

Zoe greeted her with a 'Wow!' and touched her hair.

'The long part at the back is a hairpiece till my own hair grows. I felt like a change.'

'It suits you much better than the bright red did. Older faces don't show to their best advantage against harsh colours. And I like the jaw-level look too. It's more flattering than the short style was because your chin's starting to sag a bit.'

Cassie had forgotten how frank her sister could be. Such utter honesty came as a bit of a shock each time they met, though Zoe never said anything malicious so you couldn't exactly take offence.

She shrugged. 'I must admit it's nice not to be recognised when I go out and about, and it's going to be a lot easier to maintain this hairstyle.'

'Have you had much trouble with the press since the incident? I found out about it in a newspaper article so they must have tried to poke their noses in further.'

'Yes, they did. But the fuss seems to be dying down now. At least there wasn't someone parked outside this morning, waiting for me to come out.'

'I'm glad to hear that. Must have been hard to be at the other side of the camera.'

'Mmm. It was.'

Zoe patted her arm. 'Buckle up your seat belt. You can relax today and I'll play chauffeur. No one will be looking for you in Wiltshire.'

As they headed west, Cassie tried to think of something safe to chat about, but Zoe stopped her. 'You don't have to force conversation. You're not the only one who wants a restful outing.'

'Something wrong?'

'Not wrong, exactly, but I'm feeling a bit wobbly about committing to one man for ever.'

'I thought you loved him.'

'So did I. But I didn't realise how keen he is to settle down and have children – the whole shebang. And he's the one who wants a white wedding. I'm not nearly as certain about that part of it. It's all happened so quickly, I feel like a spinning top.'

After a slight pause, she added, 'And he's got an offer of a job in the Midlands, the sort of offer you don't refuse. I'll have to give up my job and find something else. No use getting married and living apart. So lots to think about.'

'Are you going off him?'

A sigh, then, 'I may be. I don't want children yet and as for parading around in a big meringue of a dress, he can forget it. I'm definitely not into white weddings.'

'I thought it was usually women who wanted all that fuss.'

'George is an old-fashioned guy in some ways. I thought I liked that. Mum and Dad still think he's perfect, but he isn't. No one is. But he comes pretty close to it, compared to other men I've gone out with. I think he must have been born amiable. And kind. And he's interesting to talk to. But . . . oh, who knows?'

'I wish you well, whatever you decide.'

'Thank you. Will you come to the wedding if we do get married? And be my matron of honour? It'd not be for a few months, but I'd like to have you there.'

'Oh. Well, I'll definitely try. But I'm not so sure about being a matron of honour.'

'I'd really like you to do it. I know you'd need to grit your teeth about Mum and Dad – and yes, I have noticed and been saddened by how they treat you, and it's got worse since you and I started seeing more of one another. But maybe it won't happen anyway. I am so confused.'

She reached her left hand across from the driving seat to pat her sister's arm quickly.

That simple touch felt good. Perhaps Brett and Michelle were right about not keeping people at arm's length.

A short time later Cassie found herself telling Zoe about her idea of selling her house in London and moving somewhere cheaper. 'Like Wiltshire, actually,' she admitted. 'I've been researching house prices online, so it's a nice coincidence that you wanted to go there today.'

'Are you really giving up work?'

'Probably.'

'Because of the incident?'

'Partly. It's made me think. The past few years have been great but stressful and – well, it's not just the incident. I think I may have run out of steam.' She didn't tell Zoe about searching for her daughter. Nothing might come of this second attempt.

They drove in silence for a few miles, then as they turned off the M4 motorway, Zoe suggested, 'Why don't we look at some houses while we're there, then? I love having a poke round. Shall you buy one with a garden and then get a dog? I've never had a pet.'

'I asked for a puppy once but Mum and Dad wouldn't allow it.'

'No. You've got to keep your house immaculate all the time, haven't you, or the world will come to an end. Perhaps that's why I'm so untidy, in reaction.'

'Do you think George will accept the job?'

'Oh yes. I wouldn't try to stop him. But I'm not having the wedding till that's all settled and I'm sure of myself.'

'I thought you'd fixed a date.'

'Mum pushed us into doing that.'

'What did she say to postponing it?'

'Told me to stop being precious and snap him up or someone else will. If I read her correctly, she wants to rush me into marriage in case I change my mind and wind up single or divorced like you. It's the only future she sees for a woman, marriage, and she doesn't believe in divorce for any reason whatsoever. Let's face it, Cassie, her and Dad's views come right out of the Ark.'

Cassie envied the way Zoe could chuckle at that. She'd never learnt to be light-hearted about her parents' old-fashioned views or the way they seemed to see only her previous faults and had never stopped criticising her for any other mistakes she'd made. No wonder she'd taken refuge in studying hard as a key to the longed-for independence from them.

And no wonder her recent relationship had broken up. Brett had once told her she didn't know how to be part of a loving couple.

Chapter Six

When the sisters arrived at Marlbury, it proved to be a small town, not the village they'd expected from what Zoe's friend had told her.

They dropped the little table off first, but Zoe refused an invitation from her friend's aunt to have a cup of tea and came straight back to the car. 'Let's grab a quick coffee in town then go and look in estate agency windows. I saw one as we drove through. I'd much rather look at houses than antiques.'

The window display of the first estate agent's gave them a very helpful start, as it was full of photos of houses of all shapes and sizes, and all prices too.

'Wow, the prices are wonderfully low compared to my part of London.' Cassie pointed. 'Look at that one.'

After a while Zoe said, 'Let's check that other agency

over there on the other side of the road, see if this really is the correct price level.'

It was she who wandered round to the small side window and called, 'Come and look at this display.'

'Penny Lake Leisure Village! I don't want to live in an old folks' home,' Cassie said indignantly.

'It's not, you idiot. It's a leisure village. Haven't you heard of them?'

'Sort of. Not the details.' She was starting to find a lot of gaps in her knowledge of everyday matters, Cassie decided. Small picture stuff for living in the real world.

Zoe clicked her tongue in disapproval and explained. 'Listen and learn, oh sister mine. They're places adults move to when they want to lead a more chilled-out life. And yes, some people do retire to them, but they aren't usually based on a retirement ethos.'

'Good. I did an interview in a retirement complex once and it left me shuddering, the flats were so small. It felt as if they were storing old people in cupboards. And there was hardly anyone to be seen, as if they were all cowering inside their death nests.'

Zoe threw her a puzzled look. 'That's a strange way to look at them and a horrid way to describe them. George's aunt lives in a retirement village and she loves it. Lots of people to chat to if you want company, privacy in your own flat if you don't. No garden to maintain, but places to sit outside if you feel like it.'

Cassie shrugged. She wasn't old enough to need either type of place. How decrepit did her sister think she was, for heaven's sake? Fifty-six wasn't old.

'Anyway, let's go and look at this place, Cassie. It says it's attached to a golf course and there's a hotel on-site which serves meals. We can grab a late lunch there.'

'If we're going to be practical during this short visit, I'd rather grab a quick sandwich in town and look at proper houses than spend all our time in some little enclave. Might save me a trip in future to Wiltshire, if I don't like this area or the sort of homes you can buy round here.'

Zoe stopped dead. 'You know, for someone who makes her living interviewing people, you display some very fixed and limiting views at times. You've never even seen a leisure village so how do you know what one is like? I've noticed you making that sort of snap judgement before. Black or white, no shades in between. Surely if you do retire, you'll want to meet people and make new friends? Surely it's worth looking at *every* option?'

Cassie shrugged. 'I haven't thought that out properly yet and to tell you the truth, since the incident I'm still having trouble thinking clearly. And speaking the word "retire" out loud freaks me out big time. I hadn't planned to do that so soon – if ever.'

She stared into the distance. 'That explosion has turned my whole life upside down.'

Zoe gave her arm a little squeeze. 'Sorry. I shouldn't scold you when you're still upset. But since we have to eat and I don't fancy a high street café full of shoppers, let's go to this hotel and give ourselves a leisurely meal. I doubt it'll be crowded midweek.'

So Cassie let herself be taken to this Penny Lake place. What did it matter? Her sister wasn't trying to force her to buy a property there, after all.

Well, she wasn't buying anything anywhere till she'd had a good look round some of the nicer rural areas with easy access to London. She was determined to be sensible about this move, research everything carefully.

After delicious and innovative salads followed by a not so healthy shared piece of chocolate gateau at the hotel, the two women strolled across from its car park to the sales office to get some information about the type of houses being built here.

As they walked Cassie glanced to the right, where a smallish lake was glinting in the sun a short distance away. That was at least one thing in favour of this place, she had to admit, and what she'd seen of the Wiltshire countryside so far was lovely.

They picked up a brochure each and studied the site map on the wall. The woman sitting behind a desk didn't attempt a sales pitch beyond suggesting they might like to look round the two houses that were on show and open today.

'Both houses are for sale, of course,' she added as they started walking out of the display centre.

Cassie turned round. Might as well do the research properly. 'How much are they?'

'Here's a price list and details of other types of house that can be built as well.'

The woman held out a leaflet and she took it, amazed all over again at how cheap the houses were compared to London property prices in decent areas. Why, they were only about a third of the cost of her home, even for the larger of the current two show homes.

As she followed Zoe down the road and turned to the right past some occupied houses on their left, a woman came out, gave them a friendly smile and began to water the big pots of flowers that stood on either side of her door.

It was such a peaceful scene, Cassie thought wistfully. No crowds or sounds of nearby traffic, clear sparkling air, birds fluttering amongst the trees. She stopped to watch a wagtail bobbing up and down as it pecked up who knew what from the lawn. How long was it since she'd seen one of those? Years. They were her favourite birds, so tiny and always seeming happily busy.

Zoe waited for her. 'I'm enjoying this place. There's something about looking at water that soothes the soul, don't you think?'

'It's nice, yes.'

Her sister gave her a disbelieving look at this lukewarm response but didn't comment, thank goodness.

The first house that was open was the end one in a row of three. It was a neat little place, about the same size as Cassie's present home, and even less than a third of the price. It was well designed, but going round it and mentally planning how she'd live there made her realise that if she were spending most of her time at home, writing articles to bring in a little extra money, she'd need more space than this so that she could have a proper office.

The other house open for viewing was detached, much larger, with a spacious entrance and larger rooms.

'Nice family home,' Zoe said.

Cassie didn't respond but moved ahead to explore the interior, which had several linked living areas, one of which could easily be used as a home office. This house wouldn't make her feel as if she were shut up inside a rabbit hutch as some so-called office spaces had done at work, and her present house was doing since she'd been mostly confined to it.

Outside at the rear there was a sunny patio where you could have a table and chairs. All it needed were a few pots of flowers and it'd be perfect.

She went back inside, shooting a quick glance at Zoe, but her sister was opening and shutting cupboard doors. 'I'll just nip upstairs.'

'I'll follow you in a minute. I love looking at kitchens. I'm going to have a big one someday.'

The rooms upstairs were just as light and airy, with a big master bedroom with en suite.

Cassie fought a battle with herself and lost. She could imagine so clearly what it'd be like to wake up here.

And then a daring thought crept into her mind: why not buy it?

No! The idea was utterly ridiculous. Had she lost all common sense? She mustn't allow herself to go too far with her visualisations about the houses they went round. Doing that might lead to stupidly impulsive acts.

Zoe came up to join her and after they went down, she slipped her arm into her sister's. 'You like this house, don't you?'

Cassie debated whether to admit that, then sighed and gave her sister's arm a return squeeze. 'I do. Very much. I didn't expect that. I'd definitely want to buy something similar.'

Zoe stared round. 'I like the situation and the interior layout, but surely you'd be more interested in the smaller house with only yourself to bother about?'

'No, no. That one's too small. What I like best about this one is the sense of space.'

She surprised herself with her next words. 'I'm tired of being shut up in small places: aeroplanes, radio station interview booths, cars, trains, tents, people's front rooms. I hadn't realised how much I'd like the feeling of freedom that a big house and having open countryside nearby gives you. Anyway, if I do retire, I'll need a decent home office, because I'll still be doing some writing, you know, articles and opinion pieces. They pay quite well.'

She grinned and added in a mocking tone, 'I might even write a great English novel.'

'You can do what you want.'

Those words were fatal. They seemed to breach the wall of reason Cassie was trying to build round the temptation to buy this beautiful, near-perfect house. She stood stock-still, the words seeming to echo in her brain.

Yes, I really can do what I want from now on.

Eventually, after what seemed a very long time, she turned to Zoe and said, 'You'll probably think I'm mad, but I'm seriously considering buying it.'

'Wow, that's quick.'

'It's perfect for what I'd need, you see. Even the setting, with that lake, is gorgeous.'

Zoe gave her a nudge. 'Well, snatch it up then. I could recognise love at first sight when I saw how you looked as you walked round, which is why I stayed downstairs and let you continue exploring on your own. But I didn't think you'd let yourself buy it.'

Let herself?

Zoe studied her sister for a minute or two, then said, 'I'm looking for the same reaction in myself when George talks about weddings and searching for a house. The only trouble is – I'm not getting it.'

'Ah.'

'I'd intended to do some travelling before I got married. Or even try living in London for a while.'

'You should have told me. You could have stayed with me for a while and had a taste of life at the hub.'

'I wasn't sure what you'd say if I invited myself to stay for a weekend, even.'

'I'd have been delighted.' Then Cassie added something as blunt as her sister's remarks often were, 'You and I are like two distant relatives, not sisters, aren't we? There aren't only fifteen years between us, but there's the way our parents feel about me letting them down and how they've tried to keep us apart.'

'Well, I found out you were raped and how could that have been your fault?'

Cassie sighed. 'Apparently I must have been encouraging it with my wanton behaviour.'

There was dead silence, then Zoe added, 'Did they really tell you that?'

'Yes.'

'Damn them! They're worse than I thought. Have you tried to find it? Sorry to say "it". I don't know whether it was a boy or girl.'

'I had a daughter. And yes, I have tried to find her but nothing came of it. I'm, um, trying again at the moment.'

'Oh, Cassie! I do hope you succeed.'

Zoe suddenly gave her a rib-cracking hug and they stood together for a few moments, rocking slightly. It was comforting. When they pulled apart, Cassie had to wipe her eyes and she didn't mind her sister seeing that, even.

'I'd really like us to get together more often from now on.' Zoe looked at her, head on one side as if asking whether that was acceptable.

Cassie felt her throat fill with more tears and said huskily, 'I'd like that too. I really would.' She fought for self-control but more tears escaped her. 'Sorry.'

'What for? Being human?'

After she'd pulled herself together, Cassie said, 'Let's go and talk money to the sales lady. It's about time I learnt to follow my instincts.'

'Don't you have to sell your present house first?'

'No. Not to buy one at this price, anyway. I've never been extravagant with what I've earned, and I've earned rather good money in the past few years. You wouldn't catch me wasting hundreds of pounds on a pair of shoes as some women do. But I will have to sell my current house to give me enough to invest and live on long term.'

'You could rent it out.'

'I don't want the bother of doing that. I want to shed my worries, not add to them.'

'So you *are* going to retire?'

She tried saying it aloud to make it seem more real, and all of a sudden, it did, it really did. 'Semi-retire, yes. Definitely. I'm quitting the public eye and giving myself time to recover.'

'Was the bombing very bad?'

'I missed the worst because I was knocked unconscious and yet it's still hit me hard, made me feel off balance, afraid. I was so close to being killed, you see, so very close. And there were a lot of photos on the TV so I felt as if I'd been there, even though I'd been knocked unconscious.'

After a pause she asked hesitantly, 'Am I mad to consider buying it, Zoe?'

'Yes. Beautifully mad. And you know what? I'm going to be a bit mad, too. I'm not going to get married to George. I'm not ready to settle down yet and I want to see a bit more of the world. If you buy the house, I warn you, I'll visit you here often.'

'Good.' She took the initiative, linking her arm in Zoe's. 'Let's go and do it.'

What a strange day this was! She couldn't remember being quite so frank with anyone, ever. She really did feel like she had a sister now.

How wonderful was that!

She tried to tell herself to wait before buying a house, but it felt wrong. And why should she?

That was wonderful too. Well, it was worth a try. She really did need a change of scene.

In the sales office the woman looked up with a smile as if ready to talk but she waited for them to speak first.

'I'm interested in the larger of the two show houses,' Cassie said.

'Buying it, you mean?'

'Yes. Buying it.' There. She'd said it aloud.

Zoe grinned and dug an elbow in her side.

'Then do take seats and we'll go through what that involves. I'm Molly Santiago, by the way. My husband and I own this development.'

After that, it all seemed easy, as if it had been meant to happen. Molly was certainly highly efficient, which boded well for the quality of the house, Cassie thought.

When they got back to her home, Cassie turned to her sister and said, 'Thank you.'

'What for?'

'Pushing me out into the real world. I think I've been a bit stuck in the London bubble.'

'Would you say I *pushed* you?'

'Not exactly, perhaps "led me gently outwards" would be more accurate.'

Zoe gave her a wry smile. 'Well, perhaps a bit. I'm rather concerned about you buying a house at the first place you looked, though. It's a really rash move. Still, you've time to get out of it if you change your mind.'

'I'm not worried and I feel sure I won't change my mind.' It was surprising how certain she felt about that. 'It felt good in that house and I can't bear to stay in this one if I give up work.' She gestured behind her to her house, frowning at how cramped it looked after the other one. 'Do you want to come in for a coffee or something?'

'Not this time, but on another occasion I'd love to spend more time with you. I've arranged to meet a friend tonight for dinner. I wasn't planning to catch up with you today, you see, but I'm so glad I did.'

When she'd waved her sister goodbye, Cassie went into her present home and waited for reality to hit her over the head and that inner voice to tell her how stupidly she'd acted today. Only it didn't. Instead she got out the brochures and smiled at the mere sight of the photos of the house like hers. She went through the details again, just in case she'd missed something. But actually, she could remember the layout of the house exactly and mentally walk round it.

It made her feel excited, with something to look forward to.

That night she slept better than she had for ages, only waking up a couple of times, once with a start because a vehicle misfired nearby. It took a while for her heart to stop pounding but she fell asleep again quite quickly.

The second time she had to use the bathroom and then lay smiling into space at the thought of how much more peaceful it would be at her new home.

In the morning she tried to go through reasons why she shouldn't rush into buying the house. She had to be sensible. This would change her whole life.

But she stared at the pictures in the brochure and all she felt was a longing to be there again. Some would say it was sensible to live where you'd be happy, that buying a house was as much an emotional act as a financial one.

Ah, she was making too much of this. If she wanted the house, she could afford to buy it. There was only herself to consider. Simple. No, there was no reason for not carrying through the purchase. She could always sell the house again later if she didn't like living there and wanted to come back to London.

Her many years' lack of interest in spending money extravagantly and her ability to invest it carefully was paying off big time now, though she'd still be careful not to waste money.

What's more, doing this seemed to be helping overcome the impact of the incident. Once she moved, she felt sure she'd settle down again quickly and completely.

And the prospect of not going back to work with Terry made her feel good. She hadn't expected to feel quite as happy about that. He was such a twerp about people, so irritating to deal with, even though he had excellent ideas for features. It was amazing he'd been so successful, given how frequently he rubbed people up the wrong way.

So that was that. She was buying the house. Starting a new life. Moving on.

Once she'd set in motion the rearrangement of her finances to provide the money for the house purchase and hired a firm to oversee the settlement process, Cassie started going through her cupboards. If she was going to move in as soon as feasible, she had a lot to do.

She'd neglected this home recently and allowed clutter from all sorts of work-related travel to pile up. This place would have to be in a much better state to sell quickly. And there wasn't a lot she wanted to keep.

Good. She needed something like this mini-project to occupy her time.

To set the crown on her improved mood, Cassie had a phone call from the agency to say they'd located her daughter and sent her the prepared letter.

They hoped to hear something within a day or two, but sometimes it could take longer for a person to respond, so she wasn't to worry.

She did worry, of course she did. They'd located her daughter as quickly as they'd said they might, but would that daughter refuse to see her again?

No, she had to hold on to the hope that this time there would be a good outcome.

And if there was still no reply, well, it'd end the suspense she'd lived with for so long and she would just have to find a way to get past it.

She so regretted not having had any other children. Too late for that now.

Did all people feel like this as they grew older? Was it normal to have a hunger for family and passing on one's genes? She'd have to research it.

In the meantime she'd got plenty to keep her busy, preparing to move house.

Hal was packed and expecting to move to Wiltshire in a couple of days when he was asked to follow up a rather important but unexpected outcome to the last project he'd undertaken. It was something he'd be able to fix in a few days but others might take several weeks to get up to date on all the legal details before they could be sure of everything.

He didn't really want to delay his move but agreed to this small project on condition they not only paid him the juicy sum offered, but covered any extra expenses which cancelling his move would cause. He wasn't happy about it, but there you were. He'd always prided himself on doing a good and thorough job, in whatever he undertook. It was called professionalism.

But this was the last time anyone did this to him, however urgent their need, and he made that absolutely clear, too.

He camped out in his flat, which he'd not yet sold fortunately, leaving most of his goods and chattels in the boxes in which they'd already been packed ready to go.

Then he set to work to get the project finished as quickly as possible.

Never had the work seemed so fiddly and boring. He realised how much he'd changed his attitude already, something which had started with the cancer diagnosis. He was still changing, wasn't sure where it would lead, but he hoped to enjoy every precious minute of the new stage of his journey through life.

Chapter Seven

Fran moved in with Keith as soon as Evie had settled down with Cousin Amelia. They were going to get married while her daughter was away, so that they could stop her protesting and make her realise this was for keeps.

She was more nervous than she'd told anyone about this and living permanently with a man again after all the years of managing on her own, and nearly backed out of it at the last minute.

Only, Keith was being so kind and helpful, she couldn't do that to him. And when they turned up at the register office to get married, he had friends waiting to act as witnesses – not his friend Ryan, thank goodness; he knew she didn't get on well with him. And Keith had a lovely meal booked after the ceremony.

It would all work out, she was sure it would. He was

so kind to her, loved her so much. *He* wouldn't let her down as James had.

They went back to her house the next day to move the rest of her personal possessions. He'd insisted she didn't need to take any of her furniture with her but she hadn't sold it as he'd suggested, had put it in storage instead. She'd worked so hard to buy it, had restored old pieces bought cheaply at charity shops. *He* might want all new stuff, but she intended to persuade him to let her bring a few of her own near-antique pieces once they'd settled into marriage.

He had flowers waiting, a meal simmering in the crockpot and candles ready to be lit when she got back from cleaning her house ready to hand it back to the agent to rent out again.

When they went to bed, he was a tender and caring lover.

Things were going to be all right, she thought as she slid happily into sleep. Well, they would be once Evie got used to the new situation. The only thing marring her happiness was being at odds with her daughter.

When she got home from work the following day, she phoned Evie to check that things were going all right at Amelia's and they got chatting. That made her late starting the preparations for the evening meal.

To her surprise, Keith went suddenly grim-faced about that.

'We did agree to eat at six each evening,' he said.

'So we'll eat at seven instead tonight.'

He opened his mouth to say something, then snapped it shut, but he remained rather distant and disapproving all evening, especially as she'd burnt the steaks in her hurry to get them finished.

The following evening he came home earlier than usual and caught her chatting to Evie on the phone again.

'Dammit, does that girl still rule your life? You're married to me now.'

She ended the call and put her phone into her bag, then turned to go into the kitchen.

To her astonishment, he grabbed her by the shoulder and swung her round, throwing her against the wall. For a moment or two she thought he was going to hit her, then he let go, took a deep breath and stepped back.

'I thought you might put us first for a while, Fran. This is supposed to be a honeymoon period, after all.'

She rubbed her shoulder. 'That doesn't give you the right to manhandle me.'

He smiled and grabbed her again, still using his strength against her but this time taking care not to hurt her as he persuaded her to take her clothes off.

She wasn't sure she liked that way of starting to make love, but it seemed to put him in a good mood.

She woke in the middle of the night and found him gone from their bed, heard a low voice from downstairs and realised he was talking on the phone.

It soon became obvious who to – his friend Ryan. The two were as thick as thieves.

She was about to go back to bed when she heard him say, 'I soon persuaded her to pay more attention to me.'

Then a minute later, 'No, of course I didn't hit her. That's no way to make a woman want to be with you. You and I will never agree about that. Anyway, I have to go back to bed now. I need my sleep, got to keep my strength up.'

She crept back into bed and pretended to be asleep.

He didn't try to snuggle up to her, just settled down and was soon snoring slightly, something that had annoyed her both nights.

It wasn't so much what Keith had said to his best friend, but his tone of voice when he'd spoken about her that had annoyed her.

She yawned and told herself she was imagining things. It had been a rush into marriage, so it was bound to take time for them to settle down together.

But it was a long time before she got to sleep.

A couple of days went past smoothly. She kept her calls to her daughter short and got dinner ready by six, but wasn't feeling comfortable about pandering to him about that. In his own home, he seemed . . . well, different, somehow. More bossy, needing to show his dominance. Which wasn't something she'd expected after the way he'd been before.

'I shall be glad to hand this over to you at the weekend,' she said as she waited for him to offer to help her clear up. He hadn't done that on the previous few evenings.

'What?'

'The cooking. Since I'm cooking during the week, I think you should clear up afterwards. I'll do the same at weekends: you cook and I'll clear up.'

'I have work to do sometimes in the evenings. I've had to put things on hold as we were getting to know one another, but I must start catching up now. And really, Fran, you can take this women's lib business too far. I doubt you'll be volunteering to do the heavy work about the house.'

She stared at him open-mouthed.

He gave her a hard stare back. 'I asked the guys at work before we married and none of them do that sort of thing, whatever they claim in the media. There are still women's roles and men's. It's always been like that and it always will be. This women's lib stuff is just a phase.'

He started to walk out on her as if he'd won the argument, and she felt suddenly furious. She rushed after him and grabbed his shoulder. 'Just a minute.'

He gave her a back swipe with one hand, sending her sprawling.

She lay there in sheer disbelief for a moment or two, then started to get up.

He rushed across to help her. 'I'm sorry, love. So very, very sorry. It's been a hell of a day at work and I let my temper take over. I won't do it again.'

She let him hold her and then watched stony-faced as he did the washing-up.

If he ever laid one finger on her again, she'd walk out. Only, she'd rented out her house, so where would she go?

Had she walked into another abusive relationship?

Surely not?

He continued to be so apologetic that she decided to give him a second chance.

But there would be no third chance if it happened again. She didn't say that, though.

How could things have turned chancy so quickly?

Why had she let him persuade her into such a hasty marriage?

What was her daughter going to say when she found out?

Evie had been settled in at Amelia's for a few days when without warning she received a visit from her mother and Keith one evening.

After a few minutes' chat, she tried to claim homework to do, but they insisted on taking her out for a meal at a local pub. And it was no use trying to pretend she'd eaten because Amelia had left the bag of groceries lying on the kitchen table while she 'just had to' add a few touches to her latest painting.

Amelia refused to come with them, saying she'd grab a sandwich and go on with the painting.

At the pub, they ordered and sat waiting for the food to be served. Evie's mother looked at her uncertainly. 'I've been worrying that you feel pushed away by us sending you to stay with Amelia. We've never been separated for more than a weekend before. Wouldn't you rather come home now, even though there's still a mess on the top floor at Keith's house? There's another bedroom you can use temporarily.'

Panic ran through Evie. Was this the start of him manoeuvring to get her under his roof? She knew her mother cared about her, but she could be so credulous when she was in love, she seemed to stop thinking for herself. Evie had seen this a couple of times before.

She wasn't quite sure how the two of them were getting on. Was it her imagination or was there a little less lovey-dovey between them tonight? Perhaps they'd had a quarrel about her.

She realised her mother was waiting for an answer and shook her head. 'No, thank you, Mum. Though it's, um, kind of you to think of me. I'm finding it easier to study at Amelia's than I would somewhere with builders coming and going.'

'But what about the longer time you have to spend travelling to and from school?'

'I'm using that to keep up with my reading. It's very helpful, actually. No one to interrupt me. And school's nearly over now anyway.'

Keith leant forward and took her hand.

Evie jerked hers away and watched him exchange rueful glances with her mother.

He said in a soppier voice than usual, 'I really do want you to live with us, dear, to make us into a proper family. Though of course, Fran and I are hoping to have children of our own after we're married, as I'm sure you must realise. We don't want to leave that too late.'

Fran relaxed a little at those words. It was so important to her to have another child before it was too late. She smiled at him and he smiled back, but she had to ask her daughter again, 'Are you sure you want to wait till school ends, love?'

Evie nodded vigorously. 'Very sure. I have important exams coming up at the end of next school year and I'd really like to get through them without hassle, so I've started laying the foundations already. Having nowhere quiet to study wouldn't be a good thing at the moment. You know I want to become a doctor, Mum. I always have done. I need to get top results for that.'

Fran sighed, wishing her daughter wasn't so set on this. 'And *you* know I'm worried about how we can afford that.'

'There are student loans and I can get a part-time job. I'll find a way to keep the burden off you, I promise. There are scholarships I can go in for next year as well, which is even more reason to study hard. And of course I'll get jobs in the holidays while I'm at uni.'

Keith turned to Fran and shrugged, as if to say that he'd tried.

Evie repeated, 'I do need my quiet study time at the moment. I'm working on a couple of special projects.'

'I'm really missing you, love.'

'I'm missing you too, Mum. But you and Keith need time on your own to settle into your relationship.'

'I suppose if you're sure you'll be all right with Amelia, we'll leave it at that for now, then. I'll, um, be at Keith's all the time now.'

It was Keith who'd pressed her to make this offer before the date they'd agreed on and convinced her it was the right thing to do. Now she wasn't so sure and was glad her daughter had turned it down. She wanted to be more sure of Keith, didn't want Evie watching them in that sharp, disapproving way she had. Her daughter could be all too perceptive.

Besides, she had to learn to stand up to him. When she was with him, he convinced her of things she didn't agree with when she had time to think them through on her own.

She saw Evie push her plate away, with half the food uneaten and that reminded her of another worry Keith had raised about girls that age. 'Are you trying to lose weight, Evie Milner?'

'No. I don't need to lose weight. I like the size I am. You gave me good genes for weight control, and I'm not stupid enough to want to look like a human stick insect. I'm simply not hungry tonight. And I have an essay to finish so I don't want to be late back.'

Fran gave her a searching look and glanced at Keith, who frowned and shook his head as if not convinced by this.

* * *

When they got back to Amelia's, Evie again claimed she had an essay to write and gave her mother a farewell kiss.

'How about giving Keith a hug?'

Evie backed away. 'No. He's your boyfriend not mine.'

'Apologise for that at once. It's very rude.'

'It's all right, darling,' Keith said. 'I know better than to take offence at a teenager's moods.'

Evie backed towards the door, leaving the three of them chatting. But she started to worry because they did this in hushed voices and when even these faded, she looked over the bannister next to her bedroom and saw that they'd closed the door of the front room, closed it without making any noise, something Amelia never did normally.

So they must be plotting something. What?

She went to sit on the bed, really upset by this visit, especially the smug way Keith looked at her before they left, as if he'd won some point or other.

In fact, she was so upset and so worried about what he might do that she lay awake fretting. First thing in the morning she decided to pack an emergency bag in case she had to run away. She'd meant it when she said she'd do that rather than live with him, and each time she saw him only made her more certain it was the safest thing to do.

Was she over-reacting? She shook her head. No. Already it seemed as if he'd brainwashed her mother into being an obedient slave. She was so much quieter since Evie had come to stay with Amelia.

What on earth was going on?

The trouble was, if he and her mother came here with an ultimatum before she'd worked out what to do, he was stronger than her. Would he go as far as forcing her into his car? She wouldn't put it past him.

But he wouldn't be able to keep an eye on her every minute of the day.

Her eyes were accustomed to the semi-darkness now and she stared round. She usually enjoyed thinking 'What if?' and working out how to deal with situations but this time she felt it was a genuine necessity.

There was only one way out from her bedroom once he was downstairs and he could easily block the stairs. She looked across at the window, then got out of bed to go and open it as far as she could and stare down. This was the only other way out.

Oh, she was being stupid and melodramatic.

Then she remembered the smug look on his face as he stared at her, and her mother's unusual quietness. No, she wasn't being stupid.

She had to work out a way to escape from Amelia's house in case he was waiting for her downstairs. It had to happen without them realising what she was doing, too. She was *not* going to move in to his place, not under any circumstances.

Think! she told herself. If they came with an ultimatum about moving in to his place, they'd have to send her upstairs to pack her things. She looked at the door, which already had a bolt on it. Good. Then she went back to look out of the window. Could she climb out and escape across the back fence before he broke the door down?

All this made her feel as if she had suddenly been transported into a children's adventure story, the sort she'd read when much younger. It felt surreal but her instincts said to have an escape route planned, just in case. And her instincts weren't usually wrong. She hadn't been brought up with a protective father, only a rather weak mother.

She'd need a rope, could buy one the very next day from the sports goods shop. She'd tie knots in it and hide it in her wardrobe. Looking round it was easy to work out exactly where she could anchor a loop of rope if she created one at the end of the line, round the foot of the old-fashioned, iron-framed single bed. The rope would have to be long enough to dangle out of the window with knots tied in it at intervals, right down to the ground.

Good thing Amelia didn't go through her things like her mother now did!

The next morning Evie got up early and took her old backpack out from the back of the old-fashioned wardrobe. Thank goodness their cousin had inherited all her grandmother's furniture with this house and never bothered to change most of it!

She put a few sensible changes of underclothing in the backpack, as well as an extra sweater and pair of jeans. As an afterthought, she stuffed in the scruffy dark wig she'd once worn in a school play, then fastened an old anorak, one her mother had told her to throw away, to the backpack strap.

The anorak was a faded red and frayed at one part of the bottom edge. But if anyone were searching for her, it would look very different from her usual outer clothes, especially if she wore the wig.

She sighed as she set the things ready. She really, really hoped this would be unnecessary. The last thing she wanted was an adventure.

Finally, she wrote a note and put it in an envelope addressed to Amelia. She'd post it if she had to flee, to make sure *he* couldn't find it if he went through her things.

She shoved the old backpack and anorak into the wardrobe then tested out grabbing it in a hurry. If she moved her winter shoes, it was the work of seconds to pull it out.

She turned to look at the bedroom door, an old-fashioned one, quite sturdy. She thought it might be best to find an additional way to secure it. That bolt was rather flimsy. When she bought the rope she'd need to find something to wedge the door shut.

Could she persuade Amelia to let her live here permanently? Would her mother even consider that? It might be worth trying because even if nothing ever happened and she didn't need to escape, she'd still have to find some way of refusing to move in with him once the attic conversion was finished. But that wouldn't be for some weeks yet, thank goodness.

She was worried sick about her next year's schooling

and the all-important final exams, so she had to sort her life out before then, had to.

She dreamt that night she was struggling against a fast-running river that was trying to wash her away.

Things had started going wrong when her mother got together with Keith. How had he managed to make her mother like him so much she didn't seem like the same person? It was as if he knew exactly what to do to manipulate her.

Well, he isn't going to manipulate me! Evie thought. *Not a chance, you horrible, slimy creature.*

The next day Evie managed to slip out of school during a study period on the excuse of having an upset stomach. She nipped across the playing field to the local shopping centre without being seen. At the post office she withdrew a large amount of money from her savings account, just in case she had to run away.

On her way home from school, she stopped off at the sports store and bought the correct length of rope and then at a hardware store where she found a wooden wedge for holding doors open. Only, she'd be using it to help keep the door shut if someone was trying to break in from outside.

Back at the house, she ran upstairs to put her schoolbag away and hid the things she'd bought at the back of the wardrobe next to the backpack. Summoning up a calm smile and checking it out in the mirror, she then went back down to make herself a cup of tea.

Amelia joined her in the kitchen and began fiddling with a teaspoon before saying thoughtfully, 'You know, I don't really like your stepfather-to-be, even though he says all the right things.'

Evie shrugged.

'And you don't seem to like him, either. You actually shied away when he touched you.'

'Well, all right. I admit I don't like him, but I'm not the one who's going to marry him, am I?'

Amelia seemed to be struggling with herself as if she wanted to say something, then she shook her head and a minute later said, 'Is there something you haven't told me about him? There must be some reason for you to feel such strong antipathy towards him.'

Evie shook her head. She was quite sure if she told Amelia it'd go straight to her mother, who wouldn't hear a word spoken against her darling Keith.

Their cousin gave her a strange look and said only, 'Well, if you ever need to tell me anything, don't hesitate. I'm on your side, not his, believe me. Just because your mother loves him, doesn't mean you have to.'

Evie opened her mouth then closed it again. No, she'd thought and thought about telling someone, but simply didn't dare say anything without proof. 'I won't hesitate. Thanks.'

When she went up to study she used the time to tie the knots in the rope and since Amelia was busy in her studio, she tested out the length. Good. It would work.

* * *

To Evie's shock and dismay, the need for her to act happened sooner than she'd expected.

Keith turned up the very next day soon after she got home from school. She was grateful that Amelia was around and though she saw him arrive from her bedroom window, she didn't try to join them.

Eventually Amelia called up the stairs, 'Have you got a minute, love?' and she couldn't delay going down any longer.

She stayed next to Amelia and only nodded at him when he said hello.

'I've got to nip to the shops,' Amelia said. 'Don't go before I get back, Keith. I want to say goodbye to Evie properly.'

Alarm bells rang in Evie's brain. *Don't go. Say goodbye to Evie properly.* What did that mean? He must be planning to take her away.

'Aren't you going to sit down?' He patted the couch beside him.

'I've been sitting all day. I'd prefer to stand.' She made sure there was a stool between them.

'I'll get straight to the point. Your mother is fretting about having sent you away, thinks it's putting a barrier between you and her, so I've come to take you to my house, to stop her fretting. There is a spare bedroom, even if it's small. We'll manage, I'm sure.'

'I don't want to go there. I've got studying to do and that's far easier here.'

'I'm not taking no for an answer, Evie. I intend to

keep your mother happy in every way I can. And you, if you'll let me.'

He glanced at her figure as he spoke. Whenever they were alone, he did that without attempting to hide his focus, though he never made the mistake of doing it in front of people. She didn't try to hide her shudder and watched him smile in response to that, as if it pleased him. Ugh! What a total and utter creep he was!

'Go up and pack your things.' He glanced at his wristwatch. 'I'll come up in a few minutes and see if you need any help.'

No way was he coming into her bedroom when they were alone in the house!

How did he think he'd get away with all this? If he laid one fingertip on her, she'd scream the place down. Or was he planning to drug her? She'd read about date-rape drugs and how you didn't remember what had happened to you under their influence.

She couldn't see any other choice now about what to do.

She locked the bedroom door and put the wooden wedge she'd bought under the bottom of it, kicking it tightly into place. Then she got the backpack out of the wardrobe and opened the window fully. It was the work of a minute to put the rope in place and climb up on the bed. She tossed the backpack down onto a soft patch of soil and squeezed out of the window.

Thank goodness she'd always been good at gymnastics and could shin up and down ropes 'like a monkey' as her PE teacher had once said. And thank goodness the sitting room was at the front of the house so *he* wouldn't see her leave.

She was so thankful she'd not waited to work out this escape plan, even though she'd only thought there was an outside chance of it being necessary. It was lucky the weather was fine today, too. That would help.

Chapter Eight

Keith ran lightly up the stairs, smiling. It was all coming together. He knocked on the door of Evie's bedroom, but there was no answer. After knocking a second time in vain, he tried the door. Locked, of course.

'Evie! Open up. This won't solve anything. Think about your mother. She needs you at home. She's worried.'

Again there was no answer.

He tried to bump against the door, but it didn't give and he didn't want to damage anything.

It was a further quarter of an hour before Amelia came back and when he told her what was going on, she rolled her eyes. 'I have a ladder in the shed. I'll go up it and see what she's doing.'

But when they went round the back, they saw the

rope before they even got as far as the shed. Cursing, he went to tug on it as it lay flapping against the wall in the light breeze that was blowing.

'Can you climb up the rope?' Amelia asked.

'No, of course I can't. What do you think I am, a monkey? Where's that ladder?'

He pushed her out of the way and climbed it. 'The room's empty.' He tried to open the window wider, but gave up when it stuck. 'I'm not trying to climb through that because I'm no good with heights. I'll have to break the door down, see if she's left a note.'

'You're not breaking my doors down. Let me come up. I'm pretty agile. I bet I can get into the room.'

He watched Amelia carefully manoeuvre her way into the bedroom and disappear from sight. A couple of minutes later she stuck her head back out of the window and gave him a cheerful wave.

'Come back into the house. I've got the bedroom door open.'

Muttering under his breath, he went into the house and walked up the stairs. But though he searched the drawers, there was nothing to tell them where she had gone, let alone a note.

'Damn her!' he exclaimed.

Amelia scowled at him. 'I don't know what you've done to her, but when we get her back, she can come and live with me if she can't stomach living with you.'

'That will be up to her mother.'

'We'll see. You'd better phone Fran and tell her what's happened.'

He did that and then rushed home.

As soon as he left the house, Amelia phoned Fran and again offered to have Evie to live with her till she went to university.

'Keith won't want that. He wants us to be a real family.'

'It isn't just up to him. Evie can't stand him and frankly, I haven't really taken to him, either. He must be very good in bed to have won you over so quickly.'

There was silence at the other end.

'If she doesn't come back, you'll have to call the police.'

'She'll be back.'

Amelia wasn't so sure. 'Well, if you're not going to let her come to me when you get her back, I'm not going to delay my trip to Italy. I don't want to be caught in the middle of a family row. But I think you're wrong, very wrong, to let Keith dictate what you do.'

'He doesn't dictate anything.'

It was no use arguing. Fran was besotted with the fellow. But Amelia couldn't help worrying about Evie. She tried phoning the girl, but there was no answer. She left a message on Evie's phone but wasn't at all sure she would get a response.

Oh hell, she was fed up of being piggy in the middle.

There was only one more day of the school term for her to work. She was going to pack her things and go to Italy as soon as she could arrange it. She planned to drive to the villa she and her friends were going to stay in. It'd be wonderful.

Evie walked quickly down the road, wanting to get as far away as possible before they found she was missing.

When she'd got out of her bedroom, she'd crept across the garden, not sure where she was going to sleep that night only that it wouldn't be in *his* house. What did homeless people do at night?

As she walked, she reviewed her options again, worried at this drastic step. Her friends' parents would just send her back to her mother if she tried to stay with any of them. No, her only chance was the unknown grandmother, who sounded so anxious to catch up with her daughter. Oh dear! She hadn't brought the torn letter with her. Thank goodness she'd memorised the address.

If the stranger didn't want her and tried to send her back to her mother, she'd have to become a street kid till she was a legal adult. That wouldn't be anything but the last choice of utter desperation.

Maybe there was a late bus that would take her closer to the London suburb where this grandmother lived. It was too far to take a taxi, even if one would accept her as a passenger at this late hour. And anyway, she didn't want to use her phone, wasn't sure whether they'd put an app on it to trace where she was. She'd checked, didn't think they had.

She had to believe this Cassie Bennington, who was so eager to contact her daughter that she'd paid a private agency to find her, would also want to meet – and help – her granddaughter.

This stranger was still the only person Evie could think of who might, if she was really lucky, help provide a long-term solution to her problem.

She found a bus that took her to the outskirts of their small town and the only other passengers didn't even glance in her direction. When she got off at the terminal, she saw a post box and hesitated, but decided not to send the letter yet. Give them a day or two to hunt for her, then maybe she'd send the letter to Amelia, who wouldn't give it to him, but to her mother, as she'd asked their cousin to do on the back of the envelope.

She began making her way along the road that led to a village on the outskirts that she'd found on an online map. She hadn't visited it before but knew if she went straight through it, she'd be going in the right direction.

Strange how little she knew even about the area where she'd always lived. If there were any teenage girl who'd had less chance to travel and see other places, it was her, thanks to her neurotic homebody of a mother. The only exceptions had been school camps.

She stuck to the verges, hiding whenever she heard a vehicle approaching. There was hardly any traffic. Anger at being forced to do this fuelled a fast pace of walking at first, then she gradually slowed down.

But the anger wouldn't go away.

Her mother had made another bad choice and must have done the same thing all those years ago as well, because Evie's father had left them, hadn't he, and no one on his side of the family had seemed to know where he could have gone. Or if they did, they weren't telling.

At least her mother hadn't given her up for adoption and she knew that she did love her. In her own way. She was more like a rather dopey older sister than a parent.

Maybe being adopted was what made her mother so clingy to anyone who seemed to offer her love and security. Evie would have to research that properly once she started her medical studies and had access to better libraries as well as better online access to medical sites.

Her grandmother's recent letter had explained why she'd given her baby up, and Evie had felt there was a warmth behind the words. Surely the person who'd written like that could be trusted?

She hoped she wasn't wrong. She was staking her whole future on it.

After just over an hour's walking, she came to a transport café and couldn't resist going inside to buy a hot drink because she'd missed her evening meal. Only, it was full of people, mainly men, who stared at her as if they'd guessed she was running away from home. A horrible old man even came over and asked her if she needed a lift anywhere.

She answered as cheerfully as she could manage. 'No, thanks. I'm being picked up by my dad soon.' She glanced at her watch and forced a smile. 'In a couple of minutes, actually.' She picked up her takeaway coffee and left the warm interior of the café reluctantly.

After waiting behind a clump of bushes to make sure no one had come out to follow her, she finished drinking the coffee and continued along the road.

A little further on she found a country bus shelter near a junction between two roads and put the empty container into the rubbish bin there. A quick glance at the timetable with the tiny torch on her phone showed her that there would be no more buses tonight, so she decided to spend the night there.

She put on her extra sweater under her anorak, jammed her beanie down over her ears, then sat on the ground, leaning into the corner of the bus shelter. As there was glass only in the top half and the bottom panels were solid metal, she was out of sight of passing traffic, and surely no one would be wandering along such a minor country road at this late hour?

She huddled down with the backpack on her lap, trying in vain to keep warm.

What was her mother doing? Were she and Keith making a fuss? Had they reported her going missing to the police?

The night seemed to go on for ever and she felt far colder than she'd expected. She didn't sleep much, just a few uneasy dozes, because she had to get up from time to time. She jogged up and down the road near the shelter to warm herself up, but hated the feeling of being alone in the windy darkness which was full of night noises. She went back to the bus shelter as soon as she was warm because it was slightly less frightening there.

It was a relief when the sky started to lighten. But that also meant the occasional car coming past. According to the timetable the first bus would arrive soon, not going in her direction unfortunately. She needed to get to a railway station and into London.

She couldn't sit here any longer, was shivering with cold, so decided to walk openly along the side of the road again, wearing the dark wig and ratty old red jacket.

Even if they were looking for her, they wouldn't be looking for a scruffy brunette, surely? She was banking on that.

And on the help of a complete stranger.

Chapter Nine

Cassie had done everything she could think of to get ready for her move to Wiltshire and was feeling a bit at a loss as to how to fill her time on the last day. Why did house settlements always take so long, even on a new build? She hadn't liked to put her present house on the market till the final settlement was complete in case something went wrong with her purchase and she had to stay here. It always paid to keep an eye on the worst-case scenario.

She'd been more than ready to go last week, and it was a new home so there was no chain of buyers and sellers to slow things down, so she was probably worrying needlessly. She'd done a lot of worrying since that damned incident. And a lot of nearly jumping out of her skin at sudden loud noises.

Last night she'd again slept badly and this morning she felt weary, unable to settle to anything.

Towards lunchtime she was standing at the bedroom window looking down the street for the postman when her eye was caught by a shabby woman in a red jacket walking along towards her end of the street.

As the figure trudged closer she realised it wasn't a woman but a teenage girl. What's more, the poor thing looked as if she were homeless and had slept rough the night before. Cassie had interviewed a few similar people for one of her TV reports the previous year and recognised the signs.

What was someone like that doing round here at a time of day when the street was usually like the land of the dead? This was a quiet, middle-class suburb and most people were at work or school now.

The girl was looking at house numbers and as she got closer, Cassie could see how utterly exhausted she was by the droop of her body. *Join the club!* she thought, easing the tension from her own shoulders.

A police car came cruising along the street. It passed the girl and stopped. The poor creature glanced back at it then speeded up, looking terrified now, giving out all the wrong signals to the officers inside it.

Cassie's heart went out to her. She wasn't doing any harm, after all. On a sudden impulse she ran down the stairs and opened the front door just as someone opened the passenger door of the police car and started to get out. She called at the top of her voice, 'There you are, Mary! Where on earth have you been? You're late.'

She beckoned vigorously and after an initial surprised look, the girl hurried across to her, hesitating at the door, then glancing back at the police car and going inside.

Cassie closed the door, saying, 'You looked as if you needed rescuing.'

'I did. Thank you.'

They stood staring at one another in the hall for a moment.

'I'm not going to hurt you. Are you in trouble?' she asked gently, not moving, afraid of sending the girl fleeing.

'Are you Cassie Bennington?'

'Yes. How do you know my name?' And it was her real name too, not her working name.

'You wrote to my mother about getting in touch.' The girl took a deep breath and added, 'I think you're my grandmother.'

The phrase seemed to echo round the stairwell. *Grandmother!* Cassie gaped at the stranger. Was this for real?

The girl sagged suddenly against the wall just inside the door. 'Sorry. I'm feeling dizzy. I'll be all right in a minute. *Please* don't call the police.'

But she was far from being all right. Her eyes rolled upwards and she fainted, letting go of the backpack dangling from one hand and crumpling slowly to the floor like a graceful rag doll. Luckily her head came to rest on the backpack, because Cassie had been too frozen with shock for a few seconds to catch her.

She knelt by the girl who was already coming to. The tatty dark wig had slipped, so she pulled it off to reveal red hair exactly the same colour as hers had once been. That shook her.

Is it possible? she thought. *Is it really possible she's telling the truth?*

Then she realised this wasn't the time to worry about anything except that the girl needed help, whoever she was. She seemed to have regained consciousness, thank goodness, so Cassie slipped one arm round her. 'Can you stand up? I want to take you into the front room so that you can sit comfortably.'

The girl jerked, half sat up and looked round with fear written all over her face as if she couldn't at first remember where she was. She sagged in visible relief at the sight of Cassie and clutched her arm. 'Don't let him catch me.'

'No one's going to catch you but we do need to get you off the floor.'

When she had her visitor sitting on the couch with the backpack by her side, she decided the first priority was probably food. 'Haven't you eaten today? Is that why you fainted?'

'I've had nothing since yesterday lunchtime.'

'Mug of tea and a piece of cake suit you – for starters?'

'Yes, please.'

As Cassie turned to go into the kitchen, the girl said, 'Can I come with you? I – I don't feel safe anywhere on my own at the moment, but I do feel safe with you.'

Cassie could relate to that feeling of constant danger looming after her recent clash with terrorists. Oh boy, could she!

'Of course you can.' She walked along the hall into the kitchen, gesturing to one of the two wooden chairs at the tiny table where she ate most of her meals. After putting the kettle on, she took out the cake she'd made yesterday to use up an ageing packet mix, for lack of anything better to occupy her time. How lucky! Cutting a piece, she put it on a plate and shoved it across the table.

'Thank you.' The girl waited, looking at her as if out of politeness.

'Do start. I'm not hungry.'

'Could I have a drink of water first, please? My mouth's a bit dry.'

'Yes, of course.'

Her guest drank the whole glassful, so Cassie refilled it, then made them both mugs of tea.

By that time the piece of cake had vanished. The girl cradled the warm cup in her hands, sipping it slowly and with obvious relish.

'Do you want to tell me why you think I'm your grandmother?' Even to say that aloud made Cassie feel strange.

'You wrote to my mother, Frances Milner.'

'I don't know your mother's name. I hired an agency to trace my birth daughter and they forwarded a letter from me to her. Did she show it to you?'

'Not exactly. I'm sorry but she threw it into the rubbish bin. I fished it out and read it. I saw the bit about you being forced to have her adopted because you were very young, so I could see why you'd done it. Mum's always been angry at you for giving her away, you see.'

She frowned as if thinking back, then nodded. 'That's right. You didn't address her by name in your letter, it was just typed on the envelope.'

Cassie stared at the girl hungrily. This really was her granddaughter. Must be. Her voice came out choked. 'How wonderful!' She wiped away a tear then reached out to clasp the girl's nearest hand. 'I'm so glad you came to me.'

The girl nodded, holding that warm hand tightly. Her eyes were also brimming with unshed tears.

'I'm sorry your mother threw my letter away, though, more sorry than I can say. I tried two years ago to contact her and heard nothing back from her then, either.'

'Well, I want to get to know you and . . . I really need help. In fact, I'm desperate.'

Cassie saw more tears gather in the girl's eyes and roll down her cheeks, so sat down next to her and reached out to take her other hand as well. 'Anything I can do to help you, I will, I promise. Let's start with your name. I don't even know that.'

'Evie, short for Evelyn, Milner like my mother's maiden name.'

The girl struggled against tears then started sobbing. 'Sorry. I didn't know where else to turn for help. I've been so frightened.'

Cassie moved her chair so that she could take her granddaughter in her arms. She cuddled her close till the tears slowed down, not speaking, letting her cry her anguish out.

When the girl pulled away, she let her go reluctantly. 'Finish your tea now then we'll go back into the living room and sit more comfortably while you tell me all about it. Most of all I need to know why you need help so desperately. I'll do anything I can to help, I promise. Will that be OK?'

'Very OK.'

When they were comfortably settled, the story came out, with extra details prompted by a question here and there.

Every word Evie spoke rang true. Cassie felt quite sure of that and she'd interviewed enough people over the years to be able to judge it with a fair degree of accuracy. For one thing, the story was awkwardly put together, coming out in short spurts. She didn't expect what she heard about recent events, though, and felt furious that someone like that sleazy fellow could treat a young girl in such a disgusting way and expect to get away with it.

Some men did get away with it, though. She'd done a story on paedophilia and it had upset her big time. It felt even worse when it happened so close to home, to her own newly found granddaughter. She'd felt a sense of anger in the past; now, she felt absolutely sizzling with fury.

The girl finished her tale and fell silent, looking at her. 'You really believe me when I say I'm your granddaughter, don't you? Can I ask why?'

'Give me a minute.' Cassie went to the corner and took out the cardboard box of photo albums she'd packed away so carefully a few days ago, slitting the sealing tape on it without hesitation. She flicked through one particular album till she came to a page with photos of herself as a teenager then handed it to Evie.

The girl stared at it then gaped at her. 'Oh! This could be me! Or a photo of Mum at the same age.' She touched her hair.

Cassie glanced ruefully towards a mirror. 'Red hair is lovely when you're young but unfortunately it seems to go white earlier than other colours of hair. I've recently stopped dyeing mine.'

She saw the moment Evie figured out who she was, or rather who she had been.

'Oooh! You're Cassandra Benn, aren't you? I've seen you on TV.'

'I used to be on TV. Not any longer.'

'I watch your programmes whenever I can. Mum's not much into serious stuff. You've investigated some very interesting topics. Oh!' She snapped her fingers as something else occurred to her. 'Weren't you caught up in that terrorist incident not long ago? At the block of flats?'

'Yes.' Cassie couldn't hold back an involuntary shudder, fighting to keep calm, which took an embarrassingly long time.

Evie watched her knowingly, then asked quietly, 'PTSD?'

'Sort of. And it's also given me a nudge to review

what I'm doing with my life. How did you guess? They didn't put how I've been affected on the news, surely? I've tried to stay out of the limelight.'

'I did a project about it once. I want to train as a doctor if possible, you see.'

'Wow. My grandfather was a doctor, your great-great-grandfather, that is.'

'So it runs in the family?'

'Yes, definitely. His father was a doctor, too.'

Evie's face lit up. 'That's cool. And it's the sort of thing I've always wanted to know – what sort of ancestors I come from.'

'Intelligent ones.' Even her parents with their very limited view of the way the world should function ran a small business very successfully. Cassie waited a moment, then heard the girl's stomach rumble. 'Would you like a proper meal now?'

'If you don't mind. I am a bit hungry still.'

'Mind? I'm over the moon that you've come to me.'

'Good. I'm not going back to my mother and *him*, not for anything.'

'I wouldn't ask you to. Not without . . . an intervention of some sort, anyway, one you'd have to agree about. I'm happy to have you stay with me for a while till we've worked out what's the right thing to do.' She'd have to wait till she knew Evie better to organise something permanent, though. She didn't intend to rush into anything. If she got into trouble with the law about that later, so be it. Her granddaughter's safety came first.

'Thank you. I doubt Mum will remember your address from that contact letter. She hardly even glanced at it. I forgot to bring it with me, but I hid it, so I should be safe here.'

'Won't matter if she does remember. I'm moving house tomorrow and I don't know the neighbours except to smile at because I've been away so often. They won't have any idea where I've gone. You can come with me and if it's all right with you, I suggest we take a few days together in my new place to work out what to do before we get back to your mother.'

Evie let out a huge, heartfelt sigh. 'That'd be great. I don't want to upset Mum, but she's too besotted to see any harm in him.'

Cassie was already trying to work out how to find a good lawyer who specialised in this sort of thing because they'd undoubtedly need legal help, but she didn't tell Evie that. She didn't intend to do anything immediately. She was sure a peaceful country setting would help them both work out some reasonable steps to take that would still keep Evie safe.

In the meantime, there was food to be thought of and catering wasn't her strong point. 'I'm sorry, Evie, but apart from the cake, I only have bread, frozen ready meals, tinned stuff or packaged goods. And a few elderly pieces of fruit. I'm not a mad keen cook at the best of times, and I've let supplies run down lately because of being about to move house.'

'Where are you moving to? You didn't say.'

'A leisure village in Wiltshire. Near a lake. It's very peaceful there.'

'Sounds lovely. I enjoy cooking, so I can do some of it, if you like. Mum sometimes lets me into her kitchen. She's a great cook but she always follows recipes to the letter. I like to add new touches sometimes.'

Already her granddaughter's colour had returned and she was looking less stressed, thank goodness. 'Let's go and see what there is to eat.' Cassie opened the freezer and they inspected its meagre contents.

After they'd eaten, she suggested Evie take a shower and have a nap, and her granddaughter hesitated.

'You won't . . . contact the police or anything?'

'I promise I won't contact anyone at all. And as you'll find out, I always keep my word.' She made the crossing the heart sign, then gave her granddaughter another tentative hug.

It was returned, just as quickly and shyly. Cassie had to swallow hard to rid her throat of the lump emotion had dumped there.

'I'd love a shower. I did bring clean underwear.'

Cassie unpacked some sheets for the spare bed she'd bought and gave Evie a nightdress to wear. That brought a smile to her granddaughter's face.

'I can't remember ever wearing a nightie before.'

'I find them comfier and freer than pyjamas.'

Cassie peeped into the bedroom a few minutes later, worried by the silence, and found Evie fast asleep, her face smooth and unlined, her hair so bright red, it was like looking at a younger self.

She tiptoed downstairs and sat for a while staring into space, trying to come to terms with the ramifications of this. She had no doubt now about their being related, none whatsoever, given their close resemblance to one another, not just their hair but the shape of their faces and even the fact that they were neither of them tall.

And oh, to have found a granddaughter was like a dream come true. Would her daughter still refuse to meet her? She was hoping desperately that she wouldn't refuse again. Fran. That was her daughter's name, short for Frances. Nice name, one she might have chosen herself.

Was she doing the right thing in not contacting the mother immediately, though?

Legally, probably not.

Emotionally, she hoped she was, for the girl's sake. It was her best guess and anyway, she'd given her word.

She bounced to her feet and went to stare at herself in the long mirror that was now leaning against the wall, ready to be taken away.

I'm a grandmother! She felt she ought to look different. No, that was silly.

Her phone rang and she rushed into the kitchen to snatch it up before it woke Evie. 'Yes?'

'Zoe here. Just wanted to wish you happy moving day tomorrow.'

Cassie relaxed. 'Thanks. You must come and visit me soon.'

'I'll do that. Stay in touch.'

She almost told her sister about Evie, but something held her back. If their parents found out, she had no doubt they'd report the matter to the police. To them, parents' rights to control their children were immutable. They had few nuances in their view of life.

Another thing occurred to her and she frowned. It'd be better not to use Evie's real name when they got there, in case the police put out a missing person call.

Could they maintain their secrecy? Keep Evie's identity hidden? For a time, surely?

Unable to settle, she fiddled around as the girl continued to sleep. When they said truth could be stranger than fiction, they were right.

Evie didn't wake up till late afternoon. Cassie heard her stirring and put the kettle on, but waited for her to come down in her own time instead of going up to check she was all right.

She turned round when she heard footsteps on the stairs. 'Hello, sleepyhead.'

'Sorry. I didn't sleep well last night. I was cold – and frightened of someone attacking me.'

Cassie ventured another quick hug. 'I'm very glad no one did. Are you hungry again?'

'I am rather. I'm sorry to be such a nuisance.'

'You could never be a nuisance to me. You're more like a dream come true.'

She saw the girl's mouth shape an O of surprise and

then a smile creep across her face, making her look suddenly younger and more vulnerable.

'Let's get you some food. I took a few things out of the freezer. I hope you don't have any problem foods. I forgot to ask.'

'No. I can eat anything, and without putting weight on luckily.' She assessed Cassie. 'You're quite slim.'

'I'm lucky, like you. I have a friend who has an underactive thyroid and she puts weight on if she so much as looks at a piece of cake. This stuff about calories in, calories out and how much to eat to lose weight is rubbish. One size doesn't fit all in any aspect of human life, I've found. I was meaning to do an investigation into it when—' She shrugged and finished, 'When the bomb went off.'

'It tore your life apart, didn't it? Just as Keith has torn mine.'

'Yes. Since then I've been regrouping but I may get to do that article one day. I've come to believe that people are being conned about many aspects of life, and made to feel guilty for things that aren't their fault.'

After clearing her plate and topping up with some cheese and biscuits, Evie sat back, prepared once again to chat. 'What time do we leave in the morning?'

'The movers are coming at seven. I think it'd be better if they didn't see your hair. Could you wear that wig, do you think, and maybe sit outside on the back patio while they take everything out to the removal van?'

'Yes, of course. I'll do whatever you think best.'

'When we get to Wiltshire, you won't be able to keep wearing the wig, but I wonder if we should use another name for you, just for the time being? What do you think?'

'Good idea. It felt like being in an adventure story running away from home yesterday and it still feels like one. They're not as much fun as they sound in books, though! I didn't mind climbing out of the window and shinning down a rope but I got very cold at night. And afraid.'

'What made you prepare like that?'

'I don't know. Everything just felt wrong about him and I grew frightened. It felt as if he were a predator moving in for the kill. I just wish I'd thought of food, though.' After a pause, she added, 'Everything still feels a bit unreal, even now I'm with you.'

She stopped talking, frowning, reliving her memories of escaping, if Cassie guessed right.

She gave her a little time then changed the subject. 'Shall I think of a new name or will you?'

'We-ell, I rather like the name Lacey. How about we use that?'

'Fine by me. I like it too. Don't forget to answer to it when other people are around.'

'I won't.'

No, anyone who prepared a successful escape rope in advance could be trusted to remember details, Cassie was sure. She saw Evie studying her, head on one side, and smiled at her. 'Something wrong?'

'No. It's just, you don't seem as old as I'd expected. My mum's adoptive parents used to be a bit old-fashioned in their ways. Mind you, now I come to think of it, they were older than you by about twenty years if you were only fifteen when you had my mother.'

'Were older?'

'They were killed in a car crash.'

'Oh. I'm sorry.'

'Yes, I was too. They were really nice.'

'Well, thank you for the compliment. I don't feel old in my head and it's nice to know I'm wearing well on the outside too.' *Bless!* she thought. Her granddaughter was still a child in some ways and anyone past forty no doubt seemed old to a teenager.

Within a couple of hours, Evie-Lacey was yawning again.

'Why don't you go to bed?' Cassie suggested. 'We'll have to be up very early tomorrow.'

'Would you mind?'

'Of course not.'

Evie stopped at the door to say, 'Thank you, Grandma.'

'You're welcome, darling.'

'Or should I call you Gran?'

'Mmm. Yes. I think I'd prefer that.'

'I do too. Gran it is.'

That brought happy tears to Cassie's eyes as she checked that everything was ready for the move, before following her granddaughter's example and going to bed early.

What an eventful day it had been! Who'd have thought life could change so drastically in such a short time? Surely this relationship would now form part of her new life? Or was she being too optimistic? Would her daughter be cruel enough to keep them apart?

Perhaps one day she'd even get to meet Fran. Or would she continue refusing to see her birth mother, even after they'd sorted out Evie's problems?

It hurt to be rejected. Twice it had happened now, so it wasn't just a whim on her daughter's part.

Please let that change now! she prayed desperately as she slid into sleep. *Oh, please!*

Chapter Ten

Hal was relieved when he finished the extra project, which had taken longer than he'd expected. He was lucky enough to catch the removal company with a day when they had a crew and vehicle free, so within twenty-four hours he had everything ready once again for the move. Well, he'd never unpacked most of his stuff.

He went to bed on the final night in his flat feeling happier and more relaxed than he had for a good long while. It was over. He was free to choose his own path from now on.

The following morning, the movers were on time and packed everything into their truck with speed and efficiency. He watched them drive away, did a final check that everything was clean and tidy and locked up the flat one final time.

He set off at once for Wiltshire, not looking back. He wouldn't miss the isolation of living in a block of flats where no one did more than nod at a neighbour in passing and silence was more common than the faint daily noise of fellow humans nearby.

He soon overtook the movers' vehicle. Good. He'd be able to open up the house and have everything ready to let them in. To crown it all, a lovely day was forecast, sunny but not too warm, the weather report had said.

'Perfect!' he said aloud, not switching on the radio because he was enjoying the feeling of driving quietly into the future. He absolutely craved peace and quiet these days.

An hour and a half later, as he was leaving the M4, the car engine misfired.

'No! Don't do that!' he begged it aloud. To his relief the engine picked up and he continued.

But the car misfired again just after he'd passed through Marlbury and was on a narrow stretch of country road with no places to stop. This time it continued to misfire and when the car began to lose speed and move jerkily, he looked ahead for somewhere to pull off the road. To his dismay, before he could find a suitable place, the engine cut out altogether.

The best he could do was pull over to the very edge of the road before he totally lost momentum. Unfortunately his car was still blocking most of one lane and to make matters worse, he'd been forced to stop just after a bend. He sat there for a moment or two, feeling a strong sense of aggrieved disbelief. It wasn't an old car, it had low mileage and he had it serviced regularly. What the hell could have gone wrong?

He had no idea, of course. He'd never been into cars and because he lived in a fairly central part of London, he'd used public transport much of the time.

He phoned his breakdown service but they said it'd be about an hour before they could get someone out to him.

Sighing, he put his phone away and decided to get out and stretch his legs by moving up and down by the roadside. There was just enough room for one person to walk along the overgrown verge.

He was closing the car door when a yellow van whizzed round the bend, moving far more quickly than was safe. In fact, it had crossed the middle line into his lane as it hit the bend and passed so close it caught him on the shoulder, sending him sprawling forward onto the road.

He lay there, squinting at the registration plate.

The driver must have seen him fall but didn't stop. He murmured the registration to himself as he lay there, feeling dazed and trying to pull himself together. He was shocked at how suddenly it had happened.

He was vaguely aware of another car coming to a halt in front of his. A woman's voice, low and pleasant in tone, brought him back to the situation.

'Are you hurt?'

He managed to find some words. 'Only bruised, I think. Can you write this down? It's the registration number of the van which hit me.'

'Tell me. I'll remember it.'

She repeated it after him then said, 'We have to get you off the road before another lunatic whizzes round that bend. My granddaughter's keeping watch.'

He tried to get up and found it difficult. She tried to support him, but had difficulty because she was much smaller than him. A teenage girl ran to join them and together the two helped him round to the verge side of his car just before another car whizzed by, luckily on the right side of the road this time.

He leant against his vehicle, feeling shaky, but remembered enough to say, 'Please – can you write that number down?'

She fished in her car and wrote it down, reading it to him and getting his approval of it. 'What exactly happened?'

'My car's engine cut out so I let it roll to the side of the road and had just got out when a speeding van came round the bend in the middle of the road. Yellow, it was, with some sort of logo on the side. In red.'

She wrote on her pad again.

'Something, maybe the wing mirror, clipped my shoulder, sending me flying. The van didn't stop.'

As she scribbled again, he tried to straighten his body and winced. 'Oh hell, it hurts to move my right shoulder.'

'But you can move it?' the girl asked.

'Yes.'

'Then it's probably not broken or dislocated.'

He stared at her, surprised that a teenager would venture to comment so confidently.

She must have realised what he was thinking. 'I did a first-aid course, an advanced one. We should get you to the nearest A&E and let them check you properly, though.'

The woman nodded agreement. 'I'm Cassie, by the way, and this is . . . Lacey.'

'Hal Kennedy.'

She studied him. 'You look pale. I'll call an ambulance.'

'No, wait. I'm already feeling better. And Lacey's right. I can move my shoulder.' He eased it cautiously forward and backward, but though it hurt, it wasn't a major pain and he was quite sure nothing was broken. Relieved, he leant back against the car again, because that felt more comfortable.

Another car drove past and pulled up just beside them. A man stuck his head out of the window.

'Anything wrong?'

So Hal explained what had happened again.

'Have you called for help?'

'I called the breakdown service before I got out of the car. They're on their way but they said it'd take an hour or so. I think my shoulder is only bruised.'

'Well, if I can't do anything, I'll be on my way. Good luck!'

Hal continued to lean against the car, feeling like an idiot. The movers would get to his new house and find no one to let them in. And they wouldn't be likely to use this narrow lane as a shortcut, as he had, because of the size of their vehicle, so he wouldn't be able to flag them down. He'd have to phone Molly Santiago and see if she had a key to his house, and then heaven knew where they'd dump his things.

'I'm going to be late,' he muttered.

'Where were you going?' Cassie asked.

'Penny Lake Leisure Village. It's not far away. Do you know it?' The woman looked vaguely familiar, now he came to think of it, but he couldn't work out where he'd seen her before.

She let out a huff of laughter. 'That's where we're going.'

'Really? Then perhaps you could give me a lift? I have to open my new house and let the removal crew in.'

'What about your car?'

'I'll put my key under the passenger seat and phone the breakdown people, ask them to tow it to the nearest garage and let me know where that is. After all, no one can drive off in it if the motor won't start.'

'If you give me the key, I'll put it in place for you,' the girl said.

'Thanks. I appreciate that.'

The woman opened her rear car door and rearranged some bags. 'You'd better get in, Hal. You can phone the breakdown service again while we drive.'

She was about to close the car door on him when he suddenly remembered something. 'Oh! I've just remembered. I have one of those gadgets to warn people of a hazard ahead in the boot. Can you wait until I've put it near the bend on the other side? I don't want someone smashing into my car.'

'I can do that for you,' Cassie said. 'I know how to set one up.'

Before he could say anything, she'd opened his boot, found the triangle and got it to flash. She placed it round the bend, out of sight from here but giving more warning. As she went back to close the boot, she asked, 'Do you need anything else from your car, Hal? We can't squash much in, I'm afraid.'

'Could we take that small suitcase and the bag of frozen food from the boot? I don't want to leave that out for too long and the suitcase has important documents in it.'

She went to rummage and held them up. 'These?'

'Yes.'

'I'll have to put them in the back with you. Our boot is full up.' She had to put the suitcase on his knee and the food bag on top of that.

By the time he'd phoned up and told a disapproving despatcher what he'd done with the key, they'd reached a wider road.

He switched off the phone. 'The breakdown service will bring the car to my home if it's a simple fix, since it's not far away. I've got my fingers and toes crossed.'

'Good. And we've only five minutes to go now, according to my satnav. It's a real coincidence that we're moving into that leisure village too. Oh, look. We're nearly there.'

They all stared at the hotel as they turned off the road and drove slowly past it, then moved away from the car park and across to the group of houses.

'This development isn't really big enough to be called a village, is it?' Cassie said as she slowed down. 'Which house is yours?'

'That one at the far right.'

'Ah. We're going to be next-door neighbours, it seems.'

'Amazing coincidence you stopping for me, isn't it?'

'Coincidences happen more often than you'd think.'

Once she'd stopped outside his house, the girl came to take Hal's bag of food out of the car and he turned to her grandmother. 'Thanks for your help, Cassie. I owe you a drink for that.'

He tried to pick up his small case, but winced as the weight tugged at his sore shoulder and let the case drop to the ground again.

As he was reaching for it with his other hand, Cassie said, 'I'll get that.' She picked it up and walked him to the front door.

'I really am grateful to you both.'

'Our pleasure. If you open the door, we'll bring your things in.'

When they'd deposited the food on a kitchen surface, Cassie looked round. 'Yours is completely different in configuration to mine.'

'You must come round for a thank you drink one evening.'

'Happy to.' She switched on his new fridge and freezer, then they left.

He waited at the door to wave goodbye, then closed

it on the world, leaning against it, feeling as if he were watching an out of focus film. He had to admit to himself that his head was aching and he still felt rather shaken. But as the girl had said, he could still use that shoulder, so surely it must only be badly bruised?

He really didn't want to visit a hospital, not now with the movers due, and not ever again, if he could help it. Which was silly when the medical system had helped him beat cancer, but there you were. That was how he felt.

He moved around the kitchen area, aching for a cup of strong tea, but of course, although the cooktop was fitted and came on when he tried turning a knob, he had no utensils to boil water or brew tea in.

Still, the movers mustn't be far away now. As soon as they arrived, he'd retrieve a kettle or saucepan and boil up some water.

He went to sit on the stairs, *faute de mieux*. At least he had arrived at his permanent home now, and if it wasn't quite the triumphal taking possession he'd imagined, well, he was here. That was the important thing.

Cassie moved her car to the drive of her own house next door and sat for a moment, smiling at it. She had the same feeling of coming home that she'd had on her first visit. Strange how quickly she'd fallen for this place.

She'd remembered it so clearly that she hadn't come back for a second visit, too afraid of someone from the press following her here. With a bit of luck she was safe from them now, and since she wasn't hot news any longer, she doubted they'd go to any great lengths to trace her.

She was getting over her desire to stay hidden in a bunker now, thank goodness. She turned as her granddaughter spoke.

'They're lovely looking houses. The inside of Hal's place was all big spaces. Is yours the same? Mum and I have only ever lived in small houses or flats.'

'Let's go inside and walk round mine, then you can see for yourself. Though it'd make sense to carry a few things in as we go. It's a wonder we fitted Hal into the back of our car, we'd stuffed so many stray bits and pieces into it.'

Evie followed her round, wide-eyed, murmuring, 'Wow!' in a whisper as she walked through the downstairs spaces, then up to the bedrooms.

'This front one is mine,' Cassie said. 'You can have any of the others you like.'

Evie chose the larger of the two that looked towards the back. 'If I lean out of the window, I can just catch a glimpse of the lake. And I have my own en suite bathroom. My very own. I can't believe that.'

'Believe it. But keep it clean, please.'

'I'm very clean and tidy in my ways. I've had to be, because Mum isn't and I hate having to hunt for my school things amongst the piles of dirty washing she leaves for ages. I can do my own washing, don't worry. I'll try not to cause you extra work.'

'Good. But sometimes extra work is worth it.' They exchanged smiles, then she said, 'Now, let's make a cup of coffee or tea. I don't think Hal will have anything to make a drink with, so I think we'd better take him a cup, too.'

But just as they were about to do that, their removal truck arrived and Cassie said sharply, 'Put that wig on, quick! And don't start chatting to them. Stay out of their way as much as possible.'

'Play the moody teenager?' Evie asked with a smile. 'I don't normally do that but I've seen others do it.'

'Perfect.'

Afterwards Cassie was kept busy deciding what went into each room and she noted with approval that Evie took a chair outside and sat there with a book.

She'd have to buy some more furniture quite quickly. Thank goodness she had a studio couch for Evie to use as a bed.

Hal watched enviously as a removal truck arrived next door. Then, to his surprise, a van with the logo of the emergency service on it pulled up outside his house, towing his car. Oh, thank goodness! It must have been something simple that went wrong.

He went out eagerly to find a cheerful woman on her way to his door.

'Mr Kennedy?'

'Yes.'

'Do you have some ID?'

He got out his wallet and showed her his driving licence and she noted the number of it because it didn't have this address on it.

'It was only a blocked fuel line and a loose connection, so I fixed them and brought your car back here. You can move it onto your drive yourself after I've gone.'

'Thanks. I'm so grateful.'

'Well, the despatcher said you were moving into a new home, and I know what that's like. Here you are.' She held out his car key. 'Can you sign this, please?'

He read the form then signed it willingly, writing 'Excellent service' in the comments section.

After the van had pulled away, he got into his car and moved it. Before he even reached his half-open front door, he was further cheered by the sight of a second removal truck arriving in the narrow little street, so turned to wait. It could only be for him.

'Yesss!' he murmured happily.

It edged skilfully backwards into his short drive, stopping in exactly the best position for unloading.

He saw Cassie at her kitchen window and gave her a thumbs up as he went to greet the removal crew.

Within half an hour, he'd retrieved his kettle, found some mugs and made them all cups of tea. He didn't keep coffee, the smell of which seemed horribly strong since his various hospital treatments and made him feel slightly nauseous.

In just under two hours, the crew had unloaded everything and driven their empty vehicle away. He looked round at the chaos and felt happiness bubble up inside him, for all that his shoulder was still aching.

He really was home now and it didn't matter if he

had to take the unpacking slowly. All he needed was somewhere to sleep, sit and eat. The rest could be tackled as and when he felt up to it.

He walked to the doors leading out onto the back patio. He'd have to buy some better outdoor furniture than the few shabby pieces he already had. It'd be a great place to sit and chat to friends, or just read a book.

He hoped to spend his final years here. Life was good.

Keith had worried about leaving Fran on her own but he had an important meeting that he couldn't afford to miss.

When he got home from work, his new wife greeted him with tears in her eyes. She hardly gave him time to close the front door before saying in a wobbly voice, 'There's still no sign of Evie and last night was the second without her. Keith, we'll *have* to go to the police now. She may have been murdered!'

He put his briefcase down, hiding his annoyance about that stupid girl. 'Not her. She'll have found someone to stay with, I'm sure. She's a sly one, I'm afraid, darling. You have to face facts about her. We'll only be pandering to her prima donna antics if we go to the police. And she's bound to tell them lies about why she ran away. That's what teenagers do. Then there will be a huge fuss. You don't want them taking her into care, surely?'

'Take her away from me! Surely they wouldn't do that?'

He put his arms round her and kissed her cheek then her lips, something that usually won her over, but though she clung to him, it only calmed her slightly today. He'd never met such a needy female. Or one with such a pretty young daughter. He'd fallen lucky there. If he played his cards right, he'd be getting two for the price of one.

Pity Fran didn't have much money to contribute to the family purse now they were married, but there you were. He'd make sure she continued working and as for having other children, forget it. Babies and small brats were a pain to live with as he had found out the first time round. He'd had the operation years ago to ensure he couldn't have any more.

With a sigh, Fran pushed away from him. 'Well, Amelia will still be there. She's not going to Italy till tomorrow. I'll just give her a quick ring and see if she's heard from Evie.'

He bit back a sharp response as the two women chatted on and on, then he led the way upstairs and made sure Fran had something else to occupy her mind and body before she cooked his tea.

Females! What a pity one couldn't live without them. And he had an especially strong need for what only they could give him.

Fran pretended to be asleep, angry with herself for giving way to his skilful lovemaking yet again.

She couldn't get it out of her mind that Amelia was worried about Evie too, had said in no uncertain terms that she should have gone to the police. But her cousin wouldn't agree to stay in England, was still planning to leave soon. She'd said Fran must sort things out herself.

Fran sighed. She had a key to Amelia's house, after all, so she could check whether Evie came back and took refuge there. But she wished her cousin was going to stay around, just in case Evie needed her.

Somehow Fran didn't dare to go to the police, not now. Keith had been very emphatic about that, had shouted at her when she persisted. Somehow she felt a girl as clever as her daughter would keep herself safe. She had to believe that.

Why had Keith tried to force Evie to come and live with them when she was so set against it? She didn't think Evie had agreed, but he'd claimed she had because he'd persuaded her to think of her mother.

Why had Evie run away when he'd sent her upstairs to pack, then?

Anyway, Amelia had told a different story, saying Evie had begged to be allowed to stay with her the previous evening. Fran had begun to wonder why the girl was so frightened of him.

If her daughter had persisted in objecting to moving in here, she'd have let her stay with Amelia for that crucial final year at school, even though it wasn't her favourite option.

Fran chewed one of her nails, then stopped herself because she'd promised him to give up nail biting. And she'd managed it. Well, most of the time.

Why, oh why, had she rushed into marriage with Keith? He wasn't always as nice when they were in his house.

What if her marriage alienated her from her daughter permanently? She couldn't bear the thought of that.

Lying in the darkness, listening to Keith's steady breathing, Fran admitted to herself that she was – not exactly frightened, but definitely nervous of upsetting him. He'd proved what anger could drive him to do when he hit her.

She ought not to have married him till she knew him a lot better. He might be OK, but . . . he might not.

Only, her house was now rented out and her furniture in storage. If she decided to leave him, it'd be hard to arrange somewhere else to go without him finding out. And, oh hell, what a fool she'd look if she left him after such a short time married!

It occurred to her that he had poked into every aspect of her life and she was only just realising how much he had started controlling her. The only thing she'd held out about was them keeping their bank accounts separate. She wasn't sure yet that she wanted to have a joint account. It was early days and they were both a bit on edge. He could be so nice at times, charming and caring.

But he had hit her. He might think she'd put up with that occasionally, but he was wrong. He'd better not do it again, even. It was her sticking point. She'd seen a TV programme about how battered women got sucked in and persuaded it was their fault for provoking their partner, and had never forgotten its lesson.

She wasn't going down that track. Another show of

violence would prove that he wasn't trustworthy and she'd end their relationship, however humiliating that was.

She snuggled down, feeling she'd taken one good decision, at least: separate bank accounts was something she'd not give way on.

The rest had been put on a rather wobbly footing.

If she only knew for certain that Evie was safe, she'd be able to concentrate better on sorting out her own situation.

Chapter Eleven

Cassie strolled up to the hotel, which took only a couple of minutes, and found out that the snack bar did takeaways, so she took a menu home and rang through an order for the two meals they'd chosen.

She and Evie walked up to collect them but she left her granddaughter outside, because that really was a dreadful wig, not only an obvious fake but well past its use-by date.

They walked back quickly and sat in the middle of partially organised chaos, eating. For the first time in ages Cassie was truly hungry and cleared her plate.

Evie pushed her empty plate away with a happy sigh. 'It's lovely here. Could we go for a walk round the lake after we've cleared up, do you think?'

'Why not? As long as you put that wig on again. In fact, let's go now before it gets dark. We can clear up the kitchen later.'

'I'll ring him at home tonight, then, and you can phone him at work just after nine. Here's his number.'

'Thanks, Judy. I'm so grateful.'

When she'd put the phone down, Cassie smiled, feeling as if fate were on their side. She could drive to Chichester easily and it would be safer for both of them not to have to travel on public transport as they would in London.

But the smile soon faded because she doubted from what Evie had told her that things would go easily with the girl's mother and her husband-to-be. And she knew from checking online that a mother's rights usually trumped a grandmother's when it came to making arrangements for the care of children.

Well, it did unless you could prove there was a problem such as Evie had described, which she doubted would be possible in this case. She believed what her granddaughter had told her about that horrible man, oh yes, because the way Evie said he was acting fitted the type. Only, he'd been clever and had managed not to alert anyone else so far to what he was really after, damn him to high hell!

She didn't think she could bear to send Evie back into he lion's den – but would she have any choice?

She'd have to wait and see what the lawyer said.

But if necessary, as a final resort she'd break the law. e even knew one or two people who would shelter girl temporarily, people she trusted who hated erts just as much as she did. She wasn't letting Evie

Evie did as she'd been asked and tugged on the stupid wig, rolling her eyes at her reflection in the mirror.

They stopped at the other side of the lake to look across at the group of new houses.

'Do you have any plans yet for what to do about me, Gran?' Evie asked suddenly.

'Not really. I'll have to contact a lawyer before we make any important decisions. I'd better do that as soon as possible, tomorrow if I can find one. I don't want to be charged by the police with abducting you.'

Evie stared at her in dismay. 'I never thought of that! I don't want to get you in trouble, Gran.'

'I wouldn't be helping you if I didn't want to do it, or if I felt it was morally wrong.' She put her arm round the girl's shoulders and gave her a hug. 'Truly. You really are the best thing that's happened to me for years.'

Evie nestled against her. 'Well, that's the nicest thing anyone's said to me in a long time. *He* does nothing but complain about me. It's as if he's trying to come between me and Mum.' After a slight pause, she added in a near whisper, 'I, um, feel the same about you, too, Gran.'

That brought a lump into Cassie's throat.

They finished their walk and as they passed Hal's house, he came to the front door. 'I'm just about to take a break. Do you fancy a cup of tea? I don't have any coffee, I'm afraid.'

'I'd love a cup of tea,' Cassie said at once and they joined him inside.

'Did you enjoy your walk?'

'Loved it.'

'I saw you go past and would have liked to join you, but my shoulder is aching and walking jolts it too much, so I've postponed that pleasure. Look, I feel like celebrating moving into my new home. How about a glass of wine instead of the tea, Cassie? We can drink to your new home as well.'

'Sounds perfect.'

'And I can offer a choice of tea, drinking chocolate or a can of ginger beer for you, Lacey.'

It took a few seconds for Evie to remember her new name and realise he was addressing her. 'Ginger beer would be lovely, thank you, Mr Kennedy.' When he turned to get it for her, she shot a guilty glance for her lapse at her grandmother.

Cassie grinned and winked at her, and she relaxed again.

They sat in Hal's lounge for nearly an hour chatting and toasting their new homes, then the two women headed next door.

Cassie yawned. 'Another early night for us both, I think.'

When they got inside, Evie flung her arms round her grandmother, surprising her. 'What a lovely day it's been! Thank you so much for saving me.'

'My pleasure. Will you be all right on that old couch? We'll go and buy you a proper bed tomorrow.'

'I could sleep on the floor, I'm so tired.'

Cassie didn't spoil the moment by reminding her that staying here was only a temporary fix for her

problems. She wished it wasn't, wished Evie could stay with her permanently.

But the law might decree otherwise.

When her granddaughter had gone to bed, she got out her phone and called a friend she hadn't been in contact with for a while, apologising for that.

'I heard about the terrorist incident and called you, but when you didn't answer your phone, I guessed you were being hounded by the press. Are you all right, Cassie?'

'Yes.'

'Really?'

'Well, I'm getting there, Judy, because something good has happened to balance the scales.' She knew Judy well enough to explain about her granddaughter turning up and her need for a lawyer to help her deal with this.

'Don't you have a relative who is a lawyer?'

Her friend laughed. 'Yes. And what's more, my cou specialises in family law. I'll give Thomas a ring ton and tell him he absolutely must fit you in tomorrow

'Thanks. I'm truly grateful.'

'The trouble is, he's moved down to Chichest you be able to get there?'

'Actually, that's better for me. I've just m new house near Swindon, so I'm not too far a enjoy a drive there much more than a tra London.' She'd decided to say 'near Swi of 'near Marlbury' and not mention the village' to hide her actual location.

join the homeless and have to sleep rough regularly.

Her granddaughter's safety came before anything else.

Evie proved to be an earlier riser than Cassie had expected for a teenager and was up and showered by 8 a.m., hungry and ready to continue helping her sort out the house.

If only that was all they needed to do today, what fun they could have had going shopping together.

After breakfast Cassie couldn't put it off any longer. 'Don't get up from the table yet. I have something to tell you.' She explained about phoning her friend and finding out about her lawyer cousin.

She hated to see the happiness vanish from her granddaughter's face. 'I'm sorry, love, but we have to find out where we stand. I'd prefer not to flout the law. That wouldn't help our case at all.'

'Our case?'

'For you to stay with me. If you want to, that is?'

'You really mean that, don't you?'

'Oh, darling, of course I do!'

'I can't think of anything I'd like more, but they'll make me go back to Mum, I know they will. I'll run away if they do and live rough if necessary. I love her but I'm *not* living with *him*.'

'Let's find out first where we stand before we panic, shall we? Then we'll make plans together – for all eventualities. If the worst comes to the worst, I can help you do better than live on the streets, believe me.'

She rang Thomas Wutherington (why did lawyers so

often have weird names?) just after nine o'clock and was put straight through to him by his secretary when she gave her name.

'Judy rang me at home last night, Ms Bennington.'

'Did she explain my problem?'

'Yes. Well, she gave me a broad-brush outline anyway. Why don't you come in and see me today? I have an hour free at eleven. Can you and the girl get here by then?'

'Yes, definitely.'

He checked that she knew his address and told her where best to park, which was very thoughtful of him, before he rang off.

Evie looked at her, just looked, but it hurt to see the fear on that young face.

'We need to leave immediately. And you'd better wear the wig till we're away from here, then you can take it off. We don't want him to see you looking like that. I'm so sorry to have to put you through this, love. And I can lend you a smarter jacket than that red thing.'

'You don't need to keep apologising, Gran. I don't want you to be arrested.' She accepted the jacket, but clearly didn't care about clothes at the moment.

'You can tell the lawyer that you won't live with Keith, but remember, it makes a better impression to speak your piece calmly and not sound hysterical. And always tell the truth. This is not about pleasing me but getting the best outcome for you and what you really, really want.'

Evie frowned, then nodded slowly as she thought about that. 'You're right. I'll do my best to stay calm. I'm pretty good at it usually. I've had to be, because Mum can get a bit, um, excitable.'

Remarks like that made Cassie wonder what sort of woman her daughter had grown into, let alone what sort of mother she'd been. Evie spoke of her fondly, but sometimes she sounded to have played a more adult role than Fran had.

They were on the road within ten minutes. Thank heaven for satnavs.

Thomas Wutherington was about forty, a big teddy bear of a man, which seemed appropriate for someone specialising in family law. His expression however was distinctly shrewd and Cassie liked that. She wanted the best advice she could get, the very best, not waffling and kindness.

She outlined the situation, then he turned to Evie and offered to speak to her privately if she preferred, but she shook her head.

'I can say anything I need to in front of my grandmother. She's not forcing me to do anything; it's my mother who's trying to do that.'

He then asked a few more detailed questions about her wishes, after which he sat frowning for a while before speaking to Cassie. 'If you were the acknowledged grandmother, Ms Bennington, it'd be a lot easier, because she's nearly sixteen and that's usually the age where a child is considered old enough to decide where to live. But in your case you'd never met Evie until she turned up on your doorstep – what? – two or three days ago? So if the mother creates a fuss about parental responsibility, I doubt it'll be straightforward.'

'What should we do, then?'

'First, I'd advise you to take a DNA test, so that you can prove there's a genuine relationship. Ask them to send a copy directly to me. Their clerk will bring it round, it's so close to here and my clients use their services regularly. That way, there will be no doubt that I got the real results if we have to go to court. Secondly you *ought* to return Evie to her mother's care in the interim.'

Evie leant forward. 'I'll run away if anyone tries to force me to go back, Mr Wutherington. It's not Mum so much as *him*. I'd go back to Mum but I daren't live with him.'

'You may just be imagining this problem, you know.'

She immediately shook her head. 'No. I'm not, Mr Wutherington.' Her shudder spoke volumes, as had her quiet sureness when she answered his questions.

Cassie had watched her intently all the time, ready to step in if necessary. But she was pleased that the girl was continuing to speak calmly and sound convincing. The truth often was its own best advocate when people stayed reasonable, she'd found.

He'd been studying her granddaughter openly. 'I must admit, you seem very level-headed to me, Evie, and mature for your age. Of course, if you've been classified as "gifted" educationally, as you say, that might make a difference to the decision. But unfortunately, nothing can hide the fact that you don't know this woman properly yet, even if she is your grandmother.'

'I'm getting to know and love her, and I trust her absolutely. She's straightforward, tells me the truth and doesn't treat me like an idiot, as *he* does. It's my mother who is the idiot, not me. She's been a bit like this before with a couple of men, but never as bad. She does whatever Keith tells her and seems to believe every word he says. She really needs a husband, but not one like him.'

The lawyer's look was meant to be neutral, Cassie thought, but if you asked her, a couple of times his expression had betrayed a flicker of sympathy. She glanced surreptitiously at a big clock on the wall and tried to move the discussion on, knowing they only had an hour. 'So what else do we need to do, Mr Wutherington, besides getting our DNA tested?'

'I think you should make every effort to stay out of the courts and legal system, and try to settle this informally, which will mean contacting them, preferably voluntarily. I can help you with that, if you wish. I'm not at all sure you'd get a Special Guardianship Order if you went via the courts, you see. Hmm. There's another thing that may help: I gather you want to go to university, Evie.'

'I'm going to go there, whatever it takes. I'm planning to become a doctor.'

'Well, then perhaps that might give you another argument in favour of staying with your grandmother. If you want to go to university, you'll need financial support and it doesn't sound as if your mother can afford to help you much with that – especially for such a long and expensive course.'

When he paused and looked questioningly at her,

Cassie didn't hesitate. 'I can support Evie, and I'll do that whether she's allowed to live with me or not. Or I'd be happy to go and live near the relevant university so that she can stay with me, if that's a requirement.' A granddaughter was more important than a house – far more important than anything else in her life.

'That sort of offer might help show your commitment, especially if the DNA proves your relationship.' After a pause, he added, 'What about this cousin you were living with, Evie? Could you go back to her in the meantime?'

She didn't even pause to think but shook her head. 'As soon as school ends she's spending the rest of the summer abroad, doing her art thing. I wouldn't go to her anyway because I'd be too vulnerable there. If my mother came to take me away, Amelia would let her. And Mum has already moved in with *him*.' She shuddered. 'So I don't have another home to go to.'

'I see.' The lawyer glanced at his watch. 'Any more questions? No? Well, then I'm afraid that's all the time I can offer you today. I suggest you think it through carefully and come to some conclusions about the path you want to take. Make a few plans, then come back and discuss the legal implications of them with me.'

Cassie nodded. 'We'll certainly do that.'

'Don't forget to ask my clerk for directions to the place nearby where you can get your DNA tested.'

'I won't. We'll call in there straight away. And we'll definitely come back to you for any further legal advice.'

'It'd be an interesting case and your being famous

would add another layer to how it played out, assuming the mother kicked up a fuss.'

'He'd make her kick up a fuss,' Evie said bitterly. 'He controls everything she does nowadays. His attitude towards women is antediluvian from what I've seen!'

Cassie lingered to say, 'I've given up the TV work. I'll be more out of the public eye than in it from now on.' She hoped she hadn't shown her brief feeling of panic at the mere thought of returning to her old role in the world.

'But people will still know Cassandra Benn, so we'll have to make allowances for them regarding you as famous. And it could prove an advantage.'

'In the meantime you won't tell anyone about us, will you – where I live, I mean?' Cassie asked. 'Our personal information will be kept confidential?'

'Definitely. I'll not give it to anyone unless a court demands it or you give me permission.'

He smiled so reassuringly, looking at her in a way that made her suspect he'd noticed her sudden near panic.

'That's not likely to happen at the moment, is it, Ms Bennington? How would anyone even know about me being involved in advising you?'

'I suppose you're right. I'm just trying to be hyper-careful. Thank you for your help today.'

She hated these flashes of panic that struck without warning, had never been vulnerable in that way before.

Chapter Twelve

When they got outside, Cassie needed to get her thoughts straight, so suggested they go into a nearby café for refreshments.

When they were sitting at the table after placing their order, Evie looked at her thoughtfully. 'Are you all right, Gran?'

'Yes.'

'You're still reacting to that terrorist attack, aren't you? Just mildly. From what I've read, anyone would, and you seem to be doing better than most.'

'It hits me occasionally out of the blue, I'm afraid. It certainly takes some getting over.'

'That's another reason why you don't want anyone finding out where you're living, isn't it? Because you really do want to change your life. That often happens, by the way, after a traumatic event.'

'Yes. But I think a change was long overdue.'

'Mmm, probably. You must have led a super-stressful life because you tackled some really difficult topics. From what I've read, there's a limit to how long most people can cope with high-stress lifestyles and jobs.'

Cassie felt surprisingly comforted by her granddaughter's words and also by the quick pat on the arm that accompanied them. This was definitely an old soul in a young body. Evie would probably make a brilliant doctor and she was already a decent, caring and mature human being.

Her mother must be very proud of her.

Evie was clearly waiting till she was paying attention again to continue speaking.

'I want to make it clear, Gran, that I'll do my very best not to involve you, if there's any trouble.'

'No! I want you to involve me. Please promise me you won't run away without at least telling me.'

'How can I when it'd put you in the wrong legally?'

'Evie, I am involved now, fully involved, and I intend to continue helping you. In case you're worrying, I'd not try to stop you running away if there were no alternative, only I could give you some money, arrange how we could contact one another, that sort of thing. In fact, I think we should start a bank account straight away, one that you can just dip into without asking me.'

'I already have a bank account.'

'Does your mother know about it?'

'She encouraged me to start one. But it's my own account and she doesn't know the details.'

'Well, it wouldn't hurt to have another account that she doesn't know anything at all about, and if we make it a joint bank account, we can both access it and I can put in more money as necessary, as well as seeing what you're doing. There will be no need for you to become a street kid, believe me. Also, I am not short of money.'

Evie gave her a look that was both tearful and happy. 'You're wonderful, Gran. You make me feel I'm not alone any more, that there's hope.' She sniffed and then fumbled for a tissue, mopped her eyes and blew her nose.

'You're making me feel the same.'

'I promise faithfully that I'll tell you first if I feel I have to go. If I can, that is. If not, I'll be in touch as soon as it's safe.'

'I'll give you my secret email address and phone number. They're very secure and only people like my sister and my very closest friends know about them.'

'Shall I be able to meet your sister? She's my aunt, isn't she? No, great-aunt! Wow, imagine having an aunt as well as a grandmother!'

'I hope you'll meet her. I think you'll get on well with Zoe. She's fifteen years younger than me and will be tickled to know she's a great-aunt, I'm sure.'

Evie beamed at her. 'I've always wanted family.'

'I have a brother as well, but Michael's more like my parents, rather narrow-minded and unforgiving of what he regards as wrong behaviour.' She sighed and got another pat on the hand.

'Sorry about that, Gran.'

'If you've finished, let's go and arrange for our DNA to be tested and then open the bank account. Oh, and we'd better buy you another wig. That one is absolutely scruffy and if I have to look at you wearing it much longer, I'll scream.'

Evie giggled, suddenly looking years younger. 'It is rather tatty, isn't it?'

The DNA test was accomplished without any glitches, and they signed a piece of paper allowing a copy of the results to be sent to Mr Wutherington as well.

As they came out, Cassie stopped and took Evie's hand in hers. 'I want you to know something else: even if the DNA says we aren't related, I'll still help you. But given your appearance and hair colour, I doubt that will prove to be the case. I just wanted to say it because I find it best to work on the principle of covering all possibilities in a situation.'

'You're wonderful.'

And for all her years of experience at dealing with the world, Cassie could feel herself blushing.

Evie chuckled. 'I'm growing very fond of you, Gran, even if you're not my grandma, but I think you are.'

Evie felt warm inside as they got into the car but was glad they didn't speak much as they drove back. She glanced sideways a couple of times but her grandmother was looking so thoughtful, she didn't try to chat. It seemed to her that they both needed some thinking time.

She couldn't help worrying about what the future would bring, but she was sure now that her grandmother really did want to help her and get to know her. Wasn't that wonderful?

Why did her mother keep turning down the opportunity to get to know her birth mother?

'Let's go in there.' Cassie turned off the main road just outside Marlbury into a shopping centre they'd passed earlier. She pulled into the car park and nodded as if pleased. 'It's bigger than I'd remembered, which is going to be useful. Let's go, kid. Shop till we drop, eh?'

Evie stared round as they walked. 'Wow, it is huge. I don't know about shop till we drop, though. I don't usually enjoy shopping for no reason.'

'Me neither.'

'But I do need a few things today, Gran.'

'Well, I need a lot of things, so please bear with me.'

They started by buying a proper bed and a small chest of drawers for Evie, which made her feel guilty again.

'I shall continue to need a spare bed, whether you're with me or not, Evie. I do have a few friends who'll come and visit once things are settled. I'm just buying it sooner, that's all.'

'Oh. Yes, of course.' That made her feel better.

'As the rear car seats fold down, we'll be able to take these with us, so you'll sleep more comfortably tonight.'

Her grandmother gave her an assessing glance. 'I know we need to buy you a few clothes but first of all let's get a wig if there's somewhere that sells them. I can't stand the sight of you in that thing any longer.'

Evie glanced at her own reflection in a shop window and gave one of her rare girlish giggles. 'It does look awful, doesn't it?'

'Ghastly. Plus we'll need all sorts of fresh food. I like to eat healthily, even if I'm not a very good cook. Wig first, furniture second, clothes third and food last, eh?'

They asked an attendant at a help kiosk and were given directions to a shop selling wigs. They had a hilarious time trying on a few, and settled on a mid-brown in a nondescript, jaw-length style, and a darker one similar to the one that was due to be 'filed under R for rubbish' as her grandmother called it.

Evie poked her tongue out at herself in the mirror in the mid-brown one, which wasn't particularly flattering. That might be a good choice strategically, though, because it certainly wouldn't attract attention or be easily remembered, as her own vivid red hair would. And the darker one was a cheapie fun wig, which didn't even attempt to look real, just in case they needed a different look in a hurry.

As they went into the large store to look for clothes, Evie fumbled for her purse.

Her grandmother reached out to stop her opening it. 'This is my treat.'

Guilt shot through her. 'I don't want to keep costing you money.'

'It's nothing, darling. I'm not short of money, but I am short of buying treats for a granddaughter. Where shall we start?'

As they shopped, Evie soon realised how much her grandmother was enjoying doing this and stopped worrying. It occurred to her that for all the fame and fortune she'd achieved, Cassie must have been lonely a lot of the time.

Well, look at what she'd said about the terrorist incident. Why, she hadn't even had anyone to call to pick her up from the hospital. If her ex hadn't come round, she'd have been utterly alone. He must be a nice man.

What must it be like to be so close to being blown up? Evie felt a chill run down her spine at the mere thought and couldn't help looking round the shopping centre for the nearest exit.

They had fun trying on clothes and came away with several large bags. They even bought some jeans for her grandmother, not skin-tight ones, which the salesperson tried to persuade them to buy because they were very popular. Evie had watched other girls at school parade around in these, regardless of whether they were flattering or not – which they usually weren't. She was glad her grandmother had good clothes sense.

Then to crown the pleasures of the day, they found a large bookshop in the complex. Her grandmother led the way inside without even asking her, urging Evie to buy several books. She didn't complain when her granddaughter chose mainly non-fiction, as Evie's mother would have done in yet another attempt to stop her 'being such a swot'.

As if you could switch off your brain or stop feeding it with interesting things that broadened your understanding of the world! As if she should want to limit herself in that way!

She had a peep at the books her grandmother had bought, one about the history of Wiltshire and a couple of cosy mysteries.

Cassie grinned at Evie. 'I still prefer paper books to ebooks.'

'So do I. And I'm not the only one in my class to feel like that. You can cuddle a paper book and it doesn't break if you drop it, but it's not much fun cuddling an ebook reader.'

Cassie held the books out for her to see the titles. 'I have to confess to a weakness for this sort of story, Evie love, cosy mysteries. It's all Agatha Christie's fault. I found her books when I was much younger than you and enjoyed them very much.'

'I haven't read any of hers.'

'We'll unpack some of my books when we get back, then you can borrow any of them you fancy. Christie's stories are a bit dated now but if you read them as being set against a historical background, they're still good reads.'

'You're very generous.'

She watched her grandmother blink rapidly, to clear away tears.

'I'm thoroughly enjoying having someone to buy presents for.'

It was out before Evie could stop herself. 'Don't you buy them for your sister?'

'I shall do now Zoe and I are getting closer, but our parents kept us apart as much as they could and I'd left home well before she even got to high school.'

'All that because of you having my mother after being raped? That's so unfair.'

'It was because I refused to get rid of the baby, I think.

They hate to be seen as unconventional in any way. They tried to impose their own view of the world on their children and failed with me and my sister. Only, Zoe smiles and somehow manages to go her own way. She's more tactful than I could ever be. Anyway, that's water under the bridge now that I'm getting to know her.'

Evie didn't ask any more questions because she could hear the lingering pain in her grandmother's voice. Well, although her mother had never put her first when there was a man around, Fran did love her, she was quite sure of that.

'What does your brother do for a living?'

'He's a civil servant, not sure where he's working at the moment. He hasn't made any effort to get to know me even though he left home a good few years ago. But my sister took the initiative to improve our relationship, to my delight. Zoe's lovely, so kind. You'll like her.'

Later, as she snuggled down in her new bed, Evie thought through what she'd learnt about her grandmother today and decided that no one had a perfect life. Well, no one that she knew anyway.

Perhaps that's why there were so many books with happy endings. You could put anything you liked into a story.

She could put a light on and read herself to sleep if she wanted to here, she was sure. But tonight she didn't need that. Tonight everything felt good. Mmm. She closed her eyes and let the world fade away.

Chapter Thirteen

The following day Hal's phone began to ring and he picked it up, sighing as he recognised the number.

The voice was hesitant. 'Dad?'

'Oliver. Nice to hear from you, son.' It probably wouldn't be nice at all. His son usually only phoned when he wanted something.

'How did the move go?'

Hal rolled his eyes at the thought of what he could say about his recent hassles, but didn't get into that, contenting himself with, 'Pretty well on the whole.'

'Good, good.'

'How are you and Mandy?'

'Um – that's what I'm calling about. We haven't been getting on for a while and – well, we're splitting up.'

'Oh dear. Is there no hope of, you know, mediation?'

'She won't even try that. She's met someone else at work.'

Hal whistled softly. 'I'm so sorry.'

'Yeah, me too. I wondered – could I come and stay with you for a week or two? I know it's a big ask, but I need to get away. I'm moving out of the house and I'm going to transfer to a branch in another town. The company's been very, um, helpful and it's nearly settled.'

'Goodness.' Oliver didn't seem to be seeking advice, only wanting to talk about it, so Hal waited for him to offer further information.

'I've looked at flats to rent near my new job, which is in Swindon, so I'll be quite close to you. But I can't sign up for a place yet in case something goes wrong with the move. I should be a shoo-in with my experience, but you know how chancy it can be when you change your job. And it costs a lot for the deposit and stuff, so I can't afford to waste money.'

'Why can't you stay in your own home till you're sure of where you're going?'

'It's a bit far away, and Mandy's new guy is going to help her buy me out of my share but he'll only do that if he can move into the house straight away. So the sooner I can move out of there and get the money for a new place, the better.'

'But you loved that house! You did so much work on it when you bought it. Can't Mandy move out for a while? Her new guy must already be living somewhere.'

'Yeah, well. We've argued so much that I've stopped feeling good about that house but *she* really wants to stay there. As long as I get a reasonable amount of money for my share – and they're being fair about the finances, I must admit – I'd prefer to start over somewhere else. I should have enough for a deposit on a small place and I'll rent a flat while I look round for a fixer-upper.'

'What does your mother say? Can't you stay with her? I've only just moved in here, haven't even had time to unpack.'

'She's found a new guy as well. You know how she chops and changes. She's too busy with him, so she can't put me up and anyway, she's still friends with Mandy, takes her side against me. They always did get on well.'

'Ah.' Hal didn't really want this complication, had been looking forward to some quiet time.

'Is that OK, Dad? Me coming to stay with you for a couple of weeks, I mean?'

Hal heard his son's voice wobble and when Oliver suddenly blew his nose, it was obvious he was fighting tears. Hal simply couldn't say no. A marriage break-up could be harrowing as Hal knew from experience. Oliver was clearly very upset, however much he was trying to hide it. 'Yes, I suppose you can stay. But there will have to be some ground rules.'

'What? I'm a bit old for rules, don't you think?'

'Not in someone else's house you're not. I don't care what you do when you're away from here, but I'm going to set rules for when you're at home. Frankly, you don't seem to have changed much since you were a teenager and you still tend to make a lot of noise, regardless of other people's needs, not to mention leaving a mess wherever you go.'

'Why do you say that? I'm not a slob.'

'You were last time you stayed with me, never cleared up after yourself. I'm not going to act as your servant. Plus, I've not only got a brand-new house, I desperately need some peace and quiet myself.'

'Yeah, yeah. That'll be fine. I'll just fit in with you.'

'Oliver, did you hear me?'

'Mmm?'

'I'm not sure you did listen properly so I'll say it again to make sure it's absolutely clear what I'll expect. If you don't tidy up after yourself while you're here, I'll throw your stuff out of the house – literally. I won't put up with *any mess whatsoever.*'

'But—'

'No, let me finish. If you clear up as you go, there is never any need to do big clear-ups because it never gets bad, which is how I choose to live.'

His son's voice was sulky. 'That's the sort of thing Mandy used to say. Has the whole world gone tidy-mad?'

'I don't care about the whole world, just my little part of it. So there you are. If you decide to come and stay, you'll know what to expect.'

'I'll do my best, Dad. But I'm still a bit upset, so you'll have to cut me a little slack here.'

'No. I won't cut you any slack whatsoever where cleanliness is concerned.'

He heard a muttered exclamation, but since his cancer, he'd found that keeping control of his surroundings had become important to him and he wasn't giving in about this.

There was dead silence for a few moments then Oliver said, 'Oh, all right. I'll fit in as best I can. Look, I've a few things to do here. I'll phone and let you know when I'm arriving.'

When he put the phone down, Hal stood staring at it for a while before he moved. He couldn't help feeling upset at the confrontations to come. Oliver was in for a few shocks. And he would lose his precious peace for a while.

Hal knew he'd changed a lot in the past couple of years and was equally sure his son hadn't. It'd take a lot of effort to ride shotgun on Oliver about his slovenly habits, but he wasn't going to compromise on this. He looked round. This place was brand new, after all. Oh hell, he really didn't want to share his living space. And much more important, he didn't want to mess up his brand-new chance of life.

One of the worst aspects of this was that his family didn't know about the cancer and now it'd probably come out.

He should have said no to his son coming to stay. Only, he couldn't.

Anyway, he loved Oliver, even if he didn't enjoy living with him. And his son had sounded deep-down upset about his marriage break-up. Well, who wouldn't be, if they were honest? Marriages usually started with such high hopes. Hal remembered how upset he'd been when he split with Oliver's mother after a few years of marriage, even though that had been by mutual agreement and had gone relatively smoothly.

The only thing he and Gillian had disagreed strongly about afterwards had been how to bring up Oliver. He should have interfered more. But would she have let him? He doubted it.

He heard voices and looked outside to see Cassie and her granddaughter get into the car and drive away. Shopping? Or something else?

They both looked worried and it occurred to him again that they had some problem they were trying to hide from others. Though why that girl was wearing such an appalling wig, he had to wonder. It slipped sometimes and showed the red hair underneath.

Was she hiding from something? Or from someone? She must be.

Well, he had enough on his plate without taking on other people's worries, so he didn't want to get involved. His new neighbour seemed a decent sort and he wished her and her granddaughter well.

It was a rare person who didn't have a problem or two to deal with.

Hal went out soon afterwards. He wanted to stock his house with healthy fresh foods and basic supplies. He'd also have to buy a single bed and bedding for Oliver, because he doubted his son would have thought to commandeer any of the marital household goods. But he wasn't buying junk food or even having it in the house. His son could either put up with healthy meals or go out to eat on his own at food outlets.

There was apparently a big shopping centre on the outskirts of Marlbury, so he found it online and set his satnav to take him there. He had no trouble finding a bed, bedding and a wide range of fresh food, then was tempted by the bookshop. Now that he'd stopped working he'd be able to catch up with the latest bestsellers and any new books by his favourite authors. Oh, the bliss of that freedom!

By the time he got home, his shoulder was throbbing, so he carried the bags of food into the house one at a time using his other hand, put the frozen stuff away, then sat down in his recliner chair and switched on the TV.

He'd just have a short break and catch up with the news before he unpacked properly.

He was woken a couple of hours later by someone banging on his front door. He jerked to his feet, nearly knocking his half-empty mug of cold tea off the small table beside his chair and wincing as he moved his shoulder incautiously.

When he opened the door, he found his son standing there, looking truculent.

'All right if I come to stay now? The bitch threw all my things out into the garden because she didn't like the way I was packing up.'

Hal didn't let himself sigh as he held the door open.

'Can you give me a hand with a few things, Dad? They're a bit heavy.'

'I'm afraid I can't. I hurt my shoulder yesterday.'

'How am I going to get them into the house, then?'

'You may have to leave some of them in the car.'

'But I've got my sound system and it's an expensive one.'

'I'm not having it set up in the house anyway, so you might as well leave it where it is. Your car will be safe enough on the drive.'

'But—'

Hal wasn't going to get into an argument. He turned and went back into the house, hearing a muttered curse behind him as he put the kettle on.

Oliver came in and dumped a big backpack on the floor in the living area. 'Which bedroom am I in?'

'None of them till the bed is delivered. I've not worked that out yet. I was tired when I got back from the shops, so I had a nap.'

His son gave him a puzzled look.

'Cup of tea?'

Oliver peered at the kitchen area. 'I'm not much into tea. What sort of coffee-making equipment have you got?'

'Kettle and tea-making ingredients only.'

'I'll bring my coffee maker in from the car. At least she let me take that.'

'I'm not having it set up. I've developed a very acute sense of smell these days.' One of the strange after-effects of his treatment. 'As far as I'm concerned, coffee stinks the place out and fancy coffee is even worse.'

That got him another puzzled look.

'Cup of tea or I think I've got some instant drinking chocolate?' He waited, hand on the cupboard door.

'Tea.' Oliver's voice was sulky. 'Though I don't know why you won't take advantage of my gadgets.'

'Because I don't want them. I've moved here for some peace and quiet.'

'Are you . . . all right? Your health I mean?'

Hal hesitated, then shrugged. Why try to hide it? 'As it happens, I'm recovering from cancer.'

'*What?*'

'You heard me.'

'What sort of cancer, Dad? Why didn't you tell anyone? Are you going to be all right?'

'Colon cancer. They think they got it in time. It's been over a year since it was found and it was early stage, so they've more or less turned me loose now, except for the regular check-ups.'

His son's voice was soft and hushed, as if he were talking to an idiot. 'That's why you've retired early. Are you *sure* they've sorted it out?'

'It's never one hundred per cent certain even with the more treatable cancers but in my case, it's far more likely than not that I'm clear.'

Silence greeted him and when he turned, Oliver was staring at him with what he'd begun to think of as *that look*. You'd think everyone with cancer metamorphosed overnight into infectious and moronic aliens, the way some people treated you, and yet roughly one in two people would get it at some stage of their lives.

He turned away and finished making the tea. 'Come and sit down for a few minutes. Tell me about your new job and what your plans are for the future.'

'It'll be much the same as the old job, except it'll be in Swindon. I was lucky. They wanted someone there so I, um, volunteered to transfer. Things just need finalising.'

'But what will you be doing there?'

'Same boring old stuff, answering queries about our products, doing market research, you know. But it brings in the money for my real life.'

'Which is?'

'Chilling out with my mates, gaming online and now, I suppose, I'll have to start pulling chicks whenever I need their services.' He patted himself complacently.

Hal found that disgusting and had made his feelings plain about such attitudes towards women before but didn't waste his breath saying so again. It'd be water off a duck's back with Oliver in his present mood. He wasn't having stray 'chicks' brought back here, though. No way.

Oliver took another sip of tea and grimaced. 'I'll have to bring in my coffee maker, Dad. I don't usually do tea and it tastes as bad as ever.'

'Didn't I just refuse to live with coffee? If you don't like my tea there's plenty of water in the tap.'

'*Tap water!* Don't you even buy proper spring water? Honestly, Dad. No one drinks out of the tap these days.'

Hal prayed for patience, didn't find it and once again spoke his mind. 'Well, if you bring bottled water inside my house, I'll chuck it out again. All that plastic isn't good for the environment and it's daft to pay so much for water anyway. Get it through your head, son, that this is *my* home and as I told you earlier, if you stay here you'll have to live *my* way.'

'But—'

The doorbell rang and it was just as well. Hal couldn't help scowling as he went to answer it. He wasn't giving in to his son. He was going to live in his new home the way *he* wanted. It was one of the things he'd promised himself.

He found a couple of guys delivering the new bed and other packages. 'Great. I'll show you the way. It's upstairs.'

When they'd left, he stood at the top of the stairs and called, 'Oliver! Come up and I'll show you your bedroom.'

There was no answer, which surprised him. He went downstairs and found Oliver with earbuds in, beating time to some music that was so loud Hal could hear the tinny sound of it from across the room even though it wasn't on the speakers.

He went across and stood in front of his son, arms folded.

It took a couple of minutes before Oliver noticed him and reluctantly pulled out the earbuds.

'Come up and see your bedroom, then you can take your stuff up and unpack. And please don't play your music so loudly in future. If you want to damage your hearing, that's your own business but I need peace and quiet in my home. How many times do I have to tell you that?'

'I'll take the stuff up later.'

'Now, please. You've already scattered some of your things in my living area.'

'Aw, stop fussing, Dad. Chill out.'

Some devil had got into Hal, a devil he'd been holding in rein for years. No wonder they called some of his son's contemporaries 'the entitled generation'. Oliver clearly belonged to that group. He quickly gathered together the mess of objects and mainly dirty clothes that Oliver had dumped out of his backpack when searching for something, and before his son could stop him, he'd thrown them out of the front door.

That got Oliver out of the chair in one leap.

'What the hell did you do that for?'

Hal folded his arms and leant against the wall. 'As I told you earlier on the phone, I keep my home tidy. Any mess you make goes out of the door the minute I set eyes on it.'

He saw Oliver's hands clench into fists and waited, unable to believe that his son would turn on him.

As a stand-off, it was a non-event. The fists unclenched, Oliver took a deep, growling breath and brought his stuff in, then followed Hal upstairs and helped put the bed together and make it up with the brand-new sheets.

Scowling, he went down again and began unloading the car.

Hal followed him, warning, 'Not your sound system and coffee maker, remember.'

Oliver glared at him, but put the box he was holding back into the boot.

After his son had taken up the last load, he came down and said sulkily, 'You've certainly changed, Dad.'

'Cancer does that to you, son, makes you realise what you value in life, gives you the courage to go for it, too. I shall keep saying it till I get through to you: this is *my* house, and you're always welcome to visit, always, but we do things *my* way here. And the tidiness edict covers your bedroom, too, not just the living areas. I'll chuck out anything left lying around.'

Oliver gaped at him, not seeming to know what to say, so Hal left him to sort out his things and went to sit out on the patio, which was a trifle chilly but at least peaceful.

He was shaking with reaction to their spat because his emotions were still rather fragile and he couldn't cope as easily with conflict, even minor conflict. He hated that weakness, absolutely hated it, but couldn't seem to alter how he reacted at times. Not yet, anyway. He was hoping he'd settle down here and gradually achieve some sort of equilibrium and rhythm to his days.

He didn't know Oliver as well as he'd have liked. Well, let's face it, he'd never had the chance. He'd not been allowed much say in how his ex had brought up their son and you couldn't change much on occasional visits. He was sorry to start off Oliver's stay with a row, but he wasn't backing off.

How would he cope with a couple of weeks of this, though?

Then he felt a smile slowly creep across his face and he began to relax a little. How would Oliver cope with living with his neat and tidy father for that long?

Had his son taken on board properly how much Hal had changed? He didn't think so. Not yet.

He wasn't giving in about how he ran his home. Or about anything else. What did they say nowadays? *My way or the highway*.

No, he couldn't throw Oliver out, but his son might leave in a huff.

Could he even afford to set himself up in a flat? From what he'd let drop he was a bit short of cash till the money from his house came in.

Chapter Fourteen

That evening Cassie looked out of the back window of her house, wondering whether to sit outside for a while. Would she be too cold? No, the patio was quite sheltered and she could put her shawl round her shoulders.

Evie was watching some soap on TV that she'd confessed to being addicted to. Good luck to her. For a teenager, she was surprisingly good about keeping the volume low, hadn't even needed telling.

Cassie ran up to get her shawl, opened the rear doors then turned back. She fancied a glass of wine. Why not? Having one glass wasn't setting a bad example.

She poured a glass of dry white from her favourite Australian vineyard, a place where she'd once done a 'behind the scenes' programme on a round-the-world series about wine making.

Taking her glass outside, she sat down with a long

sigh of relief and felt herself immediately start to relax. There was the sound of a chair being moved next door and when she looked round, she saw Hal coming towards her across the newly laid lawn between the houses. It was nice not to have fences. Well, unless you were lumbered with a bad neighbour.

'Refugee from the TV?' He rested his hands on the back of the next outdoor chair, smiling down at her.

'Yes.'

'Me, too. My son has come to stay for a couple of weeks. He's just split up with his wife.'

'Oh, that's sad.' She could see his wry smile in the light from the back rooms of her house.

'Actually, I'm surprised she put up with him for so long. He's a slob. Leaves a trail of mess wherever he goes. I need to warn you about one thing: I've threatened to throw anything he leaves lying around out of the house, and I've already done it once. So if you see piles of what looks like rubbish or old clothes in front of or behind my house, ignore them.'

She chuckled, not even trying to hide her amusement. 'I'd like to be a fly on the wall. Will you really keep on doing that, do you think? It takes a lot to change an untidy person's habits, as I found out when I tried to live with one otherwise nice guy.'

His expression grew very determined. 'You've got to believe it. Living in this house is my dream for the rest of my life. What do oldies call it these days? My death nest.'

'What a horrible concept. You're far too young to be thinking of death.'

He hesitated then said quietly, 'I'm a cancer survivor, Cassie. I've grown used to the thought of dying, though they tell me I'm clear now.'

She'd reached out to clasp his hand before she knew it and he didn't pull away. 'That's tough, Hal. I did a programme on surviving cancer once, and I so admired the people I interviewed. Facing a premature death while you make plans for the family you'll be leaving behind is one of the highest forms of bravery, if you ask me, Hal.'

'Is there anything you haven't done an article on?'

'Oh, lots of things, but I've covered many of the big issues of life over the past twenty years.'

'Especially the last five years of *Life with Cassandra* on the first Friday of the month.'

'You've watched my programmes?'

'Quite often, yes. You have an incisive yet tender approach to your topic and show a respect for the people you involve.'

She was touched by the compliment. 'Thank you. I've had enough of other people's problems, though, and even of their achievements. I want to concentrate on my own life from now on.' She glanced at the glass she was holding and waved it towards him. 'Like to join me?'

'I'd love to.'

'I don't know why I've left you standing there as we talk. Do sit down, please.'

While he made himself comfortable, she went into the house, found another glass and took the bottle out with her. Evie was still glued to the TV and the two people whose lips seemed fused together. She didn't even seem to notice her grandmother coming and going.

Hal didn't say a lot nor did she try to force conversation, but it was nice to have someone her own age to chat to and Cassie felt relaxed enough with him to pour them both a second glass. Although the rear patio was nicely sheltered, it was getting a bit chilly, but she didn't want to break up an interesting conversation. She might have a conservatory built on, so that she could use the area whatever the weather.

She didn't even switch on the outside lights. The rising moon added a soft glow to the scene that was more than enough.

Hal was quite good-looking for a man of his age, she decided, after a surreptitious study of him as he talked, eyes alight with interest first in one thing, then in another, and hands waving to emphasise important points. She hoped the moonlight had blurred the wrinkles on her face, as they had on his.

What attracted her to him most of all was his intelligence and the kind yet not wimpy way he seemed to interact with the world. It was as if he were quietly sure of his own place in the universe and didn't need to prove anything to anyone.

Hal broke off in the middle of a discussion as he heard the sound of a phone ringing several times then cutting off inside his house.

A few moments later the back patio door slid open and a figure peered out into the darkness. 'Dad? Are you out here? There's someone on the phone for you.'

He sighed in annoyance. 'Tell them I'm busy.'

'You didn't even ask who it was.'

'I don't care who it is. I'm enjoying the peace and quiet out here.'

'They'll have heard your voice, Dad.'

Hal sighed and put down his glass. 'Don't go in yet, Cassie. I'll be back shortly.'

Once inside his own house, he picked up the phone and glanced at the number, muttering, 'Oh damn!' Taking a deep breath, he said, 'Hello?'

'Hal, it's me, Sabine. Surely you recognise my number? I've been chasing you for a couple of weeks. Where are you?'

'I've retired to the country, as I told you I was going to do.'

'That doesn't mean you don't want to see old friends, surely? How about I come and visit you for a day or two?'

Her voice had gone low and throaty, a device she employed when she wanted to sound sexy. Hearing it after a few weeks, he decided it had the opposite effect on him now that he knew it for a deliberate trick. 'I'm living a very quiet life these days, Sabine. It'd bore you to tears.'

'Try me.'

'Thank you but no. Look, there's no easy way to say this. We had a nice fling but I thought we'd both moved on.'

'I don't agree. I was just giving you time to recover. I

saw you in the distance the other week and remembered how good we'd been together.'

Make that, she'd been waiting to see if he did recover. 'Well, there you are. I've certainly moved on. Thanks for calling, Sabine, but I'm not picking up the past again. Have a good life.' He clicked the phone off, then looked up to see Oliver staring at him.

'She sounded a sexy piece. Why did you turn her down?'

'She's a rather predatory woman. I'm not interested in getting together with her again.'

'Mum always said you were a babe magnet.'

'Then your mother was wrong. And please don't answer my phone again. Or listen to my phone conversations.'

Oliver shrugged. 'Whatever. Who were you talking to outside?'

'My neighbour. And I'm going back to continue our conversation, so I'll leave you to your TV watching.'

'I could come and join you for a glass or two.'

'No, you couldn't. Cassie and I are enjoying each other's company in a very peaceful way that will bore you to tears. And you haven't brought any wine with you.'

'You've got plenty. Surely you don't grudge me a glass or two?'

'I buy good wine. You guzzle it as if it's lemonade and I'm not wasting mine on you. I know exactly how many bottles I have, so don't go taking any after you finish that bottle you've pinched without asking me tonight.'

He had the satisfaction of seeing his son's mouth drop open in shock as he moved outside again. He pulled the sliding door firmly shut behind him and sat down again, trying to switch off his annoyance as decisively as he'd switched off the phone. Only, it was still there, humming away inside him.

'Unwanted caller?' Cassie murmured.

'Definitely unwanted. I went out with Sabine a few times, but that was BC – before the cancer. She vanished quickly after I was diagnosed. She must have heard that I'd recovered. She's probably between men and I'd guess she's looking for a husband now that she's getting older, to help maintain her expensive lifestyle. And she'd prefer one who'll die while she's still youngish and leave her a nice chunk of money.'

'Is she really that bad?'

'I'm afraid so. Gorgeous-looking, good conversationalist but no heart behind the façade.'

She was thinking aloud before she knew it. 'The old Cassie would have wondered about doing an article on predatory women who deliberately marry for money.'

'And the new Cassie?'

She shrugged. 'The new Cassie is much more interested in helping her granddaughter and making a few carefully selected new friends.'

'I'd love to count myself a friend of yours.'

'It's a bargain.' She raised her glass to him and clinked it against his to seal their agreement, and they smiled gently at one another as they each took a sip of wine, then put their glasses down.

'So, Cassie, how's it going with Evie?'

'Really well. She's a great kid.'

'She seems to be. Very capable too, from what you've told me.'

They chatted about the current political news, then Hal couldn't hold back a yawn. He savoured the last mouthful and put his glass down. 'I think I'll call it a day. Nice wine, that one.'

'One of my favourites. And I must say, I was thinking of doing the same thing. I'm not a late night sort of person.'

'Thanks for inviting me across.'

'I've enjoyed your company.'

'I've enjoyed yours, too. My turn to play host next time.'

When Cassie went inside, she found Evie sitting reading a book and the television switched off.

Her granddaughter greeted her with, 'I can see by the expression on his face that he likes you.'

'And I like him. But not in that way.'

'Not yet.'

'That isn't the first thing I think of when I meet someone, Evie. It doesn't matter to me whether they're male or female, what I want to know before I make friends is that they're decent human beings with a well-exercised brain between their ears. Doesn't even matter whether they're particularly intelligent, as long as they keep the brain they were born with active.'

'Those sound like good criteria for judging someone.'

'I reckon so. Now, I'm going to bed and you should too, don't you think?'

'I was just planning to do that. I'll need a glass of water to take with me. Can I get you anything, Gran?'

'No, darling. But a goodnight cuddle wouldn't go amiss.' She held her breath, waiting. Had she gone too far, expecting too much too soon?

But Evie came across to her smiling and they had a nice hug, swaying to and fro for a few moments before drawing apart.

'Sleep well, darling.'

'You sleep well, too, Gran.'

Cassie was still smiling as she got into bed and listened to her granddaughter making similar preparations for sleep. What a lovely evening it had turned out to be.

Things were going so well. Fingers and toes crossed that nothing went wrong and Evie's mother didn't find out where she was. Well, not yet, anyway. They shouldn't postpone a reconciliation for too long.

But first, Cassie wanted so much to get to know Evie. She liked – no, make that loved – what she'd seen so far.

Surely her daughter must have some good qualities to have produced and raised such a delightful girl? Cassie hoped she could meet Fran and get to know her as well.

Chapter Fifteen

Fran didn't have to go to work that day and after waving Keith off, she went to sit down with a cup of tea and have a think, not only about Evie but about . . . well, everything.

Whatever Keith said, she was still worried about her daughter. Surely Evie could have found some way to email her by now?

She was worried about Keith too. She'd promised herself when she split up with her previous guy that she'd never let herself be manipulated again. And now look at her, married in a blind rush and afraid to do openly what she felt to be right.

For a start, she knew for certain that Evie wasn't sly. Why did Keith keep saying that? If anything that girl was too straightforward about how she interacted with people and hadn't yet developed much tact. Wait till Evie got interested in boys. She'd have to learn to deal with them more tactfully or she'd never keep a boyfriend.

Only, perhaps you could be too tactful. Fran had lain awake worrying each night that Evie had been away. Keith didn't seem to understand a mother's love and just kept brushing her worries aside and distracting her.

And she still hadn't gone against his wishes and contacted the police! What did that say about her? Only, maybe she'd needed this breathing space, this chance to see what Keith was like in an emergency.

Not as good as she'd expected. Let's face it, not good at all. Of course no one was perfect, she knew that. But – she was beginning to add a lot of buts when she thought about him. Why had she let him push her into marriage?

Well, Evie came first at the moment, then she'd deal with her own problems.

She'd racked her brain about where her daughter could possibly have gone. Amelia was no longer around to take her in. She'd just left for Italy even though Fran had asked her to delay her departure in case the poor girl turned up looking for help.

Amelia had always been like that, avoiding trouble at all costs.

So had she, Fran admitted. She began to pace up and down, trying to set her thoughts in order.

She was off work today. Ought she to go and check Amelia's house, in case Evie was hiding there? She didn't think her daughter would break into someone else's home – not unless she was utterly desperate.

What Fran couldn't understand was why Evie would

be desperate enough to run away in the first place?

What was it about Keith that upset her so much? What had she missed seeing in him?

Fran remembered introducing him to her daughter, how kindly he'd spoken to Evie. And afterwards he'd complimented Fran on how pretty her daughter was. He cared more than most men did how people and things looked, fussed over the house, needed everything just so, had even shouted at her for leaving things lying around.

And . . . I have to admit it, I let him shout at me! That was . . . pitiful.

When she'd finished her drink, Fran rinsed out the mug and went up to her daughter's bedroom, or at least what had been intended for Evie to use as a bedroom till the attic was ready. She and Keith had simply dumped all her daughter's things here in piles when Fran moved in. Then, after Evie ran away, they'd brought back what had been left at Amelia's house, which had added another pile or two.

That was something else that was puzzling Fran. She knew exactly what Evie owned. Her daughter had left nearly all her clothes behind when she vanished. How was the girl managing without a proper change of clothing?

As she stood in the doorway of the bedroom the anger faded and tears welled in her eyes. Evie wouldn't like her things to be dumped in untidy heaps like this. She was good around the house, always tidy, giving little trouble.

In fact, she was much easier to live with than Keith!

Evie could be stubborn, though, when she believed in something. Would she ever agree to live with him? That was, if she came back, if she didn't stay away. Fran pressed one hand to her mouth but the sobs would come out and she fumbled for another tissue to wipe her eyes.

Was it worth losing her daughter to marry Keith? The answer surprised her. *No. Nothing is worth losing Evie for.*

She had to believe that things would improve between herself and Keith. They'd built up a nice life as a couple and developed a circle of friends, most of whom were useful to him for business purposes – which didn't stop them being very pleasant people to socialise with.

The only one she didn't like was his best friend, Ryan, who was a bit creepy, if you asked her. Keith changed when Ryan was round, grew more bossy and, yes, scornful towards her.

She had a sudden memory of seeing Evie through a half-open door slapping Ryan's hand away from her. Evie claimed he'd touched her breast. Keith had laughed it off and said Ryan had only been joking and his hand had slipped.

Had Ryan upset Evie more than once? Was that it? And if so, why hadn't Keith seen it as a problem?

Heart sinking at what this might imply, Fran walked across to the window and stared down into the garden. No, no! Keith was nothing like Ryan, wouldn't defend him if he really was harassing Evie.

She shouldn't be wasting time like this. There was so much to do in their new house. Keith had left her with a list of things to be sorted out today. Only, it was more important to her to find her daughter, so the list could damned well wait.

Should she go to the police? What would they say if she reported Evie missing now? *Why didn't you come to us sooner?* That's what they'd say. They might not even take her seriously.

She screwed up Keith's list and left it lying on the floor. She'd take the day off housework – or the morning anyway – give herself time to think more clearly and decide what to do about Evie.

She turned away, then turned back. The mess in her daughter's bedroom annoyed her. It wouldn't take long to clear this lot up then she'd go out for a stroll.

As she put things away tidily, she checked once again for any hint of where Evie might have gone. They must have missed something the first time they'd searched her daughter's things, must have.

Keith had insisted on them searching Evie's room regularly, saying everyone who had teenage children did it and the girl would never know. But she could see by Evie's hurt expression whenever they did it that she did know someone had been through her room.

When Fran had plucked up the courage to ask a colleague at the office if she did that, Carole had been horrified by the idea of doing that to an older child unless there was a very good reason, which there wasn't with

Evie. She was nearly sixteen and wasn't troublesome in any way except her antipathy towards Keith.

Fran suddenly felt deeply ashamed. It wasn't right to have kept invading Evie's privacy like that, and letting a man finger all her underwear.

It occurred to her again as she sorted out the clothes that if Evie had been *planning* to leave, she wouldn't have left nearly everything behind. It looked, it really did, as if she'd left in a hurry, grabbing just a few things.

All Amelia had said about that day was that she'd left Keith on his own with the girl, at his request, and when she got home, he'd told her Evie had run away and shown her a makeshift rope ladder.

He'd later told Fran her daughter had run away in a fit of anger at being told to go and live in his house so that her mother wouldn't worry. He hadn't mentioned the rope ladder to her. Amelia was the one who'd told her about it.

Only, Evie didn't usually do fits of anger.

Fran stared out of the window, appalled at herself for being manipulated. Had she made another big mistake in her choice of a man? She wiped away more tears at that thought. She was such a loser.

Evie would be all right, surely she would? She was clever enough to find some way of surviving. Fran had to believe that or she'd go mad with worry.

Thank goodness it was the school holidays now and her daughter wasn't missing school, so no official need know.

Evie was such a brilliant student, a daughter anyone would be proud of. And though there was no way Fran could afford to support her through medical school to avoid those horrible debts, she might just about manage to stretch her money to helping with accommodation.

Except that Keith wanted to take her money into a joint account and use it to pay off the mortgage. He referred to it as 'their mortgage' but it wasn't. She'd never been able to afford to buy a house. She hadn't agreed to a joint account because her first husband had run off with most of their money from one of those, money that had taken a lot of earning.

She was so glad she'd done that because suddenly she wasn't sure she was going to stay with Keith. If she did, he had to understand that she wasn't going to be a doormat. She'd been reading a book about that sort of thing, one a friend at work had given her, saying she sounded as if she needed it.

She'd been offended at the time, but she'd started to read it anyway in her lunch breaks and it talked a lot of sense about equality and respect in life partnerships. One saying had stuck in her mind: *If you want to be treated as a doormat, first you have to lie down and let people wipe their feet all over you.*

She had been a doormat, she admitted that to herself now. Keith had even said last night that running away might actually do the girl good, allow her to get some real-life experience under her belt before she became a student. And Fran to her shame hadn't even contradicted that.

Then he'd surprised her by adding that the girl was being unrealistic about what she wanted to do with her life. There were enough female doctors around and what the country needed was more males enrolling for such courses. Before she could take issue on that he'd begun making love to her and she'd forgotten all else.

What would he be like as a father if they had children? No, not *if* they had children, *when*, she told herself. She loved children and it was one reason why she'd desperately wanted to get married again, to have a couple more kids before she got too old, and to bring them up in a stable home environment.

As soon as they set the date, she'd given up taking the pill, in the hope of surprising Keith with an unexpected wedding present. To her amazement nothing had come of it so far, yet with the baby she'd lost and with Evie too, she'd fallen pregnant very quickly.

Had her fertility decreased badly already? She was forty-one after all. Or was there something wrong with Keith's sperm count? After all, he was even older than her and he'd had only one child with his first wife.

As she was stacking Evie's school things in the bookcase, the large art file fell out again, scattering sheets of paper across the floor before she could catch it. Clicking her tongue in annoyance at her own carelessness, she bent to pick them up.

As she picked up the last sheet of paper, she gasped in shock. It was a letter, stained and torn in two, then sellotaped together. She recognised it instantly, of course she did. It was from an agency hired by her mother asking her to get in contact. This was the second time she'd been contacted and the second time she'd refused to respond. She didn't want to meet the woman who had given her away at birth like an unwanted package, whatever the reason, definitely not.

Yet she distinctly remembered that after tearing the letter in half, she'd tossed it in the kitchen rubbish bin. Yes, and she'd tied up the liner bag for Evie to take out when she cleared up the kitchen. Had the bag burst, or had Evie seen her doing it and wondered what it was all about? Whatever the reason, her daughter must have retrieved it and kept it hidden.

Surely she hadn't contacted this agency?

Fran scowled as she reread the letter, realising that Evie wouldn't have needed to contact them. Her birth mother's address was freely offered at the end of it.

Evie can't have gone to the woman; surely she hasn't done that?

Only, this might be the way she'd managed to disappear without a trace.

Fran's first reaction was to phone Keith at work and share this with him. She'd even picked up the phone when something stopped her. She hadn't told him about the letter. He'd be furious about that. He liked to know everything she did.

Besides, this was something she ought to manage on her own, to show herself *and* him that she could stand on her own two feet. Putting the phone down, she looked round Evie's bedroom. She ought to finish off the tidying up. Only, she couldn't settle to anything, not now.

She was very tempted to throw the letter away again, only if she did, she'd be throwing away what might be an important clue. After some thought she memorised the woman's name and address and put the letter back in the folder. That was as good a hiding place as any.

She looked out of the window and saw patchy grey clouds, but it wasn't raining. She'd go out for a walk. Fresh air and different surroundings often helped you think more clearly.

Chapter Sixteen

The following morning, Evie fiddled with her breakfast then pushed the half-eaten bowl away and looked across the table. 'What are we going to do about it all, Gran? Long term, I mean.'

'I'm not sure. One option for the short term is to send a letter to your mother by recorded delivery. I'll ask for a response to a PO box I have under another name. Do you think she'll reply?'

'Probably. It depends on what Keith tells her to do, though. He seems to control everything about her. I've watched him gradually take over till he's just about telling her how to breathe.'

She frowned in thought; she said slowly, 'I'd like to send a letter to my cousin Amelia without giving her our address, just to say that I'm all right. Would you mind? Only, I'll have to do it quickly because she'll be going to Italy any day now.'

'I think that might be a good thing to do. I've been worrying about how your mother is feeling, I must admit. You can simply leave the letter at the hotel and they'll put it in the post with their mail, I'm told. They seem very obliging about such things for people in our village.'

Evie heaved a big loud sigh of relief. 'I'll do that straight away then.'

'Perhaps we should see if we can find out more about this Keith person as well.'

'I've tried researching him online already, Gran, but he doesn't seem to have a past.'

'What do you mean?'

'There aren't any mentions of a Keith Burgess of his age, not that I could find, anyway. And I couldn't find that name and his birth date in the census records, either. He never talks about his family background, told Mum he was an orphan brought up by the state.'

'That's . . . not a good sign.'

'No. But I knew better than to say anything about not believing that to Mum. I thought perhaps he'd fallen out with his family.'

'Well, how about I call in a favour from a friend who's very savvy about tracing people online and in other ways? We'll see if Mitch can trace Mr Elusive before we do anything else about contacting your mother directly, shall we?'

Evie nodded, sagging back in her chair as if a load had been removed from her shoulders. Indeed, her whole body language said more about how she was feeling than words could ever have done.

'How about I go and phone Mitch about helping us this very minute while you write the letter?'

'Yes, please.'

Evie soon had a letter written, then could only fidget and wait for her grandmother to return from the still-messy open space she called her 'office'.

When Cassie did rejoin her, she said only, 'I've left it with Mitch. He's a whiz at tracing people. He's just finished a job and is able to give it his immediate attention. He hopes to get back to us by the end of the day, if not earlier.'

'So we'd better hang around the house.'

'Yes, but we could walk up to the hotel to ask them about putting the letter in with their post. I have a stamp.'

'Might it be best to take a photocopy of the letter before we do?' Evie asked.

'Good idea. If it comes to legal troubles, at the very least it'll show I'm not trying to keep you from communicating with your mother.'

'Isn't it awful that we have to do this so sneakily?'

'Yes.'

They walked up to the hotel and handed the letter over to a smiling young man on the reception desk, then strolled back home.

When they got inside, Cassie said, 'I wouldn't mind a quiet day and I have a few business matters to attend to. Have you enough to do to keep yourself busy? I can lend you an old laptop if you like.'

Evie beamed at her. 'That'd be brill! I couldn't bring my own laptop with me because it's old and quite heavy, but I hid it at the back of the wardrobe before I left. I doubt Amelia will have found it. I definitely don't want it getting back to Mum and Keith.'

Cassie set her granddaughter up in one of the smaller bedrooms, made sure she could get online and left her to it. She had her own office to sort out and would welcome a chance to put things away and also to come to terms with her new role.

She had a feeling that this was just a lull before a storm so she'd better make the most of it to organise her new home.

Oliver spent the morning in the living room playing some sort of computer game, and when this went on for quite a while, Hal was puzzled. It seemed a childish way for a man of twenty-nine to spend his time.

As they ate lunch he asked, 'Don't you have to go to work?'

'No. Compassionate leave.'

'Do you really need it?'

'I'm entitled to it, so why not take it and have a bit of a rest at their expense? This is a nice place. I may go out for a stroll later, or drive into town and get a real coffee somewhere.' He scowled at his father as he said that.

Hal didn't rise to the bait about that. He cleared his crockery and watched his son walk away from the table without doing the same. 'Hoy!'

Oliver turned round.

'You need to clear up after yourself.'

'Oh, for goodness' sake!'

Hal folded his arms and waited.

Muttering under his breath, Oliver dumped his crockery on the draining board and turned again to leave.

Hal put out his arm to stop him. 'They need a quick rinse and then you put them into the dishwasher. *Voilà!* Clearing up all done, house tidy.'

Their glances met for a second time, but Hal was adamant. He corrected Oliver about where to put the dirty dishes in the machine and watched him do it, then made him wipe down the splashes of tea and milk from the surfaces.

After that they separated. Oliver went back to slump down on the sofa in the living area and started fiddling with his mobile phone.

Hal took refuge in his home office, sighing. This visit was obviously going to be very wearing, but he wasn't giving in on the tidiness side of things.

Half an hour later he saw Cassie come out on her back patio and sit there with a mug of something. He gave in to the temptation to ask if he could join her for a while because the atmosphere in the house was upsetting him.

The postal van arrived earlier than usual at the hotel and the driver went inside to pick up the letters.

The woman on reception looked round for the pile of letters and rolled her eyes when she saw them scattered in one corner. The envelopes hadn't even been stamped with the hotel's name and address. The new young man wasn't doing his job properly.

'Won't be a minute.'

She stamped all the envelopes quickly and passed them over, then started to sort out the incoming mail.

Cassie saw the little red van pull away from the hotel and nodded in satisfaction as she finished her lunch. The letter to Evie's cousin would be on its way.

Evie finished her apple. 'I'll clear up. You go and sit out in the sun and enjoy your coffee.'

'Thanks.'

'Afterwards I'll go back online, if that's all right. I've found a really interesting website about black holes.'

Cassie sat down outside, enjoying the sun on her skin. She was enjoying not having to rush around seeing lawyers today and they had enough fresh food to manage for the time being.

When she heard the outer door next door open and close, she turned her head and raised one hand in greeting to Hal. As he walked across to join her, she was surprised at how stressed he looked.

'If I'm not intruding on you, I'd welcome a little sane, adult conversation.'

'Isn't your son an adult?'

'Only physically.'

She gestured to a chair, studying him, head on one side. 'Still not getting on with him?'

'No, I'm not. I made it a condition of him coming here that he keep the place tidy but I have to stand over him even to make him put his dirty dishes in the machine or pick up after himself. He's twenty-nine, dammit, not seventeen. And I'm not giving in. I can't bear to live in a pigsty. So it's making for a very bad atmosphere.'

'Wow.' She waited a minute and he stared blindly into the distance as he continued to talk.

'I hadn't realised how utterly lazy Oliver is. After they were married and bought a house, he worked hard on it for a year or so, and I thought he'd grown up at last. But he's always liked working with his hands so either that kept him going, or else Mandy kept him at it. Since he got here he seems to have nothing constructive planned, only to laze around and play games on his tablet.'

He picked up his mug, stared at it as if it were an alien artefact before putting it down again without taking a drink. 'I know from my ex that he's been told to get some more qualifications but he's made no attempt to do any studying. His former wife has just got her Master of Business degree apparently.'

Hal looked so stressed, her heart went out to him. 'I don't guarantee that my conversation will be fascinating but I think I'm fairly adult and you're welcome to come across and chat any time I'm sitting out here.'

'Thanks. Am I making too much fuss about details, do you think, Cassie?'

She had no hesitation in reassuring him. 'It's your house and up to you to choose the way you want to live in it. I think any guest should automatically respect that. How old is your son, did you say?'

'Twenty-nine.'

She whistled softly.

Hal sat in silence staring at the lake in the distance then looked at her. 'Will you do me a favour?'

'If I can.'

'Will you and Evie come up for an evening meal at the hotel with me and Oliver, as my guests, tonight or tomorrow, whichever you prefer? That ought to make for one pleasant evening, at least.'

'You don't need to pay for us. We intend to go up there occasionally for dinner anyway. I'm not the world's greatest cook.'

'If I'm the one inviting you, I'd prefer to pay.'

'Very well. You can pay this time, I'll pay next. We'd love to accept, but Evie will have to wear her new brown wig.' She hesitated, wondering whether to explain.

He seemed to read her thoughts. 'You don't have to tell me why you called her Evie if you don't want to.'

'I think perhaps I ought to, in case there's trouble.'

'Trouble?'

She explained the whole story and saw that she'd distracted him.

'That's terrible for the poor girl. If I can help in any way, Cassie, you've only to ask. If you don't mind, I'll mention it to Oliver, so that he doesn't put his foot in it.'

'Yes, we'd better tell him. And thanks for the offer of help. That's kind of you, but we're going to wait and see what my friend finds out about this Keith Burgess fellow before we do anything. In the meantime Evie has sent a message to her cousin Amelia, asking her to tell her mother that she's all right. And then we wait for Mitch to turn something up.'

'What if he doesn't?'

She grinned. 'That's like saying what if the sun doesn't rise tomorrow. Mitch is the best at finding things out about dodgy people, the very best. Keith is a living, breathing human being and must have left some sort of trail through life.'

'You know, it sounds as if the fellow has deliberately taken on a new identity. But why would he do that? What could he be running from?'

'Wow. I hadn't thought of that.' She frowned, thinking it over. 'You may be right.'

'I've met it once or twice in my work as a lawyer.'

'Well, he's not going to hurt my granddaughter and I—'

Just then the back door of Hal's house slid open and his son stuck his head out.

'Oh, there you are, Dad. Look who's turned up to visit. Your friend Sabine.'

As Oliver pushed open the door and gestured to someone inside to come out, Hal gasped in dismay and in anger too. How dare that woman pursue him down here! He leant closer to Cassie and despair made him ask for her help. 'Can I pretend you're my new girlfriend? I can't shake off this woman with words. She's the one I told

you about, the one I think is intending to marry me –
well, marry my money, anyway.'

For answer, Cassie leant forward and took hold of his
hand. 'Of course you can ask for help. Let's have a bit of
fun with her. Give me a kiss and pretend you didn't hear
what your son said.'

Her eyes were dancing with mischief as he pulled
her into his arms and started to kiss her. His anger
was suddenly diluted with amusement and as the kiss
deepened, that turned into something else that neither
of them had expected – a proper kiss, one filled with
passion and promise.

Hal really did forget about Sabine for a few
moments and was furious when someone broke the
spell by tapping him on the shoulder. He pulled away
just a little, but kept his arms round Cassie as he glared
sideways at his son.

'What do you want?'

'Didn't you hear me?' Oliver asked. 'Honestly,
Dad, what a way to behave! Aren't you a bit old for
sitting out snogging in full view of the whole world
and his wife?'

'No, I'm not too old at all to enjoy the pleasure of
that. What the hell do *you* mean by interrupting us?'
Only then did he look beyond Oliver and pretend to be
surprised. 'Oh.'

Sabine was glaring at them from his own back patio.
'Sorry to have interrupted,' she snapped and swung
round. She went back into his house, heels clicking on

the paving of the patio and then fading away across his polished wooden floors.

He didn't attempt to follow her but kept hold of Cassie's hand.

There was the sound of a door slamming and a car starting up at the front of his house then the person drove away.

Oliver was still standing there, gaping at them both.

'Go away, damn you!' Hal exclaimed. 'And stay away.'

He watched his son jerk round and vanish into the house, sliding the door shut with a bang. Taking a deep breath Hal turned back to Cassie, who was still leaning into the circle of his arm, making no attempt to move away.

'Do you mind if we try that again?' he asked. 'It's a long time since fireworks have gone off inside me when I kissed someone. I thought . . . I thought the cancer treatment had put paid to such reactions.'

'It's been a long time for me too, Hal, and yes, I'd really like to try it again.'

So he kissed her gently and she responded tentatively. And since no one interrupted them this time, it turned slowly into an enthusiastic kiss.

When they pulled their heads apart, gasping for breath, he traced a line down the soft curve of her cheek, making no attempt to move away.

'I didn't plan that, Cassie, but I'm very glad it happened. It not only reassured me about my masculinity but gave me great pleasure.'

'I'm glad too. For similar reasons. It's been a long time since I've enjoyed being with a man. I'd been worrying that I was past it.'

Reluctantly, he let her pull away and as she leant back in her chair, he did too. But they kept hold of one another's hand.

'I don't think that was a one-off physical reaction to an attractive woman; I think I'm as attracted to your mind and personality as your body, Cassie.'

'I'm attracted to you in that way too.' She gave a soft chuckle. 'Some would say that sharing a few kisses is a rather old-fashioned way to approach a relationship, but I think it's what we both need just now. Softly, softly.'

She looked at him uncertainly before adding, 'After my marriage broke up, I vowed to give up men. And I didn't find that particularly hard. Today, well, it took me by surprise how much I enjoyed it.'

He flourished a mock bow. 'I'd be grateful, then, if you'd give one hapless male a chance to prove himself worthy of your attention.' He waited again.

Slowly, very slowly she smiled and inclined her head. 'Yes, please. Only, could we not rush things, Hal? I'm still recovering from that terrorist incident and there's Evie to think of. Who knows where that will lead me? She has to come first till her mother and I settle what to do about her future.'

'Of course she comes first. And I'm a bit hamstrung at the moment by having Oliver hanging around, as well as by my surprise at being able to react like that to you.'

'What a pair we are! We'd never fit into a romance novel, would we?'

'I've never read one.'

'Some of the modern ones seem to be more about bedding one another than falling in long-lasting love. I've read quite a few. When you're travelling and things go pear-shaped, you pick up any books that are lying around in hotels in desperation.'

He didn't attempt to let go of her hand and she smiled back and continued to hold his just as firmly.

A short time later his hand slackened and she saw that he was frowning again.

'What is it now?'

'Oliver. I don't know why but I get the feeling he hasn't told me everything.'

'Do they ever? Oh damn.' Her phone was ringing from inside the house and she ran to answer it, then poked her head out to say, 'I have to take this. See you later.'

He walked slowly back to his own house, feeling pleased. When he'd thought he'd lost the ability to be roused by a woman, he'd grieved about that. Surely tonight's reaction couldn't be a fluke?

He paused on the threshold, realising abruptly that he was also happy because the one to stir up such feelings was Cassie, a woman he'd admired on the television for years, and who was even more impressive in person.

She seemed to be a good person, too, which was equally important to him. He thought about the way she was looking after her granddaughter and how fond of one another they seemed already. That aspect was particularly important to him, because he'd had to deal officially with some conniving cheats in his working life, people who believed business laws, or indeed any laws, didn't apply to them and that other people were only there to be used.

Some had sickened him with their callous disregard of other people's life savings, like the one he felt pretty sure his recent work had helped to catch at last, who must surely be facing and deserving a jail term.

He forgot about that and smiled again. In his retirement, he'd hoped to enjoy the company of decent people and lead a simple, quiet life. But to have the companionship of a woman like Cassie would be way beyond what he'd aspired to.

Surely it wasn't too late for love to bloom again?

He hoped not. Though like her, he wanted to take things slowly. Just in case.

But oh, he wished Oliver wasn't here to complicate matters!

Chapter Seventeen

As always, Fran felt better in the fresh air. She began walking, striding out along a road she'd driven along only once since she moved here. If she remembered correctly, there had been a small park at the far end. She would give herself the time to explore it today, time to think without being interrupted by the phone.

Ah yes, there was the park. After walking in through its elegant wrought-iron gateway and up the slight slope, she stopped near some flowering bushes to admire them then stayed there to watch the children playing on the swings in the small playground to one side. Some mothers were sitting on a bench nearby chatting while keeping a watchful eye on their offspring.

On the other side of the path an older couple was occupying another bench, chatting animatedly if their hand gestures were anything to go by. As she watched they stood up and strolled away hand in hand.

It all looked so innocent and peaceful. It made her feel more relaxed, but as she was about to continue her stroll she noticed a man hovering at the far side of the play area. His strange behaviour drew her attention and she began to worry about what he was doing there.

He was half hidden behind some bushes that were similar to those near her, but he'd had to step off the path deliberately to get amongst them, while she was still on the path. His attention was focused on the children and his expression was – well, avid was the only word to describe it – as if he could see something that made him hungry.

He had a beanie pulled down but she still recognised him and to her surprise it was Keith's friend Ryan. He hadn't noticed her, thank goodness. What was he doing here at this time of day, watching children?

Watching them like that! Alarm bells rang in her brain.

A woman jumped to her feet suddenly from one of the park benches near the swings, her phone in her hand. Her voice floated across to Fran.

'That pervert's back again. I've just taken a photo of him and I'm going to report him to the police. Will someone else take a photo too?'

Ryan must have heard her because he immediately swung round, pushing into the bushes, not going back onto the path. As he hurried away, he tugged his collar higher in an attempt to hide his face.

Fran stood there for a few seconds unable to move, so shocked was she. No! Surely he wasn't one of those horrible types you read about who preyed on children?

Only – his expression while watching them hadn't been right somehow.

'I got him too,' another woman said in a satisfied voice, showing her phone to the one who'd drawn attention to him. 'He's been here a few times now. I'll come with you to contact the police. Maybe they'll be able to find out who he is. You can't be too careful these days.'

Before she realised what she was doing, Fran had moved forward to join the duo of angry young women. 'I saw what happened. I know who that man is and where he lives.'

'Really? That's wonderful.'

She gave them his name, even gave them her own before she realised how that might pull her into the mess if Ryan was proved to be acting wrongly.

Keith was going to be furious, whatever came of it.

But surely her husband wouldn't protect Ryan if he was proved to have those disgusting tendencies?

Only . . . the two of them were very close friends and had been for years.

She'd often wondered why an intelligent man like Keith would be so close to a dull man like Ryan. She clapped one hand to her mouth as one reason occurred to her. Keith had often said, 'Oh, we like the same things, Ryan and I.' Surely he couldn't mean . . .

Before she could pursue that unwelcome line of thought, a sudden heavy shower took everyone by surprise.

The women collected their children and Fran ran for shelter to a nearby rotunda, standing near the entrance staring out in dismay at the rain sheeting down. She hadn't brought an umbrella, had been too eager to get out into the fresh air.

'Who'd have thought it'd rain so soon?'

She turned with a jerk at the sound of a voice behind her.

An older woman was there and she gestured outside. 'This morning's weather forecast said showers this evening but clear this afternoon. Who'd have expected it to rain like this when it started off so sunny?'

'I certainly didn't.'

'Haven't seen you in the park before and I know just about everyone who comes here regularly by sight.'

It was only then that Fran realised the woman was wearing overalls with a motto on the front pocket and behind her there was a trolley containing tools and a rubbish bin, also bearing the same motto. She must be a council gardener.

'I've just moved in nearby,' she explained. 'The park is so pretty, I'll probably come here regularly.'

'Good. I hope you enjoy your visits. We pride ourselves on our flowers.'

'They're lovely.' But Fran hadn't really looked at them after she'd seen Ryan. She was about to turn away when the woman grabbed her arm and tugged her to one side.

'Stay quiet. He's back and I don't think he's seen us.'

There was a man peering sideways from behind some bushes at the rear of the rotunda, not looking at them but back at the now-empty play area: Ryan again.

'What's he doing hiding there?' the gardener wondered aloud.

'He's been watching the children. He must be waiting for them to come back. It made me shiver to see the look on his face. Their mothers saw him and two of them took photos. They said they'd seen him round here before and were going to report him to the police.'

The woman became very still. 'They're sure it's the same man?'

Fran nodded. 'Yes. And I was able to tell them who he is because I know him. He's a friend of my husband's. Not my friend, though.'

The woman pulled out an ID card which showed she was a police officer. 'I've been sent to act like a gardener and watch for suspicious activity because a couple of people have already reported a man loitering near the children's playground.'

'Oh dear.'

'Give me your name and address, please. I'm going to follow him and I'll want to interview you afterwards.'

Fran did this but was beginning to feel afraid. What had she started? How would Keith react to this?

Only, she didn't like the idea of why Ryan might still be loitering here. And how could she not help the police to protect children?

'I can wait for you here, if you like,' she offered.

'I'd rather come and visit you at home later. I don't know how long it'll take me to follow him and question him.'

Fran watched her stow the tools behind the rotunda and leave.

Keith would be furious if she'd helped catch his friend, whether Ryan was guilty or not. She was quite sure of that. He didn't have a very high opinion of the police, she'd never understood why.

She was suddenly glad that Evie wasn't living with them.

If she was with Fran's birth mother, would her daughter be safe? She had to believe that her birth mother was a decent person because now she knew why Evie wouldn't live with Keith, she didn't want her daughter coming anywhere near him. No, there would be less risk with her birth mother, surely?

What was beginning to worry her was whether she herself would be safe once Keith found out that she'd identified his friend. If he got into one of his rare tempers he might hit out at her again – and really hurt her this time.

Did she want to risk that? No.

How quickly her feelings for him had shrivelled away. What he and Ryan were doing was . . . horrible.

The worry for her own safety sent Fran hurrying home, heedless of the rain which was still pouring down.

When she got home, Fran was soaked through and shivering. She glanced at her watch. It was only two o'clock.

She couldn't face a confrontation with Keith, just couldn't. Seeing Ryan spying on children had pushed her another step towards ending her relationship with Keith. A possible decision to leave him had suddenly turned into an urgent desire to do so.

It wasn't just because he was Ryan's closest friend, but because she was starting to feel frightened of him. He'd hit her once, and hard too. And even though he'd apologised, that had left her nervous of him.

She might have been stupid enough to rush into marriage but she wasn't stupid enough to live the rest of her life in fear – or put her daughter in danger. If she hurried, she'd have time to pack most of her clothes and leave.

Where could she go, though?

She had a key for Amelia's house and had promised to check on it a couple of times, but Keith knew about that so it'd have to be a B&B.

Since she'd married Keith and moved into his house, he'd changed so quickly she couldn't believe it was the same man who had been so charming over the past few months. He'd grown rougher and hadn't hesitated to show his anger and take it out on her. It was as if he now felt sure of being able to control her.

Was what had driven Evie away fear of Ryan hurting her? Or was it worse? Was Keith like his friend Ryan where children were concerned?

She couldn't forget the look on Ryan's face today, kept seeing it again in her mind's eye. She'd done the right thing giving those women and the police his name.

But what was the right thing to do for herself?

That was a no-brainer. She needed to leave.

Why was she such an utter fool about men? Never, ever again!

As Fran was packing her final bag a couple of hours later there was the sound of a car pulling up in the drive. She peered out of the bedroom window and her stomach muscles clenched in fear. Oh no! Keith had come home an hour early, something he rarely did.

He stormed up the stairs and burst into the bedroom. 'You rotten bitch!'

She didn't need telling why he was angry. How had he found out about Ryan so quickly?

He studied her final suitcase and the other two standing ready. 'What's this in aid of?'

'I'm leaving you.' She was upset at how her voice wobbled, but the look on his face terrified her.

'Oh no, you're not. You're married to me now, remember? That gives me rights. But I'm going to make sure you don't tell lies about my friends again. Enjoy your trip to the park, did you?' He gave her a hard shove, sending her staggering backwards.

'No. I got caught in the rain.'

'Was that before or after you'd been maligning a decent man?'

He took another step towards her and she edged back till she bumped into the dressing table.

He smiled, not a nice smile. 'Well, we're going down to the police station in a few minutes and you're going to tell them you've made a mistake in identifying Ryan.'

'I didn't make a mistake.'

'Oh yes, you did. You'll say you were upset because you and I had had a row, and you hadn't been thinking straight. And you'd better make it convincing.'

His fist suddenly shot out and he punched her in the belly. It hurt so much she screamed and backed into the bay window, gasping in pain. He smiled as if he had enjoyed doing that, such an evil smile that she started throwing the items off her dressing table at him, yelling for help all the time.

When the front door opened, he didn't seem to hear it, because he had just punched her again, sending her sprawling on the floor. But she had heard it and yelled for help again, trying to curl up to protect herself. This time he kicked her, making her cry out, then drew back his leg to do it again.

As she cowered in terror, waiting for another blow, he jerked away from her instead.

Then she saw the woman from the park holding him with his right arm shoved up behind him. Only, this time the woman was wearing a police uniform and there was a male officer standing beside her.

'I'll look after him, you see to the lady,' he said.

'Thanks, Ali.'

Keith began to struggle and yell as she shoved him towards her companion, but though the male officer was no bigger than him, he somehow managed to use the arm lock to stop him. After that he held Keith with his face against the wall, jerking on the arm and making him yell when he tried to get away.

'You all right, love?' the woman asked, holding out one hand.

Fran let her help her up and subsided on the bed, clutching her stomach. 'No. He – hurt me.'

'Show me. I'm Janice, by the way.'

Fran looked across at the two men, reluctant to have a strange man see her undressed.

'I presume that man is your husband?'

'Yes.' She moved incautiously and winced.

'It'd be best to show me what he's done to you immediately and in front of my colleague, then your husband won't be able to claim it was done somewhere else,' Janice said.

Feeling deeply ashamed of what had happened, Fran lifted her skirt. She winced as she moved to show her belly and side, both of which already had big bruises showing on them.

'Can I photograph them?'

'She came home with those bruises!' Keith shouted. 'She'd fallen in the park, could hardly walk.'

Janice winked at Fran. 'Good thing you and I had already met in the park, eh? You were showing no signs of being in pain then.'

Sickened by this behaviour from a man who had been pretending to love her for the past few months, Fran allowed Janice to take a couple of photos, then straightened her clothes. 'Can you keep him here while I finish loading my car?'

'I think it'd be best if we take you to a doctor and get you checked.'

Fran almost refused. She just wanted to get away and never, ever see Keith again. Then she saw him glaring at her, mouthing something that looked like, 'I'll get you.'

Something snapped in her and she turned to the woman beside her. 'I'll need to take my possessions away from here, but then I'll go and see your doctor. My husband and his friend have to be stopped.'

A sigh of relief escaped her companion and she said in a low voice, 'Thanks, love. So many women don't carry through on getting their abusers to face justice.'

'I've read about it. But it is frightening. He's only just started treating me roughly. We got married recently and after I moved in with him he changed. Believe me, I'd not have married him if he'd done anything to hurt me sooner. And I'm not staying with him, whatever he says or does.'

Keith cursed her as he again tried to escape from the policeman's hold, but failed.

'Let's get things organised then,' Janice said. 'I'll carry your suitcase out.'

'Don't let her steal my things!' Keith shouted. 'She's loaded up the car with my possessions already. I demand to see my lawyer.'

Janice merely smiled and said politely, 'We'll see that everything is done properly, believe me, *sir*. Ali, I'll help you get him into the car, then I'll take Fran to the station and meet you there.' She took handcuffs from her belt.

It took the two police officers a while to subdue Keith and get him safely downstairs.

'Good thing we came in this car, eh?' Janice said as she shut the rear door on the compartment they'd locked Keith into.

She turned back to Fran and said in a gentler voice, 'Anything else you want to take with you?'

'My books and music stuff. Oh, and there are some things of Evie's too.'

When they'd carried those out, Janice said, 'Come on, love. Let's go and see the doctor.'

Fran turned at the car to look back. How happy and hopeful she'd been when she came here. How quickly dreams could crumble.

Four hours later, Janice came to talk to Fran, who was feeling numb. She'd seen a doctor and the woman had said it was only bruising. They'd taken photos of it, though, which she found utterly humiliating.

Janice came back to join her after that was over. 'Where are you going now, Fran? You'll need to keep in touch.'

'I don't know where to go.'

'Haven't you got any friends who'll take you in?'

Fran stood thinking then stared at her in shock as the truth sank in. 'We only see his friends now. We moved away from where I was living and I've lost touch with most of my old friends and neighbours over the past few months.'

'Family?'

She was about to shake her head when it occurred

to her that she did have one family member that Keith wouldn't know about.

'There may be someone I can ask for help. But I'm not sure.'

By the time Janice had escorted her out of the police station and they were standing near her car, she'd changed her mind. No. She just couldn't do it. She couldn't go and ask her birth mother for help after she'd hated the woman for years, refused to see her twice and vowed never, ever to speak to her.

She didn't know why she was so reluctant to meet her, but she was.

Janice waited patiently. 'Something else wrong?'

'On second thoughts, I can't ask the person I was thinking about. The connection is too distant. And anyway, I need to go somewhere *he* can't find me.' She was on the verge of tears again. How could she have been so weak, let him walk all over her?

'Let me call someone to help you temporarily, then. You're in no state to drive anywhere.'

'Who?'

'Someone from the women's refuge. They have emergency beds there.'

And heaven help her, Fran agreed to it.

Anything to keep her safe from Keith. She was so sore from his punches, it hurt to move her body.

Most of all she needed time to come to terms with this sudden change in her circumstances. And there was Evie. She was still worried sick about her, prayed that her guess about where her daughter had taken refuge was correct. What if Evie came to Keith's house looking for her and he was there?

It didn't bear thinking of.

'I'll drive you there,' Janice said quietly. 'Ali will come and pick me up afterwards. Just let me tell him.'

Fran could only nod acceptance of that offer and get into the passenger seat.

Chapter Eighteen

Zoe phoned Cassie later that evening. 'Doing anything in particular at the weekend, sis?'

'Um, no.'

'I'm in London and I have to be down here for a meeting next Monday as well. I thought rather than going back to the north for such a short time I could come and visit you in Wiltshire.'

Cassie didn't know what to say. Of course she wanted to see her sister. But there was Evie to think about.

Zoe's tone of voice changed, grew stiffer. 'If you're busy, I can come another time.'

'No, no! I do have a guest, but when I think about it, it's someone I'd really like you to meet. It'll be a nice surprise. Do come.'

'You're sure?'

'Very sure. Trust me, you'll be interested.'

'OK. I'll be down tomorrow evening, then.'

Cassie went to find Evie and hurry her out to purchase another single bed.

They walked round the shops arm in arm, happy to be together.

'I never thought I'd need other spare beds so quickly,' Cassie said. 'I'm amazed by how my life is changing.'

'It seems to me you're enjoying having people you care about with you in a quiet place, both friends and family.'

'Yes, I am. But most of all, I'm enjoying having you.' She glanced sideways and added, 'Something's worrying you, though, isn't it, Evie?'

'Yes. I wish Mum could be with us. I'm sure she'd love you if she gave herself a chance. But—'

'But what?'

'If I could only find out how she's getting on, I'd feel a lot better. I don't trust him to look after her. She gets so anxious sometimes.'

'She'll have received word from her cousin that you're safe by now, surely?'

'I hope so. But I'm afraid *he* might get hold of the letter first. If he did, he'd destroy it, I'm sure. And then he'd come after me, which is why I didn't tell her where I was.'

For an intelligent girl like Evie to believe that this man was so threatening to her safety made Cassie sure there was something very wrong with him. She'd never met such a mature youngster. Was he really the sort of pervert his focus on a young girl seemed to indicate?

Surely her daughter couldn't have married a man with such a warped mind? But Evie had said he could be charming when he wanted. What a mess!

Fran let Janice take her to the women's refuge and park her car, then she got out a bag into which she'd slung some overnight things. Janice escorted her inside and they went into the matron's office, where she gave a few particulars, feeling utterly humiliated to be here. She'd never expected to wind up in a place like this, never.

'I have to go now,' Janice said. 'You'll be all right here, I promise you. He won't be able to get to you.'

'Thanks for your help.' She watched the police officer leave then followed the matron upstairs to her bedroom, a very small space with a shabby duvet on the single bed and one tiny wardrobe.

'I'll leave you to settle in then you can join the others downstairs. There's a toiletries pack in the top drawer, if you need it. The bathrooms are at each end of the corridor.'

Fran used the bathroom, but couldn't bring herself to unpack let alone go downstairs, just couldn't do it. She flopped down on the bed, sitting hunched on the edge, not wanting to face anyone, thank you very much.

A few minutes later, however, someone knocked on the door. She didn't answer, but when there was another knock, she sighed and straightened up. 'Come in. Oh, it's you, Matron.'

'Call me Tracy. We don't stand on formality here. I gather you've been hurt. Is it something I can help with?'

Fran shrugged, not wanting to go into details, not really knowing what she wanted, if truth be told.

'Would you let me look at your bruises before we join the others? I have a salve that helps bruising get better more quickly. No need to prolong the pain, eh? You won't be the first to need it.'

Fran nodded, feeling like bursting into tears at the kindness in the older woman's tone and expression. She let the matron tend to her sore belly and side, trying not to whimper and not always succeeding.

Afterwards Tracy screwed on the cap and handed the tube to her. 'Keep it. And Fran – you were right to come here. This beating was done to hurt you as much as he could without it showing or creating permanent damage. People like that can go on to do far worse.'

'I figured that out. I'll never forget the look of pleasure on his face as he thumped me.'

'There are some warped people out there. Now, one more thing. The police weren't sure how long you'd be staying when they called in for an emergency bed. Do you have any idea at all? We won't throw you out on the street, I promise, but it helps if we have some understanding of your situation and whether you have someone else who'll be able to help you.'

'I'm not sure. This has all blown up so suddenly. I've only been married to him for a few days, though we've been seeing each other for several months.' She couldn't hold back a sob. 'How could I not have realised what he was like? I must be the stupidest person who ever had to take refuge here.'

'You'll only be stupid if you go back to him. Some women do that, believing the promises of no more violence. One or two have died because of it, sadly.'

Fran gasped then bowed her head. 'That's terrible. I definitely won't be going back to him, though. I'd already decided that. It's the only thing I'm at all sure of. But I shall need to find somewhere to live and . . .'

She hesitated, then told Tracy about her daughter running away. 'My birth mother is looking for me, you see, and I'm hoping Evie may have taken refuge with her. It's the only thing I can think of, unless my daughter's sleeping on the street. I'm adopted, so don't have any close blood relatives.'

'Then isn't it a good thing your birth mother is looking for you?'

'Not really. She gave me away in the first place. I'll never forgive her for that.'

'How old was she when she had you?'

Silence, then Fran muttered, 'Fifteen.'

'She might not have had any choice.'

'I still don't want to see her.'

'Didn't you say your daughter is fifteen? Can you imagine your Evie keeping a baby with hostile parents refusing to support her in that option, when she's legally too young even to leave school? If your grandparents had done as they threatened and pushed your mother out onto the street, she'd probably have had the baby taken away. It wasn't as easy in the past for underage girls to find help. Not that it's *easy* now. Having a baby with no support never is.'

It was the thought of Evie in that dilemma that hit home hardest of all and that only added to the confusion Fran was experiencing.

Tracy waited a few moments then stood up. 'Let all that go for now. This is no time to make important decisions. You look utterly exhausted. I think what you need most is to rest in peace and quiet. How about I bring you a cup of coffee and a snack, then you take a nap?'

She was back within a few minutes. 'Here you are. I'll leave you for a while, but do come down if you want company or feel hungry. Just follow the noise of people chatting at the rear of the house.'

'Thanks. I think you're right. I'm way beyond exhausted.'

'Just a word about tomorrow. A cooked breakfast is served from 7 to 9 a.m. If you miss it, you can find something in the kitchen in the fridge and cupboard marked with red tape. Same if you're hungry later. Anyone will show you where to go.'

'I'm not really hungry.'

'Well, just bear it in mind. The women here are very supportive, you'll find. Well, those who have enough emotional energy left to support someone else are. Some of the more recent arrivals are like you, stunned by what's happened to them.'

Fran watched the door close, then ate half the piece of cake and drank some coffee. But she was too tired to be hungry, so visited the bathroom, put on a nightdress then curled up in bed.

She'd expected to cry herself to sleep, but she didn't cry at all. She felt too numb.

It was bright daylight when Fran awoke and she was amazed to find that she'd slept right through the night. She had to rush to find a bathroom, after which, since it was past nine o'clock, she went back to get her towel and took a leisurely shower. She was horrified by the size of her bruises and avoided looking at them as much as she could while she put on more of the salve.

When she was dressed, she took the tray downstairs and found a group of women sitting chatting in a shabby room full of armchairs, sofas and small tables.

As she stood hesitating by the door, one of them got up. 'I'm Polly.' She waited, head on one side.

'Fran. I, um, got here last night.'

'Yeah, we heard another woman had come in. Welcome. This is a good place to find your feet again. Now, I bet you'd like a cup of coffee or tea to start with?'

'I'd kill for one. And I'm hungry, too.'

'I'll show you the kitchen. Here, give me the tray.'

With Polly's help, Fran got herself something to eat, still expecting questions. Only, they didn't come. Indeed, the other woman sat sipping a mug of coffee opposite her at the small table, staring towards the window, clearly giving her the choice of talking or not.

'Are we allowed out?'

Polly chuckled. 'Of course we are. Do you think you're in prison or something?'

'I don't know what to expect. I didn't think I'd end up in a refuge, that's certain. I only got married to him a week or so ago.'

'Known him long, had you?'

'Several months.'

'I bet he was taking the time to separate you from your friends first so that he could get you to depend only on him.'

'How did you know?'

This time Polly's laugh was totally mirthless. 'Because that's how my ex started off with me. Ah, to hell with men like that! Where do you want to go? Not to see him, surely?'

'Heavens, no!'

As the silence lengthened, Polly said, 'You don't have to tell me anything, but you should know I'm a part-time counsellor here. I understand what it's like, you see. I was training to be a real counsellor until I met my ex. I'm working on my studies and earning my keep here by helping out. Up to you if you want to chat any time. Do you have a car?'

'Yes.'

'Just a warning. He'll know it by sight if you go to any of your former places.'

'I hadn't thought of that.'

'If you pay for the petrol I can drive you where you want to go in mine. It's old, not much to look at but reliable. Besides, you'll be safer if you're not on your own. He's likely to be angry.'

'Oh yes. He was absolutely furious with me for identifying his friend.'

'Then let me take you round.'

'Can it be that easy to get on with things?'

'What's easy about picking up the pieces and trying to start a whole new life? It's hard going, especially when you leave here and face the world.'

'Yes. I suppose it is. I'm not really thinking straight yet.'

'Which only shows you're normal!'

'Normal but stupid.'

'Don't put yourself down.'

'I have to face facts. No one forced me to let him take over my life.' After another moment's thought, she added, 'Look, I can not only afford to pay for the petrol but I'd really welcome some company.'

Polly smiled. 'Good. I like going out for drives – as well as helping other women in the same situation as me. Let's find you some clothes that are nothing like what you'd usually wear and a beanie to pull down over that hair of yours. It's a dead giveaway, red hair is.'

Fran gaped at her. 'Is that necessary?'

'Who knows? But if it is, we'll be prepared, eh?'

Chapter Nineteen

When they arrived at Amelia's house, Polly parked a little way down the street. 'Don't get out yet. We'll watch the house for a few minutes before we even go across to it.'

Her companion sounded as if she'd experienced this situation before and been caught out, so Fran would rather be too careful than sorry. Her bruises reminded her of that at regular intervals.

There were no signs of life so Fran pulled her borrowed beanie right down to hide her hair and they got out of the car. As they were approaching Amelia's gate, Fran was sure she saw a curtain twitch in the front bedroom upstairs. 'Don't go in!' She tugged her companion past the house. 'I saw the curtain move.'

'So did I,' Polly said. 'Let me take over.'

She turned in at another house a few doors along and knocked on the front door, saying brightly, 'I'm very sorry to trouble you, but is there someone called Svenson living in the street?'

'Not that I know of.'

'Oh dear, I must have got the address wrong. Thank you so much for your help.'

'You're welcome.'

The door closed and they returned to Polly's car.

'What is your ex's car like?'

'A red Ford with a slightly dented boot.'

'See if you can spot it.' Polly drove slowly up the next street and down the one after.

'That's it!' Fran exclaimed, shocked because she hadn't really expected to see him near here and had almost persuaded herself that they must have seen the curtains move slightly by a stray current of air. 'It must be him inside the house, looking for me. Who else could it be? Amelia's away.'

'Good thing we were careful. We'll get a police escort to come back to your cousin's later. We're not risking any more physical violence. Look, I don't know anything about your background, but is there absolutely no one else you think your daughter could have gone to for help?'

Fran bent her head, feeling sick that it had to come to this, then admitted in a choked voice, 'There is someone. My birth mother.'

Polly let out a soft whistle of surprise. 'Could you not have gone to take refuge with her last night?'

'I've never met her and I don't want to. I only know her

address from when she tried to contact me recently. Evie must have found it when she was clearing up the kitchen because the letter I'd thrown away was hidden amongst her art things. I'm hoping she took refuge with her grandmother. She'd be far safer there than on the street, whatever the woman's like. I suppose we'd better try her house.'

'You're sure you want to go there? From the tone of your voice, you don't sound as if you're ready to face the woman.'

'Since she's been trying to contact me, I'd guess she would have been happy to help Evie.'

'Perhaps you'd better think carefully about it before we go any further.'

'No. I don't have any choice now. It's the best chance I have of finding my daughter, I'm sure, because there's nowhere else Evie *can* have gone.' Nowhere else Fran could go, either, that Keith wouldn't know about. But she didn't like to admit that aloud yet.

'You're sure your ex doesn't know where your birth mother lives?'

'Pretty certain, yes. I doubt he'd have left the letter amongst Evie's things if he'd spotted it. Knowing him, I'm sure he'd have burnt it so that I didn't have anywhere else to turn . . . don't you think?'

'Your guess would fit the behaviour pattern of men like him. Come on, then, tell me where your birth mother lives.'

The address Fran had memorised turned out to be in a very nice suburb, with rows of well-maintained houses, neat gardens but few people around at this time of day.

Fran scowled at it. 'She's not short of money, then.'

'Did you want her to be?'

She didn't even try to answer that, but felt a bit ashamed of being so surly.

They stopped outside the house and studied the façade.

'It looks empty, with all the blinds drawn like that,' Polly said. 'Are you sure this is the place?'

'Yes, I'm sure. Let me do this on my own.' Fran summoned up all her courage and got out of the car, knocking on the front door with an old-fashioned brass knocker in the shape of a cat, for lack of a doorbell. There was no response and the sound seemed to echo inside.

She knocked again, but to no avail.

Polly came to join her. 'She could be at work.'

'But Evie wouldn't be and if she were inside and saw me knocking, she'd have opened the door, I know she would.' Fran went to try and peep in the window, but the blinds were drawn and covered the window completely.

They tried the tall side gate that led to the rear, but it was locked and fitted the gap so closely they couldn't see what lay behind it.

'Whoever lives here really values their privacy,' Polly commented.

As they went back towards the car, a woman walking a dog along the street stopped to call, 'She's moved out.'

'Oh. Do you know where she's gone?'

'Sorry, but I don't. She kept herself to herself. Well, famous people usually do, don't they?'

Fran looked at her in puzzlement. 'Famous people? I'm looking for Cassie Bennington.'

'Yes. But she's Cassandra Benn when she's on TV. Didn't you know?'

'No. I've seen Cassandra Benn on TV, but I didn't know it was her I was looking for. I've been checking my ancestry, you see, and we may be related. You don't know where she's gone?'

'No, sorry. And I don't think anyone round here will, either. She was away a lot and didn't do more than nod when she passed you in the street, even when she was at home.' She raised one hand in farewell, gave the dog's lead a little tug and walked on.

Fran stared at Polly. 'Cassandra Benn can't be my mother, surely!'

'I've seen her on TV. She has your colour of hair.' She studied Fran. 'Could be, you know. There's a resemblance, same shape of face, if I remember correctly, same slender build, too.'

'Let's go back to the refuge. I don't know what to think or what else to do.'

'We could contact the police when we get back and ask if they'll help you visit your cousin's house safely.'

'Not today. I'm just . . . gobsmacked by what that woman said.'

It felt as if not only her present life but her past had been turned upside down, somehow. Could Cassandra Benn really be her mother?

* * *

When they got back Fran once again went up to her room, claiming to feel exhausted. All she wanted to do was come to terms with what she'd found out, only her thoughts seemed to be in a worse tangle than ever. How could she be the daughter of the famous journalist? The woman didn't look old enough to have a daughter approaching forty-two.

And as she lay on the bed, a picture of Evie came into her mind. She had the same red hair as her mother and grandmother – same resemblance to them both!

The only thing Fran was sure of was that she should have gone to the police as soon as her daughter went missing. Why had she let Keith persuade her not to?

It was inevitable that she went on to wonder what she would have done if Evie had been assaulted and made pregnant as her own mother had. The answer was a no-brainer: she'd have helped her, that's what. She might be useless at choosing a man worth falling in love with, but she'd never, ever threaten to throw her daughter out on the street, whatever the circumstances.

Her mother's parents had done that and forced her to have the baby adopted. How cruel!

Fran sighed. The more she looked into this, the more uncertain she became about what was the right thing to do next, or even how she now felt.

All she was sure of was that she wasn't going back to Keith. She was utterly certain of that, and her decision was reinforced every time her bruises hurt.

She would probably give up men for ever, and with it

the chance to have another child. She couldn't face any more catastrophic relationships and break-ups.

In the middle of the night, she woke with a start and couldn't get back to sleep. She lay thinking for a while, coming to the conclusion that she was being cowardly. It was obvious that she needed to go into Amelia's house because if there was one place Evie would send a message, in order to make sure Keith couldn't intercept it, that was it. Finding her daughter was far more important than anything else in this mess.

The curtain at Amelia's house had definitely moved even though the window hadn't been open to let in a breeze. They'd both seen it. Had Keith already broken into the house? Got hold of any messages?

She shivered. She wouldn't be surprised if he had. Nothing he did would surprise her now. How was she going to protect her daughter if she couldn't even find Evie?

She rolled over without taking care and whimpered as she hurt her bruised belly. That made another shiver run through her. She didn't want to face her ex again. He was much stronger than she was. She definitely had to ask for a police escort before she went anywhere near Amelia's house, just in case he was waiting for her there.

Even if there was a message from Evie asking for her help, she didn't even have a home to take her daughter to now.

She couldn't think beyond going back to Amelia's house and praying that she'd manage to find her daughter.

It was a long time before she got to sleep again and she woke feeling utterly exhausted.

The next day dawned with heavy grey skies and the damp feel of rain threatening. After she'd showered and dressed, Fran tried in vain to phone Amelia's mobile. There was no answer and no answering service either, which was unusual. Usually when Amelia went overseas she kept in touch with her friends.

She gave up trying in the end and sent an email without much hope of a reply. She made it down to the kitchen by half past eight. Polly waved to her to come across to the table where she and three other women were chatting.

'Dump your handbag and get some food. It's self-serve.'

Fran went to fill a plate, but could only face toast and jam.

When she rejoined the group, Polly introduced her then said, 'You don't look as if you slept well.'

'I didn't.'

'Now why am I not surprised?'

'I didn't sleep all night through for weeks after I got here,' one woman said. 'Give it time. You'll gradually settle down and start thinking more clearly.'

Fran nodded, managed to force a half-smile and tried to eat her toast. Only, it seemed to stick in her throat and eventually she pushed the last half of it aside.

'How about a stroll round the garden before it starts raining?' Polly suggested. 'Daylight's good for you when you're feeling depressed.'

Fran didn't even bother to deny that she was feeling down. The other women seemed nice, but she didn't want to chat to them, so she put her dirty dishes away and contented herself with nodding to them as she left.

When they got outside she breathed deeply, enjoying the freshness of the damp air, in spite of the lack of sunshine. 'I did decide one thing last night, Polly. I want to go to my cousin Amelia's house today in case there's a message. How do I arrange for the police to come there with me?'

'We can get Tracy to phone them. You're sure about that?'

'Yes. It's the only place I can think of where Evie might try to contact me. I tried to phone Amelia this morning but there was no answer.'

'I'll go and sort that out now.'

It seemed a long time till Polly came back. 'The police can meet you there at about eleven. They don't want us to go inside till they arrive, not even into the garden.'

'Not until then?'

'We aren't exactly their first priority.' She smiled sympathetically. 'I know. There's a lot of hanging about to put up with while you sort things out, but we'll gradually work through it all and find a way to help you.' She led the way back into the kitchen. 'How about another cup of tea? And maybe a piece of fruit?'

Feeling guilty about taking up so much of Polly's time, Fran took a banana, peeling it slowly and carefully, not really wanting to eat. 'You must have better things to do than babysit me.'

'Not today, I don't. You really need me.'

'I always seem to be needing someone. You'd think by my age I'd be able to manage my own life.' She took a small bite of the firm, white banana and forced it down.

'You're just going through a bad patch. Just one more thing. Tracy asked me to check whether you've contacted work to let them know you won't be in.'

She gaped at Polly. 'No. What was I thinking of? I have to do that straight away. I don't want to lose my job on top of everything else.' She dropped the banana on the wooden bench and took her phone out of her handbag, then paused with it in her hand. 'What shall I tell them?'

'Say you had an accident and will need a few days off to recover. We'll get you a doctor's note.'

She made the phone call, dissolved in tears when she tried to explain and had to let Polly finish for her.

Only, the call continued and Polly's expression grew grimmer and grimmer. 'No. He doesn't speak for his wife . . . That man is the *cause* of her present problem, for heaven's sake . . . Please tell him nothing in future. No, not even whether she's still off work.'

The person at the other end seemed to be protesting and Polly cut the conversation short. 'Her husband is dangerous. He attacked her yesterday and the police had to get involved to stop him. Do you want to be responsible for him hurting her again?'

The voice started up, louder now, and after a few seconds she interrupted the speaker. 'Is there someone in HR I can speak to? I think they'll have a better idea what to do. As you say, this is not your area of expertise.'

She sighed and waited, rolling her eyes at Fran, then speaking earnestly to someone else, explaining yet again that Keith was the cause of Fran's indisposition and that the assault was now being handled by the police. This time she nodded a lot and the grim expression lightened gradually.

When she put the phone down, she said tartly, 'The human resources person was much more understanding than your section boss, thank goodness.'

'I didn't want them to know.'

'I had to say something. The guy you're working directly with hasn't a clue about this sort of situation and he'd actually agreed to let your husband know if you turned up to work. We needed to stop anyone there giving your ex information about you. The guy in HR was very angry to hear your section head had done that, so I'm pretty sure he'll take care to prevent that from now on.'

Fran nodded. She couldn't see herself going back to work there now that she knew what her boss had done. She'd never really taken to him but now, she'd not trust a single word he said. Besides, she didn't want to go anywhere she might run into Keith and he not only knew where she worked but where she usually had lunch. There wasn't even anyone on duty at the entrance to the building to vet those coming in.

She might have to start all over again, finding a job in another town and building up a life from nothing. She'd done that a couple of times before, hated the stress and loneliness of it. She'd be even lonelier without her daughter to look after and love. And there had never been such a dire need for secrecy as there was now. She wondered if she'd ever feel safe again – ever *be* safe.

Thank goodness she'd still kept control over her savings and bank accounts. It wasn't only a matter of having the money but of knowing that she hadn't been totally stupid.

And when she'd eventually realised the danger she was in, she'd had the sense to try to get away from him quickly, too. From what the other women here had told her she'd done well there.

Those were signs there was still hope for her – weren't they? That she wasn't totally brain-dead?

She hoped so.

Chapter Twenty

Hal finished his breakfast and cleared his things away, sitting over the remains of his cup of tea to keep an eye on his son, who had got himself a mug of drinking chocolate but hadn't yet eaten any breakfast.

Oliver finished his drink and went to sit in the living area, caught his father's eye and without saying a word, went back to put the mug in the dishwasher. Then he sat down and started fiddling around with his smartphone.

Must be bad news, judging from his son's expression as he glared at his messages. Hal didn't say anything, waiting to see if he would share the news.

Fists clenched, Oliver sat scowling into space for a few moments, then looked round, opened his mouth as if to speak then snapped it shut again.

'Is something wrong?'

Oliver came across to join him at the table, still clutching his phone.

Sometimes, Hal thought, those phones seemed more like children's toys or even children's security blankets than communication devices.

'They want me to go on a course before I start work at the new place.'

'An interesting one?'

'No. Interpersonal skills.'

'Grooming you for a promotion perhaps?'

Oliver stared down at his phone, then switched it off and scowled at his father. 'No. If you must know, the new job is a demotion and this is an update of a course I did a couple of years ago. I already know all the blah-blah politically correct crap in it by heart.'

Hal waited a moment or two to ask, 'Why a demotion?'

'Some stupid bitch complained that I was sexist and anti-gay.'

'And are you?'

Oliver stared down again. 'I don't think so. Not really. I was just a bit . . . well, a lot angry and spoke without thinking. She took exception to it and we got into a row. You can't open your mouth these days without upsetting someone.'

'You must have done something more serious than that to have got yourself demoted.'

'Yeah, well, I was having a bad day and needed to be on my own, only she kept following me around and talking at me. I apologised afterwards for shoving her out of the way, didn't I? And I didn't *hurt* her. She didn't fall over or anything. What else do the HR people want from me, a pint of blood?'

Hal watched him thump one fist down on the table but couldn't help noticing that his son's eyes were over-bright.

'Sounds to me as if you need counselling and an anger management course more than interpersonal skills training.'

'Oh, they want me to do that as well. The latest email also gave me details of my first appointment with a counsellor. The new lot who bought out the company last year pride themselves on helping their employees through bad patches in life, you see.'

Hal didn't know what to say to that. No one had helped him through his recent close brush with death. He might have been glad of a little help because it shook you up good and proper to face cancer.

Mind, it was probably his own fault because most of the people he'd worked with hadn't even known what he was going through. Would he have welcomed counselling? Who knew? He'd just got on with things.

He realised Oliver was glaring across at him.

'Well? Not got anything to add to it, Dad? No little lectures from a fond parent?'

'Only that if there's anything I've learnt in this life, it's not to let bad news swamp me. I've had to find ways to stay calm in the past year. You're not the only one who's been facing problems, you know. What'd happen if we all lost our tempers and hit out at others?'

The silence lasted a long time, then Oliver muttered, 'Sorry. I was forgetting. I should have been there for you.'

'That's all right. You didn't know about my problems.'

'No. Nor you about mine. So just to keep you informed now, I definitely don't want to take this job at a lower level. It's far less interesting. And all the people there will know I'm *in remediation*. That's what the people huggers who took over a perfectly good company call it. Hah!'

'Then find yourself another job.'

'I can't.'

'Oh?'

'Not in my area of work and at a decent salary, anyway. Not till I'm able to get a full reinstatement and a good reference. I'm a great salesman, in case you're interested, and they know that or they'd not go to this much trouble.'

'You could take casual work for a time?'

'No way. Anyway, I can't go back to serving in a bar or any of the casual jobs I did when I was a student, because I have a big credit card debt to pay off.'

'I thought you were getting a payout for your share of the house.'

'I won't use the money I'm going to get for that or I'll not have enough left for a deposit on a new place. Besides, I'll need a steady job to get a mortgage. That's important to me. I don't intend to lose owning my own home on top of everything else.'

'Then you'll just have to bite the bullet, go back to work and face the new people.'

A growl was his only answer.

'Why don't you get some breakfast, and after you've cleared it up, go out for a nice, long walk? It always helps me to get out in the fresh air.'

Oliver shrugged, gave him a dirty look and made several pieces of toast, slathering them so thickly he used up the last half-jar of his father's favourite black cherry jam.

This wasn't the time to talk about nutrition, or selfishness. Indeed, Hal couldn't think of anything he could say to help. It was up to his son to make the necessary decisions about his own future. But if Oliver was trying to preserve his house money, even if he wasn't going the best way to lower interest payments, that surely said he hadn't completely lost all common sense?

He stayed at the table, pretending to read an article in yesterday's newspaper and waiting to make sure his son cleared up after himself. He intended to keep reinforcing the lesson about how he wanted his home treated, because control over his surroundings was important to him – ridiculously important perhaps, but hey, this was his beautiful, brand-new home.

From the scowls shot in his direction, Oliver was well aware of why he was lingering, but at least he did what was necessary before slamming out of the house.

There was the sound of a car starting up outside and Hal let out a long, slow breath, then another. Phew! His son's visit was going to be harder than he'd expected.

He wasn't going to offer to lend Oliver the money to pay off the credit card debt, even though he could have easily afforded it. His son had to take charge of his own messed-up life and work his way through it, learning from the experience, hopefully.

Only if absolute disaster threatened would Hal step in.

A little after eleven o'clock, the police turned up to meet Fran and Polly outside Amelia's house. It was a different pair of officers but just as kind, and their mere presence made Fran feel safe.

She had her key ready but when she tried to insert it into the lock, something seemed to be blocking it. When she bent to try to peer into it, she saw only darkness. The officer who did the same thing said something must be obstructing the inner end.

'Let's go round the back and see if we can get you into the house that way,' he suggested. 'I'll go first.'

When he opened the side gate, a box that had been hidden on a nearby shed roof was pulled down by a rope attached to it and fell on him. It must have been heavy because he yelled and jumped aside, kicking it and rubbing his shoulder as if it hurt.

His companion yanked the two women quickly back out of the way. 'Booby trap. Stay there and don't touch anything.'

Fran stared after him open-mouthed. She could guess who was to blame for these problems. But why?

Had Keith gone completely mad? Was he so determined to hurt her further that he'd planted a booby trap for her cousin? Or did he know Amelia was away and had meant it for his wife?

Well, if he'd wanted to further stiffen her resolve not even to consider going back to him, he had succeeded.

The officer who had been with them returned. 'You can come round to the back safely but stay on the path.'

They both stopped dead as they saw that the other officer, who looked as if he had the beginnings of a bruise on his cheek, was now standing beside a broken kitchen window, which had a hole in it big enough for an adult to get through. Fran could see shards of glass littering the surfaces inside the room as well as outside the house.

'I'm presuming this wasn't done before?'

'No, of course not. Amelia wouldn't go away and leave a broken window. What's it like in the rest of the interior? Has Keith done anything else?'

'You sound sure it's him.'

'I'm quite sure.'

The officer tried the sliding door and it opened easily. 'The intruder must have come out this way and not been able to lock it again, or not bothered to try. I'll have a quick check of the inside before anyone else goes in.'

He walked round the dining area and vanished into the front of the house. When he came back, he said, 'Well, there's more damage but it seems to be on a smaller scale. You know the place well, so we're hoping you can tell us if anything's been touched apart from the obvious vandalism.'

Fran had been nervous until now, but as she looked round the interior, that feeling began to give way to anger. Most of the big room next to the kitchen hadn't been trashed but one beautiful art glass vase that Amelia had particularly treasured, and had shown with pride to Keith the first time he came here, had been smashed in the centre of the floor, sending multicoloured splinters of glass everywhere. It was as if he'd wanted to make a threat about what he could do to her by destroying a precious possession.

She pointed to the side. 'Amelia's studio is in the conservatory over there and it also contains her office equipment and files.'

The other officer had found a sweeping brush and led the way across to the conservatory, brushing glass aside when necessary, though some smaller pieces still crunched underfoot.

They all stood in the doorway, staring in disgust at more vandalism. A beautiful painting of a meadow of spring flowers on an easel had been daubed with a cross of white gloss paint, then the tin of paint had been upended on the floor nearby. All three drawers in the filing cabinet had been pulled open, with papers and art materials scattered nearby.

'He could have been searching for something specific from the looks of this,' one officer said.

She knew now, oh yes – she might have let love blind her before but now she was utterly certain Evie had been right to fear him. 'Keith wants to find my daughter. She said he made her feel uncomfortable and I didn't realise – didn't listen. Well, you don't expect that sort of thing from someone who has always been charming to you, do you?'

'No.' The officer's voice was gentle. 'People like that can be quite clever in manipulating people.'

'I should think Keith wants to get hold of both me and my daughter now. The police took his friend and business partner Ryan in for questioning yesterday for hovering near little children at the playground in the park. I was the one who gave them Ryan's address and I can give it to you.'

'If you're talking about Ryan Ogle, we have it already, because that wasn't the first time he'd been taken in for suspicious behaviour near children.'

'No!'

'We searched his house yesterday but there was no sign of anyone else living there nor was there any evidence of wrongdoing on his computer. We'll check out your ex's house in more detail after this and see if there's anything untoward there. We'd be grateful if you'd help us by asking us to go in to help collect the rest of your things.'

She nodded. 'Of course. There are some books I wouldn't mind getting, but I put my furniture in storage when I moved in with him.' Thank heavens she'd told Keith she'd sold it. He'd said it was rubbish, but she loved her old pieces, some of them genuine antiques which she'd refurbished with loving care.

'Good. Now, let's have a good look round here and see if there's anything else out of place.'

She sighed as they studied the carefully targeted destruction of items. 'Poor Amelia. It's not fair. It's as if Keith's punishing her for what I've done.'

'No, it isn't at all fair, if it is him and that's what he's doing. Shall we go and look at the front door next to see why you couldn't get the key in the lock?'

It was immediately obvious that glue had been used to block the keyhole.

'I should think he did this to make sure you went round the side.' The injured officer rubbed his shoulder.

'I'll have to get someone in to fix this for Amelia, since it's my fault he did it,' she said.

'Not yet. Keep trying to contact your cousin and in the meantime we'll get a team here to see if we can find any prints or DNA samples. Keep your fingers crossed that he cut himself. We'll take your prints to eliminate you before we let you go back to the refuge, if that's all right.'

She nodded.

They'd just turned to go out through the back when there was the sound of something falling through the letterbox into the hall. One of the officers went to check it and called, 'It wasn't the post, but an envelope must've been stuck in the letterbox.'

He came back holding it by one corner. 'It's marked "Delivered to no. 15 by mistake". It's from some hotel in Wiltshire. Is the hotel somewhere you go to or know?' He held it out.

The envelope caught Fran's attention immediately, not the explanatory scrawl but the handwritten address. 'This letter must have been written by my daughter. I'd recognise her handwriting anywhere. Can we open it? I'm hoping she's asking Amelia to pass on a message to me.'

He handed her the envelope and when she turned it over, she saw that it had indeed been stamped with the name and address of a hotel in Wiltshire. She answered his earlier question. 'And this isn't a hotel I've ever heard mentioned, let alone stayed at.'

She memorised its name and address quickly before opening the envelope and pulling out a letter. 'It *is* from Evie.' Tears of relief came into her eyes as she read it.

> *Dear Amelia,*
> *Will you please contact my mother and tell her I'm safe?*
> *I won't give you my address because I don't want her letting Keith know where I am. But I'm with someone who cares about me.*
> *Love,*
> *Evie*

Fran looked at the envelope in puzzlement. 'She said she wasn't giving her address but there's the hotel information on the back of this.'

'She might be staying there and have handed it to them to post. She'd not have known that they stamped the back of the outgoing letters,' Polly suggested. 'When we go back we'll look up the hotel online.'

'And then I'm going to phone and ask if she's there, so that I can drive down to get her.'

'You shouldn't go there yet,' one of the policemen said hastily. 'Your ex is very determined to cause trouble and you shouldn't go anywhere on your own till we're sure you'll be safe. We'll get in touch with the police down there and ask them to check out the hotel first.'

Fran shook her head. 'No. I've not been the best of mothers but I love my daughter and I've let her down badly recently. I have to see her . . . just have to, and take her somewhere safe.'

'I can come with you, but we'll have to go in your car,' Polly offered. 'Mine's a bit old for long journeys.'

'I can't ask you to do that.'

Polly grinned. 'It's no sacrifice, believe me. I've not been out for a drive in the country for ages.'

'Does your husband have any idea about this hotel, do you think, Mrs Burgess?' the younger officer asked.

She shook her head. 'I can't see how he could, because until now I'd not even heard of it. And could you call me Ms Milner from now on, please? It's my maiden name. I don't want to use his name any more. I'm going to divorce him as soon as it can be arranged.'

'We can't stop you going to look for your daughter, but we'll call the police in that part of Wiltshire and let them know about your situation. That way, if you need to call for help, you'll get it more quickly. You're not going there today, are you? It's too late for that, surely?'

'No, but I'm going to phone them today and see if she's staying there. Maybe I can even speak to her.'

'Why don't you try now?'

She nodded and took out her phone, dialling the number stamped on the back of the envelope and adding it to her phone number list. But the person who answered said there was no one of that name or description staying at the hotel.

'I'd have noticed if a young woman with red hair had visited us recently, madam.'

Fran had a sudden idea. 'Are there any holiday lets nearby?'

'There is a leisure village attached to the hotel, but I don't think any of the houses in it is used as a holiday let. It's not a big place and they're still building. All that have been completed are owner occupied.'

After Fran had ended the call she gave the two police officers a very determined look. 'I'm going there tomorrow. Evie has to be nearby, surely, if this was posted from the hotel?' She shook her head sadly, even more worried about her daughter. It was dusk now but she'd set off at first light. Why was Evie in Wiltshire, for heaven's sake? That wasn't even near to where her birth mother had lived before. Or had the woman moved right out of London?

Cassandra Benn might have taken Evie to Wiltshire, for some reason. Two redheads should be easy for people to remember, surely? She wouldn't phone again, though, she'd turn up at the hotel in person.

After seeing what Keith had done, she was even more certain that she was never getting romantically involved with a man again. She'd made a lot of bad choices in men over the years, but none had proved as terrible as Keith. She was getting worse at it, not better.

She knew men weren't all bad, of course she did. But that was beside the point. The biggest weakness lay in her. She clearly didn't know how to distinguish good males from bad. Her track record had proved that conclusively.

Nope, no more romances for her.

Chapter Twenty-One

It was just after seven when Zoe drew up outside her sister's house. Cassie peered out of the window, then came hurrying out to greet her with a big hug.

That was the first time her sister had been openly affectionate of her own accord, and it made Zoe glad she'd fudged the truth about having a meeting in London on Monday as an excuse to come down here, instead of obeying her parents' command to go home for the weekend.

'For goodness' sake, forget about your older sister,' her mother had ordered. 'She hasn't been a credit to the family and our careful upbringing, so we don't owe her anything. It's about time you showed *us* your loyalty. I don't know what's got into you lately.'

Zoe had had more than enough of being nagged by them, enough too of them trying to keep her away from Cassie.

'I love my sister and intend to see a lot more of her, whatever you say or do.' She'd stormed out, sick of their hypocrisy and cruelty to poor Cassie.

She'd left home decades ago, even though at first she'd lived in the same town, but they'd still tried to control her, so she'd left her friends and reluctantly moved to Manchester. Though she dutifully phoned her parents now and then, and even visited them once or twice a year, when she couldn't put it off any longer, distance had enabled her to see them even more clearly. They were cold and more concerned about appearances than other people's troubles. Especially when it concerned their elder daughter.

They weren't even proud of how successful Cassie had been, always putting her down when people commented, saying the topics she featured in her TV programmes were disgusting and should be kept out of the limelight.

Zoe stared in surprise as Cassie grabbed her arm to prevent her from going into the house.

'I have such a wonderful surprise for you, Zoe. Let me tell you about it before we go in.'

'OK. I'm all ears.'

'I have my granddaughter staying with me at the moment.' She paused and stared challengingly at her younger sister.

'*Your granddaughter?* You have a granddaughter?'

'Yes. The agency found my daughter only once again she turned down seeing me. Her daughter did want to see me, though, and she's here.'

'That's great! I can't wait to meet her.' She turned

away to get her suitcase out, but as she closed the car boot, Cassie grabbed her arm again.

'There's more. The guy my daughter married recently upset Evie so much she ran away and came to take refuge with me.'

'That's a bit of an overdramatic reaction, don't you think?'

'No. He sounds like a paedophile to me, from what she's said.'

'Oh no!'

'My daughter wouldn't believe anything was wrong, but since Evie saw the letter from my agency, she knew my address so came to ask for my help. She didn't want to live with him, didn't dare.'

'Dear heaven, what a terrible situation for the poor girl! And for you.'

'It was such a close-run thing, it makes me shiver. Evie turned up seeking my help the day before I moved down here. If she'd arrived two days later, she'd have missed me and would probably be living on the streets now because I didn't leave any information about where I was going with the neighbours.'

She shuddered then gave her sister a watery smile. 'She's a great kid.'

Zoe gave her a hug. 'I couldn't be more pleased for you. Aw, love, don't cry.'

Cassie swiped at her eyes. 'I'm so happy to be able to get to know her and help her. And what am I doing standing out here, blubbing like a big baby? Come and meet our newest family member, Zoe. You'll like her.'

'I'll *love* her, I hope. Hey, just think, I'm an auntie to a girl, no, great-auntie. Michael's only got little boys and they're a subdued pair who never say much when I visit. He's nearly as bad as our parents for being strict.'

'Yes. I pity them. Anyway, here we go.' She flung open the door. 'Evie, darling, this is my little sister, Zoe.'

Evie looked across towards the door apprehensively, but Zoe simply held open her arms and moved forward. 'You're my very first great-niece.'

They met in the middle, hugging, then separating to stare at one another.

'You've got the family hair,' Zoe commented. 'Do you get called "carrots" at school?'

'Yes.'

'Used to drive me mad.'

'Cup of tea, you two?' Cassie asked. 'Or do you want to do some more hugging?'

They laughed and moved apart.

Zoe beamed first at her sister then at her niece. 'A glass of champagne would be more appropriate, don't you think? This is something to celebrate big time. And I'm sure a half-glass wouldn't hurt our Evie, who's almost grown up. It's such a wonderfully special occasion.'

She saw the girl mouth the words 'Our Evie' and could have wept all over again for the wobbliness of her niece's smile, which said a lot about her hunger for family. It must have been as strong as Cassie's hunger to find her daughter.

What a mess their family was in! Well, if Zoe had

any say, she and her sister were going to stay together and help build a real, loving new family. Their parents might be sadly lacking in parenting skills but she'd been lucky to have her father's spinster sister living nearby. Mary had showered her with love, so she hadn't grown up without experiencing genuine affection.

Poor Cassie had left home before Auntie Mary came to live nearby, so she'd missed that affection. Well, when things settled down, Zoe would bring Mary to meet the others. Her aunt would love that. Mary sure gave the lie to the idea of old women sitting around needing to be helped as they tottered towards death. She still helped others, volunteering at a couple of charities, and she had loads of friends.

But that was for another time.

Cassie went to the fridge and took out the bottle of champagne she'd bought on their big shopping trip. It had been chilling there, waiting for a happy occasion, and lo and behold, that had happened sooner than she'd expected.

She poured two full glasses and one half, then put it away again, passing the glasses to the others.

Zoe raised her glass. 'To us! Family for ever.'

They each clinked their glasses against hers and took a sip.

'This is a very nice drop.' Zoe put her glass down and looked from one to the other. 'My goodness, you two are so alike! Why didn't I get that lovely colour of hair instead of this faded mousy brown?'

'Mine's completely white now,' Cassie protested.

'Silver. And it looks as good on you as the red used to. You have a very elegant bone structure. Evie's got it too.'

'Took me a while to stop colouring my hair. The sort of people I worked for weren't openly sexist but they definitely preferred to hire female journalists who didn't look too old on the TV screen. I wonder if the current fashion for grey hair will change that?'

'My mother has the same colour of red as me.' Evie patted her short, wavy hair and stared across the room at her own reflection in the mirror. 'Though she has one or two silver threads now and boy, does she hate that.'

'I'm so looking forward to meeting her,' Zoe said. 'I hope she'll come round to the idea of extending her family to include us.'

'Evie told me that what her mother desperately wants is to have a husband and more children, even though she's over forty. Only, she shouldn't have them with a creep like him.'

'No more talk about him today, please,' Zoe said firmly. 'This is a time for celebration. Here's to aunts and grandmothers everywhere!' She took another sip and smiled at her sister. 'Can you sit down comfortably now? We all need to chill out.'

'I will and—' Cassie snapped her fingers as something occurred to her. 'I'd better go and cancel our evening out with Hal and his son before I relax, though.'

'Who are they?'

After this had been explained, Zoe shrugged. 'Why not ask them instead if it's OK for me to join you? I'm happy to pay for my own meal.'

'I'll go and see Hal straight away, just to make sure it's OK. He's relying on us to keep the peace between him and his son so I don't think he'll mind another person. Oliver turned up yesterday and seems very unhappy about something. I won't be long.' She got up and left the house by the back door.

Zoe took another sip and smiled across at her niece. 'Tell me about yourself.'

'What do you want to know?' A guarded look replaced the smile.

'Anything and everything. Let's not focus on why you ran away, though. Let's concentrate on good things tonight, like what you want to do with your life and what you want to know about our side of the family.' She lowered her voice dramatically and added, 'I know all their dark secrets and am willing to sell them to you for money.'

Evie was surprised into laughter.

Zoe grimaced. 'I'd better warn you, though. Our parents won't welcome you into the family. They don't have anything to do with your grandmother.'

'I've gathered that. It's cruel. She's such a lovely, kind person.'

'Yes. I agree. But Auntie Mary will want to know you and I'm sure you'll love your great-great-aunt.' She explained about their oldest relative.

* * *

Cassie found Hal sitting on his back patio in the sheltered spot he seemed to have made his favourite retreat. He was staring across the garden, his expression so bleak she paused, hesitating to interrupt him.

The minute he noticed her, the unhappiness vanished from his face. Jumping to his feet, he held out one hand, smiling. 'Cassie! Do come and join me. I was in need of cheering up and the mere sight of you lifts my spirits.'

'Just for a minute. I have a visitor.'

'I noticed the car arrive.' He let go of her hand to pull a chair out for her, giving her a quick hug before he allowed her to sit down.

'What brought on your fit of the dismals, Hal?'

'Oliver.'

'Ah.'

'Turns out he's been demoted and has to attend a course on interpersonal skills before he can take up his new lower-level job, as well as undergoing counselling.'

She let out a soft whistle. 'Did he say what he did to upset people?'

'Sounds as if he bad-mouthed women and gays, and shoved a female colleague out of his way.'

'Bad tactics but he must have been upset about his marriage breaking up, so can't they give him a little leeway?'

'It seems not. The new owners of the company are extremely politically correct.'

'It's not a good way for him to behave but I know I was very upset when my last relationship ended, and that was a reasonably amicable split – though Brett initiated it, not me.'

'The guy must be crazy to have dropped you.'

She smiled. 'You say the nicest things. But actually, he was right. At the time, I was too focused on work to make a good life partner. It took the terrorist incident to shake me out of that and point me back towards being a normal human being, not a work-focused automaton.'

'His loss, my gain – I hope.'

'You're good for my morale too, Hal.'

'Well, that's a great start for our relationship, don't you think?'

They sat smiling at one another for a few seconds then she told him about Zoe's arrival. 'So is it all right if my sister joins us for dinner?'

'Of course it is. The more the merrier. Moreover, if she's closer to Oliver's age, perhaps he'll find he has something in common with her and show us all his better side, which I admit I haven't seen much of so far this visit.'

He paused for a moment then asked, 'No word from your daughter?'

'No. But hopefully she's received Evie's message and isn't worrying about *her* daughter's safety. Only, from what Evie has told me, I think it's Fran we need to worry about now. Her new husband sounds to be a wrong 'un, as an old friend of mine used to call unsavoury folk.'

She got to her feet. 'I really have to go, Hal. Zoe's not been here long and we have a lot of catching up and bonding to do. You should have seen Evie's expression at having a great-aunt as well as a grandmother. That girl is hungry for love, someone to give it to as well as someone to receive it from.'

'We all need both of those in our lives.'

The world seemed to stand still for a precious moment and she could have sworn that she could feel his affection for her already, a tangible presence. He was such a nice man, would be so easy to love.

Was she reading too much into their friendship? She thought not.

At seven o'clock they met outside the front of the two houses and Zoe gasped in surprise. 'Oliver Kennedy.' Her exclamation was hidden by the voices of the others.

'Zoe.' He glanced quickly towards his father, then looked back at her apprehensively and lowered his voice. 'Can we please start our acquaintance again? I'm sorry I was so rude to you. I do remember that evening, the beginning of it anyway. My wife had just told me she was leaving me, which is why I drank way too much and acted up.'

She sighed but held her hand out to shake his. 'Here's to second time lucky, then. You certainly didn't make a good impression the first time and I shan't give you a third chance to get the social niceties right, if you mess up again.'

He took her hand. 'I can't remember much, though I do remember your face and how disgusted you looked. Was I very bad?'

'Yes, very. The things you said about me and all women were . . . horrible.'

He swallowed hard. 'Oh hell.'

His father turned towards them. 'Nice to meet you, Zoe. Did I hear that you and my son have met before?'

'Only once, and it was at a party, so we didn't interact much.'

He waited till his father had turned away to whisper, 'Thanks.'

Oliver watched in admiration as Zoe turned away any other questions about their previous meeting, then she stayed next to him to walk across to the hotel. He must have upset half the world in recent weeks. What a pity he'd picked on her. Her attractiveness didn't come from make-up and expensive clothes, but from her face and personality. She was lovely in a girl-next-door way, all warm and friendly – 'bubbly', people might call her.

What would they call him? The word 'grumpy' sprang into his mind. That's what his father had called him tonight as they were getting ready to come out, anyway.

'What do you do for a living?' he asked.

'I'm a commercial artist.'

'Do you have a speciality?'

She laughed. 'What is this? Practice for Starting up Conversations, Unit 101?'

He could feel himself flushing. He didn't usually have trouble talking to people but it had thrown him to find he'd made such a bad impression on such an attractive woman. Her sister must be much older than her, but she was attractive too, and the niece was going to be good-looking when she grew out of her gawkiness. Only, tonight she looked as if she were worried about something and why on earth was she wearing what was obviously a wig? Who was going to know her here? She was overreacting to the situation if you asked him.

He followed the others into the hotel, pleased that they'd got a round table to sit at. It was always easier to chat on those though he intended to let his father lead the conversation most of the time. He didn't want to stuff up.

The menu wasn't at all bad, he soon decided. 'What do you recommend, Dad?'

'The beef and ale pie. One of the best I've ever tasted. They don't go for fancy stuff here, thank goodness, just good, hearty fare.'

A woman came across to greet them. 'Hi, Cassie and Hal. How are you settling in?'

'We're starting to sort ourselves out. Everyone, this is Molly Santiago, one of the owners. Molly, meet my sister Zoe and my granddaughter – um, Lacey.' She shot a quick warning glance at the others.

Curiouser and curiouser, Oliver thought. An assumed name as well as a wig. Things must be bad. She had lovely red hair, he'd seen her sitting out on the back patio, but whenever she went away from their house, she put on that wig. Why buy one that didn't flatter you, though?

He looked sideways at Zoe.

'Don't ask her anything,' she ordered in a low voice. 'I'll answer your questions another time, those that I can, anyway.'

'OK. I know a rough outline, was just thinking she was overreacting. Um, I've seen your sister on television, but she had red hair then.'

'She got fed up of dyeing it and after she got caught up in that terrorist incident, she didn't want to be recognised. She needs peace and quiet to recover.'

'Oh yes. I remember seeing it on the news. Rotten luck, eh, but at least she survived.'

'Yeah. I'm pretty glad about that, I can tell you.'

She raised her voice and joined in the general conversation and he followed suit, though he didn't contribute as much to it as she did. She was a lively one. He enjoyed just watching her.

What had he got into here, though?

He'd have to ask his father to explain the details more fully when they got back. He didn't want to put his foot in it. And maybe whatever it was would add interest to a rather boring stay. He wasn't going to start the new job until he had to.

But he couldn't avoid the damned counselling session, more's the pity, had to go to the first one tomorrow in Swindon.

They sat chatting till half past nine, then Zoe yawned. 'Sorry. Been a long day. I think I'll stroll back home.'

'We all will,' Cassie said. 'It's not good to be walking about after dark with half-built houses and piles of junk to provide hiding places for troublemakers.'

Zoe looked at her sister in surprise. 'This village

doesn't seem the sort of place where you'd be in danger of getting mugged after dark.'

'No.' She took a deep breath and her voice grew sharper. 'Neither did the block of flats where I was interviewing that poor woman seem dangerous, and that incident happened in broad daylight, killing some people.'

Which was when Zoe realised that her sister had been left even more upset than she'd realised by the incident. Minor PTSD at least, but Cassie was trying to hide it. She leant across to give her a hug. 'We'll all stroll down together, then.'

'I might stay up here and have another beer,' Oliver said. To his surprise he caught Zoe giving him a scornful look and to his even greater surprise realised he didn't want to be on the receiving end of that scorn.

He shrugged. 'On the other hand, it's no fun drinking alone, so I'll head home with you, Dad, and borrow one of your books.'

His father had also been scowling at him, but now he nodded as if in approval. And when Oliver followed his father's next glance, he saw that it was focused on Cassie. He suddenly realised there might be something serious going on between the two of them. Hey, who'd have thought?

Chapter Twenty-Two

As they strolled across to the houses, Oliver tripped because he was again staring at Zoe instead of watching where he was going.

He was brought to a sudden halt as he grazed his hand on a concrete bollard at one edge of the storage area for the building works. Wincing, he steadied himself on the stupid object and that was when he caught sight of a guy sitting in a car staring at their group. There was little doubt about what he was doing because there was nothing else to see in this direction except the group of people on the lighted footpath.

Since Oliver had very good distance vision, he could even see that the guy had a very sour expression on his face. Was he Evie's stalker? No, surely not!

Then the man must have suddenly noticed Oliver looking in his direction, because he slid down in his seat as if trying to hide. That made Oliver even more interested in him. He tried to hide that, however, by setting off walking again, using his eyes to glance sideways but trying not to turn his head.

He definitely hadn't imagined it. The guy was still watching them. Oliver walked slowly after the others, letting them get further ahead, and saw that the man was still staring at the women leading the group. He was positioned lower in the car to do it. Must be uncomfortable.

Should he say something to his father about the watcher or not? Oliver wondered. He was watching. Why else would anyone be sitting in a poorly lit car park without trying to start up his engine?

He stopped again, pretending to refasten his shoe, while staring at the stranger. He was pleased to see that the car's number plate showed up clearly from this angle, so memorised it on principle.

Nothing else he could do, so he speeded up to join the others who had almost reached the houses now. He said a general goodbye and went into the house. He'd definitely ask his father what he thought and whether they should mention this to the women.

This looked rather serious, because if he were watching them the fellow would have had to come down from London. You didn't drive for two hours on a whim. And stalking could be a prelude to violence, everyone knew that.

Oliver didn't usually forget details about people, which was why he was such a good salesman, but while he was thinking about it, he scribbled down the car's registration number on a receipt which was the only piece of paper he had on him, and stuffed it back into his pocket. Numbers were too easy to get wrong.

Yawning, he waited for his father to finish saying goodbye and join him in the house.

Hal was beaming happily as he came in. 'Cassie and I are going to sit outside and have a quiet chat on the patio because neither of us is sleepy yet. You get off to bed, son. Don't wait up for me.'

Which meant his father wanted time alone with her. Strange to see the old man so taken by a woman. Oliver didn't raise the matter of what he'd just seen. More important to give his father a chance to spend time with his neighbour. Ah, he was probably just imagining that the guy in the car had been watching them, anyway.

But as he sat there alone, Oliver continued to worry about what he'd seen. Could this be the stepfather? Surely not? How would he have found out where Evie was?

He waited for his father to come in again, but fell asleep in the chair and was woken by someone shaking his shoulder.

'You'd be better sleeping in bed, Oliver.'

'Dad, wait.' But he must have mumbled it too softly and by the time he'd come out of his grogginess, his father had gone up to bed. He could hear him humming happily as he closed the bedroom door.

Never mind. He'd tell him about the watcher in the morning. It couldn't be all that urgent. No one was going to kidnap that girl tonight. They'd have trouble snatching her anyway, because she never strayed far from her grandmother and he'd never seen her even sitting out on the back patio on her own for more than a minute or two. Now that the aunt had turned up as well, Evie was well guarded.

He smiled. Very attractive woman, that aunt. He'd have to find out if she were seeing anyone.

Then he shook his head. No, better not get involved with her or anyone else for the moment. He didn't want to upset his father and lose this place of refuge. He desperately needed a few days to pull himself together and have a think about his future, still missed being married, to his surprise. Though he didn't miss the quarrels with Mandy.

He didn't really know what he wanted to do with his new life as a single chap, if truth be told. But he felt to be calming down a bit already. This evening had helped. Nice group of people.

It suddenly occurred to him that in the past he'd mostly gone out to drink with his so-called mates after work. And rather than chatting, they'd poured down drinks and watched sport on TV. Sometimes when he'd had a bad day he'd gone home drunk. Only, those guys weren't long-time mates, just chance acquaintances and friends of fellow workers.

He definitely hadn't paid enough attention to his wife; he admitted that to himself now and regretted it. He'd been upset big time when Mandy had told him she wanted to split up because she'd met someone else.

Even more upset when she'd refused to go for marital counselling because she was in love with the new guy.

It had taken a while before sheer honesty made him admit to himself that he hadn't been a particularly good husband in several ways. You could see things more clearly when you moved out of the picture – and also, when you stopped drinking so much.

He wasn't sure he'd want to try marriage again for a good long time. It was too complicated living with someone and finding out it was different in so many ways from what you'd expected.

And splitting up hurt like hell. He hadn't anticipated things going so very wrong. How could you ever tell for sure that things were going to turn out OK?

With another sigh at how complicated relationships were, he went upstairs, flung off his clothes and crawled into bed. It was a long time before he managed to fall asleep. He kept nearly dropping off then jerking awake and listening for a prowler.

The man sitting in the car park watched them go inside, taking note of which houses the various people went into. He hadn't tried to get a room at the hotel or even buy something to eat there because he wanted to stay anonymous. No one had seen him, unless that fellow who'd been staring had. No, the distance was too great to see anything clearly at the best of times, let alone after dark.

It'd mean a long, hungry drive home again now, but it was worth it. He'd be better prepared for his own needs next time he came here and would bring a snack and a bottle of water.

Pity he'd have to stay home to open the shop the next day, but he had no choice. Ryan was still too upset to deal with certain special customers.

Ah, he'd manage to stay awake. Mind over matter, that was it.

He let out a soft chuckle as he started the car. They'd be sure he hadn't seen that letter at Amelia's. He'd not opened it, too risky, but he'd noted where it came from when the neighbour pushed it through the door while he was at the house, because he'd recognised Evie's handwriting on the front. It was a very showy script, all dark ink and slashing strokes.

And he'd found her quite easily from the hotel stamp he'd seen on the envelope, hadn't he? She might be wearing a wig but he'd recognise her anywhere. And who was the old biddy she was with, someone even older than his stupid and ungrateful wife?

He intended to make Fran sorry she'd not done as he told her, very sorry.

She'd not get away from him. Neither of them would. She belonged to him now and so did her daughter. The stupid bitch would never out-think him. Nor would the police. He'd learnt through a very hard lesson to be extremely careful what he did.

Fran would come down here soon as well, bound to. Then he'd work out how to get her back.

There was no way he was going to act immediately,

though. This had to be planned with meticulous care. He would never let his anger rule him again.

Oliver wandered downstairs in the morning to find the house empty and his father's car gone from the front of the house.

Damn! He'd missed another opportunity to tell him about the guy in the car park. And today he had to go to Swindon to see the counsellor.

He found a note from his father, who had gone shopping, glanced at the clock and forgot about last night. He'd have to hurry to get to his appointment on time. Why was he sleeping so badly lately? He should be relaxing now he'd finished sorting out the many bits and pieces of business connected with ending his marriage.

He grabbed a couple of pieces of bread, slathered them with butter and searched in vain for a jar of jam.

Then he remembered that he'd finished one off yesterday. Oops! Must have been the last one. He hoped his father hadn't wanted any for breakfast.

He drove into Swindon, had trouble finding a parking place and arrived for his appointment five minutes late, breathless from running. Hell, he must be way out of condition. Another reason to cut down the drinking.

He was shown straight in and found himself facing a motherly woman, which was not what he'd expected. He'd rather have spoken to a guy. He was still panting. 'Sorry! I hadn't realised – how hard it'd be – to find a parking place. I don't know Swindon very well.'

She gestured to a chair. 'Well, as long as you don't make a habit of being late, I'll let it go this time.'

She waited till he was settled. 'Now, tell me why you think you were sent to chat to me.'

He tried to answer briefly, but she dragged more and more details out of him, piling one intrusive question on another. To his utter horror, it revealed feelings that had him brushing away a few tears, then a few more. He couldn't remember the last time he'd cried in front of anyone.

'Here.' She passed him a box of tissues. 'In case you're interested, I think it's hopeful that you're so upset.'

He gaped at her. 'It is?'

'Yeah. Shows you haven't put up your barriers against emotion too high.'

What did that verbal garbage mean?

By the time he left, he felt wrung out and exhausted, and he wasn't at all sure he could face coming back for his next appointment. The counsellor might look motherly but she was as sharp as a razor – or an axe!

He stopped on the way home at the big shopping centre he'd passed before and bought a few supplies, which included a couple of jars of cherry jam to replace the one he'd eaten. It must still be his father's favourite and was one of his, too. He'd eaten a lot of toast since he'd set up on his own in the flat. He'd better learn to cook or he'd not get fit again, and it was cheaper than buying meals out.

He slapped his midriff. Oops! He really needed to shape up a bit. So he nipped into the bookshop and found a cookery book for guys setting up on their own. Who'd have thought there would be exactly the sort of book he needed? There hadn't been any in the supermarket.

As he got back he saw the three women from next door setting off in their car and waved to them. They looked happy and very much together. He envied them that.

His father still wasn't home yet and the silence inside the house seemed to echo around him. Where had the old man gone?

He had a sudden horrible thought. Surely his father wasn't still facing cancer and going for treatment? He'd said the doctors had cleared it up.

What if they hadn't? He couldn't imagine life without his father to turn to.

He clutched his head in his hands for a moment, trying to calm down again. As if he hadn't got enough to worry about!

The three women had decided to do some sightseeing so went to visit Avebury, which wasn't too far away. The massive grey stones, erected so long ago for who knew what reason, spread out in a half-circle and were also dotted about in the village, singles mostly. And unlike those at Stonehenge, you could go up and touch them.

Cassie watched Evie approach a huge stone, lay her hands on it, palms down, and touch her forehead to the rough surface as if communing with it.

'I wonder how they found the strength and

endurance to build them without modern machinery and equipment,' the girl commented as she rejoined the others.

'Driven by faith of some sort, I suppose,' Zoe said. She'd been unusually quiet since they got here and seemed affected by the stones as well.

She fitted in so well with them, Cassie thought. How lucky she was to have a sister who'd taken the initiative of bringing the two of them closer. And such a lovely granddaughter as well.

Evie came to walk next to her, to Cassie's delight. Without thinking about it she gave the girl a quick hug and got a smile in return.

'This place puts our human worries into perspective, doesn't it, Gran?'

'It certainly does.' Not for the first time, Cassie thought that Evie had a wise old head on her shoulders. Had she been born with such common sense about the world, or had her upbringing brought out those qualities in her? Common sense wasn't as common as its name suggested. It sounded sometimes when Evie talked about her life as if she were the mother and Fran the daughter.

Ah well, they could all have done things better with the benefit of hindsight. Cassie had made a mess of her personal life, too, even as recently as in her relationship with Brett. The important things were firstly to learn from your mistakes and secondly not to hurt people if you could avoid it.

* * *

When they got home there was a letter waiting for them.

Cassie picked it up. 'It's the DNA results.' She couldn't wait, tore open the envelope and dragged out the contents as soon as she got inside the house.

When she looked up with tears in her eyes, she realised they were all of them still standing just inside the door and the other two were waiting to find out the results.

'Why are you crying? Is something wrong?' Evie faltered.

'Everything is wonderfully all right. These are happy tears, so very happy, darling! We are definitely closely related, you and I.'

With a shriek of joy, Evie grabbed her and danced her round the spacious, partly furnished room, chanting, 'Grandmother, grandmother, grandmother mine!' in a very loud voice.

Then she let go and grabbed Zoe, doing the same to her, except she changed the chant to, 'Auntie Zoe, Auntie Zoe, *my own* Auntie Zoe!'

After that, they pulled themselves together and made lunch. But none of them stopped smiling.

As they ate, Cassie explained to Zoe the details they'd discussed with the lawyer, and why it might be very important indeed to be able to prove that they were related.

Chapter Twenty-Three

That same morning, Fran and Polly went out to her car which was parked just in front of the building. They were chatting happily, ready to load it for the journey, when they saw it.

'Oh no!' They stopped in dismay. All four tyres had been slashed and were not only flat but clearly beyond repair.

'How did anyone get close enough to do that without being seen on the CCTV?' Polly asked.

'Must have crawled round, I suppose, hiding behind the other cars.'

Fran clutched her companion as this sank in. 'This means he's found me.'

'Looks like it. Let's call the police.'

'What can they do? I need to call for help getting the tyres changed and then move right away from here.' She clapped one hand to her mouth. 'Only, I have to find Evie first. What am I going to *do*?'

'We really do need to call the police first. He may have left some traces. And you'd be a fool to leave the refuge. He might have got into the car park, but he won't break into the building without getting caught, believe me. Our inside security system is second to none and there are always other people around to help you.'

'I doubt Keith will have left anything to trace him by. He's clever as well as cunning.'

However, Polly insisted on phoning the police so Fran humoured her new friend, who had been so incredibly supportive already, and waited till after their visit to call for help with the tyres.

The police turned up an hour later, checking everything out carefully. There were no fingerprints anywhere on the car around the tyres, but there was a strand of blue fluff, which looked as if it came from a knitted garment, caught on the wheel arch. There was also a half-footprint at the edge of the gravelled area that might have belonged to whoever did this. Someone must have been kneeling there and made the mark when moving away.

When the woman officer shone a blue light slowly over the car, she also found a partial set of fingerprints on the edge of the boot. Beneath them and to one side the paintwork had been wiped clean recently and again there was another tiny piece of blue fluff caught in a crevice. It was amazing that this partial set had been left. The person must have missed it when wiping the area clean.

'Do you have any blue gloves?' the officer asked Fran.

She shook her head. 'Mine are black, but Keith has some that he keeps in his car and yes, they are blue.'

'He must have been fiddling with something delicate and taken them off, then thought he'd wiped the area clean afterwards. Strange, that, because slashing the tyres doesn't require any particular dexterity. Why would he have to take his gloves off? Hmm. We'll need to check this out properly, so I'm afraid you won't get your car back for a couple of days. There's a new push on stalkers since that woman got murdered by one last month.'

Fran mouthed the word 'murdered', not even wanting to say it aloud! 'Oh no!'

'We're rather wary of stalkers who go to such lengths to upset one particular person, because research has shown them to be possibly on their way to committing much more serious acts. I reckon you're in more danger from this guy than we at first supposed, Ms Milner. If he's nearly fifty, as you say, it's amazing that he's stayed so completely off our radar for this long, though.'

They took Fran's and Polly's fingerprints and waited for a tow truck to take the car to an investigation centre for vehicles involved in crimes to be more thoroughly examined.

Left alone, the two women looked at one another and let out simultaneous sighs.

'That's mucked up our trip.' Polly gave her a sympathetic pat on the back and turned to go inside.

Fran didn't move. 'No, it hasn't. It's only delayed our

starting time, that's all. I'm going to see if I can hire a car and we'll drive down as soon as we can get hold of one.'

'But the police want you to stay at the refuge, where you'll be safe.'

'How can I be safe here unless I never poke my nose outside? And that won't help me to find Evie, will it?' After a moment or two's thought she added slowly, 'Keith found out where my car was. How the hell did he do that?'

They looked at one another and Polly asked, 'Is he good with technology?'

'Yes. Very good. He always mocked my mistakes and that made me nervous of doing anything.'

'Didn't want you learning to help yourself.'

'And I let him do it to me.'

'He might have put an electronic tracker in your car. And isn't there a tracking app you can put on people's mobile phones?'

'I'd never have let him put one on mine.'

'He might have done it without you knowing. We'll have to check it. One of the women is good with technology. We'll ask her.'

Dead silence then Fran followed her reluctantly inside. 'I must be the world's biggest fool to have thought myself in love with him.'

'No, you're not. You've been conned by an expert. I hope the police can trace those fingerprints or find a tracking device in the car. It'll all build up against him. I'm going to phone them and suggest they look for one.'

'They're not stupid. They'll have thought of that.'

Polly got a stubborn expression on her face. 'I'm not relying on anything, better to be sure.' She took out her phone and made a call to the woman they'd been given as their first contact.

When she ended the call, she smiled at Fran. 'You were right. They are wondering about that, too. She said we should definitely wait here for further news.'

'Keith can't possibly know where Evie is. That letter with the hotel's address on it wasn't delivered till after we got into the house. I very much doubt that even he can get into the post office depot where the letters are sorted.'

She stiffened her spine. 'I'm determined to find my daughter and make sure she's all right, Polly, or I'll go crazy worrying. I'm going to hire a car and we'll know for certain there won't be a tracker in that. You can come with me to Wiltshire or not. Up to you.'

'I'd better come and keep an eye on you. But I'm telling the police what we're doing, and Tracy.'

Polly could tell the whole world, Fran thought, but she wouldn't stop her going to find her daughter.

But first they went to find Leanne, who did find the tracking app on her mobile phone and was able to delete it.

'Thanks. I owe you for that,' Fran said as she took it back.

'I'm happy to stop these rats treating women like possessions.'

To Fran's disappointment, it took much longer to hire a car than she'd expected because the hire companies wouldn't accept the women's refuge as a suitable place of residence, it being temporary and from the tone of the person's voice on the phone, not approved.

In the end she took a taxi and went in person to a third car hire place, a smaller company. She didn't mention the women's refuge and gave her former address at Keith's house, for which she had IDs with her photo on them.

Even then, this company couldn't find her a car until the next day, but she still had to pay the hire fees into their bank straight away and wait to have the payment confirmed before they would finalise the transaction.

Then she had to fill the long, slow hours of the afternoon and evening. It seemed to go on for ever, and though she joined a group watching television, she couldn't have said what programmes had been on.

That afternoon Hal was cornered by Oliver. 'I have something to tell you, Dad, something important.'

He listened in increasing dismay as his son told him what he'd seen and what he suspected had been happening.

After Oliver had finished, he said, 'I hope you're wrong. If you're not, that chap is more seriously crazy than we thought.'

'I could be wrong, Dad, but I don't think so. I have very good distance eyesight, as you know, which is why I have to wear glasses for reading and close work. I probably saw more than he realised, more than most other watchers would have done. Do you think we should tell the ladies or not? They all went out earlier but they're back now.'

'I think we should definitely tell them. Come on, then. No time like the present.' He led the way out.

Cassie opened the door to them, looking happy and relaxed.

Hal hated to spoil her mood. 'I'm sorry to disturb you and I know it's nearly teatime, but there's something we need to tell you. It's to do with Evie's problems.'

Her smile faded to be replaced by apprehension. 'Come in.'

When they were all seated, Oliver explained what he'd seen and the three women listened to him, looking more and more horrified.

'What was the car's registration number?' Evie asked when he'd finished.

He fumbled in his pocket and it took a minute or two to find the crumpled receipt and read it out.

'That's Keith's car.' She turned to her grandmother. 'He's found me. I have to get away as quickly as I can.'

'Actually, I think you'll be safer if you stay here,' Hal said. 'You'll have four people to protect you.' He glanced at his son for confirmation that they'd both be up for this and was pleased when Oliver nodded without hesitation.

'What do we do, then?' Cassie asked. 'Just sit and wait like bait in a trap?' She couldn't repress a shiver at the thought of facing more violence and still woke in the middle of the night sometimes feeling panicky after a dream of the bomb incident.

'I'm not sure. Maybe we could set a trap of our own.'

'How would we do that?'

Hal couldn't come up with anything quickly. 'I don't know. It's, um, not something I've ever had to do before. We could have a think then brainstorm it, see what we come up with.'

'He's going to make for this house,' Cassie said. 'He must have seen us come in last night.'

'Maybe . . .' Hal hesitated, then completed his sentence, '. . . you should come and stay with us?'

'He'll have seen you two walk across with us and go into the house next door,' Evie said. 'It'd be the next place he looked for me, I should think. It's what I'd do, anyway.'

'How about we ask Molly to let Evie stay at the hotel? They must have a room there that'd be safer than here?' Cassie suggested. 'And lots more people to call on for help, including a security guard.'

'Molly's the owner of the hotel, right? Do you trust her that much?'

'Yes. She and her husband Euan are both great to deal with. Everyone speaks well of them and they can't do enough for their guests. Talk about service. I'm quite sure they'll help if we decide that's the way to go.'

But Evie was frowning. 'I think I'd prefer to stay here, at least tonight. I don't want to be left in a hotel on my own.'

'I'd come and stay with you,' Zoe said at once.

'There would only be two of us there, but there are three of us with two neighbours within call here.'

'Anyway, there's another problem with the hotel. If he's still watching, he'll see her leaving the house and where she goes,' Cassie said thoughtfully.

'I can stroll up and check out the parking area for a car with that registration,' Oliver offered. 'He might just have moved it.'

'Even if he's not there any longer, he could have parked at the other side of the lake and from there he can easily come back to the leisure village on foot.' Evie shivered at the thought of Keith creeping around.

'I have some night binoculars I used to use for bird watching. I know where they are and can use them to keep a check on the public car park across the lake,' Hal offered. 'There aren't usually many cars left there by the end of the afternoon and it's rare to see any at all after dark.'

'Do that now, please,' Cassie said.

'I will.'

She turned to her granddaughter. 'In the meantime the only thing I'm certain of is that you shouldn't go anywhere on your own till this is over.'

'Definitely don't wander off,' Oliver said firmly.

Hal nodded in approval, pleased that his son was joining in so wholeheartedly and trying to offer help and advice. He was even sounding more like a younger Oliver had sounded, caring and full of energy. He stood up. 'I'll go and get my binoculars and have a look.'

Welcome back, son, he thought as he walked across to his own house.

Oliver had been watching Evie, and it upset him to see how frightened she was now looking. 'We won't let him hurt you.'

'It's not just him hurting me physically. I don't know where my mother is. She may be in hiding somewhere for all we know. Or he may have fooled her into doing things his way. And he may hurt her if I upset him further. Even if we call the police, what if he persuades them that as my stepfather, he's now a suitable person to act as legal guardian for me and they agree?'

'I don't think the police would do that if we all protested strongly,' Cassie said.

'Who knows? He's cunning. I've watched him manipulate my mother. One of the neighbours saw them at the register office and posted on Facebook that they'd got married. How he persuaded her to marry him so suddenly, I can't imagine. She was trying to take things slowly last time she and I talked.'

'If that happens, I'll spirit you away and take you to a friend's house in another town,' Oliver offered.

'Thanks.' She shrugged a sort of acceptance, but looked unconvinced at its feasibility.

'If I could get her into my car unseen, I could take her up to Manchester, but then I'd have to leave her alone in the daytime while I went to work.' Zoe sighed.

'Every alternative we look at means getting her away from here without him seeing it happen, and finding somewhere to keep her safe. At the moment we don't know whether he's still around or if not, when he'll return.'

A glum silence followed.

'I shall never read a mystery novel again without feeling cynical about what it takes to outwit villains,'

Zoe said bitterly. She stood up and added, 'How about I make us some sandwiches? I'm hungry, even if you guys aren't.'

She and Oliver were the only ones who ate with any enthusiasm because the other three said they weren't hungry and only picked at the sandwiches. Evie took a mere couple of bites and gave up the pretence, leaving the rest of hers on her plate.

'I'll go out and look across at the car park again soon,' Hal said.

'Perhaps we should contact the police?' Cassie suggested.

'I'd rather not unless we absolutely have to. The lawyer said we were on shaky ground about custody,' Evie reminded her.

'We can't afford to drink alcohol, because we have to stay alert, or I'd offer you a glass of wine, but I've got some lemonade if anyone's interested,' Cassie offered.

'Thanks, Gran, but I don't feel at all like eating and I don't fancy anything fizzy, either. I can get myself a glass of water when I'm thirsty.'

The others simply shook their heads to her offer as well.

All they could think of to protect Evie in the short term was to make sure the girl was never left alone. Evie nodded agreement to that. Surely it would be enough to keep her safe?

'We're too tired to think clearly, let alone come up with something innovative that he won't suspect,' Cassie said in the end. 'Let's go to bed and Evie, I think you should bring your bed into my room. I don't want you to be on your own at all.'

Evie nodded. She didn't want to be on her own, either.

When they'd moved the mattress and got ready for the night, she could tell that her grandmother was listening to her, so breathed softly and slowly hoping the rhythm of that breathing would lull Cassie to sleep.

Evie heard the moment when her gran fell asleep and smiled.

She couldn't manage to get to sleep, tossing and turning for a long time. She didn't make the mistake of getting up and wandering round the house, though. She was *not* giving *him* even half a chance of catching her on her own.

Eventually she fell asleep, not waking until dawn started to brighten the world. Things usually looked better by daylight, she'd found.

When she looked across the room, she saw her grandmother still sleeping although the tangled bedcovers said she hadn't spent a peaceful night. But the sight of her made Evie relax and fall asleep again.

Next time she woke, Zoe was lying on the other bed. 'Cassie's gone to have a shower. I'll stand guard outside the en suite if you want to use it. Might be a good time for you to have a shower as well.'

'Thanks. And thanks for caring about me.'

Zoe blew her a kiss and she blew one back.

In the en suite she brushed tears away from her eyes. She felt so loved when she was with them but she missed her mother and was worried sick about her.

How long was this going to go on for?

What was needed now to make life better than ever before was for her mother to leave that horrible creature and join them. But would she? He seemed to have pulled the wool right over her eyes and hidden his true nature.

He'd tried to charm Evie too when she was first introduced to him but she hadn't trusted him. She didn't know why, but she'd found that it often paid to listen to your instincts about the people you met.

And as his subsequent behaviour showed, Keith had proved to be a sleaze when her mother wasn't around. His slightest touch made Evie shudder with loathing.

If her mother refused to leave him, what was going to happen to her? Would she be able to get away from him permanently? If she couldn't, she'd never feel safe again.

She let the shower water pour down on her, hoping it would wash away the worries about what he might do. Only she felt just as worried afterwards.

Chapter Twenty-Four

That evening, Keith drove home from a tedious day at the shop, detouring via the women's refuge because it made him feel good to see the shabby place where his wife was reduced to living. She liked her comforts, Fran did, so that place would teach her a preliminary lesson on where her best interests lay. And he'd reinforce that lesson in various ways till she learnt to obey him. He'd done it before with other women, knew exactly how to set about it.

Her car wasn't back yet. He frowned and checked the tracking device he'd placed in it. The vehicle wasn't nearby, so he followed the electronic trace to the location where the device indicated it had been taken, stopping just down the road.

All he could see from the outside was a big shed with high walls round a yard at one side topped by barbed wire. There were no signs to indicate who the place belonged to. Was her car in there having new tyres fitted? It didn't look like a tyre dealer's. He didn't like not knowing what lay behind all that secrecy.

But she was too stupid to have discovered his device, he was sure of that, any more than she'd discovered the tracing app on her phone for weeks. The bitches in the refuge must have spotted that though, because it had suddenly stopped working. He had to get her away from there.

Ah, he was seeing problems where there weren't any.

Well, she'd have the car taken back to the refuge once new tyres had been fitted, and even if it were parked in the secure area round the back, he'd find a way to get at it again. He'd enjoy figuring out how to do that.

But first he wanted to make another trip down to Wiltshire to see what that girl was doing. Maybe he could snatch her and use her to get the mother back. That'd make it easier to control Fran.

Unfortunately he had to get Ryan back at work minding their shop before he could go away again, because he was expecting a few important deliveries.

His next visit was to his so-called best friend. He grinned. Most helpful friend, more like. Another simpleton. They came in useful.

Ryan opened the door and for the first time ever didn't look happy to see him. 'Come in.'

Keith followed him back inside and accepted a cup of coffee, watching Ryan mix it with meticulous care and then sipping it appreciatively. 'Delicious. You make the best coffee I've ever had.'

After a little more judicious flattery, his friend had relaxed a little, and he risked saying, 'You need to get back to work, mate, because I have to go to Wiltshire again. It really is time to get my wife back.'

Ryan stiffened. 'Get real. You're pushing your luck if you pursue her now she's brought the police into it. You'd be wise to let all that drop.'

'I'm married to the bitch so she *belongs* to me now. You've never been married so you don't understand how much effort I've put into getting Fran used to doing as I wish. Why should I have to train someone else?'

'Up to you, but don't ask me to help you in that sort of thing. I've had a formal warning from the police about keeping my nose clean, so I'm going to stick to photos and online porn sites from now on.'

'They'll catch you if you put them on your computer.'

'I've got somewhere else set up for that.'

'Well, chicken out if you're such a coward, Ryan, but I still need you back at work tomorrow.'

'Oh, very well.'

And with that Keith had to be satisfied.

Ryan was an idiot – but such a useful idiot, he was worth staying friends with. It was another case of managing people so that they did what you wanted.

* * *

During the night Polly started feeling feverish, with a runny nose and watery eyes. By morning she had developed a heavy cold and looked so ill, Tracy insisted she stay in bed so as not to pass it on to the other residents.

'I'm sorry to let you down,' Polly croaked when Fran went up to see her. 'Stay over there by the door and cover your mouth with a handkerchief. You don't want to catch this cold, believe me. It's a real stinker. We'll have to postpone our trip for two or three days till I'm feeling better. It'll probably be safer for you to wait and go then anyway.'

'You're probably right.' She tried to sound casual, but Polly looked at her suspiciously.

'You're taking that too calmly . . . Oh, Fran, you're surely not intending to go on your own?'

She hesitated but couldn't lie to Polly. 'Yes, I am. It's too urgent. I have to find Evie before *he* does.'

'Don't do it. You'll be putting yourself in danger.'

'Keith won't know about that Wiltshire hotel. Also, I won't be driving my own car and we've had that app taken off my phone, so he won't be able to track where I go this time.'

'It's still too risky. That man's dangerous, a real sicko.'

'I know that now. I'll be extremely careful, I promise you. I'll go to pick up the car by taxi, and I won't even try to use public transport.'

'Fran, *please* don't—'

'I'm going!'

She got ready quickly and left before Polly could think of any way to stop her. She rang for a taxi, waiting for it at the front door, with overnight necessities stuffed anyhow into her backpack.

She was outside the car hire place before it opened and was the first customer to go inside as soon as the doors swung back. Even so it seemed to take ages to go through the formalities for taking the hired car and then a young guy had to drive her out to where it was parked to hand it over to her.

She watched him leave and set off at last, groaning aloud in relief that she was on her way to find her daughter.

Even though she was anxious to get to Wiltshire as quickly as possible, she didn't make the mistake of speeding or doing anything that might infringe traffic regulations. No way did she want the police stopping her, didn't intend anything or anyone to prevent her from finding Evie.

And if that meant finding her birth mother too, she'd just have to put up with it. She'd be polite, of course she would, but she'd get Evie away as soon as possible. She'd hated the thought of that woman giving her away like a parcel ever since she found out she was adopted. Having a child of her own had only reinforced that feeling.

Surely someone at the hotel would know what had happened to Evie? She must have been there or they'd not have posted her letter. And red hair was so often a dead giveaway. Fran touched her own neat locks. She'd tried dyeing it various colours when she was a teenager, hating that it was so conspicuous, but had eventually come back to her own shade of red. Dyed hair didn't have all the lovely coloured glints in it that natural hair did. And it was easier when you grew up. Other adults didn't mock it as some mean children had done at school.

'Just let me find my daughter,' she murmured over and over as she drove westwards along the M4 motorway. 'Just let me find my Evie.'

Once she'd done that, she'd be able to work out the next steps. It felt as if everything was suspended until then, even her ability to think clearly.

Polly slipped out of bed and stood shivering by the window, watching Fran's taxi leave the refuge. Should she or shouldn't she report this? She didn't want to cause trouble for Fran, but she decided she'd have to report what her friend was doing because it was so stupid.

She'd seen it before in the refuge, women acting irrationally, fixating on something, anything that would make them feel as if they were doing something to get out of the trap – a few times with sadly brutal or even in one case fatal results.

Suddenly certain that this was the right thing to do, she dialled the number of their police contact with a steady hand and croaked out an explanation of what Fran had done.

'She's gone off on her own?' her contact exclaimed. 'That's utterly insane. Couldn't you have stopped her?'

'No. I'm in bed with a cold, or maybe flu. I'm dizzy if I stand up. And anyway, I have no right to try to control her movements.' She began to cough and it was a few moments before she could continue speaking again. 'The women aren't prisoners here, you know.'

'Yeah. I know. Sorry. I just have a bad feeling about this guy.'

'So do I. I begged her not to go but she's absolutely desperate to find her daughter.'

'What mother wouldn't be? Look, I'll pass the word to the Wiltshire police to keep an eye out for prowlers near that hotel and to answer any calls for help promptly.'

'Thanks.'

'Look after yourself.'

Polly crawled back into bed, shivering uncontrollably. She had no choice but to look after herself. She couldn't even stand up without the room spinning. She'd rather be looking after Fran but it seemed that wasn't going to be possible for several days.

She waited till someone was going past and called out to ask them to send Matron up to see her.

One look at her and Tracy ordered her to stay in bed and not even try to get up till she was truly better.

Evie felt restless that day. She helped Cassie clear up the kitchen then tried to settle down to read a book, but couldn't – which was rare for her. She kept worrying about what her mother was doing.

Even when she got out the laptop her grandmother

had given her, she couldn't think of any site she wanted to visit or even any game to play.

'I wish I could go out for a good long walk!' she said.

Cassie looked across at her. 'Feeling restless?'

'Yeah.'

'I have some business stuff I need to clear up, I'm afraid, so we can't go out for a drive. You can't keep the tax people waiting for too long.'

'I know. I'll be all right.'

Cassie grinned. 'Yeah, and cats will take up knitting. Look, how about we ask Oliver to drive you and Zoe somewhere in the country and take you for a good long walk. She's nearly as restless as you are.'

'Where is she? I didn't see her go back upstairs.'

'That's because she went outside at the back, and Oliver came across to chat to her. They're discussing antiques. Seems they're both into restoring antique furniture. Who'd have thought? If they're still out there, it'd be safe for you to join them.'

Evie went to peer out at the back. 'They're laughing together. I don't want to interrupt.'

'Go on with you. They're not a pair of lovers. His divorce isn't even final yet. Oh, leave it to me. I'll call them in and suggest you all go off somewhere. Why waste your time indoors while you're in this beautiful part of the world?'

When she called them, Zoe and Oliver came in, still arguing about the best way to clean dirty old wood carvings.

Cassie waited till they'd agreed to disagree to say, 'How about you three going out and doing some sightseeing? With three of you, you'll be safe enough and poor Evie is bouncing off the walls after being cooped up indoors for so long.'

'I'm a bit twitchy too,' Oliver confessed. 'I'm not used to being so inactive, but I didn't want to risk leaving Evie. Where should we go? Any ideas?'

She considered this. 'You could go back to Avebury – or no, I have it! How about Salisbury? The cathedral there is magnificent.'

He looked from Zoe to Evie. 'I'd be up for that. What do you two think?'

Evie frowned at her grandmother. 'That'll leave you on your own. You might not be safe, either.'

'Easily solved.' Oliver took a step towards the door. 'I'll go and ask Dad to come and join you, Cassie. He's not doing anything special today. He'll sit and read if you've got work to do.'

When he winked at her, she realised he'd guessed that she and Hal were getting more than friendly. 'Only if your father can spare the time.'

'Oh, I think he'll enjoy a bit of company.'

He was out of the back door before she could protest, so she turned to Zoe. 'Let me give you some money and you can be in charge of the finances for today.'

Her sister frowned. 'I don't need subsidising.'

Cassie jerked her head towards Evie and said firmly, 'My treat for you all! I insist.'

Luckily, Zoe took the hint.

Within half an hour, they'd gone and Cassie looked at her visitor. 'Are you sure you had nothing better to do this morning, Hal?'

'What's more important than keeping you safe and maybe getting to know you a little better?'

She was annoyed to feel herself flushing at that. 'I'll be about an hour working on my taxes, then we'll have a nice chat. I feel lazy today.'

'Me too. But being lazy here with you sounds nice.'

She could feel herself flushing again. It was a long time since a man had affected her in this way. She smiled as she sat down at her computer again. It was rather nice, made her feel young again.

It seemed to Fran to take for ever to reach Wiltshire. It was only just over two hours, but she hadn't driven so far on her own for a long time, or even done much driving, now she came to consider it, because Keith had always insisted on taking the wheel.

Why had she let him? She usually enjoyed driving but in the past few months she seemed to lose some of her confidence about handling a car in traffic.

The more she was away from him, the more clearly she could see their relationship and how it had eroded her self-esteem and positive attitude towards life.

Why had she married him? That annoyed her most of all. She must have been utterly crazy. It'd cost her a fortune now, and a load of hassle, to get a divorce. And what would he do to stop her? Something, she was sure. She shivered, shaking her head at her own stupidity.

She saw a signpost for Marlbury and drove straight through the town, following the satnav's instructions to the hotel. When she stopped outside it, she sat in the car for a few moments, glad to have arrived safely.

She studied her surroundings and decided the hotel was a pleasant-looking building, not a huge place but big enough and nicely proportioned. A housing development seemed a strange thing to site so close to a hotel. Or perhaps the owners hadn't had any choice? Who knew with builders and planners what was going to be proposed and approved of next.

She went inside the hotel and was tempted by the wonderful aroma of food in the snack bar area, so ordered coffee and a toasted sandwich before she did anything else. She was suddenly ravenous and realised she'd missed her midday meal completely.

Besides, she was nervous about taking the next step and felt she needed a few moments of peace to gather her thoughts.

However, even though she still felt confused about what exactly would be the best approach to solving her problem once she'd eaten, this couldn't be postponed, so she went across to the reception desk.

The woman stared at her. 'Hello. I thought for a moment you were Ms Bennington. You look so like her.'

'Cassandra Bennington?'

'No, her sister Zoe.'

Was Evie pretending to be the woman's sister? No, she couldn't be. There was too great an age difference between her and her grandmother for it to be at all credible. Where had an aunt come from, then? Was this person really a relative? She realised the woman was waiting for her to continue, so said hastily, 'Well, I'm looking for both of them, actually. Are they staying here?'

'Are they expecting you?'

'No. I wanted to surprise them.' To add to her confusion, the reception clerk was now looking at her rather suspiciously.

'Look, I'll fetch the owner. Ms Santiago knows them better than I do.'

Fran wondered if she'd gone too far and nearly left the hotel, but that would have been stupid. She had to find and face the woman who'd given birth to her, and it'd be best not to delay it any longer than she had to, for Evie's sake. The last thing she wanted was for her daughter to get too attached to the woman.

She took a few deep breaths to calm herself as she waited.

A lively looking woman who seemed to be only a little older than herself came out of a side door and joined them at the reception desk. 'I'm Molly Santiago, one of the owners. I gather you want to see Cassie. Shall we discuss this in my office, Ms . . . ?'

'Milner.'

When they were seated in her office Ms Santiago

studied her. 'You look very like the people you're seeking. How are you related to them?'

'I'm not quite sure. I've been, um, trying to trace my birth mother.' She hadn't intended to reveal this but it had just popped out.

'Hmm. How about I phone Cassie and let her know you're here? I'll do it from another room, if you don't mind.'

Fran nodded and watched the woman walk out into the lobby again.

Why was this woman acting as if she were suspicious of someone asking for these people? Had something happened here? Surely Keith couldn't have found them? No, of course he couldn't.

The minutes passed very slowly as she waited and worried.

What had she got herself into? What if they refused to see her?

Chapter Twenty-Five

Cassie picked up the phone. 'Hello? Oh, Molly. Hi, there. How can I help you?'

'You have a visitor asking for you at the hotel. She looks so like your sister and Evie, it's clear she's a relative, but she doesn't seem sure of anything except that she's looking for her birth mother.'

Dear heaven! This must be Evie's mother. How had she found them?

'Cassie? Are you still there? Do you want me to send her down?'

She took a deep breath. 'Yes. But thanks for checking, Molly. As I've explained, we have to be very careful what we do.'

'If my opinion is of any interest, your visitor looks extremely nervous and not in the least threatening.'

'Thank you.'

'I'll send her down to you, then.'

After she'd put down the phone Cassie quickly brought Hal up to date on what was about to happen.

'Do you want me to stay or leave?'

'I think this is one thing I need to face on my own.' Only, she wished she'd had more notice or felt more confident about the likely outcome of this meeting.

'I'll sit out on my back patio, then you have only to call out if you want me to join you, or if there's trouble.'

'Thanks, Hal.'

He cradled her cheek in his hand for a moment and said in his quiet way, 'You're not on your own now, Cassie, unless you want to be. Anything I can do, you have only to ask.'

She clasped his hand and pulled it to her lips, pressing a kiss on it. 'Thanks, Hal. That means a lot to me.'

When he'd gone out the back way she hurried to stare at her reflection in the hall mirror and grimaced at how untidy the hairpiece was before going to peer through the living-room window.

A car was turning out of the hotel parking area. It made its way across to the leisure village, moving slowly as if the driver were uncertain where exactly to turn.

She waited till it had drawn up outside her house, then braced herself and opened the front door without waiting for her visitor to knock.

The woman who got out of the car did indeed resemble Evie and Zoe: same colour of hair, similar features and slim build. But she didn't have their basically cheerful expressions. In fact, she was scowling and looked as if she hated being here, which didn't bode well.

Evie had said her mother didn't want to meet the woman who'd borne her and Cassie's hopes about the potential for their relationship shrivelled to practically zero as she watched her daughter stare coldly back at her. Well, they neither of them had any choice today.

'I'm Cassie.'

Fran stared at the older woman, feeling emotion well up inside her. This was her mother. But she didn't want it to be. Did she? All she could think of to say was, 'Your hair was red on the TV.'

Cassie looked surprised. 'Is that important now?'

Fran shrugged.

'I've stopped dyeing my hair now that I've retired from public life. Um, do come in.'

Reluctantly Fran followed her into the house. 'Is Evie here?'

'No, but she will be later. She's gone out sightseeing with her aunt and a neighbour of ours. You might as well wait for her here.'

That was another thing that puzzled Fran. 'The receptionist mentioned an aunt. Who would that be?'

'My younger sister.'

'Ah. I see. Well, I'm Fran – Fran Milner.'

'Yes, I realised that. Evie has told us a lot about

you. She'll be delighted to see you again. She's been so worried about you.'

Fran's emotions were still in turmoil and she couldn't think straight. 'Perhaps I should wait at the hotel till she gets back.'

'I think you'd be safer waiting here.'

Fran gaped at that. '*Safer?*'

'Yes. We think your husband is stalking her. A man was seen in the car park here in a car with his registration number.'

'How could he have found this place?'

'We don't know, and we can't be one hundred per cent certain it was him, though it's highly likely.'

'It's me he's stalking.'

'I think he's been stalking your daughter as well and his behaviour even before she ran away upset her greatly. Had you no idea?'

'I knew he had been a bit of a nuisance.' Guilt shot through her. She'd not paid the attention she should have to the situation.

'More than a bit, surely?'

'Yes. I can see that now. It took me a long time to admit to myself how uneasy he made her feel. I only started to realise how bad it was when she ran away at the thought of having to live in his house.'

'Yes. She told us why she'd left.'

'But I still don't understand how he could have found her. There was a letter from her posted from this hotel here and sent to my cousin's. It asked Amelia to pass a message on to me, but it only arrived after Keith had been there and it hadn't been opened, I'm sure of that.'

'How did you know he'd been to your cousin's?'

'He'd trashed Amelia's house, I suppose in revenge for me leaving him. Oh, there's no proof it was him, not that satisfies the police, anyway, but who else could it have been?'

'Evie will be upset about that happening to her cousin. The more I find out about this Keith, the more dreadful he sounds. Please – whatever you think of me, do come inside properly and let me close the door. It's better not to stand here in the doorway in full view of anyone who passes.'

She led the way into the living area and to her relief, her daughter closed the door and followed.

Cassie had a sudden thought. 'Will your husband recognise your car if he comes back? If so, you should perhaps leave it up at the hotel.'

'He won't recognise this one because it's a hired car.'

'Oh, good.'

'And I'd rather we referred to him as my ex, not my husband. It may have taken me a long time to realise what he was really like, but I'm not stupid enough to stay with him after he bashed me.'

Fran looked round. 'What about the back door? Is that locked?'

'No. My neighbour is keeping watch and needs to be able to reach us. He'll see if anyone tries to get into my house by the back way.'

Cassie gave her a searching gaze. Fran still looked as if she felt awkward. And Cassie felt she wasn't doing her best at handling her daughter. She was too anxious about the whole situation, too involved. Had she really been a vibrant TV presenter, followed by many? She didn't feel at all like that now, just an anxious older woman worried about her family.

Fran took another couple of steps into the living area, then seemed to give in mentally and accept the seat Cassie had indicated, sitting down on it with a sigh.

'You're sure Evie is all right?'

'Yes. There are three of them and Oliver is a strapping young fellow. Even I don't know where exactly they've gone sightseeing.'

'That's the most important thing to me, Evie being safe.'

'I agree. But it's also important to keep you safe from him.'

'And you. I think he'll lash out at anyone who gets in his way. He doesn't often get angry, but when he does, he's – terrifying.'

Silence fell again and Cassie asked, 'Would you like a cup of tea or coffee?'

'No, thank you. I grabbed a quick snack at the hotel before I came to see you because I'd missed lunch.'

'Then we'll stay here in the front living area, so that we can watch the approaches. There's only the one road from the hotel to the leisure village. We'll not only see the others when they get back, we'll also be able to see anyone else if you've been followed into the hotel grounds.'

Fran frowned across at her. 'I still don't see how Keith can have found out where Evie is.'

'You may have let something drop without realising it.'

'No. I left him a couple of days ago. He hit me a second time and I won't put up with being treated like that. Luckily the police had come to see me about giving a witness statement on an incident at the park and I screamed for help. They stopped Keith and took me to a women's refuge.'

'That still doesn't explain how he found his way here.'

Fran was still trying to work out how that had happened and went through it aloud. 'A letter from my daughter dropped through the letterbox at my cousin Amelia's house while I was there with the police, looking for Evie. It had the hotel address stamped on the back of the envelope. It wasn't the postman but a neighbour who pushed it through, so we thought it'd been delivered next door by mistake.'

She looked at Cassie, feeling swamped by anguish at how he was out-thinking them at every turn. 'Keith must have intercepted it, mustn't he, and seen the back of the envelope? He'd trashed Amelia's house before we got there but the police couldn't prove it was him though he's still in the picture as a suspect. I knew it was him, though. I was quite sure.'

She couldn't understand why she was volunteering all this information. It was the last thing she'd expected to do. She studied her birth mother, who was still looking drawn and anxious. 'Did Evie run away to you?'

'Yes.'

'But why did you bring her here? The address on the letter you sent me was in a London suburb.' She hadn't memorised it intentionally, but it seemed to have stuck in her mind.

'I was about to move house when she turned up. She caught me just in time so came with me. We didn't know whether you were still with Keith, you see, so she didn't come back to you straight away. My neighbour and I have been keeping a very careful eye on her, I promise you. And my sister has too, of course. Evie's a wonderful girl. You've done a brilliant job of raising her.'

'Have I? I wonder sometimes.'

'I don't. I'm sure you did your best and if there's one lesson I've learnt over the years, it's that no one can do more than their best. No one. She loves you dearly. I so envy you that.'

Fran sagged in relief. At least this woman didn't sound as if she'd been trying to come between her and her daughter. And her last words had been poignant. She didn't want to feel sorry for her birth mother, but that feeling was sneaking into her mind.

'We all love Evie,' Cassie went on, 'but she's fretting about whether you're all right, Fran. When she gets back, she'll be over the moon to see you here. And if you've left that fellow, well, maybe you can both settle down again somewhere else.'

'If he'll let me go.'

The silence was fraught with tension.

'I've done programmes about violence against women and men stalking their former partners. Not all men go to that length. Is your ex that bad?' Cassie asked.

'I think he is. I didn't realise for a long time because he was so nice to me – most of the time anyway. Except occasionally when I behaved stupidly, which he teased me about but in a way that emphasised it. Only, I wasn't behaving stupidly, I can see that now. Except by letting him brainwash me.'

'That sort of person can be very clever how they set about their campaigns to control people.'

'Tell me about it. I think he could have persuaded me that black was white – until recently. He certainly persuaded me to marry him when I'd not wanted to do that until we'd tried living together.' She flushed and added painfully, 'I've not got a good track record at choosing men.'

Cassie moved instinctively to comfort her, arm outstretched, but Fran held out her hand in a stop sign.

'Don't touch me! I can't bear you to touch me.' She watched her birth mother flinch but didn't move from her 'keep off me' stance. She'd already said too much, given too much ground.

What was there about this woman that made you feel you could confide in her? Whatever it was, it must be a very integral part of her and had probably helped make her such a well-known interviewer. Did she mean what she'd said? Was she really concerned for Fran as well as Evie? How did you tell what was true and what was false? She'd believed Keith's lies for months.

Cassie stood up. 'Do you mind if I get myself a cup of tea?'

Fran waved one hand permissively but didn't let herself speak. Only, she couldn't help noticing that Cassie surreptitiously wiped tears from her eyes once she'd turned away.

'I'd better let my neighbour know about you.'

She watched her open the back patio door and beckon to someone, then an older guy came across to join them.

'This is my, um, daughter, Fran. This is Hal, my neighbour and friend. As I told you, he and his son have been helping me watch over Evie.'

Fran liked the look of him. He had a kind expression and it was obvious that he cared for Cassie from the way he looked at her.

'I'm pleased to meet you,' he said in a low, pleasant voice. 'And I'm sure Oliver and Zoe will keep your daughter safe today. If you like, I could phone him and suggest they come home straight away? Though it won't make much difference because they were planning to be back in an hour or so's time.' He looked at her questioningly.

'I don't want to upset her. Just . . . leave it be, if you really think they'll soon be on their way back, that is.'

'If all goes according to plan, they will. So OK, we'll wait for them.'

'Would you like a cup of tea?' Cassie asked him.

'Thanks but I just had one.'

She saw him to the back door and hesitated.

'Everything all right? You look – upset.'

'It's difficult with my daughter, Hal. I think I'd be better talking to her on my own. It's – awkward, worse than I'd expected. Can you carry on watching the back of the house?'

'Of course.'

A vehicle drew up at the front just then and they both peered down the gap between their houses to see a big delivery van. A man got out and went towards Hal's front door. Hal called out to him.

'I'm here. Can I help you?'

'Got some paving to deliver. Where do you want it?'

'Round the side.'

'OK, mate.'

Hal shook his head. 'I'd completely forgotten about the paving coming today. Everything happens at once, doesn't it? Look, you go back inside. I'll stay on watch at the back and let them bring the paving round.'

When Cassie came back from speaking to her neighbour and sat down again, Fran said, 'He seems nice. Are you and he – you know, seeing one another?' She was surprised to see Cassie flush slightly. Was her birth mother always so nervous when she wasn't facing a camera? Then she suddenly remembered the terrorist incident and wondered how it had affected her and made her jumpy.

Oh hell, she didn't know what to think about

anything. She realised her birth mother was struggling to find suitable words.

'Hal and I are getting to know one another. It's early days. I haven't been with anyone for a while, so I'm treading carefully.'

When they were both seated again, Fran sought for something else to talk about. 'I was surprised to find a housing development so close to the hotel.'

'This is a leisure village, not a normal housing development, with strict rules to govern living here in peace and quiet. It'd be a lovely place to live normally.'

Silence fell again and Fran couldn't think of anything else to say. She didn't usually struggle to chat to people, but casual small talk was impossible, given how anxious they both were about Evie.

Chapter Twenty-Six

In the end Cassie broke the silence. 'Evie looks very like you.'

'Except she's slim and I'm overweight.'

Cassie gaped at her. 'Overweight? You're not too heavy by any standards I know.'

Tears filled her daughter's eyes and she clapped one hand to her mouth. 'Oh! That's another thing Keith has made me think. I keep realising how he's been sapping my confidence.' She got up and went to stare in a full-length mirror near the front door as if she'd never seen her own body before.

'Some men are horrible towards women. What does he want you to be, a walking skeleton?'

'A slave, unable to think for myself. And he nearly succeeded in brainwashing me.'

'Yes. That happens with some men who have bad attitudes towards women.'

'You sound as if you've experienced it.'

'Not in the same way as you have, but my father seemed to hate me after I got pregnant, even though it was because I was raped. He never lost a chance to put me down. I only stayed with them for a few years, just till I'd got a qualification. For the whole time they were – ridiculously strict.'

She took a gamble and added a piece of information. 'I was quite ill after I'd had you and they persuaded me to give you up for adoption, made me feel I could never cope with being a single mother. And in one sense they were right, I suppose. I was too young even to leave school, let alone find and hold down a job.' After a pause she added without thinking, 'Though I could have coped if they'd helped me.'

But her daughter's frown didn't change and she didn't say anything, so Cassie gave up trying to break down the barriers between them and let herself fall silent again.

Was it really going to be impossible for the two of them to get to know one another? She could weep at the mere thought of that.

And surely Fran wouldn't keep Evie away from her now?

The thought made Cassie sag against the back of her chair. She wanted to cover her face with her hands and sob her heart out. But what good would that do? She'd done it many times in the early days after she'd had her child and nothing had changed.

* * *

When the phone rang both women nearly jumped out of their skins.

'I'd better take it.' Cassie picked up the phone and heard a voice speaking quickly at the other end: 'We've broken down. Well, run out of petrol . . . then there was a power cut because of the storm and the next place couldn't access the petrol pumps. We thought we had enough to get back . . . Don't know where we are . . . called for help. Poor connection . . . get back to . . . soon and—'

The connection cut off abruptly and she was left staring at the device then looking across at her guest.

'That was my sister Zoe. They've run out of petrol and they're waiting for help. There were power cuts, then even that poor connection was cut off completely. How infuriating!'

'Oh dear. I'd better book a room at the hotel for tonight then.'

'You'll be safer here. I've got a spare bedroom.' She saw her guest's expression turn stubborn, then dubious.

'I can't impose.'

'You can't *not* stay, now. We don't have any idea where they are or when they'll come back, and we don't want you or Evie wandering round the hotel grounds after dark.'

There was a long silence, then, 'Very well. Thank you.'

'I'll get something out of the freezer for tea, but I'd better warn you that I'm not the world's best cook. Evie's been doing most of the cooking. She said you taught her.'

'We both enjoy finding new recipes – or we did till I met Keith. He has a set range of meals and doesn't like foreign foods.' Short silence, then, 'I can do the cooking, if you like. I'm pretty capable, I've had to be.'

'Thanks. Let's explore the freezer. I won't offer to feed Hal. I want him to stay in his own home and keep an eye on the rear approaches to these dwellings. Anyone can walk round Penny Lake to get here and you must have noticed the piles of building materials which would provide cover for a person trying to approach from this side without being seen. I prefer to keep the front curtains open and all the exterior lights on so that I can see anyone coming towards the house. Hal prefers to sit in the dark and stare out, says it gives him good thinking time and his eyes get used to it.'

Fran got up and went across to peer out of the rear sliding door and nodded. 'I can see what you mean.'

'I often sit outside at the back because it's quite sheltered, but it looks as if it'll rain again and hopefully that'll help deter intruders.'

A few minutes later it did indeed start to rain, at first a few large drops pattering against the windows, then a steady downpour.

These sounds punctuated the awkward silences and stray remarks that never seemed to lead to any real conversations, or to reveal much personal information about Fran.

In the end Cassie accepted defeat in breaking that icy

barrier and offered her daughter a choice of books to read or switching on the TV. Fran picked a book out, but though she held it open on the arm of her chair, she didn't seem to do much turning of pages.

Neither did Cassie and eventually she put her book down again.

They both glanced out of the window quite often.

The weather cleared up for a time then, as it grew dark, it started to rain again, more heavily than before.

'Looks like it's setting in for the night,' Fran commented at one stage.

When it grew late, they investigated the food choices, then Fran put a simple meal together and they sat down at the table.

Cassie tried to force herself to eat, but couldn't do it, so pushed her plate aside. 'I'm sorry. I'm a bit anxious about Evie. I can put the food in the fridge and heat it up again later.'

'I'll do the same if you don't mind. I'm – rather anxious too.'

It was as near as they'd come to complete agreement about anything.

When the car faltered to a halt Oliver called for help and the trio had to stay in it to shelter from the heavy rain. They managed to call Cassie and let her know they'd be delayed, but it was a very poor connection and then it cut out completely.

Oliver stared at his phone. 'Oh hell. Good thing we

phoned for help first. Everything's gone dead now. This must be a bit of a black spot.'

A full hour passed and still, the rescue service didn't turn up. And they still couldn't get any of their phones to work at all.

'Well, at least we managed to get through to my sister earlier,' Zoe said. 'So she won't be worrying about us.'

'I think Gran might be worrying now, though,' Evie said. 'She's more fragile than people realise since that terrorist incident. I do wish we could get through to her again. Could you just try it again?'

But there was still no signal.

'I think there must have been a big local breakdown for all our phones not to work,' Oliver said grimly. 'It's been thundering in the distance for a while now. Perhaps something got struck by lightning. Let me try the car radio again.'

But they could only get static.

Zoe sighed. 'We shouldn't have taken this country road, only it was so beautiful as the sun was going down. Didn't the rain come on quickly? And it's turned into a real storm.'

When headlights appeared coming towards them, they all sat up expectantly. And cheered loudly as it proved to be the rescue service.

The poor driver was soaked but he remained incredibly cheerful as he had a quick look under the bonnet. 'You need some petrol. I've just given my last can to someone else. I'll turn round and tow you to the nearest garage.

Good thing you called me before the power outage, eh?'

The garage was also without lights.

The owner said, 'I can give you a couple of litres but that's all I have to hand. I can't get at the pumps till the power comes on again.'

'Just do whatever you can,' Oliver said. 'We'll pray we can get home on that.'

Just after dusk a car slipped into the hotel entrance, hidden behind a large van and with its lights switched off. It turned in to the car park and moved slowly across it to the side farthest away from the hotel, stopping in the deeper shadows beneath a huge tree.

The man driving it didn't get out at first but sat watching the houses through some night goggles, smiling grimly at how clearly he could see everything. His determination to get his wife back had built up as the day passed. He'd set off far too early, so had been forced to wait for a couple of hours in a motorway service station. No use getting here before dusk.

But that had only made him angrier. Still, he'd learnt to control his rages, so it didn't really matter if he was simmering a little with anger. He always thought more clearly when he felt strongly about something.

He wasn't going away again without Fran and, if he was lucky, her daughter too. His stubbornness sometimes got him into trouble, but more often than not, it got him what he wanted. And at the moment he very much wanted to tame his wife and her daughter, whatever it took.

He noted that one of yesterday's cars was missing from the parking area in front of those two houses, but another car was parked there today instead. There was no one walking around in such heavy rain and few houses had lights showing so were presumably unoccupied at present.

He walked round the further edges of the car park, checking everything. At one stage he wiped away the rain from his eyes, but mostly ignored the moisture plastering his clothes to his body.

When he was sure he was the only person out, he crossed the car park but stopped again to check all round him, making utterly certain there was still no one nearby. Satisfied, he left it and moved closer to the houses, staying away from the only road into the group of dwellings.

This time he went past the house he was heading for at a distance, approaching it obliquely from the side furthest away from the lake. They'd expect an intruder to come via the lake or from the hotel, he was sure, not from the part that was still like a building site.

He found himself a good vantage point behind a pile of timber near a new building that was only built to waist height, and stayed there to check out his surroundings again and make sure he was still alone.

Oh yes, he knew how to be careful.

Inside the lighted windows of the house were two women and surely one of them was – he blinked. Yes, it was her: Fran. His wife.

The other was much older, grey-haired. Who was she? And where was Evie? There was another woman who'd been there last time he watched and she was missing too.

There was no sign of the two men from next door, either, and their house was dark. Good. If they weren't at home that was one potential problem solved.

Fran had said she had no close relatives. It had been one of the useful things about her. No one to interfere. But this old biddy seemed to be very at home here, so she must be involved in this somehow. He continued to watch carefully, but she and his wife seemed to be the only ones in the house.

One or the other of them kept coming to peer out of the front window. That probably meant the others were away and due back soon. Well, he could modify his plans and take only his wife home today, but he'd better do it straight away. He smiled. The courts would give her custody of her daughter if she asked for their help – and he'd see that she did.

He still had to cross an open piece of ground, but had a bit of luck when a large combi van pulled up at one of the half-built houses and two men began unloading window frames in the beam of their headlights and a nearby street light. The van gave him the chance to cross the road and hide behind some piles of bricks, which were much closer to the house where Fran was skulking.

From his new vantage point he could see into it much more clearly and he could also walk partway round the row of houses, to peer along the rear gardens. There were no lights, not even a table lamp, inside the house next door.

Really, things couldn't have worked out better.

He was glad now that Ryan had delayed him by a day. Fate seemed to be on his side in all sorts of ways, and about time too. He was due a bit of luck. Triumph swelled within him, waiting to be let loose as his careful planning came to fruition.

She was going to learn not to trifle with him!

Chapter Twenty-Seven

Keith waited for the van driver to leave then moved quickly forward, crouching down as he managed to reach the rear door of the house.

He waited a moment but clearly he hadn't been seen. Reaching out, he tried the sliding door and nearly laughed out loud. It wasn't locked. Pitiful security, ladies! Well, the older woman could be left tied up. He had no use for women who were past their best. She would no doubt regret her carelessness over the long, uncomfortable hours of the night.

He could see how it would all work out, like a brightly lit movie playing in his mind.

He still had his balaclava tugged down to cover his face from the security cameras and he tugged it off quickly because it was annoying him and he couldn't see a camera here. Taking a deep breath, he edged the rear sliding door back and it moved along silently. He had to work quickly now because the sound of rain and cooler air would warn them of an open door.

The two women swung round suddenly and he stood up and started to move steadily forward across the open-plan space. 'You're coming with me, Fran. You're *married* to me, and we're staying married.'

As he'd expected she froze and took a step backwards, cringing. His training was showing nicely and paying off.

He stepped forward more confidently but to his intense annoyance the other woman stepped between them, barring the way.

'Leave her alone. She's not coming with you. She's left you.'

He grabbed her and took hold of her shoulders, trying to shove her aside, but someone must have taught her a few tricks, because she ran one foot down the front of his shin, her shoe connecting painfully with the bony part.

He shouted in pain but his anger about that seemed to lend him extra strength. He tugged her slightly forward and hurled her to one side, in a move he'd learnt at a self-defence class. She stumbled helplessly across into the kitchen area and then fell. He heard the thump as she banged her head on something, after which she lay still.

Stupid cow! Deserved what she got, didn't she? Very useful to have her knocked out.

He turned back to his wife. 'Come here, Fran. *Now!*'

She backed away from him. 'No. I've left you. I'm getting a divorce. I'm *never* coming back to you.'

He moved forward step by step as she backed away. She'd not even moved towards the front door, but had let herself be trapped against the front window. He couldn't help laughing. What was she going to do against him? She couldn't even think straight when he threatened her.

Suddenly she screamed for help at the top of her voice and continued to yell. Annoying. But who was to hear in the group of deserted or half-built houses? Still, he'd better stop her.

But as he reached her, she half turned and brought something out from behind her back, thumping it down on his head, smashing it.

The room whirled about him for a few moments and her shrill screaming seemed to set his head spinning even worse.

He tried to struggle to his feet. Time to get away and take her with him.

The trouble was, he felt dizzy and had to grab the windowsill to stay more or less upright.

As Fran jumped away from Keith, who was swaying, she noticed the headlights shining into the house from the parking area. Had the others come back? Or had Keith brought someone to help him? For a moment or two she didn't know what to do.

Then the neighbour she'd already met rushed in through the back door and a few seconds later the front door burst open as well. They must have seen through the window that there had been trouble.

A younger man stood by the front door as if trying to work out what to do.

'Phone the police and ambulance, Oliver,' Hal yelled to him. 'And then help me stop that fellow getting away. He's hurt Cassie.'

Fran sagged in relief. The newcomer was on their side. Then she knelt down by Cassie.

Hal knelt beside her.

She was terrified by the cut on Cassie's forehead which was pouring blood. Her birth mother groaned and didn't seem fully conscious.

She was also terrified when Keith straightened up and looked round for a way to escape.

The younger man had his phone out and passed it to the person behind him. 'Call the police and an ambulance.'

Then he moved towards Keith, as did his father and there was a brief moment of confrontation as he tried to push his way past them. Then they both grabbed hold of him.

For a moment there was silence in the room except for the sounds of the men scuffling, then Fran gasped, 'Quick, we need to tie him up somehow or he'll get away.'

Evie had been standing in the doorway but now she moved forward. 'There's some duct tape in the bottom drawer. That's what they use in movies, isn't it?'

She found the grey roll of tape and though it was a struggle, they managed to fasten the intruder's hands behind him.

Keith cursed and struggled but he was outnumbered. When they got his arms taped together behind his back, the younger man managed to stick more tape round his ankles, not without difficulty.

Only then did Fran smile across at her daughter. Evie was safe. She'd needed to see that with her own eyes.

But she was worried about Cassie and went across, bending down and then grabbing some tissues to staunch the blood. 'She needs medical help. It'll probably need stitching. I hope she's not got concussion. How long will the ambulance be?'

The other woman, who must be the aunt, spoke. 'The police said they'd be here quickly. They'd been alerted to the fact that there might be trouble here by the police in London apparently. And an ambulance is on its way, shouldn't be long either.'

'This is my aunt Zoe. My mother, Fran.'

The two women nodded at one another.

'How did Gran get hurt?'

'She stepped in between Keith and me.' Fran knelt beside Cassie and held her hand. 'She was protecting me. I didn't expect that.'

'She's always cared about you. It was her parents who caused the trouble.'

'But why did Pop and Nanna tell me she didn't want me?'

'My mother and father must have told them that,' Zoe said sadly. 'Cassie said after she got pregnant they seemed to start hating her. No wonder she left home as soon as she could. I was too young to remember much but over the years they've said some dreadful things about her to me. Which even my older brother admitted weren't true.'

Cassie opened her eyes just then and stared dopily up at them both, giving them a particularly sweet smile and saying, 'You are so alike, my darlings,' before closing her eyes again.

Evie turned to her mother. 'Are you all right?'

'Keith probably bruised my arm but that's nothing. It was Cassie who got the worst of it. I did manage to smash a heavy ornament over his head, though, and that slowed him right down,' Fran added with great satisfaction. 'He came after me because I ran away from him. He was determined to take me back.'

Evie brightened. 'You hit him?'

'Yes. Took me long enough to figure out what he was doing to us both, didn't it? Can you ever forgive me?'

Evie gave her a lop-sided hug. 'Of course I can. Especially now you've come to your senses.'

She looked down at Cassie then sideways at her mother. 'You were wrong about her. She didn't give you away willingly. My aunt told me how she kept your first bootees and used to cry over them.'

'Giving away – all my secrets – Evie?' Cassie whispered.

She leant forward to kiss her grandmother's cheek. 'Only the ones that Mum needs to know about. She thought you gave her away willingly.'

'No. Never willingly.'

* * *

A couple of minutes later the police car turned up and the officers came inside.

One officer checked Cassie. 'You'll need to go to hospital to get that properly stitched or it'll leave a bad scar. The ambulance won't be long.'

'Well worth it,' she said, still smiling and holding Fran's and Evie's hands.

'Keith threw her across the room,' Fran said. 'That's how she hit her head.'

'Did he now?'

As she was explaining exactly what had happened, and how her ex had been stalking her, the male officer kept looking at Keith and frowning.

'They're telling lies,' Keith called out. 'It's all lies! I love that woman and they're keeping me from reconciling with her after a row. Everyone has rows and they have no right to do this to me.'

The officer snapped his fingers as if something had occurred to him and went right up to where Keith was lying on the floor propped against the wall. 'Now I know why you seem familiar. I never forget a voice. Ricky Bottrell, by all that's wonderful! I wondered what had happened to you.'

Keith stared up at him in horror. 'I don't know what you mean. My name's Burgess.'

'Easily checked. You have a small tattoo on your left shoulder blade if I remember correctly, a whirling comet.' He began to pull Keith's clothing open and though the man squirmed, he was still securely taped and couldn't prevent the officer from uncovering the mark.

He laughed out loud. 'Told you! You're nicked, Bottrell, on top of whatever you've done today and recently.'

'He not only attacked my grandmother,' Evie said, 'but he's been stalking my mother, who is his wife but left him recently.'

The officer grinned even more broadly and looked down at Keith. 'Another wife? Last I heard, your first wife was still living in Bury and hadn't divorced you because she doesn't believe in it. And you can't have divorced her because you vanished off the face of the earth and I've kept an eye on divorces and you've definitely not been amongst them. Seen Hazel lately, have you, Ricky?'

Fran took a quick step forward. '*He's got another wife?*'

The officer nodded. 'Hazel. She phones the local police station regularly to ask if he's turned up. I still have a friend up in the north who lets me know. He'll be delighted to pass the news on to her.'

'Well, he married me recently but when he thumped me, I left him.'

He hadn't stopped grinning since he recognised who Keith really was and now he clapped him on the shoulder. 'Oh dear, that means we'll have to add a charge of bigamy to the list of whatever other charges are brought against you.'

'I was going to divorce him.'

'No need to do that. Your marriage isn't valid. I'd get a lawyer to sort out any details as necessary, though.'

She ignored Keith's scowl and beamed at the officer. 'That's wonderful, absolutely wonderful.'

Evie came to throw her arms round her mother, then they both knelt and kissed Cassie's cheeks from either side.

'All forgiven?' Cassie whispered to her daughter.

'Nothing to forgive, just errors to be corrected. As far as I'm concerned, new page, new life.'

Happy tears were running down Cassie's cheeks and mingling with the reducing trickles of blood. 'That's the best news *I've* ever had in my whole life.'

There was the sound of a siren and more headlights raked across the window.

The first responders came hurrying in and knelt by Cassie, then one ran out again to bring in the wheeled stretcher and they soon had her installed on it.

'I'm coming with you,' Evie said at once.

'So am I.' Fran moved forward to stand beside them.

'You should follow us in a car, so that you can get back home afterwards. Don't worry. We'll look after her, but that's a bad cut and it definitely needs medical attention.'

So Fran got into the car and drove off after the ambulance.

She didn't think she'd ever felt so happy in her whole life. She wasn't married to Keith! And now she had a mother, an aunt and her daughter back – a real family.

She glanced sideways at Evie and her daughter gave her a smile.

'Life is going to be wonderful.'

'You won't stop Gran seeing me.'

'On the contrary, I'm going to move to live nearby and we'll see a lot of one another.'

Evie's voice was choked. 'That's – just – absolutely wonderful.'

'Yes. It is. And I'm never getting involved with a man again.'

Evie hid a smile. She didn't believe that, but surely with her gran's help they'd manage to stop Fran making any more big mistakes?

The hospital came into sight and they parked the car.

'It's like walking into a new life,' Fran said softly, taking her daughter's hand and moving to find where Cassie was.

Epilogue

They planned it carefully and made the necessary phone calls. Two days later Hal went to bring Cassie home from hospital while the others got everything ready that they could.

He made a shooing gesture when he brought Cassie back. 'Go inside. This is a family time for you.'

'Thanks, Hal. But you'll come round for a drink tonight, eh? And bring Oliver.'

'Good idea. I'd like that.'

Evie ran to greet her at the door and after a slight hesitation, Fran followed and even gave her mother a hug. Their welcome brought tears of joy to Cassie's eyes.

'Everything all right?' she asked.

'Brilliant!' Evie handed her a tissue. 'No crying. This is a happy time!'

'I'll do my best. I'll have a rest after lunch because I've

invited Hal round for a drink tonight.' As Evie opened her mouth, Cassie held up one hand. 'I'm not an invalid, so I insist on having a little celebration.'

'All right, Gran. If you're sure. We could even put out a few nibblies.'

'Good idea. Get a selection delivered from the hotel. We can make it a bit of a buffet meal. Go and tell them while I'm asleep. I don't want you slaving over the stove. I want us three to talk. I've photos to show you, all sorts of things to ask.'

'That'll be fun.' She watched them smile at one another and exchange glances. There would be a lot of smiling from now on if she had her way.

'How about they come at about six o'clock?' Evie suggested.

'Yes. Nice time to start a celebration.' Cassie stretched. 'I must say I wouldn't mind something tasty to eat then a little nap. Hospital food is awful and you can never sleep well there. They're always waking you up to take your pulse or check your dressing.'

'We'll go up to the hotel and order the food while you rest,' Fran said.

Luckily, the food was delivered while Cassie was changing into more flattering clothes.

'That's another hurdle got over,' Evie said. 'She'd have been asking why we ordered so much.'

Fran nodded. 'It's as if fate is on our side.'

'You all right?'

'Yes. I'm still getting used to my new status, that's all, and getting angry at myself for being such a fool.'

'Well, you'll know better with the next man.'

'There isn't going to be one.'

Evie hid her smile. Of course there would be, eventually. Especially after she'd gone off to university.

When the food delivery was complete, they quickly set the food out on the table and covered it with a tablecloth just as Cassie came down.

'You look great, Gran,' Evie said, leading her into the sitting area. 'Very elegant.'

'And that top suits you better than it ever did me.' She held out one hand to her daughter and Fran joined them. 'That dress suits you too.'

'You have a lot of clothes. It was fun choosing.'

She shrugged. 'They were working clothes as far as I was concerned. I mostly lived in kaftans that I'd picked up overseas when I was at home in the evenings.'

There was a knock on the back door and Evie went to let Hal and Oliver in.

Hal leant close to whisper, 'They're waiting at the hotel, coming down in five minutes. Does she suspect anything?'

'I don't think so.' She led the way in and poured them both a glass of wine, taking a lemonade for herself.

'How lovely to have neighbours who are also friends,' Cassie said.

There was a knock on the front door and she frowned. 'Who can that be?'

'You'll only find out if you let me answer it,' her granddaughter said.

Six people were waiting outside and as Evie showed them in Cassie gaped. 'Brett! What are you doing here?'

'Celebrating your new life and the fact that you're safe. I've been worried sick about you.' He gave her a hug.

His partner smiled at Cassie and did air kisses. 'We both have. Am I allowed in, too?'

'Of course you are. Life's too short to hold grudges and you kindly lent Brett to me after that incident.' She turned to Molly and Euan.

'We've been invited to celebrate with you as well,' Molly said. 'We like to make friends here as well as build houses, and we hated that you were attacked on our property.'

Cassie hugged them both. She felt like hugging the whole world tonight.

She didn't recognise the other two women, but Fran moved to join them. 'May I introduce Tracy and Polly from the women's refuge. I couldn't leave them out of this celebration, since they helped me so much at a very bad time.'

Polly flapped one hand. 'I'm just recovering from a cold, so I'm not doing kissy-kissy, but I hope you'll let me join you.'

'I'm delighted to meet you. Fran mentioned how helpful you two were.'

With a grin Hal and Oliver brought in the garden chairs they'd sneaked across and left outside ready for the extra guests, and Zoe whipped the tablecloth off the refreshments, shouting, 'Ta-da!'

Cassie pretended to be angry. 'You sneaky creatures!'

'Did you want to cook?' Evie asked with an expression of fake innocence.

She had to chuckle. 'Of course not. I never get the desire to cook.'

'Then you sit down at the head of the table and we'll all enjoy that delicious food.'

When they'd finished eating, Hal poured everyone a glass of champagne. 'As self-appointed toast master, I'd like you all to raise your glasses to our hostess. Cassie!'

They all echoed her name.

Fran surprised herself by calling out, 'And I'd like to add another toast. To my birth mother and Evie's grandmother, Cassie. I'm so very glad we found her.'

They all echoed that as well and as they did so happy tears welled in Cassie's eyes and she thrust her glass at Hal. Standing up, she put one arm round each woman. 'Can someone take a photo, please? Lots of photos. This is the best night of my life.'

'I'll do it,' Oliver said. 'First family photographs of many for you, I hope.'

She could only nod and smile blissfully at the camera. First of many indeed.

Thank goodness Evie had found her that day.

ANNA JACOBS is the author of over ninety novels and is addicted to storytelling. She grew up in Lancashire, emigrated to Australia in the 1970s and writes stories set in both countries. She loves to return to England regularly to visit her family and soak up the history. She has two grown-up daughters and a grandson, and lives with her husband in a spacious home near the Swan Valley, the earliest wine-growing area in Western Australia. Her house is crammed with thousands of books.

annajacobs.com

The
HIDING
PLACES

KATHERINE WEBB

An Orion paperback

First published in Great Britain in 2017
by Orion Books
This paperback edition published in 2017
by Orion Books,
an imprint of The Orion Publishing Group Ltd
Carmelite House, 50 Victoria Embankment,
London EC4Y 0DZ

An Hachette UK Company

1 3 5 7 9 10 8 6 4 2

A CIP catalogue record for this book
is available from the British Library.

ISBN (Mass Market Paperback) 978 1 4091 4858 6

Typeset at The Spartan Press Ltd,
Lymington, Hants

Printed and bound in Great Britain by Clays Ltd,
St Ives plc

www.orionbooks.co.uk

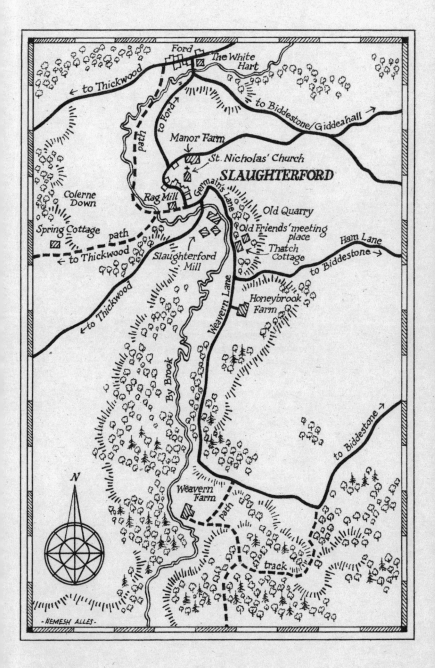

Ford

The White Hart

← to Thickwood

to Ford

to Biddestone/Giddeahall →

Manor Farm

path

St. Nicholas' Church

SLAUGHTERFORD

Coleme Down

Rag Mill

Germain's Lane

Old Quarry

Spring Cottage

path

Old Friends' meeting place

← to Thickwood

Ham Lane

Thatch Cottage

to Biddestone →

Slaughterford Mill

← to Thickwood

Weavern Lane

Honeybrook Farm

By Brook

to Biddestone →

N

Weavern Farm

path

track

- HEMESH ALLES -

Firstly

On the day of the killing the sky above Slaughterford dropped down – almost to the treetops – and it poured with rain. Lavish, drenching summer rain, the first in weeks. The villagers all claimed, on having woken to such weather, to have known that something was very much amiss. They were superstitious people, prone to seeing signs and portents everywhere, and to suspecting the worst of every one. Sid Hancock, out at Honeybrook Farm, swore he saw the By Brook run red. Heads were nodded, ruefully, though the murder hadn't happened near enough to the riverbank for blood to have reached the water. Woolly Tom, who kept a flock of sheep on a small-holding up on the ridge, said he'd known a death was coming ever since one of his ewes had birthed a two-headed lamb back in the spring. He'd been carrying a desiccated rabbit's foot everywhere with him since then, in case the shadow tried to fall on him. Death was common enough, in Slaughterford. But not this kind of death.

What troubled people most was the sheer *blamelessness* of the victim. Nobody could think of a single bad thing to say of them, or recall a single cruel or shameful thing they'd done. There was a *wrongness* about it that shook them. Grave illness could happen at any time, as could a fatal accident. Only the year before, six-year-old Ann Gibbs had climbed over the cock-up stones designed to prevent exactly that, and had fallen into the well at the top of the lane to Ford. She'd drowned because her brother had told her the fairy folk lived inside. Fits, flu and seizures took their annual tithe of loved ones, but if your time was up you could hardly argue with that. Tragedy and ill-luck abounded, but for one of their own to be cut down with such savagery, for no reason at all ... It simply wasn't natural. They were people of the land, and struggled with anything that wasn't natural. They channelled the shock of the murder into the rocks beneath their feet, just like lightning rods. And they all wondered whether one such act of violence could help but lead to another.

I
Three Girls

The morning before it all began, Pudding paused by the little window at the top of the stairs and saw her mother outside on the lawn. Louise Cartwright was near the back wall, looking out over the drenched tussocks of the paddock that sloped away down the valley, and fiddling with something in her hands that Pudding couldn't see. It was early, the sun not yet clear of the horizon; the sky had an immaculate, pale clarity, and it looked like being another hot day. Pudding felt the little thump of dread she was coming to know so well. She waited for a while, but when her mother didn't turn or move, she carried on down the stairs, more slowly now. A gentle snore came from the darkness of her parents' room, where her father was still asleep. In earlier days he'd been the first to rise every morning. In earlier days he'd have fed the stove and put the kettle on, and been shaved and buttoned into his waistcoat before Pudding and Donald stumbled down to the kitchen, rubbing the sleep from their eyes. Now Pudding usually had to go in and wake him, feeling guilty every time she did. His sleep was like a stupor.

The kitchen at Spring Cottage was more chaotic than it had used to be – the bowls on the shelves were no longer stacked in exact order of size; the hop garland looked dusty; crumbs in the cracks and splashes of grease made the smell of stale cooking hang about. Donald was waiting at the kitchen table. Not reading, or mending anything, or jotting a list. Just sitting, waiting. He'd stay like that all day if nobody roused him up and sent him on his way. Pudding squeezed his shoulder as she passed behind him, and saw him swim up from the unfathomable depths inside himself to smile at her. She loved to see that smile – it was one of the things about him that hadn't changed at all. She kept a tally in her head: things about Donald that were just the same; things about him that had changed forever. It was the *forever* part she struggled with. She kept expecting him to shake it off, get up from the table with his old abruptness, quick with energy, and say something like, *Don't you want some toast with your jam, Pudding?* They'd spent the first two years after he'd come home watching, waiting to see what would return to him. A few things did, in the first year: his love of music; his love of Aoife Moore; his fascination with machinery; his appetite – though he sometimes struggled to swallow, and ended up coughing. But during the past year, nothing else had come back. His dark hair was just the same – soft, shiny, unruly. So very lovely. And that ironical curve to his mouth, though irony was one of the things he'd lost.

'Morning, Donny,' said Pudding. 'I'll just see what Mum's up to, then we'll have some breakfast, shall we?' She patted his shoulder, and was already by the back door by the time he managed to reply.

'Good morning, Puddy.' He sounded so normal, so like her big brother, that Pudding had to take a deep breath, right down into her gut, to stay steady.

She pulled the door to behind her, then looked up for Louise with that stubborn optimism she couldn't suppress. She hoped her mother would have moved, hoped she'd only been picking parsley for the scrambled eggs, hoped she'd been on her way back from the privy and had stopped to watch hares boxing in the field. But her mother hadn't moved, so Pudding distracted herself by noticing other things instead. That her breeches were getting too small again already, the waistband dragging down at the back so that her braces dig into her shoulders; that one of her socks was already sagging, bunching infuriatingly in the toe of her shoe; that her shirt was pinching under her arms because her chest seemed to get bigger every day, however much she willed it not to. It felt like her clothes were at war with her – delivering a constant, unnecessary commentary on her unwelcome expansion, upwards and outwards. The air was glassy-cool, fresh and green. Louise's footsteps through the dew showed up dark green against the silver. Pudding stepped into them exactly, shortening her stride.

'Mum?' she said. She'd planned to say something jovial, to brush off the oddness of the scene, but it wouldn't come. Louise turned her head sharply, startled. For a moment, there was no recognition in her face. That blank look, tinged with trepidation, was becoming the thing Pudding feared most. She found she couldn't quite breathe. But then Louise smiled, and her smile was only slightly vague, slightly hollow.

'Pudding! There you are, love. I've been looking for you,' she said, and in her eyes was that struggle to catch up, to guess at the truth of her statement. There was nothing in her hands, Pudding saw. The constant fiddling had been with the bottom button of her yellow cardigan. She always started at the bottom, but she'd got no further with doing them up that morning.

'Have you, Mum?' said Pudding, forcing her clenched throat to swallow.

'Yes. Where have you been?'

'Nowhere, just up in my room. I can't have heard you calling. Come on.' Pudding rushed on, before this fiction had time to bewilder her mother. 'Let's go in and get the kettle on, shall we? Make a nice pot of tea?'

'Yes. That's what we need.' Louise sighed slightly as she turned to walk back beside her daughter. They obliterated their original footsteps; the dew flicked up and soaked through Pudding's socks around her ankles. Still, she felt an irresistible surge of cheeriness as a phalanx of swifts shot across the sky above them, screeching out their joy, and the Manor Farm dairy herd, on the other side of the valley, lowed as they were let out from milking.

'Did you see hares in the field, Mum?' she asked, recklessly.

'What? When?' said Louise, and Pudding rushed to retract the question.

'Oh, nothing. Never mind.' She took her mother's arm and squeezed it, and Louise patted her hand.

Dandelions were crowding the back step, and the ash pail needed emptying; the blackcurrants were going over, unpicked except by blackbirds, which then left purple droppings on the path and down the windows. But when they got back into the kitchen Pudding's father, Dr Cartwright, was there, stoking up the stove, and the kettle was hissing on the hot plate, and he'd combed his hair and dressed, even if he hadn't shaved yet and his eyes were still a little sleepy.

'Two roses, fresh with dew from the garden,' he greeted them.

'Morning, Dad. Did you have a good sleep?' Pudding put the butter dish on the table; rattled open a drawer for knives; fetched yesterday's loaf from the crock.

'Far too good! You should have woken me sooner.' The doctor rubbed his wife's upper arms, smiling down at her. He pushed some of her unbrushed hair back from her forehead, and kissed her there, and Pudding looked away, embarrassed, happy.

'Toast, Donny?' said Louise. She'd done up her cardigan, Pudding noticed – every button in the right hole.

'Yes please, Mum,' said Donald. And they moved around each other as breakfast was assembled, perhaps not quite as they always had, but in a version of old habit that felt blissfully familiar. Her family strayed in the night, Pudding thought. They scattered like thistle seeds, carried here and there by currents she couldn't feel, and didn't understand. But she understood that it was up to her to gather them together again in the morning. As she sliced the bread she sang a snatch of 'Morning Has Broken' in her worst possible singing voice, to make them smile.

❧ ❧

When Irene heard the rattle of Keith Glover's bicycle her heart gave a lurch, walloping into her ribs, and she was careful not to look up or twitch – so careful not to react at all, in fact, that she wondered whether her extreme stillness would give her away instead. She felt as though her guilt were written all over her face in bright red letters for Nancy to read; Nancy with her eagle eyes and her disbelief in everything Irene said and did worn quite openly. She was sitting opposite Irene at the breakfast table, putting the merest scraping of butter on her toast and frowning at any overly large pieces of peel in the marmalade. The sun glanced as brightly from her silver hair, combed back into its usual bun, as it did from the rosewood tabletop. She was small, slim, hard as iron, and sat with her tiny feet crossed at the ankle. She flapped the page of the news-paper to straighten it, read for a moment and then grunted in derision at something. Irene had already stopped expecting her to elucidate, but Alistair glanced up, expectantly. He glanced up every time, with half a smile on his face, ready and waiting. His optimism appeared fathomless, and Irene marvelled at it. It made his eyes sparkle above the soft pouches in which they sat, and made him look younger than his middle years – younger than Irene's twenty-four even, though she was almost fifteen years his junior. She felt she'd aged a decade in the six weeks she'd been in Slaughterford.

Boot heels sounded on the yard; the brass flap on the letter box squeaked. Irene stared at her fingers on the handle of her coffee cup, and forced them not to tremble. The diamond in her engagement ring and the yellow gold of her wedding band stared back at her. As usual, after the guilt came the anger – at herself, at Fin, at blameless Alistair. A rush of bright, hot anger at the situation she was in, and at those who had put her there – herself most of all. She rejected her new role completely, even as she played it as best she could. The anger burnt out as quickly as it flared, and despair came hard on its heels. Despair like a pit she could drown in, without something to save her, something to cling to. The lifebuoy of a word, a sign, a token. Some proof that, even if her misery couldn't end, she was not, at least, alone in it. What she would do if she actually saw Fin's writing on an envelope, she had no idea. She wouldn't be able to keep still then – she'd probably fly to pieces. Her stomach writhed, tying itself in knots. She remained perfectly still.

'Well, it looks like being another beautiful day,' said Alistair, suddenly. Irene glanced at him, startled, and found him smiling at her. She tried to make her own face respond and couldn't tell if it moved or not.

'Yes,' she said. Flick, flick, flick went Nancy's eyes – from Alistair to Irene, back to Alistair.

'What are your plans, darling?' Alistair asked Irene. He put his hand over hers on the table, and her coffee cup rattled as her stiff fingers fell away from it.

'Oh, I . . . I hadn't thought.' Irene heard Florence coming along the hall to the breakfast room – her light, apologetic tread on the boards. The girl had the beady eyes and pointed nose of a mouse, which matched her personality well. Irene's heart escaped her control, and went bounding up into her throat.

Florence knocked softly, came in with the letters on a tray and put them on the table by Alistair's elbow, bobbing awkwardly before she went again. Alistair flicked through them – four envelopes. Irene couldn't breathe. Then he picked them up, straightened them, and slipped them into his jacket pocket as he got to his feet.

'Well, enjoy the day, anyway, both of you. I'll be back for lunch – if it's as fine as yesterday, we should have it out on the terrace.' He pushed his chair away tidily and smiled at Irene again. His smiles seemed in endless supply, like his optimism, when Irene felt like she'd run out of both. His whole face was geared for it – that softness to his eyes, and the upward curve of his lips and cheeks. Without his smile, his face looked bereft. 'You might visit Mrs Cartwright, and see how she is.'

'Mrs Cartwright?'

'Yes – the doctor's wife. You know. Pudding and Donald's mother.'

'Yes, of course.' Irene knew she should be learning all these names, and matching them to faces – the wheelwright, the smith, the vicar's wife, the woman who ran the shop and her son who brought the post. She knew that in a village as small as Slaughterford it was unforgivable not to know. She seemed to have done much that was unforgivable of late, but, just then, she couldn't face paying a call to the doctor's wife – a complete stranger and an invalid, she vaguely remembered being told. She hadn't the first clue what she should say to her. But then Alistair left, and Irene was alone with Nancy again. The long day yawned ahead of her, a void to be filled. She looked up at her husband's aunt, knowing that Nancy would be watching her, judging her openly without Alistair to moderate her. Sure enough, there was the knowing look, the arched brows, the mocking half-smile. Nancy seemed a particularly cruel part of Irene's penance. She was in her seventies but lean and well-preserved; the lines on her face were thin, faint, refined. When Alistair had told Irene his aunt lived with him at Manor Farm she'd imagined a separate cottage and a pleasant old bat filling her time arranging flowers for the church, and holding charity luncheons. A separate wing of the house at least. Not this constant sharp edge, everywhere Irene went, waiting to cut her. When she remarked on it – on her – to Alistair, he'd looked hurt.

'My mother died the day I was born, Irene. Nancy has raised me as her own – she's the closest thing to a mother I have. I don't know how my father would have coped, if she hadn't been here with him. Well, he wouldn't have.'

Irene took hold of her coffee cup again, though she had no intention of drinking the contents. It was stone cold, and filmy on top. Eventually Nancy folded the newspaper away and stood.

'Really, Irene, my dear, you must eat something,' she said, offhandedly. 'It may be all the rage in London to look at death's door, but you'll stand out like a sore thumb down here. Anyone would think you weren't happy – unthinkable for a new bride, of course.' Nancy kept her pinned for a moment longer, but Irene knew that she wasn't expected to reply. Unthinkable, unforgivable. All these new words for Irene to describe herself, and for others to describe her. 'You're a Hadleigh now, young lady. And Hadleighs set the standard around here,' said Nancy, as she turned to go. Only when she'd shut the door behind her did Irene let her chin drop, and her hands fall lifelessly into her lap. The silence in the breakfast room rang.

❧ ❧

Kingfisher, wagtail, great tit, bunting. Clemmie kept a list in her head that almost became a chant as she walked, keeping rhythm with her steps and her breath puffing in and out as she climbed. *Kingfisher, wagtail, great tit, bunting.* The early sun was a glorious flare in her eyes, and sweat prickled under her hair – her mad pale curls, so like her mother's, which defied any attempt at order. She was climbing the narrow path that cut between the field hedges from Weavern Farm to the lane that led down to Slaughterford. The path was tolerable then, early in the morning. By the afternoon it trapped the sun, and hummed with gnats and horseflies, so she came back along the river's edge instead – the longer way, and winding, but cooler. The hedges were full of dog roses now, laden with flowers and baby birds. Her father's cattle tore up the grass to either side of them; she could hear them, and smell their sweet green stink. *Kingfisher, wagtail, great tit, bunting.* The bottles of milk and rounds of cheese in the baskets yoked across her shoulders clanked as they swung. The yoke was almost too wide for the path; cow parsley flicked her arms, and foxgloves, nodding with bees, and wild clematis.

Her parents no longer bothered urging Clemmie to come straight back from her errands; she got back when she got back, sooner or later, depending on how long she spent with Alistair Hadleigh, or watching the river, or caught suspended in a daydream. She usually tried to hurry – she knew there was always work to be done. But even if she set off fast she tended to slow down by the water, or in the woods. Sometimes she saw things that stopped her, and absorbed her, and she didn't even realise it – didn't even realise time had passed until she noticed where the sun was in the sky, or the way her sisters rolled their eyes when she finally did get home, greeting her with varying degrees of resentment, depending on the hour, saying, *Here's our pretty ninny*, if she hadn't been needed, or *Look what the cat dragged in*, if she had. But Clemmie would wander. She had to wander. So they set her to delivering the milk to the mill canteen, though they knew they might not see her for hours. Like the other, larger, dairy herds in the area, Manor Farm, which also owned the mill, sold its milk by the gallon to the butter and condensed milk factories, which left the local deliveries to the smaller Weavern herd.

'At least she gets that one errand run,' her father said, ruefully. He set off in the cart at dawn, twice weekly, to take the bulk of their milk, cheese, butter and eggs to Chippenham market.

Flies circled in the shade of Germain's Lane, despite the early hour; the air hung heavy with the garlicky stink of the ramsons gone over and the fox-musk foliage of wood anemones. The white dust lane ran down the wooded northwest slope of the hill that Clemmie had just climbed, out of the sunken pocket of land that cradled Weavern Farm, bypassing several large loops of the By Brook river. Clemmie tipped back her head to watch the torn fragments of sky, painfully blue, beyond the branches. A dark shape circled there; she added buzzard to the morning's list, and then squirrel, as one leapt between trees overhead – an agile flash of bright red fur. Beech and oak and elm; a thick new canopy that had caused the spring flowers to die back. Only honeysuckle remained, scaling a young elm and blooming among the high branches. When she walked on, imprinted scraps of the bright sky stayed in her eyes and half-blinded her.

Clemmie had walked this route, and carried this aching yoke across her shoulders, more times than she could count, but when Slaughterford Mill appeared at the bottom of the slope, it always made her stop to look. An array of buildings and sheds, hunkered on the river; the tall, steaming chimney; the thrum of noise from the paper-making machine, thudding down into the ground and then up through her feet. As she crossed the little footbridge over the river she heard the roar of the overshot waterwheel, hidden in its pit below ground. The sudden smell of metal and steam and grease, of men and brick and labour, so unlike anything else in the world. And there was a new reason, too, that the mill made her senses prickle. The boy. She might walk around a corner and catch sight of him, and knew her thoughts would both scatter and narrow in, onto him, to the exclusion of everything else. She couldn't forget what he'd done, and wanted to see him exactly as much as she did not, so, in confusion, she stopped to listen to the wheel for a moment, tipping her forehead against the wall to feel its constant beat, and the crash of the water, vibrating into her skull. She was still there when the foreman happened to pass, and roused her.

'Up you get, lass, and take that milk out of the sun.' He smiled kindly beneath his thick moustaches, which were redder than the rest of his hair, and bushy like a fox's tail. Clemmie trusted this man. He never came too close, nor tried to touch her.

She did as he said, walking on into the mill yard, but it troubled her, this looking out. This watching; this hoping to find. She had never done it before; she liked to simply see, not to look. Only a few women worked at the mill, in the canteen and in the bag room, a long, low building close to the water's edge. It was immaculate inside, but freezing in winter – swept elm floorboards and polished walnut benches, not a drop of machine oil or ink anywhere to spoil the finished paper as it was stitched and glued into strong bags for sugar, flour, suet. In summer it smelled deliciously of beeswax, cotton and wood, but Clemmie wasn't really allowed inside – not with her filthy feet and her muddy hem. A couple of the female workers were on their way to clock in as she passed, and one waved to her – dark-haired Delilah Cooper, who was in Clemmie's memories of long hours spent at the dame school in Slaughterford, when they were barely old enough to walk. Watched for a fee by an old woman with a sour face, in her cottage; kept out from underfoot during the working day and eventually taught the bare basics of the alphabet, some songs and prayers. Delilah's face conjured up the smell of ten small children, kept all day in one room; of watery porridge and smuts and the cold stone floor. The other woman eyed her flatly, suspiciously, but Clemmie didn't mind. She liked the scrape and clatter of the women's pattens on the yard, and the clonk as they kicked them off at the door, carrying on in their boots and shoes. She shut her eyes to listen.

'Not right in the head, that one,' said the scowling woman.

Clemmie took the milk to the canteen, then went across to the old farmhouse, a substantial stone house around which the mill had grown up and taken over like unchallenged nettles. Few now remembered Chapps Farm before the mill, and the farmhouse, in which Clemmie's great-aunt Susan had been born – suddenly one morning, on a straw mat in front of the range – now housed the mill's offices, where the foreman and his clerk had their desks, and Alistair Hadleigh too, from Manor Farm, who owned it all. He was a kind man; Clemmie liked his face, which was always ready to smile, and the way he nodded and spoke to the men when he inspected their work. As though he respected them, even though, to Clemmie, his wealth made him seem another order of being altogether. The clean glow of his skin fascinated her; he seemed to breathe different air. Sometimes she carried on walking, through the yard and out the other side. That morning, she went up the old farmhouse's stairs and knocked at the door to Alistair's office. He looked up from his desk, his forehead laddered with worry lines.

'Ah, Clemmie. You've caught me quite unawares. Had we arranged for a lesson?' he said, in a vaguely distracted manner. Clemmie turned to go. 'No, no – do come in. Fifteen minutes won't make or break a thing today.' He got up to shut the door behind her. She caught a whiff of his hair oil, and the very masculine scent that hung about his jacket. No one else in Slaughterford had hands as clean as his. The surface of his enormous desk was hidden beneath piles and piles of paper – some samples that the mill had made, some finer than that, and typed upon. Clemmie couldn't have read the words even had she been inclined to try. She went to her usual place by the window and turned her back to the glass. She liked to stand in silhouette, knowing that her face was partly obscured. 'Now,' said Alistair, perching on the edge of the desk. 'Have you been practising?' Unabashed, Clemmie hitched one shoulder to tell him that she had not. Alistair didn't turn a hair. 'Well, never mind. Shall we start with the breathing exercises I showed you?'

The lesson did not go well. Clemmie swayed her weight from foot to foot, and wished she hadn't bothered. The time was not right; she couldn't concentrate, and tired easily. Looking defeated, Alistair patted her shoulder as she left. 'Never mind,' he said. 'We shall get there in due course, Clemmie. I'm certain of it.' Nancy Hadleigh was climbing the stairs as Clemmie went down. Instinctively, Clemmie turned her body away slightly, clamping her arms to her sides, and avoided her gaze. Nancy was difficult, and hard. Nancy had a stare like iron nails, and only ever spoke past Clemmie, never to her.

'Really, Alistair, what do you hope to achieve?' said Nancy, at the office door.

'There's no earthly reason why that girl shouldn't talk,' said Alistair, quietly. 'She only needs to be taught.'

'I don't understand why you must take it upon yourself to be the one to do so.'

'Because nobody else cares to, Nancy.'

'Well, you must realise that speech is not all people say you're teaching her, shut away in your office together. It's hardly wise, to make yourself the subject of such rumours. Least of all now.'

'Really, Nancy. I'm sure nobody thinks any such thing.'

'I doubt your hothouse flower would approve, if she knew.'

'You make it sound like something seedy, Nancy, when it's nothing of the sort.'

'Well, I just hope you're not giving the girl ideas, that's all.' Their voices faded as the door closed, and Clemmie carried on down the stairs, unconcerned.

She went over to the shop to collect any letters for Weavern Farm – there were generally precious few. The shopkeeper gave her something small – sweets or cheese or an apple – for saving her son the long walk out to Weavern to deliver them, and that day Clemmie chewed a toffee as she carried on her way. But the boy. The boy. His name was Eli, and his family were bad – the Tanners. The worst on God's green Earth, her father, William Matlock, had once said, as he forbade any of his girls to fool about with any of their boys. They'd had a Tanner in to help cut the hay one year. He'd made several attempts to corner Clemmie's sister, Josie, who'd been twelve at the time, and in the end left her with a cut lip; and when he was told to go he'd gone with two of their hens. Now William's face curdled dangerously at any mention of a Tanner. But Clemmie couldn't help thinking about the thing she'd seen the boy do – the thing he'd done for her. She couldn't help but picture his face, so at odds with itself that she hadn't quite worked it out yet – her instincts, normally good enough at guiding her, went blind and were no help. There'd been blood beneath his fingernails, and deep scratches on his hands. He'd smelt of beer and sweat, of something hard and mineral, but, underneath that, of something better. He'd told her his name – defiantly, as if she'd challenged him: *I'm Eli*. And then not another word. The silence had been painfully loud.

But he was nowhere around; if he was working at the mill that day then he was already inside. Sometimes he worked at Rag Mill, the smaller mill, just a little way upriver, which pulped rags for the paper mill. Clemmie remembered seeing him leading the shaggy pony that pulled the cart of sloppy stuff between the two. Tugging at its bridle as it twisted its head in protest, his face screwed up in anger. So much anger in him – so at odds with what he'd done for her. She gazed towards Rag Mill, but had no call to go further upriver. The malty smell of Little & Sons brewery – one of her favourites – drifted down to her, but she left the mill yard troubled. She would go back along the western side of the river, through the trees. There was no path but she knew the way. She felt watched as she went; she was used to the feeling and knew it at once: the weight of eyes. This time, though, she looked around and tried to see who it was – tried to see if it was the boy. *Eli.*

2

The Doll

Pudding did her best to look smart. The new Mrs Hadleigh was – finally – coming to the stables to see the horse Mr Hadleigh had bought for her, in the hope that she would take to riding. Irene Hadleigh had been at Manor Farm for almost six weeks already, as spring had swelled into summer, and the fact that few in the village had seen or met her was causing mutterings. The most sympathetic rumour was that she was an invalid of some kind. There'd been enough of a hoo-hah already, when they'd married up in London after a whirlwind courtship, rather than in St Nicholas' church, squat and solitary in a field in the centre of the village. When the old Mr Hadleigh had been married, the whole village had been invited to a fête in the orchard at Manor Farm, with beer, bunting and apple bobbing. Not that Pudding had been alive to see it, but she'd heard it talked about; and recently she'd overheard Mrs Glover, who ran the tiny shop, complaining to Dolores Pole about the lack of a celebration. Before she'd even arrived and apparently shunned them, the villagers had felt cheated by the new Mrs Hadleigh. Pudding liked the idea of this sudden wedding though – she imagined a passion too urgent to be borne, the need to possess and be possessed, and the thought gave her a hungry feeling. She yearned to yearn for somebody, and to be yearned for; a puzzle of feelings she couldn't yet decipher. Such passion must surely have left traces on Irene Hadleigh. Some kind of glow from within, perhaps. And since Pudding had only caught brief glimpses of her – sitting out on the back terrace with her face down; or blurry, gazing from a window of the house – Irene Hadleigh had become a kind of distant, glorious, near-mythical figure. At the thought of actually meeting her Pudding's heart galloped absurdly.

Manor Farm had five loose boxes and a larger stable they called the cob house – where the two-seated gig and the cob pony who pulled it lived – arranged around a small yard to the west of the farmhouse. It was all built of the same golden limestone as the rest of Slaughterford, quarried out of the hillside above the mill in some earlier century. This yard was where the riding horses were kept, and it was Pudding's domain. The farm's three pairs of working horses – six mighty shires, all feathered feet and muscle – were kept together in skillings behind the top barn, and looked after by a short, wiry man called Hilarius. He wore the same long canvas overalls every day, come rain or shine; nobody knew his age but he was ancient, and had been at the farm since he was a child – far longer than anyone else. His parents had come from some-where in Europe, originally; his eyes watched the world from within a network of creases, and he didn't say an awful lot. In summer he slept on a straw mattress on a mezzanine in the cavernous great barn; in winter he moved into the loft above the cob house. It was his job to get the working pairs harnessed by seven o'clock every morning, ready for the carters to take out; and to rub them down, feed them and turn them out when they returned from ploughing or sowing or whatever at the end of the day. With nods and gestures and demonstrations, Hilarius had taught Pudding a lot of what she knew about stable work, and the rest she'd taught herself from a book called *Sound Horse Management*, which she'd got from the library in Chippenham.

Hay was fetched from the rickyard, up the hill, where it was stacked and thatched on staddle stones to keep it dry. One of the farm's many small sheds had been put aside as a tack room and fitted out with a pot-bellied stove, to prevent the leather blooming, on which Pudding could boil a kettle to make tea. There was an ancient stone water trough outside which doubled as a handy mounting block. Pudding kept the tack room as spotless as the yard – so spotless that the laundress had joked, one day, that the sparrows would have no scraps to build their nests. After that she'd taken to scattering a few wisps of old hay onto the muck heap each morning. Just during nesting season. At least there was plenty of mud around the field gates for the swallows and martins – they'd arrived a few weeks before and set about patching up their nests in the eaves of the stables, and were so sweet Pudding didn't even mind it when they dropped their mess in her hair. Pudding's charges were five: Mr Hadleigh's towering brown hunter, Baron; Tufty, the pony he'd had as a child, now implausibly saggy and ancient; Nancy Hadleigh's hack, Bally Girl – though Nancy rode less and less frequently, with her hip; Dundee, the cob that pulled the Stanhope gig when someone wanted to go into town; and now Robin, the gelding for Mrs Hadleigh. He was only just bigger than a pony and as mild as anything, but not heavy or a plod. Even his colouring was gentle – honey brown. Irene Hadleigh couldn't fail to like him.

Pudding brought him out onto the yard just before eleven and gave him one final polish. She nudged him to straighten him up when he slouched, tipping a back hoof, wanting to show him in his best light. He was a reflection of her work, after all, and Pudding wanted more than anything to be the best girl groom possible. Well, not more than *anything*. She thought of Donny, and her mother too; and of the mystery of yearning. But otherwise, it was what she wanted most. Her father still wanted her to go on to secretarial college, or perhaps even university, as Donny had planned to, once upon a time. Donny was meant to have been an engineer – he had a natural talent for it, and understood machinery of all kinds – but the Great War had changed all that. Dr Cartwright called this summer a *trial run* at being a groom, but, at fifteen years old, Pudding knew exactly what she wanted. She was going to excel. She was going to make herself indispensable to the Hadleighs, and she was going to stay in Slaughterford with her family. For a minute or two she wondered who on earth she would marry, there in Slaughterford, but then the clip on one of her braces popped open as she bent down to pick up Robin's foot, and she blushed even though there was nobody to see it, and reminded herself that marriage was the least of her concerns. Then she heard footsteps and voices from the house, and, flustered, refastened the clip and brushed the horsehair from her sleeves as best she could.

Manor Farm was the most northerly house of Slaughterford, on the steep lane that headed off to Ford, the next village north along the By Brook. From the farm there was a wide, sweeping view of the rolling valley, almost impossibly green with summer, with the church on one side, the mills down on the water, and the cottages in between. The valley was too steep for crops – it was all woods and grazing, and the far fields were dotted with sheep and bronze cattle. The riverbanks to the south were so thick with trees that the water was only visible down by the bridge, where three lanes met – Germain's, which joined Ham Lane to Biddestone; the lane to Ford in the north, and the lane towards Thickwood in the west. All the lanes were narrow and made of crushed limestone, and anyone travelling along them caused a cloud of white dust. The weather had been hot and sunny but it had been raining at night, so that the field gates and water troughs sat in churned mud. The air was slightly damp, the By Brook ran swiftly, and there were insects everywhere. With this glorious backdrop

Nancy and Irene Hadleigh walked across to the yard from the house. For an idiotic moment, Pudding felt she ought to stand to attention, and clean forgot what to say. Luckily, just as the women arrived alongside him, Robin broke wind quite loudly, and she couldn't help but laugh.

Irene Hadleigh recoiled, and kept her distance, watching Robin as though she half expected him to lunge at her, all teeth and fury. It gave Pudding the chance to have a good look at her. She was medium height and whip-thin, with the kind of elfin delicacy that Pudding longed for. Her dark hair was cut into a glossy bob across her ears; her eyes were similarly dark, with smudges underneath them, stark in her pale face. And there was something so immobile about her face, something so frozen, that Pudding couldn't imagine her laughing. She was like a china doll, and quite unreadable. She was dressed in immaculate riding clothes – white breeches, a tweed jacket and a stock – and Pudding racked her brains in panic, having no recollection that Robin should have been tacked up for riding.

'Well, that's a charming welcome,' said Nancy, stepping forwards. She wore her usual shirt and slacks, tidy but just slightly faded; her old, creased boots; a silk scarf over her hair, knotted under her chin.

'It's all the summer grass after the rain, Miss H,' Pudding blurted out.

'I'm well aware of that, Pudding.' Nancy slapped Robin hard on his neck, and ran practised eyes over him. 'Nice enough creature. Not too big. Nothing to alarm – a bit fat, mind you.' With this she gave Pudding a stern look. 'What do you say, Irene?'

'Well,' said Irene, starting slightly. Her voice was subdued. She clenched her hands together. 'He seems fine.' There was a pause while Nancy skewered Irene with one of her smiles, which Pudding knew well, so she stepped forward and held out her own hand.

'It's a pleasure to meet you, Mrs Hadleigh. Mr H mentioned that you haven't done very much riding before, but I've been out on Robin a few times now, and he really is as gentle as a lamb. He didn't even spook when the charabanc passed us in the lane on Monday, and heaven knows it makes enough smoke and racket. You'll be as safe as houses on him, I promise you.' She shook Irene's hand perhaps too vigorously, and faced down her nerves, even though Irene's eyes were as glassy and blank as ink spots. For a moment Pudding baulked, and felt a pang of puzzled sorrow that lovely, sunny Mr Hadleigh should have wed such a cold creature. But then it dawned on her that Irene simply looked fagged. Utterly exhausted.

'Well,' said Irene, pausing to clear her throat. 'In fact, I've never even sat on a horse. I've never quite seen the point, when I've two good legs of my own.'

'Yes, and a car to drive you everywhere,' said Nancy. 'Come the winter, not many things with wheels are any use around here.'

'Oh, and riding is so much fun! And such a wonderful way to see the world,' said Pudding.

'The world?' Irene echoed, with a trace of something bitter in her tone.

'Yes. Well . . . that is, this corner of it, anyway,' Pudding amended. 'Shall I saddle him up for you? I could walk you out on the lead rein, if you like, just to get a feel for it? Or even just around the paddock.'

'Now?' said Irene, alarmed.

'Yes, why not hop up? Only way to find out if you like it. Alistair would be thrilled to hear you'd given it a go,' said Nancy, brightly, and Irene looked horrified.

'I just thought . . . since you'd dressed for riding . . .'

Pudding trailed off. Two spots of colour had appeared on Irene Hadleigh's cheeks. She looked as though she'd like nothing better than to turn tail and flee. 'But you needn't, of course,' Pudding added.

'Nonsense. No time like the present. How are you ever going to hunt at Alistair's side if you won't even get on?'

'I just . . . hadn't thought to . . .' Irene floundered, and Nancy stared at her meanly, and didn't help at all, so Pudding came to her rescue again.

'Well, why don't I ride him in the paddock for a bit, so you can see his paces?' She saw Irene's shoulders drop in relief, and with a small noise of derision Nancy went over to feed Bally Girl a carrot from her pocket.

So Pudding rode Robin in some large circles, loops and figure-eights; in walk, trot and canter. She even popped over a few small jumps, and was enjoying herself so much and concentrating so hard on showing him off that she didn't notice at which point Nancy and Irene stopped watching and left – Nancy across the field to the churchyard, and her brother's grave, and Irene presumably back to the house. Puffed out and sweaty, Pudding let Robin walk on a loose rein back to the yard. The horse was puffing too, and Pudding worried that if she got any bigger, she'd be too heavy to ride him. She spent the next hour scouring off the last of Tufty's winter coat with a curry comb – clouds and clouds of greasy, greyish hair; something for the swallows to line their nests with – and tried not to be disappointed by this first meeting with Irene Hadleigh. She'd been tentatively looking forward to having someone a bit closer to her own age to ride out with, even if she was a Londoner and very upper. Or at least to hearing a bit about London life – the constant parties and balls and bohemian salons and jazz dancing of which she imagined London life to consist. But Irene Hadleigh, though she'd married one of the nicest and best men for fifty miles in any direction, had looked as though she'd rather have been anywhere else than at Manor Farm. A china doll who longed to be back in her box.

At one o'clock, Pudding went to fetch Donny to go home for lunch. Her brother worked at Manor Farm as well, helping the head gardener Jeremiah Welch, whom everyone knew as Jem. He'd been the gardener at Manor Farm for forty years; his body was a strip of bone and sinew, stronger than tree roots and just as brown, and he kept ferrets – there was usually one about his person somewhere, and if there wasn't then their particular smell remained.

'Hello, Jem, are you well?' Pudding called to him, waving.

'Lass,' Jem replied, his Wiltshire drawl stretching out the word. 'Your Don's hoeing the rose beds.'

'Right you are.' The rose garden was behind high brick walls, sheltered and hot. The perfume of the flowers was as rich as their mad profusion of colour. Donny was in the far corner, with his shirtsleeves rolled up and a brown apron over the top. Pudding was always surprised by the breadth of his shoulders, the solidity of him through the hips and waist that told of his strength. A man's strength. She still half expected to see the lanky boy he'd been when he'd gone off to enlist. He'd been tall enough, and his brows heavy enough, for his lie of being eighteen to pass, but he'd been only sixteen. Pudding remembered being on fire with admiration for him that day, and could hardly bear to think of it now. She hadn't had a clue what going to war meant. Donny was sweating, and though he held the hoe ready to work, he was standing stock-still. It happened sometimes – if something made him pause, he might remain paused until somebody came along to restart him. Pudding made sure she'd stepped into his line of sight before she touched his arm to rouse him, but he still flinched. 'It's just me, Donny,' she said, and he smiled, reaching out to pinch her chin between his thumb and forefinger. The sun threw the scar on his head into relief – Pudding could hardly look at it. A flat depression the size of her palm, on the right side of his head, mostly under his hair but coming onto his forehead too, surrounded by knotty scar tissue. 'Time for lunch,' she said. Donny straightened up, bringing the hoe to his side.

'Right you are,' he agreed.

'Looks like you've been working hard this morning.' Pudding looked around at the neat beds and the fresh, weed-free soil Donny had worked between the rose bushes. Then she looked down at the bushes nearest to them, and said 'Oh!' before she could stop herself.

The two rose bushes at Donny's feet were in shreds. Mature bushes, two and a half feet high, one white, one pale yellow – the colours Nancy Hadleigh liked for her brother's grave. Their petals, leaves and green stems had been chopped to pieces by the hoe. Pudding stirred the sad confetti with her toe. 'Oh, Donny, what happened here?' she said quietly, immediately trying to think of a way to conceal the damage. It would be impossible, of course. She felt a tremor go through her brother and looked up at him, fearfully. 'It's all right,' she said, but it wasn't. Donny's face had clouded with rage – that anger with himself that was so terribly destructive for having nowhere to go; no object other than his own intangible frailty. His mouth worked, his skin flushed carmine, and he shook. His hands on the shaft of the hoe were white with the strain of gripping it, and Pudding had to ignore the urge to step back, out of its range. Donny would never hurt her. She knew that so deep down it was written on her bones. But sometimes, since Donny had come home, he stopped being Donny, exactly, and got lost inside himself. Pudding stepped closer, so that he had to see her, and rubbed her hand on his forearm. 'Well, Donny, they'll grow back, won't they?' she said. She could feel the tension in him, like the vibrations in the ground near the beating house of the mill; like the way she could feel when a horse was about to bolt – that shuddering of pent-up energy that had to go *somewhere*. She could almost smell it. 'What do you fancy for lunch?' she said, refusing to show the least concern.

She kept on talking to him, and after a while his breathing slowed and the tension left him, and he shut his eyes, covering them with one muddy hand, squeezing tears into the lashes. 'Come on, then, or we'll miss out,' she said, and he let himself be led away. She would see Jem and Alistair Hadleigh about it after lunch, when she was sure that Donny was calm again. Jem would chew his lip and set about tidying the plants in silence; Mr Hadleigh would smile that sad, sympathetic smile he used when these things happened, and say something like, *Well now, there's no point crying over spilt milk*, and Pudding would struggle to keep herself together. Even Nancy Hadleigh was kind when it came to Donny – although Pudding had long suspected that Alistair's aunt was kinder underneath all the bristle than she liked to let on. Pudding had once seen her wring the neck of a duck the fox had got hold of – it had been left with big, bloody holes in its breast, one eye gone and a wing twisted, hanging limply behind it. Nancy had despatched it quickly and flung it onto the bonfire heap, wiping her hands on a rag, saying, *No point trying to nurse it*, but Pudding had seen the way her eyes gleamed, and the sad set of her mouth.

They walked down into the village, across the bridge at Rag Mill and up the steep footpath through the field that led home. The field was still called Bloody Meadow by the villagers, after the legend that King Alfred had defeated the Danes in battle there, centuries before, making the river run red with the blood of fallen warriors. They said that was how Slaughterford got its name. Donny had told Pudding the story over and over when she was little, before the war – re-enacting long, fictional accounts of the battle, blow by hideous blow, complete with sound effects and swoops of his hazel sword. She'd loved the excitement of it, the imagined glory and wonder of such an ancient time. Magic and thanes and treasure. It was on the tip of her tongue to ask Donny for the story again, or to tell it to him; to bring back that time. But battles weren't as alluring any more, and heroic death meant something now – it meant fear and pain and broken lives. Too many other boys had left Slaughterford for the war, from its precious population of eighty-one, including two Tanners, a Matlock, two Smiths and three Hancocks. Only Donny had come back. Alistair Hadleigh too, of course – but he hadn't been a boy, or a Tommy. Instead, as they climbed and started to puff, Pudding told her brother about Irene Hadleigh, and how she hadn't wanted to ride. She wasn't sure Donny was listening until he stopped walking, frowning, and said:

'You never could understand a person not wanting to ride, could you, Pud?' He spoke slowly, concentrating hard, and Pudding grinned.

'No, Donny. I never could.'

Spring Cottage was named after the rill of freshwater that bubbled up from the ground in front of it, trickling through a swathe of luminously green duck weed into a stone trough, and then down pipes to give Slaughterford its supply of drinking water. The house was Georgian, not particularly large but handsomely square and symmetrical, with sash windows and a big brass knocker on the front door. Inside, everything was wonderfully normal – Louise had made pea soup from the garden, and gave them a half-proud, half-annoyed list of the chores she and Ruth, their daily, had got through that morning: new paper and pink disinfectant powder in the privy, all the beds changed, the blackcurrants picked and jellied – and Dr Cartwright came bustling in late, as he always did, apologising profusely. Their house was up too steep a hill for his consultations to be held there, so he rented a room in the schoolmaster's house in Biddestone, and cycled to and fro. Pudding surreptitiously checked her mother for signs of mishap. That was how she and her father termed what was happening to Louise. *Mishaps*. It was a terrible misnomer neither one of them could bring themselves to drop. But her mother looked fine, if a little tired. Her blond hair was fading as grey invaded it; there were deeper lines around her eyes and mouth than a woman of forty-eight should have, but most of those had appeared the morning Donny went off, seven years previously. It wasn't a beautiful face, but it was wide and appealing. She was soft and rounded and perfect for hugging. The first sign of mishap was when she began to look around the room with the beginnings of a frown, as though she couldn't remember why she'd come in, or – worse – which room she was in. Pudding was always watching for it. She never again wanted to be as unprepared, as frightened, as the time she'd come down for breakfast and found her mother standing at the stove with an egg, still in its shell, smoking in a dry pan. Louise had turned to her and smiled politely, and said, *Oh, excuse me, young miss – perhaps you might help me? I'm rather worried I've come to the wrong address.*

Pudding remembered their kitchen table from her earliest memories – gouging ancient crumbs from its seams with her thumbnail when she was bored of practising the alphabet; the cutlery drawer that jammed; the slight stickiness to the wood that no amount of scrubbing could get rid of. There was a dining room as well, with a far nicer, polished, table, but they used it less and less. The kitchen table was like the enamel pans on their hooks above the stove, and her mother's yellow apron, and the brown teapot with the glued-together lid – anchors; things Pudding could rely upon. Ruth, who refused to give her age as anything but *somewhere in the middle*, sat down to lunch with them and gave the doctor the usual report of her large family's ailments. Pudding's father did his best to advise.

'And my Teresa's acne never gets any better,' said Ruth, as they dipped their spoons into the pea soup. 'Poor thing's got a face like wormy meat. How's she supposed to find a husband, looking like that?' She appealed to the doctor as if there was something he could have been doing to help her daughter, yet wasn't. Louise put down her spoon in protest; Donny slurped away, unconcerned. The doctor nodded kindly.

'A girl of Teresa's sunny disposition should have no trouble there, Ruth. These things are often simply grown out of. But she mustn't pick at them, and damage the skin.'

'Hilarius put a tincture of witch hazel and ash on Tufty's infected bot bite last month,' said Pudding. 'It was miraculous. The boil was as big as a walnut, and really smelly, but it dried out in three days flat.'

'Oh, good grief, Pudding, *not* at the table,' said Louise.

'Sorry, Mum.'

'Witch hazel, you say?' said Ruth.

Pudding wondered whether to mention the rose bushes. The last time something like that had happened, Donny had got into trouble soon afterwards. His frustration seemed to build gradually, as though the daily fight to get back to himself wore him out, and weighed him down, until it grew too much to bear. The incident at the White Hart in Ford the year before had been the worst. Patches of sticky blood on the dark stone flags, and a broken tooth; the police sergeant fetched out from Chippenham when Pete Dempsey, the local constable, couldn't hold Donny by himself. But it hadn't been Donny's fault – none of it was Donny's fault. He'd seen Aoife Moore earlier that afternoon. Aoife with her black hair and green eyes, and the dimple in her chin, who he was supposed to marry. They'd been sweethearts since they were twelve, and got engaged before he went away, but when he got back she managed ten minutes with him, and the crater in his skull, and the way he struggled to speak and eat, and ran away crying. She got engaged to a carrier's brawny son the following month. Then Donny saw her buying black and white bull's eyes for her little sister – five for a farthing – from the widow who sold sweets through her front window in Ford. Aoife had struggled to reach through the window, what with her pregnant belly so huge. And then the man she'd married was in the pub, with some others, and had goaded Donny. Pudding hadn't been there, of course, but she was sure Donny *must* have been goaded. But the rose bushes were just a slip-up. Just a loss of concentration – his arms still working the hoe though his mind and gaze had drifted off. Pudding decided not to say anything about it.

Her father stopped her as she went upstairs to bed that night.

'A good day today, Pudding?' he asked, softly. Upstairs, Louise was putting Donny to bed. In some ways he'd become an oversized child, needing prompting through the bedtime rituals. *Brush your teeth, Donny. Into your pyjamas, now*. Their footsteps made the floorboards squeak. Pudding didn't like to think what might happen if her mother ever didn't recognise Donny, or forgot what had happened to him. The idea of their confusion clashing, and frightening them both, was sickening. Dr Cartwright was a gentle, smallish man – shorter than both of his offspring – with a neat face and grey whiskers. Behind round spectacles, his eyes were sad. When Donny had absconded to join up he'd gone into his consulting room in Biddestone and hadn't come out, or admitted anyone, for the rest of the day. When he'd finally returned home he'd hugged his daughter tightly, and his eyes had been pink, and he'd said, in a tight voice, *The boy'd never forgive me if I sent a telegram with his real age, would he?* And Pudding, still star-struck by her brother, had said, *He's going to be a hero, Daddy.* The exchange still haunted her. She was sure it haunted the doctor too. The hope in his voice, when he asked Pudding about their day, was painful to hear.

'Yes, Dad,' she said. 'A good day.'

At night, Pudding read. She still had books of pony stories she was far too old for, as comforting as slipping under the blankets and finding the warm spot where the hot water bottle had been. Or she read the tuppenny story papers – love stories and lurid accounts of true crimes. Ruth sometimes passed on well-thumbed copies of *Weldon's Ladies' Journal* and *Woman's Weekly* for her to read as well.

'Since your own mother's in no state to teach you,' she'd said the first time she'd brought one over, pursing her lips afterwards and colouring up. Pudding did like to read about clothes and hosiery and lipstick, and what she should be knitting, or doing to her skin to make it bloom (in fact, her skin was perfect), but at the same time she felt that none of it was really relevant to her. It was interesting, but like reading the romances or the murder stories – not something that would ever happen in real life. She had bobbed her hair the year before, though, in imitation of the cover star of one of the magazines, and much to her mother's upset. But it hadn't hung in a straight, glossy line like Irene Hadleigh's, with razor edges and a halo of reflected light. Pudding's hair was thick and bushy, so it'd stuck out from the sides of her head in a triangle, and made her look even wider. Appalled, she'd let it grow back, and in any case it spent most of its life in a hairnet, held back with clips or crushed into the shape of a riding hat and sweaty at the edges.

That night, though, she picked up *Murder Most Foul – true*

stories of dark deeds in Wiltshire; a book she'd found in a junk shop in Marshfield. It contained fifteen stories of horrible things that had happened in the county throughout its history, two of them in Slaughterford itself, most fascinatingly, albeit years and years ago: 'The Maid of the Mill', the murder of a local girl; and 'The Snow Child', which told the terribly sad story of a family of tinkers (*beautiful as exotic animals are, and similarly devoid of morals*, the book said) who had perished from the cold one bitter winter night, having been refused shelter by everyone in the village. Only a little boy had survived, and was found lying half-buried by snow, between his dead parents who'd huddled around him and his sister, trying to keep them warm. Pudding normally couldn't read it without shivering in sympathy, and being grateful for her warm bed, but she couldn't seem to concentrate on it that night. She read to the end anyway, then put the book down and wondered, for a moment, how different life might be if one were slim, and beautiful, and married to Alistair Hadleigh.

When she was little her mother had marked her bedside candle with her thumbnail, and once the flame had burnt down to that point Pudding would know it was time to blow it out and go to sleep. Now it was up to her when she twisted the knob on her gas lamp to extinguish it, and she was usually the last one awake in the house. She liked to be. Her father worked so hard, and worried so much, he was exhausted. And Donny and her mother needed to be watched over, so watch over them she would. Sometimes, on windy nights, she felt like crying. Which was stupid, she told herself, when there was nothing to cry about, really. She had her home, and her parents, not like the little boy in 'The Snow Child'. And what about the Tanners and the Smiths, whose sons and brothers hadn't come back from the war at all? What about Maisie Cooper, whose mother had been kicked in the head when her pony was stung by a bee, and had lain unconscious ever since? Maisie had to be back from college for the holidays by now, but she hadn't come up to see Pudding. Of course, Pudding had far less free time now she was working, and she understood why some of her other friends stayed away – not everybody knew how to talk to Donny any more, or to Louise, and it made them nervous. But she'd thought Maisie, out of everybody, wouldn't have minded as much. Pudding refused to cry, not when it was only the wind, making her feel like the last human being on earth.

❦ ❧

In the circle of light cast by the bronze lamp on the desk, Irene's hand cramped over the paper. She'd been gripping the pen too hard, as though she might have been able to squeeze words out of it. *Dear Fin*, she'd written. *I don't think I can carry on much longer without a word from you. Just a single bloody word*. After that, her hand had stalled. She'd meant to write with a lighter tone. Something more conversational, as though they might manage to pretend a friendship. She'd meant to write something dry about Nancy's ever watchful presence, or about the absurdity of life in Slaughterford – what kind of name was *Pudding*, anyway? – or that there only seemed to be four different surnames to go around, or that when Alistair had told her about Manor Farm, she'd heard the 'Manor' part louder than the 'Farm' part, when the reverse was closer to reality. But those words wouldn't come. They'd have been false, anyway. Irene shut her eyes and he was there at once. A quiet, diffident presence behind Serena, who was anything but serene. Not overly tall, not overly handsome, but with something warm and deeply compelling about him, so much so that once they'd exchanged a word and a glance, weeks after meeting, Irene had felt both – glance and word – travel right through her like a wave rolling ashore, and hadn't afterwards been able to want anything but him. Serena had towed him here and there behind her, by his hand, like a child. He'd been so silent, so overshadowed by her for the first few weeks Irene knew them that she hadn't heard his Scottish accent, or realised that Fin was short for Finlay, a name she'd never heard before.

Serena was a different kettle of fish. All bright, all sparkling, all smiles and loud laughter. Irene had first met her at a costume party, dressed as a peacock – sequins and paste jewels twinkling everywhere, iridescent feathers wafting as she moved, blue and green, turquoise and silver. From then on Irene always saw her that way – even when Serena was wearing brown wool, she dazzled. It took a long time to see that it was armour, in fact, to hide what was going on inside her. Serena had bowled Irene over. She bowled everyone over. She didn't so much make friends as assume that everyone she met was already her friend – and they usually turned out to be, sooner or later. It seemed impossible to resist Serena; so impossible that, later, when Irene asked Fin why he'd married her and he hadn't been able to explain it, she'd understood at once. She remembered clearly the first time she hadn't been able to eat in Serena's presence. Just as she couldn't in her mother's presence. It had been in a restaurant in Piccadilly, over a lunch one Tuesday. Sole Veronique. A group of seven or eight of them, some Irene knew, some she did not. Fin sitting opposite her at the far end of the table. She'd caught his eye by mistake and looked away quickly. *Irene has a secret pash, you know*, Serena had announced, smiling with her eyes ferocious, drawing attention to Irene when she knew Irene would hate it. *Look at her blush – isn't it adorable? Tell us who it is or we'll make it up!* When the food had arrived Irene's hands had refused to touch the cutlery, and her mouth had refused to open; just like it did when her mother was watching.

She blinked and took a deep breath, looking down at the scant, wretched words of her letter and hating herself anew. The gas lamp hissed and she thought of all the things she missed about London – not just Fin, or the motor taxicabs Nancy had mentioned earlier. Electric lighting, for one thing, and indoor lavatories; the theatre, and the flicks; music that didn't involve a squeeze box, washboard or fiddle. The comforting, anonymous throng of busy people; the ease with which new clothes – new camouflage – could be got. The sense, stepping out of the front door, that an infinite variety of things to do, places to be and people to see lay within easy reach. In Wiltshire, there was nothing beyond the front door but mud and animals. The only motor vehicle she'd seen attempting the steep, stony lanes was the lumbering chara-banc bus that brought mill workers in the morning, and took villagers off to Chippenham and Corsham. The only thing that both places had in common was the unnatural dearth of young men, and the blank eyes of those who had made it back from the trenches. Carefully, Irene tore away the page with her short letter on it, and was about to screw it up when she heard Alistair's step outside the door. She quickly slid the page beneath the blotter and arranged her hands in her lap as he came in. He smiled and crossed to her, kissing her cheek.

'How are you now, darling?' he asked, solicitously. 'You gave us quite a scare.'

'Rather better, thank you. It was really nothing – that sauce was just a little rich for me.' A cream and sherry sauce, laced with walnut oil. It had coated the inside of her mouth and throat, and she'd felt her cheeks water in protest as her head began to cloud.

'Yes. Well . . .' Alistair trailed off, looking awkward. 'Irene,

I can't help thinking . . . I can't help wondering whether, if you ate a little more, perhaps your system would be more used to . . .' He fell silent again.

'I'm simply . . . not hungry, a lot of the time. That's all,' said Irene. She tried to say it lightly, but it sounded as phoney as it was – her empty stomach clawed at her from morning to night. Yet the thought of food closed her throat. Alistair crouched down by her chair, and took her hands. Guiltily, she noticed the ink on her fingers. Alistair had long hands, pianist's hands, with very neat fingernails. Not like Fin's, all bitten down in frustration. Her new husband was undeniably handsome; tall and slim, his hair a muted gold, his eyes half green, half brown. And that way his face was always either smiling or about to be.

'But you're so thin, Irene.' He shook his head slightly. 'I'll call Dr Cartwright in the morning, and get him to take a look at you. Just to be on the safe side.'

'There's really no need. I'm perfectly all right. Really,' said Irene.

'Are you, though? You promised to always tell me the truth, remember? That's all I ask.'

Alistair looked up at her in a beseeching way, full of the love she felt so unworthy of. How could she possibly keep that promise? She reached out and ran a hand over his hair and down the side of his face, feeling the beginnings of stubble on his jaw. Alistair shut his eyes and turned his face into her touch, kissing her palm, and Irene froze, caught between duty, gratitude, and the urge to flee. Alistair caught her hand tightly and pressed kisses along the inside of her arm, where bluish veins showed beneath the skin. He took a long breath, and shut his eyes, and Irene fought not to pull away.

'Alistair, I—' she said. He laid his face along her arm for a moment, then stood up, letting it go, smiling a strained smile.

'No. I quite understand, what with you under the weather, you poor thing,' he said, and relief swooped through her. 'Could you stomach a little Bovril, do you think? Just a small cup?'

'I think that might be just the ticket, thank you.' She breathed more easily as Alistair reached the door, but then he paused, and turned. He looked at the blank paper in front of her, and her pen discarded to one side, and the ink on her fingers. He opened his mouth but it took a moment longer for the words to come.

'I ... I do understand how difficult this must be for you, Irene. People are quick to lay blame but ... I personally think *he* treated *you* abominably. I don't expect you to forget it all right away. I don't.' He swallowed, and met her eye with a wounded gaze. 'I only ask that you try.' He shut the door and left her alone again, in the circle of light by the desk, surrounded by the darkness.

In the morning Irene was woken, as she was every morning, by the racket of the heavy horses' feet on the yard, the incomprehensible banter of the strappers and carters as the teams went out to work, the mooing of the dairy herd, the geese honking with a sound like metal hinges, and the collie dogs barking to be fed. She felt surrounded by baying animals of all kinds. After breakfast, she went down to what was going to be her writing room and hovered outside the door, not announcing her presence at once. It was a small room, half dug into the rising ground on the north-east side of the house, where there was little natural light and the flagstones were so cold, even then in summer, that they felt damp – and possibly were. The walls were painted a faint pink – no panelling, no cornicing, no ceiling rose. The plainest of rooms. The two ancient metal casements were crooked, and the curtains were simple, chequered affairs. The fireplace had been boarded up with a wooden frieze showing an arrangement of flowers and fruit. Overall, the room felt like one that nobody had used in a very long time, and Irene had been drawn to it immediately. In every other part of the house she felt that she was trying to make space for herself in somebody else's life, somebody else's house – and that *somebody* was Nancy.

'I still don't see why she need do anything so drastic,' said Nancy, looking on disapprovingly as Verney Blunt, the village builder, and his lad carried in their ladders and sheets and metal boxes of tools. Verney tipped his hat in a bid to get her to move out of his way, as he struggled to find room for everything, but Nancy ignored him. 'And why this room, of all of them? She might as well set up camp in the cellar.'

'I loved this room when I was a boy,' said Alistair, standing by the window with his hands behind his back.

'No you didn't, you goose. You only loved escaping from it. What boy loves his schoolroom?'

'All right, but I did love it in some ways. Especially when I had Mr Peters. He used to bring me toffee, you know.'

'I do know. You'd come out with it all over your chin.'

'Well, Irene likes this room, so as far as I'm concerned she can have it. It's quiet, and cosy. Quite suitable for a writing room.'

'Cosy? Tosh. She'll go blind in here – there's no light. And she'll change her mind come winter – that chimney has never done anything but let the wind howl down. Why do you think it was blocked up in the first place?'

'I know. But look, Aunt Nancy, she needs a room to make her own – no small thing when everything else in this house has been here for centuries. She's chosen this one, so let's just say no more about it, shall we? It's not as though it's being used for anything else.'

'But new furniture? New fabrics? New everything?'

'Why not? It's about time at least one corner of this old place was brought up to date. I hope she might take on some of the other rooms, in due course. She has quite the eye for it, you know.'

'Does she indeed. Well.' Nancy sighed. 'You're as soft as my dear departed brother was before you, Alistair.'

'We can afford to be soft with you to watch over us,' Alistair told her, smiling.

Irene put her shoulders back and lifted her chin before she entered the room, and refused to let any hint of an apology suffuse her face or voice.

'I'm really very grateful,' she said.

'There you are, darling,' said Alistair. 'Mr Blunt here is ready for your instructions.'

'Mornin', Mrs Hadleigh,' said Verney, grudgingly. He was stout, red-faced, white-haired.

'Hello,' said Irene. The younger of the workmen, who only looked about fifteen, eyed her curiously, and Irene wondered what account of her was making it out into the wider realm of Slaughterford. The lad had dark, unwashed hair and a thin face, almost ferrety. His eyes were guarded, his whole body poised to flinch.

'You're one of the Tanner clan, aren't you?' Nancy said to him. The boy nodded, ducking his head.

'Get on, then, and fetch the rest of the gear,' said Verney brusquely, sending the boy scuttling from the room.

'Is the silver quite safe, Mr Blunt?' said Nancy. Verney Blunt swelled his chest, but looked a little uneasy.

'I reckon so, Miss Hadleigh. He's a good lad, not as bad as some of them. And I'll be keeping my eye on him, you've my word on that.'

'What is he – a Noah? An Abraham? A Jonah?'

'A Joseph, madam.'

'One of Slaughterford's little jokes,' Nancy said to Irene. 'That the least godly family in the whole county should decide to opt strictly for biblical names for their offspring.'

'Oh? But they don't attend church?' said Irene.

'Some of them do. When they aren't too drunk to stand.' Nancy shrugged. 'Well, I shall leave you to your artistic endeavours in here. I must see Lake about the new fencing in Upper Break.' She strode from the room with her hands thrust hard into the pockets of her jacket.

In her absence Alistair smiled, and pulled Irene into a quick embrace before the workmen's footsteps approached along the hall again.

'Who is Lake, and what is an Upper Break?' said Irene.

'You met John Lake – remember? The farm manager. Huge chap.'

'Yes, of course.' Irene remembered the man's towering height, and bullish shoulders all but blocking out the sky, but she couldn't recall his face; she remembered the bass growl of his voice, but not what he had said. She found the Wiltshire accent of the villagers all but unintelligible, and in the first few weeks after their wedding she'd been more of a shell than a whole person. She dreaded meeting again the few of Alistair's acquaintances she'd been introduced to, since she'd forgotten their names at once.

'And Upper Break is the high field – the one that goes over the hill towards Biddestone, where the ewes are at the moment. Good pasture, rocky as anything but it drains well.'

'Nancy's rather indispensable around here, isn't she?'

'I suppose so. Well, not indispensable, but very involved. The farm and Slaughterford are her life.'

'The farm, Slaughterford, and you.'

'Yes, I suppose so. Especially since we lost my father.'

'She must have had suitors, in her day? I've seen her deb portrait. She was very beautiful.' The portrait hung in the study, opposite those of Alistair's parents – Nancy's brother and sister-in-law. There were early photographs as well, ghostly and pale, including one of Nancy with long dark hair, piled up high, cheekbones like a cat and flawless skin. Something cool and angry in her eyes.

'There were. But the one she really wanted got away, and it seems as though that was that for Aunt Nancy. That was before I was born, of course, and she's rather prickly when you ask her about it.'

'You do surprise me.'

'Do you feel up to coming down to the mill later today? Then I can show you what I get up to all day long.'

'I was always given to understand that most men don't want their wives to know what they get up to all day long,' said Irene.

'Well, I am not most men, and you are not most wives. This is your home now, as it's been my family's home for generations. My dearest wish is for you to come to know and love it as I do, and be happy here. I know it will take a bit of time to adjust, but you'll see ... There's a good life to be had here.' He took her hand and gave it a squeeze, and Irene saw how badly he wanted her to see it, and how she had become a feeble thing, an invalid, who needed to 'feel up to' things.

'All right, then. I'll come to the mill with you after lunch.'

Irene hadn't known what to expect of the mill, but a place of such size and complexity certainly hadn't been it. With the rest of the village so sedate and bucolic, she'd half pictured most industry being done by hand. Instead, the place was powered by steam and electricity, and the din and smother of it all was shocking. She drew curious glances from the workers as Alistair led her from building to building, but when she met their eyes they jumped and went back to work with extra vigour, as though she were some sort of visiting dignitary. Which, perhaps, she was. She was introduced to the foreman, George Turner, and to his second in command, the paper-maker. Alistair talked her through the process as they went into the vast machine room – how scrap paper and old rags were cooked down, pounded into pulp and then pumped onto the Fourdrinier machine. This behemoth was near enough a hundred feet long, and six feet wide. The stuff – as the pulp was called – went onto an endless mesh that drew out the water before it rolled onto felts and proceeded, at a steady walking pace, through a succession of huge, steam-heated cylinders to dry it out. It ended up on a vast reel at the end, as finished paper. Irene nodded a lot, and tried not to sweat too visibly in the clinging heat.

Light poured into the machine room through tall metal-framed windows; the floor was awash, the air was a ruckus and the walls and every surface were spattered with paper pulp. Irene was happy to leave it for the smaller rooms where the paper was cut and stacked, and the bag room where women, whose scrutiny was more calculating, were sewing and gluing. Plain metal lanterns hung down from the ceilings, and there were large time clocks on all the walls, where the workers punched their cards in and out at the change in shift. These reminded Irene of the station clock at King's Cross, and one of the worst days of her life, just a few months before. She struggled to keep listening, and keep smiling. Alistair took her hand and squeezed it.

'Come along outside, darling,' he said. 'A breath of fresh air is what's needed.'

'Yes,' said Irene. 'But thank you very much for explaining it all to me.'

'What do you make of it all?' he asked, as they returned to the sunny yard and walked slowly towards the old farmhouse that served for office space.

'It's very impressive. Far ... bigger than I'd imagined.' Alistair looked dissatisfied with this answer, so Irene sought about for more to say. 'So much machinery and noise and ... and steam. It looks like hard work for the men. And it must be dangerous – I mean, it must all take careful management.'

'In fact, Mr Turner keeps it running almost as smoothly as the Fourdrinier itself, as a rule. He's jolly good; been here for years, like a lot of the more senior men. As for dangerous – not as much as you might think. There's only been one serious accident, but that was years ago, before I was born.'

'What happened?'

'It was just along at Rag Mill. The villagers used to roast apples and potatoes in the coals beneath the boiler. By pure ill-luck, some of them were fetching theirs out when the boiler exploded. It's a very rare occurrence, and the man in charge was fired at once for not having replaced a faulty valve.'

'And people were hurt?'

'Three were killed, in fact, including a young boy, only ten years old. He was blown clean across the river, by all accounts. A terrible tragedy. I can assure you that I take the safety of my workers very seriously.'

'How awful,' said Irene.

'Yes, but other than that – and one robbery, also years ago, when an office boy was hit over the head – we've never had any trouble. Now, what shall I show you next?'

'Oh, I don't know,' said Irene, struggling to muster the enthusiasm Alistair seemed to need. 'You choose.' He looked down at her for a moment – he was a good head taller – then smiled.

'I know,' he said. 'My office, and a cup of tea.'

Irene looked in on Verney and the Tanner boy when she got back to the farm, but there wasn't much to see in the old schoolroom except mess, and she felt awkward, as if checking up on them, so she left them to their work. The walls would be bright white; there'd be a translucent marble surround for the fire; curtains sent down from Liberty; a red lacquered table by Eileen Gray; a gold chair by Jean Dunand; the turquoise and grey silk Persian rug she'd inherited from her grandmother; her black Underwood typewriter and a stack of immaculate bond paper. Things the likes of which Manor Farm had never seen before. She would make herself a corner of her old life to retreat to, when the reality of the new one became unbearable. Maybe then she would be able to start writing again, and have that solace as well. Her newspaper column – just society gossip, really, even if she'd tried to make it more than that – had ceased, of course, with her departure from London, and the manner of it. The novel she'd begun – a romance – had stalled at four chapters. Whenever she tried to write now, she was faced with a blank page, a blank mind, and feelings of profound futility. She drifted through the rooms of the farmhouse, making Florence the maid and Clara Gosling, the housekeeper, dodge about her as they tried to work, always polite but radiating impatience. The main body of the house was long and narrow, with low ceilings and bulging plaster. The rooms followed each other along a corridor in steady succession. Sunlight flooded through the windows, onto the comfortable carpets and furniture, all of which were from some previous century. Elm floorboards creaked beneath her feet; the turgid air parted for her then swirled to stillness again.

Irene went into the study, a deeply masculine room of dark oak and leather books, and stood for a while in front of the portrait of Alistair's parents. Alistair looked a lot like his father – after whom he'd been named – and very little like his mother. Tabitha Hadleigh had been short and serious; her eyes fractionally too close together, her mouth fractionally too small. In their wedding portrait she was swathed in a very Victorian dress involving mounds of ruffles, lace and ribbons, yet still managed to look sombre. Irene wondered how she would have felt if she'd lived to see her son grow up, and seen how little of her there was in him. Alistair was no memorial to her whatsoever. In a photograph of him as a boy of about seven, his arms wrapped around a wire-haired terrier, the features he would have as a man were visible, if unformed, and the warm light in his eyes was already there. Alistair senior must have been chipper, she thought – or young Alistair must have had a kindly nanny; surely no child raised solely by Nancy could look so happy.

From a south-facing window she watched the wind ripple the long grass between the apple and pear trees in the orchard. Down the hill to the south-west sat the church of St Nicholas, its graveyard aglow with buttercups. Beyond that rose the smoke and steam of the mill, seething on the riverbank like some vast creature. She saw the girl groom, Pudding Cartwright, sweeping the yard with vigour. None of the girl's clothes seemed to fit her – she always looked as though she might be about to burst out of them. But then, that had been the overall impression she'd given Irene – of being about to burst out. With words or enthusiasm, or energy; or perhaps something else. There'd been something eager about her that was almost desperate. Now she was sweeping the yard as though, if she swept it well enough, good things would happen. Pausing to catch her breath, Pudding turned her face to the sky, to the sun and the breeze, and closed her eyes, and Irene wished she herself knew how to be outdoors. Here, in the countryside, surrounded by endless fields and grass and trees and water and mud and animals. It was all alien to her, but unless she could find a way to love it, Manor Farm would close its walls around her, forever, and she didn't think she would survive that. There was a knock at the front door, and the sound of Nancy greeting a female caller and taking her into the back sitting room, which was unofficially Nancy's, for tea. Irene was not asked to join them. She dithered a while in the corridor outside, wondering if she should knock and introduce herself, but then she heard Nancy say:

'The girl's quite useless. Honestly, I don't know what my nephew was thinking, in marrying her. He's always had a soft spot for birds with broken wings, but as far as I can tell, this one hasn't even *got* any wings.' So she left them to it.

Sometime later Florence came to find Irene, leaning on the door handle in the way that Nancy always berated her for, as though, at sixteen, her body was exhausted.

'Beg pardon, ma'am, only that Verney Blunt asks for 'ee, down in the schoolroom,' she said. 'Reckons he's found something.' Her accent made the last word sound like *ʒome-urr*, and *down* had two syllables: *dow-wun*.

'Thank you, Florence.' She felt the girl watching her as she left the room ahead of her. They all watched her, Irene realised. Perhaps they, too, were wondering how on earth she'd got there, and why. She tried not to be nervous of talking to the workmen by herself, and when that failed she tried not to let it show. 'What is it, Mr Blunt?' she said, as she came into the room, surprised by how frigid she sounded. The old furniture had been removed; the floor was covered in dust sheets; the ceiling gleamed whitely, wetly, and the frieze that had covered the fireplace was off. On the hearth, on another sheet, was a slew of soot, fragments of mortar, and the broken remains of birds' nests. Verney Blunt and the Tanner boy stood to either side of this pile, their faces tense and their bodies braced. They looked up as though startled.

'Excuse me, Mrs Hadleigh, but it's *that*,' said Verney. He pointed at the mess from the chimney as though a live snake lay there. Irene's pulse picked up.

'What?' She followed his pointing finger with her eyes.

'*That*, missus! The votive!' said the boy.

Puzzled, Irene stared down at the pile. Then she saw it. Blackened, dishevelled, incongruous amidst the dreck, was a doll. However it had once looked, it now looked hideous – whatever had been used to give it a face had shrivelled beyond recognition; its wired limbs were all twisted and broken. But it was still recognisably a doll; it had a bonnet and a rough dress of blue fabric, held together with big, neat stitches, and someone had also stitched a simple daisy motif on its front. Irene crouched down and reached for it.

'Don't *touch* it, yer daft cow!' said the Tanner boy, urgently, and Irene's cheeks blazed.

'Joseph, watch your lip!' said Verney. 'Sorry, Mrs Hadleigh, but he might be right about not touching it.'

'Why on earth not? It's just somebody's old doll,' said Irene.

'It may be, but when dolls is put up chimneys ... well, round here, that can be witchery, ma'am,' said Verney.

'Witchery? You're not serious?'

'I'm proper serious, ma'am.' Man and boy went back to staring at the doll, as though daring it to move or hex them in some way. Irene decided that they were pulling her leg. Mocking her. That this would become a funny story, told in the pub at her expense. She swallowed.

'Well, I don't believe in witchcraft, so I suppose I'm safe.' She reached for the doll and picked it up, ignoring a frustrated hiss from the boy.

'That's gone and done it,' he muttered, darkly.

'It's filthy, Mrs Hadleigh. You'll spoil yer nice things,' Verney grumbled.

Irene turned the doll over gently in her hands, feeling bits of twig and soot come away onto her fingers. It was only about eight inches tall, and its little head, which once might have been canvas wrapped around some kind of fruit, had been painted with a rudimentary face – blobs for eyes and nose; a rough, uneven smile. Beneath its dress, its body felt like lumpy rags. It looked like a doll home-made for a child out of whatever could be found, and though Irene wanted to find it charming there was something about it that was not. Perhaps it was only the men, still watching her intently, waiting for whatever would happen next, but Irene began to feel uneasy. She stared into the doll's smudged face and noticed a slip in time – the moment stretching out too long, and the silence in the room ringing in her ears with a high bell tone. She felt something shift, though she couldn't tell if it was within her or without; she felt that she had passed a mark of some kind, and that things must change thereafter. Troubled, she curled her hands carefully, protectively, around the grotesque little doll.

3
Nature's Child

Sometimes, Clemmie's sisters turned on her. She had three: Mary and Josie, who were older, and Liz, who was younger by a year. They'd had a brother too: Walter. But he was five years dead and they rarely spoke of him – the gap at the table where he should have been was enough of a reminder of the hole he'd left in all of them. None of them needed reminding of the way he'd died. Blown to pieces; barely enough left to bury. His room stayed empty, when the girls could have spread out into it. Instead, they remained in their loft room, like pigeons, sharing two vast old beds with their monthly cycles perfectly synchronised and their moods like a single tide of ebb and flow. But sometimes the others reached a point of saturation with Clemmie being the most beautiful, the most strange and often forgiven, the most talked about. Even Josie, with whom Clemmie had always had a special connection. Past that point they couldn't stand it any longer – they lost their individuality, like water droplets merging, and became a single entity of sibling rivalry that turned hard eyes on its mute sister. How long this would take to pass varied a great deal.

When it happened on Friday morning Clemmie was wise to it at once: Liz's glower, putting a crease between her dark brows; the way Mary snatched the hairbrush away when Clemmie reached for it; the way Josie rolled her eyes and ignored her when she signed good morning. It hurt, every time, but Clemmie knew she had no choice but to weather it; no choice but to wait for it to break. At breakfast, Mary put salt in Clemmie's tea instead of sugar, and handed her the cup with a smirk. Liz and Josie refused to 'hear' any of her requests for things to be passed – the gestures she used that the whole family knew. Then Liz grabbed Clemmie's favourite black kitten from her lap and dropped it out of the kitchen window, leaving it squeaking in fright on the yard. At this, Clemmie slapped her palm on the table top in distress, which made their father look up sharply.

'Was there a beetle, Clem?' Mary asked, innocently.

'You wenches pack it in,' said William Matlock. He was grizzled, weatherworn, his skin like creased bronze leather around a salt and pepper thatch of beard. His wife, the girls' mother, Rose, drifted from stove to table, bringing fried eggs and bread soaked in dripping, and slices of ham and cheese. There was grease in the whiskers on William's chin. Once, he'd been hard on the outside and soft on the inside – Clemmie remembered his rough hands under her arms, lifting her onto his shoulders when she was very small. But since Walter's death he seemed to have gone hard all the way through, and his teenaged daughters seemed to plague him like gnats around his head.

The kitchen table was scrubbed, bleached by years of sun and wear; every wall and low beam of the room was hung with tools and pots and utensils, some related to cooking, some to farming – sieves, drenching funnels, coils of wire, scythe blades, shears, rasps and branding irons. Some things were so rusted and ancient they'd been forgotten about, and colonised by spiders. The door was so often left open in the warm weather that a robin had nested in the top of an old jar of nails, and the hens wandered in and out, hopeful of scraps. The room faced south-west – the whole farm faced south-west – and was still shaded. By noon, sunlight would burnish every surface. Clemmie's hands smelled of milk, muck and coal tar soap – all of the girls' hands did, after morning milking.

They cornered her as she hunted for eggs in the small barn, where the hens nested in the hay and fouled it up with feathers and droppings. Mary and Josie wrestled her down and held her, and she fought them pointlessly for a while, her face pounding with blood and injustice. She knew nothing truly bad would happen, but still felt traces of unease and remembered fear – the man at the edge of the woods on the way to Ford, a year ago, holding her wrists in one hand as he groped her with the other, saying, *You want it, don't you, girl? Tell me I'm wrong.* She wondered if her sisters realised that they reminded her of this, as they gritted their teeth with the effort, and let their fingers bruise her arms. She kicked for a while but they stayed out of range, and when she fell still, Liz, with her cute pug nose and bow lips, knelt beside her with an egg in her hand.

'If you don't want this in your hair, you've only to say,' she said. She'd have to wash it out in a bucket of water; go through the painful process of teasing the knots out of her wet hair all over again, fall far behind with her chores, risk the back of William's hand.

'I think she wants it,' said Mary.

'You've only to say, Clem, if you don't,' Josie urged her.

'Perhaps she's tired of being so pretty,' said Mary.

'Perhaps she's tired of being so strange.'

'Or perhaps she loves it. Perhaps she loves being nature's child.' This was a term their teacher had used, during the few brief years they'd gone to school in Biddestone, as she'd petted Clemmie's pale frizz of hair and not scolded her silence or lack of attention.

'If she's *nature's* child then she can't be our sister, can she?' said Liz.

The egg slapped into her scalp with a wet crunch. Clemmie screwed her eyes tight shut as the gluey liquid rolled down towards them. She was aware of making a sound in her throat, a strangled sound which, in anyone else's mouth, would have come out as words; as *get off me*.

'Oh dear, what a mess,' said Liz, finding a glob of chicken shit on a wisp of hay and adding it to the egg. This done, the three girls went still, and silent. For a while the only sound in the barn was of their rapid breathing, and, from high in the haystack, the fussing of a worried hen. Then they let her go and stood back as she struggled to her feet. The four of them glared at one another and Clemmie felt the shift, as they watched her shake and the mess drip down her forehead – the subtle shift from triumph and spite to sheepish defiance, and the inevitable onset of contrition. Josie broke first, as she always did. She held out her hand to Clemmie, rolling her eyes and blowing a lock of mouse-brown hair off her forehead.

'Well, come on. I'll help you wash it out.' And, as always, Clemmie's anger disappeared in an instant. Feelings were like that with her – they flashed and fired, and then were gone again. Traces of the hurt stayed in her memory, but she forgave without hesitation.

'Well, you do ask for it sometimes, Clem!' Mary called after her, still angry, but mostly with herself by then. Later on they would be kind to her, to make it up; Mary would plait her hair before bed so it wouldn't knot; Josie would whisper secrets to her in the darkness, and make her laugh; Liz would leave her alone.

One of Clemmie's first memories was of being held in her mother's lap in front of the inglenook at Weavern Farm, in the capering light of a fire, listening to her soft humming, and then her saying, close to Clemmie's ear so no one else could hear:

'You cried when you were a baby, you know, my Clem.' Rose had wrapped strong arms around her, squeezing her sleepy body. 'The day you slithered out you set up a wail they heard in the mill, above the paper machine. So I know you've a voice in there, whatever folk say. And you'll use it when you're good and ready.' Clemmie remembered wanting to answer her, and the utter relief of not having to. She guessed, looking back, that she'd been around three or four years old, and that her lack of speech was becoming impossible to ignore. She remembered trying to talk, and something happening to the words between her mind and her mouth – a disconnection that made her impatient, then frantic, then panicky, and got worse the harder she fought. And the more she tried, the bigger the gap between her mind and her mouth got. It cleaved her tongue to the back of her teeth, and froze her lips, so that she ended up lowing like a cow, or making some other sub-human sound that made her schoolmates laugh but filled Rose's face with fear. And so she stopped. She didn't take to her letters at school – her mind was too ready to wander, and the teacher didn't try very hard with her. However carefully she copied out the alphabet the letters were often back to front; when put together into words they shifted and changed their shapes, *p* becoming *q*, *d* becoming *b*; and they jumped around, refusing to stay in order. Clemmie was mystified by how easily her classmates came to recognise patterns in them, when she could see none. So they sent her home at twelve, saying she was simple-minded, and left her with nothing but gestures to tell the world what she thought. What she wanted; what she didn't want. Clemmie didn't mind it, though. There was precious little she wanted, and the world seemed precious unconcerned to know her thoughts. From the age of five, when she had stopped trying to talk, until now, rising eighteen, Clemmie hadn't been troubled by any of it. But she was troubled now.

Once her hair was clean, and she'd listened to Josie prattle on about Clarence Fripp, an apprentice to the stonemason who was courting her with a kind of bawdy sweetness – all winks and laughs and suggestive remarks with his mates around him; all shyness and posies when he came to walk with her to church on Sundays – Clemmie finished her work as quickly as she could. A bucket full of eggs boxed for market; a shift at pressing Monday's washing; the cheeses turned; the butter pats scoured and a portion of the twenty pounds of butter, summer-yellow instead of winter-pale, that they would churn each week done. A hapless old hen who'd stopped laying needed to be drawn, plucked and jointed for stewing, and wringing its neck was the only thing Clemmie wouldn't do. She'd done it once, years before, and felt such a barb of sorrow as the inconsequential life ended in her hands that she'd burst into tears, and refused to do it ever since. It had been before Walter died, so her father had chucked her chin wryly, and called her a mollycoddle, and Mary had elbowed her aside declaring that she wasn't scared.

The work was never done, of course; there was always more. Mending, scrubbing, sweeping, shovelling; putting away, getting out. Walking the cows from one pasture to another, through air ripe with their flatulence; watering the vegetables in the kitchen garden and hoeing out the weeds; kneading bread dough; skimming curds from whey and bagging up fresh cheese to drain. And since there was always *something* to be done, Clemmie slipped away. The farm work was a constant stream that had flowed without pause through every one of her days, and to wait for a break in it would be like waiting for the sun not to rise. Breaks had to be made, else it was a long wait for the Sunday school summer outing; the harvest home; the Slaughterford revel.

She got up before dawn and slipped away into the half-light, as she had often times before, when the course of the By Brook was shown by the white ghost of mist hovering over the water. She took the hump-backed bridge across the river to the south of the farm, and then the path up onto the ridge. From the top of the hill she could look down at Weavern Farm: the squat farmhouse three storeys high, its top floor nestling into the mansard roof. The yard was surrounded on three sides by stone barns and stables and skillings, and opened south onto pasture dotted with cow pats. Behind the house were the vegetable patch and privy, and then the land rose steeply up to Weavern Lane. Her sisters and her mother often complained about how cut off they were – how they only ever heard news from the villages second- or third-hand, at church or via their neighbours at Honeybrook Farm; or when William had been to the pub – and that was rare enough. But Clemmie loved it. She wasn't interested in what other people did, generally; she liked the fact that there were no passers-by at Weavern – few callers, few intruders.

She'd all but stepped on the boy, at the edge of the steep woods near the Friends' chapel, opposite the mill. She'd had her eyes on the sky; he'd been hunkered down behind a thicket of birch saplings, with a young rabbit – just a kit really – kicking in his hand. He'd had two more rabbits, tied by their feet to a length of twine, slung over his shoulder. An intake of breath and they'd both frozen, eyes locked. Clemmie had recognised him as a Tanner from his cornflower eyes and long face – his cheekbones making hard, slanting lines beneath his skin – and she'd got ready to run. They were thieves and thugs, the Tanners. Everybody knew. They were drunks and cheats, and murderers, and there were more of them, connected by blood ties as tangled as a bramble thicket, than anyone but the Tanners themselves really knew. The chapel wasn't far from Thatch Cottage, where twelve members of one branch of the family lived, so Clemmie guessed he'd come from there. One of his uncles had beaten his wife to death, two years before, for no other reason than drink. The beatings were commonplace, but that time he'd delivered one too many blows when he should have left off. Gin had dethroned his mind, he said in court, but it wasn't much of a defence and they'd hanged him for it, not that he'd seemed to mind, by all accounts. Another one – a woman – was hanged for killing her baby with a draught of opium. She'd mixed it herself, from the pale pink poppies that grew along the top and shivered in the morning breezes. She said she'd only meant to keep it sleeping while she got on with her work.

Clemmie had looked down at the little rabbit. Kicking away in terror, every bit of its strength in every futile movement, ears flat to its neck. One of the rabbits hanging over the boy's shoulder had had a bubble of blood gleaming at its mouth, and a deep wound around its neck, but the little one had only been caught by the foot, so the snare hadn't killed it. The boy's fist around its neck had been filthy and thin, all tendons and smears, and something about it brought on a deafening roar of feeling in Clemmie – as though it were *her* hand about to crush the quickness of life from the animal. She'd seen enough animals go to their deaths and felt nothing much about it as long as she hadn't done the killing, but suddenly she'd felt the rabbit's manic heartbeat beneath its fur, and its unthinking terror; the briefness of its life and needlessness of its death – the butcher certainly wouldn't pay the usual sixpence for such a small one. Nothing on it to eat. She'd felt her eyes fill up and her mouth gape in horror, and hadn't been able to run even though he was a Tanner and she should have got away. But the boy had frowned slightly, never breaking off his gaze, and when the long moment had passed he'd lowered the rabbit to the ground and let it go. It had darted off into the undergrowth, leaving a dark pearl of blood behind on a burdock leaf. Then the boy had stood up, and she'd seen from his height and the bony width of his shoulders that he wasn't really a boy, but almost a man.

'I'm Eli,' he'd said. And when, a moment later, she'd found her feet and hurried away, she'd felt her own name poised behind her teeth. *I'm Clemmie*. She'd turned to look back before the trees hid him and he'd been in just the same spot, still watching.

That had been a week ago, and she hadn't seen him since. But she'd been looking, and the more she didn't see him, the more important it became that she should. As yet, she had no idea why this should be, but she had never worried much about the whys in life. She could picture his hand around the rabbit kitten so clearly – a starving, damaged hand. In an abstract way, she wondered if her need to see him again would be explained in the doing so. She walked a long route on high ground, going wide of the river and the mill's long tail race, coming down past Spring Cottage and crossing the river north of Rag Mill. This was far smaller than Slaughterford Mill: three slope-roofed buildings with whitewashed walls, housing a big iron boiler to cook down old hessian rope, twine and grain sacks, and a small waterwheel to run the beaters that would pummel them for days, reducing them to the pulpy half-stuff that could then be turned into brown paper packaging. Clemmie liked to watch the spoked hammers turning in the tanks, and the beater man resting a cane on the drive shaft and putting it to his head, to feel from the vibrations when the half-stuff was ready.

From Rag Mill she went on to the big mill, and walked from building to building, always staying outside, always peeping from a place of shelter. Trying to find him. Her stomach dropped oddly when she saw a tall, thin figure at the bottom of the big winch, fastening a bale of old paper scraps to be hoisted up to the sorting floor. But when she blinked, and looked again, it wasn't him. She peered into the bag room, and the canteen, and the machine spares sheds, and even spent a while watching the privies. There was no way to see into the machine room or beating house without going inside, and getting sent out with a flea in her ear. Frustrated, she slunk around the back of the old farmhouse and hunkered down in a spot beneath a window where she could see the workers coming into the yard. She picked daisies and threaded them into a garland, as the day got older and brighter, and heard Alistair Hadleigh come into the office to have his morning meeting with the foreman. They spoke of things that didn't interest her, but when Alistair Hadleigh's voice began to sound anxious, she paid more attention.

'But what about Douglas and Sons? Have they still not placed their usual order?'

'Not yet, sir. I wrote to them again last week, but they've yet to reply.'

'It'll be a close-run thing.' Mr Hadleigh sighed. There was a long pause. 'I'll find a way, never worry.'

'I don't doubt it, sir. This mill has run without pause for centuries. Run on a while longer, it surely shall.'

'Well spoken. Let's hope you're right.'

After that, they spoke more of customers and orders, of the problem of dye leaching into the By Brook downstream, and the poor quality of the last lot of rags from Bristol, and Clemmie stopped listening. As the sun began to burn her scalp through her hair, she got up and went back the way she'd come, towards Rag Mill. On the hill behind it, the brewery breathed out its ripe, yeasty smell, and alongside it was a long open storage shed, jammed to the rafters with rag scraps tied into bales, ready for pulping. As Clemmie headed for the trees beyond it all, she saw him at last. Tall, raw, angry. He came striding out of the mill and lit a cigarette, then held it between his teeth as he hauled out a bale and wrestled it into a handcart.

Clemmie took a step forward, then stopped. Eli Tanner turned the handcart and wheeled it back into the mill, cursing through his teeth as it stuck in the hard ruts left after winter. He was lanky and angular; his nose was crooked, and looked like it had been broken more than once. She thought of the boy's father, called Isaac but known simply as Tanner – patriarch of the lot who lived at Thatch Cottage.

He was a brute of a man, everyone knew. You didn't cross him, and even then it didn't make you safe. People edged back from him like sheep from a dog they didn't know. He sometimes worked as a strapper on one or other of the farms; sometimes in the mill, doing unskilled work – sorting scrap paper or rags, scrubbing out the stuff tanks between runs, stoking the boilers. He worked wherever he could get work, and until he was dismissed for fighting, or stealing, or drinking. Once for passing out drunk and letting the steam generator go out – something that ought never happen. Mrs Hancock at Honeybrook Farm swore that the last time he'd gone to church the water in the font had boiled. They said his wife had given birth to twins over the winter and he'd drowned the littlest like a rat in a barrel, because they had too many mouths as it was. Only it couldn't be proven because no one had attended the birth, or seen both babies, so Clemmie had no idea how the story got about. When she'd asked her mother – raised eyebrows, the tilt of her head that signalled a query – Rose had pursed her lips and said, *There's no smoke without fire*. Clemmie couldn't imagine what it must have been like to live beneath the cosh of such a man. Her own father could change the mood at Weavern Farm with a mere look or a word, and he never did anything worse than put the back of his hand across their faces now and then.

When Eli came back for another rag bale, he saw her. Clemmie twisted on the spot, uncertain of herself. Uncertain of him. With a glance back over his shoulder, Eli came across to her. He opened his mouth to speak but then didn't, and scowled instead. He looked so angry, and she wondered why. She would have been afraid of that anger if it hadn't been for the rabbit, and the conflict she saw in his every move and gesture – the suspicion, the doubt; of her, of himself. She wondered if his anger were somehow a means to survive.

'Hello,' he said at last, looking down at his bare feet, then up at her through the roughly cut ends of his fringe. He stank of the soda solution the rags cooked in. She raised her fingers to say hello back, and thought she saw disappointment in his face. As though he'd half hoped the stories weren't true, and she wasn't mute. She smiled a quick apology and saw him blush, and then how angry that made him. 'You're Clemmie Matlock. From down Weavern,' he said, curtly, and she nodded. 'I seen you before. Bringing the milk. And out walking, in the woods and that. I like it out there too. I like being out on me own.' He stood askance, his weight in his toes, his arms loose at his sides. She got the feeling that if she made too sudden a move he might run. Or lash out. His hands were as restless as his gaze; always moving. In the pause where she should have spoken the boiler roared inside the mill, and steam plumed from the chimney, and the beaters thudded and rumbled. A blackbird in the trees behind them sang as loudly as it could; bees hummed in the ivy and the sun streamed down, gold and green. Clemmie wished she could say, *Why did you let that rabbit go for me?*

'Eli, where's that bale?' came a shout from inside. Eli flinched, then glowered again. Clemmie wanted to put her hand on his arm, to still him. As soon as the thought occurred to her, it took over – sending its roots down into her bones. More than *anything*, she wanted to touch him, and still him. He looked back at her and shrugged one shoulder, shifting his weight.

'I'd say you're the loveliest thing I ever saw, Clemmie Matlock,' he said, and even then he sounded angry. As though she'd taken the advantage, or insulted him. 'I've got to get back to it. Maybe I'll see you again though. Out walking.' He pinched a fleck of tobacco from his lip and flicked it away, and then his hand hesitated in the air between the two of them, not dropping back to his side, not reaching for her. The tips of his fingers were stained, the nails all broken away, and they shook slightly. Almost too slightly to see, but Clemmie saw. 'Maybe I'll walk along this way when shift's over,' he said awkwardly, his cheeks burning. 'Towards Ford; about sundown.' Before he turned to go, Clemmie smiled again.

❧ ❧

Alistair Hadleigh came to find Pudding one morning a little later in the week, and she felt a familiar little flood of happiness at seeing him approach. He had a diffident way of walking that she loved – he never just came striding up, even though he owned the place, and was usually busy. Instead he joined his hands behind his back and moved with a measured step, looking around as though taking in some magnificent garden, not the muck heap or the pig skillings, or Jem Welch's baby leeks in their parade-day rows. She supposed it had to do with knowing that he owned it all, in fact – that whatever was happening, it would wait for him. Pudding's father always seemed to be in a hurry – except when he was with his patients. Dr Cartwright galloped between house calls, bag swinging; he galloped to his consulting room in Biddestone – pedalling frantically, puffing as he pushed his bike up Germain's Lane. Only once he was actually face to face with a patient was he calm and soothing – even if he hadn't quite caught his breath.

Pudding had been stropping the cob, Dundee: whacking a

folded cloth into his meaty parts, over and over, to promote circulation, muscle tone, and, as witnessed by the great clouds around them, beat some of the scurf out of his coat. It was probably unnecessary, given the amount of work the sturdy pony did, up and down the hills between Slaughterford and Chippenham, but it was what old Hilarius had taught Pudding to do, so it was what she did. She was pink, rather sweaty, and her nose was running, but there wasn't much she could do about that. Alistair smiled as he reached her. That was something else she liked about him. The sun was bright in his fair hair, and on the shoulders of his tweed jacket. He gave Dundee a hearty pat on his neck.

'Good morning, Pudding. Looks like you've your work cut out for you there,' he said.

'Rather. It's not very different to beating out a carpet, if truth be told,' she said.

'Indeed. Poor Dundee. A rather ignominious comparison.' Alistair rubbed the cob's neck for a while longer, and Pudding recognised his slight hesitation. Whenever he had something to say about Donny, he showed this gentle reluctance to do so.

'Donny was most upset, and very sorry about the roses, Mr Hadleigh. Really, he was,' Pudding rushed in, to help him.

'Of course he was. And, really, it's not important.' Alistair looked at her frankly. 'My wife doesn't seem to care for the gardens overly much. Chances are the bushes will have quite recovered by the time she goes out to see them. And Nancy only cuts them for my father's grave each week. She doesn't really like them for themselves, if that makes sense.' He sounded so sad that Pudding searched desperately for something cheering to say.

'Well, perhaps it's only roses Mrs Hadleigh doesn't care for? My aunt can't stand the things – they make her eyes stream. They were so bloody and swollen when I saw her last year, she looked diseased.' Pudding stopped, sensing she'd gone too far with this description.

'Yes? Poor woman,' Alistair murmured. 'Well, perhaps that's it. In any case, they'll all have gone over in another week to two, so Donny really needn't worry about . . . what happened, and neither should you.'

'Thank you, Mr Hadleigh. It's . . . jolly good of you to be so understanding.'

'As I've said, your brother will have work here as long as he wants it,' said Alistair, gently. 'I know something of what he went through, over there. In the war. I went through some of it myself . . . That he returned to you at all is miracle enough. One cannot expect . . . wholeness. One cannot expect there to be no changes in a man who has witnessed such things.'

'Thank goodness *you* came back whole, at least, Mr Hadleigh,' said Pudding, and then regretted it at once. Alistair's expression turned pained, and he didn't reply. 'I mean, where would Slaughterford have been if you hadn't? With the farm and the mill, and everything,' she carried on. 'That is to say—' But she couldn't think what to add, so she lapsed into a silence she wished she'd found sooner.

Dundee sighed the exaggerated sigh of a bored horse warming its rump in the morning sun. Sparrows hopped along the gutter of the cob house, chattering and scavenging for barley; the mills rumbled in the valley and something set the geese in the rickyard off into outraged honking.

'That'll be Keith with the letters,' said Pudding, pointlessly.

'I wondered if I might ask you a favour, Pudding,' said Alistair, at almost the same time. He looked sheepish, and Pudding blushed on his behalf, busying herself with the exact fold of her strop cloth to cover it.

'Of course, Mr Hadleigh. I'd be happy to help.'

'Irene – that is, Mrs Hadleigh – has found something rather

odd in the chimney of the old schoolroom. A doll, it appears to be. Which is odd, because there wasn't a little girl here for a hundred years until Aunt Nancy, and she's quite adamant that it isn't hers. Anyway. Verney Blunt and the Tanner lad think it might be some kind of votive.'

'A votive, I see,' said Pudding. 'What's a votive?'

'Well, something placed in the chimney as a kind of . . . offering, I suppose. A charm, or a spell.'

'Like the children's shoes you find in old thatch?'

'Exactly like that. Only the Tanner boy is saying she should take it to show his grandmother – apparently, she's some kind of expert on these things, and will be able to tell if it was left for good or evil, and can take steps against any . . . ill effects that may come from removing it.'

The glance Alistair gave her was steeped in embarrassment, and Pudding couldn't decide whether to pretend credence of such things when she had none, or to scoff when perhaps it would insult Mrs Hadleigh if she did.

'Well. I have heard that Ma Tanner's the person to see, about all kinds of things. You know that when people are ill and can't afford to call my father, they go to her instead – she mixes up all kind of things from herbs.' Pudding was careful not to betray her opinion of this in her tone, but her father had described the state of Teresa Hancock after she'd taken one of Ma Tanner's white bryony draughts to get rid of an unexpected baby. No more than fourteen, writhing like a snake on her sheets with her insides doing their very best to be on the outside. Her little boy, Micky, was now a sturdy toddler, spoiled rotten by everyone despite being born of shame and all that.

'Well, I'm quite sure it's all bunk. The witchery, I mean,' said Alistair.

'Oh, yes. Probably.'

'Only ... my wife has rather taken to the idea. Not of it being witchcraft, per se, but of going to see Mrs Tanner and asking her. The boy – Joseph – has her quite convinced. Of course, she doesn't know ...' He gave Pudding another careful glance. 'She doesn't really know about the Tanners. Their troublesome reputation. And I have rather been carping on at her to get out and meet some of the neighbours, you see. Nancy refuses point-blank to be involved in any way, which only seems to make Irene more determined ... Well, I was wondering, Pudding, whether you'd mind awfully going down with her? To the Tanners, I mean? I'm sure it won't be a lengthy visit. Safety in numbers, you understand; and they do know your face, at least.'

'Of course I will! I'd be happy to,' said Pudding. Alistair looked relieved, and she swelled inside.

She would, of course, have agreed to whatever he'd asked, even if it had been to roll in a muddy puddle, or spend the rest of the day hopping on one foot, or change her name to ... Well, in fact she couldn't really think of a worse name than Pudding, so changing it would have been a blessing. Her loyalty and obedience towards her employer were partly down to the way he was with Donny, and partly to do with the fact that he was constant – he'd been at Manor Farm since before she was born, like some benevolent overlord – which, of course, he was; at least to the men who worked in the mill. He was a steadying presence, and a reliable smile, and he was fairness and moderation when a lot of other people seemed to be shifting, and unsteady, and unpredictable. Even the people she loved best in the world.

'Thank you, Pudding. I'm most grateful,' he said, interrupting her thoughts. 'I'll be going into Chippenham this afternoon, to talk to the bank, so if you could have Dundee hitched up by two, I'd be much obliged.'

'Of course, Mr Hadleigh.'

'Then perhaps you and Mrs Hadleigh could go visiting, after lunch?' He turned to go. 'Ah, yes, Pudding, I meant to ask after your parents ... Are they well?'

'Oh,' said Pudding. The words *perfectly well* died on her lips. She found it impossible to lie to Alistair Hadleigh, and most especially impossible when he would know the lie at once. At Easter, he'd greeted Louise Cartwright outside church, as he greeted everyone – holding out his hand, saying her name. Pudding's mother had backed away abruptly, shaking her head in panic, not recognising him, or the situation, or what was expected of her. She'd worn an expression of complete perplexity throughout the service, as though the vicar had delivered it in Latin, and hadn't sung any of the hymns. Everyone had seen; everyone knew. Things amiss. 'Muddling through,' she said instead, trying to sound easy. She couldn't bear the pity in Alistair's eyes – it seemed to melt all her strength away, and as though he realised it, he backed away at once.

'Splendid,' he said, nodding. 'Jolly good. Well, Pudding, back to work for both of us. And ... should you need anything ...'

'Thank you, Mr Hadleigh. In fact, I could rather do with a new head for the yard broom,' she said, knowing that this was not at all what he'd meant.

When Pudding was about five years old, back before the war, the Hadleighs had invited Biddestone Sunday School, which most of the Slaughterford children attended, to have its summer picnic in the great barn at Manor Farm. It had become clear that a spell of wet, dreary weather that had been slouching over Wiltshire for a fortnight wasn't going to shift. The children, young and old, had been generally downhearted to begin with, since the picnic usually involved a long ride in a horse-drawn bus, with wooden benches down the sides and a canvas roof, either to the station for a trip to the seaside, or to some high hill miles away, with a view they didn't know, to have their games and sandwiches in the waving grass of a meadow. Blind Man's Buff and Thread the Needle; I Sent a Letter to my Love and Twos and Threes. Now they just had a short walk up the road to a muddy farmyard they all knew anyway, where the geese hissed and ran at them, and the collie dogs nipped at their calves, trying to herd them. And it wasn't even lambing season.

The cowslip posies in their best straw hats got damp and bedraggled on the way. Admittedly, few of them had ever been inside the great barn, but the general consensus was that a barn was more or less a barn. But the Hadleighs, particularly Alistair, had done their best to make it magical. Bunting and paper lanterns, and the trestle tables used for the church fête covered with checked cloths, and cream from that morning's milking for the scones, and – a thrill beyond everyone's ken – ice cream from the farm's own kitchen, rich and flecked with strawberries. Disconsolate foot scuffing had turned to excited fidgeting. The great barn was ancient, from some earlier time when Slaughterford and its mills were granted to the monastery at Farleigh Hungerford by a king with the deeply un-kingly name of Stephen, and a tithe was collected there from every farm and mill. The roof soared, its hammer beams twisted with age; it had wood-mullioned windows eaten away by beetles, and crumbling stone walls that nevertheless gave the impression of being immortal, indestructible. There was at least a century's worth of farm junk built up at one end, which had been pushed back as far as possible and strewn with more bunting. Doves roosted in its dusty entanglements, cooing and flapping at the intrusion of twenty-three children, in various states of cleanliness, driven wild by more sugar than they usually had to eat in a month.

In spite of being the doctor's daughter, and therefore higher up than the farm and mill children, Pudding was always the butt of jokes because she was so round and so plain. She'd felt the disappointment of not getting out of Slaughterford particularly keenly, and consoled herself by touring the tables, licking every last smear of ice cream from the bowls and picking the last crumbs from the plates. She was well-liked, since she was cheerful and eager to please, and had no trouble making friends – even with the little Tanner girl, Zillah, who was so skinny that her arms at the shoulder weren't as thick as Pudding's wrists, and who had been known to kick and bite with very little provocation. One of the farm boys from Ford, Pete Dempsey, was chubby too, but instead of being Pudding's ally he was usually the first to start the teasing – perhaps to be sure none of it came his way.

When Miss Wharton announced Pig-in-the-Middle, and asked who would be the first pig, everyone laughed and pointed at Pudding. When Nancy Hadleigh called them to attention and demanded to know who had been into the back kitchen and taken half a loaf of bread from the crock, everyone laughed and pointed at Pudding, even though it was far more likely to be Zillah Tanner (and it was – the loaf dropped out from under her skirt as they trooped from the barn at the end of the afternoon). And when they began the treasure hunt and Pudding got stuck between the broken slats of an old manger, nobody helped her, but stood laughing instead as she struggled and bruised herself, and tears drenched her scarlet face. They stood and they laughed until Alistair Hadleigh appeared, forced the slats wider so Pudding could wriggle free, then picked her up and set her on her feet – not without effort – and brushed the dirt and chaff from her dress.

'There, now. All pretty again,' he said, even though there was snot running down her chin, and her hair had come out of its ribbons. 'Shame on you, children,' he said to the others, who shuffled crossly. 'You must learn to be kinder to one another – especially today, when you've all been having such a lovely time.'

Her classmates' eyes went wide as they absorbed this reprimand. Alistair Hadleigh was the most important man in the village. Alistair Hadleigh was clean and handsome and rich. Alistair Hadleigh employed, one way or another, near enough every one of their fathers. Alistair Hadleigh had picked Pudding up and tidied her dress and called her pretty, and she loved him without question from then on. The other children spent the rest of the day being as conspicuously nice to Pudding as they could, even though by then Mr Hadleigh was nowhere around. The spell didn't last, and they soon went back to laughing at her, but it didn't matter. Pudding's heart was his.

She was brought out of this reverie by going into the tack room and finding Hilarius inside, sitting on a stool by the stove in spite of the heat, with an open book in his hands. He never normally came to the tack room, since the work harnesses were all kept in the great barn, and she wondered if he'd run out of leather soap or clean cloths, or needed to borrow the hole punch. Then she saw that the book he'd been reading was her copy of *Murder Most Foul*, which she'd brought with her to read on her tea break. Pudding was ashamed to admit to herself, just then, that she hadn't supposed Hilarius knew how to read.

'Oh! Hello, Hilarius. You made me jump,' she said. The old man nodded and stood up. He frowned, but he didn't look annoyed – more puzzled by something, or troubled. 'Is everything all right?'

'Ar,' said Hilarius, distractedly. His accent was unique to him; an odd mixture of Wiltshire and something else – something foreign, left over from the land of his birth. Pudding had asked, once, where he was from, but he'd let his eyes rebuke her, and had changed the subject in a way that had made her feel very rude, so she hadn't asked again. He closed the book and turned it over in his hands, frowning down at it, his face as cracked as oak bark.

'What is it, Hilarius?'

''Ee shouldn't read such things,' he said, putting the book down on the stool behind him. It was an odd thing to do; Pudding had expected him to hand it back to her. He stood there, between her and the book, and folded his arms as if guarding her from it. 'Bad things'll come to bide in 'ee.'

'Oh, you mean it'll give me nightmares? Yes, my mum says the same thing whenever I read the dreadfuls. But don't worry, it doesn't seem to happen to me,' said Pudding, brightly, to reassure him. She smiled but old Hilarius kept his frown. He looked past her, down at the floor, and there was a long pause that Pudding wasn't sure she should break.

''Ee shouldn't read the likes o' it, girl,' said Hilarius, then nodded as though he'd said his piece, and went out. Feeling a bit guilty about it, even though there was no reason at all for him to be upset, Pudding tucked the book away out of sight, and tried to remember why she'd gone into the tack room in the first place.

        ❧ ☙

Irene had wrapped the fragile, dirty doll in an old scarf, and was being as careful as she could not to break it. Truthfully, her interest in it might well have waned as soon as it had sparked in spite of the vehemence with which Nancy had scoffed, and the look of genuine consternation on Joseph Tanner's face, if it hadn't been for her own odd intuition about it. The feeling wouldn't let her drop it – it nagged at the back of her mind like the tiny glimpse of a memory from earliest childhood; amorphous and tantalising. She couldn't put her finger on what it was, and didn't know what she wanted to know about the doll, only that she wanted to know *something*. 'Our Ma'll see it right,' Joseph Tanner told her, quietly, when Nancy was out of earshot. As if determined to offer her help he was sure she was going to need, despite the impropriety of it. It had felt like the kind of offer that would only be made once, and then never again. There was something compelling about that, and about Joseph Tanner, with his nervous energy and his dark, dirty hair.

Nancy gave one last opinion on the mission as Irene came downstairs after lunch, dressed for her outing in her least city-like clothes – a beige skirt and a long ecru jacket, and her sturdiest leather shoes. Nancy was wearing breeches and a linen shirt; buttoned in, creaseless. She swept her gaze over Irene's outfit before she spoke.

'I feel I ought to warn you, since my nephew is too soft to speak ill of anybody,' she said, 'the Tanners are a bad lot. Thieves and murderers, for the most part – including the women. You've managed to select the one set of people it most ill-behoves you to become acquainted with.' She raised her eyebrows in that way she had, and Irene tried to see the least bit of good humour in her face. Nancy with her straight jaw and her diamond-hard eyes.

'Well, I'm sure they won't murder me just for knocking at their door. And I do have an invitation,' she said, trying to sound unconcerned. Nancy replied with a quiet scoff.

'They just might, you know,' she said. Still no humour. Irene's resentment flared.

'Well, Pudding Cartwright will protect me. Or, if needs be, I can use her as a barricade,' she said, and regretted it at once. Nancy's gaze hardened even further.

'That girl works hard, tells the truth, and carries her entire family. You'd do well to emulate her, Irene, rather than mock her.' She turned on her heel and left the room before Irene could retract the remark. It was not the kind of thing she would ever say, normally. Heat bloomed across her face and neck, and as she stared at Nancy's retreating back she realised that she had no idea who she was any more. It was the loneliest feeling.

Pudding Cartwright talked a lot, as she stomped alongside Irene. *Stomped* was the best word Irene could find for the way the girl moved – it was a kind of economical, ground-covering, wide-set stride; entirely unfeminine, and not unlike the horses she so doted on. She wore long rubber boots caked in mud, and didn't bother to step around puddles or piles of manure in the lane, so that she frequently drew ahead and had to turn and wait as Irene caught up.

'Has Mr Hadleigh told you how the village got its name?' she asked, as Irene walked gingerly down the steepest section of lane from the farm. She wasn't used to the feel of dust and pebbles beneath her shoes; wasn't used to slopes that hadn't been fashioned into steps. The day was warm but overcast, the air humid and thick with smells – Irene couldn't remember London ever smelling so much, even when the tide was out. It smelled . . . alive, and not necessarily in a good way. It was like being breathed on by some huge animal.

'Something about Vikings, wasn't it?' she said, distractedly.

'That's right. Shall I tell you?' said Pudding, proceeding to do so without waiting for Irene to answer, and obviously enjoying the gorier bits of the battle story. Irene stopped listening. She was trying to think about Fin, trying to remember exact words he had said and the exact way he had said them, trying to see his face without Serena's appearing to obliterate him – her eyes with their slight slant, her teeth glittering, and hidden things flickering inside her like flames.

'And then the river ran red with the blood from so many horrendous wounds and dead men,' said Pudding, and Irene failed to think of an appropriate response. 'Of course,' the girl went on, 'some people also say that *sleight* means water meadow in some ancient language, and that's the origin of Slaughterford. But I like the river-of-blood story better, don't you? I do admire your hair, you know, Mrs Hadleigh. I tried mine cropped like that last year but it looked frightful. Everybody said so. But yours looks simply perfect.'

'Thank you,' said Irene.

'You know – it might be an idea to pop into Mrs Glover's here and get something to give the Tanners,' said Pudding, halting beside some steep steps that led up the bank to a crooked stone cottage.

'Get them something?' Irene echoed, confused. She looked at the cottage and saw the downstairs window thrown wide open, and a hand-painted sign propped outside, reading *Groceries*. This was what passed for shopping in Slaughterford. Pudding thumped up the steps and stuck her head through the window.

'Shop!' she called, loudly, then turned back to Irene again. 'Yes – doesn't matter what, really. They have little enough of most things. Some soap, perhaps?'

'Wouldn't that be a little tactless?'

'Would it? Oh, yes – I see what you mean. Not soap then. Some tea, and barley sugars for the littlest ones. Or biscuits? Mind you, Trish Tanner makes the best lardy cake you've ever tasted. She sells it at Biddestone fête sometimes; we might get a slice if we're lucky. Mrs Glover had some lovely boxes of

Huntley and Palmer's last week, though, with Jackie Coogan on the tin. Dad took us all to the cinema in Chippenham last month, to see *The Kid*. Have you seen it? I expect so – I expect you went to the pictures all the time in London, didn't you, Mrs Hadleigh? You must miss it terribly.'

'I do,' said Irene. It was finally something she could say with feeling.

'But you gave it all up for Mr Hadleigh,' said Pudding, with a kind of wistfulness. 'It's all terribly romantic. That he swept you off your feet like that.'

'Yes, I suppose so,' said Irene, sensing Pudding's disappointment when she didn't elaborate.

In fact, her courtship with Alistair had been far more a case of him picking her up and setting her back on her feet, rather than sweeping her off them. It had begun the first and only horrible time her parents had induced her to go out with them after it had all happened, after everybody knew. They decided to put on a front, to feign unconcern until unconcern could be achieved. Irene remembered the looks and the laughs, the muttered remarks, the invisible circle around their table that nobody was willing to cross. She remembered mottled colour on her mother's rigid cheeks, and the flush of alcohol across her father's; not enough air and time grinding to a halt, and then Alistair appearing, crossing the line and asking Irene to dance. The horror of it all had been so loud inside her head that she was up and in his arms before she knew what had happened, or whether she had spoken. His hold around her offered some protection but she'd still felt naked. Her steps had been stiff and clumsy.

'Just keep dancing, dear girl,' Alistair had said, as a ripple of laughter chased them across the floor. 'Forget them. People are quick to enjoy the misfortunes of others; it doesn't make them right.'

'Please,' she'd whispered back, wretchedly. 'Please, can't I just leave?'

'Yes. Perhaps you shouldn't have come out so soon, but you must finish this dance first. Don't let them beat you.' If it hadn't been for his hands, his arms, holding her, she'd have fled and caused another scene.

He walked them out after that, and came to call on her the next day. This had been back in March, and there'd been sunshine on the window with a promise of spring at last. It had made him seem bright as he'd crossed the room to her, like he'd brought the light with him, and Irene had turned her face to the glass because it was too much. She wanted Fin. She wanted to be somewhere else – anywhere else – with him. She wanted to understand. Those were the only things she wanted. Alistair had sat down across from her, with his trousers riding up over his ankles and his gloves in his hand, and she'd felt his optimism, his care and his regard, as he glowed there, in the corner of her eye. She wanted none of it – rejected it outright, and ignored him when he asked how she was. Surely he would see, when he looked again, how worthless she was. How lost. And then his pointless visit would come to a merciful end.

'I learnt a lot of things during the war, Irene,' he said, after a pause. 'Most of them of no use whatsoever. But there's one thing I can't unlearn, even if I wanted to, and it's that life is very short, and very precious, and if we can't find a way to be happy in the one brief span we're allowed, then there really isn't a lot of point to any of it.' He paused again and Irene finally turned to look at him. He smiled slightly, kindly, and she knew he lived in a different world to the one she did. 'So I've a proposition for you, and I don't want you to think about it too much. We get so tangled up in knots, we humans, trying to think everything through, trying to guess at outcomes we can't possibly know. So please just listen. I adore you. Marry me.'

Irene thought she'd heard him wrong, but then an odd noise burst out of her mouth, which might have been the mangled beginnings of a laugh – at him, at herself, at the mad words he'd just spoken. She stared at him for a while, from what felt like many miles away, and decided there and then not to inflict herself on this absurd, kindly lunatic, who clearly had no idea what he was saying. When she shook her head he smiled again, sadly, and looked down at his hands.

'No,' she said. It was all she could find to say. Alistair stood to leave.

'You need to get away from here. You need to start again. You need rest, and someone to care for you.'

'No, I don't.'

'Only until you're feeling better. Only until . . . the shock has passed. Because none of it matters, Irene. None of it really *matters* – don't you see? What people say, and what they think. I've seen it so many times . . . The absurdity of it all. Most people don't have the first idea how fragile it all is. How fragile *they* are. The only thing is to be kind, and to love, before it's all over. Marry me, and I'll show you.'

'No,' Irene murmured, exhausted by him, deadened to it all. 'I did love. I do love. But I don't love you.' She saw him wince a little, and swallow.

'I know you don't. But perhaps – for now at least – it might suffice that I love you. That I want to help you.'

'If you want to help me,' she said, turning her face away again, 'then leave me be.'

The Tanners lived in the only thatched cottage remaining in Slaughterford; the others had been stone-tiled as the straw had rotted off, or in some cases covered with tin. It was entirely unadorned; a rectangular box of a place, none too large. As close as it was to the mill, the rumble of machinery was constant. The thatch looked dark and mouldy, even now in summer; the cobbled path that ran around the base of the walls was furred with moss, and the yard was an obstacle course of junk – boxes and crates, broken wheels and tools, rolls of wire, piles of stone and tiles. Three small children were playing on a simple rope swing hanging from an elm tree behind the house, and as she and Pudding walked up to the front door Irene felt eyes following them. She looked around and saw a boy of about six, peering out at them from the makeshift den of a tea crate, his eyes glossy in the shadows. Irene repositioned the basket in which she carried the doll, and felt uneasy. She had no idea what she was going to say, and hoped that Pudding would fill in the gaps. It seemed entirely likely that she would.

'I've never been inside this house before. I think it might be the only one in the village I haven't been into, in fact, at one time or another,' said Pudding, excitedly, as though this was what passed for an adventure in Slaughterford.

'But I thought you knew them? And they knew you?' said Irene.

'Well, sort of.' Pudding led the way to the door and knocked without the least hesitation. Irene thought back over what Nancy had told her, and felt her unease grow. Pudding lowered her voice. 'Mostly from all the many stories one hears. Everyone knows everyone here, but the Tanners aren't the overly sociable sort. Most people steer well clear of them. They ought to know who I am, at least. Oh, hello,' she greeted the thin, grubby girl who opened the door. 'I'm Pudding Cartwright, the doctor's daughter, and I've brought Mrs Hadleigh here to see Ma. Joseph invited us, so hopefully she's expecting us. And we've brought you some biscuits.' Without a word, the thin girl, who was perhaps only thirteen or so, stepped back to admit them. Irene's heart began to pound.

Inside, the cottage seemed bigger than it looked from outside. It was split into two rooms, the first leading to the second; from the first, steep stairs led to the upper floor, and in the second a large iron range was running at full chat, so that the heat was suffocating. The girl led them through to this second room, where a smell unlike anything Irene had met before was rising with the steam from a huge crock pot on the stove. In one corner, an ancient man watched from a truckle bed, with a thin blanket pulled up around him. Irene risked only the briefest glance at him – a fleeting impression of sunken cheeks and eyes, wisps of grimy white beard, hands of a size and strength that even age couldn't wither, and the emanation of a powerful hostility, incongruous given his obvious frailty. At least eight other people were arranged around the room – three barefooted children sat on the floor in watchful silence; two older teenaged girls were at a butcher's block, skinning rabbits and adding the iron smell of blood to the air. An older woman was sitting near the bedridden grandfather, mending a shirt, and the person Irene took to be Ma Tanner was seated in regal solitude in a carver chair nearest to the stove, her skin waxy and flushed. Pudding and Irene approached uncertainly, and under the scrutiny of so many eyes, Pudding turned pink.

Little light penetrated, since the windows were hung with thick felt that was obviously awkward to tie back; and what light there was was greenish from the algae on the glass. It could have been any hour of the day in there, any season, and Irene wished more than anything to go back in time and undo the stupid decision to come. Even Pudding had gone quiet, and was looking around the room with a slightly frantic smile, her hands continually fussing and smoothing her clothes. Irene took a deep breath and stepped in front of her chaperone. She hated her own fear of people, and where it had led her; it was running though her every fibre just then, but she rejected it.

'I'm Irene Dal— Hadleigh,' she said, stumbling slightly over her maiden name, Dalby. She carried on quickly, but the old woman in her carver chair noticed the mistake. 'How do you do?'

'Well enough,' said Ma Tanner, in a voice far more melodious than Irene had been expecting, and not in the least bit eldritch.

'I've come to show you a thing that was found in one of the chimneys at the farm. Your boy Joseph thought it might be significant.'

'Yes, he said you'd be along. New bride, aren't you? Not yet truly wed, are you? Not wed with your heart,' said Ma, peering up at Irene in a relentless way that wasn't unkind. Irene stared back at her, at a loss. Behind her, she felt Pudding shift her weight, and could practically feel the girl's curiosity burning through the back of her jacket. The old woman grunted, and smiled. 'Not like the doctor's lass, there.'

'Who, me?' said Pudding, in an overeager way. Ma Tanner's smile got wider.

'Perhaps you'd like to see what was found?' said Irene, hearing how cold she sounded.

'Yes, your ladyship,' said Ma Tanner, with a chuckle. One of the teenaged girls with the bloody hands scowled at Irene, but the old woman shifted up straighter in her chair, her hands gripping the arms in obvious interest. Her outfit was an amalgamation of garments from several prior generations, patched in and repaired; layers of rough cotton, lace and linen beneath a green woollen shawl. How she hadn't expired from the heat, Irene couldn't guess; a trickle of sweat was twisting down her own spine, and she longed to take her jacket off. But she stepped closer to the glowing range and took out the doll, unwrapping it carefully.

More bits of dirt and thread dropped off the doll as the old woman turned it over in her hands. She brushed them off her lap and peered at it, screwing up her eyes so that her face followed, crumpling like paper in a fire. For a while, the only sound in the room was the scrape and slither of the rabbit carcasses, and the rattle of air behind the old man's ribs. The attention of everybody in the room was fixed upon the old woman and the doll in the ratty blue dress. The fire in the range seethed; the pot bubbled; one of the children had a perpetual sniff. Pudding, who looked mesmerised, stepped forwards next to Irene to see better. Nobody spoke, and the moment dragged on. The old woman sucked her lower lip. The smell in the room made it hard to breathe; Irene took shallow sips of the air until she began to feel dizzy.

'Pinned up the chimney, or just tucked behind the baffle?' said the old woman eventually, so suddenly that they all jumped.

'I don't know. By the time I saw it, it was on the floor in a mess of soot,' said Irene.

'Hm. Probably just hidden up behind the baffle then.'

'Does it matter?'

'It might.' Ma Tanner went back to her silent contemplation, and the rest of them went back to waiting, and Irene's impatience to leave grew and grew. She fought to stifle it.

When the front door banged open again they all jerked – all except Ma Tanner. Three men came into the room, and Irene felt Pudding trying to be smaller. Two were just lads, perhaps not yet twenty, but the other, Irene guessed, was Tanner himself, the master of the house. He was tall, not thickset but broad at the shoulder, with a kind of lean, knotted strength to his frame. His face was a mass of suspicious frown lines, and there was something sour about the set of his mouth. His nose and cheeks were mapped with the broken red veins of a heavy drinker, and his hair had plenty of grey through the dark. The lads flanking him were thin and restless, their eyes watchful and angry; one had a split lip surrounded by livid purple bruising.

'Who's this, Trish?' Tanner demanded, nodding at Irene but addressing the middle-aged woman at her mending.

'The new Mrs Hadleigh, down from Manor Farm,' said the woman, in a voice entirely without tone.

'Is it now?' he said, his expression turning even uglier – suffusing with something like contempt. Irene felt the weight of it and refused to buckle. She lifted her chin, but couldn't quite bring herself to say 'How do you do' into the face of such open hostility. 'And what does the new Mrs Hadleigh want with us?'

'Peace, man, she's come to see me,' said Ma Tanner, and the man was stilled, though he didn't seem to like it. Then he caught sight of the doll the old woman was holding, and his face changed at once.

He crossed to the old woman and reached for it as though he would take it from her, then seemed to change his mind. He began to turn away but only made it halfway before something stopped him. He couldn't take his eyes from the dirty, broken doll. Ma Tanner squinted up at him, speculatively.

'Where in hell did that come from?' Tanner asked. His voice was a growl, but it shook.

'Up at the farm,' said Ma, always watching him, never blinking. 'Hidden away a good long while. In a chimney.' Pudding and Irene exchanged a glance of bafflement at the scene.

'*Garn!*' a voice said suddenly, and, startled, Irene turned to find the old man glaring at her from under his blanket. She blushed, embarrassed both by his sudden rousing and because she didn't understand him. He raised a thick, trembling finger and pointed it squarely at her. 'Garn, and get!' he said, and this time she understood. She was being told to leave. Pudding pulled at Irene's sleeve.

'Should we go?' said Irene, to Ma Tanner, but the old woman was still staring at her son, and he was still staring at the doll from the chimney. A moment later Tanner broke off his study to glare at them with such ferocity that they both took a step backwards.

'Peace, man,' said the old woman again, but she handed the doll back to Irene. 'You'd best be on your way with this, Mrs Hadleigh. Pudding. Take it and go.'

'But . . . what is it? What does it mean?' said Irene, bewildered.

'It's no votive, no spell, so don't worry about that. As to what it means . . .' She looked up at her son again, who was standing stock-still, staring into the shadows in the corner of the room as though stupefied. Ma settled back into her chair and said, without expression: 'It means change is coming.'

4
Touched

Alistair's best friend, Charles McKinley, lived with his sister Cora and their elderly father, Gerry, in Biddestone Hall, a sprawling Tudor house of gables and mullions and creaking doors. It sat back from the village green in Biddestone, behind gates and a high stone wall. The front door was lit by a pair of torches as Alistair and Irene climbed down from the Stanhope, and two of the McKinley footmen appeared to take the horse and usher them inside. It felt odd to be in evening dress. Irene's shoes pinched across her toes in that way she remembered so well. She hadn't worn her fox stole since London; hadn't worn her debutante diamonds since London. Since her wedding day, in fact, when she'd presented herself to Alistair with the numb, guilty sense that she'd sold him something broken; something faulty, that wouldn't work. The trouble was, she knew that Alistair had known it already. And he'd wanted her anyway.

'Don't be nervous, Irene,' he told her softly, as the door of Biddestone Hall swung open. He kissed the back of her hand. 'They're jolly nice, and they're going to love you.' An immaculate butler admitted them, but a woman of perhaps thirty appeared behind him at once, giving the immediate impression of huge eyes and a huge smile, with perhaps slightly too much tooth and gum. Her chestnut hair was close-cropped, with a wave; she had a long neck and long arms, and the overall effect was instantly appealing.

'There you are, Alistair!' She gave him a hug on the door-step.

'How are you, Cora? You look ravishing,' said Alistair.

'Oh, you know – simply *melting* in the heat. Thank heavens for the pool. And you must be Irene.' Her handshake was hearty. 'I just *know* we're going to be the best of friends,' she said, with such bulletproof conviction that Irene immediately wondered who she meant to convince. Cora was a war widow, Alistair had told her; she'd married a childhood sweetheart called Bertram, only for him to be shot dead on more or less the same day he'd arrived in Belgium. Since then, she hadn't found anybody eligible to marry amongst the ranks that stumbled back from the war. But within half an hour of seeing how she beamed at Alistair, and glowed whenever he looked at her, and laughed his way, Irene had an idea about where Cora might have put her stock.

The inside of Biddestone Hall was as imposing as the outside – all Turkmen carpets, gleaming silver, mirrors and liveried servants. Gerry, into his eighties, was a quiet, dignified sort of man, clearly quite deaf, and Charles was as vivacious as his sister; a handsome man, if running a little to fat. They ate an enormous dinner, served at one end of a vastly long dining room table.

'The next time you come we'll invite more people,' said Cora, leaning towards Irene. 'But this time, we wanted you all to ourselves, didn't we, Charlie?' Irene smiled, but couldn't think of a reply. She wondered whether Alistair had told them she was shy, or unwell, or otherwise feeble, and felt small. She dropped her eyes to her salmon mousse and kept them there for a while. But Cora was undeterred. 'Tell me everything about London – I do so miss it, between seasons! Not that it isn't divine down here in Wiltshire, and nobody in their right mind would want to be in town in this weather. But one does feel so out of it, after a while. Have you met the St Iveses yet? Johnny and Maria? Alistair! What *have* you been doing, closeting her away like this? Their house near Malmesbury is *the* place to be when it's this hot. We're going for a Friday to Monday next week.'

'Cora, take a breath, old thing, and let Irene fit a word in,' said Charles, laughing.

'Oh – am I talking too much? I do do that, it's true,' said Cora, not in the least abashed.

Irene was perfectly happy to let them talk and, like Gerry, contribute little. There was little she could contribute, since they'd clearly been primed not to question her about her London life, or her swift departure from it, and she didn't know any of the people or places they wanted to talk about. Gerry met her eye over dessert and gave her a benign, tolerant smile, as Cora dissolved into laughter at the shared memory of a Christmas party when they'd all been in their teens, and Charles had drunk too much rum punch, and they had to hide him behind the curtains until he was less of a giveaway. After the meal the men went off together to smoke and play poker.

'Not that it's worth it, with Alistair. I can never get your husband to bet more than a shilling, Irene,' said Charles.

'He's exaggerating,' said Alistair. 'Will you be all right?' he said to her, quietly. Irene had little choice but to nod.

'Of course she will,' said Cora, taking Irene's arm and giving Alistair a knowing look. When the men had gone she toned it down a little, draped herself languidly over a sofa and lit a cigarette. 'Good,' she said. 'Now we can get to know each other properly.'

'Yes,' said Irene, more stiffly than she'd intended. Cora took a deep breath of smoke and blew it out through painted lips.

'So tell me, how are you getting along with Aunt Nancy?' There was a definite glint in her eye, but Irene couldn't tell, yet, if it were directed at Nancy or at herself.

'Nancy is . . .' she began, thinking carefully. 'I don't think Nancy has warmed to me terribly much, yet.'

Cora tipped back her head and laughed delightedly.

'I should think that's the understatement of the century!' she said. 'Gosh, I do feel for you, really. I'm sure Alistair would have been married five times over by now if it wasn't for Aunt Nancy. I know of at least one girl she chased off.'

'She's like a mother to him, I suppose. And rather picky.'

'She's a demon! And don't pretend otherwise,' said Cora, frowning at Irene's reticence. 'Why else would it take a sweetie like Alistair so long to find a wife? We were all *terrified* of Nancy as children – I still am a bit, I don't mind admitting. And as for her being like his mother,' she tipped her head to one side, and cocked an eyebrow, 'you don't know how right you are.'

'How do you mean?'

'Well.' Cora shook her head and reached for her brandy. 'Far be it from me to spread scurrilous rumours. But perhaps I will, just this once.' She chuckled. 'You know Alistair's father was Nancy's twin brother? They were inseparable as children, by all accounts – nothing unusual there. But I've heard it remarked upon that perhaps Nancy remained a trifle *too* devoted to her brother, as they got older. She only let him get married because it was that or lose the estate, since he'd all but gambled the whole lot away, and Tabitha Hadleigh brought her whopping inheritance with her from America – her parents owned half the goldmines in California. And when Tabitha died Nancy came back in a flash, and devoted her whole life to taking care of her brother and her new nephew. Almost more like a wife than a sister.'

'You can't mean to say . . .' Irene trailed off, aghast. Cora waved a hand through the cloud of smoke around her head.

'Oh, nothing *biblical*, I'm sure. But more than one new

acquaintance mistook them for husband and wife until it was pointed out that they were brother and sister. And since old Alistair died, your Alistair has been the sole focus of all of her energies.' Irene didn't miss the slightly strained way in which Cora said 'your Alistair'. 'So I'm not at all surprised that she hasn't taken to you.' Irene wondered how much of what had gone on in London the McKinleys knew, and whether Cora knew that her disgrace formed part of Nancy's distaste for her.

'I don't think she ever will,' she said, heavily.

'No,' said Cora, not without sympathy. 'I fear you've your work cut out for you there.' She swilled her brandy around in its huge glass. 'But if any man were worth putting up with her for, it's Alistair, isn't it?' She leapt up before Irene could reply. 'Come on. Why should the boys have all the fun? Do you fancy a swim?'

'I . . . I haven't a costume.'

'Me neither. Don't worry, it's dark as pitch out there. Come on, it'll be a hoot!'

In the end, Cora swam and Irene perched on the side of a steamer chair, smoking, watching moths batter themselves against the lamps and the way the profusion of stars turned the night sky mauve. The air filled with the smell of swimming pool water on still-warm stone. It was a dream of a night, too benign and beautiful for words, but Irene noticed the way it failed to move her, and felt a kind of creeping despair that she would never feel anything properly, ever again. She'd expected Alistair to be half-cut by the end of the evening, but he seemed quite sober. He put his jacket around her shoulders on the way home, and his arm around that, and held the reins easily in one hand.

'Was it all right?' he said. 'Did you like them?'

'I think it would be impossible for anybody not to like them,' she said, and he smiled.

'I'm glad.'

'How did you do at poker?'

'Oh, not very well. I never do, that's why I refuse to bet real money. I really only play to keep Charles company. It's one way in which I'd prefer not to follow in my father's footsteps,' he said, and Irene remembered Cora's remark about the estate being almost gambled away.

'He liked cards too much?'

'He did. Not that I ever saw it – one of Nancy's looks was enough to keep him in line when I was a boy, as I recall it. But I've heard she wasn't always able to rein him in when they were younger.' They drove on in silence for a while; the Stanhope's lamps only lit a few feet in front of them, and a barn owl swooped overhead on silent wings.

'I think Cora carries a torch for you,' said Irene, in the cover of darkness.

'Perhaps,' said Alistair, uncomfortably. 'She's a lovely girl. But my heart belonged to you the moment I saw you, Irene.' He pulled her closer, and kissed her hair.

When Alistair made love to her, Irene noticed all sorts of things. The well-worn softness of the sheets, and the slight itch in her eyes of dust from feather pillows that could have done with replacing. The odd creaks and knocks of the house as it cooled down with the night outside, the shadows cast by the sinuous beams that wriggled across the ceiling, and the rasp of Alistair's cheek against her own. The way his face seemed to blur as he was carried away by sensation, and emotion; the way her mind did the precise opposite – calling everything into sharp, unforgiving focus. She wished she could stop feeling as though she were betraying Fin, each and every time; and she wished she could stop hoping, in the exact same moment, that he would feel that betrayal wherever he was, and be wounded by it. In his bed, she supposed; Serena sleeping beside him. Or perhaps not sleeping at all. She knew deep down that it was only herself she was hurting with such thoughts, and she knew that, to the rest of the world, that would seem entirely just. She didn't mind Alistair's touch. He didn't repel her – he was wonderful in his own way. She liked the smell of him, and the width of his hips, and the rhythm of his movements. Her body ignored her, treacherously, and responded to him. She wondered if, were she whole, she wouldn't come to feel for him what she should, and fall in love. She wondered if she could ever do that again. If she had any love left.

Afterwards, Alistair got up for a glass of water, climbing back into his pyjama trousers. He was boyish, with his flushed cheeks and tousled hair. Made light by happiness. His limbs were long and smooth; neither muscled nor soft, but lean, economical.

'Is there anything you need, my darling?' he said, lying down beside her and propping himself up on one elbow, and she shook her head, though there were many things. She could hardly bear his efforts to please and the guilt they made her feel. 'Oh, I meant to say – I hear we're not about to be struck down by voodoo,' he said, lying back, letting his hand rest on her midriff. His smile put gentle creases around his eyes, and smoothed out his brow.

'What?'

'The doll you found. Pudding told me Ma Tanner confirmed it: no witchcraft.'

'Oh, yes, that's right. No witchcraft.'

'Well, that's a relief.' He smiled. 'I'm afraid I can't think of any other way to establish who it belonged to, or what it was doing there.'

'It really doesn't matter,' said Irene, truthfully. She'd been tempted to throw the doll away once they'd escaped from the Tanners, but that weird sense of significance had persisted, and in the end she'd rewrapped it and put it away in a drawer. The whole expedition annoyed her now – pointlessly putting herself in such an uncomfortable situation. Shouted at by a bedridden old man in front of a herd of unshod children. The thought made her hot with shame, and she had to keep reminding herself that it hadn't been Nancy's idea, but her own. One more way in which she'd managed to do the wrong thing. 'I've forgotten all about it already,' she said.

'Well, anyway, I'm happy you went out and met some of the villagers. Even if it was old Mrs Tanner and her nefarious brood.'

'There did seem to be a lot of them.'

'Who did you meet?'

'Well, "meet" is perhaps an overstatement. Ma, of course, a lot of children and some older girls, and a woman called Trish, who looked past fifty. And an old grandpa. Then after a while Tanner himself came home, with two older lads – but he didn't make a point of introducing himself or them, so I didn't get their names.'

'Well, Trish is Tanner's wife. The older lads were probably their two eldest sons, Jacob and . . . Elias? Elijah? I forget.'

'It doesn't matter. I don't think I'd have gone at all if it hadn't been for your aunt Nancy, telling me so many times I shouldn't. And I don't think I'd have knocked at the door if it hadn't been for Pudding. She's quite fearless, isn't she?'

'About a lot of things, yes. I suppose it comes from so long being teased by her companions. I imagine she's had to develop a thick skin.'

'What on earth possessed her parents to call her Pudding? Surely she can't have been *born* fat?'

'Goodness, that's not her real name. Just a nickname from early days that has hung on ever since. Rather a pity for her. No, her real name is . . .' Alistair frowned. 'Do you know, I've quite forgotten it? It's something very grown-up – perhaps that's why it never took. Does it begin with an L? It's no good – you'll just have to ask her.'

'It doesn't matter.'

Irene realised then how many times she'd said *It doesn't matter* since moving out of London. She glanced at the clock as Alistair turned out the lamp; it was a little after midnight. The witching hour – she hadn't called it that since she'd been a child. As soon as she'd turned seventeen, most of her witching hours had been spent out, at the Embassy Club or some other night spot; with her parents and then with friends – groups made up of young marrieds, young hopefuls, her cousins and a schoolfriend or two. Crammed elbow to elbow at tables that encroached onto the dance floor in the middle of the huge room; snatching a course of dinner and washing it down with gin and tonic before getting up to foxtrot again, to visit another table, to watch and be watched while the band played up on their balcony, all but lost in the haze of smoke. Talking, shouting to be heard above the din; dancing and laughing with that mad energy, that frantic need for joy, that swept through England after the Great War. Unemployment wasn't an issue for the members and guests at the Embassy, but the shortage of young men was. It gave the single women an edge of desperation, of constant questing, and made the remaining young men feel hunted – which some of them relished. It made some young women, the shyer ones, too terrified to even talk to a man, since it would be immediately assumed that she wanted to marry him.

Irene had been one of this latter group. She was shy to begin with, anyway. Added to that her parents' continual mania that she be married to the first young man in whom she took an interest, and she determined to show an interest in none of them. Irene's mother, who approached fashion as a matter of life or death, decided that her lack of confidence stemmed from not being thin enough for the dresses coming across from Paris, and put her on so strict a diet that Irene passed her days in a daze of dizziness and detachment, weak with hunger. Her mother watched her so sternly whenever she did eat that Irene soon found she couldn't at all, in her presence. Many nights, she felt she didn't have the resources left to make any effort at overcoming her shyness. The very last softness disappeared from her body, leaving a boyish shape with knobbly knees and arms like pipe cleaners, and a bloodless face in which her mascaraed eyes bloomed like black flowers. She took up smoking; it helped her not to think about food. When she didn't have the energy to dance, she simply sat; when she didn't have the energy to talk, she stayed silent, watching the room with the dispassion that was all she could muster, hoping that nobody would attempt to engage her. And they did try – because she looked the part, and because of who her parents were, and because they mistook her fatigue and fear for a glamorous kind of *ennui*. So she sat there, night after night, draped in silk and strings of beads, smoking through a tortoiseshell cigarette holder and wondering how and when it would all end. But that was life, and that was what passed for enjoyment, and to be anywhere else – to be at home – felt like stepping off and leaving the whole world to turn without her. Like dying.

The first time Serena and Fin came to the Embassy was on Irene's invitation, in 1920, after they'd met at the costume party – Serena as a peacock; Serena just as vivid without her feathers. Irene had no idea what Serena saw in her as a friend. Whether it was her connections, or the way the Paris fashions hung perfectly on her starving body; or whether she, too, mistook exhaustion for a fashionable disdain that she envied. Or perhaps Irene was a blank canvas onto which Serena might paint colourful images of herself. She towed Fin around behind her, always holding his hand, taking him from group to group, table to table: a husband, a rarity, as a dress accessory. And then he touched Irene's arm for the first time, sitting side by side on an upholstered bench, late in the evening, well after midnight. The witching hour. Beached together to one side of the shifting sea of people – the maelstrom of the dance floor, the high-tide line of tables all strewn with the detritus of a five-course meal and too much to drink. Irene hadn't had a thought in her head that she knew about, other than that it was entirely comfortable to have him there, with the sleeve of his jacket just brushing her bare shoulder, giving her gooseflesh. Not really noticing him, as people generally seemed to not really notice him. She remembered a vague sense of there being safety in numbers; of it being unlikely that she would be approached while he was there. She noticed the discomfort of the sequins on her dress more, cutting into the skin on the undersides of her arms. Did he speak before he touched her? It seemed likely, and she just hadn't heard him. His touch was to get her attention.

She couldn't pick the single thread of it out of the tangle of what came next. It seemed, in her memory, that his touch had roused her from a nightmare. Pulled her out of a cage she'd built for her own protection. Four fingers on her forearm, and through the quagmire of champagne and stress she'd felt easier. A little unlocking inside. She couldn't even remember exactly what he said. Was it, *You mustn't mind Serena, when she says things like that*? Or was it, *Will you dance with me one evening, Irene?* Or was it, *I wish I knew what you thought about all this*? It didn't matter. Of course it didn't matter. She lay there next to Alistair as his breathing deepened towards sleep, and remembered that he'd been there that night too. Alistair Hadleigh, up from the country for a visit with some other old Etonians; old – almost forty – but still handsome. She remembered being introduced to him, then seeing him at a few parties – one might even have been at his apartment in Mayfair – and driving about in his brand new Alvis. A tall man with straight fair hair, kind eyes and a slightly weak chin. She'd danced with him, she thought, if not that first night Fin touched her then another, soon afterwards. She remembered thinking that his laughter lines made him, conversely, look a little sad. But Fin's touch on her arm. The feeling of being woken, and shown the way out, was far stronger than the unreal sense of danger that came with it. That was easy to ignore.

%% %%

Eli Tanner wanted to touch her, of that much Clemmie was certain. She wondered why he didn't. It seemed entirely obvious to her that he loved her, and she thought it must be obvious to him that she loved him – that she was on fire for the love of him. The kind of love that came into being a full-formed thing, living and breathing, strong, and needing no more explanation than the sun or the wind. They met most days – walking through the water meadows beside the river up towards Ford, or down towards Box, as far as Widdenham Mill, which had made paper until ten years earlier but now sat still and empty. Water rushed busily over its weir, unaware of its redundancy. The summer grass was lush; the cows stood over their ankles in mud at the By Brook's edge, pulling up greedy mouthfuls of it, swatting endlessly at the flies on their flanks. Eli and Clemmie always stopped short of civilisation; they kept to the quiet curves of the bank, and the shade of trees, and the hidden paths tucked between the high, ancient banks at field edges, where the bluebells were dying back. Climbing through squeeze-belly stiles and gaps in the hedgerows, they made sure they weren't seen. This was agreed mutually, in silence. Clemmie didn't know if Eli's father's objection would be to her specifically, or only to Eli not working. Eli taking time for himself, out from under his father's heavy hand. She knew her own family's objections would be to Eli, and his Tanner blood. And perhaps to the very idea of her having a suitor – she didn't know, since it hadn't happened before, despite her pretty face. Because she didn't speak; because they thought her touched.

Touched. Simple. Nature's child. All it meant was that Clemmie had been set aside and talked over all her life, and was not expected to have thoughts or plans of her own. She was expected to always stay exactly where she was. Perhaps it was this that made her appreciate all the other living things around, which many people didn't. The birds and the vermin and the livestock – they were also speechless, also very much alive. Like them, she preferred to go her own way, unnoticed; like them, she was largely left to do so. Exempted from the expectations other people had for one another; occasionally approached by men and boys, but never considered for a wife. Never considered as a mother to somebody's children. So Clemmie hadn't considered herself that way, and had never needed to challenge this assumption that she was flawed.

The touching should have been simple; she couldn't understand Eli's hesitance. When he waited too long, Clemmie took his hands in hers, meshed their fingers together, pushed his palm against her stomach or her thigh or chest. If he wanted to touch, then she wanted him to. There was no explanation for this other than an innate trust, a feeling of complete safety and understanding. His whole body shook, and his breathing got quicker, and his eyes seemed to catch alight. The taste of him in her mouth was heaven. She didn't seem to have enough skin on her whole body to press against his. She wanted to say his name. She wanted it so much she even practised at home, when nobody was around – using the exercises Mr Hadleigh had taught her, breaking the word into pieces, letting her mouth get used to each one before moving on to the next. Like learning the steps of a dance. She practised behind the barn, or in the dairy when everyone else was outside – tucked away amidst the churns and scrubbing brushes, the pails and pans and the wooden box of salt. The stress of it was incredible. Just a few minutes left her panting, damp with sweat, heart pounding like she'd been running. The first sound was all right. She could do it, the E. But switching from E to L made everything lock, and her brain jar against the stone wall of her tongue. It had been so long since she'd tried to speak, without Mr Hadleigh to help trick herself, that she'd forgotten the horror of it, and after fifteen minutes or so she stopped, spent. One day, she tipped her head back against the dairy wall to rest and said the one part of his name that she could, drawing out the sound:

'Eeeeeee . . .' A soft footstep made her gasp, and there was Josie in the doorway, a bundle of clean smocks in her arms, wide-eyed at hearing her sister make a sound.

'Go on, Clem. Go on, you almost had it,' she said, but Clemmie shook her head, scattering tears of frustration from her eyelashes.

Once she had the knack of it, if she ever had the knack of it, she would whisper it into his ear, with the animal smell of his unwashed hair in her nostrils and the impossible softness of the skin at his hairline. *Eli*, she would whisper, and feel the shock of it run through his body like a delicious kick. The sun catching in his eyes brought out the blue; flashes of bright colour like the kingfishers that arrowed away along the water's surface. He was so gentle with her she couldn't believe anything bad about him, even though she still saw the anger in him sometimes, when they were first reunited. Anger that soon ran out of him and left him almost dazed, as though the relief of being free of it made him drunk. He shut his eyes and concentrated when she put her hands through his hair, on the back of his neck, on his face. Like he was memorising how it felt to be touched in that way – with kindness.

'We should marry, Clemmie,' he whispered, as she lay back, as she reached for him. A bed of grass and curtains of fox-gloves, cow parsley and figwort; the sound of the river nearby, and the rattle of a big green dragonfly darting back and forth, spying on them. 'We should marry first.' But he shut his eyes as he said it, rapturous, and his shoulders blocked out the sun above her, and she closed his mouth with kisses. If she could have spoken, she'd have said, *Why wait?*

❧ ❧

On Sunday afternoon, after a deeply tedious morning service during which the vicar had droned on about constancy in the face of adversity, Dr Cartwright and Donny went fishing, and Pudding and her mother went along simply to sit on a blanket in the sunshine and eat the picnic they'd made – cheese and tomato sandwiches, small pork pies made by Ruth the day before – greasy in the heat but delicious – apples and short-bread fingers. They spread their blanket on the flat meadow upriver towards Ford, in the shade of a gnarled hawthorn, where the water was wide and deep, and moved with smooth insistence down towards the mills. The current tugged at bright green weeds along the riverbed. Pudding and Donny had swum in the same spot every summer as children; Pudding might have quite liked to swim that day, but having to appear in a bathing suit when anybody could walk past had robbed the fun from it. As he unpacked his rods and tackle, Dr Cartwright pointed.

'Look, there! Donny, look – the fattest trout I ever saw, just waiting for us. The cheeky blighter – I swear I saw him wink,' he said, just as he would have when his offspring were much younger.

'Did you, Dad?' said Donny, after a while. It took him a lot longer than it used to to get himself set up, but his first cast was smooth, effortless, and sent the fly arcing out across the water to land softly, silently on the surface. Donny's muscles remembered some of the things that his brain had forgotten, the doctor had explained to Pudding.

'That's my boy,' he said. 'All in the elbow, just like that.' And then the doctor had to look away, so that the brim of his boater hid his face. Donny could fish for hours without getting bored, squinting at the shining water from underneath his cap – for even longer now than before he went off to the war. And just like then, he didn't seem at all bothered about actually catching a fish.

Louise Cartwright sat with her legs tucked neatly to one side, and tapped Pudding's arm to correct her when she sat cross-legged.

'You're not a little girl any more, Puddy,' she said. 'Try a smidgen more form.'

'Sorry, Mum,' said Pudding, too pleased to be noticed and spoken to by her mother to mind being corrected. The four of them, just then, were perfect. No hint of anything amiss. If Pudding concentrated, she could pretend that nothing was. The sun flamed down at them, so that the grass seemed to steam; swallows swooped, a pair of swans sailed by, and a robin watched them from the hawthorn, waiting for crumbs. Pudding picked a blade of grass, clamped it between her thumbs and whistled with it. Donny drew in his line and cast again, and the doctor fiddled with a tiny carp he'd hooked, ready to throw it back. Pudding watched a two-spot ladybird climb the whole length of a red campion stalk and then stop at the top, and her mind drifted back to a day before the war – a day of similar chalk sky and languid heat – when they'd caught the early train from Chippenham down to the coast at Swanage. Pudding had only been six; already sturdy and round enough to have the nickname that would never leave her. It had been the year before the war broke out; Donny had been a strapping fifteen; all long limbs and burgeoning strength. Pudding remembered his skin in the sunshine, so different from her own – darker, and freckle-free; deepening in colour the second his shirt was off. He'd caught the eye of many a young lady on the beach that day, and along the quayside where they'd gone to tea; but he'd already fallen in love with Aoife Moore by then and had hardly noticed.

Pudding watched the easy way her brother cast his line, and remembered his hands around her ribs, sliding up to her armpits, tight with the effort of lifting her. But lift her he had, again and again, lobbing her as high as he could into the waves while she shrieked and laughed so hard she got water up her nose and they had to stop. She remembered him kneeling on the sand in front of her while she coughed and spluttered and her eyes streamed, grinning, saying, *You're not supposed to drink the sea, silly Pud; you're supposed to swim in it.* The sun gave his hair a deep mahogany glow; the beginnings of whiskers just shadowed his jaw. She stayed in the sea for hours – her puppy fat kept her warm. She heard her mother calling her in, but pretended not to. Her father wore the same straw boater to keep the sun off his pate; her mother wore her blue dress with the sailor collar, and never went further into the sea than her ankles. The day had seemed endless and joyful; like the summer, like life. Try as she might, Pudding could no longer feel quite the same way, in spite of the beauty of the day, and her mother's lucidity, and Donny's calm contentment, and a picnic. The careless feeling of being a child had slipped beyond her reach. She felt herself at a point of fine balance between happiness and fear.

'Can't we eat the picnic yet?' she said to her mother, to stave off sombre thoughts. She knew what the answer would be, and longed to hear the familiar words, spoken in her familiar voice.

'Certainly not! Good gracious, Pudding, it's not yet one.'

'Well now, I think you've a bite, my boy,' said the doctor. 'Donny? Did you hear me?'

For something to say, Pudding began to tell her mother about Irene Hadleigh, and their trip to see Ma Tanner at Thatch Cottage. Pudding had hoped that it might have marked the start of a thaw in Irene Hadleigh, of her coming out and talking to Pudding a bit more, and riding, but it didn't seem to be happening. Pudding had been alight with curiosity after Ma Tanner said that change was coming. She was desperate to know what Ma had meant, and how she could tell, and what kind of change. But when she'd said all that on the walk back up to the farm, Irene hadn't shown the least interest. Something else the old woman had said was plaguing Pudding. She'd said that Irene wasn't married *in her heart*. Pudding wondered if that could possibly be true. It seemed inconceivable to her that anyone – least of all his new wife – might not love Alistair, given the chance to. But then, Irene did seem a bit of a *cold fish*, as Ruth might have said. However many times she told herself that it was none of her business, Pudding couldn't seem to leave the thought alone. She'd been quite happy when Alistair got married – happy to think he'd found someone to cherish him as they ought. The thought that he'd married someone who didn't cherish him was just deeply *wrong*, in a way she couldn't quite put her finger on. She'd also hoped, in some abstract way, that Alistair being married, and bringing a new resident to Slaughterford, might jolt the world from the rails it seemed to be on, and alter its course, because she didn't like the way it had been going. The growing certainty that Donny was as recovered from the war as he was ever going to be. The inescapable fact that her mother only ever got a little worse, never a little better.

On Monday morning Pudding hacked out on Robin, the horse meant for Irene Hadleigh, and took a hilly route to work some weight off him. But as the lane climbed and Robin began to puff, she felt a bit guilty – he didn't have a lot of bone, and, really, she was probably too heavy for him. Her lower legs dangled down, clear of his flanks. She sat as well as she could, as though that might somehow mitigate her inexorable growth. She'd had to ask Nancy to buy some wider stirrup irons for the ladies' saddles, since by now her feet were far closer to man-sized. Not like Nancy's tiny, neat feet, which even looked delicate in boots. She knew for a fact that by the autumn, when the hunting season began, she wouldn't be able to fasten her one decent jacket over her chest any more.

When she got back to Manor Farm, Pudding saw Irene Hadleigh at one of the upstairs windows and gave her a wave, but Irene didn't seem to see her. For some reason that, and thoughts of her hunting jacket being too small, ruined Pudding's fragile good mood, and when the farrier's lad turned up, asking where she was since he'd been expecting Dundee and Baron down at the forge, it took her by surprise. She would never normally forget such a thing, and had to run to bring the horses in from the field and wash the mud off their feet. Baron was outraged and refused to be caught, swinging his hindquarters at Pudding and laying back his ears, until she almost wept with frustration, and Hilarius had to come across to help her.

'What ails thee, girl?' he asked her, squinting shrewdly at her red face and harried expression.

'Oh, nothing! Nothing,' she said.

'Can't lie to the beasts,' he replied, with a shrug. 'They smell the truth on you.' The old man caught Baron without mishap, murmuring incomprehensible things in the language he'd learnt as a child – he always did this so softly that Pudding never heard it clearly enough to have a guess at where he might have been born – then handed her the lead rope without another word.

'Wench must be in love,' said the farrier, aptly named Smith, as Pudding finally towed the horses into his rickety shed. He gave her a lopsided flash of his brown teeth with the perfectly round notch where the shaft of his pipe sat. He had hands thick with scars, and a limp where he'd been kicked once; he only ever called Pudding wench, but she didn't mind. She smiled vaguely, feeling too distracted to blush.

'Are you, then?' said Ben, Smith's apprentice, who was only a year older than Pudding and as awkward with his new body as she was. His face was a series of misshapen features, on the move, not yet settled where they finally would; he had spots on his cheeks and watched the world sullenly through a messy fringe of hair, but he had a way with horses that Smith called 'the touch' – any animal he handled immediately fell calm, and was at least grudgingly cooperative as its feet smoked beneath the hot metal shoes.

'Am I what?' said Pudding.

'In love?' The question had an accusatory note, as though love were an act of gross stupidity.

'Hardly,' said Pudding, airily, assuming she was being teased about Alistair Hadleigh. 'Who on earth is there to fall in love with around here?' At this Ben flushed crimson and glowered, and turned away to top the forge embers with a shovelful of slack. Smith observed the exchange and grinned again.

'Reckon the wench ain't the only one,' he said, but Pudding wasn't really listening.

At the end of the day she went to collect Donny to walk home, but he was nowhere in the grounds of Manor Farm, so she made her way down into the valley, and along to the mill. The sky had clotted by then, and the air felt thundery. Tiny black beetles appeared from nowhere to dot Pudding's clothes and skin, and the river's surface teemed with gnats. Donny loved the mill, and all its machinery and steam and smoke and racket. He'd understood the workings of it, apparently inherently, from the age of about ten, when to Pudding it had always been a mysterious, alarming catastrophe of a place. Not somewhere she belonged at all. She only liked the bag room, where the women stitched and glued with an air of quiet industry, and everything was spotless. On bad days she saw the mill as a cancerous blot on the beauty of the By Brook, and wished it didn't even exist. Such intrusive modern industry was wrong in such a timeless place, and it seemed to grow all the while. Like the massive brick building and towering chimney Alistair had built just two years earlier, to house the new steam boilers and generator; a 1920 date-stone set proudly into the wall. Pudding could hardly guess what the building and all the new equipment it housed must have cost, and it stuck out like a sore thumb. But then, she couldn't mind it too much, because it was Alistair's. And because the mill employed men from villages all around, when many of them would be impoverished otherwise, their families along with them. Without the mill, Slaughterford wouldn't be Slaughterford.

The beater man gave her a nod and a wave as she passed the doors to his domain. With the Fourdrinier machine and the beaters running full tilt, and the agitators in the stuff tanks turning, and the water turbines thundering, it was easier to gesture than to talk. Most of the workers were used to Donny and Pudding, and knew that their occasional presence was to be expected and tolerated. Still, Pudding knew that the men had work to do, and that it wasn't a safe place to be, and she made it her business to extract Donny as swiftly as she could when he paid one of his visits. The engineer pointed at the new generator house, and Pudding waved to thank him. She found Donny in front of the huge Belliss and Morcom steam engine, which – somehow – made electricity for the whole mill. It was still shiny in spite of all the soot and smoke in the air, rearing fourteen feet above the tan and white tiled floor. Donny was standing with his arms loose at his sides and the machine looming over him like some great black animal. To Pudding's eyes it was all pipes, belts and cylinders, and pressure dials with trembling red needles. She wondered if Donny still understood how it all worked, or if, like her, he simply saw metal and mess now. She didn't know which would be worse – she hated to think that he stood there in full knowledge of his new, flawed existence. There was sweat on his brow, but whether it was from the heat or some internal struggle, she couldn't tell.

Then, with a jolt, Pudding noticed Tanner. He was behind them, tucked into a corner near the coal heap, asleep with his cap pulled down low over his face and a brown bottle nestled tenderly in his arms like a baby. She caught her breath, filled with dread at the thought of him waking up and finding them there, as witnesses. His clothes were all sooty and dark; smuts had settled into the creases of his face so that he looked like an old, old man. He'd been let go more than once before, she knew, for just the same thing. Drinking on the job – or drinking and being incapable of the job. Or, once, drinking and throwing a junior beater into the mill race during a row over an imaginary insult that had nearly ended with the other man drowned. Somehow, Alistair always managed to give him another chance, but the last time, six months earlier, Pudding had overheard Nancy and Alistair arguing about it in the mill office when she'd passed on the way to find Donny.

'No more, Alistair. The man is a liability,' Nancy had said, at her most adamant, which was when she usually went unchallenged.

'Nobody else will employ him, Nancy.'

'And there's a good reason for that.'

'What of his family? All those youngsters?'

'Enough youngsters to send out to work, and cover his lost earnings. Of all the inbred peasants we're forced to employ, he really does take the biscuit – he will be the death of himself, or somebody else. Or of the mill.'

Alistair's subsequent silence had been telling, but perhaps he'd spoken to Tanner because the man's presence in Slaughterford had been relatively unobtrusive for many months, and Mrs Glover'd had it from Trish Tanner – his wife, who rarely spoke a word and trudged through life with the air of a woman who'd abandoned hopes and dreams at a young age – that he'd given up the drink altogether. He'd come back to work at the mill again, and now he was passed out drunk in the coal heap. One of his sons, one of those Pudding and Irene had seen at Thatch Cottage, was shovelling coal into the two boilers. He gave her a black glare when he saw her looking, and Pudding jerked her eyes away. Whether the man was found out or not, it wouldn't be her who reported on him; it could hardly be her business, when she wasn't even supposed to be there. She roused Donny with a hand on his arm.

'Time to go home now, Donny.' The steam hissed, the boilers roared. The gentle summer day outside was lost and forgotten in that building, with its alien machinery and high metal rafters, and suddenly Pudding longed to escape from it. She tugged at Donny's arm but, in spite of her size, there was no way she could move him until he wanted to move. He looked down at her in that underwater way of his.

'I used to know all this,' he said. 'Didn't I?' Pudding's heart sank.

'You did, Donny. Yes, you did.'

'It's like I still know it, Pud. Only . . . I can't remember what I know.'

'Never mind, Donny,' she said, trying not to show her dismay. 'You've other work now, haven't you? In the gardens.' He nodded, turning back to the steam engine. His brow creased with thought – with the effort of thought.

'Yes,' he said. 'But I used to know all this.' Pudding didn't know what to say. The Tanner boy watched them, suspiciously, resentfully; he was filthy from the coal and the sweat, and Pudding could see his exhaustion at that late hour of the day – a judder in his muscles with each dig of the shovel.

When she finally managed to coax Donny out, the evening had mellowed, and the western sky had a bruised, yellow look. Pudding crossed her fingers behind her back and hoped there wouldn't be a thunder storm. The noise terrified Donny, and left him wild-eyed and piteous, unable to escape from himself or the fear. Last time, Pudding and her father had played records for hours to drown out the weather, but Donny had flailed and crashed about, attempting to barricade himself into his room by heaving the furniture about, and when Pudding had looked into his eyes it had seemed as though her brother were no longer in there at all. She didn't like to remember it.

'I dreamt I was back in the mud in France, Pud,' Donny had said, quietly, the morning after. 'Stuck there near the lads on the washing lines, and the smell they had. And I couldn't get away; I couldn't.' They walked up the hill to Spring Cottage in silence, since every time Pudding thought of something to say, a glance at her brother's closed-off face silenced her. Buzzards wheeled above, with their high, lonely cries; rabbits scattered into the bank, and glossy black bumblebees milked the clover. Change was definitely coming, Pudding thought then. She could feel it gathering, drawing in its breath. She was just no longer at all sure that it would be for the better.

                                        ✺

However early Irene got up in the morning – and she had been getting up earlier each day, with the noise of the farm and the sun streaming through the crack in the curtains – Nancy was up and dressed before her. Irene wondered if she needed sleep at all, or merely carried on throughout the night, being impenetrable and efficient and entirely correct. Now, only a single place remained at the breakfast table, for Irene; Alistair's and Nancy's had been used already and cleared away. On the sideboard, the mushrooms and kidneys had gone cold, and the house already had the left-behind air of a place abandoned by busy people. Irene was completely unprepared for the letter that had been left for her, beside her place setting. She knew the handwriting at once, and her face flooded with blood, knowing that Alistair and Nancy must have seen it already, and known exactly who it was from. She stood staring at it for a long time, listening for anyone approaching, wondering whether to open it there, as she ached to do, or to take it somewhere private. Somewhere she could revel in it – her writing room, perhaps, where the paint wasn't quite dry. She could hide herself away and let his words – his voice – wrap themselves around her. When she picked it up, her hands juddered uncontrollably. There could be nothing in the letter that would change what had happened, nothing that could undo the fact that she was married to Alistair Hadleigh, and living in a different universe to the one she knew. Nothing that could undo the fact that Fin was still married to Serena. Yet seeing his handwriting felt like being given air. She held it to her face and inhaled, hoping for a trace of him.

Nancy came in so quietly it was as though she'd simply materialised. She was dressed for going into Chippenham, in a calf-length skirt and matching jacket; her heels had hardly made a sound on the rug. She stood with one hand on her hip and a revolted expression on her face, and Irene felt like a child caught picking her nose. Or worse. Nancy's judgement weighed more than a millstone, and Irene took a breath.

'May I not have a letter from a friend without being castigated? Must I *always* be castigated?' she said, not caring that her voice shook. Nancy cocked an eyebrow.

'We weren't born yesterday, you know, my dear. If it were simply a letter from a friend, believe me, nobody would castigate you. But then, from what I gather, you have few enough friends left. I've always taken it as a good measure of a person – how far back in time they can trace their friendships. It implies a constancy of character, wouldn't you say?'

'It must be nice to be unimpeachable in that regard, Nancy.'

'Yes. It is.' Nancy sounded amused at this, in her hard way, which only made Irene feel more wretched. More angry.

'Perhaps it's easier to achieve when one feels nothing whatsoever, for anyone. What gives you the right to . . . to treat me with such *disdain*, Nancy?' said Irene, forcing out the words in little more than a whisper, terrified, knowing that they could never be unsaid. Nancy pursed her lips for a minute and studied her, as if she were having the same inward battle. There was no trace of doubt in her voice, though, when she did speak.

'Because as far as I am concerned, Irene, you entirely

deserve it.' In the pause, the mantelpiece clock ticked, and a horse kicked at its stable door outside. 'My nephew is one of the best men you'll ever meet. One of the best men anyone will ever meet. Goodness only knows how he turned out as kind and loving as he did, having been raised by me, but he did. Goodness only knows how he came through the war without it ruining him, but he did. And he deserves a far better wife than a chit of a girl, starving herself for fashion, who's only married him to dodge a scandal of her own creation, and hasn't the slightest idea how to behave.'

Shocked into silence, Irene stood rooted to the spot with Fin's letter in her hands. Something flickered in Nancy's eyes, and it might have been the acknowledgement of how far she had gone – a seed which might have germinated into repentance, in another person. But Nancy was too stony ground for that.

'I see,' said Irene, too shaken to say anything else.

'We Hadleighs set the standard, as I told you before. This family's good name is sacrosanct, and I'm damned if I'll let you make a laughing stock of us. Had Alistair's mother been alive, you'd still be under house arrest in London, you know. Tabitha was very Catholic, and you'd have been quite beyond the pale. She might have been a papist delusionist, whom I never much liked, but we saw eye to eye on certain things. Why do you think Alistair married you in such a hurry?'

'Because he . . . loves me.'

'Perhaps he does, silly boy. But he also knew I'd have put a stop to it, if I could. I'd got him out of an inappropriate engagement before, and I'd have got him out of this one, too. I have always done what needs to be done around here, even when others may not see it, to begin with. It would certainly have been better for this family if I'd had a say in your . . . union. But, here you are.' She sighed slightly, through her nostrils. 'But this isn't a game, you know, Irene. You're married to Alistair now, so I suggest you get on with it.' Her eyes flicked to the letter. 'I simply won't have you embarrassing my nephew. Besides, only an idiot would cling to ... flotsam, when a ruddy great lifeboat was sailing right by.'

The front door thumped shut behind Nancy, and Irene sank into a chair at the table. It took a long time for her pulse to slow. She wondered how on earth she was supposed to go on living under the same roof as Nancy; how she was supposed to cope with the woman reiterating every bad thing she thought about herself on a daily basis. Clenched in her hand, the envelope of Fin's letter had grown damp. Irene opened it, reeling with the mad hope that whatever he'd written, it could somehow save her. It could make her feel again the perfect rightness of being with him – a rightness that had flooded out and encompassed the whole world around her. *Dear Irene*, he'd written, *I hope this letter finds you well. We are both quite well, and will be leaving London soon to spend the remainder of the summer in France, with Serena's parents, so I thought I would take this opportunity to write. Serena had wanted to do so herself, but I persuaded her to let me. It just won't do, you see, Irene. Your continuing to write to me. It bothers Serena terribly, when everyone is trying so hard to carry on with life as it ought to be lived. It makes the servants smirk, and you know how she can't bear that. And you are a married woman yourself now, after all. I can't imagine your husband welcomes the knowledge that you and I continue to correspond, if, that is, he is aware of it. I hate to write a letter such as this, but thought it for the best, in the long run. Your letters pain me more than I can say, and must stop. I wish you all the best, Irene. Kind Regards, F. S. Campbell.*

Irene stayed at the table for a long time. At some point, she became aware that the remainders of breakfast had been cleared away, though she hadn't noticed it happening. The buttery sunshine outside seemed, like everything else, to deride her. For the first time in weeks, she wished her mother were there; but even though she had come to Irene and Alistair's wedding, her mother hadn't forgiven her yet either. More judgement. More castigation. She sat, without moving, and felt as though she were drowning – cold waters of despair closing over her head. It was the feeling of all her hopes dying; the snuffing of that last final spark inside, the one that had whispered, treacherously, that love would somehow save her. If it were a good thing, she couldn't believe it just then. Outside the window, Pudding Cartwright rode past on Robin, the horse that had been meant for Irene. The girl looked too big on him, and the horse looked put upon, and the absurdity of it was as bitter as everything else. Irene wondered where the lifeboat was, that Nancy had mentioned. She wondered if she were simply blind to it, or incapable of reaching it, because the drowning feeling continued, unabated, however long she sat there, and she didn't think she could be expected to carry on that way. She could not carry on that way.

Towards lunchtime, Alistair came to find her in her writing room. She had little memory of making her way there, but when he appeared at her shoulder and roused her she found herself in front of her typewriter, with a clean sheet of paper loaded and Fin's letter open on the desk beside her, for anyone to see. She didn't know if she'd planned to write anything, and when she realised that Alistair would see the letter her heart gave a jolt, but it was too late to hide it. She couldn't even look at him.

'Irene . . .' he said eventually, quietly.

'I'm sorry,' she said.

'Were you going to write back to him?' His voice was unsteady.

'No. I wasn't,' she said, truthfully.

'To whom, then?'

'No. No, I was just . . .' She looked up at him, numb, guilty. 'I honestly don't know what I was going to do.' For a while, neither of them spoke. The air in the old schoolroom was cool and clammy; in spite of all her expensive new furnishings, the prevailing smell was of mildewed books, old wood, forgotten things. The sounds beyond the walls – of animals, labour, life – seemed to come from very far away. Alistair pulled up a chair and perched beside her, taking her hand. His expression was heavy, weary and sad, and suddenly the thought of being the cause of that, the thought of him giving up on her, made Irene feel even more wretched.

'I know you're lonely, Irene. I know . . . I know you're unhappy here. I just wish . . .' He shook his head, opened her hand and dropped his forehead into her palm. 'I just wish I could help.'

'You are! You do . . . Alistair, You do. I just . . . I don't feel I belong here.'

'I know. And we won't always have to stay here in Wiltshire, we can go up to London. It just might be better not to until . . . the dust has settled.' He sighed. 'I thought I could make you happy. I thought coming here would make you happy.'

'No, Alistair – please don't say that. Please. I can't bear it. I'll get better, I know I will. It will get better. I'll . . . try harder.'

'No, you're right, I ought not to say that. And you mustn't *try*, Irene. Nobody can try to feel anything – we either feel, or we don't feel. We must both be patient, that's all.'

'Yes,' said Irene, trying, nevertheless, to feel hopeful. Alistair smiled.

'You could . . . invite a friend down to stay. Or your mother . . .' He trailed off, having never got along with Irene's parents. 'Or anybody, really. Anyone you like. If it'd make you feel more at home.'

'Perhaps I will,' said Irene, not wanting to say that she had written to all her friends, repeatedly, and to her cousins, and had asked them all to come to stay, or to have her stay with them. She'd had few replies, but those she'd had had been full of apologies that people were far too occupied with their summer plans already.

'Or Cora – why not invite her around, or take a trip into town together?'

'Town?'

'Yes, Chippenham. It's not exactly the West End, I'll grant you.' He smiled again. 'But it has coffee shops, a cinema, shops. People who might have travelled beyond the bounds of Wiltshire now and then . . . It would be a change of scene, I suppose.'

Alistair stood, and pulled Irene up by her hands. She looked up into his face, and her relief at seeing that the heaviness had vanished from it surprised her. Her shoulders dropped, and she felt a little of the tightness behind her ribs ease.

'Why do you love me, Alistair? Why did you want to marry me?' she asked.

'Why?' He shook his head. 'I really don't think love needs a *why*. Some things simply are. I saw you, and I watched you dance and smoke . . . always with that lost, embattled look in your eye, and I knew that you were kind, and bright, and different . . . and it simply happened. It came into being. And I am so, so happy that it did.' He touched her face, smoothing back a lock of her hair.

'But how can you be? How, Alistair?'

'Because I get to see you every day. And every time I see you, I feel better.'

'Better about what?'

'Better about everything.'

'Oh, Alistair . . . I just feel so . . .' Irene hung her head and felt her eyes fill with tears, stinging and hot. 'I just feel so . . . *stupid*. And so pointless.'

'Well, you're neither. Irene . . . I know that just now you don't believe you'll ever feel right again, but you will. I promise you. One day, you will have forgotten him – it might take time, and it won't happen all at once, but gradually your thoughts of him will lessen, and the pain will fade along with them. I can promise you this, because I have also been forced by . . . circumstances . . . to separate from somebody. It was a long time ago now, but I also felt, for a while, as though the world had come to an end. But it hadn't, Irene. It hadn't. And now I have you, and I'm so, so glad.' He held her for a long time while she cried like a child; she couldn't seem to stop, and she wondered how long the tears had been building up. Thinking back, she realised she hadn't cried once since the storm had broken over her. She'd been numb, she'd been angry; desperate and in terrible pain. But she hadn't cried once. Alistair simply stood, and rested his face against the top of her head, and waited it out with perfect patience.

∽ ∼

On a day so sweltering hot that the cows could hardly be bothered to graze, and the horseflies were legion, and biting, and Rose Matlock had turned puce halfway through mangling the sheets and gone for a lie down, Clemmie and her sisters swam. Just in front of the farm was a lazy curve in the By Brook; the water slowed as it swung round it, and had carved out a pool about five feet deep in places. It was bone-achingly cold, but, once the shock of it had passed, blissful. They filled the air with their voices as they plunged in – squeals and laughter and, from Mary, some salty curses. Clemmie took a deep breath and dived straight in, shivering at the cold touch of it on her scalp, which the sun had scorched through her pale hair. They swam in their underwear, which clung to their chests and hips; their hair smoothed to their necks, their skin gleamed. The vicar, walking past with his laced-up gaiters, alpine boots and thumb stick, and sweating profusely, gave them a peculiar, strained sort of smile, and muttered something awkward about naiads in a crystal stream before hurrying on his way. Liz stared after him a moment too long.

'You're not serious?' said Mary.

'What?' said Liz, colouring.

'Liz has a passion for the vicar!'

'I do not! You shut your mouth!' said Liz, lunging at Mary, who waded away, laughing.

'It'd be no fun at all, Lizzie!' she called over her shoulder. 'He'd have to say so many prayers before and after he laid you down, you'd nod off!'

'I wish Clarence would lay me down,' said Josie, wistfully. 'When he holds my hand, I swear, it sends me into shivers all over.'

'Don't let Father hear you talking like that or he'll tan the hide off you,' said Liz, obviously grateful for the change of focus.

'I'm not daft,' said Josie.

'Are you sure?' Mary grinned at her, and Josie put out her tongue. 'You wouldn't catch me letting on who's caught *my* eye. After what happened with Tom, I'm dead set on being quieter than Clemmie about it.'

The three girls turned idle gazes to their mute sister, and found her smiling. She couldn't help it. Eli Tanner was never far from her mind, and their talk had brought him right to the fore – all the shuddering delight of him moving inside her, and the taste of him, and the way he looked at her and melted into her touch. She was saturated with him, but only ever wanted more. There was no way she could not smile, even when she sensed a single thought coalesce in her three sisters, and felt a tingle of danger. Liz, Josie and Mary paddled closer to her, dripping water from their chins, watching her with their expressions changing from teasing to consideration, to incredulity.

'Clemmie Matlock!' Mary exclaimed. 'Have you got a sweetheart?'

'She can't have . . . she's touched,' said Liz, outraged, always jealous.

'Boys don't care what comes out of your mouth, only what goes in,' said Mary.

'Have you, Clem?' said Josie. 'Tell us!' They came closer, circling her; a moving wall of sunlit ripples on skin. 'Tell us who.'

'How's she going to do that, you dunce?' said Mary. 'For all those lessons the squire has given her, she's still not once uttered a proper word.'

'Well then, nod us yes, Clemmie – is there someone?'

She could have shaken her head. She thought about doing it, but for some reason she *wanted* to tell them, she wanted to share it – she wanted to shout it out. It felt too big to keep inside, and for once she wanted to be on equal footing with her sisters, not different to them, not behind in some way. Happiness made her giddy, and gave the illusion of safety when she wasn't safe, and neither was Eli. But there was no way her sisters could know or guess who it was, and no way they could make her tell them. The sun burned down on their skin, and the water soothed, and the world was as benign a place as she could imagine, just then. She nodded. Josie gasped, her fingers flying to her mouth, her eyes lighting up with excitement; Mary's face was incredulous, Liz's too.

'Oh, that's so wonderful, Clemmie! Is he handsome?' said Josie.

'Wonderful? Are you mad?' said Mary. 'Someone must have taken advantage of her! Who is it, Clem?'

'Leave her alone – why shouldn't she love someone?' said Josie.

'We'll have to tell Father,' said Liz. Her fingers were splayed in the water, near the surface, as though to keep her balanced. As though to catch Clemmie if she tried to escape. Panic flooded through Clemmie; she shook her head, her mouth dropping open in fear.

'Don't you dare!' Josie flared. 'Don't you dare tell, or I'll tell him you tried to coax the vicar out into the woods – I swear I will!'

'You wouldn't *dare*!' Liz gasped. Clemmie whined in her throat and grasped at Mary's hands, silently pleading: *Don't tell, don't tell!*

'Is he married, Clem?' Mary asked. Clemmie shook her head vehemently. 'And he's your own age, thereabouts, not some dirty old man?' She nodded just as hard. Mary thought for a moment longer. 'We won't tell on you, Clem. And if you say a word,' Mary rounded on Liz, 'we'll make you wish you'd never.'

However many times she told herself that it was fine, and that her sisters would keep their word, Clemmie felt uneasy. She wished she'd shaken her head, but it was too late. It was out there now, and couldn't be got back. That moment of wanting to share – to boast, really – and now her precious secret was only half a secret. She made her way through the woods opposite the mill, towards Thatch Cottage, stopping now and then to listen, to look behind her. She wasn't being followed, by her sisters or by anybody else, but the nagging feeling remained. A shadow of unease. The sun was sinking as the afternoon aged, but the heat was still stifling; the air between the trees was sluggish and overripe. There was sweat in her hair and between her thighs; she could smell the river water on her skin – dank now, vegetal. Clemmie climbed up onto the ridge, panting, sliding on loose soil; she waited a while then slithered back down again, watching for him, waiting for him. A bluish shade gathered beneath the trees. She sat down on a gravestone at the Friends' chapel, with a view of Thatch Cottage's roof, to empty the stones from her shoes. She was restless, impatient for him to appear. Then there was a loud crash from the cottage, and the sound of Tanner shouting, his voice so huge and full of rage. Clemmie's heart flung itself against her ribs.

She knew who was responsible for Eli's nose being so crooked, and for the split lip he'd had recently, when he'd stayed out too late with her and returned home after dark – they'd fallen asleep beneath the wizened roots of a fallen tree, tangled up together. She was suddenly afraid that he was in trouble because she'd revealed their love, before remembering that there was no way her sisters could have guessed who, or told anyone. Frightened for him, outraged for him, her blood raced in her veins. She dodged nearer, keeping close to the trunks of trees, the cover of bushes, then a pile of broken stones, and then the Tanners' privy, which stank and buzzed with flies. The cottage's windows were open, so the voices inside were clear.

'I'll have his bloody guts!' This was Tanner – bitter, hard, furred with drink.

'Christ, but he gave you enough chances, Dad!' A boy's uneven voice, newly broken; not Eli's. There was the sound of a blow and a woman's cry, and the scrape of shoved furniture.

'Don't hit the boy! It's none of his fault!' A woman – Eli's mother, Clemmie guessed. There was more shouting, more thumping. 'Stop it! Lay off!' the woman said again.

'You're all of you naught but wasted space! I should have drowned you each as she whelped you!'

'And what does that make you, Dad? Passed out drunk on the job again, where any bugger could see you?'

'You come here, you little shit! You're no son of mine.' The front door banged wide and a thin boy ran out, arms pumping, head down, dodging the detritus in the yard. Tanner followed but lost his footing and sprawled to the ground. He stayed down a while, ribs heaving like bellows, until his wife came to his side, looking too weary to be frightened. Tanner let her help him up then pushed her away, staggering back inside.

Clemmie still hadn't heard Eli speak, but if he wasn't inside and he hadn't come to find her then she didn't know where he could be. There was no more shouting for a while, no more crashing. Clemmie sidled closer, watching every footstep, so careful not to make a sound that her head began to thump. She crouched down below the back window. The smell of stewed carrots and bone stock drifted out to her; a baby cried for a moment and was quickly hushed; there was the sound of a plate being put down on a table.

'Here. Eat something,' said Mrs Tanner. For a long time after that, nobody said anything. There were at least ten or twelve Tanners living there; many of them little. Clemmie found their silence unnatural, ominous. She wished she had the courage to peer in at the window, just to see if Eli were there, but she didn't dare. 'What'll you do, then?' said Mrs Tanner, at last. Tanner grunted.

'I'll have his bloody guts.'

'Alistair Hadleigh's always been good to us,' she said, cautiously.

'He was itching for an excuse to get shot of me this time. Rich folk are all the same. They're all slippery bastards; holier than the likes of us, they think.'

'Perhaps he'd have you back again, given a bit of time . . .'

'I'll not work for that grinning idiot again.'

'But . . . the money, Isaac. We can't do without it.'

'I'll get money.' Another long silence followed his words.

'What do you mean?'

'He's got more than he needs, especially now, with all the wages due to be paid. Reckon it's time I paid him a visit.'

'You can't mean to rob him . . .' Her voice was hushed, frightened now. 'It'd be madness, right here in the village! We'll be hounded out, Isaac—'

'Shut your mouth, woman. I weren't planning on leaving a calling card. Me and Eli and John'll do it, just like always. Haven't been caught yet, have we? We'll take care of him, and your bloody money. Nobody calls me what he did today and gets away with it. Ain't that right, boy?'

'When do you want to do it, Dad?' Clemmie went cold. He sounded frightened, he didn't sound himself. But it was Eli who had spoken.

5

The Change

Pudding tried not to notice the way Irene Hadleigh's hands shook as she gripped the leather strap around Robin's neck. Her face was pale, her jaw clamped shut. Pudding wondered whether to say something specific about there being no need to worry, or whether that'd only make Irene feel worse. Like when people pointed out that she was blushing – as if she might be unaware of the hot blood thumping in her cheeks – which always made her blush harder.

'That's right. Now, he's not going to move until we're ready for him to, I promise; I've got hold of him.'

'You're sure?' said Irene.

'Perfectly sure. Now, left foot into the stirrup, right leg over the back and you're on. That's the way.' Pudding had never taught anyone to ride before. She felt proud, knowledgeable, and under a terrible weight of responsibility. Now that Irene had finally decided to try, Pudding supposed it would be her fault if she didn't take to it. 'Comfortable?' she asked, having adjusted the length of the stirrups.

'Not remotely,' said Irene. Pudding glanced up with a smile, thinking she was joking, but Irene's fixed expression made her change her mind.

'Oh. Well, er . . .' she said. 'It does take a little bit of getting used to.' Except that Pudding remembered first sitting on a horse – a pony, in fact – and her reaction had been instantaneous joy and excitement. She busied herself for a while, showing Irene how to hold the reins and where to have her legs and feet. 'But for now, just hold onto the neck strap if you feel wobbly, and we'll go for a bit of a walk. All right? Ready?' Irene took a short breath, re-clamped her lips, and nodded.

She sat stiffly, swaying awkwardly with every step Robin took, as Pudding led them across to the flattish paddock where she normally schooled the horses. She wasn't sure how to continue the lesson. It didn't seem fair to start drilling Irene about keeping her heels down or her thumbs to the top – *you're holding teacups, not pushing a pram* – as her own instructor had done – not when Irene seemed to be concentrating so hard on simply staying sat, and not giving in to panic. They made a few sedate loops of the paddock, until Pudding couldn't stand the silence any longer. 'What made you decide to give riding a go, Mrs Hadleigh?' she said, smiling up at her. Irene flicked her eyes at Pudding for the briefest second, as though keeping them fixed on the horizon were essential to success.

'Oh. It was high time, I suppose,' she said, tonelessly. 'Or rather, Nancy and my husband thought it was high time.'

'Well, you do have a super horse to learn on. I learnt on a pony so fat I could barely straddle him. We should count ourselves lucky we're allowed to ride astride at all, though. A lot of ladies Miss H's age still think it's obscene. And a lot of chaps.'

'In London, most ladies still take the side saddle.' Irene's tone left Pudding none the wiser as to whether she approved of that or not.

'Really? Well, astride is infinitely better, and easier.' Pudding wondered, once she'd said this, about her own authoritative tone. 'That is, I think it is,' she amended, but Irene didn't seem to have a strong opinion about it.

They went on in silence for a while. Irene was so quiet that Pudding glanced back now and then, half expecting her to have toppled off some way back and be sitting among the daisies. The saddle creaked; Robin chewed his bit thoughtfully; from further down the hill came a loud curse and the delighted squealing of a pig. Irene cleared her throat carefully.

'Have your family always lived in Slaughterford?' she asked.

'Oh yes. It's the best place, really.' Pudding thought about that for a moment. 'Well, I like it anyway. But I should like to see London, one day. I truly would.'

'You've never been? Why not?' Irene sounded surprised.

'Oh. Well. We just . . . live here.' Pudding's mother had always said they would take a trip up to London when Pudding was old enough to appreciate it. Pudding felt that that time had definitely come, but now, of course, her mother might not enjoy it as once she might. And Donny certainly wouldn't like all the noise and people.

'But . . . you must have been away before? Away from Slaughterford, I mean?' Irene sounded vaguely appalled.

'Oh, yes! Of course.' In fact she hadn't gone anywhere in ages – not since Donny had come home from the war, in fact. 'We used to go to the seaside all the time, when we were little. Three or four times, every summer. And I've an aunt in Porlock – we go to visit her quite often.'

'Oh,' said Irene, and Pudding guessed that it sounded very parochial indeed to her. She felt caught between defending her small corner of England and naming all the many places she would love to visit. 'Well, I've been planning to pay a call to your mother. I . . . ought to have done so sooner,' Irene added. 'So perhaps I could mention it to her – that a visit to London is a very good thing for a young person. If you'd like me to, that is? I'd be very subtle.'

'Well . . .' said Pudding, her heart sinking. Clearly, nobody had explained the nature of Louise Cartwright's illness to Irene. She hunted around for the right words to do it, but soon gave up. 'That's very kind of you, Mrs Hadleigh,' she mumbled instead, and to change the subject completely, pointed at one of the rounded hills on the horizon. 'That's Cold Tump. It's probably an old barrow – did you know that when a place is called "cold"-something around here, it means it's haunted? Or rather, that whoever named it thought it was haunted. Which usually means it was named by some Celt or Saxon settler who was superstitious about the prehistorical bits and bobs left behind – burial mounds and things. Old bones in old tombs. There's a Cold Harbour Farm on the way to Chippenham, and people still say it's haunted.' She went on to describe the spectral procession of dead warriors, all with spears, helmets and ghastly empty eye sockets, who'd been seen marching past the farm on frigid, moonlit nights. She kept on with the story, even though she wasn't sure if Irene Hadleigh were even listening, or wanted to know about it all, because when she stopped talking the silence seemed to rebuke her. It was something like guilt that made her rattle on – guilt to have said nothing about her mother's illness; nothing about how Donny's injury had made trips away even rarer; and guilt to have implied, even to herself, that she might wish for things to be otherwise.

❧ ❧

Irene walked stiffly back towards the house after her lesson, feeling relieved it was over until she reminded herself that riding just once was not going to wash. She would have to do it again, and again, and try to master it and enjoy it. She fought against the sinking feeling that gave her, and paused in the yard to pull off her gloves, a finger at a time. There was movement from one of the farmhouse windows, and Irene hoped Nancy had been watching, and had seen her on the horse. Just then, the old groom, Hilarius, came out of the great barn, and since

Irene's first impulse was to turn away, go indoors and pretend not to have seen him, she made herself square up and introduce herself. She hoped that Nancy were *still* watching.

'Hello,' she said, holding out her hand for Hilarius to shake. 'I'm Irene Hadleigh.' The old man paused in his progress, and peered down at his filthy palm before apparently deciding not to take Irene's. She let her hand drop, feeling foolish, and hoped Nancy had stopped watching.

'Ar,' said Hilarius. Irene couldn't guess his age. He was bald on top, with straggles of grey hair around his collar; she couldn't tell the colour of his eyes – they were merely a glint through narrow gaps in his eyelids. She noticed that his eyelashes, though they were few, were still jet black.

'You . . . look after the work horses, is that right?' she tried, floundering. Her mouth had gone dry and she didn't feel right. Something fluttery and strange was inside her head, making it hard to think, or focus her eyes. She blinked rapidly, and every time she did a shadow seemed to coalesce around the old man, receding when she tried to see clearly. The sun was high in the sky, and her own shadow was stunted, close to her feet. But the old man somehow seemed to cast a huge shadow. Far bigger than himself, and fathomless. He watched her with that distant glitter of his eyes, and Irene found herself backing away.

'Ar, that's right,' he said, but Irene hardly heard him.

'I'm sorry,' she murmured, powerfully unwilling to look him in the eye, or to be near him. The fluttering inside was getting worse, and she felt cold. He seemed to radiate cold. 'Won't you please excuse me,' she whispered.

Inside, Irene sat down on the horribly uncomfortable chair that lived in the hallway, and had been designed to be looked at but not sat in. She took a deep breath, and swallowed.

'Everything all right?' said Nancy, coolly, as she came along from her sitting room.

'Yes. Quite all right. Thank you.' Irene rose, smoothing her gloves between her fingers.

'Jolly good. Excuse me.' Nancy went past, and up the stairs.

'Is that my good lady wife?' Alistair called, from the kitchen.

'Alistair! You're home,' said Irene, relieved to find she wasn't alone with Nancy.

'A bit early for lunch, I know, but I couldn't wait to hear how you'd got on. Well?'

'Oh, I don't know – you'd have to ask Pudding. I didn't fall off, anyway.'

'Well, that's a start.' Alistair laughed. 'But how did you like it?'

'Well enough, I think ... I wasn't sure what to expect. Pudding's talkative, isn't she?' she said, to head off any questions about when she would next ride.

'Oh, yes.'

'And rather ghoulish. She always seems to want to tell me some hideous story about a battle or a ghost or something.' At this, Alistair chuckled again.

'Yes, she always did like the more blood-curdling stories. I once caught her and a companion – little Maisie Cooper, I think it was – under a hedge, dissecting a rat. They'd each brought a paring knife from home to do the job. They can't have been more than eight or nine years old.'

'That's hideous!'

'Thoroughly. They told me it was *anatomy*, in fact, and insisted that the rat had been run over by a wagon full of beans, so it was quite humane.' He smiled at Irene's disgusted expression. She thought about Hilarius, and when she did the fluttering returned, albeit in a weaker way. She'd decided against saying anything when the words came anyway, unbidden.

'I just met Hilarius, the horse groom.'

'Oh yes? Solid as a rock, that old chap. People have never taken to him, in the village; they can be so spooked and peculiar at the idea of a foreigner, at times. But he's a good sort.'

'Yes, of course,' said Irene, not in the least bit surprised to hear that the man was not well liked.

She'd written to Cora McKinley, since Alistair had been so keen that she write to *somebody*, and Irene found herself wanting to try harder for him. Besides, doing all these things that scared her was proving a good way to distract her from Fin's last letter and what it had said. She very much still needed to be distracted from that. Her letter to Cora had been rather vague, suggesting that they might go into Chippenham or Bath together one day, and the morning after her riding lesson, Keith Glover brought Cora's reply. Her handwriting was a series of exuberant swoops in black ink. *We must! Or – even better – how do you fancy the coast? My cousin Amelia has a little villa – well, perhaps I'd better call it a hovel, to manage your expectations – in the hills near Lyme Regis. I'd been thinking about descending upon her, with it so terminally hot. You must come with me! There's simply nothing like sea bathing for whipping up the spirits. Write back immediately and say you'll come. Just us girls.* Alistair looked delighted when she showed him.

'Good old Cora,' he said. 'You'll have a lot of fun, I'm sure.'

'You think I ought to go?'

'Well, yes.' He looked surprised. 'If you'd like to, that is. I'd miss you, but if you promised to come back again before very long . . .' He smiled, pleased, and gave her a kiss. Irene attempted to stifle her reluctance to go. Cora had been easy enough company – garrulous enough to make up for Irene's lack of conversation. But she wasn't sure if she could pretend to be all right in front of Cousin Amelia; she wasn't sure how they would take her, how it would go. She imagined hearing whispered conversations, and stifled laughter behind her back. It caused her a flood of nerves, but she went to her writing room and took out a note card, and penned her acceptance of the invitation. Her mother had often instructed her, growing up, to feign the proper feeling, the proper form, until the proper feeling arrived. Or simply to keep on feigning if it didn't.

Every time Irene did one of these new things – went for a ride, introduced herself to somebody, exchanged a civil word with Nancy – Alistair seemed happy. Happy that she was trying, that she seemed to feel better, that she was making herself at home, at last. And Irene had started to find that making Alistair happy made her feel a little better too. She wavered, frequently. Twenty times a day she told herself that she couldn't do it – she couldn't accept that Manor Farm, and her marriage to Alistair, were her life from now on. They were her present reality, and they were the only future she had, and she had no idea how she would ever be reconciled to that. Twenty times a day she felt despair lapping, dangerously, around her ankles – a rising tide that would drown her if she let it. If she stood still, and watched it rise. So, twenty times a day she tried to take a step towards higher ground, even though it wasn't always obvious where that might be. But Alistair – and the ease with which she could please him – seemed a reliable stepping stone. The following morning, when Irene announced that she was going to visit Louise Cartwright, the doctor's wife, she let Alistair's warm smile of approval be her reward in advance. It also prevented her from backing out.

'Bravo, Irene,' he said. 'She always did love Clara's raspberry lemonade – you might take her a bottle from the pantry.'

Following Alistair's careful directions, Irene went on foot, which was the best way until she was confident enough to ride on her own. The lane up to Spring Cottage was too steep for the gig; the only way to reach it by road was by making a huge loop through Ford. The sun beat down and Irene walked incredibly slowly, ostensibly so that she wouldn't arrive sweating like a shire horse but mainly because, now she was out and on her own, she was horribly nervous. She tried to think of at least five safe topics of conversation she could rely upon if it all dried up: the weather, of course; Pudding teaching her to ride; how very busy the doctor must be; the best places to shop in Chippenham. Try as she might, she couldn't think of a fifth, and was terrified that she'd mention Pudding's brother Donald. She'd tried to talk to him about flowers for the house a few days before, and his terrible scars had been such a shock that she'd recoiled before she could stop herself. When she'd realised that the young man was simple she'd retreated, loathing her own inadequacy. What could one possibly say to a mother about a son who'd been so damaged by the war? Irene prayed that Louise wouldn't want to talk about it.

However, once the Cartwrights' hatchet-faced housekeeper had led Irene to where Mrs Cartwright was sitting, limp, in a garden chair, it became abundantly clear that she wouldn't want to talk about Donald. Or about anything else. When none of her overtures met with any response she could understand, Irene sat in terrified silence, entirely wrong-footed. Her heart hammered and her mind, though it churned and sped, drew a complete blank as to how she should proceed. In the end Mrs Cartwright sat forward, shaking her head, and said:

'But who *are* you, young lady? I don't understand why you refuse to tell me.' Irene repeated her name but Mrs Cartwright simply shook her head again, looking lost.

'Not a good day,' said the housekeeper, as she ushered Irene out. 'Try back another time, why don't you? Good of you to call. I'll tell the doctor, he'll be sorry to have missed you.'

But Irene walked a few yards down the hill, until she was safely out of sight of Spring Cottage, and burst into tears. The despair swilled around her feet. She felt shocked, exhausted; the tremulous relief of having survived a situation far out of her depth. And then she thought about Pudding, coping with her mother being so confused as well as her brother being so altered, and forced herself to stop crying. It wasn't herself she ought to be pitying. Cringing, she remembered offering to nudge Pudding's mother towards taking her up to London.

By the time she got back to Manor Farm, Irene was angry. She was angry with herself for being so useless, and not knowing what to say; for being frightened by the unfamiliar, and for adding to Mrs Cartwright's puzzlement and obvious unease. But she was angry with the others too. She might have coped – or at least coped better – if somebody had let on to her that Mrs Cartwright's illness wasn't physical. Alistair might have told her. Clara, the housekeeper, might have told her. Nancy certainly might have – she'd merely smiled thinly as Irene had announced her plan to visit. Perhaps there *had* been a glimmer of amusement, or malice, in her eyes. Quite possibly, now that Irene came to think about it. Still shaky, she went in search of Nancy, not sure what she would say but thinking of something along the lines of it possibly being easier, in future, for her to maintain the *Hadleigh standard* if Nancy didn't set out to deliberately sabotage her, and make her look a fool. Nancy would doubtless find it highly amusing, but she resolved to say it anyway. She went through to the back sitting room, where Nancy had her desk and books, but Nancy wasn't there. The room was incredibly hot and stuffy. Puzzled, Irene looked at the hearth, where the remains of a fire was burning low. She sat down in the fireside chair, took the poker and stabbed at the ashes. Why Nancy had thought she needed to light a fire on such a fine day was a mystery. There were shreds of paper in the ashes, and traces of something blue – a colour that tugged at Irene with its familiarity for a second.

She stirred the glowing embers about and stared into them, searching for something she would recognise, waiting to understand why she didn't feel she could simply walk away and forget about it. She had that same distracting feeling of something being wrong, or perhaps merely familiar, as when she'd first handled the doll in the old schoolroom – a discordance that was almost like a déjà vu. The sense that there was something to notice, but she wasn't quite able to see it. Staring hard, she remembered the day her cousin Gilbert had died, and how her greatest shock, when she'd been given the news, had come from realising that she was not surprised. She had known. She'd been to visit him the day before, with her parents. She'd been twelve, Gilbert seventeen. Blond-haired and lithe, and so full of himself Irene hadn't liked him much at all. She'd played tennis with him on the lawn outside her aunt and uncle's imposing house in Richmond – a wildly one-sided match, since Gilbert wouldn't hold back his shots or his serve just because his opponent was so much younger and smaller – and when they'd shaken hands across the net after his inevitable victory, Irene had scowled up at him and seen something flicker in his eyes. A shadow of something passing, like a shred of cloud across the sun; and from the way his nostrils suddenly flared, whatever it was had made Gilbert take a breath. Irene hadn't thought of anything specific happening, at all – she'd only known that it was significant. That something important was going to happen.

When Gilbert died the next day, from what the doctors eventually decided was a catastrophic and hitherto concealed defect of the heart, Irene had felt peculiar. And not surprised. She'd said nothing about it to anyone, and it was only as she got older, and was able to think about it more, that she wondered.

She wondered if sometimes a hindquarter of her mind took more from the things her eyes saw and her ears heard than the main part of her brain was aware of. She wondered whether that hindquarter sometimes jumped up and down and waved its hands, metaphorically speaking, and did its best to be heard, to no avail. So she sat a while longer, sweating, in Nancy's overheated room and tried to put her finger on what it was she'd noticed without realising it. Then again, there was always the possibility that Gilbert had been a complete fluke, and the feelings she sometimes got were the self-aggrandising delusions of a child. After all, nothing whatsoever had come of finding the old doll. Feeling cross and exhausted, Irene gave the ashes a final stir. She got up and tried to open a window to let in some air, but couldn't get it to budge.

In the kitchen, Clara and Florence the maid were shelling peas.

'Excuse me,' said Irene, distractedly. 'There's a terrible fug in Nancy's room and I can't find the key to open the window.' Clara blinked at her, then exchanged a glance with Florence, who shrugged.

'A fug, Mrs Hadleigh? What kind o' fug might that be?' said Clara.

'The kind that makes it hard to breathe. Why on earth did she want a fire lit, on a day like this?'

'A fire, Mrs Hadleigh?' Clara frowned. 'There's no fires lit; not been for weeks.'

'Well, I'm quite sure I didn't imagine it, Mrs Gosling.'

'Miss Hadleigh never would take it upon herself to light the fires. They weren't even laid up ready. And certainly no one's been to ask us to do it. I don't believe Miss Hadleigh has even been back since lunch.' Clara glanced at Florence, who shook her head.

'Well, I can assure you there is a fire going in her sitting room, and if neither you nor she lit it, then who on earth did?' said Irene, exasperatedly.

'Well,' said Clara, giving Florence a look that might have been meant to imply that Irene had gone peculiar. 'I'm sure I don't know, Mrs Hadleigh.'

'Never mind.' Irene sighed. 'Is there a key to the window?'

'Ar. 'Ee bides zomewur hind o' the shutter,' said Florence. Irene stared at her. 'Cassn't thee follow I?' said the maid, incredulously.

'It'll be hanging on a nail behind the shutter, ma'am; same as with all the windows,' Clara translated, speaking slowly, as if to a child.

At the end of the day, Irene told Alistair about her difficult visit to Louise Cartwright, and he looked pained.

'But I did tell you, darling. I explained that she suffers a degradation of the mind, right back in the beginning,' he said.

'Oh.' It was quite possible. Irene had almost no memory of her first weeks in Slaughterford, back in early May. Alistair took a sip of his gin. They were out on the terrace, which was alight with late sunshine beneath a vast span of clear sky.

'I . . . spoke to you about Donny as well. Do you recall? That he was injured in the war and is . . . well, somewhat slower, these days.'

'Yes, I remember,' Irene lied.

'Have you met him properly yet? Donny, I mean?'

'Sort of. I . . . went out to ask about flowers, but I didn't get much of a response.' She sensed what was coming next, and was about to say that she wasn't up to it, but just then Nancy came out onto the terrace and gave her a measuring look.

'Yes, you're better off speaking to Jem about anything you'd like brought in from the gardens. Would you like to meet Donny again now?' said Alistair. 'He's just over in the potting sheds, though I expect he'll be heading home for supper soon.'

'Yes, all right,' said Irene. Happily, with Alistair at her side, the conversation with Donald went far better than the one with his mother had gone. The scars of his wound were still terrible, and at first Irene didn't know where to look, until she realised that Donny himself wouldn't notice anyway. He seemed sweet; there was something soft and almost childlike in his slow responses, and the careful way he moved and spoke. Alistair seemed delighted that it had gone so well, and Irene felt again that delighting Alistair might in fact be a worthwhile way to spend her time. She decided, as they returned to the aperitifs on the terrace, that the day hadn't been a complete bust after all.

In the evening, she and Alistair played cribbage while Handel's *Water Music* played on the wireless, and Nancy read a book on the sofa, her legs crossed at her elegant ankles. Irene won three times in a row.

'You have me quite licked, darling,' said Alistair. 'Excuse me while I nip out to greet the prince.' By this he meant visit the privy, which, whilst it could only be reached by going outside, did at least flush – with such a roaring, gurgling thunder of water that it had been nicknamed the Royal George, after the ocean liner. As soon as he left the room, Irene felt Nancy's presence grow. Sure enough, she heard the book close, and the creak of the sofa as she rose.

'I owe you an apology, Irene,' she said, coming to stand beside the card table. Irene was struck dumb. 'I ought to have explained to you about Mrs Cartwright's condition. It was unkind of me not to – to the pair of you.'

'Well,' said Irene, fingering the green baize of the table. Nancy grunted.

'It seems to me that, as much as anything, you're frightened of people.' There was mild exasperation in her tone as she said this. 'You'll grow out of it, I'm sure. But there we go. I ought to have said. It can't have been an easy visit for you.' With that she went back to the sofa and her book, and Irene steeled herself to continue the conversation.

'Nancy, did you light the fire in your sitting room today?' she said. Nancy peered at her across the top of her book.

'I beg your pardon?'

'I looked for you in your sitting room earlier, and found the fire lit. It was dreadfully hot in there. Clara and Florence both say they never lit it. I was just . . . wondering, I suppose.'

'Well, why on earth would they? Why would anyone, on such a glorious day?' said Nancy, looking back at her book, and Irene still hadn't decided whether or how to go on by the time Alistair returned. 'What did you want me for, anyway?' Nancy asked.

'Sorry?' said Alistair.

'Irene was just saying that she came to look for me, earlier.'

'Oh, nothing. It doesn't matter,' said Irene, relieved beyond words that she hadn't found Nancy and tried to tell her off over Louise Cartwright, when this apology had been in the offing.

'Shall we go up, darling? I don't think I can take another pasting at cards tonight.' Alistair smiled and held out his hand, which Irene took gratefully.

It had been so long since a day had dawned dark and wet that when Irene woke the following morning, she thought it was still night-time. Alistair was gone, and she hadn't been aware of him getting up; she was becoming accustomed to sleeping beside him, and to the small sounds and movements as he rose and disappeared into his dressing room, as softly as he could. She turned over and looked at the clock, and even though it was late in the morning, she settled her cheek back into the pillow for the last peaceful half an hour before she would have to rise and face another day. To her surprise, she found that the thought of the day ahead wasn't so very bad at all. Her stomach growled hotly for some food; she put out her hand to feel if any warmth remained between the sheets on Alistair's side of the bed, and wished she'd seen him before he'd gone out for the day. She'd started to look forward to his smile, and the way he cared for her in spite of it all – when it felt like nobody else did. She lay a while and thought about that, wondering why her first impulse was to resist it. Something her mother had shouted at her – during one of the many rows once she and Fin had been discovered – came back to her then. *Why do you actively seek to destroy yourself, Irene? You always have. Ever since you were five years old and took scissors to your own hair.* Neither at that time, nor at any time since, had Irene been able to explain that it was because she had never felt good enough. But she didn't want to resist Alistair. There and then she decided not to, and shut her eyes to pledge it to herself.

She got up and peered out at the rain – a steady downpour that draped a curtain across the valley, muting the trees and fields to grey. It washed the smoke and steam from the mill chimneys before it could rise, and the sound of it hitting the window drowned out the thud of the machinery. It was like waking up in a wholly different place. Irene dressed, ate some of the dried-out scrambled eggs in the breakfast room and sat down with the paper, and it was a while before she began to feel as though something might be amiss. The quiet was too quiet; the house felt as though it were holding its breath. For no reason she could trace, the skin prickled restlessly at the back of Irene's neck. She got up and went to the window again, and was still staring out when Nancy came in and stood beside her. Irene braced herself, but Nancy was looking down at the mill and seemed lost in thoughts other than Irene's failings that morning.

'Good morning, Nancy,' said Irene.

'Good morning. Did you see Alistair before he went off?'

'No, not this morning.'

'Me neither. Odd.'

'Is it?'

'He hates rainy days. Always has, even when he was a boy. I used to have to chivvy him up, and now he's a man he still uses it as an excuse to lie about in bed.'

'I can't imagine that, somehow.'

'No, well.' Nancy shrugged.

'Will the river flood?'

'If it keeps this up much longer, it just might,' said Nancy. It was the closest they'd yet come to an easy, civil conversation, and Irene was pleased, even if it was about the weather.

'You can't even see the smoke from the chimneys, or hear the Fou . . . the paper-making machine,' she added, and Nancy frowned.

'The Fourdrinier. No,' she said. 'You can't. And that *is* unusual.'

They stood side by side for a while longer, and Irene searched for something else to say – something pertinent – but had come up with nothing by the time Nancy turned to leave again. She paused by the door, and seemed to weigh something up. 'I'm going down to stick my nose in,' she said. 'Are you coming?' She fixed Irene with an accusatory look, as though daring her to decline, or perhaps to accept. Irene nodded.

'Yes, all right,' she said. 'Only . . . I haven't a raincoat.'

'Not to worry. I've an oilskin mackintosh that will fit you, since there isn't a shred of flesh on you.'

'I've had some eggs this morning,' said Irene, and then loathed herself for trying so blatantly to please.

'Well, good. Let down your hair and have some lunch later as well, why don't you? Come along. You'll want a hat as well.' Nancy strode off along the corridor towards the back kitchen where coats and boots and walking sticks waited in their ranks, and Irene went along in her wake, with the anxious sense of having found a point of balance that might very easily be lost again.

A torrent of muddy water poured down the lane outside the farm, towards the village; fast and deep enough to roll small stones along with it. Pudding was newly back from a hack on Baron, Alistair's hunter, and looked as wet and bedraggled as a drenched cat. Water dripped from the peak of her cap, but she hallooed them as they passed.

'Dismal day for a walk!' she called. Steam rose from the horse's flanks.

'Don't be ridiculous, girl,' said Nancy. 'We're off to the mill. I think the machines have stopped.'

'Not really?' said Pudding, looking aghast, and Irene wondered how bad it could really be, since presumably the machines could simply be started up again at some point.

'Seems so, but I'm not sure. Do get that horse in and thatched, Pudding.' They carried on into the village, where they didn't see a soul. The beaters of Rag Mill were audible, and ragged pennants of steam rose from the brewery in spite of the rain, and Nancy's face darkened.

'Is it so very bad, if the machines stop?' Irene asked, tentatively. Nancy grunted.

'Not life and death, no. But it usually means the boilers have been allowed to go out, and it takes an awful lot of fuel and effort to get them back up again. It ought not to happen at all, and if it has I shall very much want to know why.'

The mill was eerily still. Outside the bag room, two women were standing idle, holding a coat over their heads as an umbrella. They stared at Nancy and Irene with wide, fearful eyes, and though Nancy drew breath to interrogate them, the words died on her lips. Most of the rest of the mill workers appeared to be gathered around the huge sliding doors to the new boiler house. The rain had soaked their shoulders darkly; they stood hunched, hands in pockets, staring across the yard at the old farmhouse. A few more men clustered at the door to the offices. Standing in the rain as though they'd been prevented from going inside. 'What in hell's name is going on here? Why is nobody at work?' said Nancy, as she strode over to the farmhouse door. Irene hastened after her, the rain pattering loudly on her hat. One of the men put out his arms to block their path, and Irene recognised him as the paper-maker she'd been introduced to. The look he gave her was so grave that Irene's throat went dry.

'Best not to go in, Miss Hadleigh, Mrs Hadleigh,' he said, sombrely. 'Best not to.'

'Get out of the way, man,' said Nancy.

'Miss Hadleigh—' Nancy pushed past the man and, with Irene on her heels, walked into the dry warmth of the offices. And there she stopped.

For a few moments, Irene could make no sense of what she was seeing. Something was heaped on the floor near the old inglenook; spilt dark liquid had puddled there, lustrous as oil, and more men were standing in the way, so that the thing could only be glimpsed through their legs. There was an odd smell, metallic but fresher than the hot, greased metal of the steam engine and boilers. A butcher's shop smell that made the hair stand up along Irene's arms, and her stomach start to turn. Nancy rushed forwards, fell to her knees, then froze. Irene took two steps after her, but her legs felt numb and watery, and she no longer trusted them to carry her. She stopped, and stared. In the weird hush of a roomful of people not talking, Nancy started up an awful keening. It sent a shiver right through Irene, but she couldn't react. She had no idea how to react, as her eyes registered what they were seeing.

It was Alistair, lying on the floor, and the dark, lustrous stuff was his blood. His neck was a ruin of deep, ugly wounds, and one had cut into his right cheek as well – there was a grey-white flash of bone, a ghastly flap of skin, hanging loose. He was sprawled on his back with his arms flung out and his legs at odd, uncomfortable angles. His eyes were open, gazing up at the metal lamp above his head as though mesmerised by it. It seemed, to Irene, far too gentle an expression for him to wear, when he had been subjected to such violence. But then, that was Alistair, she supposed. Had been Alistair. She swallowed. There was no chance that the broken thing on the floor was a living person any more. Irene felt a hand on her shoulder, but couldn't turn her head.

'He was found this way soon after the first shift started, Mrs Hadleigh,' a man told her, softly. 'We've sent Kenny – the office boy – to Biddestone to fetch the police constable, and they're sending to Chippenham for more men, too, in case he gives us any trouble. They oughtn't to be much longer.'

'Why weren't we told?' Irene whispered. She pictured herself feeling Alistair's side of the bed for warmth; sitting at the table, eating scrambled eggs. 'Why weren't we told right away?'

'Nobody wanted to be the one to . . .' The man trailed off. 'There didn't seem to be anything to be gained by it,' he said, heavily.

'But I should have been told,' she said, her voice shrinking. She felt as though she were shrinking. Nancy was still weeping, kneeling beside her nephew, and Irene knew she ought to go over and try to comfort her. But it was a ridiculous idea. Nancy couldn't possibly be comforted in the face of such a loss, and the sight of her bent and broken on the floor was almost as bad, almost as unnatural, as the gentle expression on Alistair's face.

Then they all just stood, for a while. Nancy cried, and Irene didn't blink, and one of the men coughed, and the rain hammered down outside, trickling musically along the guttering. The implausibility of it all robbed Irene of the slightest idea of what to do, and from the way the men fidgeted and glanced at one another, they were all similarly stupefied.

'Someone ought take the women away,' one of the men muttered, but nobody moved to. The idea of making – or even suggesting – Nancy do something was alien to them all. Irene was steeling herself to be the one to try, and had even managed a step forwards, with her heart hammering so loudly she could hardly hear above it, when she was barrelled from behind by the wet, breathless form of Pudding Cartwright.

'Here you all are. See! Keith came up to the farm to tell us, but I knew it couldn't be . . .' she said, but halted abruptly when she saw. Irene turned to her, and saw her face contort into an expression of such utter agony and disbelief that Irene felt it in her own bones. With a small cry, Pudding seemed to deflate, and she sobbed unashamedly, like a child, with her chin on her chest and her shoulders heaving. Behind her, Jem Welch the gardener appeared, and old Hilarius the groom – servants who'd known Alistair since he was a baby. Their lined faces were heavy and afraid, and neither one of them spoke. The smell of it all wormed its way inexorably into Irene's nose – wet bodies and blood and horse and earth and hair. A cacophony that her mind reeled from. Black blotches crowded in at the sides of her vision, and she staggered to one side, reaching out for balance.

'That's quite enough, now,' said George Turner, the foreman, finally taking charge. 'You men – take these three ladies back up to the farmhouse, and get Mrs Gosling to make them sweet tea. It's a terrible shock, and none of them ought to have seen him this way. I'm sure the police constable will be up to call on them very shortly. And Pudding ought not see her brother carted away in irons.'

Pudding's head came up in an instant. Her face was blotchy and red.

'What? What did you say?' she gasped. George pressed his lips together until his moustache all but hid his mouth.

'Best you get on home, Pudding. Or up to the farm with Mrs Hadleigh here. We've sent for your father but he's attending a difficult birth in Yatton.'

'Yes . . . a doctor. My father could help . . .' said Pudding, hopefully. Then she looked at the blood and the wounds again, and that hope vanished. 'But what did you say about Donny?'

'Now, Pudding—'

'Is he hurt too? Tell me!'

'Girl's going to find out sooner or later,' said another man, gruffly.

'Speak up, man,' Jem told George, curtly.

'It seems that . . . Donald was the one to attack Mr Hadleigh.'

'No.' Pudding shook her head. 'He wasn't.'

'He was found in the machine room with bloodied hands, and shirt, and . . . holding a shovel, also bloody. One of the coal shovels, it seems. He was just standing there, and still is, and he'll not speak a word in his own defence.' George's reluctance to give this news was evident. Jem Welch's face went through outrage and disbelief to a kind of resigned sadness, but Pudding shook her head madly.

'But that's just what he does – he likes to watch the machines! That's just what he does. It doesn't mean a thing! You can't *possibly* believe he would hurt Mr Hadleigh?'

'Perhaps he didn't intend to ... inflict such injuries as he did, but nevertheless—'

'He didn't do it,' said Pudding. 'I know he didn't. I'll ask him and he'll tell you!'

At that point the sound of an engine came into the yard – the police superintendent from Chippenham, with the Biddestone constable beside him and two other young officers, in a steaming, spluttering car with mud splashed all up its sides. A wave of palpable relief went through the men in the room, and they began to file out like some kind of sombre welcoming committee. Nancy hadn't moved from Alistair's side; Pudding was still gabbling, struggling to breathe through her tears – Hilarius had hold of her arm and was trying to lead her outside. The superintendent came in, wiping rain from his spectacles, and began at once to order them away from the corpse, out into the rain. On sudden impulse, Irene struggled forwards through the moving wall of shoulders and chests. She knelt down close to Alistair's head, and was careful to look at his eyes, which were going dry and losing their shine, rather than at his terrible wounds. They drew her gaze with a hideous, irresistible fascination. There was blood in his fair hair, matting it. His mouth was soft, lips slightly parted; Irene's skin still had the memory of their touch from the night before. It was all so impossible – what she was seeing, what had happened – that it felt like a terrible, terrible ruse. She reached for one of his hands, wanting to hold it, tightly, as though he might still feel it, but it was cold and oddly hard, and didn't feel right at all. She dropped it and recoiled, losing her balance, and when she put her hand down to steady herself it smeared the pool of his blood, and that was cold too. The room receded behind the deafening crash of her heart, and the black blotches crowded in again. Then she felt hands grasping at her arms, lifting her up.

*

Pudding and her mother sat at the kitchen table with their tea gone cold. Outside, the rain had cleared and the sky had turned an ugly, incandescent white as the sun set about burning through the cloud. Pudding wondered how it could dare to. How it could show such disrespect. Louise's eyes were red and puffy; Pudding was sure her own were worse, but she was at least grateful that when she'd told her mother what had happened, Louise had understood – Pudding hadn't had to explain it three different ways, when she could scarcely believe it herself. It felt like a nightmare she should wake up from at any moment. She prayed that she would. They'd only let her see Donny for a second before they'd taken him away. She wished more than anything that her father had been there – he would have made them wait; he would have made them see sense. Somehow. Donny had gone as quietly as a lamb, climbing obediently into the car and not seeming to mind when nobody answered his question about the type of engine it had. Pudding had told them that they didn't need to put handcuffs on him, but they hadn't bothered to answer her either. The rain had begun to wash the blood from Donny's hands but it still daubed the front of his shirt, and was smeared up his sleeves. Alistair's blood. It had made Pudding's throat close up in horror.

'Donny – you didn't hurt Mr Hadleigh, did you? Tell them,' she'd said.

He'd given her a faraway look, and said: 'I tried to get him to safety, Puddy. Just like I tried with poor Catsford.'

'But it wasn't you that hurt him.'

'I found him there. I found him.'

'There! You heard that! It wasn't him!' she'd said to the superintendent, who was very tall and thin, with black hair, a pale face and a steady, unsettlingly gaze. He'd asked who

Catsford was – another young Tommy, Donny's new best friend, who'd died in France, Donny had written home to tell them, draped on the barbed wire like dirty laundry – and then told Pudding to move out of the way. He wouldn't have treated her father in such an offhanded manner, and if she'd had room to feel it, she would have been furious. She reached across the table and took her mother's hand again, and gave it a squeeze.

'It'll be all right, Mum,' she said, for perhaps the tenth or eleventh time. She knew it was mostly for herself that she said it, and wished she could believe it. 'Dad will make them see sense. And they'll find out who really killed Mr Hadleigh, and they'll...' She had to stop, and swallow a fresh storm of tears. Mr Hadleigh, dead. Alistair, murdered. Gone. The pain of each reminder was terrible. She sat there, shuddering, utterly helpless.

When Dr Cartwright got home he looked bedraggled and exhausted. His hair was messy and damp, as were his clothes. His face had a grey heaviness to it that Pudding had only seen once before – when he'd got back from visiting Donny in the convalescent hospital where he'd spent the first two months after returning from the front. She leapt up and took his coat and hat and bag, and put the kettle on to boil again, as the doctor sat down wearily and took Louise's hands.

'Well, well,' he said, softly. 'A day we won't soon forget, however much we might wish to.'

'Where's our Donny?' said Louise. 'Is he not back with you?' Dr Cartwright glanced up at Pudding, but she could only shake her head.

'I'm sure he'll be back soon, my dear,' he said, quite calmly, though his knuckles, as he held his wife's hands, were white. For a long time, they didn't speak. Pudding passed her father a cup of tea. Warm, damp air drifted in from outside as the sun finally broke through, and the birds began to sing. It was mid afternoon, Pudding supposed, but that didn't seem to mean anything any more – neither did what day it was, or what month, or what year. She felt it ought to be night. It ought always be night from then on.

'Well, I'd best get the supper on, I suppose,' said Louise, rising and brushing her skirt. 'I've got some pork loin, and there are finally enough broad beans to make a meal.' She paused, frowning in thought. 'Does Donny like broad beans? It's quite gone out of my head.'

'Yes, he loves them,' said Pudding, dully.

'Of course he does.' Louise smiled. 'What a thing for a mother to forget!' She hummed as she put on her apron, and stood at the sink to wash her hands. Pudding sat down opposite her father.

'What have they done with Donny, Dad? Where is he? Can he come home?'

'He's in the holding cells at the police station in Chippenham, Puddy – he can't come home just yet. They've given him something to eat, and dry clothes. I asked for his others to bring back and wash but they . . . said that they'll be kept as evidence.'

'Evidence? You mean . . . they still think it was him? Didn't you tell them it wasn't?'

'Of course I did. Of course I tried.' Dr Cartwright sighed, and rubbed his chin. 'But they still think it was him – and we must try to be patient with them. They don't know our Donny; they can only go on the evidence as they perceive it. They say he was holding the very shovel that was used to kill Mr Hadleigh, and nobody else was seen at the mill who could have done it.'

'But he just *found* Mr Hadleigh like that – he told me! He said he tried to help him, and that must be how he got blood on himself. And . . . and he was probably just taking the shovel back to where it belonged, in the boiler house – you know what he's like about odd things like that, and—'

'Hush now, Pudding; you don't need to convince me!' The doctor took Pudding's hand and tried to pat it but she gripped it so hard he winced.

'But we have to make them *see*. We have to make them realise he would never do such a thing.'

'And we will. We will.' But with a sinking feeling, Pudding realised how tired her father sounded already; how defeated.

'You look exhausted, Dad. You need to rest. How did the birth go? The one that kept you from coming to the mill?'

'Not well. The child was lost,' said the doctor. 'A dark day indeed.' He took a sip of his tea, carefully, because his hand was shaking.

Pudding was so beset by the urge to be up and doing – something, *anything* – that it was soon impossible to bear it another second. It felt as though something were creeping up behind her; she didn't know what it was, but it was frightening, and she was sure she didn't want to let it catch her. Everything was wrong, and Pudding's first impulse had always been to put things right.

'I'm going down to the mill to talk to whoever it was first found Donny. And whoever it was first found . . . poor Mr Hadleigh,' she said, pulling on her boots.

'Pudding, you can't. The mill's closed off. The police are still talking to the workers,' said her father. She paused with one boot on and the other in her hands, and her eyes filled with tears again.

'Poor Mr Hadleigh,' she said, quietly. 'Who on earth can have wanted to hurt him? I don't understand.'

'Neither do I, my dear. Neither do I.'

'What's happened to Mr Hadleigh?' said Louise, from the stove. Her voice was high, and anxious.

'Remember I told you, Mum? He's been killed.' Pudding fought to keep her voice steady.

'Pudding,' said the doctor, in a warning tone.

'But we can hardly go about pretending that he hasn't!' she cried.

'Oh, how *dreadful*!' said Louise. 'Was it an accident of some kind? How simply dreadful!' Unable to bear another second of it, Pudding wrestled her foot into her other boot and went out into the glare of the sun. The spring tinkled its crystalline water into the stone trough, as pretty as anything, and Pudding felt as though a huge crack had opened up right through the middle of the world. She stood on the track and wept, and through the burn of tears saw a figure, coming slowly up the hill. It was Hilarius, his gaunt features as unreadable as ever.

'Horses want seeing to,' he said, curtly, when he reached her. He squinted into the sun, his eyes all but invisible. A watchful glitter, hard as diamonds. Pudding gaped at him for a moment.

'But... Mr Hadleigh is *dead*!' she said, anguished. 'And... and they've taken my brother away!' Hilarius considered her for a while, then nodded.

''Tis bad enough,' he said. 'Knew young Alistair afore he were born, I did, and he went a long way towards lifting the dark off that house. But those beasts don't know aught about it. Waiting on 'ee for their well-being, they be.'

'Well, I can't come now... I can't! I need to...' Pudding tried to think what it was she needed to do. 'Can't you just see to them, Hilarius?'

'Not my job, girl. It's 'ee thar kicking at doors for.' He stared at her a moment longer, then nodded and turned to make his way back down the hill, awkward on his bandy legs.

Pudding watched after him a while, rubbing her face where the salt made it itch. Then she followed behind him, and went to work.

❧ ❧

In the sultry nights that week, Clemmie couldn't sleep. She fidgeted and turned and kicked off the sheets, until Josie sighed and Liz threatened to strangle her if she woke her one more time. Clemmie slid out of the bed and knelt down by the open window, low beneath the eaves. Their room trapped the heat of the day and exhaled it at night, and the air outside was only a little cooler. Bats wheeled and twisted along the river and across the yard, feasting on moths; a tawny owl called across the valley, and was answered by another. The river's soft rush was constant; the sky was blue-black, and a crescent moon turned everything else to grey. Clemmie didn't know what to do. The police constables from Biddestone and Chippenham had been lingering at the mill for days, eyeing everyone with such suspicion and gravity that Clemmie, with her guilty heart, fled from them as soon as she saw them. She could feel their scrutiny like a physical touch, and felt utterly transparent. On one of her visits she'd tried to take the milk into the canteen as usual, and been turned back. She'd overheard one of the women who usually worked in the bag room complaining at having been asked to clean the blood off the office floor.

'Can't be my job, can it?' she'd muttered, with a sickly, buttoned-up look on her face. 'How can it be my job to do it?' On another occasion, Clemmie had overheard someone talking about Isaac Tanner.

'Got an alibi, so they say, but hasn't he ever? They're a bad lot, all them Tanners, and I said as much to that copper when he asked me.' Her heart had got into her throat then, and all but choked her.

She hadn't seen Eli since it had happened; she didn't know what she would do when she did. She was torn in two, knowing what he had done, even if his father had made him, but loving him so completely. She'd been to Thatch Cottage and lingered for a while, half hoping he would come out and half hoping he wouldn't. Then, beneath the window, she heard one of Eli's brother's say, shakily: 'Why'd he have to hit him so hard? I don't see why . . . I don't see why he had to go at him so hard.' Clemmie didn't know who the boy was speaking to, and she didn't hear the reply, if there was one. She'd shut her eyes, feeling cold, hot, and full of fear. She prayed that the words had been spoken about Isaac, and not about Eli. But Isaac had infected all the Tanner boys with his anger, and his violence. She had seen it.

Her thoughts, as she knelt by the window, were in constant, kaleidoscopic shift. She had overheard their plan; she hadn't known how brutal it would be, how serious, but she had known something bad was coming. She could not have spoken of it to anyone, and she didn't know if she would have done so even if speech had come easy to her. She didn't think she could ever say anything to bring trouble down on Eli. But she felt culpable; she felt a liar of some kind. She hadn't even let on to Eli that she knew of their plan, or tried to discourage him from taking part – she'd let him kiss it away, and carry her out of herself with his touch. But she also knew she could not have stopped him – not if his father was set on it. She'd felt Eli's anger, worse than ever, and seen the cage he lived in, and had felt only love, only desperation on his behalf. But now there was blood to be scrubbed from the mill office floor, and nothing would be the same again, and the weight of what she knew would not go away. She would do nothing to betray him, yet she could not do nothing. She gripped big handfuls of her hair, yanking at it till it hurt, trying to force the thoughts to come clearer, and make sense. Her skin was as softly clammy as the night air, and her breath felt too hot in her mouth. There was no peace to be had, and as if in agreement a vixen shrieked, down by the river's edge, a harsh sound echoing against Weavern's walls, and in Clemmie's ears.

By morning she was dull with fatigue. She seemed to be tired all the time lately as it was – nagged by a lassitude that dragged at her steps and made everything seem like harder work than it should have been. There were purple shadows under her eyes.

'Buck up, my Clem,' said her mother, Rose, as Clemmie stood staring at a jug of yesterday's milk, gone sour because she'd forgotten to scald it before bed. 'What's got into you?'

'Got other things on her mind, I reckon,' said Liz, and Mary shot her a dark look that wiped the smirk off her face. They all glanced at their father to see if he'd noticed anything, but he hadn't. He hunched over his plate of food, ate with a mechanical rhythm, and paid them no attention. The look on Rose's face as she watched her husband was sad, exasperated, and a little lost. Clemmie lingered around the farm that morning, unsure whether to go to the mill again, or to look for Eli. Still unsure what she would do if she found him. She helped Rose put the rhubarb through the mangle, to squeeze out the juice for wine. They did it in the shade to one side of the house, turning the ground sticky and pink with juice, the air impossibly sweet. They covered the crushed stalks with sugar and packed them into earthenware jars to macerate out the last of the juice they would ferment.

'*Is* anything amiss, Clemmie?' Rose asked her, as they finished the job. 'You needn't be frightened – I won't be angry with you, my girl, whatever it is.' Clemmie held her eye for a moment before shaking her head. For once, she was glad to have no voice with which to have to try to explain.

It had taken a few days for work to resume at the mill, but farms were different. Animals couldn't wait, and neither could crops. Farms were living things, systems that had to carry on breathing or die. Everywhere, as she walked along the high ridge to the east of Slaughterford, Clemmie saw teams of horses, with their glossy mahogany coats and their leather collars black with grease, turning the first cut of hay, or pulling great carts loaded with timber, or beans, or women and children being taken out to walk the fields and pull the weeds and wild oats from the wheat. She usually liked the clank of the box bells on the horses' harnesses, and the hair flying around their feet, and the stink of their sweat as she pressed to the hedge to let them pass by. But now she couldn't enjoy anything, because of what had happened, and what she knew about it. Knotted thoughts, and fear, and missing Eli like air. Driven by those three things, Clemmie found herself in the yard of Manor Farm. The cob pony looked out over its stable door at her, the chickens peered side to side at her, and swallows arrowed above her head. Mrs Kent, a widow, was doing the laundry in big vats beneath the half-portico at the front of the house. She gave Clemmie a little wave then stood with her hands on her hips, taking the chance to straighten her back. When Clemmie neither gestured nor approached, she went back to work with a sigh, stirring the sheets with a wooden paddle. Clemmie stared at the farm's front door, the date stone above it and the iron knocker, hanging there, waiting.

But what could she do, if she could neither speak, nor write? She'd always relied upon people asking the right questions — and they couldn't possibly know the ones she needed them to ask now. She wished she could see Alistair. She wished she'd seen him in time. He might somehow have been able to coax the words from her, in the quiet seclusion of his office – he had come closer than anyone at showing her how to master it. She could have warned him of Tanner's plan to steal from him, at the mill, which had gone so horribly awry. Guilt came over her in a wave, and galvanised her to act. But Alistair wasn't there, and Nancy Hadleigh was another thing altogether. And then there was the chance that Eli would be arrested because of her. In an agony of indecision, she paced back and forth by the yard gate. She could not ignore what she knew, but could do nothing about it either. She ground her teeth together and moaned in her throat, and then, out of the blue, as if to surprise herself, she tried to say, *I know about what has happened*. The *I* was fine, but by the *n* of *know* her mind had caught up, and the rest of the word gathered behind her teeth and stuck there, an immovable thing she could neither swallow nor spit out, blocking everything. Her heart raced and she felt her face reddening with the effort, and she balled her hands into fists, and when she finally gave up it was with a cry of pure frustration.

'What in heaven's name's up with 'ee, hen?' called Mrs Kent, but at the same time the farm door opened and Nancy Hadleigh came striding out.

She moved with such angry purpose that Clemmie took an involuntary step backwards. Nancy was slight but her body was hard and her will was like thorns all around her that you ran into at your peril.

'What do you want?' she said, barking out the words. Clemmie flinched and dithered, shifting from her left foot to her right and back again. She saw Nancy's red eyes and pale face, her mottled skin and bitten lips; saw then that she was in anguish. The strain of it was making her wiry form thrum. 'Oh, what is it? What do you *want*?' Nancy cried. 'Alistair told me that there's no reason why you can't talk, so go on. Talk!' But Clemmie couldn't. Nancy's eyes narrowed, her face went tight. 'Perhaps I can guess what you want, in fact. Perhaps I can.' Her voice dropped as she said this, and Clemmie waited, hope kindling. 'Is it not enough to haunt the mill, and have your . . . *lessons* – is it decent to come and bother us here as well? Is it?' she demanded. Clemmie shook her head, confused. 'Go away. Alistair isn't here. Don't you understand that, you stupid girl? He's gone, and it's too late. You can't have him!' Tears choked off these final words, closing Nancy's throat so that she had to wait and catch her breath. Clemmie watched her cautiously, waiting for whatever would come next. The misunderstanding was so huge that she couldn't bring herself to go, and let it remain. She shook her head, but Nancy was dabbing at her eyes and didn't see, and then she threw up her arms and shooed Clemmie back, pushing her when she resisted. 'Go on, why don't you? Go!' she said, not looking up, her face shining wet. Defeated and afraid, Clemmie hurried away.

In the afternoon, William Matlock put the back of his hand across his mute daughter's face, after she lost control of the herd between fields and they jogged off happily, raiding the hedgerows along Weavern Lane towards Honeybrook Farm. Hedgerows still full of wild garlic that would taint their milk for at least a day, maybe two. Clemmie tried without success to get ahead of them and turn them, and they were only turned back by lucky chance, when Honeybrook's dogs barked and sent them into a panic of blown breath and clattering hooves.

'Will!' Rose exclaimed, as the blow landed, then said nothing more as her husband strode out into the yard and Clemmie stood with her hand pressed to her throbbing face. It was a good blow and she could taste blood where her lip had split a little. 'He don't mean it, Clem, you know how he is,' her mother said, dabbing at the blood with a wet cloth. Clemmie nodded, not even minding. Her lip had soon swollen up and felt odd – huge, numb and sore at the same time. She batted her mother's hands away, then went around the kitchen searching until she found an old chitty for cattle drench and the stub of a pencil, then sat down at the table and tapped the paper urgently with one finger. Rose frowned slightly. 'You want to write something down? You've something to tell me?' she said. Clemmie nodded emphatically. 'But . . . we've tried you with learning your letters before, love, and not managed it,' she said, gently. Clemmie jabbed the paper even harder, tears in her eyes. 'All right, all right; don't get in a lather. We'll find a way.'

Rose sat down beside her, and began, laboriously, to write out the alphabet, as she had done a hundred times before; sounding out each letter as she wrote it. She glanced at Clemmie, to see if she would echo the sounds, but Clemmie wasn't going to start trying to talk – it would only confuse things, and make it harder. She stared hard at the shapes her mother drew, and tried to learn them, tried to keep all their lines and curves in order in her mind, but her eyes seemed to dodge away from them, without her bidding, and when she looked again she could not recall which one she had been looking at, and they all seemed subtly different. She pointed to the sky outside, and then gestured for her mother to write it down. The three letters Rose chose were not at all what Clemmie had expected. She got up and pointed to other things around the room – the door, a pan, a dish, a spoon, a knife. *Niffe*, Rose wrote, obediently, carefully.

Try as she might, Clemmie couldn't spot a pattern between the sounds and the symbols. She dropped her chin, ground the heels of her hands into her eyes in exasperation. 'Oh, don't cry, my Clem! Whatever it is, it can't be as bad as all that, can it?' said Rose. 'Are you in trouble? Are you in any danger? Or one of your sisters?' she asked, and Clemmie shook her head. 'Well then, whatever it is will work itself out, I'm sure of it. Only don't get yourself in such a stew over it, it won't help.' Rose held her at arm's length and thought for a moment. 'Are you still upset over what happened at the mill? That's it, isn't it?' Cautiously, Clemmie nodded. 'I know it was terrible, but you're in no danger, I'm certain of it. I heard it today from Libby Hancock that the police have arrested someone, and they're sure they've got their man. He's locked away fast, so that's that. He's not at large no more; he can't hurt you.' Clemmie stared at her mother as this news sank in. 'I can get Josie to make the milk run instead, if you want? So you don't even need to go over to Slaughterford. There'll be no more of your lessons with Mr Hadleigh gone, in any case,' she said, but Clemmie shook her head to that.

In the evening, after supper, she sneaked away and went to Thatch Cottage. Hopes had bloomed like flowers inside her – the hope that Isaac Tanner was locked away for good, and Eli was free of him; free to be happy. The hope that she was free of her terrible dilemma. She made her way closer, tree to tree, and then to the back of the privy, trying to be cautious but too eager to know, too eager to have her hopes confirmed. She was just crossing the patch of ground between the privy and the wall of the cottage when the privy door banged open. Clemmie gasped and turned around as Isaac Tanner emerged, fastening his flies. She froze. He hadn't looked up or seen her yet, but it would be a matter of seconds. She had seconds. She knew she should run but couldn't decide which way; her feet faltered, pulled in all directions at once. Tanner looked up, and stopped; his face registered surprise, and then suspicion. He had such heavy brows, such a cruel mouth, such stony eyes. He moved like a fighter, always ready to react.

'Well? Who are you?' he said, flatly. 'What you doing back here? What do you want?' He didn't sound drunk, or angry – yet. Clemmie's breath whistled out of her and she couldn't seem to get more in. 'Well?' he said again, louder, harder. He started walking directly towards her, and with a stifled sound Clemmie darted away, towards the front of the cottage and the gate out to the lane. 'Oi!' Tanner shouted behind her, and now he sounded angry. 'I asked you a question, girl! You come back here and answer it!'

Clemmie ran until her heart was bursting and a stitch had stuck a knife into her left side. Then she walked, gasping, her fingers burrowing into the pain, trying to stifle it. When she had the breath for it, she cried for a while. Whoever the police had locked away, it wasn't Isaac Tanner. She didn't understand how they could have got it so wrong; she thought that surely they must know, surely there must be some evidence, pointing to Tanner's guilt. Clemmie found a safe place to sit – on the raised roots of a massive elm by Cold Tump, high above the village – and thought. If Isaac Tanner had not been arrested for the crime, then she could only suppose that either John or Eli Tanner had. All her hopes were replaced by fear; a dry-mouthed, queasy kind of fear. *They've got their man*, her mother had said. So just one of them, not both. She hated the idea of Eli hurting anybody; hated the thought of that anger boiling out of him as violence. She knew it was not who he really was – it was something that had been done to him. And whoever the police had taken, that person might hang. Eli might be hanged. Clemmie put her face into her hands and moaned, wordlessly. She longed for the power of speech. She longed to be able to walk up to the police and say that, however it was Tanner had managed to escape suspicion, he was the architect of it all. *He* was the source of all the pain. However he had managed to escape the blame. Clemmie thought about that. She wondered if her Eli could possibly have done such a terrible thing. Beaten a man down like that. The thought brought more tears, more sickness.

Later, she went to a place on the river where she and Eli had once lain down together. She tried to find the exact spot – tried to see the grass still crushed – but the summer growth was too vigorous for that. With her knees drawn up and her chin resting on them, she sat and watched gnats dipping and careering over the water, and realised that without Eli she was lonely for the first time in her life. Horribly so. It had only been days since she'd seen him but it felt like weeks. If he was taken away from her, if he was hanged, she didn't know how she would carry on living. She shut her eyes to the gloaming and wished for Eli to find her there – wished for it so hard that it came true.

When she heard his footsteps, swishing through the long grass, she got to her feet with her heart speeding, weak with relief. She knew the rhythm of his walk exactly, she didn't need to open her eyes to know it was him but she was hungry for the sight of him. Tall, angular, hunched; he had shadows under his eyes and his clothes were dirty and creased. He looked exhausted but restlessly alert. He radiated his hostility for the world, so much so that as he reached for Clemmie she almost flinched. However she longed for him, she still knew he'd been a part of it, and she still didn't know who had struck the blows. But the police didn't have him; the police weren't blaming him. She realised there and then that nothing else mattered. Whoever had been arrested, whoever might hang, it was not Eli. She reached out her arms to him. A moment before he kissed her, Eli noticed her split lip, and she noticed that some of the shadows and smudges on his face were bruises. He turned her chin to the last light in the western sky. His mouth was slightly open; eyes harried.

'Who hit you, Clem?' he said, his voice so hard the words seemed to take shape in the air between them. She shook her head minutely to say it didn't matter. 'Who? Your father?' he pressed, and she stayed still. 'I'll knock his bloody head off,' Eli whispered, and Clemmie shook her head, urgently. His hand on her jaw tightened painfully, and she whimpered. At once, he softened; his fingers loosened but stayed on her skin, resting gently. 'Sorry, sorry,' he whispered. She put up her own hands and felt the knots at the corners of his jaw, shifting as he ground his teeth together. 'What gives them the right?' he said. 'What in bloody hell gives them the right?'

Eli let go of her and stepped away, putting his hands over his face for a moment, pacing here and there. There was no stillness inside him. He stifled a loud cry, and Clemmie murmured her anxiety. 'God, I hate him,' he said, the words muffled through his hands. She tipped her head at him, tried to take his hands. *Who?* she asked, without a word. 'I hate him so much. Isaac. My *father* ... I want to kill him. I'd happily kill him, Clem!' There was something wild in his eyes as he said it, and she believed him. His pain and anger broke the quiet night apart, and suddenly Clemmie saw that part of him was broken, and might never be mended. She might never be able to mend it. She couldn't help but start to cry. She wasn't afraid, just awash with sadness – drowning in sadness – that the world had done such a thing to him. 'The things he does; the things he makes *us* do . . .' Eli was just talking now – not to her, not to anyone, just talking because he had to. He shook his head wildly. 'Perhaps I will kill him. He wouldn't expect that, would he? Won't make much difference to me now, but it might to the others . . .' Clemmie watched him and wept, filled with ill-defined longing. Perhaps it was the longing to take his pain from him. In the silence her stifled sobs were loud, and so was Eli's breathing, and the nervous cough of a moorhen they'd woken, and the gentle push of the breeze in a willow tree. There was no way she could reject him; no way she could turn away from him – he had filled her heart to brimming.

But when he finally looked up at her again, and then walked towards her, quickly, decisively, she took a step backwards. She couldn't help it. She'd been pushed and shouted at by Nancy Hadleigh; she had been hit by her father, chased away by Isaac Tanner. She'd been tormented by her own thoughts, and by the terrible stain of violence at the mill; she was weak and bewildered from lack of sleep, and desperate. He had perhaps only meant to kiss her, or gather her into his arms, but when she took a step backwards Eli froze. The disbelieving shock on his face was terrible to her. 'Are you frightened of me, now, Clemmie?' he said quietly. She shook her head and stepped towards him, and put out her hands, but he held her back. 'Why would you be scared of me? When I've never made any move to hurt you – me, who loves the very bones of you?' He grabbed her wrists, gave her a shake. 'I haven't slept with a roof over me head in three nights, Clem, did you know that?' Clemmie took a huge breath. She shut her eyes to concentrate, and tried, as Mr Hadleigh had taught her, to think of the parts of the word as stepping stones – not reaching for the next one too soon, but going steadily, one at a time.

'Eee . . . l . . .' she managed, before stopping to recover.

'What? What do you know, Clem?' he said, not recognising the beginnings of his own name. But with his breath hot on her face, and the grip of his hands on her wrists, and the anger burning in him like a fire, she could not concentrate, or be calm. She could only weep. 'Why would you be frightened?' he said again. 'Look at me, Clem.' She did, and could no longer tell if he were cross with her, or hurt, or confused. His eyes were strange to her. 'Why would you be frightened? What do you know?' And what she wished for then, as she saw his anger ignite, right before her eyes, was that she could simply open her head, and her heart, and let him see inside. But she couldn't.

Irene got up when she heard the farmhouse door thud shut. She'd been lying on the bed upstairs, hiding from Nancy. After the rain the woods and fields had exploded with renewed growth when the sun returned, a frenzy you could almost see happening, and which seemed menacing to Irene – as though the human world might soon be smothered by swathes of foliage and writhing roots. And then she couldn't help but think of those roots going down into Alistair after his burial the following day, which would be nine days since his death. His eye sockets, and the soft gap between his knuckles; his ears and nose and mouth; all the cavities not protected by bone. Her stomach swooped in protest at this, but she couldn't keep the thoughts away. To Irene, the worst travesty of Alistair's death was not that he was now absent, but that his body would be violated in such a way. It was the only tangible way she could comprehend his death – she could not miss him, yet, could not mourn him properly, honestly. Not the way Nancy could, and was. The gulf between the two of them seemed unbridgeable now; perhaps, eventually, Alistair would have bridged it. Irene felt adrift again, she felt homeless. Even though she hadn't had a chance to fall in love with Alistair, he had become a place of safety. In vulnerable moments deep in the night, between islands of fitful sleep, the feel of his dead hand appeared, like a ghost, in her own hand, and she sometimes sat bolt upright with a gasp, and ran her fingers through her hair, certain that it would be matted, stiff with blood.

Clara and Florence responded to the shocking death of their master by working with a kind of silent expectation that only served to keep the house on edge. They watched Nancy and Irene constantly, as if seeking validation, or expecting some extraordinary instruction or announcement. Perhaps they, like Irene, questioned the point of doing any of the things they had done before. There was no point cooking meals for a household that wouldn't eat. There was no point cleaning rooms that nobody cared about, or was using. Their aimlessness was too much for Nancy, who was like a raw nerve – impossible to touch. She snapped at them frequently, when she wasn't so closed off that she didn't even see them. She veered from businesslike stoicism, as impenetrable as stone, to an excess of emotion so alien to those who knew her that it sent them scattering like hens. She'd sent Pudding away more than once, damp and red-faced, when she'd tried to come inside and talk. Jem Welch had caused an explosion by asking if he should cut white roses or red for Alistair's wreath. The old man had gone away as steadily as he'd come, but his face had shown his distress, and Irene gathered it was as much down to Donald Cartwright being arrested as it was to Alistair being dead. Nobody was talking about Alistair's killer much; people seemed in the uneasy position of wanting to condemn the sin but not the sinner – that it had been Donald, it seemed, was as big a tragedy as that it had happened at all. He'd been damaged fighting for king and country, after all; nobody was in any doubt that the Donald who went off to war would never have done such a thing. Irene peered out of the window at the top of the stairs on her way down and saw a figure in poor clothing walking away across the field towards the church with a crabbed, uncertain gait – head down, arms clasped around herself, pursued by a mad mess of pale, frizzy hair.

Nancy was in the hallway, going through the letters and cards that had come that morning. She was crisply dressed, with a black cotton cardigan buttoned over her shirt; her pose would have been entirely normal had it not been for the tears on her cheeks and her hollowed-out eyes.

'Did somebody come to call?' said Irene.

'No. It was just that odd creature from Weavern, hovering

around, as she's always done,' said Nancy, curtly. 'I sent her on her way. Not the full ticket, that one.'

'Oh. And how are you this morning, Nancy?' Irene hadn't once tried to hug the older woman; hadn't once tried to take her hands. She'd been watching, as closely as she could, for any sign whatsoever that Nancy would welcome the gesture. Even at the inquest, which had opened the day after Alistair's death and returned a verdict of unlawful killing almost immediately, Nancy's hands had remained in her lap, fingers laced. Now she looked up at Irene with an expression so flatly hostile that Irene's mouth went dry.

'This morning? It's half past three in the afternoon, Irene. Most of the day is over, and as usual you have contributed nothing to it whatsoever. As to how I am, I . . .' Here her rancour failed her, and for a moment she looked so lost it was painful to see. She glanced down at the white envelopes in her hands, some of which were edged in black. 'So very Victorian, some of our acquaintances,' she murmured. 'Most of these condolences are addressed to you. I suggest you get on and answer some of them before they pile up too much. You have such a lovely new writing room, after all, as well as all these others.' She thrust the envelopes at Irene and moved away.

'All which others? Nancy, wait,' said Irene. 'Please. Look, I . . . I know we've not seen eye to eye over much since I got here. I know you don't think I deserved Alistair. I don't know if it matters now, but I really didn't think I deserved him either. I know I didn't. He offered to rescue me from a horrible situation, but perhaps I wouldn't have married him, even so, if my mother hadn't made it my only option. And I know I didn't . . . love him the way you did. But I just wanted to say . . . I just wanted to say . . .' She realised only then that she didn't know what she wanted to say.

'What?' said Nancy, with a wintry smile. 'That you share

my pain? That we are united in our grief? That we are *in this together*?'

'No. No, not that. I'm sorry. Perhaps that's it – I'm sorry you've lost him, and . . . however hard this might be for you to believe, I'm sorry *I've* lost him, too. I just . . . I just don't know what to do next.'

'Don't you?' Nancy stopped smiling. She slipped her hands into her pockets and lifted her chin. 'I should rather think the world is your oyster now, Irene.'

Irene did as she was told and took the cards into her writing room, slitting each one open with a knife and trying to place the names of the senders. Some she knew, most she did not; none at all were from any of her own friends or family. She smoked until the air was hazy, and answered each one as best she could, noticing the un-summery chill in the air and the draught from the chimney that Nancy had foreseen. She stared at the hearth, with its new marble surround, and thought again of the strange broken doll that had been found there. She thought, with a shiver, of Ma Tanner's pronouncement of change, and the odd feeling of prescience she'd had herself. She felt as though she'd been at Manor Farm for years, decades – like her unhappiness had trapped time, and slowed it down. And then she realised, with a jolt, that she was free to leave now. There was nothing to keep her there – that was what Nancy had meant about the world being her oyster. The desire to be gone was a sudden, irresistible craving, even if it came with an ill-defined taint of failure. She could go back to London; she could go home, as soon as the funeral was out of the way. No doubt the residents of Slaughterford would denounce her for abandoning the home Alistair had intended for her, but she could hardly start caring about what the residents of Slaughterford thought of her now. There was no good opinion to risk losing. Finally, one of the cards she opened was from her parents, who'd probably read about the murder in the papers. Irene quickly wrote a reply, asking to come home to them in London as soon as possible after the funeral. She wrote so fast that she smudged the ink, which her father would hate, sealed the envelope and got up to walk it down to the post box in the shop wall herself, not caring if it was decent or not for her to be out and about; not caring if the scarf she draped around her neck was emerald, rather than black.

Superintendent Blackman, from the Chippenham branch of the police, had his hand raised to the knocker just as Irene dragged the front door open. Tucked away in the old schoolroom, she hadn't heard the rattle and growl of the car, pulling into the yard. Constable Dempsey from Ford, a fresh-faced young man with clear green eyes, stood at Blackman's shoulder. Startled, caught off guard, Irene's first instinct was to smile. Just as she had always been taught to. But the superintendent's face was so firmly chiselled into an expression of respectful gravity that he could do nothing to alter it; Constable Dempsey smiled before he could help it, but then fell serious again. Irene blushed and took a step backwards, dropping her eyes. Her levity, her green scarf, her ridiculous smile. As Nancy had once said, she really had no idea how to behave.

'Mrs Hadleigh,' said Blackman. 'My continued condolences at this tragic time for you, and your household.'

'Yes. Thank you,' said Irene.

'Have I called at a bad time? I've come to keep you – and Miss Hadleigh – appraised of the progress of our investigation.'

'Oh? I'd understood there wasn't to be much of one,' said Irene, and straight away wished she hadn't. The two policemen stood in silence until she stepped back to admit them. 'Won't you please come in? I'll ask Clara for some tea.'

She took them into the drawing room at the far end of the house, where there was too much floral fabric – swathes of curtain and pelmet, cushions, rugs and upholstered footstools. The air smelled of dust, dog, and the rankness of the vase of flowers in the swept-out fireplace, where the water had gone murky. The two police officers looked ill at ease in their setting, clasping their hats in their hands, and Irene remembered that Nancy had taken them into the front kitchen before, and seated them at the long pine table. 'Please do sit down, gentlemen. I'll go and find Nancy,' she said, awkwardly, but then heard Nancy's smart footsteps coming along the corridor anyway.

'Why on earth have you come in here?' she said, from the doorway. 'Hardly fitting. Shall we up sticks?' The young constable got to his feet.

'Well, since we've already settled, perhaps we might remain?' said Irene, with a flutter of defiance, and the constable glanced at Nancy before sitting down again.

'Hardly matters, I suppose,' said Nancy, going to stand by the window with her back to them. Superintendent Blackman cleared his throat.

'As you know, ladies, the jury at the inquest into the death of Alistair Hadleigh returned a verdict of unlawful killing, for which Donald Cartwright has now been formally charged. He will soon be moved from Chippenham to Devizes prison to await his appearance before magistrates, where he will, I have no doubt, be committed for trial at the next assizes, in six weeks' time.' The superintendent paused as Florence came cringing into the room with the tea tray. Irene found her hands shaking as she poured. The policeman's words returned her to the inquest, and the horror of listening to the doctor – Dr Holbrook of Chippenham – describe the post-mortem examination he had carried out on Alistair, and the violence of his wounds: a blunt trauma wound to the back of the head, significant but not having caused the skull to fracture; five deep lacerations to the neck, severing the major blood vessels there; a further laceration to the face, most likely caused by the same instrument – consistent with the weapon being a heavy shovel, used first flat, and then with its edge to hack at the neck. The attack was hurried, passionate, and carried out by an assailant of significant physical strength. The cause of death was loss of blood. Now, as when she had heard the words spoken, Irene had to swallow down a hot rush of nausea that swept through her. The exact feel of the cold, slippery blood, sliding beneath the heel of her hand, returned with horrible clarity.

Blackman watched her carefully, and with more sympathy now, as she handed him a rattling cup and saucer. 'Are you well enough for me to go on, Mrs Hadleigh?' he asked gently, at which Nancy snorted, then waved a hand for him to continue when he looked across at her. 'Young Cartwright claims innocence, in the vaguest terms, but the evidence against him is as clear-cut as any I have encountered before. Such grievous injuries could only have been inflicted by a man of some strength, and in an outburst of rage, to which, many will testify, the young man is prone. The case is as open and shut as any I've known.'

'He was such a gentle lad before the war damaged him,' said Nancy, shaking her head. 'And very bright. He'd been planning on going up to Oxford to read engineering.'

'I didn't know that,' said Irene, thinking of Donald's slow movements, and the faraway look in his eyes. As though the air were thicker for him, as thick as water, and he was forced to swim rather than walk.

'Anyone would have told you, if you'd asked.' Nancy shrugged. 'He destroyed some rose bushes, recently. Hacked them to pieces with a hoe. For no reason – just one of his lapses. I don't know if Alistair spoke to him about it, or perhaps rebuked him. Perhaps Donald felt aggrieved.'

'Perhaps. It is most tragic,' said Blackman, perfunctorily. 'But the fact remains that the young man has now proven himself a danger to others. The judge may be lenient, given the circumstances of his . . . alteration, but then again – as with a mad dog – perhaps it would be wisest and kindest all around to . . .' He was interrupted by a gasp from the doorway, and there was Pudding Cartwright, face stricken, mouth open in shock.

'Good grief, Pudding!' Nancy cried. 'You can't just come wandering *in*, child!'

'How can you let him say such things about Donny?' said Pudding. 'You're talking about hanging him, aren't you? Aren't you?' she demanded of the superintendent, who had the grace to look uncomfortable.

'Now, Miss Cartwright, it—'

'My brother is *not* a mad dog! Or a murderer! Tell them, Miss H – he would never have hurt Mr Hadleigh! He just wouldn't! There's been a terrible mistake – this is all a terrible mistake. Donny has always been as gentle as a lamb, and—'

'But that's not entirely true, is it, Miss Cartwright?' said Blackman. 'Constable Dempsey here was called out to an incident only last year, in which your brother attacked another young man—'

'He didn't *attack* him! He just . . . it was just . . . he was provoked!'

'Indeed. An altercation over a young lady, as I understand it.'

'Aoife Moore. Donny was supposed to marry her, but after the war . . . They were goading him about it. It wasn't his fault.'

'Young miss, I'm afraid that violence is always the fault of the one who perpetrates it, whatever duress they might be under.'

'But what possible reason could Donny have to hurt Mr Hadleigh? I'll tell you – none at all! He always loved Alistair! And Alistair was always so kind to him ... to everyone ...' Huge tears brimmed along Pudding's eyelashes. Constable Dempsey got to his feet, drew out his handkerchief and offered it to her clumsily.

'Here you go, Pud— Miss Cartwright,' he said, but she looked at the handkerchief as if she didn't know what it was for.

Horrified by the scene, Irene folded her arms tightly and perched on the edge of her chair. She was so ashamed that Pudding, the girl groom, was visibly more upset about Alistair's death than she was herself that she could hardly stand to witness it. She stared down at the faded rug and imagined herself far away, in London, with the reassuring drone of traffic and a throng of anonymous faces in which she might hide. No longer on display, no longer watched all the time, no longer always wrong. At that exact moment she realised she hadn't had any word from Fin, when he must by then have heard about Alistair's death.

'This is ridiculous.' Nancy's hard voice interrupted her thoughts. 'Pudding, do stop that din, child. I know how desperate it all is, I really do, but you must brace yourself up. Wailing won't help.'

'But, Miss Hadleigh, I can't bear it! I can't! Donny would never have hurt Alistair; he had no reason to. Alistair wasn't at all cross about the roses ... He's innocent – he told me so himself!' Pudding's voice was drenched in misery. Constable Dempsey hovered near her, uneasily, and seemed uncertain whether he ought to pat her shoulder or not.

'As far as anyone can tell me, Miss Cartwright, *nobody* had any cause to harm Mr Hadleigh. Which, I fear, only makes it all the more likely that the attack was carried out by someone beyond reason,' said Blackman. For a moment, Pudding simply stood, panting, the breath hitching in her chest.

'I saw Tanner passed out drunk at the mill! Just a couple of weeks back ... I saw him. I'd gone in to fetch Donny out of the generator room. He was asleep in the coal heap with a bottle in his arms! I bet Alistair spoke to him about it. Maybe he even threatened to fire him from the mill – he'd been drunk so many times before! And everybody knows what he's like – he's a brute! He—'

'He has an alibi, Miss Cartwright. And I have checked up on it. You aren't the only one willing to point the finger at Mr Tanner, and—'

'An alibi from some member of his own family, I bet!'

'Indeed not. From Bob Walker, the landlord at the White Horse in Biddestone, who informs me that Mr Tanner was so drunk by closing time the night before the murder that Mr Walker felt obliged to carry him out to a storage shed at the rear of his premises and leave him to sleep it off, where Mr Tanner was still to be found when he was ejected at nine the following morning, by which time Mr Hadleigh had already been slain.'

'But ... he might have come away, and gone back again, mightn't he?'

'It's highly unlikely, given the distance involved and the state of incapacitation he was reportedly in. And, let us not forget, there simply isn't a single shred of physical evidence that he was involved in any way.'

Pudding's chin sank to her chest for a moment, and she took a deep breath. Then she looked up, and her eyes landed on Irene, and they were lit with desperation.

'What about her?' she said, wildly. There was a pause, and Pudding raised her hand to point at Irene. 'What about Mrs Hadleigh? She didn't love Alistair! Anyone could see that – Ma Tanner said as much, right to her face! And . . . and she inherits everything, doesn't she? Manor Farm and the mill and all of it – it's all hers now, isn't it? And she can do as she pleases!' The air in the drawing room seemed to curdle. Irene was stunned. A hindquarter of her brain was amazed that this matter of inheritance hadn't occurred to her sooner, and noted that the cause of much of Nancy's continued hostility, and her sideways remarks, were now a good deal clearer. The thought of what she had inherited settled onto her with the weight of a millstone. There could be no scot-free escape to London; she was far more tangled up in Slaughterford than she'd realised. But mills and farms could be sold, she reminded herself – or tenants found. Which left Nancy without the home she'd lived in all her life – evicted from the last place where she might surround herself with the ghosts of her family.

'But . . . I don't *want* it!' said Irene, like a child.

'See?' said Pudding, her conviction seeming to grow. 'See? She doesn't even deny that she didn't love him!'

'Pudding, that's enough. Irene was here all that morning, as the servants can testify. And she's so thin she's practically feeble – there's no way she could have . . . hurt Alistair in that way,' said Nancy.

'She might have sneaked out! She didn't love him, but she was stuck with him until death, otherwise, wasn't she?' Pudding was trembling all over, though Irene couldn't tell which particular emotion was shaking her. Superintendent Blackman got to his feet.

'Miss Cartwright, it doesn't do to go about flinging accusations at innocent people,' he said, severely.

'But ... but that's exactly what you're doing to Donny!' she said.

'No, indeed it is not.'

'Of course it wasn't me! How could it have been? I could never do such a thing.' Irene sprang to her feet and found her voice.

'Mrs Hadleigh, nobody is accusing you of anything,' said Blackman.

'I am! I'm accusing her,' said Pudding. 'I knew there was something not right about her when I first met her. How could anybody not love Alistair? She probably planned this all along – she probably planned it when she married him.' This said, Pudding dissolved into uncontrollable sobs.

'Clara!' Nancy called sharply down the corridor, and the housekeeper, who'd clearly been loitering within earshot, appeared and led Pudding away. Constable Dempsey watched her go, his expression full of concern until he noticed his superior watching him.

Irene sat back down again, tingling, feeling naked; Nancy stood across from her with her arms folded, and the two policemen exchanged a glance.

'Perhaps that's enough for now,' said Blackman. 'We'll see ourselves out, Mrs Hadleigh, Miss Hadleigh. I'm sure we will meet again before long.' He nodded to each of them, politely enough, but Irene noticed that his eyes, as they settled on her, were different from before. A good deal of the sympathy had gone from them, and something harder had come in its place. Something questioning, and watchful, and a lot like suspicion. Irene thought of the way she'd smiled as she'd opened the door to them, and the emerald scarf around her neck, and went cold.

6

Allies

The holding cell at Chippenham police station was small and sparse, with a grubby stone floor gored here and there with deep scratches, and bars on the tiny window. An officer from the front desk led Pudding and Dr Cartwright through, though every line of his face read of disapproval. The brass buttons on his uniform gleamed, he smelled of boot polish and camphor, his breath of onions, and Pudding was glad her father had come with her. It seemed unlikely that she would have been admitted on her own. The officer made a big show of checking, through the hatch, that Donny wasn't waiting just inside the door to ambush him, before rattling his keys in the lock and steadily pulling back the bolts. Once Pudding and her father were inside, he locked the door behind them, and the sound of it gave Pudding a shudder. The foul smell of the slop bucket was strong. Donny was sitting on the edge of his narrow bed wearing the same shirt and trousers Dr Cartwright had taken him days before. They were well creased, and looked stale, and Pudding's first thought was that when Donny got home he'd need a damn good scrub in the tub. It was still beyond her comprehension that he might never get home. She refused to think it.

'Hello, Donny,' she said. She didn't want to sound tremulous, or grave, or too perky, so in fact she didn't know how to try to sound. Normal was out of the question. Her brother smiled fleetingly, and got up to come closer to her. He held her arm in his right hand, squeezing it gently.

'Hello, Pud, Dad,' he said, shaking his father's hand as he had always done. But this time Dr Cartwright pulled him into a quick, tight embrace, clapping a hand on his shoulder as he let him go. Donny didn't like to be hugged, though he had done, before the war. This time, however, he didn't pull away. 'Can we go home now?'

'Not yet, Donald. I'm afraid not. Soon, I hope,' said the doctor, and Pudding heard how he hated to lie. 'But it could be a goodly while yet. You've to go before a judge first.'

'And the judge will say I can come home?'

'We hope so, Donny. We do hope so.' Pudding saw the way her father's smile refused to kindle, repeatedly sparking but then dying on his lips. She saw the desperate sorrow in his eyes. Donny nodded slowly, and sat back down on the bed.

'I used to like Chippenham. But I don't like it here much,' he said.

'No,' said Dr Cartwright. 'I don't suppose you do, son.'

There was a long pause then, in which Donny merely sat, and Pudding and her father merely stood. Noises came from the street outside, and it seemed obscene to Pudding that life should just carry on as it always had – with farmers carting in their produce to sell, and livestock being driven to market, and travelling quacks and salesmen proclaiming their latest miracle cure or must-have gadget, and newspaper boys shouting the headlines, and children bickering over cigarette cards. Chippenham was carrying on as normal, as though nothing was wrong, when nothing was normal and nothing was right. With a sudden loud roar of machinery and clanging of bells, they heard the fire engine approach and fly past, on its way to some emergency, and instinctively she and Donny looked to the window. It had been one of their favourite things, before the war – seeing the big, shining pump engine go flying past, with the men and their ladders clinging to its sides, cheered on from the street, shouting at people to move out of the way. Back then it had been pulled by horses, now it was horseless, which Donny liked even better. But they couldn't see out of the tiny, high window, and so they turned away again. Pudding refused to start crying, so she went and sat down next to her brother, and took his hand.

'What's the food like, Donny?' she asked him. He shrugged one shoulder.

'It's not up to much, Puddy. Stew with too many carrots, most days. Not like Mum's cooking.'

'Well, we've brought you some bits and pieces to keep you going – a coffee cake, and some fruit.' Donny nodded absently, and Pudding wondered how much of his situation he really understood. The hope that where there was ignorance there was bliss was tenacious, but Pudding had been caught out, time and again, assuming that just because her brother didn't react, he didn't realise.

'I didn't hurt Mr Hadleigh, Pudding,' he said then.

'I know you didn't.'

'I've been thinking and thinking, and making sure I remember it right, and I do remember. I went over to the offices because the door was open and the rain was getting in. And I found him lying there. I don't . . . I don't remember exactly what came next. For a while I . . . got lost. I thought about Moggy Catsford, my friend in France. And then I was in the generator house, looking at the machines, and I must have picked the shovel up, I suppose, and then.' He stopped talking suddenly, as though he'd simply run out of words.

Pudding gave her father a significant glance, and couldn't understand the doubt in his eyes. It made her feel she needed to try harder, go faster, push further.

'Did you see anybody else in the offices, Donny? Did you see anybody . . . perhaps running away?' she said. Donny stayed quite still for a long moment, and then shook his head. 'Did you see Mrs Hadleigh?'

'Pudding, that's quite enough.'

'Mrs Hadleigh?' Donny's brow furrowed in confusion. 'No. Or if I did, I don't remember. They think I did it, don't they?'

'Oh, Donny. They do, at the moment – but I am going to change that.'

'Pudding—' Dr Cartwright shook his head, but added nothing else.

'Mr Hadleigh is always kind to us. He's kind to everybody. I should never want to harm him.'

'I know, Donny. And I am going to make sure they realise that. I am going to prove who it was that *did* hurt him, and then they'll let you come home. All right?' She squeezed his hand hard, until he looked at her, from that far-off place, and nodded.

'Right you are, Pud,' he said, and her heart swelled up to bursting.

'Now, son, they'll be taking you to Devizes jail soon, so you can see the magistrate there. I don't want you to worry about that. You just do as they ask you, and always tell the truth, and we'll come and see you there very soon, all right?'

'All right, Dad. Will Mum come next time?'

'Well, we'll just have to see about that. It might upset her, you see, and we wouldn't want that, would we?' Donny shook his head, and Pudding smiled at him as best she could. She stared into his eyes, searching, and recoiled when she saw, deep in the depths of them, a flicker of fear. She stood up quickly, because she couldn't bear it and didn't know what else to do.

'I shall find out the truth of it, Donny, and you'll be home with us soon. I promise,' she said, with her heart hammering and a feeling like she might overflow. The camphor and onions man came back then, rattling his keys again.

'Time's up, I'm afraid,' he said curtly. So they left Donny perched on the edge of the bed as he had been upon their arrival, and went back out into the heedless, sunny day.

'You must be very careful, Pudding, who you go about accusing. You will lose your job at the farm,' said Dr Cartwright. Pudding hadn't told him that she'd already named Mrs Hadleigh to the police. And right in front of Nancy. Her gut gave a spasm when she thought about it. 'But then,' her father went on, 'perhaps that wouldn't be such a terrible thing. Perhaps we ought to think about you continuing on in college somewhere. Somewhere away from all this.'

Pudding kept her silence as they walked back to the bus station, not stopping to eat or go shopping or to watch the busy street life – it had not been that kind of outing. She could feel her father's reprimand, his fear for her and for her brother, and part of her did indeed struggle to picture Irene Hadleigh – frail, tired, immovable Irene Hadleigh – picking up a shovel and attacking Alistair with it. It was hard enough to imagine her leaving the house to go down to the mill in the first place. But she had all but confessed to not loving her late husband, Pudding reassured herself, so she was clearly flawed in some significant way, and she was the only person with any kind of motive. Pudding took a deep breath, trying to marshal her thoughts when they threatened to scatter out of control. She would make it all come right, she swore to herself. She felt again the shudder as the cell door had locked behind them, and the terrible, unimaginable horror of Donny never coming out of there again. She would not allow herself to fail.

She didn't like to think about the immediate consequences of her accusation. With Hilarius's wisdom still fresh in her mind, she went to fetch in the Hadleigh horses in the afternoon, just as she normally would, and rode Baron, Robin and Bally Girl in succession, by the end of which her legs were tired and she was as grimed with sweat as the animals. She rubbed them down and mixed their feed, then stood in the blessed shade of the tack room, cleaning all the bridles, and all the while she cast furtive glances at the house, expecting to see Nancy or Irene Hadleigh coming across to tell her to leave, permanently. Each time a door opened or closed, her heart jerked. But neither woman appeared, and she was left to wonder whether they even knew she was there, still at work. Whether they assumed she had resigned, after her sensational performance. She sat a while to think whether or not she should announce her continued presence in some way, until she realised that they must know, since, clearly, no other provision had been made for the care of the horses. Then she was left with the simple realisation that they'd disregarded her words, her outburst. That nobody had taken it seriously. That nobody took *her* seriously. She went to muck out the cob house and found a swallow's nest that had dropped from the rafters and smashed against the cobbles. Three naked baby birds were dead amidst the wreckage, and their oversized yellow beaks were so tragically clownish, and Pudding felt so powerless, that she surrendered to tears for a short while.

At the end of the day she trudged up the hill towards home, watching the daisies disappear beneath her big, booted feet and not knowing whether to be happy or angry that they merely sprang back upright once she'd passed. She stopped, realising that she was angry, and was deliberately grinding one into the sod when movement in the woods to her left caught her eye. Startled, she looked hard into the dappled shadows and tangled undergrowth beneath the trees, and then relaxed when she saw a woman in rough, peasant clothes – a long skirt snagging on the brambles, a collarless blouse with the sleeves rolled up – with a familiar thatch of thistledown hair obscuring her face. Pudding didn't bother to call out to her – she knew from experience that she'd get no reply. But there was movement and the sound of a twig snapping underfoot from further down the hill as well, and when Pudding refocused her eyes she saw a man moving away in the opposite direction. She couldn't make him out clearly, but he was tall and angular, and moved with a kind of steady, resigned tread that spoke of hardship. A Tanner, perhaps. Pudding waited until they were both out of sight and earshot, and wondered about the secret, other world they lived in, so different to her own. A world of clandestine meetings in summery woods; a world where you were wanted, and your brother was not in jail, wrongly accused of the murder of one of your favourite people in the whole world. Her envy of them was like a sudden, sharp pang of hunger.

She was so surprised to see the police superintendent's car parked outside Spring Cottage – spoked wheels dusty, headlamps like wide, alarmed eyes – that she stopped and stared at it for a moment, trying to imagine what it meant. They were all at the kitchen table, stifled by an uncomfortable atmosphere, with cups of tea in front of them. Superintendent Blackman and Constable Dempsey, and her parents. Ruth, their daily, was at the stove with a pan full of acrid piccalilli, her ears and eyes practically on stalks. Louise Cartwright looked clear-eyed and harried – like a mother missing a son ought to look, though Pudding couldn't be pleased about that just then. The silence as she came into the room rang, and she blushed crimson at once, feeling as though she must have transgressed in some hideous way and not even been aware of it.

'Hello, Pudding,' said Constable Dempsey, and was silenced by a glance from his superior. Just then Pudding remembered a game of Assassin, played one Sunday afternoon when she was about eleven: a group of Ford and Slaughterford's youngsters, standing in a circle in silence, the assassin winking at people to 'kill' them, and everyone else trying to see them do it and denounce them before they themselves got killed. She'd looked across at Pete Dempsey and found him staring at her, and she'd stared right back, and they'd kept it up for a long time, each one waiting for the other to wink, until the look of constipated intensity on Pete's face had given her a fit of the giggles.

'Miss Cartwright, I wonder if you and I might have a further conversation about recent events,' said Blackman, without preamble, and it wasn't a question.

'Well. Yes,' said Pudding, dry-mouthed, wondering if it was in fact a crime to accuse somebody of another crime; wondering if the Hadleighs were going to prosecute her for it, and how on earth she would save Donny if she herself were in jail.

'Good,' said Blackman, getting to his feet. 'Is there some other room we might use?' He addressed the question to Pudding's father, who also got to his feet.

'Yes, of course. We'll go into the sitting room,' said the doctor, but the superintendent held up one hand.

'That's quite all right, Dr Cartwright. I am sure your daughter can guide me there. Perhaps you might remain with your wife for the time being.' He nodded to Pudding to lead on, and with an anxious glance at her father, and at Ruth behind him, she did just that.

Blackman closed the sitting room door behind them, and Pudding waited to be told to sit down, even though they were in *her* home. The policeman had such an impenetrable watchfulness about him that Pudding could hardly bear to be alone with him; though she had nothing to hide, he made her feel as though she most decidedly did. The reflection of light on his round spectacles made it hard to see his eyes clearly. His hair was darkly oiled, and his skin was smooth – in spite of his air of authority, Pudding wondered if he wasn't much older than Alistair had been.

'Now, Miss Cartwright—' he began.

'Oh, everyone calls me Pudding,' she said, trying to smile, trying to relax. He gave her a steady look, and she decided not to interrupt again. He spoke with the deliberate elocution of a man trying to lose a regional accent.

'Miss Cartwright, I understand that this whole business has been very upsetting to you. That it continues to be so. For a child such as yourself to have witnessed the terrible scene at the mill of last week is to be most deeply regretted. I understand that you were fond of Mr Hadleigh, and are very fond of your brother as well. I can imagine that to lose both of them in such a way is distressing.'

'I'm not a child, I'm almost sixteen, and I haven't lost Donny,' said Pudding, resolutely. 'Donny didn't kill Mr Hadleigh.'

'So you keep saying. Now, Miss Cartwright, I need you to listen very carefully to the questions I am about to ask you, and I need one other thing to be wholly clear: it is imperative that you answer them as truthfully as you possibly may. That means with facts that you are certain of, not with ideas that you wish to be true. Do I make myself clear?'

'Yes, Mr Blackman.'

'It's Superintendent Blackman. Now, Miss Cartwright. What can you tell me about the relationship between Mrs Hadleigh and your brother, Donald?'

'Their relationship? What do you mean?'

'Were they close? Were they perhaps ... on friendly terms?'

'Well ... no. I don't think so. I don't think Irene Hadleigh is on friendly terms with anybody here.'

'Yes. I've been told that she hasn't cared to involve herself with the village since her arrival. That she doesn't seem to care overly much for ... making Slaughterford her home.'

'Well, that's certainly true.'

'So you never saw Irene Hadleigh and your brother to-gether?'

'What do you mean, together?'

'Talking together, for example. Or perhaps was Donald invited into the house? For tea?'

Pudding stared at the policeman in bewilderment. He stared right back, and didn't blink.

'No, of course he wasn't,' she said.

'You're quite sure of that?'

'She wouldn't invite anybody in, least of all Donny. I saw her talking to him once and she looked horrified – she looked like she was afraid of him. Which is stupid, just because he has a scar on his head, and—' Pudding cut herself off, beginning to see what Blackman was driving at.

'So you did see them talking together?'

'Just that one time, but it was out in the garden, and I think she was asking about some flowers for the house.'

'You overheard the conversation?'

'No, I just—'

'Stick to facts, please, Miss Cartwright.' Superintendent Blackman made a note of something in a small black jotter. 'Mr Hadleigh spent much of each day at the mill, or in town. Nancy Hadleigh is also out a good deal of the time, on farm business or on social calls. Which means that Irene Hadleigh has often been left alone in the house. Would your brother have told you if he'd had any other kind of contact with her? She's a very attractive woman, after all. And very fashionable. Did Donald ever tell you that he found her so? Did you ever see him, perhaps, watching Mrs Hadleigh? Do you think he would still notice . . . such a thing, since his injury?'

'No. I don't know,' said Pudding, dumbly. 'How could he watch her? She almost never comes out. He never said any such thing to me, and the only thing he likes to watch is the machines in the mill. He was going to be an engineer, before it happened – did you know that? He was so clever.'

'Yes, your mother told me as much. Now, are you quite sure you can tell me nothing whatsoever about a friendship between your brother and Mrs Irene Hadleigh?'

'Donny doesn't have any friends,' said Pudding, quietly. 'None but old Jem Welch. And Alistair Hadleigh. All the other people he used to know find it too hard now.'

'And you, of course,' said Blackman, staring at her again. 'A most loving and loyal sister.' He made it sound like a bad thing to be.

'A loving and loyal sister is not the same as a friend.'

'Indeed.' Blackman snapped his jotter shut and stood up.

'Wait – do you think Irene Hadleigh is involved, then? Please tell me – have you realised it wasn't Donny? Because I *know* it wasn't him!'

'However hard it may be, Miss Cartwright, I fear you've little choice but to begin to accept that your brother, though he may have been out of his mind at the time, did kill Alistair Hadleigh. All the evidence points to it. What is puzzling to me is the reason why. As you say, nobody has a bad word to say about Mr Hadleigh, and every man in the mill tells me that your brother only ever went into the machine rooms at the mill, never the offices.'

'Yes! You see? It can't have been—'

'I'm also told by those who have worked with Donald since his return from the war that he rarely takes anything upon himself. That he has little initiative, though he works hard and steadily at a job when somebody sets him to it.'

'That's right, yes. So you see—' But Pudding cut herself off again, as she began to see. 'You think Irene Hadleigh put him up to it?' Disbelief made her voice rise.

'She has inherited the estate in full, and she does seem

curiously unmoved by her husband's untimely death. And she is a beauty . . . I wonder if she might not have found out a way to persuade your brother to act on her behalf.' The policeman clamped his mouth shut and blinked rapidly three times, as though realising he'd said too much. 'But this is merely a theory voiced aloud, Miss Cartwright, as yet entirely uncorroborated and certainly not to be bandied about.'

'If . . . if it's true, would they let Donny go?' Pudding asked, her mind racing ahead.

'No, indeed. I fear not, Miss Cartwright. Whatever the reason he did it, the fact remains that he has murdered a man. There can be no doubt about that — Mrs Hadleigh's servants confirm she did not leave the house that morning, and in any case it is inconceivable that she would have the strength to inflict such wounds.'

'But . . . if it was all her idea? If she coerced him somehow . . . or tricked him?'

'I presume she would need to have his trust, or his . . . admiration, in order to achieve such an aim. And you have just finished telling me, Miss Cartwright, that there was no such close relationship between the two of them. I suspect this theory of mine will prove to hold no water whatsoever. I merely wanted to see if you could give it any credence, and you have answered me well enough.'

He opened the door and held out his arm to usher her back through it, and Pudding rose reluctantly. She didn't want to return to the kitchen, and let the moment pass. She felt that, somewhere in the conversation they had just had, there was a glimmer of hope for Donny, though she couldn't quite catch it. She was loath to leave in case she missed it altogether.

'My brother did not kill Alistair Hadleigh, Superintendent Blackman,' she said, weighting the words with every ounce of her conviction. 'And the worst part of it is that the person who *did* kill him is out there somewhere, right now, knowing that they are getting away with it. Knowing that *you* are letting them get away with it.' Blackman paused, letting his arm drop back to his side. Behind his glasses, his eyes were entirely impenetrable; his breathing was so soft and slow it was imperceptible, and beside him Pudding felt like a gasping, wobbling, helpless thing. But he was considering her words, she could tell. Eventually, he gave a minute shake of his head.

'One must always try to find the *why* in these things, Miss Cartwright,' he said. 'Who else has a reason to kill Mr Hadleigh? The answer is nobody. But your Donald, since his injury, does not seem to need much of a why at all.'

'You're wrong about that. And somebody did have a reason,' said Pudding, and saw interest light Blackman's steady eyes. 'The real killer had a reason,' she said, and the interest vanished. Blackman turned away from her, and she knew she had failed.

❧ ❧

Clemmie's sisters were so desperate to know the identity of her lover that when they saw the alphabet Rose had written down, they made Clemmie sit at the table and tried again to teach her to write. Clemmie had been apathetic towards the letters at school, but the fact that she now had cause to learn made no difference. The letters fought her, just like spoken words did, and she certainly wasn't going to let them coax a secret from her that she was more determined than ever to keep.

'What's this nonsense?' said William, coming in for his lunch and seeing them there, three girls huddled around the fourth. 'Haven't you lasses enough work to do?'

'We'll do it, Pa. Only it's wrong that Clem can't even write her own name,' said Mary.

'Or anyone else's name,' added Josie.

'She's no need of it,' said William, ruffling Clemmie's hair, sitting down heavily. They all stared at him. It had been a long time since he'd touched any of them in kindness, or with affection. He glowered at their scrutiny so Rose broke the silence hastily with sliced bread and ham, and pickled onions. But the girls were on Clemmie's side now – even Lizzie, who'd spotted a bite mark on her neck, and woven her mad hair into a loose braid on that side to hide it. Perhaps they hoped to encourage her confidence with such displays of loyalty, but she remained resolutely uncommunicative. In the night, disembodied whispers came through the darkness.

'Is it Bobby Silcox, Clem?' This was a slow-witted Biddestone boy who worked in the sawmill there, stacking cut planks, sweating all day long.

'Is it Jared Hinckley?' A thin young man with a wall eye, who appeared at Honeybrook Farm now and then, looking for work. Clemmie didn't know whether to be happy or sad that they never once thought to suggest a Tanner.

When they'd met at the river, for the first time after what had happened at the mill, Eli had asked enough of the right questions to work out that Clemmie had overheard the plan to rob Alistair Hadleigh.

'I didn't want to, Clem. I swear to you, I never would have, left to my own devices,' he'd said, and Clemmie had taken his face in her hands to show that she believed him. 'And then with what happened . . . I wanted more than anything for the coppers to take the old bastard in. Even if it meant taking me and John as well . . . I wanted them to finger Isaac for it. But you can't count on 'em for a bloody thing.' He'd had to pause and breathe, slowly, through his anger. In the fortnight since then, and since Eli had realised that Clemmie still wanted him, and wouldn't betray him, things had changed. His passion for her had crystallised into something deeper, and less childlike; something so intense it gave her a shiver along her spine when she saw it, and a seasick feeling, like the ground was tilting.

'No one's ever been as good to me as you have, Clem. No one's ever been as true,' he told her, with kisses so strong they bruised her lips, and left them puffy and red. 'You're an angel. You're *my* angel.' She couldn't tell if the shiver were a warning or a thrill, but it was addictive, utterly addictive. It made her feel like a different person to the one she was before – more awake somehow. More real. And she needed his salt-metal taste in her mouth like she needed to breathe; she craved the unexpected softness of his skin in places nobody else knew; she was fascinated by his eyes – older than the rest of him but blue and beautiful, when everything else about his face was ferocious.

And when the police did not return to hound the Tanners, when the investigation seemed closed, she began to wonder if she'd got it all wrong. If she'd misunderstood what she'd overheard at Thatch Cottage – if the robbery at the mill had been aborted, or had happened sooner than she knew, and had nothing to do with the violent attack. If the Tanners had had nothing to do with that, and news of their robbery had been lost in the sensation of the worse crime, or attributed to whoever had dealt the blows. She wished she could ask Eli, wished there was some way she could find out for sure. When she thought back to what she had heard, and what Tanner was like, and how Eli had been afterwards, it seemed obvious to her that it had gone just as she feared it had. But the notion that Eli had no part in it was tempting, and seductive, and as long as she didn't think about it too much, it remained a possibility. Sudden rushes of emotion assailed her all day long, bringing strange physical side effects – a dizziness, the feeling that she was receding from the world into some wrong-moving tunnel; tastes in her mouth that came from nowhere, stemmed from nothing, and made her either ravenous or nauseous; overwhelming surges of love for her family, accompanied by a wobbling weakness in her legs, which then quickly ebbed into a kind of simmering hostility she had never felt before, which somehow made her notice that her clothes were too tight, and cutting into her.

With Isaac Tanner safely away from home during the day, or safely at the pub in the evening, Eli began to take Clemmie home to meet his mother and younger siblings at Thatch Cottage. They were nervous; there was a watchful uneasiness about them all – except for his grandmother, who slept in a chair by the stove the whole time Clemmie was there. At first she thought they were unsure of her, or bothered by her silence. After a while she saw that they were scared for Eli. Frightened that he was there, where his father might catch him not working, might catch him bringing an outsider into their home. Mrs Tanner looked up sharply at any sound from outside – a pheasant coughing in alarm, a snapping twig, any sudden noise from the mill. She had long, bushy hair that stayed in a bun at the back of her head without the help of pins, and a weary, knowing look in her eye. But her smile was ready enough, though it was wry rather than warm. Whenever they were there she made sure that the windows stayed covered with the thick felts that the mill gave away when they got too worn for the paper-making machine. So for Clemmie the inside of Thatch Cottage was a place of shadows, with dark corners and watchful inhabitants moving in them, whatever the time of day. A place that had turned its back on the rest of the world. She could hardly bear it when it was still daylight outside. She fretted and fidgeted, feeling the walls close in around her. But once it was dark the cosiness drew her in, and the candlelit dimness seemed soft and cosseting, and Clemmie stopped feeling as though she had walked willingly into a den of thieves.

Clemmie knew that her family were poor – God knew there was never any money for anything – but compared to the Tanners she saw that her life was blessed in many ways. That at Weavern Farm they had eggs and milk and cheese and fresh vegetables, and clean air and space, and the reassurance and rhythm of constant work. Thatch Cottage was dank amidst the trees, and dirty for having too many people inside, trying to live, trying to breathe. The patch of ground they had outside was muddy and too shaded to grow anything; it stank of the privy and the pigsty, from which the sow gazed out, unhappily, through her white eyelashes. There was never enough food, and the food they had was unappetising, and monotonous. The children had coughs and snivels, even then, at midsummer. Two of the littlest had angry skin rashes, all red and scaly, which they scratched at constantly. Mrs Tanner cut their nails as short as she could and mixed up an ointment of tea leaves, comfrey root and pork dripping to rub on, though they grizzled as she did. The smallest child, a little boy called Jacob, took an instant shine to Clemmie and crawled into her lap whenever she was there, knotting his fingers into her hair and sucking his grubby thumb. The child, not yet two years old, smelled of earth and leaves, and Clemmie remembered the story she'd heard, that Tanner had drowned this baby's twin sister in the river at birth. Seeing the way their mother was with them, and the way she made do, Clemmie knew it was nothing but a vicious rumour. Eli brushed his little brother's cheek with his knuckles, his expression keen, tender.

'Takes after you, this one, Ma,' he said.

'For a change,' said his mother, with a smile. She looked at Clemmie. 'Every other boy I've had has been a copy of his dad – like they were struck from the same mould. But if you marry a strong man, perhaps you'd best expect it. I'd all about despaired of having a sweet one until my Jacob there came along.' Clemmie smiled, but Eli's face had closed off, and he went to the cupboard to look for something. 'If this first of yours is a boy, perhaps you'll have a sweet one too, young Clemmie,' Eli's mother said, quietly, so that he wouldn't hear. 'My Eli has always been soft underneath, even if he can't let himself show it. Drink this, child.' She handed Clemmie a steaming cup. 'Nettle tea. It'll stop you looking so swollen up and ripe. But your folks'll work it out sooner rather than later, as will Eli – best to just tell him.' Clemmie sipped obediently, and thought little of it.

Eli returned to the table with a cloth doll of a little boy: soft, stuffed arms and legs, with dark brown wool hair and blue eyes in needlepoint – just like a Tanner. It was wearing a yellow twill waistcoat and trousers, a white shirt and tiny black shoes, which Clemmie felt sure no Tanner child had ever worn. It was dirty, but not as dirty as it could have been – the pale cream fabric of its face had been grimed yellowish from the touch of human skin, but on the whole it looked as though it had been kept safe, for special use.

'The vicar's wife gave us this, when I was only knee-high,' said Eli. 'She brought us a load of stuff – clothes and shoes the church had collected, and other toys. Dad chucked it all out. He got into such a rage, saying we didn't need their charity, and how they thought they were so godly and above us. I only managed to save this by sitting on it.' He tucked the doll under Jacob's arm, and the toddler squeezed it tight to his ribs, his eyelids drooping with sleep. 'Why shouldn't the littl'uns have a doll?' Eli murmured. Clemmie wanted to ask how they'd kept it hidden from his father all that time, and it was as though Eli heard the question. 'We keep it in a flour pot. My dad never looks there – you can't eat flour right out the jar, after all.' He smiled briefly, and it caused Clemmie's heart to clench. She realised how few times she had seen him smile.

'The two of you need to think,' said Mrs Tanner, gently enough. 'When he finds you out – and he will find you out – he'll like as not turn you out from under this roof, Clemmie, and like as not you'd be glad of that. He's worse than ever of late, since what happened at the mill. I don't know what ails him.' Mrs Tanner shook her head. 'But something ain't right. He's full of nightmares and pain, and the only way he knows how to deal with that is with his fists. But I dare say your folks'll turn you out an'all. So. You need to think.'

Eli's smile vanished. One of his sisters worked at the stove, jamming in a poker, feeding in dry twigs. From upstairs came a loud thumping.

'Go on and see what your granddad wants,' Mrs Tanner told one of the children. 'Tell him supper won't be long.'

'We'll get gone,' said Eli, rising and holding out his hand to Clemmie. She took it, and got up, and nobody argued that they should stay longer, or eat supper. They slipped out into the night together, moving quietly, assuredly, west of Slaughterford through the mill's potato fields and up the hill, until there was no chance of being seen. Then they stopped and kissed, held each other tight, carried on walking again, until Eli stopped by the bridge to Weavern Farm, with the river's rush to hide any noise they might make. 'Go on in to your bed,' he told her, pushing her gently. Clemmie held his hands and wouldn't go. He would sleep rough to keep out from under Tanner's feet – a bed of long grass under a hedge somewhere. He'd wake before dawn, drenched with dew, chilled, restlessly exhausted. He was becoming a bird, a rabbit, a fox. Becoming wild. She wanted to stay with him, and be like him, and at the same time she wanted to take him inside with her, to a feather bed and the clinging safety of the loft room, and give him that life instead. 'Go on, Clemmie,' he insisted. 'We'll think of a plan, just like Mum said. But not tonight. I'll think of a plan, I promise.'

Clemmie woke with the sun. Her head was thumping and her body felt limp. Her sisters were stirring, and she forced herself to sit up. There were small twigs in her hair and mud under her fingernails. Josie, beside her, pinched her arm fondly as she got up.

'Scarecrow,' she said. Clemmie shut her eyes and swallowed. There was a lump in her throat that wouldn't go, and a taste of iron, or blood. She tried to ignore it for a moment, then lurched over the side of the bed to reach for the pot, but it was too late and she threw up all over the rag rug and Josie's feet. 'Oh, Clem!' Josie cried in horror.

'Oh, for pity's sake,' Mary grumbled.

'What did you eat, Clem?' said Josie.

'What *didn't* she eat?' said Lizzie, always at her worst first thing in the morning. 'No wonder she's getting so fat.' Shakily, Clemmie got to her feet and patted Josie's arm in apology. She wanted to go and get water and a cloth to clean up with but couldn't quite make her legs work. Mary was watching her intently, with her head on one side; thoughts marched across her face, and the quality of her silence was such that, gradually, the other three stopped and stared at her.

'No!' said Lizzie, her face falling into astonishment.

'What?' said Josie, frowning.

'Fewer rags to wash last month, weren't there?' said Mary.

'And she's been as moody as a mare. And eating like a pig,' Lizzie pointed out. Realisation dawned on Josie. Her hands flew to her mouth, and she turned wide eyes on Clemmie.

'Oh, no . . . oh, you're not, are you, Clemmie?'

'I reckon she is,' said Lizzie, excitedly.

'Well, we can't keep *that* a secret for you,' said Mary, her shoulders dropping wearily. 'You daft cow. Dad'll go spare.'

They fell into a heated debate about when to tell Rose,

and how their mother might react, and what was to be done, and how they could find out the man responsible and whether William would force them to marry, or kill him and then beat the baby right out of his daughter, and solve it that way. There was a kind of frenetic excitement to their words, their voices, their movements. Clemmie was buffeted to one side of the flow, and drifted over to the window. She pushed the thin drapes aside, sat down on the sill and took a deep lungful of the morning air. The chickens were muttering for release from the barn, the cock was warming up his disjointed crowing, and the cows were milling at the yard gate to be let in and milked. Clemmie put her hands flat on her stomach, and thought for a while, sending her mind inwards until she found what she was looking for – the unmistakable sense of new life. Chicks and goslings, kits, kids and piglets, and now herself. Clemmie and Eli. *Hello, piglet*, she said silently, and smiled. She let the early sun fall onto her at the open window, hoping that, however impossible it was, Eli would see. It seemed to her entirely right, and entirely as it should be. She felt certain that all would be well. The piglet would become a part of their plan, and all would be well.

๛ ๛

The whole of Slaughterford turned out for Alistair Hadleigh's funeral. The mill was left to fall silent – the machines halting their endless turning, beating, stirring and drying, the hiss of steam petering to nothing. Even farm work stopped for the day. Nancy Hadleigh had refused for any work of any kind to go on at Manor Farm, bar the essential feeding and milking of animals, and the brewery and smaller farms had followed suit. Nobody could remember such a happening before, and nobody had ever heard such silence in Slaughterford. The quiet belonged to bygone years before any of them had been born. Voices were lowered outside the church, and though it might have been out of respect for the occasion, people kept turning to look down into the valley, to wonder at the gentle nudge of the breeze and the skylarks' constant song, and the incredible hush everywhere, as though they couldn't quite believe it. They searched the valley as though the view must have changed along with the sounds in their ears – the mill must have vanished, the brewery chimney toppled, the cottages swept away by some massive hand. When the breeze dropped they could even hear the river, parting sibilantly around the piers of the bridge. The stillness cast a magic spell that enthralled them all.

Alistair's body had come back from Chippenham that morning, in the undertaker's ebony carriage, its glass sides showing the glossy coffin and the multitude of white flowers inside. The horses were black, and wore black plumes; their harness had silver buckles, brightly polished, as did the carriage and the coffin. The whole sad parade was monochrome, and so wildly out of place against the greens, yellows and pinks of the flower-strewn churchyard that it might have dropped down from the sky. Or risen up from some underworld. Irene wore black from head to toe. She had a veil so thick she could hardly see out from under it, and, crucially, it was nearly impossible for anybody to see in through it – to see her face. Which didn't stop them trying, of course. Word had got about, as word will get about. Word of what Pudding had accused her of, and that the police superintendent had been up to Spring Cottage to interview her about it. Word that she hadn't loved Alistair, and that her grief was a sham. A rapid spread of incredulous words, passing through the villagers like an infection. She felt their looks, and felt them speculating. She felt, more than ever, her every move scrutinised; she felt that if she got one tiny thing wrong they would fall on her and devour her. She wondered if only Nancy were stopping them. As the coffin was carried, with excruciating slowness, from the lane to the side of the family grave, which gaped in readiness, Nancy took Irene's arm. It might only have been to keep herself standing, but it felt like unity. A show of support. Irene clasped her hand, never more grateful to Alistair's aunt, even if the gesture were not all it seemed.

Chairs were brought out for Irene and Nancy, and while Nancy sank carefully onto hers, Irene felt wound too tight to sit. When it seemed that things would not proceed until she did, she perched on the edge of the chair, her body thrumming with tension. The crowd of mourners seemed to cluster in and tower over her, like a wave that might break, and wash her into the grave along with her late husband. The black coffin was like a tear in the world. Looking at it gave Irene the same electric shock, deep in her bones, as the memory of Alistair's wounds; the same terrible lurch of dissociation from reality. She tried not to look at it because she couldn't help picturing him inside: pallid now, washed clean of blood but still broken and torn. She couldn't help picturing his sinking cheeks stuffed with cotton wadding, and his eyelids stitched shut and his lips entirely bloodless, and all the quietly violent things that would have been done to his insides in preparation for burial. As though what was left in the coffin were a doll of Alistair – a life-sized doll, put together from his remains in macabre imitation of the real man. It sent cold tingles over her scalp, and washed her cheeks with saliva, and she shut her eyes and longed for the moment when the thing in the coffin would be dropped into the ground and covered over forever. She didn't hear the sermon; she was concentrating too hard on surviving the horror of simply sitting there. When Gerry McKinley took her arm and helped her to her feet, she had no idea what he wanted. She panicked as he walked her closer to the grave, and tried to pull her arm away, until she saw that the coffin had been lowered in, and everyone was waiting for her to throw the first handful of earth over it. Then she had to fight the urge to fall to her knees and push great armfuls of it in, and shovel it in with her hands, and keep going until there was nothing left to shovel.

She and Nancy led the mourners up to Manor Farm, where there was to be a sedate wake for the higher-ups. The villagers and mill workers drifted away to their homes, or to the pubs – the White Hart in Ford and the White Horse in Biddestone – to raise a glass or several to their late master; a man they had loved, in a distant way, and respected. At the back of the crowd, their faces downturned, were Dr and Mrs Cartwright, and Pudding. No Donald, of course. The doctor looked pale and exhausted; his wife looked blank, but calm. Pudding's face was wet and ravaged, her normally bright eyes so puffy from crying that they looked piggish and ugly. Besides Irene, they were the most scrutinised of the gathered crowd. She glanced around and saw a variety of expressions directed at them, from bland curiosity to pity, anger and hatred. Pudding and her mother seemed oblivious to it all, which Irene supposed was a good thing. Only the doctor flinched from every face, every unspoken word. He looked like someone struggling to stay standing in a hurricane, and the three of them huddled together, subtly but completely cut off from their neighbours, as though such bad times might be contagious. Irene spotted Constable Dempsey, who, like most young people in Ford and Slaughterford, had known the Hadleighs all his life, and the sight of him set her heart thumping. But if he was there to watch her and report to his superiors, he was doing a poor job of it. He was watching the Cartwrights far more intently, and Pudding in particular.

They had the wake in the dining room, where the long table was laden with cold food, but people spilled into the sitting room and morning room, seeking the space to sit. Clara Gosling and Florence had extra help, on loan from the McKinleys at Biddestone Hall – two stony-faced girls who looked too smart for the farm in their crisp uniforms. They ferried out dirty glasses, ferried in clean ones, refreshed the trays of savoury pastries and petits fours and proffered them to the mourners, whose respectful silence grew less and less so as the first glasses of sherry went down. Irene stood where she was put and was commiserated with by many people, most of whom she didn't know. She neither ate nor drank, and hadn't all day, and soon began to feel the familiar lightness of being in need of nourishment. She let it carry her away from the crowd, into a vague place where she could do nothing about anything, and so expected little of herself. But then Cora McKinley appeared before her, and jarred her out of it. Cora's normally lively face was drawn, and set into hard lines that made her look older than her years.

'What will you do now?' she said, but Irene had no answer. 'I suppose you'll sell up – realise your assets, I should say. And move on to your next adventure.' Her voice cracked a little as she spoke, and she moved her glass of sherry from her left hand to her right, and back again.

'I don't know what I'll do,' said Irene, but the sound of her voice seemed to anger Cora.

'Well, you've all the time in the world to decide, I suppose.' She looked down at her feet for a moment. 'Father says it is just one of those terrible things that happen. But I can't help seeing everything that happens as part of a progression, from one thing to the next – the latter either caused by, or following on from, the former,' she said, her eyes beginning to gleam as her brother Charles appeared behind her. 'Alistair survives the war, marries you, and brings you here, and then is killed. I mean, it's one hell of a coincidence, isn't it? So I can't help wondering whether the latter might not have happened if the former hadn't either. If he would still be alive if you'd never come here. If he'd never met you.'

'Cora, that's enough!' said Charles, taking her arm. Cora wrenched herself free and stormed away, her face in her hands.

'Nobody thinks that, Irene,' said Charles, not quite able to meet her eye. 'Cora is just upset. We're all of us at the Hall so terribly sorry for your loss.'

'Everybody thinks it,' said Irene, quietly. Charles looked at her at last, his face sorrowful. 'She's only saying what everybody thinks. Isn't she? Everybody thinks I'm somehow to blame.'

'Irene ... people just don't understand, that's all. They don't understand why it's happened, and grief makes people irrational.'

'I don't understand it either,' said Irene. 'I don't!'

'Dear girl, you must only try to think of getting through these dark days as best you may, and to remember how dearly Alistair loved you. I never saw him happier than when he came down to say you'd accepted him. It stripped years from him – he looked like a boy again, hooking the biggest fish out of my father's pond.' Charles looked down, his sadness tangible. 'It's a rum do, and no mistake,' he muttered, and gave her hand a squeeze before moving away. He hadn't invited her to visit them, or offered to return if she needed company. Without Alistair, Irene doubted she would see them again.

A tray of full claret glasses went by and Irene reached for one, taking a gulp and feeling the delicious heat as it reached her empty stomach. Then she left the room as discreetly as she could. She couldn't face going up to the bedroom – the room where Alistair had slept for so many years before she'd even come into his life. She had an oddly guilty feeling, as though she, too, had begun to blame herself for his death. She remembered the feelings of prescience that had beset her more than once since she'd been at Manor Farm. She racked her brains for some connection between them all, some sign or warning she had missed. She remembered Tanner's odd reaction to the old doll, and Ma's declaration that change was coming; she remembered the darkness that surrounded Hilarius, and the unflinching hardness of his eyes. Bewildered, she went through to the study, where the Hadleigh family portraits hung, and for a second felt the blessed relief of being alone. She shut the door behind her, letting out a long breath she hadn't known she was holding, and only then saw Nancy, standing silently in front of the portrait of her twin brother, Alistair's father. She was looking up at it with a broken-hearted intensity, as though she hoped the picture would come alive and offer her some comfort. At once, the weight of her circumstances settled back onto Irene, and she thought about slipping away again, unseen, just as Nancy turned and saw her.

'Irene,' she said, obviously unhappy at the interruption.

'Sorry, Nancy. I didn't know you were in here. I'll go.'

'Not on my account,' said the old woman, turning her gaze back to her brother. 'The atmosphere in there is awful, isn't it? All those people pretending to grieve as they shovel food into their mouths.' She shot Irene a wintry smile. 'Not that they weren't fond of Alistair. But fondness doesn't translate into true grief. Does it?'

'No,' said Irene, knowing that Nancy included her beneath that umbrella.

Irene stared up at the portrait of the first Alistair, and saw again how like his father her husband had been. Same height and build and demeanour; same light in the eyes, same arrangement of the face that made it seem permanently on the brink of a smile. 'Was he like his father?' she asked. Nancy sighed deeply.

'So very much like him, in appearance,' she said. 'Especially as he got older. Sometimes, in more recent years, it was so like having my brother back that I almost forgot they were two separate men. Almost.' She looked haunted. 'But my brother and I were in the womb together. I feel his absence wherever I go, and whatever I do.'

'How did he die? Alistair's father, I mean.'

'He had a reckless streak – my nephew had it too, but in a far gentler way, and I did my best to foster it out of him. But my brother had no fear – or rather, he *loved* fear. He loved the excitement of danger – foolish wagers, foolish business deals, foolish liaisons. When we were children, on one trip to the seaside, he jumped into the water from a high cliff that none of the others would even climb up to – just because they bet he wouldn't. Broke his ruddy ankle as he hit the water, the stupid boy, but he didn't care because he'd won the bet. Always racing, always climbing, always gambling with his money and his life – and his reputation . . . He got better as he got older – his gentler side came more to the fore. But he simply couldn't resist a wager. He was racing a friend from Chippenham to Lacock when it happened – racing across country. Robert Houlgate's new hunter, which was a great black brute of a thing, strong as an ox, against Alistair's bay mare – she was lighter, built more like a thoroughbred, so not as strong in heavy going.'

Nancy stared off into the past for a while. 'It was madness. They didn't know the route or the fences overly well. The horses were green, the ground was waterlogged, and it was too long a distance – too tiring for the animals. They took a hedge side by side, as Robert described it afterwards, and didn't see the ditch on the far side until it was too late.

Both horses fell. Robert was thrown clear, and only broke his collarbone. Alistair fell underneath his mare as she rolled. And that was that. The horse had to be shot, and Alistair had been crushed to death before anyone could even try to help him.' Nancy turned away from the portrait as if telling the story had rekindled an old anger towards him.

'Perhaps that was even worse than what has happened to young Alistair now,' said Irene, with the wine in her blood loosening her tongue. 'In a way. That he could have chosen not to do it, I mean.'

'He could have chosen not to die? No, no – I know what you mean. Perhaps, in a way, you're right. I was angry with him for a long time. So angry I didn't know what to do with myself. And I made poor Robert suffer terribly – he'd suggested the race, you see. Dratted man. He knew my brother wouldn't refuse.' She shook her head, and picked up the framed photograph of young Alistair as a boy. 'Thank goodness I had my nephew to look after. I don't know what I would have done, otherwise. There'd have been little point to anything.' She held the photo close to her midriff, and slumped over it, slowly, like she'd been delivered a blow. 'And now he's gone too. And there *is* no point to any of it.' Her voice was muffled by misery. Irene tried to put a hand on her shoulder but she shrugged it off. 'No, please. I don't think I can bear to be touched just now.'

'I'm so sorry, Nancy,' said Irene, struggling to think what she could possibly add. 'I'll be gone soon. You won't have to have me around. And I . . . I won't be turning you out of Manor Farm, so please don't worry about that.'

'You're leaving?' Nancy's head came up fast, eyeing Irene intently. Irene swallowed.

'Well . . . yes. I thought you would be happy.'

'Happy?' Nancy echoed, as though the very concept were

alien to her. 'But you're the last Hadleigh, Irene. You belong here, at Manor Farm, where Alistair brought you. We're the last two. Unless . . . ?' She kept up her scrutiny until Irene felt like running from it.

'Unless what?' she asked, uneasily.

'Unless there's any chance of a . . . a new beginning for the family?' Nancy waited, then tutted when Irene obviously didn't understand. 'Is there any chance – any chance at all – that you might be pregnant, Irene?' The hope in her face, and in her voice, was pitiful. Irene knew there wasn't – as did the servants at Manor Farm, since her period had come on suddenly in the night, three days earlier, and made a mess of her bedsheets. She could hardly bear to dash this last hope of Nancy's, and fail again, but she shook her head.

'I'm sorry, Nancy, but no. There's no chance.'

'Ah. A pity,' said Nancy, quietly.

'You might have had children of your own, mightn't you? Alistair told me you had suitors . . . you were even engaged.'

Nancy didn't reply at once. She gazed off into the dark corners – of the room, of her memory.

'I was,' she said, tightly.

'What happened?' Irene asked, made bold by the awful, alien day.

'I chose my brother. And his son.' Nancy shrugged. 'I moved away when he got married. I thought I'd give him and Tabitha some space here. And besides – I couldn't stomach the woman, with her American manners and her popish superstitions. Such blind faith has always seemed half-witted to me. I went off on the grand tour; I met a boy in Rome. A man, I suppose. Frank Launceston. Nice enough; bright enough. Plenty of money.' She shrugged. 'But then Tabitha died giving birth to Alistair.'

'Your brother must have been broken-hearted.'

'Well,' said Nancy, still not looking at Irene, 'if nothing else, he was completely out of his depth. With a baby son, I mean, and with being here at Manor Farm on his own. It had never happened before, you see. He hired a nanny, of course, but Alistair needed people around him that loved him. He needed women. He needed me.'

'So you came back.'

'I came back.'

'And Frank?'

'Frank married some vapid girl who was willing to trail his coat-tails around the globe, without a care in the world. Happier for all concerned, I've always thought.' In the quiet the clock ticked, and the merry voices of the mourners came as a wordless babble through the wall.

'You've very dutiful, Nancy,' said Irene, thinking that if it had been her, and she had loved Frank, she would have married him, and been that vapid girl.

'I'm a Hadleigh, and I have always done what needs to be done at Manor Farm.'

Once all the mourners had gone, Irene kept drinking. She'd had three glasses of red wine, and was feeling much better – as though it had all happened to someone else and she might go home and forget about it, just like the people who'd been clogging up the house all afternoon. She might go home to Fin, somehow – when he saw her, he would realise how much he loved her, and find the courage to leave Serena. To her scrambled mind this seemed wholly plausible, though it didn't offer the comfort it once had. His awful letter, and the pain of reading it, had torn something irreparably; it had weakened the part of her that still cleaved to him. She sat on a window sill in the drawing room and watched the twilight gathering in the gnarled apple trees, and the bats come out to wheel and dive, and when she ran out of wine she went, unsteadily, to the back kitchen to look for more. Clara was at the table, listening to the wireless, drinking sherry and tucking into a huge plate of leftovers. She gave Irene a pinch-lipped look, half appraising and half guilty, then fetched her an open bottle of claret from the pantry.

'The master never liked to see women in their cups,' she said, flatly.

'The master isn't here to see it,' said Irene.

'No, he ain't,' said Clara, settling back into her plate as though seeking wisdom in it. Irene went out into the near-dark.

She left through the back gate in the low orchard wall and set off down the hill towards the village. The night was warm and still, the deep blue sky was freckled with stars, and a shining sliver of moon had risen. A pretty summer night, as oblivious to the events of the day as Irene wished to be. The mills were still silent, and the brewery never ran at night. The farm animals were asleep; the wild animals kept themselves to themselves. Without a torch, Irene felt quite invisible to the world. She'd meant to go down to the river. She wasn't sure why – she'd had a vague idea about bathing; river bathing, as Fin had told her he and his brothers had done as children, in the Tay, but as she passed the church she heard a noise that stopped her. Sounds of movement, and of breathing; sounds of a person, in the very spot they'd just buried Alistair. The hair stood up all over Irene's arms, and she was suddenly cold. But however strong the impulse, she couldn't run away. For a moment, the wild possibility that Alistair hadn't been dead when they buried him flitted into her mind, and the strength with which she wished him back surprised her. But she knew it couldn't be, and she pictured the Alistair-doll instead – empty of life, stuffed with other things; a grotesque mannequin, a mockery of life – somehow out of the grave and walking. It wasn't possible, but she had to see.

Shaking all over, the wine churning sourly in her stomach, Irene went through the churchyard gate and closer to the heap of flowers that marked the spot. There was a figure there, sitting on the sod alongside the grave; a figure that was clearly not Alistair. Irene's next wild thought was that the murderer had come back to revel in it, before she remembered that Donny Cartwright was in jail, and recognised his sister as the figure at the graveside, snivelling quietly. Again, she wished she could slip away, unnoticed, but at the sound of her footsteps Pudding turned with a gasp.

'Who is it?' she said, too loudly.

'It's . . . Mrs Hadleigh,' said Irene, not going any closer. She wondered if she should still call herself Hadleigh, since she felt no more of a Hadleigh now than the girl struggling to her feet in front of her.

'Have you come to gloat?' said Pudding. Her voice had a tremor of distress that belied the bold words.

'What could I possibly have to gloat about?' said Irene, and that seemed to stump the girl for a moment. In the darkness, the white flowers on Alistair's grave seemed to glow. Irene could suddenly taste her own mouth, dry and sour from the wine. She felt nauseated. 'You can't honestly think I had anything to do with . . . with this, can you?'

'Yes! Oh, I don't know. Perhaps not,' said Pudding, rubbing at her eyes like a child. 'All I know is it wasn't Donny, but nobody will listen to me.'

'But . . . he was there, Pudding. He was . . . holding the shovel,' said Irene, as kindly as she could.

'That doesn't mean he killed Alistair! It doesn't! I know you all think I'm just saying that because I don't want it to be true, but that's not it at all. I *know* it isn't true.'

'Is that why you accused me instead?' At this, Pudding hung her head miserably, then sat back down on the damp grass.

'I'm ... I'm sorry about that. I was so confused, and I ... I know you didn't love him.'

'That hardly makes me a murderess!'

'But how could you not love Alistair? And why on earth did you marry him, if you didn't?'

With a sigh, and her head beginning to ache, Irene sat down next to Pudding.

'People get married for all sorts of reasons,' she said quietly.

'Well, that's no kind of answer.' Pudding scrabbled in her sleeve for a handkerchief, and blew her nose. 'They're going to hang him, you know. Donny. If I can't get to the bottom of this, they're going to hang him.'

'Maybe not ... maybe, because of his injury ...'

'That just gives them an excuse.' Pudding shrugged helplessly. 'You heard that policeman, talking about him like he's a mad dog that wants putting down. That's not what he's like! Just because he's different now, because he's a bit slower about things than he was, and can't stand up for himself, they think they can paint him any which way they choose! And pin anything on him! Well, they can't. It's not fair.'

'No. It isn't,' said Irene. 'But, Pudding, there was nobody else around ...' She remembered again all the odd signs, and ill-defined feelings, and fought to keep the facts to mind.

'Nobody was *seen*.'

'Well, that's rather the point, isn't it?'

'I'll find out. I have to. This is Slaughterford – there are no real secrets here. *Somebody* will know. The person who did it knows, and the next person they saw after doing it – they know too. Somebody knows *everything*, here. I just have to find them.'

'How will you do that?'

'I ... I don't know yet,' said Pudding, and started to cry again. Irene felt heat radiating off the girl, and smelt the salty damp where tears had got into the hair hanging around her face. Pudding exuded a kind of irrepressible vitality, even in her denuded state, which made Irene feel hollow, a husk, in comparison. She put her hand on the girl's shoulder and squeezed it for a moment.

'Come up to the house for a while. We'll have cocoa, and there's tons of food.'

In the kitchen, now empty of Clara Gosling, Irene peered helplessly at the stove, trying to work out how to make it hotter, and where to put a pan to heat milk, and what size or type of pan she should use. She opened the hatch into which she'd seen Clara pouring coal but there was nothing to see, just a small pool of darkness, stinking of smuts. Pudding watched her curiously for a while.

'You don't know how to do it, do you?' she said, eventually, incredulously. 'You don't know how to heat milk.' Irene folded her arms and stared at the stove. She was incredibly tired.

'No,' she said. 'I've never done it before.' She couldn't quite bring herself to look at Pudding, but the girl groom got up and set about it without another word.

'Can you fetch out the cocoa and sugar?' she said, returning from the pantry with a huge covered jug of milk. 'Back there, right-hand side, top shelf.' Soon, the childhood smell of warm milk was filling the kitchen, rising with the shreds of steam from the pan, and in the soft glow of the single lamp, Irene remembered being ushered out of the kitchen as a child, when she'd been drawn down to it by the warmth and the light and the voices because she was cold, lonely and sleepless. *Back upstairs where you belong, Miss Irene. If your mother catches you* ... The servants had tried to be kind, but they knew her parents too well. Pudding and Irene sat opposite one another at the table, and in the corner of the room the tap dripped steadily into the stone sink, adding to the small stalactite of scale on its lip.

'You loved Alistair,' said Irene. 'Didn't you?'

'Everybody did. Well – almost everybody.' She glanced across at Irene. 'I've known him all my life. That is, I had known him all my life.' Having used the past tense, Pudding gulped. To ward off fresh tears, Irene spoke.

'The reason I didn't love him was not because I'm some ... heartless thing,' she said, floundering. But the night was dark and she had no idea of the time, and the wine had left her lucid and uncaring. 'I know I haven't ... got to know any of you. So, just like with Donny, people here have thought and said whatever they've liked about me. It's not that I don't have a heart, but rather that I have a ... a broken heart.'

Pudding looked up at her in wonderment, as if this were a wildly exotic thing to have.

'Have you really?' she said. Irene nodded. The girl's eyes were like headlamps. Irene shifted in her seat. The joy and terror of having said it aloud were irresistible. She hadn't spoken a word about it since leaving London. 'Superintendent Blackman said you'd run away from a scandal. He said you were a woman of dubious character.'

'Well,' said Irene, her face heating up, 'perhaps I am. There was a scandal. And I was ... I was a fool.'

'What happened?'

'I ... I fell in love with a married man,' said Irene, and Pudding's eyes grew even wider.

'Who was he?'

'His name was ... is ... Finlay Campbell. And he was – is – married to a woman called Serena. Who was my friend.' She looked up to see if Pudding would judge her badly for this, but she didn't seem to.

'And she found out that you loved him?'

'It was worse than that. He was unhappy. He'd been unhappy for years, he told me. He told me he hadn't known what love was until . . .'

'Until he met you?' Pudding breathed, wistfully, and Irene nodded. 'How *romantic*.'

'Serena was a friend but not a real one. That hardly makes sense, does it? There was every semblance of affection between us, but it was only skin deep, and underneath it was a kind of competition, a kind of . . . envy and distaste. I had the money, I was the right class, the right . . . style. She had all the ease and charm I've never had. She bewitched people – virtually enslaved them. She enslaved Fin. I don't say any of that to excuse what happened.'

'What happened?'

'We . . . had an affair. I loved him so much, I agreed to an elopement. I agreed to run away with him, and live with him until he was free of his marriage, and then we would get married ourselves. He promised me, and I never doubted him for a second. And it didn't seem wrong, because it was true love.'

Irene shut her eyes for a moment and was back there again, on the concourse at King's Cross station, with her case in her hand and her coat buttoned up to her chin, on an unseasonably chilly day in early spring. She'd been shaking all over with pent-up nerves, excitement, love. All the mad terror of what she was doing, coupled with the certain knowledge that it was right – that she couldn't be without him, and could no longer keep her feelings a secret from Serena, her parents, their friends. It was love – the love people spoke about and read about but never seemed to feel. Not like she was feeling it. Women in furs, and felt coats and hats, and plain brown drab; men hurrying to work with bowler hats and leather cases; the stink and hiss of the hot trains waiting, breathing out plumes of soot and steam. Her ears had been full of echoes – voices and footsteps and engines – all bouncing about in the iron rafters far above her head. Pigeons had strutted everywhere; a small child was on his own, crying, and when his mother found him she gathered him up, her face white. The station clock was a ponderous presence, the minute-hand moving with a reluctant clunk every sixty seconds. Irene had watched that clock for a long time. She'd been too nervous to eat breakfast, and the smell coming from a handcart selling roasted peanuts had made her stomach rumble. She'd spent a long time wanting to buy two cones of them, one for her, one for Fin, but not daring to leave the agreed spot in case he missed her in the throng.

The minute-hand of the station clock, black and ornate against a white background. How many times did she see it go around, getting colder, getting hungrier, becoming more afraid? At least sixty times, before she realised that Fin wasn't coming to meet her. Their train – to Cambridge – pulled out of the station behind her, and she simply stood and let it. She stayed a long time after that as well, chilled to the bone, just in case he had simply been delayed. And in spite of the clock she had little idea what time it was when she finally left, and walked, dazedly, to the house where Fin and Serena had their apartment. She'd been sure something terrible must have happened to him, that he'd been injured in some horrible way; she could conceive of nothing else that might have detained him. Not until she saw the look of unabashed triumph on Serena's face at the door, and, as she smiled the coldest smile Irene had ever seen, heard her say: *What on earth do* you *want?*

'What did she say?' said Pudding, hanging on Irene's every word.

'Not much,' said Irene. 'She came down, took my case and threw it into the street. All my things went everywhere, and blew about. She said Fin didn't want to see me ever again. That my attempt to steal and disgrace him had failed.'

'But . . . *he* approached you first, you said?'

'Yes. Not that it matters, really. We were in it together.'

'You can't have believed what she said! Didn't he come out to talk to you?'

'He did.' Irene recoiled from the memory. Fin, entirely cowed, Fin crushed, Fin too ashamed to look her in the eye. She still had no idea what had gone wrong, how Serena had found out, how she'd made him change his mind, and give her up. Perhaps it had only been that strange power she had over him, the corral he didn't seem able to break free from. Perhaps it was something more cast iron than that – something she had over him. She swallowed painfully. 'He told me to go. He just . . . stood there, while Serena called me such things . . . words I'd never heard her use before.'

'And he didn't defend you?' Pudding was outraged. Irene shook her head. 'The . . . the *worm*!'

'Serena was just too strong for him. And she was his wife – is his wife. She told all our friends, my parents, everybody we knew – her version of events, of course. That I'd a passion for her husband and had seduced him into my bed, and tried to get him to elope with me, and had even thought he actually *would*.' She shook her head again. 'Not that there is a good version of the events, of course.'

Pudding thought about it for a while, and Irene finished the last of her cocoa.

'He can't have loved you. Not really,' Pudding concluded, crossly. 'To give you up like that, and let you take all the blame.' If the words were meant as a comfort, they had the opposite effect.

'No . . . no, he loved me,' said Irene. 'I'm sure of it. At least . . . at least, I *was* sure of it.'

'Perhaps he did, then,' said Pudding, retracting in the face of Irene's misery.

'What does it matter now, anyway? It couldn't matter less. He's made his choice, one way or another.' Her attempt to sound resigned to it was fake in her own ears. She thought of the mad, vain hope the wine had conjured only that evening – that she and Fin would somehow be reconciled. But she wondered then if that hope were still genuine, or merely a habit of the mind.

'So you married Alistair out of . . . revenge?'

'Revenge? No, not at all! I married him because he asked me, and he . . . he seemed a nice man. And he offered me a home away from London. And I . . . I couldn't think what else to do. My parents wanted nothing to do with me, they told me to marry Alistair or I'd be cut off completely; none of my friends . . .' She shook her head, and looked up at Pudding. 'Those probably don't seem like very good reasons to you, do they?' Pudding looked down, blushing a bit.

'It just doesn't sound very fair on Alistair,' she said quietly.

'It wasn't,' Irene agreed. 'But he knew it all, at least. He was right there, and saw it all happening, but he married me anyway. As much out of kindness as out of love, perhaps.'

'Yes.' Pudding sighed. 'That sounds like Alistair. No wonder Miss H hasn't warmed to you. Are there any sandwiches left? I'm ravenous.'

'Tons, in the pantry. Help yourself.'

Pudding came back to the table with a silver platter covered with a cloth, beneath which were a mixture of sandwiches – salmon, cucumber, cheese. She tucked in eagerly, then looked at Irene.

'Aren't you having any?' she said. Irene shrugged a shoulder, and took a cheese sandwich as much out of politeness as anything. It tasted heavenly, and her stomach squeezed in utter delight as she swallowed, so she picked up another.

'So you see,' she said, 'even though I didn't love my husband as he should have been loved, I had no reason to wish him dead. He rescued me. He was the only chance I had.' Pudding nodded.

'The policeman thinks you might have seduced Donny into doing it for you,' she said.

'*What?*'

'I don't think he *really* thinks it. But perhaps he does. I thought he almost believed me, you see, when I said it wasn't Donny. But it was just that he thought it might have not been Donny on his own.'

'You don't think that, do you? That it was me, I mean. Me and Donny.'

'No,' said Pudding, without hesitation. 'You could be Queen Titania and he still wouldn't have hurt Alistair for you. I'm . . . I'm sorry I accused you. It seems stupid now. All I wanted was for them to know it wasn't Donny. But even that didn't work – even when Superintendent Blackman thought it might be you, he still thought it was Donny as well. So it was a waste of time.' They both reached for another sandwich, and ate in silence for a while, and it felt so good to have food inside her that Irene didn't know how she'd survived so long without it. The tap dripped, and their thoughts were a mystery to one another. Irene looked at the girl sitting opposite her, and tried to imagine how hard it all must have been for her.

'How old are you, Pudding?' she asked. Pudding gave a tiny smile.

'I was sixteen today, actually,' she said. Her face fell. 'My parents forgot. Not that I blame them. I almost forgot myself.'

'Oh. That's . . .' Irene trailed off, not wanting to say *awful*, or *tragic*. 'Too bad,' she opted for, lamely.

'I don't think it's been a birthday I'll care to remember,' Pudding said, quietly. Irene reached for another sandwich. 'Will you help me, then?' Pudding added then, her face lighting with sudden desperation.

'In what way?' said Irene, uneasily, feeling ill-equipped to be this girl's ally. She still felt ill-equipped to be of use to anybody.

'To find out who really killed Alistair, of course. To prove my brother is innocent of it.'

'But I . . . I don't know how to,' she said, and Pudding sank again.

'No,' she said. 'Neither do I.'

The two of them stayed at the table until all the sandwiches were gone, and the petits fours as well, and fatigue was dragging heavily at both of them. Birds were starting to sing and the sky was turning gauzy as Pudding fell into a guest bed, still dressed, asleep before she was fully horizontal, and Irene watched over her for a little while – noticing that she looked even younger in her unconscious state, with her skin so smooth and clear, and her bushy curls flung out around her, and her mouth slightly open. She saw something angelic and something animal in Pudding then; an odd mixture of guts and innocence. Then she went up to the room she'd shared briefly with Alistair, where the beams still wriggled drunkenly across the ceiling, and in the final moments before she slept realised that she felt, in some intangible way, just a little better than before.

7

The Roots of Things

The run of fair weather had gone on so long that people had begun to take it for granted – there was no need to look out for signs the night before to know how the morning would dawn. The thundery rain that had fallen on the day of Alistair's murder seemed to have been accepted as unnatural, just like his death; some people even said it had been nature's response to the killing. Now, again, the sunshine could be relied upon. Blue skies, high white clouds, the river getting a little shallower each day, the water slowing down as though tired. The whole By Brook valley seemed to be slowing down – the baby birds had all fledged and breeding was over, so the dawn chorus was a half-hearted affair; the marsh marigolds along the riverbanks had softened from their first vibrancy into a kind of leggy languor. Slaughterford basked; its residents basked; nothing was done in a hurry now that haysel was over and harvest not yet begun in earnest. In times past, mill production would have suffered with the lowering water, but Slaughterford Mill was immune to that now, with its boilers and steam generators, and production was back to normal just a handful of days after the hiatus for Alistair's funeral. George Turner was supervising the day-to-day running of things, as he had done before, and when he came up against a decision that Alistair would have made he consulted Nancy instead, who told him to do whatever he thought best.

Down by the privy at the back of Spring Cottage, the rhubarb was half as high as Pudding, with leaves two feet across in places. The stalks were a violent magenta, gone too thick and tough to be eaten, and in the dank shade underneath, slugs gorged on the soggy ruins of rotted leaves. The garden was criss-crossed with their silver trails – and those of snails as well. The hostas and carnations had been eaten into oblivion. Louise Cartwright no longer cared to keep up her war on the creatures – once, she had collected them in a bucket and walked them down into the valley to tip them into a hedge, ignoring Ruth's suggestion to apply a brick to them and have done. By the middle of the afternoon, when the sun was at its hottest, buzzards rode the thermals over the hills, so high up in the blue that their faint, triumphant cries could be heard when they were too distant for the eye to make out. It was glorious. It should have been glorious.

Pudding caught herself imagining the summer as though Alistair hadn't been killed – as though he were still alive, and Donny were at home, and life were going on as it had before. It hadn't been perfect, she reminded herself, but by God it had been better than it was now. The eleven days since his death had been like a bad dream in which familiar things looked wrong, and frightening. She kept waiting for a return to reality, only for the permanence of what had happened to reassert itself with sickening clarity. She hated to see Slaughterford returning to normal life; the shock of Alistair's murder being assimilated into its long history, like a rock thrown into the river – there were still ripples, but the surface had closed over, and the flow continued, unabated, as it ever had. People still talked of little else, but in doing so they had begun to make it commonplace. Donny's involvement was spoken of in tragic terms – a young man broken by the war. Shocking, terrible, but not shameful. Mrs Glover in the shop had even said as much to Pudding. *Nobody's blaming your family, Pudding.* As though Pudding ought to have been grateful to them for that, or reassured. She'd paid the shillings for the tea and sugar and left without a word. And she determined – increasingly, every day – to keep the water from smoothing over altogether. The mill might be running again, and the men back at work, and the crops ripening from green to palest gold; the main topic of conversation might have moved on to what Mrs Hadleigh might choose to do with the mill and land, and what that meant for the workers and tenants, but Pudding wasn't going to let it rest. She wasn't going to let the water close over Donny.

Her early incredulity at his arrest had hardened into steady dread when nobody else was caught – when nobody else was even questioned. When it became abundantly clear that the police believed they had their man. She wanted to shake them all. Their willingness to accept Donny's wrongful arrest and move on was excruciating. She didn't know how they could think it of him – Donny, who'd been captain of the boys' cricket team three years in a row; who'd once run straight into the carpenter's shed when it was on fire because the man's elderly terrier was sitting inside, stupefied by the danger; who'd once eaten an entire tray of lardy cake for a bet, and had such a bad stomach the next day he couldn't go to school. This was the Donald Cartwright they believed could pick up a shovel and batter to death a man he had known and liked all his life. Pudding remembered the white flash of Donny's smile in the gloaming, shot back over his shoulder as he'd sneaked out to meet Aoife one night just before the war; safe in the knowledge that Pudding wouldn't betray him. Safe in the knowledge that she loved him – adored him – and wouldn't let him down.

Pudding avoided talking to people as much as she could, worried that sooner or later something would burst out of her – something angry and desperate and harmful. She walked to work with her head down, watching her marching feet.

Not that avoiding people was difficult. In fact, her friends and neighbours seemed to welcome it, and paused as she passed, silencing themselves. If it hadn't been for Hilarius, Irene and Nancy, Pudding could have gone whole days without talking to anybody other than her parents. But on the morning a message came from the police station in Chippenham that Donny's hearing before the magistrate had been fixed for two weeks' time, Pudding found she *had* to talk to somebody. The magistrate would hear the facts of the case, and the evidence against Donny, and would decide what exactly he would be sent to trial for: manslaughter due to diminished responsibility, diminished understanding of the results of his actions, and the fact that he probably hadn't intended, and certainly hadn't *planned* to kill Alistair; or wilful murder, for which he would certainly hang if found guilty.

Two weeks. Pudding read the note with her heart walloping right up into the back of her throat as panic gripped her. She had just two weeks to find out who was really behind the attack, or to at least raise enough doubt about somebody else being involved that the police would keep looking, and Donny wouldn't be tried for wilful murder. And in spite of Irene Hadleigh's tentative support, she had no idea what to do next. Irene had asked, the day before, what she could do to help and what Pudding would do next, even though *she* was the adult, and eight years older than Pudding. And Pudding had no answers for her.

'Well, can't *you* think of something?' she'd cried, the last time, pushed beyond the bounds of good manners. Irene had flinched slightly, and gone away with a quiet apology, which had made Pudding feel awful. It was the twenty-eighth of July, a Friday; and on Friday, August eleventh, her brother's fate would be all but sealed.

*

Thomas Hancock turned his hat in his hands, looking profoundly ill at ease. He was a small man, bony at the shoulder, widening to a pot belly perched on skinny legs. Irene guessed his age at around sixty, but it was hard to tell with some of the villagers. Their lives were lived outdoors, in all weathers, so their faces were beaten and creased from an early age. Thomas came with a powerfully organic aroma, reminiscent of the sheep he farmed.

'Won't you sit down, Mr Hancock?' she said, and the old man cast a horrified look around at the floral furnishings of the sitting room. He was dressed for farm work in a smock from the previous century, over canvas trousers and caked boots, and Irene knew she'd brought him into the wrong room, but when Florence had announced him she hadn't had the first clue who he was or what he might want. She'd pictured some other acquaintance of Alistair's, come to commiserate.

'Beggin' pardon, ma'am, best I don't,' he said. Irene cleared her throat and tried to think of some way to put the man at his ease, difficult when she was so on edge herself. She attempted to smile, but that only made him fidget more.

'How may I help you?'

'Ar. 'Tis only this, ma'am. 'Tis this.' He paused and looked down at his hands, and Irene agonised for a moment over whether to instruct him to call her *Mrs Hadleigh*, instead of *ma'am*. 'What with our Brandon gathered to the Lord last winter, and I with the farmer's lung . . . what with all o' that, we'd fallen behind with the rent. On the cottage and land, see. Only your husband, God rest his soul, he told I 'tweren't a problem, and I could make it up through the year as best I could, see?' Thomas cast her a guilty, beseeching look, and flinched from Irene's frown, which in fact was only down to having to concentrate to penetrate his accent. 'I know we must pay up, 'twas ever my design to. Only I hadn't quite made it up when he . . . when he were taken. I suppose . . . I do suppose if the estate is sold up, such debts as mine will be called in.' He studied the hat in his hands again – a battered felt affair, dark with grease around the brim. 'Any new owner should want to begin afresh, I should think,' he mumbled.

The penny dropped, and Irene blinked. It appalled her that an elderly man should feel he had to come to her – quite literally cap in hand – to ask her for mercy. She felt, quite definitely, that she hadn't the right. She didn't belong in Alistair's place; it was a situation she had never contemplated. *There has been a terrible mistake*. She had to stop the words speaking themselves.

'Mr Hancock,' she said, shaking her head and dropping all attempts to sound authoritative. He looked up at her, and the fear in his eyes affronted her. 'You may continue to repay any arrears by whatever arrangement you had with my husband. I shan't be calling in any such debts, I assure you.' Thomas brightened.

'Then . . . you shan't be selling up, ma'am? There's to be no new squire?'

'I . . . I can assure you, you and your family will not be turned out of your home,' Irene hedged. 'I will see to it personally.'

'Well, now . . .' Thomas Hancock nodded. 'Thank you most kindly, ma'am. Thank you. You have taken such a weight from my shoulders . . . You're as good and as kind as your late husband, God rest his soul, and I shall see to it that folks start to know of it.'

'They think otherwise, then?' said Irene, and the old man looked sheepish.

'Beg pardon, ma'am.'

'No, you haven't offended me. No one could ever be as good or kind as Alistair was, in any case,' she said, quietly.

'Ar, that may be so,' said the old man. 'There never was a worse loss, round these parts.'

When the old man had gone, Irene stayed a while in the sitting room, lost in sombre thoughts that were beginning to feel like an inner blockade of some kind – one that she probed, uncomfortably, constantly, trying to dismantle. Nancy interrupted them, wrinkling her nose from the doorway.

'Here you are – what is that unholy stink?'

'Oh – one of the tenants came to see me. Thomas Hancock.'

'Woolly Tom? That explains it.' Nancy grunted, and crossed to open the window. 'I do wish the peasants would keep outdoors. They smell worse than the collies on a wet day – why on earth did you bring him in here?'

'I didn't know who he was,' said Irene, with a shrug.

'Asking for another extension on the missed rent, I'll wager.'

'It seemed kind to agree to it. He seemed most . . . anxious.'

'Of course he's anxious, he'll never be able to pay it back. Alistair knew as much, but he let them linger on. Soft as butter,' she muttered, without any real feeling.

'I intend to honour all such agreements my husband made with tenants and workers alike,' said Irene, with more heat than she'd intended. Nancy gave her a long look.

'You must do as you see fit,' she said, stonily, walking back towards the door.

'It's the right thing to do, wouldn't you say?' Irene called after her, not wanting to start a row. Nancy turned, and softened.

'I suppose it is,' she said, and left. Irene sat quietly for a while longer, and realised that her inner blockade was anger. She realised just how furious she was.

She was angry for Alistair, to have been robbed of his entirely blameless life. She was angry for all the people who relied on him for their livelihoods. She was angry with the world for letting it happen, and in some amorphous way with herself, for lying in bed while it did. She was angry that she was now alone, when for a heartbeat it had seemed as though she might actually start to live again. She was angry with whoever had killed him. Very, *very* angry. And it was at that moment she realised that she didn't believe it had been Donald Cartwright. Her anger was not directed at him but at some unknown, faceless other person; some figure on the edge of her vision; shifting, moving, always out of reach, and vanishing when she turned her head. It was maddening. She closed her eyes tightly and tried to see; tried to piece the fragments of thought and feeling and impulse into some kind of whole picture, but it wasn't long before she was forced to give up. Along with the anger came a small measure of Pudding Cartwright's desperation that her brother had been blamed, and the real killer was being allowed off scot-free. And yet, when Pudding had asked for Irene's help after the funeral two nights before, Irene had hedged, and stepped back, and been uncertain and afraid. As she had always been. She got up, and went out to the stables.

She found Pudding bent in half with one of Bally Girl's hooves between her thighs; she was smearing the inside with a sticky ointment of some kind. Pudding's eyes were red-rimmed, and her cheeks looked chapped.

'Hello,' said Irene, still keeping a safe distance from the horse. 'What's that you're doing?'

'Oh. She always gets cracked heels when the ground is this hard. See here, where the bulbs have gone all shrivelled?'

'Oh, yes,' Irene lied.

'The grease will help to soften it all.' Pudding put the hoof down and wiped her hands on a rag. 'Did you want to go riding?'

'No. Well, perhaps, later. I wanted to talk to you about...

about your brother.' At this, Pudding was immediately alert. 'I never really gave you an answer, when you asked for my help the other night. But the thing is . . . the thing is . . .' Irene paused, suddenly beset by doubt. Her feelings of unease and prescience might all be fiction; she simply couldn't tell. She might be encouraging Pudding into a false and damaging hope; engaging in a dangerous game of some kind. She might be about to interfere in serious matters that were no concern of hers, and make them worse. Irene checked herself. Alistair's murder was most certainly a concern of hers. 'The thing is, I'm really not at all sure of your brother's guilt.'

Pudding gasped, and took an involuntary step towards Irene. She simply stared for a while, as though lost for words.

'But . . . all those things you said about him being found with the shovel, and all that?' she said, in the end.

'I know. I might have been trying to convince myself, I think. Because, you see, I have a feeling about it. That sounds terribly feeble, I know. I shall try to explain.' So she told Pudding about her cousin Gilbert, and how he'd died; she told her about the other times she'd had odd feelings like that, down the years. 'It's always been quite rare – just a handful of times – but then, since I came here, there have been several. And somehow . . . I don't know how, but somehow I feel as though they're . . . connected. Connected to what's happened, I mean.' She paused, and tried to decipher Pudding's expression. It seemed entirely likely that the girl would think her mad. Irene was oddly breathless, her pulse too quick. 'It all sounds very . . . fishy, doesn't it?' she said. 'Quite fantastic. Perhaps I shouldn't have said anything.'

'Well, what feelings have you had since you got here? About what?' said Pudding, with a slight frown.

'The first one was when we found that old doll in the schoolroom chimney. That one was very strong. It was almost as though I recognised it – you know when you've seen a place or a person before, but you can't for the life of you remember where, or when? Then . . . then of course there was the very odd way Tanner reacted to it when he saw it, and Ma saying change was coming . . . That wasn't quite the same, but it must have been significant, don't you think? Change has certainly come, after all.'

'It has.' Pudding's voice sounded older than her years. Irene went on to describe the odd fire she'd found in the house on a hot day, which nobody would lay claim to having lit. 'Who could it have been, if it wasn't Nancy, or the servants?' said Pudding.

'Well,' said Irene. 'That's the thing. Who? And the other time I felt anything odd was . . .' She hesitated. 'Well, it was when I met Hilarius. The groom. And every time I have met him since.'

'Hilarius?' Pudding exclaimed. 'Well, *that* can't be right! Hilarius is fine . . . he's a friend. Of sorts.'

'I don't mean to speak ill of him, Pudding. I just . . . I felt some oddness. A darkness. That's the only way I can describe it. Like he cast more of a shadow than he ought to have done.' She stopped talking because Pudding was shaking her head.

'People have always taken against him because he's foreign, and not one of them,' she said.

'That's not the reason, and I'm not set against him. I was just trying to tell you everything. I mean . . . he could have lit the fire in the house; he is here all the time, after all.'

'Tending to the shires or sleeping, yes. I'd be willing to wager he's never once set foot inside the actual *house*—'

'He has,' said Irene, suddenly and inexplicably certain of it. 'Sorry.'

'Well,' said Pudding. She took a deep breath and let it out slowly. 'Cup of tea?'

Irene sat on a stool in the tack room while Pudding set a kettle of water to boil on the tiny stove. The small room smelled strongly of saddle soap, leather and neatsfoot oil, and Irene felt out of place in her skirt and blouse. She crossed her legs awkwardly, and clasped her hands over one knee as Pudding spooned tea leaves into a chipped brown pot. 'I didn't think you'd want to help, really,' said Pudding, not looking up. 'I only asked because of . . . of everything being so desperate. But you're the first person to say they don't believe Donny's guilty.' She looked over at Irene with such a potent mixture of hope and fear that Irene said a silent prayer that they were right. 'Even old Jem, and Nancy . . . They're all very sorry, but they all think it was him.'

'If nothing else, he had no reason to whatsoever, from what I gather,' said Irene. 'No reason to lose his temper, even.'

'Exactly!' said Pudding keenly. 'That's what the superintendent said – that he always likes to know *why*, to be sure he has his man. He's decided that Donny doesn't need a reason, but he does! He *does*! He would never have just . . . attacked him! And I know that Alistair – I mean, Mr Hadleigh – wouldn't have said anything to Donny about the broken roses. He told me as much. Not that Donny would have been angry if he had, only sad, and—'

'Pudding,' Irene said, to halt her. 'Pudding, please. There's no need to try to convince me.'

'Sorry.' Pudding took a deep breath, and Irene saw how much sheer willpower alone was holding her together. She felt a flash of admiration for the girl, and then shame at the thought of how completely she herself had collapsed in the face of adversity. Collapsed and let it all march right over her.

'Don't be. I think the superintendent is right. If we can find out who wanted to kill him, and why, then ... well, then we can't help but find the person who did it.'

'But how do we do that? There's nobody! Everybody loved Alistair.'

'Clearly, not everybody,' said Irene, quietly. There was an uneasy pause, then she went on. 'I can't help thinking about Mr Tanner. He certainly seemed ... upset about something, when we saw him at his home that time. Very upset. And he is, by all accounts, the violent type.'

'Oh, terribly violent!' said Pudding, savagely mashing the tea leaves in the pot. 'But he has an alibi, remember?'

'Yes, I heard. But it's not so very far to Biddestone, is it? Couldn't he have come back in between being put to bed, so to speak, and being put out in the morning?'

'There'd have been plenty of time. But the landlord said he was there all night; he said he was unconscious with drink.'

'But he didn't actually *see* him there all night, did he? I mean, Tanner was alone in the shed. Nobody watched over him.'

'No. I suppose not.'

Irene accepted a steaming mug of tea, dark and bitter from its agitated brewing. She sipped it and thought back to the terrible morning of Alistair's death. The odd stillness in the house that had made her skin prickle; the grey veil of rain outside; the way she'd been disappointed, for the first time since she'd married him, not to have seen her husband before he'd left for the day. It brought a lump to her throat, and a renewed flare of anger.

'It rained very heavily the morning Alistair was killed,' she said.

'Yes. So what?' said Pudding.

'Well, if Tanner had perhaps only *feigned* his drunkenness, and had crept back to the mill in the early hours to attack

Alistair, and had then returned to the shed in order to give himself an alibi . . .'

'He'd have got soaking wet!'

'He would. His boots, at least, even if he'd had a raincoat that he got rid of somewhere.'

'So . . . if he was wet when Bob Walker kicked him out in the morning . . .'

'Then holes begin to appear in his alibi,' said Irene. Pudding chewed her lip for a moment, then put her mug down abruptly, slopping the contents.

'Let's go and ask him, then.' She stood, and hitched up her breeches.

'What, now?' said Irene, startled.

'Well, when, then?' said Pudding. Irene thought for a moment, then stifled her own fears and stood up as well.

Pudding had Dundee, the cob pony, hitched to the Stanhope in no time, and drove them to Biddestone with the nonchalance of long practice, trotting briskly along Ham Lane once they were up the steep hill out of Slaughterford. Irene had an uneasy sense of transgressing, of cheating in some way, but Pudding watched the lane between the pony's ears with a kind of fixed determination, clucking her tongue whenever they slowed. Irene peered along the driveway to Biddestone Hall as they passed it, but saw no sign of the McKinleys. They had possibly gone away after the funeral, to a place less dogged by sorrow. She remembered Cora's enthusiastic response to the tentative letter Irene had sent, on Alistair's suggestion; the trip to Cousin Amelia by the sea that had never happened. There hadn't been time before everything had fallen apart, but perhaps if they'd gone they might have been friends, in spite of what came next. But then, perhaps Cora was just one more person who'd loved Alistair better than Irene had; one more person whose grief was more visceral than her own.

The White Horse was an uneven whitewashed building set back from the green by the duck pond in the centre of Biddestone. It was nearing midday, and a few men from the wood mill were sitting outside, swigging from glasses of dark beer and brushing the sawdust from their hair. Pudding and Irene drew curious glances, and Irene wondered how they looked, the pair of them – herself so very overdressed and out of place, and Pudding scowling and grubby with her chest all but popping the buttons of her shirt. Irene did her best not to look awkward. They found Bob Walker, the landlord, in the yard behind the inn, carrying a stack of old news-sheets towards the outhouse. He was massive in both height and girth, with hands like paddles, stooped shoulders and blond hair that was thinning on top but spread down his cheeks in big, wiry sideburns.

'Ar? Help you ladies?' he said, when he saw them. Buck teeth gave him a way of leaving his bottom lip hanging that made him look simple, but he seemed friendly enough. Irene and Pudding exchanged a glance, and Irene realised that she was expected to speak first.

'Ah yes. How do you do? I'm Irene Hadleigh, and this is ... Pudding Cartwright,' she said, realising that she still didn't know Pudding's real name.

'The doctor's lass.' Bob nodded, which set his chins wobbling. 'And 'ee can't be the new widow, can 'ee?' He shook his head. 'Fearful business.'

'Yes. Indeed.' Irene hated her own voice just then; hated how it turned all her words into empty things. She sounded, she realised, just like her mother. She hurried on. 'We were wondering if we might talk to you a little bit, Mr Walker, about Mr Tanner's ... recent time with you. The night before the ... incident at the mill.' At this Bob put down the papers and folded his arms, looking uneasy.

'Oh, ar?' he said.

'Yes. The thing is . . . The thing is, we wanted to ask whether you're quite, entirely certain that Mr Tanner was as drunk as he appeared to be.'

'That police 'un, the dark-haired fellow, he asked I the same thing. I'll tell 'ee like I told him – Tanner'd had enough drink to kill most men. In here all the afternoon long, he were. Sad about something, it seemed to me. Even saw him weep for a time, I did, though not a soul will believe a word o' that.'

'But he's a man well used to drink, is he not?'

'It's true he is. A most valued customer,' said Bob, with a grin.

'But doesn't he normally drink at the White Hart, in Ford?' said Pudding.

'Takes it in turns, we do, the Hart and I. He drinks here when he's barred from there; drinks there when they'll have him back.'

'Mr Walker, I wonder if you can remember, when you came to put him out in the morning . . . was he wet?' Irene asked. At this Bob pulled himself up straighter, and looked embarrassed.

'What possible cause can 'ee have to want to know that?' he asked, soberly. 'Whether a man soils himself or—'

'Oh, no! No – not in that way,' Irene said hastily.

'From the rain!' Pudding interjected.

'I cassn't follow 'ee.'

'Forgive me, Mr Walker,' said Irene, flustered. 'I know this must seem a very odd question. When you came to put Mr Tanner out in the morning, were his clothing, his boots – or perhaps his hair – wet at all, as though he had been out in the rain?'

'But he weren't out in it. He were in the shed, still sleeping like a babe, when I turfed him out.'

'Yes, I know. But can you remember specifically, at all? Whether he was wet or dry, I mean?'

'Well.' Bob squinted up at the roof of his own establishment, and appeared to think hard. 'Now 'ee mention it, I cassn't recall. He must have been dry, then, else I'd have found it amiss, and remembered, wouldn't I? Mind you, I was soaked right through from the short walk to the shed, and rain do wash in under the door of it, so perhaps if he were wet, I wouldn't have thought that amiss either.' He kept staring up at the roof, kept thinking, but nothing else appeared to be forthcoming.

'So . . . which was it?' said Pudding.

'I cassn't rightly say,' Bob confessed. Pudding deflated a bit. 'But if I had to call it, I'd say dry. I'd say he hadn't stirred an inch from when I dropped him there the night before. I s'pose that's why you're asking?' He looked at them shrewdly. 'If he slipped out and done some dark deed, and slipped back to have I give him an alibi?'

'Well . . . yes. Only please don't put it about that we were asking,' said Irene, her pulse quickening. She realised then how afraid of Tanner she was; afraid at some deep-down, gut level. Bob Walker nodded carefully.

'As far as I can tell it, Mrs Hadleigh, he was here all that time.'

The ride home had far less of an air of urgency. Pudding let Dundee dawdle so much that the pony paused now and then to snatch mouthfuls of the hedgerow. It was as though she didn't want to get back to the farm at all.

'Well, it struck me that Mr Walker was telling the truth,' said Irene, to break a long silence that was becoming strained. 'Not providing a false alibi.'

'Yes,' Pudding agreed, glumly. 'Tanner wouldn't have the

money to bribe him, anyway. And he could hardly threaten him. Bob's as big as a hayrick.'

'So . . . I suppose the next question is when did it start to rain?' Irene tried. 'I mean, if it didn't start until *after* Alistair was killed, then it doesn't matter whether Tanner was wet or dry.'

'But it also wouldn't prove one way or the other if he'd left the shed.'

'True. But if . . . but if it didn't start to rain until after he was killed, then the fact that Tanner stayed dry still means he *could* have sneaked out.'

'I suppose so,' said Pudding, and Irene gave up. It wasn't enough, as Pudding clearly knew. The white lane shimmered in front of them and clouded with dust behind; the sky was painfully bright; a few faint wisps of cloud seemed impossibly high above them. Squinting was giving Irene a headache, and she wished she knew of some way to encourage Pudding, or cheer her. What cheer there could be for her until, and unless, her brother were released, Irene couldn't think. Hers would be one more life blighted forever by whoever had stolen Alistair from them.

'Well, we still haven't got to the bottom of his motive, in any case,' she said, desperately. 'Why don't we go and talk to the foreman at the mill, about him being fired?' At this, Pudding straightened up a bit, and looked across at her.

'Good idea! Oh – but I need to get back and get Tufty in off the grass, before he explodes. I should have done it before we left, really. And Dundee will need a rub down, it's so blasted hot . . .'

'Well . . . I'll go, then,' said Irene. She could think of few things she wanted to do less than walk down to the mill alone, and return to the very place Alistair had been killed, but she refused to yield to herself. 'I'll go, and see what I can discover.'

'Right. I'll drop you at the mill, then,' said Pudding.

There was a terrible moment outside the mill offices. Irene halted at the door to the old farmhouse, caught between the prickling stares of the workers in the yard behind her and the remembered horror of the room in front of her. She stood for a long time, her eyes down and her heart thumping, entirely unable to go either onwards or back. The mill machines rumbled; the air smelled of smuts, metal and the river. They all had so many questions for her, she knew: whether she would sell their place of work, their homes and land; what she would do; what their lives would be from now on and how they would change. And, real or imagined, she felt them blame her for all of it. It felt like a huge wave about to break over her head, and it smothered the anger she needed for strength. She jumped when the farmhouse door opened. George Turner, the foreman, came out with his face full of concern.

'Mrs Hadleigh? Is everything all right?' he said.

'Yes. That is, no, not at all,' said Irene. George nodded kindly.

'Won't you come inside out of this sun? One of the girls just brought a jug of iced tea over from the canteen, and I have to say, it's not half bad. Plenty of cucumber.' He took her elbow and ushered her in.

'Thank you.'

Irene couldn't help but look at the place on the floor where, the last time she had seen it, Alistair had lain all bloody and dead. George said something else but it was drowned out by the thumping in her ears. As her eyes struggled to adapt, it looked, for a moment, as though a dark shadow remained; a patch of gloom that might have been his body, still, or the blackened crust of his blood. In a flash she was assailed by the thought of the Alistair-doll again, and the roots and creatures that would now be making their homes in what remained of him, buried in the ground. Her head swam.

'Do sit down, Mrs Hadleigh.' George touched her arm again, and Irene sank obediently into a chair, breathing deeply. 'We had the thought of closing this place up – perhaps even knocking it down. Knocking it down and building something new to house the offices. I wasn't sure . . .' He shook his head. 'I wasn't sure if Mr Hadleigh himself would have liked that. Such a dramatic gesture, and the destruction of such a traditional part of the mill. Miss Hadleigh has said she would prefer it razed to the ground.'

'Has she?' Irene had heard Nancy make no such request; she herself hadn't given the mill a second thought.

'Oh, yes. In no uncertain terms. But perhaps decisions like that aren't best made in the heat of the moment. A new building would be a considerable investment. For whoever had control of the mill.'

'Nothing's been decided yet,' said Irene, more sharply than she'd intended.

'Of course it hasn't,' said George, gently. 'Do have some of this tea, and tell me how I can help you.'

'Thank you. Sorry. I—' Irene gathered herself. 'You're very kind. I wanted to ask about Mr Tanner.'

'Tanner? What has the fellow been up to now?'

'Oh – nothing like that. Well. I wanted to ask you, was he fired from the mill? Recently, I mean. I know he has been let go before, and then rehired. Pudding said she saw him drunk on the job, just a short while ago.'

'Yes, that's right. He was indeed let go. It must be nearing three weeks ago now.'

'I see,' said Irene, trying to keep her voice neutral.

'It was a grave shame. He had kept off the drink for a goodly while, but then all of a sudden, something seemed to set him off. And he never does anything by halves, does Tanner. One drink leads to twenty or thirty, with him. Mr Hadleigh was sympathetic, but he had no choice but to let him go.'

'I imagine Mr Tanner was very angry about that.'

'Oh yes, all the usual bluster. But I know the man well enough to know that the person he's most angry with is himself. Not that he has the capacity to recognise that, of course. Mr Hadleigh told him he could have his job back again if he stayed sober a month long, and—'

'What?'

'He was told he could have his job back as long as he stayed sober a full month. It was an arrangement that had worked quite well before – the man needs a good reason to lay off it, you see.'

'So . . . it wasn't acrimonious?' she asked, sinking inside. George grunted.

'Oh, there's always acrimony, with Mr Tanner. He's the type to soundly reject any show of charity. But Mr Hadleigh had got onto his good side, over the years – as good a side as the man has, of course. He's a bad sort, and some men are just born that way. What other employer would have a man back, over and again, in similar circumstances? Precious few, I should think. I made the same point to the police superintendent, when he asked about it. But when your husband saw a problem, or a person in trouble, he took it upon himself to alleviate the situation – or at least to try to – rather than to wash his hands of it.'

'Yes,' said Irene, thinking of herself. Their hasty marriage, the new life he'd tried to give her. Her eyes swam; the anger swelled in her chest.

'If you don't mind my saying, Mrs Hadleigh, why do you ask? Are you inclined to withdraw the offer?'

'What? I don't know, I—'

'Not that a decision is urgently required – Tanner shows no signs of regaining mastery of himself, as yet.'

'I fear I have taken up more than enough of your time, Mr Turner,' said Irene, tremulously. She was thinking about telling Pudding this news; about Tanner having not only a firm alibi, but no real reason to harm Alistair. She felt a failure.

'Nonsense. Your visit has brightened my day immeasurably,' said George.

He smiled but suddenly it slid away, and his face drooped. 'There is something weighing on my conscience, Mrs Hadleigh, and I beg your forbearance while I . . . disclose it,' he said, sombrely. Irene looked at him properly and noticed the shadows under his eyes, and that he had lost weight since she first met him. 'Your husband ought not to have been here so very early, on the day he died. He had given me time off because my wife . . . Since our little one came along, she has . . . struggled. With a lassitude, and a depressed mood she can't seem to conquer.' He looked down at the desk. 'Mr Hadleigh had been most understanding. I had been late to work several mornings, in remaining behind to help Elizabeth along. He said he would come in early in my stead, to oversee the change in shift.' He shook his head, and took a sudden deep breath, as though struggling to breathe freely. 'If I had been keeping to my regular hours, he would not have been here by himself at that hour of the day. And I know I shall never forgive myself for that.'

'Mr Turner,' said Irene, reaching out to take his hand, on impulse, and squeezing it. 'Please do not berate yourself. You are not in the slightest bit to blame.'

Back at Manor Farm, Irene saw Pudding out in the paddock

with one of the horses, and slipped indoors without going to talk to her. Her visit to the mill had only made it even more unlikely that Tanner was the culprit. If he'd been fired and rehired before, then it seemed highly unlikely he should suddenly react by attacking Alistair. More bad news, although Irene couldn't quite put her finger on why it was bad, was that the police had interviewed Mr Turner about it already. Just as they had been to talk to Bob Walker at the White Horse. Pudding and Irene were simply retracing the police's steps, and finding the same lack of evidence as they had, no doubt. She found Nancy in her sitting room cum study, writing out a list of some kind.

'Sorry to trouble you, Nancy,' she said, absently. 'I wonder if you can remember what time the rain started on the morning Alistair was killed?'

'What?' Nancy snapped, and Irene shrivelled inside at the tactlessness of her question. 'Why on earth would you ask me that?'

'I'm so sorry. I wasn't thinking.'

'But why do you want to know?'

'I was just . . . I was just thinking about that morning,' she said, knowing instinctively that Nancy would not be pleased about her trying to prove Donald Cartwright's innocence. Miraculously, her half-answer seemed to suffice.

'Yes. My mind plays those games with me, too,' said Nancy. 'What if this, what if that. I find it better not to indulge such thoughts.'

'You're quite right.' Irene turned to leave her.

'It started well after sunrise. It was a red dawn.' At this Nancy paused, her eyelids flickered and she swallowed. 'I wake with the birds, as you know. There was plenty of cloud, but the rain didn't start until about half past six.'

'So late?' Irene murmured.

'About when Alistair normally rose, which was why I assumed he would remain in bed. You remember what I told you about him being a terrible layabout on wet days.'

'I do. He went in early because George Turner's wife is sick, and he'd been having some time at home.'

'Yes. I know.'

'So he was there, at the mill, before the rain started,' said Irene, relinquishing all hope of using the weather to disprove Tanner's alibi.

'It won't help, you know,' said Nancy. 'Replaying it. Wondering if it could have been prevented. Which of course it could. But it wasn't, and never can be.'

At the end of the day the shires clopped back onto the yard, their massive legs dusty to the hips and elbows, the salt of dried sweat on their shoulders and flanks. Hilarius came out of the barn to take custody from the carters, dressed as always in his canvas overalls, no hat to cover his bald crown. He moved quickly, assuredly in spite of his great age, and the horses obeyed his every unspoken command, lining up at the rail by the barn to have their bridles unfastened, shaking their necks in relief as the heavy collars were lifted off. Irene watched him from a small window in the downstairs corridor. Pudding had been adamant that there was nothing sinister about the man, but Irene couldn't help the feeling she had, looking at him. Something hung about him, something grave; something cold and heavy and deadening. A shadow, as she'd described it to Pudding; a shadow darker than the one his wiry body cast on the cobbled yard. He would have been up even earlier than Nancy that morning, Irene didn't doubt. And she knew, she *knew* he had been inside the farmhouse. She didn't know when, or why, or why it was even significant, but she knew that he had. He could have lit the unexplained fire in Nancy's sitting room. Irene just didn't have the first clue why he would, or what it meant. Or whether it meant a damned thing.

She'd been thinking hard all afternoon, and had even spent a while in her writing room, jotting a few things down on paper, trying to draw connections between things that refused to be connected. She suddenly felt, quite keenly, that it would be hard to take Pudding the bad news without offering her some good along with it. Some idea to follow, some new thought. And it wasn't just for Pudding, she was prepared to admit. As she'd gone out to tell Pudding about her uneasy feelings that morning, she'd felt, for the first time in her life, that she was doing something useful. She'd felt that, having gone seamlessly from being her parents' charge to Fin's fool to Alistair's burden, she was now in charge of herself for the first time. It was a good feeling. And even better was the idea that she was, finally, doing a good and useful thing for Alistair, when he had done so many good things for her. It was too late, of course, far too late. But it wasn't too late for the Cartwrights. But in spite of her efforts, all she had come up with was that somebody might have paid Tanner to kill Alistair. Tanner was a poor man, a drunken sot and recently laid off; perhaps he might have been desperate enough to take such a job. There was certainly enough acrimony in the man, as George had said and she herself had witnessed. But all that did was return them to square one – searching for a reason somebody might have wanted Alistair dead. Irene hated to tell Pudding as much. She hated to disappoint her; she hated, having offered to help, to fail to do so.

On the hallway table, Irene was surprised to find a letter addressed to her in a familiar hand – the first since Fin's terrible letter, which seemed now to have arrived months, years, before. She opened it hurriedly, on the spot, absorbed the contents with a feeling that teetered between happiness and dread, and then went to tell Nancy.

*

As she worked, Pudding repeatedly calculated how much time remained until Donny's hearing – how many hours, minutes, seconds. The need to act was like a terrible itch, impossible to ignore, but however hard she tried, she couldn't think what to do next. As Irene had been forced to admit, hedgingly, the day after they'd been to Biddestone, until they could find out a motive, they were stuck. At lunchtime she banged on the front door of the house, ostensibly to ask for a glass of water but actually hoping to talk to Irene, but nobody answered. She went around the back to the kitchen and found Clara Gosling and Florence having their lunch, but since they, too, fell silent upon seeing her, Pudding retreated. In the great barn, asleep in a shaft of sunshine with his battered hat over his face, she found Hilarius. He slept there in the summer – carrying up his evening meal, which Clara gave him on a plate, every night – and if he had ever had concerns beyond the gates of Manor Farm then he'd long since left them behind him. Pudding thought about the darkness Irene said she sensed around him, but it seemed ridiculous. So ridiculous that it made her doubt all of Irene's odd instincts, though she didn't want to – just then, they were all she and Donny had. But Hilarius was a harmless old man; of few words perhaps, but he had only ever been kind to her, and the horses, and he never shirked in spite of his years.

Pudding felt awkward about waking him, but she couldn't help herself. She picked up a pitchfork and began to tidy the hay, noisily – letting the metal tines scrape against the cobbles.

'Thee'll start a fire, girl,' said Hilarius in his thick accent, not moving. 'Give up on't. I heard you coming from the house.'

'Oh, hello. Sorry to disturb you,' said Pudding, sitting down near him. He smelled comfortingly of horses, and the molasses he mixed into their feed.

'Doubt it,' he grumbled, but he tipped back his hat and looked at her without rancour. 'Still fretting on't, are you?'

'Yes.' She sat on her hands to keep them still, and hunched in on herself. A childhood habit, to make herself smaller. 'Even Superintendent Blackman said that he always sought out the why, in a case such as this. Though it didn't seem to bother him that Donny doesn't have a why at all – as though his . . . as though the way he is is reason enough.'

'Are you good and sure it isn't?'

'Of course!' She flared up at once, but Hilarius had a way of watching, with such steadiness in the wrinkled slits of his eyes, that she actually stopped to think before she spoke again. She probed her own conviction, and found it watertight. 'I'm absolutely sure, Hilarius. He got into that fight last year, and he did lose his temper, and he did . . . injure that other man. But there was a very good *why* – his Aoife marrying that chap, and about to have their first child. He might have got upset or lost his temper at other times, and it might have been . . . alarming. But he never, *ever* directed it at anybody.'

There was a pause, then Hilarius nodded and put his hat back over his eyes, and Pudding wasn't sure he was going to answer her.

'Ar,' he said, in the end, which meant yes. 'I been thinking the same.'

'Really? You have? You don't believe it was Donny? Oh, Hilarius! Thank you.' For no good reason, Pudding's hope soared.

'Not a thanking matter. And nowt to be done about it.'

'But . . . there *is*. I just have to find out who really did kill Alistair, do you see? I wanted to ask you if you could think of any reason – any reason at all – why somebody might have had a grudge against Mr Hadleigh. You've been here longer than anyone, haven't you?'

'Seventy years and mounting. Some days, I can feel each last one o' them.'

'Well, there you are then – longer than anybody. Is there anything you can think of, Hilarius? Anything at all? Irene still thinks it's Mr Tanner – that perhaps somebody hired him to do it, but we can't seem to come up with a reason why.'

'Easy for folk to lay blame on that family,' said Hilarius, disapprovingly. There was a pause. 'None of much as goes on here has owt to do with me,' he said. 'Nor ever has.' He lifted his head, and gave her a slow, shrewd look. 'I've no answers for you, girl, and it'd be best left alone, on that I be sure. But I'll say this. 'T'ain't no good holding a fruit in your hand an' looking up at the leaves and sky, puzzling where it came from, an' why it tastes the way it do.'

'A fruit? What do you mean? Where should I look, then?'

'Look down to the roots of it, girl. Look to the roots of the tree.' Pudding thought about this for a while, scratching her nose as the hay dust tickled in it. But before she'd formulated her next question, Hilarius was snoring softly, so she got up quietly and left him to his nap.

As Pudding walked home, she got lost in thoughts of her brother, and the day he'd come home from the army hospital. They'd all been delirious at the sight of him, but had tried so carefully not to overwhelm him, not to crowd him or fuss too much. The four of them – Ruth included – had followed him around the house as he'd rediscovered it, his face wearing a kind of wonder and puzzlement, as though a dream he'd once had was turning out to be real. Pointing out to him things that were new – a blue eiderdown on his bed; Pudding's height and size – and things that were just the same – everything else. Waiting for him to say or do something, to show he was still their Donny in spite of the horrors he'd seen and the violence he'd survived, and in spite of Dr Cartwright's warnings that he wasn't quite the same, that he didn't like to be hugged any more, that he needed time. Four tentative people, anxiously alert, holding their breath and hoping to feel happy soon. Returning to the kitchen, Donny had frowned a little and looked down at his toes. His right hand had strayed up, as it often did in the beginning, to brush nervously across the damage on his head, then he'd looked up and said, *Well, isn't there a cup of tea for a fellow, Ruth?* And Ruth had tutted about there being no rest for the wicked, and they had all exhaled, and the happiness had indeed begun.

Heavy footfalls scattered the memory, and the sight of Pete Dempsey jogging to catch her up gave Pudding a jolt, even though he wasn't in his uniform. Her throat immediately went dry. Since Donny's return she only seemed to encounter Pete when something bad had happened. She remembered him struggling to hold Donny while he fought, and refused to be led away after the fight in Ford the year before. She didn't doubt that Pete remembered it too, and had been thinking of it recently; she wondered if he thought Alistair would still be alive now had Donny been jailed back then, as he came to stand in front of her, red-faced from hurrying in the heat. Her heart thudded as she waited to hear what bad news he'd brought this time.

'Hello, Pudding,' he said, breathlessly.

'Hello, Constable. What is it?'

'I'm not Constable now, just Pete. I'm off duty.' He smiled as though this ought to have been funny, but it faded when Pudding didn't respond.

'Is there something new about the case? What can you tell me?' Pudding couldn't seem to do anything about the flat sound of her voice, not even for the sake of keeping a policeman on side. It seemed pointless to dissemble, anyway; she'd known Pete since they were children. He'd always been there, one of her crowd of peers, even though he was a few years older. She'd once seen him throw up all over his own boots when another boy had dared him to eat frogspawn from Worthy Pilton's pond, and he'd been daft enough to do it. He had always known Donny – deferring to him due to his size and age; slightly wary of him because he was so protective of Pudding. Now Pete represented the law, which was strange enough in itself; he had power over Donny and over them all, and Pudding didn't know how to square that away. She was oddly, and enormously, embarrassed.

Pete took off his cap and scrubbed his fingers through his sweaty hair, looking uncomfortable.

'No. I'm afraid there's nothing new,' he said.

'But are you still looking for the real killer?' she demanded, not able to look him in the eye.

'Are we what?' he said, with a puzzled frown. Then, as he understood, he looked away, awkwardly. They stood in silence for a while.

'Well, I'd better be getting home,' said Pudding.

'Pudding, wait.' Pete put out his hand to stop her. 'I've been wanting to say, since all this started . . . I've been wanting to say how sorry I am. I mean . . . I know you've enough on your plate with your mum being ill, and now this.' He cleared his throat, and Pudding's face flamed. 'I know what your Donny means to you, Pudding.' He spoke in a gentle tone she'd never heard him use before. 'I wish it hadn't turned out this way. I do wish it,' he said. Pudding still couldn't look at him. She stared down at his dusty boots instead; there was grit and chaff in the turn-ups of his trousers. She wanted to say that it *hadn't* turned out this way, and that she was going to bring Donny home with his name cleared, but she didn't think she ought to say that to the law. She doubted Pete would approve of the fact that she and Irene had been making enquiries of their own. And she knew he'd dismiss Irene's prescient feelings out of hand – Pudding wasn't even entirely convinced about them herself.

'Thanks,' she muttered instead, and this time Pete let her go.

Since Alistair's death, Dr Cartwright usually got home before Pudding finished work. He had fewer patients now, and once upon a time Pudding would have been happy about that – happy that he didn't have to rush about as much, and could spend more time with them at home. But he didn't belong in the garden – he never had, beyond sitting out in a lawn chair from time to time, to read the newspaper; it had always been Louise's domain – so he merely lingered about the house in idleness. And he was so listless, and looked so lost and tired, that in fact Pudding began to almost dread seeing him at the kitchen table when she got home. Quite often he wasn't even doing anything – not reading the paper or one of his medical journals, or writing out his bills or pharmaceutical orders; not listening to the wireless; not mending anything small and mechanical, replacing the wick in the stove or drinking tea, or oiling the chain of his bicycle with his sleeves rolled up and a rag tucked into his braces. Just sitting. Just as Donny had used to do. He seemed to deflate even further with every day that passed, and every new bit of bad news that came – like the date of Donny's hearing. Part of Pudding longed to throw herself into his embrace and sob all over him, but she couldn't let herself do that. He simply didn't look strong enough. Instead she made him tea, cut him a piece of one of Ruth's cakes, and patted his shoulder as she went about the house, doing whatever she could get done before supper time.

Ruth was stalwart. In spite of being a highly effective

conduit for gossip, and highly susceptible to it, she maintained her loyalty to the Cartwrights with puffed-up defiance like armour plate.

'Most folk don't know they're born,' she said, cryptically, when Pudding thanked her for staying on. Ruth opened the door to callers with folded arms, a gingham scarf knotted tight around her hair and a thunderous expression on her unlovely face that dared folk to peer inside, offer judgement, or hang about, eavesdropping. Not that many people came to call – they hadn't for a while, because of Louise Cartwright being unwell. If Ruth had abandoned them, Pudding knew, things would have been much worse. They'd all have gone hungry, for starters, since beyond toast and scrambled eggs, she herself was a dreadful cook. Not that any of them had much appetite – Pudding least of all. It had cheered her up before: great slabs of fruit loaf, covered in butter; bacon sandwiches on a cold morning before work; strawberries from the garden, drowning in cream. Now all she could think about, when food was put in front of her, was Donny in his cell in the New Bridewell in Devizes, eating prison stew and wishing he were home. Her parents didn't seem to notice her lack of appetite, and mealtimes were largely silent affairs. That evening, her father was even quieter than usual.

'What is it, Dad? Has something happened?' she asked, when Ruth had gone home and her mother upstairs. His forehead was all furrows and his lips looked pale. He shook his head. 'Please, tell me,' she said.

'I spoke to a fellow doctor today, Dr Whitley, in Devizes. He had . . . been called out to the prison to see to Donny,' he said. Pudding gasped.

'Why? Is he all right? What happened? Is he ill?'

'*Shh* – your mother mustn't hear! He is all right now, but Dr Whitley had to give him a sedative to calm him, so that . . . he could administer some stitches.' He had been looking down, fiddling with his spectacles, but now the doctor glanced up at Pudding. She stared back, aghast. 'The account he was given was that Donny had got into a fight with one of the other inmates. He . . . he wasn't able to tell me what the fight was about—'

'But that can't be right! Donny wouldn't have been fighting, and—'

'Pudding, please, just listen. The fight wasn't particularly serious. But Donny needed stitches to his hand where he . . . struck the other fellow, and he needed stitches to a head wound . . . a head wound that he . . . that he . . .'

'That he what?'

'That he gave to himself. Once he was back in his cell. He . . . he dashed his head against the wall. They were forced to restrain him.'

For a long time, Pudding couldn't find a single word to say. She swallowed, painfully.

'Poor, poor Donny,' she said, in the end, and the words came out wobbly, half-broken.

'Yes,' said her father.

'He must hate it in there. He must hate it so much! They won't understand him . . . they won't understand how he is! And that he needs to be allowed to . . . do things in his own time! And be shown how to do them. I bet this other man – whoever he is – I bet he picked on Donny, and drove him to fight!'

'Pudding—'

'Why would he hit his own head on the wall? Why would he? He must hate it there so much!' She started to cry, and tried to stifle it. 'They *must* let him come home!' she whispered.

'I wish they would. I wish it more than anything, my dear. He's clearly not able to . . . cope.' The doctor shook his head helplessly.

'Can't we apply to the judge to let him come home? A special order, or something – special circumstances! Donny isn't the same as other men . . .'

'Our best hope is to get a charge of manslaughter from the magistrate – then, perhaps, he could be allowed to leave on bail. If it's set at a level we can manage. But if he gets into any more trouble . . .'

'Oh, no, they'll use it against him, won't they?'

'I fear they might, Pudding. I fear they might.'

'But it's so *unfair*! He hasn't even done anything wrong!'

'Pudding.' The doctor put one hand over his eyes and shook his head slightly, as if he couldn't stand to hear her. Pudding took a few breaths to calm down. She was shocked by her father's visible distress; it was crushing him, making him smaller.

'You mustn't give up on it all, Dad,' she said. 'I'm going to think of a way to bring him home. Really, I am. I promise.'

'My dear,' he said, smiling sadly, 'you mustn't make promises you won't be able to keep. Especially not to yourself.'

'But I *will* keep it.' She felt something rising up inside, something quite like anger. The doctor shook his head again.

'I'm deeply sorry any of this has happened, Pudding, and that your young life will always carry the mark of this . . . dark time. It warms my heart to realise just how loyal you are to Donald – it warms it, and it breaks it.' Then he drifted away in silence, to help his wife get ready for bed.

Pudding lay caught in the shallows of an uneasy sleep all night, plagued by thoughts of Donny injuring himself, and the idea that, at any moment, he might be goaded into doing something that would keep him locked away forever. In the morning her head felt thick, and itchy. It was difficult to think clearly, but she decided on her next course of action – Ma Tanner. A wise woman of sorts, someone who knew Slaughterford and its people like the back of her hand, and had given Pudding and Irene a warning of change. Nobody was closer to Tanner himself, or more likely to know where he had been, and what he had done.

'Are you sure that's a good idea?' said Irene, when Pudding told her. 'I mean . . . given that our prime suspect is her son, and all that.'

'Well,' said Pudding, frowning, 'is he still our prime suspect? Anyway, we don't need to let on to her about that, do we? We'll just pretend we haven't a clue, and perhaps she'll let something slip.'

'We?' Irene shook her head. 'I'm sorry, but I can't go with you now, Pudding – I've to go into Corsham. My mother is coming to visit. Finally.' Irene's voice had a peculiar tone that Pudding couldn't decode. 'But she's never been an early riser – if you hang on until tomorrow, perhaps—'

'No!' Pudding took a breath, thinking of Donny hitting his head against the walls of his prison cell. She thought of telling Irene about it, but didn't want to make her think Donny was deranged. That he was violent. She could hardly bear to think of his pain and confusion. 'I mean, no, it's all right; I can go alone, and strike whilst the iron is hot.'

'Well. Do remember to be tactful, won't you?' said Irene, sounding uncertain. Pudding nodded but couldn't bring herself to speak. Tact was no use to Donny. She checked the horses over quickly, fed them and topped off the water trough, impatient to set off down the hill. When she was doing something – *anything* – towards bringing her brother home, Pudding could carry on; she felt she could breathe, in spite of all the fear and awfulness, and the yawning gap in the world where Alistair had once been. When she wasn't doing something, it felt like drowning.

There were hasty sounds inside Thatch Cottage when she knocked at the door – the creak of the wooden floor, footsteps on the stairs, muffled whispers – and when the door was opened by Trish Tanner, Tanner's wife, her face went through a rapid succession of expressions – from fearful, to crashing relief, to a shifting uncertainty that looked almost guilty.

'Pudding Cartwright,' she said, neutrally, not opening the door much wider.

'Hello, Mrs Tanner. I'm sorry to disturb you.' Pudding paused for Mrs Tanner to say it was fine, but she didn't. 'Er. I wonder if I might come in and have a quick word with your mother about something?'

'Mother-in-law. Now's not a good time.'

'Oh. Ah. Well, I suppose it is quite important,' said Pudding. 'May I? I won't take up much of her time.'

'That the doctor's girl?' came Ma Tanner's voice from within. 'Let her in, if she's something to say.' Pudding smiled hopefully, but again that fear flashed in Mrs Tanner's eyes, and there was a thump from upstairs that made her flinch. But she opened the door wider and stepped back.

'You'd best come in then.'

'Thank you.'

There was a hush inside, and Pudding felt even more watched than she had the time she'd come with Irene, even though there were fewer children around now, and the grandpa in the truckle bed was fast asleep, his jaw hanging open and his eyeballs flicking back and forth behind his lids. The windows were covered with thick felts and the unnatural darkness was stifling, worse than before. Pudding blinked, struggling to see as her eyes adjusted from the bright light outside; she breathed more deeply, feeling as though there wasn't quite enough air. Ma Tanner was out of her chair by the stove, adding various chopped roots to a stockpot, reaching to the high shelf for herbs. Her movements were quick and sure, and Pudding stared, realising that it was the first time she'd seen her on her feet, and that she'd always assumed Ma couldn't walk. Ma shot Pudding a mischievous smile.

'Life in these old bones yet,' she said.

'Yes,' said Pudding.

'Sit. I didn't think it'd be too long till you came knocking again. I fear you'll get no joy here, mind you.'

'Oh.'

'But ask away.' She put down her big chopping knife and wiped her wizened hands on her skirt as she sat down herself. 'Something to help you sleep, perhaps? Something to help the doctor relax?'

'No, no, nothing like that. Thank you.' Pudding tried to place Ma Tanner's odd tone. It seemed mocking, but only on the surface, not all the way through. As though she were hiding something else. 'I wanted to ask . . .' She paused, thinking hard. Saying anything without giving away her suspicions was going to be tricky. Somehow, she felt she only had this one chance to ask the right thing. From the table, Trish Tanner watched, listening unashamedly. Her face was empty of expression now, apart from its usual tension. 'When we came here before, with that doll Mrs Hadleigh found, and you said change was coming . . . was it Alistair's death you saw?'

In the pause, in the stuffy dark, Pudding knew she'd asked the right question. Ma Tanner eyed her for a long time. Her eyes gleamed in the low light.

'Not exactly,' she said, at last.

'But something to do with him?'

'Yes.'

'But why? How?'

'Can't tell you that, girl.' The old woman drew back but never broke off her stare.

'Did it tell you ... did you find out anything about Donny from it? Did you know he would ... he would be accused of something, and taken away?'

'No.' For a second there came a creeping disquiet into Ma Tanner's eyes, and then her face hardened off, quashing it. 'Not quite your brother since the war, is he? Not quite the full billing,' she said, crisply.

'Well, of course he's still my brother! He's a little ... changed, perhaps. A little less able. But still Donny, through and through.'

'Easier to do without him now, perhaps.'

'No, not at all! How can you say that?' Pudding's eyes swam. She realised then that if life were a net in which to catch happiness, losing Donny would put too big a hole in hers. She had no hope of dealing with the rest of it – her mother, and Alistair – without him. 'We're desperate to have him home. And he's the gentlest soul really, whatever the war did to him. That he should have survived all of that only to hang for this ... only to be known forever as a murderer, when he's nothing of the sort ... It's unbearable.' She blew her nose on her shrivelled, overused handkerchief, and Ma Tanner held the silence. She locked eyes with her daughter-in-law, both of them stock-still, as though waiting for a sign, as though listening. 'Please,' said Pudding. 'If you know anything that might help him, please do tell me it now. Even if it's only a hunch ... an idea. *Anything*. Hilarius told me to look for the roots of the thing, but I don't really know what he meant.'

'That old tinker is brighter than he looks,' said Ma Tanner.

'Is he? Why?'

'What he meant was that all the lives in this place – here in the valley, in Slaughterford – all the lives are tangled up. Have been for years. Years and years.'

'So ... there is somebody with a ... a grudge against

Alistair? Some grievance against him, for something that happened long before?'

'Could be. Or something them before him done, maybe. You're too young to see it yet, girl, but the roots of things go deep. I do suppose you think winter was a long time ago, don't you?' She smiled. 'I do suppose you think a lot's happened of late. Well, it's a drop in the ocean. There's plenty that's well out of your reach. Things you can't ever understand. But every last thing in life happens for a reason, especially those most foul.'

'That's enough,' Trish muttered, tersely. Pudding looked across at her, and saw fear in her eyes that was at odds with her angry tone of voice. Ma Tanner grunted.

'I daresay it is, yes.' She got up.

'But hold on – you haven't told me anything!' Pudding protested.

'I've told you all I can. If you can't let the lad go, then look further afield for the cause of all this. Now, on your way. You've a job of work to go to, and I've this stew to finish. Barley cutting's started, the boys'll be back with hollow guts come noon time.'

Feeling cross and useless, Pudding got up and followed Trish Tanner back to the door. There, the woman gripped her arm for a moment.

'Let it lie, girl,' she whispered. 'Please. Ma can't help you, and you'll only stir up more trouble.'

'But . . . my family couldn't *be* in any more trouble!'

'Believe me, you could.'

'They'll hang him – they'll hang Donny. I can't let that happen.'

'Try,' said Mrs Tanner, then tried to shut the door. Pudding put her boot in the way.

'Do you know who it was? Do you know who killed Mr Hadleigh?' she whispered.

'Course I bloody don't! What are you accusing us of? Same old story, is it – there's been a crime, so it must be a Tanner? Don't come around here asking that again, if you know what's good for you.' She kicked Pudding's foot away and slammed the door.

Feeling certain that the cottage had eyes, Pudding hurried across the barren yard, where the mud had dried and cracked, and the smell of the privy was stronger than ever, and the only things growing were dusty nettles and ivy. Thatch Cottage had always been a place to be wary of, a place of slightly menacing fascination. Now, for the first time, Pudding had the notion that it was the saddest place in the valley – apart from her own home, of course. She stood a while in the parched lane, with a fat, persistent bluebottle for company, looking across at the mill. She saw the towering brick wall of the new generator house, built on top of the original mill house; the old farm-house, its barns now used to keep machine spares rather than animals, its pigsties converted into privies for the workers. She saw the By Brook carved in two, the water split between its natural course and the mill race, and even into a third conduit on the downstream side – the open pipe of the waste water, siphoned off into dye beds to keep the river pure further south. Layers of life and work and industry; roots going back years and years. Pudding wished Irene had come with her after all. She missed her opinion and the careful way she listened, and thought; but it was good, she supposed, that Irene's mother was coming to visit. Nobody else had been to visit her. Pudding went through what she'd been told, and what it boiled down to was that both Hilarius and Ma Tanner thought that the *why* of Alistair's death lay further back in the past. What it was, and how far back, she still had no idea.

She was halfway back to Manor Farm when something Ma had said replayed itself in her ears, and rang a sudden bell. *Especially those most foul.* Most foul. The realisation hit Pudding like a cosh. She stopped in the middle of the street, by the bridge, and two lads driving the little wagon of half-stuff across from Rag Mill had to swerve around her when she ignored their shouts. Her next breath was full of oily smoke from the wagon's engine. Her heart had accelerated so radically, and was beating so hard, that she could feel it knocking against her ribs. For a moment Pudding was stuck there, on weak knees, as a shiver brushed over her skin. But when the moment of paralysis passed she turned on her heel, and ran for home as fast as she could.

∽ ∽

All five women at Weavern Farm were waiting for the storm to break. As a precaution, Rose had made sure none of the girls were in sight before telling their father that Clemmie was expecting. None of them had any idea what his reaction would be, or who would be the main focus of his ire. For an entire day the farm work was done in near silence; all communication between the sisters and their mother was made by significant glance and covert gesture, as though William were omnipresent and might descend upon them at any second. As though, for that time only, they were as mute as Clemmie herself. The day was scorching. The cows stood limply in the shade, chewing the cud with their eyes closed; the hens lay stupefied beneath the coop; the river's rush had steadied, the water smoother and more sedate. Sweat beaded on their skin, and at least part of it was due to the unbearable tension. When, late in the afternoon, William came out of the house and banged the door behind him, they all froze. But he merely strode off along the steep path towards Weavern Lane, his hands in fists and his shoulders high, leaving his wife and daughters to glance at each other yet again, at a loss.

'Well, Mum, what's he said?' asked Mary, as they clustered in the relative cool of the dairy. Rose shrugged, beleaguered. She hadn't quite forgiven the girls for not telling her that Clemmie had a sweetheart, and, by extension, for letting her fall pregnant.

'He barely said owt at all. He just went quiet,' she said, curtly.

'Angry quiet? Or sad? Or what?' Josie pressed. Clemmie stood behind her, feeling odd at being the cause of so much consternation, and at it all going on with virtually no reference to herself. As though her pregnancy were a separate entity, to be dealt with by them and not by her. It didn't feel that way to Clemmie. It felt as though they were talking about her heart. Wondering what to do about her heart.

Down the years, plenty of babies had been baseborn in Ford and Slaughterford, and plenty of couples had been forced to get married in a hurry – it was usually seen as more of a misfortune than a disgrace. But it seemed to be different for Clemmie, because *Clemmie* was different. As though her getting into trouble could only have happened as the result of a misdemeanour. As though Clemmie herself were still a gormless child. Her mother and sisters tried every tone of voice they possessed to make her lead them to the baby's father, and Clemmie simply sat down in the dust when they tried to drag her. By the end of the second day, when it became clear that the explosion they were all expecting from William wasn't going to come, twin lines appeared between Rose's eyebrows. She ushered the girls out of the kitchen after supper, as the sky was turning from gold to grey outside, and they lingered on the stairs, trying to overhear the tense, hushed words that followed.

'Someone's had advantage of her – are you not going to do a damn thing about it, Will?' they heard her say, in the end, quite clearly. William's reply was too low to make out. Josie took Clemmie's hand and squeezed it, and even Liz looked troubled – disappointed, almost. Clemmie wished she could tell them that it was fine, that she wasn't worried or scared. Eli would make a plan – was already making a plan – and he meant to marry her, as soon as he could, and it would all be well. She already loved the baby almost as much as she loved Eli, and knew in her bones that nothing so loved could bring trouble.

'Mum'll set it right, Clem,' Mary told her, not sounding at all convinced. *But there's no wrong to right*, Clemmie didn't say. Later, when Clemmie set off to wander, Liz scowled.

'Shouldn't she be staying home?' she said, to anyone who'd listen.

'Let her be, if she's happy. She won't be for long. And not much worse can happen than already has, can it?' said Rose. Then she shook her head, dropped her chin to her chest, and clamped one hand tight over her mouth.

They tried to follow her, of course. They tried it more than once, but they had no practice at being quiet as they went, and no skill at it. Clemmie led them up the steepest slope to the quarry, on one occasion, and slipped into a hidden crevice to hide until they gave up. She smiled as she heard them fighting to get their breath back, Mary and Liz.

'She can't just bloody vanish,' said Liz, looking all around. 'Clemmie Matlock! You're a thorn in all our sides!' she shouted, crossly. Another time Rose tried to follow her, but her mother was even louder and more obvious than her sisters, and it was just as easy to give her the slip. Clemmie always made sure they were safely far away before she went on to meet Eli, and when she finally got him to understand about the baby, he was dumbstruck. His jaw dropped comically and his eyes emptied of thought so completely he looked confounded, and Clemmie laughed delightedly. She had no doubt that he'd be happy, once the idea had settled inside him and taken root. She was right: he held her fiercely, breathing like he'd been running, and a kind of wild triumph lit his eyes. Then he let her go abruptly.

'I shall have to handle you softly now, shan't I, my Clem?' he said. 'Though I don't know how I'll manage it.' He put his hands around her waist, which seemed, if anything, smaller now that her hips and chest had spread. Clemmie shook her head, smiling. She felt the opposite of fragile. She felt strong, alive, powerful. She felt like nothing could happen that she wouldn't be able to protect the baby from. It was still so tiny – she hadn't felt it move, and her belly was no rounder than before – but she knew it was the source of this feeling of life, this feeling of strength. It had appropriated her whole body, and was gearing her towards growing and shielding it, and she was perfectly content with that. Eli kissed her all over her face, and then cupped his hands around it and stared hard into her eyes. 'I won't be like my dad, Clemmie. I swear it, on my life. This child of ours won't ever feel the back of my hand; and I'll do right by the both of you. I'll find us a room, and I'll get work. It's going to be a good life for us – for us three. I swear it.' Clemmie wished she could say that she believed him, that she knew. Instead she nodded. 'Say nothing for now, for they'll all raise hell if they know it's us. If they know it's me,' he said, and Clemmie beamed, delighted that, such was the ease of things between them, he sometimes forgot that she couldn't say anything to anyone.

That ease of things was resoundingly missing from Weavern Farm, and most particularly with Rose, who chafed and fretted and made suggestion after suggestion as to the baby's father.

'Will you give it a bloody rest? There's clearly no point trying to make her tell us who it was, he's boggled her mind,' snapped William, finally, eyeing his daughter with an angry sadness that was almost disgust. And since that appeared to be his final word on the matter, it was left to Rose to do whatever she thought should be done next. The following morning she put on her best dress and a straw hat with a rumpled blue ribbon normally reserved for church, the harvest home and the like, and instructed her mute daughter to do the same.

'Come along, don't drag your heels,' she told Clemmie, whose silent questions about where they were going went unanswered. Clemmie didn't have any best shoes, and she generally went barefoot in the summer, but Rose forced her into her boots, ignoring her protests. Then they set off up to Weavern Lane and towards Slaughterford, and though Clemmie went meekly it was with a growing sense of unease. How people knew the things they knew was often mysterious to her – a lot of their interactions passed her by as she kept to herself. But Rose marched right past Thatch Cottage without a glance, and Clemmie relaxed just a little. Sweat soaked through the back of her mother's dress, making an oval shape in the small of her back, and Clemmie pulled on her hand to try to slow her down, only to be shaken off. 'No, Clem, this needs to be dealt with,' Rose muttered, her attention elsewhere.

They went to Manor Farm, and when she realised it, Clemmie tried again to refuse. Rose shot her a ferocious look that brought her to heel, and she fidgeted nervously as her mother banged at the door. The cob peered at them over his stable door, ears pricked; Hilarius, the horse groom, walked across towards the barn, raising one bony hand in salute as he went. Clemmie raised her hand in reply, but he'd already turned away. Then the door opened, and Rose clasped Clemmie's hand tightly, and the housekeeper showed them into a cool, stale parlour to the far end of the house. In the sudden stillness, Rose looked harried. Her face was red and wet from the walk, and she blotted at the sweat with her fingers to no effect. Frizzy hanks of her hair, as mad as Clemmie's, had escaped from beneath her bonnet, and when she caught sight of herself in the foxed mirror over the fireplace, she gaped in horror. They looked like a pair of scarecrows, and Rose coloured even more. Clemmie shrugged, to say that it didn't matter, but at that moment Nancy Hadleigh came into the room with her usual abruptness, and Clemmie slunk back slightly, looking down at the pattern of twisting vines and flowers of the rug, and her dirty boots, smudging it.

Nancy shut the door behind her and came across to sit on one of the chairs. She was wearing a plain black dress with no ornament, and no jewellery. Her hair was combed back and held, immaculately, in tortoiseshell combs, and her extreme composure created a severe contrast to her visitors. Clemmie could feel Nancy's antipathy for them – for her – sharpening her edges. She wanted more than anything to leave, and wondered what on earth her mother planned to say.

'Won't you sit down, the pair of you? Mrs Mattock, isn't it?' said Nancy.

'Matlock, your ladyship. Rose Matlock, and this is my girl, Clemmie.' Rose was clearly rattled; her wide eyes roved the room, and Nancy smiled faintly.

'No ladyships here,' she said. 'Miss Hadleigh will suffice. Yes, I know Clemmie. The one who'd been having lessons in speaking, down at the mill. Now, what brings you to see me?'

'Well,' said Rose. She nodded to Clemmie and they sat down, awkwardly, side by side on a sofa. 'I hate to disturb you, but I've been racking my brains over what to do. It's my girl here. She's... been put into the family way.'

'Ah,' said Nancy. 'And yet I have heard no wedding bells of late?'

'No. No, there weren't no wedding, as yet.'

'She doesn't look ... with child. Are you certain?'

'Oh, yes. That is, as certain as can be until she begins to round out in belly and breast. But certain enough.' There was a pause, and Nancy didn't blink.

'Do go on, Mrs Mattock.' This was delivered in a frosty tone.

'Yes. Well, Miss Hadleigh, my Clem here can't talk, as you know, in spite of Mr Hadleigh's kind efforts towards curing her of it. So she can't tell us who it was took advantage of her.'

'Yes, I can see how it would be difficult for her to do so.' Another pause, and Nancy's steely gaze fastened onto Clemmie. Rose swallowed, and Clemmie saw with sudden clarity what her mother's words, and what she was driving at, might seem to imply. Nancy Hadleigh had never liked her lessons, and had already sent Clemmie packing from the farm once before. She got up to go but Rose pulled her back down.

'Stay still, Clemmie! Well, your – Miss Hadleigh – what with Clemmie bringing the milk to the mill most days, I can't help wonder if that's where she met this fellow, whoever he might be. And I know this would have been better addressed to Mr Hadleigh, but with that not possible ... My other girls tell me Clemmie has a sweetheart, you see, but she won't tell us who it is, so we've no other way to find him out ... to make him marry her, see, and do right by her.'

'If he's free to marry, and willing to,' Nancy pointed out, coolly.

'Ar. That's so,' said Rose, miserably, as though she hadn't considered that possibility. 'I hope you understand only desperation has brought me here, to lay such a thing out in the open. But I hoped you might understand how such a thing could happen, and be willing to ... keep it close. I've no doubt the whole world would know of it, quick as you like, if I were to go and ask around at the mill. But I wanted to ask if you could help us. If you had any idea who the villain might be. We've been so blind to it all, out at Weavern, but perhaps you've seen her walking out with a young man, or perhaps talking to one of your workers, down at the mill?'

The silence in the room rang. Clemmie didn't dare to look up. She hated to hear her life, her love, described in such terms. There had been nothing shameful in what she and Eli had done, nothing in the least bit demeaning. Or at least, there hadn't been until that moment. Nancy Hadleigh appeared unmoved, yet she radiated disgust. Bewildered, Rose ploughed on, though Clemmie tugged at her hand to make her stop. 'He'd have known, you see, that she couldn't tell on him. Do you see? Whoever he is, he'd have known that, and thought he could do just as he pleased with her, and ruin her, and not face the consequences.'

'Just what exactly are you implying?' said Nancy. Rose stared, and shook her head fractionally, and when she spoke her mouth sounded dry.

'I'm not implying, your— Miss Hadleigh ... I only meant to ask if you'd seen her about the mill with anyone, or if any of the men working for you at the mill has spoken of it ...' She trailed into silence in the cold glare of Nancy's suspicion.

'No,' said Nancy, at last. 'I've not seen her about with anybody, nor heard anything of it. Not that I tend to concern myself with the grubbier goings-on of the work force. All your sort have become far too used to Alistair being kind, and overly indulgent. I daresay he *would* have tried to help you, as you seem to think he would. But it wouldn't have been appropriate, and nor is your asking it. And I really don't see how we can help you. It seems to me to be a matter for your family to deal with, perhaps with greater discretion than you have shown here today. I imagine it would be best for your family's reputation that this did not become common knowledge.' She stood up, so Rose and Clemmie did the same.

'But what should I do, then? About bringing the fellow forward?' said Rose, hurriedly, in a last-ditch attempt as Nancy opened the door to dismiss them. Nancy watched Clemmie intently, and Clemmie shied away from her.

'We've more than enough to cope with here at the moment, Mrs Mattock,' Nancy said, tightly. 'I'll thank you not to lay your troubles at our door as well.'

They walked back down the hill in silence, Rose marching with just as much purpose as before, pulling Clemmie along by her hand when she dragged behind. Clemmie wanted to say, *Stop. It's all right, Mum, no need to fuss*. When they got to the bridge, Rose turned on her.

'Oh, do come *on*, Clem! Why must you lag like that?' She took a huge breath as if to go on, but then seemed to simply deflate. 'Can't you understand it, Clemmie – what a fix you're in?' she said. 'No one'll have you now, not with some rogue's bastard on your hip. You'll be on your own.' She shook her head, and Clemmie hated to see how careworn she looked, how tired and afraid. 'Perhaps your dad'll let you stay on with us, but I don't know. I just don't know. He's so strange since our Walter died, I don't know if he'll be stormy or fair. I never know.' Clemmie tried to take her hands to reassure her, but Rose pulled them away impatiently. 'You need to find a way to tell me, Clem. You *have* to find a way to, so we can get you wed, or get the man punished. It's the only way. Will he, do you think? Is he free to wed? Please tell me the bleeder's not already got a wife?' Clemmie shook her head at once, and Rose sagged slightly. 'Well, it's not much but it's something.' Rose heaved another sigh, pressing her fingertips deep into her cheeks. A soft breeze rustled the silver leaves of the riverbank willows, and it carried the scent of flowers. Clemmie breathed it deeply, and smiled. She couldn't understand how her mother wasn't feeling all the rightness she was feeling, in spite of Nancy Hadleigh's cold comfort. She pictured her wedding to Eli, and Rose jostling their child on her knee, and William thawing – his first grandchild starting to fill the hole that Walter's death had left. She pictured the time that was coming when all would be well, and wished she could pass her thoughts directly to her mother. With an exasperated sound, Rose marched on again, back towards Weavern, and this time she left her daughter to follow on at her own speed.

A quiet few days came next, and more hushed, terse conversations between Rose and William. Josie, Mary and Liz listened at doors, and underneath windows, and from the stairs, and Clemmie left them to it. She churned the butter and strained the curds and turned the cheeses, and walked here and there as she always had, waiting to hear from Eli. She waited to hear what his plan was, and when they would begin to live it, and in the meantime she saw babies everywhere. The sow had a litter of twelve, and at dawn the roe deer fawns tottered along at their mothers' heels on legs like stilts. A hopeless squawking woke them one night and they looked out to see a vixen carrying away one of the hens, three boisterous cubs bounding alongside her. Then, on the fourth morning, the atmosphere at the breakfast table was bleak.

'What is it?' asked Mary, but nobody answered her. Rose put her husband's plate down in front of him with a bang, and the eggs had black edges while the tomatoes were all but raw. He glowered at her, and she glared back, defiantly.

'Come along, Clemmie,' she said, undoing her apron. 'We've an appointment to keep.' Clemmie rose obediently, though she would far rather have known where they were going, and who they were to see. She noticed her sisters exchange a serious look, and Josie's eyes had gone very wide. Rose shut the door behind them far harder than was necessary.

Apparently, their everyday clothes were good enough for this visit, as were Clemmie's bare, dusty feet. Rose walked with her arms folded and her chin tucked in, as though, this time, she was as unwilling to go wherever they were going as her daughter. When they got to Thatch Cottage and Rose hurried up the path, her face still downturned, Clemmie panicked. She followed her mother with feet gone numb, on legs that shook, desperately trying to think how her secret had been discovered. Eli had told her his father still hadn't found work, and was around a good deal of the time, and he already had that crushed look his father gave him, along with a bruise on his jaw and bloodied knuckles from an argument with his brother. There hadn't been any visits to Mrs Tanner for a while, because of the risk of running into Isaac; no more cuddling the little ones or cups of nettle tea. Involuntarily, Clemmie made a noise in her throat – a whine of distress and fear. She had no idea what was about to happen, no idea what Rose would say. She only knew that it would not go well. If Eli were there, if Rose accused him outright, she didn't know what he would say, or do. She didn't like to think what would happen if Isaac were there as well. She shut her eyes and gulped for air, heart hammering, her mind in too much disarray to think or react, to do anything other than follow as her mother knocked, and the door opened, and they went inside.

Clemmie darted a look around the room, struggling to see in the darkness. Eli's grandmother was asleep in her chair, and his mother was sitting at the crooked table, and besides the two of them the room was empty, the house quiet. She breathed just a little bit easier. Mrs Tanner met Clemmie's eye with a look – questioning, and pleading for calm. Shaking, Clemmie tried not to give in to her panic, or let it show on her face. She was desperate to say out loud, there and then, that she hadn't asked for any of it, that she hadn't told anyone about Eli, and had no demands to make, other than to be left be. She sensed the stiffness in her mother's body; felt how she loathed to be there. But Rose wasn't angry. In fact, there was something almost apologetic about the way she stood, and clasped her hands, and waited to be spoken to. Mrs Tanner, without getting up, gestured for them to sit.

'Mrs Matlock,' she said, guardedly. She flicked her eyes at Clemmie, who felt sweat oozing down her spine and between her thighs. She was trembling so badly she was sure they would see. 'Something I can help you with?'

'This one's got a child inside,' said Rose, baldly. Mrs Tanner let her face register just a little surprise. Clemmie held her breath, certain that her mother's next words would be to name Eli, to demand marriage and retribution. The pause boomed in her ears, filling in the gaps between the thumping beats of her heart. She waited; she could only wait, with no idea of how it would end – of what Mrs Tanner or her mother would say next. 'It wants getting shot of,' said Rose. 'I've heard you know ways of doing that.'

It took a moment for the words to make sense to Clemmie. When they did, they hit her with such force that her body jerked out of the chair, knocking it onto its back, and she stumbled away until she hit the far wall, and stood staring, aghast. Rose gave her a quick, unhappy glance. 'Her father says as much, and there's no arguing with the man,' she said, turning back to Mrs Tanner. Clemmie began to shake her head, and tears made the room wobble and lurch. Mrs Tanner looked taken aback. She said nothing for a moment, then looked at Clemmie, meeting her eyes for a second. Clemmie saw sympathy there, and something like resignation. Mrs Tanner cleared her throat.

'How far along is she?' she said.

'Not long.' Rose shook her head. 'Won't be more than a worm, still.' *Not a worm*, thought Clemmie, *a piglet. A baby. Mine and Eli's*. She clasped her hands protectively across her middle, and stared at Mrs Tanner in terror. Mrs Tanner shook her head minutely.

'Is this what you want, girl?' she asked her, and Clemmie shook her head violently.

'She don't know what she wants!' said Rose, with a tremor in her voice. 'She can't know! What's she going to do with a baby? William won't have it – where's she going to go with it? How will she live?'

'Doesn't look to me like she wants shot of it,' said Mrs Tanner. 'I'll not do it against her will. It's not right, that.'

'Not right?' said Rose. 'None of this is right, by God!'

'Perhaps it might come so, given time,' said Mrs Tanner, carefully.

'Well, do go on and tell me how,' said Rose, shaking her head.

'Look at your daughter, Mrs Matlock,' said Mrs Tanner. Rose seemed reluctant to, but when she did, and when she saw Clemmie's distress, she slumped in her chair, defeated.

'But what'll she do? William will turn her out, he says. What then?' She sounded hopeless, and Clemmie wished with all her heart to be able to explain. Just then, she almost wished Mrs Tanner would speak on her behalf, and tell her mother about Eli, and ease her misery – if news that the baby was a Tanner had any hope of doing that.

Mrs Tanner got up and went to a cupboard on the wall. She fetched out a small paper packet and handed it to Rose.

'Perhaps you can find a way to change his mind on it,' she said. 'Take this. Give it to him in his tea or his beer.'

'What will it do?' Rose took it, a strange, suspicious kind of hope kindling on her face.

'It'll ... put lead in his pipe, shall we say. He'll need you then, right enough, and that kind of need, once tended to, makes a man grateful.' Mrs Tanner smiled slightly, and Rose fingered the packet speculatively.

'Been a goodly while since he needed that from me,' she said, then shook her head. 'He was so set though, so hard, I don't think he'll change his mind and keep her and the littl'un. I don't think she can keep it.'

'But look at your daughter – see how she holds her belly! See how rabbity she is! She loves that child already, loves it right through. You can't make her kill it, can you?' Rose turned to look at Clemmie, and Clemmie saw all her mother's resolve melt away.

'Do you love that baby you've got, my girl?' she asked, and Clemmie nodded at once, knees sagging in relief. Rose sighed heavily, like she was exhausted. She got up, still holding the paper packet in her hand. 'I pray God this works,' she said. 'How much is owed?'

'Nothing.' Mrs Tanner waved one hand to dismiss the suggestion. 'Take it with my good will, since you didn't get what you came for. Perhaps you got something better, mind you.'

The thought of leaving Weavern Farm had never occurred to Clemmie before. It occurred to her now, as they walked back home. Rose took her daughter's hand and held it tightly, and didn't speak. The Tanners might have her and Eli and the baby after they'd wed, and Clemmie tried to picture that – living there with all the listless children and frightened women, all the angry men and boys; in the unnatural darkness, surrounded by barren ground. The thought of it was like a weight, steadily crushing her. Shaking off her mother's hand, she darted into the trees, away down the hill towards the river.

'Clemmie! Come back!' she heard Rose shout after her, but she carried on. Nettles stung her ankles, brambles scratched her skin; the green smell of crushed leaves and the dusty tickle of pollen rose up all around her; flies and cobwebs and watchful, darting birds in the branches overhead. The ground was steep, and she careered from tree to tree to catch her momentum until she was at the riverbank, where she sat, putting her stinging feet into the water and letting the cold numb them. To live there, in the shadow of Isaac Tanner, would be to shut out the sun. To shut out air. Clemmie closed her eyes and tried to believe that it would be enough to be with Eli, to be his wife and have his child. But however much she told it to herself, she couldn't convince herself. She knew how Eli was when his father was around – so angry at the world that even the blood in his veins seemed to harden. She thought of the trampled mud around the cottage, the scarcity of food, the scarcity of joy. She thought of waking every morning and feeling, first of all, dread. And she knew she couldn't do it.

When she'd calmed down she told herself that living at Thatch Cottage would not be Eli's plan. It could not be. He despised his father more than anybody, and certainly wouldn't tolerate him laying a hand on Clemmie, as he was bound to sooner or later – nobody under his roof escaped his violence for long. It could end in murder; it could end in Eli swinging from a rope at Cornhill Prison, down in Shepton Mallet, where those other Tanners who'd killed had gone before him. That could not be his plan. She pictured them living out, as he had been, under hedges, in hollow trees; gone wild since they were both half wild already. But that would not do for the baby; not through the winter. Never before had she looked and seen, so clearly, that Weavern Farm was a place of safety and bounty. Constancy and warmth and food, especially in the winter months; even since Walter had died and part of her father had gone with him. Thinking of leaving was like thinking of cutting out some vital part of her, and doing without it. As she walked back to the farm at the end of the day, with sore feet and her throat aching from crying, Clemmie finally felt afraid.

Most of the household had already gone to bed, and only Mary was still up, sitting by the stove with her feet up on a stool, mending one of their father's shirts. The air smelt sweetly of hay from the chamomile flowers she liked to brew into tea. She looked up as Clemmie came in, but kept on with her work.

'They had one hell of a set-to,' she said, as Clemmie sat down opposite her. 'Josie went off in floods of tears to hear them. Soft as a kitten that one – even softer than you, I think.' *And will he let me stay? And my baby?* Clemmie asked, without a word. Mary sighed. 'I don't know, Clem. He went as red as a berry – I never saw the like of it. I thought he might go into a fit. I thought the blood might curdle in him. Mum said putting you out was just the same as killing you, and the littl'un too, and she laid it all on his head. That turned him quiet a while.' She stabbed her finger with the needle and tutted, sucking at the bead of red. 'That's it,' she said, putting the mending aside. 'That's the fifth prick I've given myself in half an hour. Time for bed. Come on, dawdler.' She stood, stretching her shoulders back, and picked up the lamp. Above their heads came a creaking, and muffled, rhythmic sounds, almost-words. Mary listened for a while, then flashed a quick, rude grin at her sister. 'She's working hard on your behalf, Clem,' she said, and Clemmie nodded that she knew. They went up the stone stairs as softly as they could, and Clemmie crossed her fingers tight.

*

William was already in the kitchen when Clemmie came down, early in the morning. She moved towards him cautiously. He looked tired but there was something softer about his face, some little sadness in his eyes that was sweet and sorry but not blank, not shut off as it had been for so long. Still, Clemmie didn't quite trust it, and when he came towards her and put up his hands, she flinched. William saw it, and she saw how it hurt him. How he accused himself. He put his hands on her shoulders and gripped them hard, gazing down at her for a while. She felt the warmth and weight of his hands through the thin cambric of her blouse, and smelled his familiar smells of grease and linen and cow. She saw how they had become all but strangers to each other, and how ill that sat with the love that remained, as fixed as the bones in their bodies. Then William cupped his hand around her cheek – rough, stained fingers; the skin gone leathery hard.

'Stay on here, then, girl,' he said. 'But I won't see hide nor hair of the louse that's done this and not come forward to marry you. Mark me, now. If he comes sniffing again I'll have his guts, and no mistake.' He turned from her then, and went out without another word. Clemmie watched the door after he'd gone, feeling her flash of joy curdle.

She worked in the sun all day, not leaving the farm's own fields, letting her head ache and the skin across her shoulders sting as it turned pink. She felt too tied to the farm to roam that day; too afraid to stray in case she wouldn't be allowed to return, or wasn't able to. She tried not to picture the future – where she would end up, and the baby, and Eli. She was tormented by the impossibility of ever reconciling her family to Eli when she hadn't the words to explain; by the unlikeli-hood of Eli ever being free of Isaac Tanner. He had such hold over his son – had made him what he was with the things he'd made him do. She had no answers, and the task of finding them was so huge that she hardly dared to look straight at it. She watched the cows graze, though they had no need of minding, listening to the tearing of the grass between their teeth, the wet curl of tongues and swish of thready tails. From where she was, in Weavern's highest field on the Biddestone side of the valley, the farmhouse and barns were hidden. The land rolled so steeply that it hid the buildings in its folds, and only the river was visible, looping away to the south. Her home was a nook in the green ground, as secret as a warren. Her home was a hidden place, separate from the rest. It was easy to imagine that nothing bad could ever come there. That Isaac Tanner would never find them, and couldn't touch them. She wished, passionately, that Isaac Tanner would quit Slaughterford for good.

In the afternoon, with the sun low and blinding in her eyes, Eli came and found Clemmie. She looked around hastily as he approached, but none of her family were about. There was a lightness in Eli's step, a new urgency, and he smelled of sweat and hot skin as he held her tight.

'I've got our plan, Clem!' he said, smiling, and she realised then that she had a plan of her own. She took his hands, meshed their fingers together, willed him to see it, and understand. But he was too excited, too defiant. 'If our families don't want us, then why should we linger here?' he said, keenly. 'I can wave a jolly fare-thee-well to my dad for good, God curse him! I've a cousin in Swindon that works in a foundry there, in the engine sheds – building *trains*, Clemmie! Imagine that. He reckons there's a job for me, just waiting. Low paid, but a job, and they'd 'prentice me up for it. We can lodge with him and his missus a while, for a few pennies, until we find our feet and get a room for ourselves. I've been to Swindon and it's nice, Clem. A good place, busy, you know? And plenty of fine folk there. Do you know it?' He took a breath then carried on describing it, because of course she couldn't say that she had never heard of it, that she didn't know where it was, that she didn't want to go, that her family *did* want them. Or at least, they wanted her, and she planned to make them take him too. At last, Eli noticed her unease, and he frowned. 'This is our chance, Clemmie. Our chance to be together and start a new life, and our very own family. A chance for me to start over, where my name ain't so well known, and I'm not suspected of something by every man I meet. A clean slate. This is the chance of it.' She looked away and he caught her chin, turning her to meet his eyes. The happiness in his face was dying, the spring in him waning. 'You do still want to come away with me, don't you, Clem?' he asked, intently. 'You do still want to be mine?'

&. &

Hilarius and Irene didn't speak as he drove her, in the Stanhope, the handful of miles to Corsham station. Irene sat stiffly beside him, hoping Pudding hadn't told him what she'd said about him. The darkness about him remained; an overwrought phrase she'd read in a book kept coming to mind, however hard she tried to dismiss it: *the stain of death*. The old groom wore his battered long coat in spite of the season; it smelled of wax and animals, and there was mud and straw in the floor of the cart. Irene found herself glancing repeatedly at his gnarled hands on the reins, wondering if they still had the strength to inflict such injuries as Alistair had been given. Corsham was a small town of crooked, old stone buildings and cobbled streets, not much bigger than a village, but even so, the Manor Farm gig looked deeply bucolic in that setting. Irene shrank inwardly to think what her mother would make of having to ride in it, back through the narrow dusty lanes to Slaughterford. She'd tried to persuade Isadora Dalby to alight in Chippenham, since it wasn't such a one-horse town, but her mother had demurred, since Corsham was closer to Slaughterford and *you know how I hate to be in a carriage in the summer, with all the insects*, she'd written in her note.

Isadora's visit had come in response to Irene's hasty letter, sent soon after Alistair's death, asking to return to her parents in London as soon as possible. When an answer hadn't come directly she'd known that she would not get her wish, but that hadn't brought about a crushing disappointment – more of a neutral, disconnected kind of feeling that made her wonder if it was still her wish in any case. And now the thought of her mother being at Manor Farm was causing a steadily growing unease; the thought of her there, and of her meeting Nancy, was too odd, too unsettling. The two belonged in separate worlds, and it somehow seemed to Irene that their meeting couldn't help but bring about a cataclysm of some kind. And there was so much she would not be able to talk about – Alistair's murder, Donny, Tanner, her odd feelings, and how she was trying to help Pudding. It left her without much of an idea of what to say at all.

'I'll go down and collect her, if you'd like to wait here?' she suggested to Hilarius, as they arrived outside the small station with its cream-painted clapboard building and green picket fence. Hilarius nodded once and Irene climbed down. Deep within her, something shook at the thought of seeing her mother again. She couldn't tell if it were fear or excitement, hope or dread.

Isadora Marianne Dalby was taller than her daughter, without spare flesh but well-built. She had broader shoulders and hips than she'd ever liked, and a broader face across the jaw and forehead, so that she looked stately rather than elegant, and only ever wore shoes that she thought made her feet look smaller, even if they gave her corns. Still, she was handsome, and drew glances from the men on the stone wharf as they used winches, pulleys and sweat to load newly quarried Bath stone onto flat-bed wagons. She was wearing a calf-length fawn silk dress with a dropped waist, white kid shoes and a white sleeveless jacket with pearl buttons. Her hair was younger than she was – it was fair, not showing any grey, and she'd cut it short and set it in a permanent wave, after the fashion. Irene realised, seeing her from afar, that she herself hadn't seen a hairdresser since she'd arrived in Slaughterford the best part of three months before. Her hair grew slowly but she put up a hand and felt it resting on her collar. At least her mother couldn't criticise her outfit. Mourning was mourning, after all.

'Hello, Mother,' she said, holding out her hands. Isadora took them carefully, with her fingers only, and kissed her daughter on both cheeks. Irene caught her familiar scent – face powder, violets, the starchy smell of her clothing. London smells; smells from a previous time and place that sent Irene right back there, into echoes of her lonely childhood, her lonely adolescence, her lonely coming of age. She swallowed, and tried to smile. Isadora's expression was inscrutable, with something hard in the eyes. But then, that had always been there. 'Thank you for coming to see me.'

'Well,' said Isadora, with a minute shrug, and then hesitated. 'Perhaps it was about time,' she added, without conceding a thing.

'Hilarius has the Stanhope just up here. Where are your cases?'

'Oh, I'm not staying – did I not say? I'm sure I said.'

'You didn't say.'

'Well. Your father and I decided it would be best if I didn't impose on a household in mourning. And we've to go to the Duncan-Hoopers tomorrow, for their anniversary ball.'

'Perhaps the Duncan-Hoopers might have celebrated just as well with two fewer guests, and spared you,' Irene murmured, but her mother gave her a hard look.

'Their invitation was accepted a good while before yours arrived, Irene.'

'Well, I hadn't planned on my husband dying. Nor on you coming here – I'd planned to come home.'

'Let's not quarrel,' said Isadora, closing the subject and looking away with a tight smile as though to appease imaginary onlookers.

She took one look at the little cart, and at Hilarius, with dust bedded into the creases of his face, and suggested that they remain in Corsham instead. There was a pretty high street to walk along, and a park, though in the end Isadora declined to leave paved ground for grass, for fear of ruining her shoes. 'One forgets, living in London, that such tiny places carry on and thrive, all unobserved,' she said, looking vaguely dispirited.

'Well, they do,' said Irene, thinking that after so many weeks in Slaughterford, Corsham seemed quite lively, in fact, with its schoolchildren, butchers, and cobblers; unemployed men with tired eyes, smoking idly on corners; busy women running errands.

'What on earth do you do to entertain yourselves out here?'

'Mother, how can you ask such a thing, when I have written to you time and again of how unhappy I am here, and how much I would prefer to come back to town?'

'Well, pardon me, Irene. I was only attempting to be civil, when you've given us so much to talk about that is *un*civil. I daresay you *would* prefer to come back to us. But don't let's make believe that you are being unfairly kept away, or unfairly made unhappy – you brought this on yourself, after all.'

'I married Alistair, just as you said I should. I came all

the way down here, away from everything, just as you said I should.'

'You can hardly blame me for your current situation, dear. And I know that you continued to write to that man – oh yes, word of it got about. Serena has done her best to make sure your name raises a chuckle wherever it's mentioned – and ours, by extension.' Irene felt her face and neck grow hot, and her throat tightened at this latest betrayal – that Fin had not managed to keep her letters secret, that he had let her humiliation continue. 'Well might you blush, Irene,' said her mother. 'But your poor father's digestion torments him.'

'Father's digestion has always tormented him.'

'Well, he has always borne life's stresses and strains on our behalf, Irene. And you have always given him plenty,' Isadora snapped.

'Not always,' Irene demurred, but quietly.

They went for coffee and cake at the Methuen Arms, a large coaching inn, and Irene considered her mother's words about unhappiness, and fairness. She recalled something Pudding had said whilst they'd been out riding, two days before – just an observation; something Pudding had gathered from listening to Irene talk, but it had struck Irene. Once they'd let the subject of the identity of Alistair's murderer rest for a while, Pudding had asked a stream of breathless questions about Fin and London and love. It had been a relief, for both of them, to dwell for a while on far-off things. By now, Irene was relatively at ease hacking out on Robin, at a walk, with Pudding riding alongside on Bally Girl, one hand on her own reins and the other on Robin's lead rein. They'd gone at that sedate pace out of Slaughterford and up the valley towards Ford and Castle Combe, pursued by a cloud of dust and flies that couldn't spoil the late summer glory of the countryside.

When she had been Pudding's age, all of Irene's thoughts

had run to marriage. It had been the same for all her friends as well, though Irene's goal had been as much about getting away from her parents as it had been about getting close to anyone else. There was the agony, during the war, of fiancés being lost and killed, of hearts being broken; and for the unattached, the subtler distress, as news of the losses rolled in year after year, of realising that there would not be enough young men left for them to marry. Pudding Cartwright didn't dream of marriage, though. She dreamed of love. She dreamed of it as an abstract marvel, like a person might dream of flying; as though romantic love were something beyond the realms of her reality, and marriage therefore pointless to dream about.

'But when you fell in love with Fin, and you knew he loved you ... did it make you *happy*?' she'd asked keenly, and not for the first time, as though the answer were of vital importance.

'Yes,' Irene had said, sensing that Pudding needed this answer. And the truth was that it had, for the brief times they were alone together. The brief times when she could pretend that other people, and the rest of the world, did not exist. It had been a feeling of safety and well-being. Otherwise, their love had brought a kind of hungry, desperate fear to everything she did. Pudding had frowned, perhaps sensing that Irene was holding back. She had, by then, extracted tales of night clubs and dinners and dances from Irene; the gossipy social whirl of London; the thrills and perils of fashion; mornings spent sleeping off the drink and despair of the night before; and she always asked for more details, more words to describe how that life had actually *felt*, and what it was actually *like*. Irene knew she needed an escape from herself, an escape from the situation, and she tried to provide it. But then, as they'd ridden back down the hill in Slaughterford, Pudding, sounding flat, had said: 'I always thought London would mean all the fun and excitement a person could wish for. But it doesn't sound as though you were very much happier there than you have been here. I hope you don't mind my saying?'

Which was true, of course, and what struck Irene was that she'd never realised it herself. It was simply all she had known. Her well-to-do upbringing, her passable education and finishing, and her parents, who had never shown anything more than a detached interest in their daughter – their only requirements ever having been that she comport herself as she ought, look the part and marry well. She'd had friends, of course, with the same goals and ideas as herself; she'd been to all the right places, and known the right people; and she'd fallen wildly in love with Fin, with all the terrified joy that had brought. But, during none of it, now she thought back, had she been particularly happy. With a jolt, she found herself at a loss to think why she was in such a hurry to return to that life – a life bound to be far worse, and far lonelier, since the end of the affair. Now, watching as her mother sat down stiffly, glancing around at the furnishings and the clientele as though she were on a different planet and keen to rise above the rusticity of the locals, Irene saw clearly how life would be, back beneath her parents' roof. The constant reminders of her disgrace, her flawed judgement, her failings. The search for a new husband with whom to pack her off into semi-respectability, which she knew would commence immediately upon her return. It was an exhausting thought. Their coffee arrived; Isadora took a sip and jerked up her eyebrows in response.

'What is it, Mother? Is something wrong with the coffee?' said Irene, sharply. Isadora trained her stony eyes on her daughter.

'It's perfectly delicious,' she said.

'Good. I'm glad to hear it. You've not once commiserated with me over Alistair's death, you know. You've not once said that you're sorry about it.'

'Well, I am sorry, of course, and I'm sure it must have been a dreadful shock. But it's not as though you loved the man. Let's not make-believe, Irene.'

'No. You never were keen on playing games, even when I was tiny. And I didn't love him, it's true. But I . . . liked him. And I miss him.'

'What are you driving at, dear?'

'Am I "dear"? I've never felt it. Perhaps I might have come to love Alistair — we were married for four months, after all. Did you ever think of that? That perhaps I might have come to love him?'

'The last time we spoke of love, you told me in no uncertain terms that you would love Finlay Campbell, and none but him, until the day you died,' Isadora pointed out, to which Irene had no answer, since it was true. It was the fact of not being asked that bothered her, the fact of her feelings not even being considered.

'But then,' she murmured, 'you and Father have always simply ignored what you didn't want to see.'

'What was that? Please don't mumble and mutter. I see your manners haven't improved, during your . . . time away, Irene. But then,' she cast her eyes around, 'I suppose this isn't exactly Paris.'

They sat in silence for a while, and Irene remembered all the times she had sat in silence with her parents before. At parties, at mealtimes, playing cards. Sitting up straight, minding her manners, saying next to nothing and not even really noticing as much, because she'd had nothing *to* say. She thought of Pudding's ready chatter, and guessed that mealtimes at Spring Cottage had been rather different. She wondered what it might have been like to have a big brother to play with, even one who teased, and parents who gave hugs and kisses, and baked cakes, and read to one another. She could hardly picture such a place, and how wonderful it might have been to grow up in. Before Donny had been injured in the war, of course; before Mrs Cartwright had begun to lose her faculties, and Donny had been arrested. Suddenly, she understood Pudding's need to talk, her need to act, even more clearly. She felt a flash of impatience to be wasting time, and not helping.

'A terrible thing has happened here, Mother,' she said, as she finished her lemon slice.

'Not terrible enough to curb your appetite, I see,' said Isadora, in an attempt at levity that fell entirely flat.

'I find that eating helps me to sleep, which helps me to cope,' said Irene, levelly.

'Well, finding a new husband will be harder work, if you let your figure thicken.'

'I've no wish to find a new husband.'

'Oh, don't talk nonsense, Irene. What else are you going to do with yourself?'

'I'm needed here, in fact.'

'Needed? By whom?'

'Those of us dealing with the terrible thing that has happened, Mother. Nancy Hadleigh, and the Cartwrights.'

'The aunt? And who are the Cartwrights – retainers? I thought you were desperate to be away from here – to come back to London, to us, and to society.' Her mother sounded wrong-footed, almost disappointed, as though she had a load of arguments marshalled against it that she wouldn't get the chance to use.

'I hadn't thought it through,' said Irene. 'But I see it clearly, now. I'm quite finished with London.'

'Well!' said Isadora, her eyes going wide and a breath staying high in her chest, ready to say more. But, as if she couldn't choose which to select, none of the words got spoken. 'Are you, indeed,' she said, in the end, somewhat weakly, and Irene saw that – for the first time in her life – she'd stolen the wind from her mother's sails.

'What time is your train back to London? I'm sure you have one in mind,' said Irene, and had the sad satisfaction of seeing her mother yet further taken aback.

Hilarius took her back to Manor Farm in silence, not seeming in the least bit curious about the change of plan. Only once they'd arrived back in the yard did he climb down, with remarkable nimbleness, and offer to hand her down. He'd never made such a gesture before.

'Thank you, Hilarius,' said Irene, taken aback. The touch of his hand caused a strange ache in her own. He nodded minutely.

'Ma'am,' he said, with a nod. Then all of his attention returned to the horse, as was more usual. Irene listened to the now-familiar rumble of the mill, and the reeling of swifts, the chipping of sparrows, the fussing of the hens and pigs. She stood in the yard and turned her hat in her hands, letting the sun dry her damp hairline, and felt curiously free, almost at ease. She asked Clara for a cold drink as she went through the house and out onto the rear terrace, to sit and think. The wooden slats of the seat were warm through her skirt. She saw Nancy down in the churchyard, sitting on the bench from which, Irene knew, she would be able to see the Hadleigh family plot; she saw Jem standing in the orchard, gently wrestling one of his ferrets free from a length of twine in which it had got tangled. The ferret twisted and kicked, objecting to the process. Then she saw Pudding Cartwright, struggling up the hill towards the back gate in a fast gait that was not quite a run, her face puce and her long legs and arms apparently at war with her.

Irene sat up and shaded her eyes to see better. The girl had a book in one hand, the pages flapping whitely. By the time Pudding made it to the orchard gate, Irene could hear her gasping for breath. She waved her free hand when she saw Irene, then waved the book as well, and tried to say something.

'Pudding! Sit down – get your breath. What is it?' said Irene, but Pudding, reaching the table, shook her head, bending over and dragging at the air.

'I've found it,' she said, eventually, still breathless. 'It came to me all in a flash – something Ma Tanner said, and Hilarius too.'

'Found what, Pudding? I can hardly understand you. What did Ma Tanner say?' asked Irene, and Pudding shook her head again. There was sweat running down her face and Irene forced her to sit and cool down and have a sip of lemonade before she said anything else. Pudding did as she was told, though impatience made her restless and jumpy. 'Now tell me,' said Irene, some minutes later. Pudding looked across at her with a wild expression, an electric mingling of hope and horror.

'Hilarius said to me to look at the roots of things – at the deeply buried *why* of Alistair being killed, but I couldn't think of a thing. Then I went to see Ma Tanner and she said more or less the same thing – that there would be a reason, and it'd be something in the past, or something like that. I went away and still couldn't think of a thing. But she said that even the *most foul* things – or *especially* the most foul things – happened for a reason, or something, and then I remembered!' She held out the book she'd been carrying, and Irene took it and read the title. *Murder Most Foul – true stories of dark deeds in Wiltshire.* A chill passed over her skin. She glanced up, thinking that the weather had changed, but it hadn't.

'Pudding, what can you mean?' she said.

'It's "The Maid of the Mill", all over again! Turn to page

ninety-six.' Irene did as she was told, and found a chapter with just that heading. Pudding couldn't wait for her to read it, though, and interrupted. 'I'd read it before – before any of this happened. I can't believe I didn't think of it sooner. I'm such a dunce! Years and years ago, last century, a young girl called Sarah something-or-other was murdered right here, in Slaughterford!'

'But ... Pudding, what can that possibly have to do with anything?'

'You have to read it, but I'll tell you – she was murdered in just the same place as Alistair, in the same way as him – hit with a shovel – and ...' Pudding paused to make sure Irene was listening, 'it happened fifty years *to the day* before Alistair was killed!'

'There was another murder at the mill?' said Irene, dimly, as a creeping dread breathed onto the back of her neck. Pudding nodded.

'A girl not much older than me, killed on the seventeenth of July, 1872. Exactly fifty years before Alistair! In the same place, and by the same means. It's not a coincidence. It *can't* be! It *has* to be the same killer – don't you see? It *has* to be! And Donny wasn't even born then!' Pudding finished triumphantly, and though Irene could see her mad relief and excitement, all she herself could feel was the same shift in things – the same point of before and after being reached – as she'd felt when she'd picked up the doll on the day it had fallen out of the chimney in her writing room. She closed her eyes, and tried to see.

8
Deeper Still

The police house in Ford was empty, so Pudding asked around and was told, in the shop, that Constable Dempsey was out in the fields, helping his father bind and stack the last of the oats. She was hot from the walk through the water meadows to Ford, but she carried on northwards, propelled by purpose, up a steep, wooded lane to the field where a row of men were all toiling together. Shirt collars open, sleeves rolled up, big boots up over their calves that must have been roasting. They were covered in sweat and chaff; their hands and arms were scratched, and when Pudding went across to Pete Dempsey, his colour deepened, caught off guard.

'What are you doing here, Pudding?' he said. Pudding had to squint up at him, and had the peculiar sense of there being two of him – the big, snub-nosed boy, three years her senior, who'd once eaten frogspawn and laughed at her when she'd got stuck in the manger at the Sunday School picnic, and this grown man with solid shoulders and a crop of brown hair on his chest peeping out at the neck of his shirt. He cast a surreptitious look at his workmates, some of whom grinned, and Pudding felt conspicuous, laughed at anew. She shook it off, although it made her notice how damp she was all over, and how strongly the smell of horse lingered on her clothes.

'I've new evidence in the case of the murder of Alistair Hadleigh,' she said, trying to sound serious and not like an overexcited child.

'You've what?' said Pete.

'I've new—'

'Yes, I heard you, I just . . .' He shook his head. 'The case against your brother is pretty well closed, Pudding. Superintendent Blackman's not even considering Mrs Hadleigh any more.'

'Well, of course not – she wasn't in the least bit involved. But what I've found out is completely different and it *proves* my brother is innocent!'

'But *you* were the one to accuse her!'

'I know that, but I was wrong, Will you just listen, Pete? I mean, Constable Demps—'

'You can call me Pete. As long as the boss isn't about.'

'Well. All right.' She wrestled the book of Wiltshire murders out of her satchel. 'I found it in this book – I'd read it before but I'd forgotten, but it's all here in black and white. Alistair Hadleigh's murder is an exact replication of a murder that happened fifty years ago. An *exact* replica. A local girl called Sarah Martock was killed – Donny couldn't possibly have done that one, could he? Just like he can't have murdered Alistair. This proves it!'

Pete Dempsey took the book from her and frowned down at the page, while Pudding looked on, impatiently. She was finding it hard to keep her hands still, so she clenched and unclenched them. Her thoughts danced about, as though her brain were too hot for them.

'Are we readin' psalms or fetching in the oats, lad?' called Pete's father, Cyril. He was on foot, leading the team of four that pulled the three-ton haywain onto which the men were pitching the oat sheaves. It was a massive, hoop-raved wagon, made for Cyril by the current wheelwright's father and as solid now as it had been then; it was painted blue with the wheels done in scarlet, and Pudding had been given rides in it when she was little. The team of gentle hairy shires pulling it were sweating into their collars, and she had the sudden memory of Donny riding one of them, barelegged in his shorts, and getting so covered in horsehair that he came running after Pudding and her friends pretending to be a werewolf – with much growling and gnashing of teeth – and sent them squealing off across the field.

'Coming, Dad,' Pete called. He passed the book back to Pudding with an apologetic look. 'I can't stop and read it now, Pudding. Miss Cartwright. Pudding.' He pressed his lips together. 'I'm all sweat and mess, anyway. Can you ... do you want to meet me after? And tell me about it then?'

'Well yes, I suppose so. But isn't this an official police matter? I'd far rather—'

'Meet me after,' he insisted. 'Down at the pub, about six?'

'At the pub?' Pudding had never been before – not in the evening, when it was full of men. 'Er. That won't do – I've to get home for supper.'

'Well, we could always ... We might ... Well, all right. Eight, then,' he said, taking a breath as though the exchange had been strenuous. Pudding nodded and marched away, ignoring the half-formed comments from the others that followed her. The golden stubble whisked beneath her feet, and the ground was crumbly, studded with chunks of limestone. She walked with purpose even though, she realised, she had nowhere in particular to go.

She wondered about going back to talk to Irene again. She'd had one of her feelings when Pudding had told her about the story in the murder book – Pudding had actually seen it happen this time, since she'd been right there. Irene's face had turned almost fearful – the kind of fearful you got when you were out by yourself after dark, and thought you saw a figure moving beside you, hidden in the trees. A figure you couldn't quite see. She'd kept staring at the murder book with that look on her face, and had seemed relieved when Pudding had suggested she go at once and show it to Pete. And try as she had, Pudding hadn't been able to get Irene to say anything specific about what she felt, or what she thought; just that she agreed that the first murder was probably significant. So in the end, and with a good deal of willpower since she felt like she might burst if she didn't talk about it again soon, Pudding decided to give Irene time to digest, and went home instead.

When Pudding told her mother where she was going that evening, Louise smiled.

'What, with Cyril Dempsey's boy? There's a turn-up. But at least I know you're safe enough, I suppose, in the arms of the law,' she said. Still, Pudding wrote a note for her dad, in case her mum forgot before he got home from the call he'd answered. She had a bath and, having no idea what she ought to wear to a pub where she would stick out like a sore thumb in any case, she put on a plain skirt and a clean shirt, and did her best to coax her hair into a sensible shape. It didn't matter, anyway – she'd be flushed and clammy again by the time she got to Ford. There was no option but to walk since it was far too steep for her to bicycle. She put her satchel diagonally over her shoulder and set off. In the waning yellow light the river looked syrupy; a heron stood on its stilts on the far bank, idly preening its grey and white feathers, and a little brown and white dipper barely disturbed the surface as it fished. Towards Ford the sound of the mill died away, and Pudding heard the far-off fretting of sheep, and the whisper of the breeze in the long grasses; the swish of them as they tickled her calves. Along the final stretch of the meadow the knotweed was in flower, creating a swathe of waving pink tufts, impossibly pretty. Pudding could hardly believe such ugly things as had happened were possible, in this place of apparent innocence. She felt cheated.

The White Hart was housed in an ancient stone building that straddled the river. The By Brook ran through a leat beneath its rooms to the mill alongside, which had once turned grist and made paper before it went out of use. The pub was busy, with a hubbub of male voices inside, and warm light in the windows, and the door thumping as drinkers went in and out, releasing a belch of tobacco smoke each time they did. Women didn't usually go in in the evening – the odd one or two, of dubious reputation. Most bought a jug of whatever they fancied from a hatch in the wall, and took it home with them. There was absolutely no hard or fast rule saying Pudding shouldn't go in, she told herself. But there was convention and family law – and the throng of strange men – and her courage failed her. She perched on one of the benches outside, and waited for Pete Dempsey there. She was anxious, on edge; she'd expected her discovery to cause a wave of instant revelation, just like the one she'd experienced when she'd remembered the older murder. She'd expected Donny to be released – if not at once, then soon. But even though Irene had reacted appropriately it hadn't translated into any action, as yet; and Nancy Hadleigh hadn't reacted at all, other than to stare at Pudding from somewhere deep inside herself, without blinking. And then Pete Dempsey had just gone back to the harvest, and if she didn't manage to convince him, that evening, to take it seriously, then she'd have to take it directly to Superintendent Blackman in Chippenham. A frightening idea, but she would do it.

'Penny for your thoughts?' said Pete, sitting down beside her with a smile. He smelled of soap and his hair was still damp, combed back neatly. He'd caught the sun across his nose and cheeks, and the skin was shining and bronze. Pudding scrabbled in her satchel for the book, and handed it back to him.

'I was thinking that if you don't listen to me, I shall go and talk directly to Superintendent Blackman. But first you need to finish reading this,' she said.

'Shall I get us a couple of drinks first?' said Pete, looking crestfallen.

'Please, Pete – please just read it.'

'All right.' He frowned down at the book, and read the whole story – it was only two pages long, one of the shortest in the book, dealing mainly with the particulars of the girl's death. Pudding had all but memorised it by then, and there was little about who she'd been, or who might have killed her. Sarah was believed to have had a lover, though he never came forward, and it was thought that her murder was the result of a lovers' tryst, held in the warmth and privacy of the mill, that had gone badly wrong. *The case*, it said at the end, *remains unsolved, the murderer at large.*

'Well?' said Pudding, when Pete looked up at her. 'It *can't* be a coincidence, can it?'

'Well . . .' Pete shrugged slightly, but he was frowning, thinking. 'I think I remember my old nan talking about this, now you come to mention it – she worked at the little mill back then, sorting the rags. It's proper strange, I'll give you that,' he said.

'The murderer remains at large, it says.' Pudding flicked to the back of the book. 'This book was published nine years ago.' The year before the war began, she reflected, after which everyone lost their appetite for horror. 'Surely we'd have heard about it if it had been solved since then?'

'We would. It was most likely her fella, if he never came forward.'

'But the murderer is clearly *still* at large – the same man who killed Alistair Hadleigh. It *has* to be the same man!'

Pete was still frowning as he got up and went inside, then returned with two glasses of dark beer. Pudding chose not to mention that she'd never drunk beer before, and sipped cautiously. It tasted bitter, earthy, half good and half bad. She tried not to grimace as she swallowed. It turned warm and woolly in her stomach.

'You sure you won't come inside, Pud? Nobody'd mind,' said Pete.

'Well . . . it's easier to talk out here, where it's quiet. And it's warm enough, after all.'

'That's true.' He smiled at her in a kind of soft, inconsequential way that made her chafe impatiently.

'Pete. Constable Dempsey! Will you *please* say something about what I've told you,' she burst out. 'I can't work out why nobody I've told is *doing* anything!'

'I was thinking on it all the while, Pudding – I was. The thing is,' he said, looking uncomfortable, 'there's two ways of looking at it. One is that Mr Hadleigh was killed by the same person as killed this girl fifty years ago – although that'd make the killer past seventy now, at least, you'd have to suppose.' Pudding paused. She hadn't considered that.

'Plenty of seventy-year-olds are still fit and strong enough to . . . commit a crime,' she said.

'Plenty? I think that's a bit of a stretch, Pud.' He held up a placating hand as she drew breath to argue. 'But it's possible, I'll grant. The second way to look at it is that somebody who knew about the old murder committed this new one deliberately to make it *seem* as though the same person has done both.'

'But . . . why would anybody do that?'

'Who knows? Who knows why anybody would kill Mr

Hadleigh – or this other girl – in the first place? I know it bothers Superintendent Blackman that we still haven't come up with a good reason why.' He took a long swig of his beer. 'I shouldn't be telling you any of this, really, Pudding.'

'You mean, he's still not convinced it was Donny?' said Pudding, keenly. Pete shook his head.

'No, no – that's not what I'm saying. He's convinced it was Donny – all the evidence points to it. But he'd prefer to know why he did it. And the thing is . . .' Pete paused, and looked at Pudding for a while. His eyes were wide in the failing light, and his face wore a kind sort of look that was almost pity, which made Pudding cringe inside. 'The thing is, if we go and tell him about this book of yours, and that's it's been lying around your house for a while . . . he's going to say that your Donny most likely picked it up and read about the first murder, and took his cues from it. He might even say that . . . it gave him the idea to kill Mr Hadleigh in the first place.'

Pudding stared into the near distance as the significance of this sank in. She felt like Cassandra, condemned to be disbelieved; she felt the awful weight of not being able to help her brother. Everything seemed hopeless, and just then despair felt like a welcoming place to lie down and rest. Pudding drank her beer down – more warmth, more woolliness.

'This is all like a nightmare,' she said, quietly. 'The book was only ever in my room, on the nightstand. Mum doesn't like me reading dreadful things, so I never leave it lying about the house. Donny never goes into my room. He never does,' she said, appealing to Pete, whose face still wore the sorrowful look. 'There's no way he would have read it.'

'I know you know that, Pudding – I understand, and I believe you. Trouble is, it can't be proved, can it?'

'You've known Donny since you were born, Pete. Do you believe he killed Alistair?'

'It doesn't make any difference what I believe,' he said, looking uneasy.

'It does to me,' said Pudding. 'I need to know who's on my side.'

'I'm on your side, Pudding – course I am. But I've a job to do as well, keeping the law. And I have to do it to the letter. I can't do anything else.' Pudding thought for a while, though the beer and bad news seemed to have turned her thoughts soupy. She bit the ends of her fingers to get her own attention.

'Well, you have to tell Blackman. Will you? If not, I'll tell him myself.'

'Even if it gives him the "why" he's after? He doesn't know Donny from Adam, don't forget.'

'Even so, it might make him think . . . you will tell him my idea, won't you – that it's the same killer?'

'I'll tell him, yes,' said Pete, sounding resigned.

'And . . . will you look into the first murder?'

'Look into it? How in hell shall I do that, Pudding? The case is fifty years old!'

'There must be records – notes on who she was, who was suspected, that kind of thing? Surely there'll be records of that, at the station?'

'Well . . . I suppose there might be, not that I'd have the first clue where to look. That's if I get permission, of course. I can't just go rummaging, willy-nilly.'

'But you could suggest it to your superiors, couldn't you? That it might be an idea to look into it?'

'I'll suggest it, yes.' Pete sat quietly, seeming to wait for whatever was coming next.

'Good,' said Pudding. 'Take the book and show him – but I want it back as soon as he's seen it.'

She got up abruptly, then had to wait while her head stopped spinning. Pete stood up to anchor her.

'Steady on, Pud . . . not got much of a head for the beer, have you?' He smiled.

'I don't know. That's the first time I've had any,' said Pudding, thinking that the sky was very far away, and that the ground sloped even though it looked flat. Pete cocked his head, still holding her arm.

'I forget you're still so young, Pudding,' he said. 'What with you so . . .' He broke off, gesturing vaguely at her figure before letting his hand and his eyes drop.

'What with me so what?'

'Never mind. Come on – I'd best get you home.'

'I came on foot, and I know the way,' said Pudding, grandly.

'Well, you're not going back on foot, I can tell you. Come on – up to the farm, and we'll take the pony and trap.'

'That'll take ages; walking'd be faster.'

'Well, Pudding Cartwright, if what you say about your Donny is right, then there's a murderer on the loose. Given that, if nothing else, what kind of police officer would I be if I let a young lady walk home all alone?'

The route to Spring Cottage that was navigable by pony and trap was long, and steep, climbing to the top of the hill out west of Ford and then dropping down again. The pony huffed and puffed, the trap swayed over stones and ruts, and Pudding fought to stay awake against a near irresistible drowsiness. Twice she jerked awake to find her head resting on Pete Dempsey's shoulder, with the warmth of him reaching her cheek through his shirt. She tried to move further away along the seat, but it was a very narrow seat. 'It's all right, Pudding, you can get your head down if you like,' said Pete, his voice half-hidden by the creak of wheels and clop of hooves. Pudding shook her head.

'You'll look into it then, and you'll talk to Blackman? You promise?' she said, as he set her down outside her home.

'I promise to talk to Blackman, and to do what I can,' Pete qualified. Pudding nodded sleepily, and turned to go. 'You'll be looking into it yourself, I bet,' Pete called after her, in a knowing tone.

'What do you mean?'

'Well . . . if it's the same killer and they're past seventy, and they've been in the area before and are back, or have always been here . . . then chances are some of the old-timers might have some thoughts on who that could be, don't you reckon?'

'Yes,' said Pudding, as neutrally as she could. 'Yes – I suppose so.'

'You be careful, Pudding Cartwright. I'd tell you to leave it to the law if I thought you'd take a blind bit of notice, but you be careful. Goodnight, then,' he said, turning the pony as Pudding waved him goodnight.

She didn't realise until the morning that she had forgotten to thank Pete for the drink, and for the ride home. But it didn't really matter – she had more important things to do. The beer had plunged her into a deep sleep, and she woke with a clear head, more convinced than ever that whoever had killed Sarah Martock in 1872 had also killed Alistair. And she knew exactly where she was going.

❧ ❧

They walked a good way out of Slaughterford to catch the bus to Swindon from Castle Combe, so that the driver wouldn't recognise them. Clemmie had tied a shawl over her telltale hair, and was too hot, and her legs felt heavy all the way. Eli walked fast, with his face set, sometimes towing her by her hand just as her mother had done on the way to Manor Farm. But it wasn't just her legs that felt heavy; the heaviness seemed to be in all the muscles of her body and every bit of her head, a dragging unwillingness that she couldn't shake – the near irresistible urge to sit down and rest, and to then turn back. When she drifted to a halt, to stare at a skyline of hills that she didn't know and feel the horrible strangeness of that, Eli turned back impatiently.

'Come *on*, Clemmie!' he said, his desire to be away every bit as strong as her desire to stay. When she whimpered, he was gentler with her, and kissed her, and clamped her hands in his, like he was praying. 'Well, come on then,' he said. 'This is our new life we're running to. The three of us.' Murmuring and soothing until she carried on again. Cottages she didn't know; faces she didn't know; fields and gates and stiles she didn't know. Paths, green lanes, copses of trees; battered farmyards alive with geese and rats and children. She lost the edges of herself in the unfamiliarity of it; she felt herself blurring, getting lost. Once they were on the bus the changes only came more quickly, more alarmingly, and Clemmie had no way of saying that it felt as though the world itself had been swapped for one she had no hope of understanding. She gripped Eli's hand not out of love, but out of fear.

The bus was crowded, and spirits seemed high as they came out of the valley onto flatter ground, and the team of cobs trotted steadily along. Men with moustaches and bowler hats, some in waistcoats that had seen better days, carrying their jackets over their arms; strappers going between farms in just their shirtsleeves, stinking of sweat, work and the muck on their boots; two women so alike they had to be sisters, gossiping happily, going into town in straw bonnets and lawn frocks with old stains washed in at the hem, and offering a punnet of cherries around the other passengers. Eli scowled blackly at everybody, so nobody spoke to them. Clemmie cowered back in her shawl, too scared to look people in the eye, too scared not to look. The sun was high but she stretched her arms out from the shade of the hooped canvas roof while they changed horses in Great Somerford; reaching them into the sunshine, reaching for things she couldn't touch. Later, when Eli shook her shoulder to get her attention, Clemmie jumped. He pointed at buildings on the horizon, coming nearer – church spires, factory chimneys, tall townhouses. His face had come alive with triumph. 'We're all but there! And just think – your folks might not even have noticed you gone yet,' he said, jubilantly. Clemmie nodded, but couldn't bring herself to smile. 'Don't look so cowed, my Clem. I'm going to look after you, and it'll all work out well – I've said so. You believe me, don't you?' he said, and she made herself nod again.

Eli's cousin, Matthew, didn't look much like a Tanner. He was squat, pug-nosed and had brown eyes, not blue; his lips were too full, and had a damp, swollen look, and his hair was a greasy swathe of mouse-brown in need of a cut. But he had a wide smile, and the shiftiness in his eyes was more speculative than malicious. His wife Polly was so pregnant she looked like the moon rising. The weight of the bump had dragged her spine into an impossible-looking kink, and she kept her hands wedged there, bracing it, whenever she could. She might only have been twenty or so but her face sagged with exhaustion, and a toddler swung from her skirt as she let them in.

'Don't panic, missy,' she said to Clemmie, catching her staring in alarm at the size of the bump. 'This is due to drop any day now, and I've a feeling there's more than one in there – my ma was one of triplets, God help me. So chances are you won't come up half as big as this.' Matthew and Polly had been told that Clemmie was mute, but there was still that pause when she was expected to reply, and the slight awkwardness of moving on when she didn't. 'How far along are you?' Polly asked, before blushing, realising that Clemmie couldn't answer that, either.

'Only Clem knows,' said Eli, looking at her as though she'd worked a miracle. 'The rest of us must just wait to see.' Polly squinted at Clemmie, and, nodding for permission, grabbed her middle and gave her a prod.

'Early days,' she said. 'No more than a couple of months, I reckon.'

'Plenty of time for me to work, then, and find us rooms.'

'Ar, well,' said Matthew, not sounding too sure. 'You can stay as long as needs be. Family's family after all.'

'Well then,' said Polly. 'I'll show you where you'll be sleeping.'

Matthew and Polly had the ground floor of a cramped townhouse; two rooms, one at the front where they cooked and washed and ate, the other at the back where they slept with their first child, three-year-old Betsy. Outside the door to these rooms, narrow stairs ran to the upper rooms from a hallway with a grimed wooden floor. It was dark, and cramped, and most of the space was taken up with pots and boxes, brooms, pails and an old milk churn in a trolley that Polly used to fetch water from the pump at the end of the street. Cooking smells lingered, as did the damp and smuts aroma of neglected corners everywhere. Beneath the stairs, a thin mattress stuffed with rags had been laid, and draped with a blanket. It was just about wide enough for two people to lie side by side, shoulders tight together. Clemmie thought of the huge bed at Weavern Farm that she'd shared with Josie. It had been there long before her parents had taken over the farm, more a part of the building than a piece of furniture, and over the years the posts had been gnawed by beetles and wasps. But it had been soft and enveloping, and it had been at home. Safe. Here, people's feet would pass by in the street, not three yards from where her head would lie.

'I've had a word with old Mrs Shepherd upstairs and she don't mind. She hasn't managed the stairs in years anyway – only time she gets out is when we take her. Her daughter comes by every day to dress and feed her, and empty the pot, but you'll be up and about before she comes, I'm sure. Only thing we need to watch is the landlord. He comes by for the rent each month, usually on the first Tuesday, so he shouldn't spring us if we're careful – not that he'd put you out, only he'd be wanting more money for you staying here, is all.'

'Our thanks, Pol,' said Eli, dropping his canvas sack onto the mattress.

'Well, I'll be off on the evening shift,' said Matthew. 'I'll let the foreman know you're here. Hopefully he'll just say to bring you in with me in the morning, then he'll glance you over like he's weighing you up at market, but don't let it rile you – he's a tiny prick of a man, in all manner of ways.'

'Amen to that,' Polly muttered.

'So he likes to act big. Tug your forelock a bit, like he's cock o' the walk, and the job'll be yours, Eli.'

Clemmie couldn't sleep. It was stuffy and hot in the hallway, and there was no window to open. Betsy woke up yelling almost hourly, and upstairs Mrs Shepherd coughed, and coughed, and coughed. Eli fought in his sleep, twitching and muttering, and out in the street footsteps did pass, and Clemmie's skin crawled every time, wondering who it was and what business they could have, out in the black of night. She saw their shadows, in the gap beneath the door. She missed Mary's soft snoring, regular as a heartbeat, and the night birds outside the farm, and the quiet murmur of the river. Night after night, it got no easier. She still got sick in the mornings sometimes, and could no longer tell if it was the baby or the dizzy fatigue of sleeplessness. When Polly took her up to meet Mrs Shepherd, she and the old woman stared at one another with similar degrees of incomprehension. Mrs Shepherd was trapped in her iron-framed bed; trapped with her feeble body and her cough; trapped in her greasy lace nightcap until her daughter came to take it off. Her misty eyes, blinking rapidly, looked out at a world that she no longer understood, and Clemmie knew exactly how she felt.

Eli was gone at first light, with Matthew, to the early shift at the engine sheds. He came back tired, aching from shovelling coal and rubbing at eyes gone red and runny from airborne grit, but serene – the peace, Matthew said, of a man who'd done a day's work for fair pay. Matthew was an operator on one of the grinding machines, and paid slightly better than Eli, whose job it was to feed the furnaces, and to lift and move whatever needed to be lifted or moved. Polly spent her days moving, slowly and laboriously, between their rooms and the market place, the water pump, the draper's and her neighbours' rooms; stopping to grip her back, to wipe the sweat from her face, to catch her breath.

'Lord save me,' she said, again and again; a constant refrain, the voice of inner fear. Betsy tottered after her everywhere, sucking her thumb, clasping her wonky home-made doll to her ribs. Clemmie took it on herself to mind the child as much as she could – picking her up when she fell; taking foul things away from her before she could eat them; changing her drawers when she wet them – to give Polly a break. She also lifted, and poured, and fetched and carried, and helped fashion whatever meagre food Polly got from the market into a meal for the five of them come evening. Pies with greasy crusts made with lard or dripping; stews of peas and barley; nothing but bread and cheese, some nights. So far, all the money Eli had earned had gone to Matthew and Polly, for their food and lodging, but demand always seemed to outstrip supply. Midway through

Clemmie's ninth day in Swindon, Polly gripped her hand, suddenly, as they sat peeling potatoes, and smiled at her. 'I don't know how I got on before you came, Clem,' she said. 'I shan't ever want to let you go.'

Clemmie liked Polly, and she managed to smile, but she realised that she was merely waiting. Waiting to awaken from this disturbing dream she was caught in, in which she had to live there in the mêlée of a town, with the looming buildings and thronging humanity, the crush, the inescapable smells, and so little that was calm or green. When she shut her eyes she sent herself back to Slaughterford. To the sweep of the river and hills, the mill, and Weavern Farm. She even conjured the steady calm of Alistair Hadleigh's office – standing with her eyes shut and her back to the window, echoing his syllables as soon after him saying them as she could, a trick that sometimes seemed to help, at least with the easier sounds. She almost heard the race of the mill leat and the thud of the beaters, and smelt paper and the woollen rug from the Orient on the floor, and Alistair's hair oil and the expensive material of his suit cloth, and felt that easing of panic that had sometimes left her almost drowsy, when a lesson had gone well. She longed to feel it now, but fear clamped down on her when she opened her eyes, smearing away who she was and what she knew, and leaving no safe places. Nobody noticed her fleeing inside herself. They didn't know that even if she could have spoken, she would have been silent for days. She cuddled Betsy, and played games with her – giving her doll sips of tea, plaiting the few strands of wool it had for hair, and trying not to notice that it smelt of vomit. And she waited to be able to leave. She waited for Eli to say, *Let's go home*.

But he didn't say that. He worked, and he ate, and he went out to the pub in the evening with Matthew, and came back after Clemmie and Polly had put their heads down, smelling of beer and tobacco, burrowing his face into her neck and falling asleep in an instant. He no longer smelt of grass or earth or the hedgerows; he no longer smelt like a wild animal, but more like a machine. The town was putting its stamp on him. One night he saw Clemmie's downcast face as he and Matthew turned to leave, and took her along to the pub with him. She tried to be pleased, but it was all noise and smother, and men talking too loudly, and women with red paint on their teeth. The buildings along the street seemed to rear up too far and crowd in above, worse than they did in the daytime, and Clemmie felt crushed. She stayed for half an hour, hating it, then squeezed Eli's hand and slipped away to the bed beneath the stairs.

'Must seem strange to you, all this,' said Polly one day, when she caught Clemmie staring up at the narrow strip of sky above the street. 'What with you being raised up on a farm. And Swindon's not really a big city, you know – I went to Bristol once. By God, there's a place. All life is there; people like . . . ants in a nest, down on the docks. You wouldn't credit it till you saw it. But you can smell the sea from there – have you ever seen the sea?' Clemmie shook her head. 'Me neither,' said Polly, wistfully. 'I can't imagine it, 'cept that it must be beautiful.' She was silent for a while, and Clemmie struggled to picture a place more populous, more clamorous than Swindon. 'Clemmie is such a pretty name,' said Polly. 'Short for Clemence, is it? Or Clemency?' Clemmie shook her head. It wasn't short for either of those, but she'd no way to explain what it was short for. 'Well, it's pretty. Maybe I'll call one of this litter Clemency, if it comes out a girl.' She ran her hands as far over her bump as she could reach.

On Sunday they went along to the church at the end of their street, which had a pretty square of grass with iron railings around it to the front, and flowerbeds full of pansies and busy Lizzies. They had no Sunday best and went in what they wore most days, with the addition of hats for Clemmie and Polly. The sun beat down, and they sat with strangers in the shade of a horse chestnut tree laden with unripe conkers.

'This is the life, eh,' said Matthew, lying back and tipping his hat over his eyes. Eli smiled slightly, but Polly ignored him. Betsy was fractious and had an itchy rash that was tormenting her, and Clemmie merely wanted to say, *No. No, this is not what life should be.* 'Bet you're not missing old Isaac, now, are you, Eli?' Matthew went on, and Eli's face fell at once. He sat with his knees up, his arms resting across them, and squinted away into the distance.

'I hope never to set eyes on that man again,' he said, at length. 'And I might kill him if I do.'

'Can't say as I blame you,' said Matthew, grunting. 'I'll never forget the time I saw him—'

'Enough, Matt. I won't have him cast his shadow here,' said Eli, tersely, and Matthew shot him a startled glance before wisely dropping the subject. Isaac Tanner was what kept Eli out of Slaughterford, Clemmie realised. He may not have liked his own name, or the Tanner reputation, but he loved his mother, and grandmother, and several of his brothers and sisters; it was his father he couldn't stand to be near. If Isaac had been the one arrested for what happened at the mill – or for the robbery if the two things were separate – and if he hadn't come back, she and Eli might not have had to leave Slaughterford at all. And there was no chance of going back, she saw, whilst Isaac remained. And then, out of nowhere, she knew the answer to it. It came with a rush of nerves and hope, and at that exact moment Polly's face paled, and she gasped.

The labour lasted right through the afternoon, and right through the night. There was no doctor; the midwife was a neighbour who'd previously brought a hundred of Swindon's workers' children into the world, not counting those she'd delivered straight into little coffins. Polly held Clemmie's hand, and as the hours passed Clemmie felt her grip get weaker, her gouging fingers turning as soft and giving as fruit gone over. As she pushed, Polly was silent for so long Clemmie wondered if she'd ever breathe again. The room smelt of her sweat and urine, her dry throat and effort. By dawn there were two babies, a boy and a girl, long and skinny and crushed; the girl sucked in a breath and wailed, but the boy lay still and quiet, his skin an unearthly blue. He lived a half-hour or so then slipped away, and Polly was too spent to react. The midwife clamped Polly's new daughter to her breast, and the child drank as her mother lay unconscious.

Clemmie was never happier for a night to be over. All blood and darkness, pain and fear, life and death had been there in the room, hand in hand. The babies had fought to remain in the womb, not like animal babies that slithered out, eagerly enough. It was the city, she thought. It was all the buildings and the dirt and the crowding, the air not right, the horizon too close, the world too strange. It wasn't as it should be. When she came away from the bedside, exhausted, she carried on out of the front door and down the street, and might have carried on walking until she got home had Eli not run out after her, and fetched her back. *I want to go home*, she told him. She longed for him to hear her, and perhaps he did, a little. There was something in the way he scowled, something in the silence between them. In desperation, Clemmie took a piece of old newspaper from the privy they shared with four neighbours and drew a rudimentary map, and stick figures of herself and Eli, in between two places – a large sprawl of scribbled chaos behind them, and their faces turned towards a place with a curling river, a mill, an isolated farm.

'We can't go back,' said Eli, flatly, understanding at once. 'I can't. I won't be near him, Clem. You understand that, don't you? This is our life now. This is our home. I've got work, and we've a place to live, and family. I wish I could make you feel how I feel – to be out from under him for the first time in my life. To start over ... It's a marvel. And I won't go back to how it was. This is home now.'

But in the dark of night after the boy twin's funeral, who Matthew and Polly named Christopher, with baby Clemency crying and waking Betsy, and Polly wincing every time she moved, and smelling of milk and exhaustion, Clemmie made up her mind. Polly's need of help was like an extra set of ties, binding her, but if she stayed, she felt she would die. Not physically, perhaps, not straight away, but in some other, fundamental way. She thought of the soul that the vicar talked about; she thought about the spirit of things, the wants and needs and memories bred into each person by the generations that spawned them; and the land that fed them. People belonged in certain places, and not in others, and she and Eli – and the baby – belonged in Slaughterford. And if Eli would not return because of Isaac Tanner, then Clemmie knew a way to get rid of Isaac Tanner.

She knew what she had overheard; she knew the truth of it. Her mother often said that the simplest answer was usually the right one, and the simplest answer was that Isaac had planned to rob Alistair Hadleigh, and had taken his sons to the mill, and had done the deed. It would not be easy; she didn't want to implicate Eli in any way. She needed to find a way to say the words, or draw them, or write them. She would work it out with her mother's help – perhaps get her to ask the right questions. She might even see if she could go into Alistair's office, and recapture the calm of it to help her, even if he weren't there. She would find a way to say that Isaac Tanner was a guilty man, a criminal; the one who'd planned to rob the mill and the cause of all the violence. A man who had raised a generation of children too angry and terrorised to break away from him. Isaac Tanner was a shadow on the world, and she would give the police the chance they'd always looked for to take him away for good.

As if he could sense her intention, Eli lay close to Clemmie when he got home, and she could just see the glint of his eyes in the dark, and he spoke close to her ear.

'You won't leave me, Clem,' he said. His voice was tight, like the grip of his hands, and she couldn't tell if he was begging her, or commanding her. 'You'll not leave me.' But he fell asleep, couldn't help himself, and his hands slithered away from hers as his breathing deepened, and she edged away from him. At the last moment that their bodies touched, at the moment that they parted, Clemmie felt something tear inside, and her heart ached. He would not understand. He could not know her plan, and that she would make a home for them where they ought to be, at Weavern Farm. She hardened her heart as best she could, knowing that his might break when he found her gone. In the dark, and after the beer, Eli hadn't noticed that she was dressed. Eyes straining, Clemmie went into the front room as silently as she could. Eli slept deeply, but if he found her before she'd had a chance to vanish she knew she would never leave. And she was frightened. She knew how angry pain made him – pain of all kinds. She fetched the apple and slice of bread that she'd hidden earlier, wrapped in a cloth in the vegetable crock. In the front room the glow of the streetlight leached in through the thready curtains and outlined the furniture in lifeless grey. She didn't have any money for the bus or a train, and only a vague idea of the direction to go in – south, and west. She would walk for as long as it took, though, and try to hitch a ride. She could feel home pulling at her; she felt that this return journey would be all downhill, and easy.

Then there was movement behind her – a soft footstep, a

taken breath – and Clemmie whirled around, heart jumping. Words jammed in her throat, and behind her teeth. *I was only going on ahead, for you to follow. I have a plan too, Eli, you'll see*. But it was only little Betsy, glassy-eyed and half asleep in the doorway. Clemmie went quickly to kneel in front of her, to keep her quiet. Betsy yawned, and Clemmie smelt the sweetly awful smell of the child's tooth decay.

'Bye, Clem,' Betsy mumbled, then yawned again and rubbed at her eyes. Clemmie gathered her in, and held her tight. She had no idea how the little girl knew she was leaving; she didn't need to know, or to question it. She gave Betsy a kiss on her forehead, and put a finger to her lips. Betsy nodded sleepily, then turned to go. Before slipping into the darkness the child turned again, hesitated, then held out her doll to Clemmie. Clemmie couldn't say *you keep her*, so she just shook her head a little, but Betsy nodded, and thrust the doll out anew. So Clemmie took it, and dropped her head to one side to say thank you. Then she crept along the hallway and out into the street, and felt the tear in her heart get wider, deeper, as she shut the door on Eli's oblivious sleep. She knew what he would think when he woke, and it almost made her quail, and run back inside. She almost couldn't stand it. But she couldn't stand to stay either, and she had a plan.

❧ ☙

Nancy's daily visits to lay flowers on Alistair's grave had already taken on the feel of a ritual, just like her weekly ritual of visiting her brother Alistair's grave. The same grave, of course, beneath the same stone slab. Irene hated that thought – the newly dead lying alongside the desiccated, the eaten-away. She wondered how long it would be before the daily visit became a weekly one, and how Nancy would make that decision. Down she went after breakfast, with cut flowers from the garden to add to the still-fresh ones already on his grave, to spend time carefully clipping off any wilted leaves, any faded petals. The rose garden was running out of roses; already the only ones left were those that had begun to weep their petals onto the ground. Irene was beginning to regret having asked if she could go with Nancy one morning. She'd been pleased when Nancy said yes, but now she seemed committed to going every day, and she felt phoney, making gestures of a grief she didn't feel. But Nancy talked to her more on the walk there and the walk back, and if Irene was going to stay at Manor Farm, at least for the time being, then she needed the *entente* with Nancy to continue. A return to the spite and disdain of the early days would be excruciating.

'Did he ever tell you about the time he got lost on his own land?' said Nancy that morning. 'He was only about ten, but still – old enough to know the way home, you'd have thought. I went out as teatime came and went, and found him sitting in one of the hedgerows, crying his eyes out.' She gave a grunt, half affectionate, half incredulous. 'But do you know, the first thing he did was apologise for making me worry and come out looking for him. Dear, soft, silly boy. I'm afraid I gave him quite an ear-bashing. And now, of course, I regret every time I ever berated him.'

'I'm sure he knew it was well-meant,' said Irene. 'I hid from my parents once. It was Nanny's half day off. I tucked myself under the bed in a spare room upstairs – I can only have been about seven, I suppose. They didn't come to look for me. I fell asleep, and it was dark by the time I rushed downstairs, certain they'd have been worried about me.'

'I've a feeling you're going to say they hadn't noticed you gone,' said Nancy.

'Just so,' said Irene. 'So that taught me a lesson about my

own importance. I would far rather have been berated, I assure you.' She opened the little iron gate into the churchyard and held it for Nancy.

'I notice your mother never actually made it here, to the farm. Rather a short visit.'

'Yes. But I found it quite long enough, in the end,' said Irene.

'Good for you,' said Nancy. She sniffed. 'Let her taste her own medicine.' But then the silence that came over her at the graveside descended, and Irene went to sit on the bench, and had to resist the urge to tip her face to the sun, and let its warmth buoy her.

On the way back, when Nancy had turned sunken and grim, Irene sought to bring her out of herself again.

'Has Pudding told you about this other murder that happened, years and years ago?' As soon as she'd spoken she knew she'd said the wrong thing. Nancy's head came up but her eyes sparkled with anger.

'Yes, and I'm about ready to lose patience with the girl,' she said. 'Why on earth can't she just accept what's happened, as I have had to accept it, and let us all move on?'

'She loves her brother too much, I suppose,' said Irene, carefully, glad not to have let on about her own role in Pudding's covert investigation. Nancy sighed.

'She does. Of course she does.' She shook her head. 'Perhaps I would be just the same if my own brother had done such a terrible thing. But the fact is that *nobody* can really know a man as damaged as young Donald – or what he might be capable of. Who knows why he did it? Perhaps Alistair did speak to him about those ruined rose bushes. Perhaps he even talked to him about finding work elsewhere. But perhaps it was simply something inside his own head. We can't ever know what set him off.'

'But don't you think it's odd that the . . . killing so resembles this other one, all those years ago?'

'Everything about what has happened is odd; in the worst possible way.'

'Yes, but—'

'I simply do not wish to hear about it, Irene,' Nancy snapped, and Irene held her tongue. There was no way to make Nancy feel any of the injustice Irene was feeling on Alistair's behalf – as far as Nancy was concerned, her nephew's killer was in gaol, and would get his just deserts. Her grief was all-consuming, and didn't leave space for more considered emotions, like Irene's. She looked around at the endless sweeps of green, the endless daisies and buttercups and clover, and it felt as though it had been summer forever, and that the summer would last forever, just like when she was a child. She felt as though time had slowed there in Slaughterford – as though the extraordinary events had isolated them from the rest of the world. As if the place needed to be any more isolated, she thought.

Pudding knocked at the door after lunch, and to Irene's surprise, Nancy invited her to come and sit with them and have some of the ice cream she herself had hardly touched.

'Florence will sulk if it goes back to the kitchen, melted and unwanted.'

'Oh, thanks,' said Pudding, but Irene could see that food was the last thing on her mind. She ate a bit, dutifully, her eyes roaming the room, her body tense. Irene found herself dreading what the girl would say next, and wishing that whatever it was she'd button it until Nancy had left the room. Irene had the sense that she and Pudding were stirring a very deep, very old pond, and she was starting to feel uneasy about what they might bring to the surface. Things that might horrify them; things that might bite. She knew they couldn't stop yet, but she didn't want to be seen doing it.

'So, was there something about the horses you needed to discuss?' said Nancy.

'The horses? No – that is, not unless one of you wants to ride this afternoon?' said Pudding, but Nancy shook her head.

'I might,' said Irene, hoping to forestall Pudding, but failing.

'Oh. Good. Well, I spoke to P— Constable Dempsey about this other murder. He's going to talk to Superintendent Blackman, and hopefully he'll be looking into it.' There was silence at the table. Pudding put down her spoon and hurried on. '*He* – Pete Dempsey, that is – suggested that I look into it myself. You know, ask some of the older people in the village who were around then and now, and see if they have any idea at all who was responsible for the murders, and—'

'Oh, for heaven's sake, Pudding, you really do go too far,' said Nancy. She pushed back her chair and stood up. 'If anybody had had the first clue who was responsible for that girl's death back then, don't you think they'd have told the police?'

'Well, yes – and maybe they did.' Pudding's face reddened. 'I'm hoping that'll be in the police records, and I can go and ask them about it. If they're still around . . . But maybe there just wasn't enough *evidence* to support—'

'None of this will help your brother, child!' said Nancy. 'I hate to say it but it seems that somebody will have to. Donald attacked Alistair, and whether he meant to kill him or not, he did; and it is . . .' She paused, not able to look at Pudding. 'It is only right that he has been taken into custody.' Pudding stared at Nancy in horror.

'But how can you say that?' she asked, meekly. 'You *know* Donny!'

'I *knew* him. Before the war. Pudding, I know how hard this is for you – don't forget that I have also lost a brother I adored. Before you were even born. So if you're about to tell

me I don't understand, then believe me, I do. But one must . . .
face the facts, as they are, square on.'

'But I'm trying to *find out* the facts!' said Pudding, desperately. 'And then I'll face them. Donny told me it wasn't
him, and that he only found Mr Hadleigh lying there, and I
believe him. I need to talk to Hilarius again, and Ma Tanner.
And when did Jem start work here, do you remember? And I
wanted to ask you, Nancy – when did your family first come
to Slaughterford? Weren't the Hadleighs here at the time of
the first murder? Can you think of anybody you saw – perhaps
a stranger – who you think could have . . .' Pudding's words
broke against the cliff face of Nancy's silence.

'At a time like this, Pudding Cartwright, you're asking me
if I know who killed some peasant girl fifty years ago?' said
Nancy, quietly. 'Go back to the yard, and look after the horses,
and please stop creating more drama on top of the real crisis
we already have.'

Once Nancy had gone, Irene could breathe.

'Oh, Pudding,' she said. 'You have to tread more softly
around Nancy! I know you've known her a long time, but
she's under a terrible amount of strain. She might send you
away if you keep bothering her, and don't let her grieve in
peace.'

'I know,' said Pudding, her eyes welling. 'But I'm under
strain too . . . and my family. And poor Donny, locked away
in a cell.'

'I wish he wasn't. I wish none of this had happened! But it
has, and . . .' Irene wasn't sure what to add. 'I want whoever
really did this to Alistair to be caught. You know I do. I'll help
as much as I can, but—'

'Will you have a look through Alistair's things, and find
out if there's anything there that might . . . explain his death?'

'Would I do what?'

'Have a look... through his papers and what have you. Perhaps there was something to do with the business that he hadn't told anybody. Trouble of some kind...'

'But that would be spying. Spying on my husband.' It seemed an indecent thing to do.

'But... Alistair's dead, Irene,' said Pudding. Irene blinked. Somehow this fact made the idea even less decent. 'He can't mind.'

'But I... What exactly do you want me to look for? I'm sure there'll be nothing about the Tanners in there...'

'Forget the Tanners! I mean... perhaps it's not him, after all. I don't know. Or perhaps there'll be clues to who might have hired Tanner in there. Anything! Anything that... might help explain *anything*.' Pudding spread her hands helplessly. Irene watched her, uneasily, sympathetically, and saw the girl take a deep breath. 'It's only a week now until Donny goes before the magistrate. I only have one week to find something that could help him, and maybe make them let him out on bail. He's... he's not coping in gaol. He's suffering, and I... I *can't* stand that.'

'All right,' said Irene. Pudding's fear and need were like a fog it was hard to see through, and they were contagious. 'All right. But I expect most of the business correspondence is down at the mill.'

'Well, you could look there, too.' Pudding nodded, like it was all settled. She gripped her chair as though to push it back but then hesitated. 'Irene, you looked... frightened when I first told you about this other murder – the first murder.'

'Yes. Well,' said Irene. For some reason, the statement made her feel guilty.

'You looked as though you'd... almost expected it. Or not quite that. Like you knew already, and me telling you only reminded you.'

'That's more or less how it feels.' Irene looked away, uncomfortably.

'Has there been anything else? Do you know . . . what it was you were afraid of?'

'Pudding, if I knew anything, I would tell you. The feelings I get are just that – feelings. Intuition, at best. I'd be worried if I thought you were relying on them, overly, and—'

'But what if they're right?' said Pudding.

'They might be, but they might not. I don't believe it's second sight or anything . . . supernatural . . .' Irene shook her head. 'It's just the notion that something important has been . . . hit upon, on each occasion. It's rather like . . . when you're looking at your own reflection in a window, and then you suddenly realise there's someone else on the other side of the glass. You have to change the way you're looking at it. But it's not that specific, you see.'

'Well. Please say, won't you, if you do think of anything,' said Pudding, as she got up. 'Or find anything. I'm sorry for upsetting Miss H. Would you tell her, when you see her? And do you really want to go for a ride?'

'If it'd help, yes.'

They rode for an hour, then Irene spent the rest of the afternoon in Alistair's study, feeling horribly intrusive as she opened the drawers of his desk one by one, lifted the contents onto the top and went through it all, one item at a time. Though she found nothing that could possibly have made anyone want to be rid of him, she soon found herself drawn in, fascinated, peering through a window into the life he'd lived before she'd known him. There was a box of letters from his relatives in America, stacked neatly in order, like library cards; the envelopes getting smaller and more yellowed the further back in time they went. She took out the first one, which was dated

April 1871, and had been written to Alistair's father from his mother, Tabitha, before they were married. Curious, she took it out and read it – a very chaste kind of love letter that spoke a good deal about respect, regard and beneficial union, and very little about love or passion. But that had been the spirit of the age, she supposed; and Alistair had told her that his mother had been a very devout Catholic. She remembered Nancy calling her a *papist delusionist*, but then, given how Nancy had loved her twin, Irene doubted whether any woman could have been good enough for him.

In another drawer, in a file labelled *Sundries*, was her own marriage certificate, and behind it Alistair's parents' one, issued in New York City on July 15th, 1872. Which answered the question of where the Hadleighs had been at the time of the murder of the girl down at the mill, Irene noted. Outside, the sky curdled to grey and thunder rumbled in the distance. Then it started to rain. The light in the study went flat and dim, and Irene found her interest waning, and all the letters and papers began to feel like what they were – remnants of past lives that she had no business looking at, which brought on a stifling, almost claustrophobic feeling. She flicked through more quickly, impatient to have done with the task.

One other thing caught her attention before she finished the search. In the cupboard containing Alistair's guns, binoculars, fishing tackle and the like, she found a box file of more papers, mostly old sports log books, postcards and maps, but in the bottom – deliberately hidden – a bundle of letters with Alistair's own writing on the front, tied up with string and with a covering note wrapped around them. *Dear Mr Hadleigh*, the note read, in an elegant, sweeping script. *I do regret any pain I have caused you, but must ask you to cease writing to me. It does no good, you see, for either of us. You were kind enough to release me from our engagement, for which I will always be indebted to you. Surely you understand that no amount of debate, and no set of circumstances, can possibly cause me to change my mind, having taken such steps as I have taken?* It was signed Miss Annabelle Cross, and dated July 12th, 1914.

Irene felt a thrill as she read it, a peculiar jolt, like she'd looked up, thinking she was alone, to find somebody else in the room. She'd quite forgotten that Alistair had been engaged elsewhere before proposing to her – and Nancy's claim to have extricated him. If it were true, then she'd done it by scaring the girl off somehow, not by talking her nephew out of it – just as Cora McKinley had said. She wondered what on earth Nancy could have said or done to cause the relationship to collapse so completely; she wondered if Miss Annabelle Cross had known that war would be declared so soon after she broke it off with Alistair, or that she would be sending him into battle with a broken heart. And his heart had been broken. Irene read only a few of his letters to Annabelle, first adoring and then frantic, but they were enough. She sat with the bundle in her lap, not wanting to spy on his heartbreak any longer, and feeling strange to find he'd loved another woman. Loved her enough to keep his own letters to her hidden away – because she had touched them, Irene supposed. Because they had traces of her skin, her scent; were relics of her.

So perhaps Alistair's quiet manner hadn't only been a result of the war, but of this heartbreak; and perhaps his sympathy for Irene's plight had been based as much on understanding how it felt to be publicly dropped by a person you adored as on his infatuation with her. She wondered if he'd ever known that his aunt Nancy had been the reason for Annabelle's flight. Somehow, she doubted it. She sat and tried to decide how she was feeling, and whether or not the needling resentment at the back of her mind was a touch of jealousy. Ridiculous, given that she'd made Alistair live with her continued love for Fin for weeks, and hadn't given herself the chance to fall in love with Alistair. There were no clues as to what had become of Annabelle, and Irene hoped that Pudding wouldn't think it was relevant, and want to track her down – she had no wish to trespass any further into her husband's humiliation.

She kept the bundle to give to Pudding and put everything else back as she'd found it, then went over to where her wedding photograph stood, on the mantelpiece. She picked it up and stared hard into Alistair's face, rendered in shades of grey. The happiness in his eyes was genuine. She felt she could see his whole soul right there in the picture – his kindness, his tolerance, his capacity for joy, coming off him like a soft, pale light. Her own face looked like that of a stranger. She looked like a shell, absent from herself. She hadn't even managed a smile, just a neutral expression like one painted on a doll. Shame washed through her. She didn't know how Alistair could have stood it, marrying her when she was in such a state. Alistair had deserved to be loved, of that she was wholly certain.

'If we'd had more time, I would have done,' Irene told him, surprising herself by speaking out loud. 'I know I would. I only needed a little time.' Suddenly, she desperately needed him to hear her, and believe her, but of course he never could. She kissed his image, on impulse, leaving a smudge from her lips on the glass. As she rubbed it away with her cuff she felt her anger on his behalf burn brighter, cleaner. She hadn't been much use to him while he was alive. Charles McKinley had said that marrying her had made Alistair happy, but Irene didn't feel as though that were at all good enough. She was going to make damned certain she was useful to him now. She put her wedding picture back carefully, slipped out of the study and closed the door as softly as she could, to make up for having invaded so completely.

As the light began to fail, and cooking smells seeped from the kitchen, Irene put on boots, a mackintosh and an oilskin hat, and went out for a walk in the rain. The claustrophobic feeling of the old papers had persisted, and after so many weeks of sunshine – the weather so settled it had come to seem as though she were waking up each morning cursed to live the same day, over and over again – she wanted to feel the rain hitting her head and hear it splashing under her feet. The low sky flickered yellow now and then, but the thunder stayed quiet and distant – more of a rumbling in her bones than a sound. She walked down into the centre of the village, near to where the mill steamed and thumped, and stood a while on the hump bridge across the river, watching the way the rain pocked the water. A pair of ducks made their way upstream, paddling laboriously. The banging of an engine got louder, and she watched a lanky lad, his hat pulled down low over his eyes and his face maudlin, drive a load of half-stuff across from Rag Mill in the little motorised wagon. Then, bracing up, Irene took the path that ran right through the mill. She passed the old farmhouse where Alistair – and where the girl, Sarah – had been killed, and had to force herself to look at it. The painted wooden door, closed now with the rain, a light on inside, and George Turner at his desk by a downstairs window, carefully inserting a sheet of paper into the micrometer. The sight of the place still turned her throat dry; she had a powerful urge to be somewhere – anywhere – else. She made herself walk slowly past, and then on through the yard with the towering brick generator house on her right and the beater house on her left, across the bridge and up to Germain's Lane. There she turned back towards the village, because she didn't want to go past the Tanner place. It was getting late, anyway; the thick clouds made it darker, and seem later still.

Past High Bank, the row of three cottages with the shop

at one end, Irene turned off the lane, went through the gate and into the paddock in which the church sat, walled off, all alone. This was the short cut to the farm that Pudding often used, though it was steep and you had to dodge the cowpats. The rain shone on the grass and the ground squelched, and Irene went slowly so as not to slip. She looked over the low wall of the graveyard and saw how the onslaught was ruining Alistair's flowers – stripping off the petals, battering the foliage. She hated to think how upset Nancy would be at the sight, so even though she was getting cold, and the rain had found a way through the seams of her mackintosh at the shoulders, she went in to see what tidying she could do. She had her face down, at the graveside, and was wondering where to start when she became aware of someone approaching, and looked up with a gasp. A tall, grey-headed man was coming towards her from around the church, and with a thrill of fear she recognised Tanner. He didn't seem steady on his feet, and she wondered if he'd seen her – or would see her before he barrelled into her. There was nowhere for her to hide from him, and she stood rooted to the spot until he was within two strides of her and still hadn't slowed. Then, inadvertently, she cried out in alarm.

At the sound of her voice Tanner threw up his hands and gripped her by the arms, peering through the rain. He had no hat and water slicked his grizzled hair to his head; she could smell alcohol on his breath, hot and sour. His eyes were red and swollen, so that it looked as though he'd been crying, but it was hard to tell with his face wet from the rain, and drunk as he was.

'You're his wife, ain't you? Came to the house with the doctor's girl before,' he said, roughly. Too alarmed to speak, Irene merely nodded. 'You found it. You found that doll up there.' He pointed up to the farm behind them, and Irene nodded again. Tanner's face creased peculiarly, and Irene was puzzled for a moment until she realised that he *was* crying, and that he was furious with himself for letting her see. 'It didn't ought to have happened,' he said. Swallowing, Irene found her voice.

'What didn't?' she said. Tanner gave her a shake.

'None of it!' he said. He shook his head like he was trying to clear it, his fingers still gouging into Irene's arms.

'Please let go of me,' she said, feebly. Her heart was hammering but at the same time she felt no specific threat to herself from Tanner – only that he was unravelled with drink and what appeared to be grief, and she had no idea what he might do next.

'I was glad of it, at first; now part of me wishes you'd never found it. For what good does it do? What good is any of it?' He shook her again, and the eyes that glared into hers were raw, and half mad.

'I . . . I don't know.' She gathered her wits. 'What . . . what did the doll mean to you?' she said, but Tanner ignored the question.

'What'll happen to the lad?' he demanded instead.

'Who? What lad?'

'The simpleton they've fingered. Will he swing for it?'

'Donald Cartwright? I . . . I don't know. If he's tried for murder then he'll most likely hang. That's what Pudding's afraid of.' Tanner stared at her for a moment then dropped his hands and pushed past her, stumbling towards the gate and leaving Irene with the hiss of the rain on the grass, and the soughing of her own breath in her ears.

She watched Tanner make his lurching way down the hill and vanish towards Thatch Cottage, and only then did she begin to relax. She had to tell Pudding. She clenched her fists because her fingers were tingling peculiarly. It seemed that her prescient feeling about the doll being important, and somehow the start of things, had been completely right. But there was absolutely nothing she could think of that the Tanners could have held against Alistair – nothing that Nancy knew of, or George Turner; nothing that she'd found in his paperwork; and they had checked Tanner's alibi themselves. She looked down at the smoking chimney of the mill, and knew she'd have to do as Pudding had asked, and look for clues in Alistair's papers there as well. Tanner himself hadn't been the only one employed there, after all – several members of his immediate family worked at the mill as well. Two of his sons, in their late teens or early twenties, had been with him the day she and Pudding had taken the doll to show Ma. Irene had been so fixated upon their father, she hadn't seen what the sons' reactions to it had been. Perhaps there was something else – some other feud or dispute, not related to Tanner's recent laying-off for drunkenness.

She turned away at last, and went around to the side of the church that Tanner had come from. There was usually only one reason a person might be found weeping in a churchyard. There were four gravestones in the narrow space between the wall and the church itself; the names on two of them meant nothing to Irene, and the names on the other two had been obliterated by weathering. Only the year was visible on one – a small stone, plain and leaning forwards towards the turf – and it caught Irene's eye: *1872*. And at the foot of this neglected headstone, a fresh bunch of wildflowers had been laid – blue forget-me-nots. Irene stared, and shivered in the rain, and felt a small, anonymous piece of the puzzle find its place in her mind.

9
Dead Ends

'But that can't be it,' said Pudding, tumbling down from another wave-crest of hope. Pete Dempsey shrugged apologetically. He'd come to the farm in his official capacity, sweating slightly in his tall helmet and fiddling now and then with the strap that cut into his chin.

'I was surprised he even let me look into it, Pud. So at least . . . that's something,' he said, lamely. Pudding stared down at the sheet of paper on which Pete had written a scant summary of the 1872 case, and the hunt for the girl's killer, which concluded: *Though a member or members of the Tanner family were initially suspected and questioned, all had reliable alibis for the time of the murder. No other suspects were identified, and the case remains unsolved.*

'How can that be it, though?' Pudding demanded. 'I mean – there's a summary of her injuries here, and they were just as . . . just as awful as Alistair's. Whoever killed her – and Alistair – is clearly dangerous. But they just . . .' She waved a hand in frustration. 'Didn't even find anybody else to question?'

'Well, just like with Mr Hadleigh, nobody could think of a reason for the killing, and nobody saw anything. Her sweetheart, if he existed, never came forward to identify himself. The shovel that did for her was dropped by her body, and they weren't so good at collecting fingerprints back then. There was something in her . . . in the blood on the floor that they supposed at first to be a footprint, but then decided that it wasn't.'

'Wasn't a footprint?'

'No. So they had nothing to go on, see?' Pete ran a finger under his chinstrap again, rubbing the red welt it left in his skin.

'Oh, just take it off, Pete,' said Pudding. 'I won't tell anybody.' Relieved, Pete took off the helmet and scuffed a hand through his damp hair.

'This heat,' he muttered. 'Makes it hard to think straight, doesn't it?'

'Why did they decide it wasn't a footprint?'

'I don't know, Pudding! It was too small, or something like that. Look, Blackman – I mean, the superintendent – listened to what I had to say, and he read the story in your book, and, well, it went as I thought it would. He let me fetch the old file out of the cellar – mouldy and half eaten-away it is too – and he read that as well. But as far as he's concerned, the only thing connecting the two killings is the description of the first in your book, which was most likely read by the perpetrator of the second.'

'It isn't at *all* likely that Donny read it! Well . . . could I see the actual file?'

'No, 'ee can't, Pudding. And it don't say a thing worth noting but what I 'as put down there,' said Pete, his accent thickening with agitation.

They were standing on the yard outside the cob house, beside a handcart of mucky straw that Pudding had just loaded. She leant on her pitchfork and took a deep breath, trying not to feel defeated.

'Well, then,' she said, but she didn't know well *what*. Every dead end was exhausting, and the effect of them seemed cumulative. 'I shall have to think of something else.'

'Have you spoken to any of the older folk?'

'Yes. None of them knows a thing. They all remember it

though – they remember the girl, Sarah, mostly because she was very pretty, by all accounts. And because they were all scared for a while, thinking there was a killer in their midst – people walked their children to school for a time, and that kind of thing. Old Hilarius was here then, but he just looked at me oddly when I asked him about it, and asked to borrow my murder book again; even though he read it before and didn't seem to like it.' She shrugged. 'But if he knew anything he'd tell me. I know he would.'

'He'd read it before, but he didn't say anything about the similarity between the two murders?' said Pete.

'No,' said Pudding. 'He didn't.' She frowned, thinking of Irene's odd reaction to the groom. She thought about the first time Hilarius had seen the murder book, when she'd left it lying around the tack room – his odd demeanour, and the way he warned her off reading it. She stifled an uneasy feeling about it. 'He probably just didn't think of it, like I didn't. He is ancient, after all.'

'How old is he, anyway?'

'I don't know. Eighty? Maybe even older. I'm not sure I'd have the guts to ask him, and what does it matter, anyway?' Pudding straightened up and handed the sheet of paper back to Pete.

'No, you keep it. I wrote it out for you,' he said.

'But it doesn't say anything remotely useful,' said Pudding. Pete sagged slightly.

'No, I suppose it doesn't. But keep it anyway.' They stood for a while in awkward silence. Behind them, the swallows' nests in the rafters were now empty and quiet; Nancy and the giant farm manager, Mr Lake, walked across to the rickyard, deep in conversation. Pete nodded in their direction.

'Miss Hadleigh's back up and running then?'

'I think she needs to keep busy,' said Pudding. 'To distract herself from how awful it all is.' As she spoke, Pudding was aware of Pete watching her with that infuriating, understanding, sympathetic expression, and she suddenly saw that everybody thought exactly the same of her as well – that she was simply keeping busy, to distract herself. She blushed. 'Well, I'd best get back to work. Thanks for trying, Constable,' she said.

'Righty-ho. Well. I wanted to ask as well, Pudding, whether you might like to . . .' He turned his helmet in his hands. 'Perhaps. Another drink, perhaps, one evening. To discuss . . . everything. Or a walk?' Pudding frowned at him, puzzled.

'Well, have you got anything else to tell me that you haven't told me now?' she said.

'No,' Pete confessed.

'Well then.' Pudding shrugged, laid the pitchfork across the handcart and began wheeling it towards the muck heap. She looked back when she reached it and began forking out the dreck. Pete was still standing where she'd left him, looking down at his feet. Then he put his helmet back on and walked away at the speed of a man with nowhere in particular to go.

❧ ❧

Pudding had already gone home when Irene got back from the rain-sodden churchyard, and dinner had been ready to serve. Nancy had given her a fishy look when she'd suggested going off to find the girl groom at that hour, and then, in the morning, asked Irene to go into Chippenham with her, to visit the pharmacist, the bank and the dressmaker. She made Irene drive the Stanhope along the quieter roads.

'It's no good you always having to be driven, Irene. You're a Hadleigh, and Hadleighs can manage. If you're staying on, you'll need to learn, and it's easy enough,' she said, in that way she had that made it impossible to argue. And it proved fairly easy, in fact, even though Irene had barely got used to being in charge of a horse she was sitting on, let alone one she was only connected to by two lengths of leather rein and a whip. 'Use your voice, like I told you,' Nancy coached. 'Look – see how his ears flick back like that? He's waiting for your next instruction.' The errands took well over an hour, and then they stopped to have coffee at the Bear Hotel before setting off back to Manor Farm, so Irene didn't get a chance to speak to Pudding about what she'd seen and heard before lunch. By then, she knew better than to say anything about it to Nancy.

When lunch was over Irene watched from a window until Nancy had gone out with Lake, and Constable Dempsey had wandered off, disconsolately, and Pudding was finally by herself, shovelling horse manure onto the heap and turning ruddy with the work.

'Pudding! Hello – did Constable Dempsey have anything new?' she called. Pudding stopped shovelling and leant on her fork with two hands, catching her breath.

'No.' She thought for a moment and frowned. 'Or maybe – something he's not saying, perhaps. He keeps suggesting we go for a walk, or a drink,' she said. Irene stared at Pudding for a moment, but her incomprehension was complete.

'Does he really? And . . . you can't think of any other reason he might want to do that?'

'No. Why? What do you think he wants?'

'Well . . . Never mind that for now, perhaps,' said Irene, smiling slightly. 'I have to tell you what happened yesterday.' Pudding came down from the heap to listen, and Irene told her about Tanner, and what he'd said about the doll, and the gravestone from 1872 with fresh flowers on it. 'And then he asked about Donny, and what would happen to him. But he said "the one they've fingered for it". That means he doesn't think Donny did it, don't you think? That the police have just arrested him to solve the case?'

'Does it? Yes, I think you're right!' Pudding gripped Irene's hand in excitement, and Irene tried not to mind how filthy it was. 'He *must* know more about it. The police will *have* to speak to him again – they didn't press him, or his boys, once they'd given their alibis, they just took Donny away and that was that! Well, they'll have to now, won't they? There are still a few days until Donny's hearing – it's not too late, if we hurry!'

'But if Mr Tanner's arrested he'll know it was me that reported on him,' said Irene, alarmed.

'I doubt it.' Pudding shrugged. 'He was blind drunk, you said.'

'Yes, but still. I should hate to get on the wrong side of him.'

'Irene, the truth is *far* more important. And in any case, Tanner might end up in jail himself! Then nobody needs to be scared of him any more.'

'Well, let's not get ahead of ourselves. But isn't it just the queerest thing about the doll? What do you think it could possibly mean?' said Irene.

'It's certainly queer – and just as queer is that you *knew* it was important. I mean, right back when you found it, somehow you knew,' said Pudding.

'But I still don't know *why*,' said Irene, cautiously.

'And the flowers on that grave – he must have put them there. Do you think it was this girl, Sarah, from the first murder?'

'Well, the year is certainly a coincidence, if it isn't. Do you think we could find out?'

'Yes, of course. It'll be in the church register – we'll have to see the vicar about having a look. Do you think Tanner killed her, and is racked with guilt? Do you think he feels guilty about killing Alistair now? And about Donny being arrested?' said Pudding, avidly. She paused, counting under her breath.

'He's old enough. He'd only have been a lad in 1872, but he could have done it!'

'Now – just hold on. No more accusations without good grounds,' said Irene, and Pudding looked chastened. Her need to act seemed to fizz around her like a static charge.

'All right, but we *have* to talk to the police again – you have to go and tell Superintendent Blackman, Irene,' she said.

'Me? Can't you?' said Irene. She'd found the policeman strange, and difficult, even before Pudding had accused her of colluding in Alistair's death.

'He'll need to hear it from you – first-hand, you see. And, anyway . . . I don't think he'd listen to anything else I had to say.' Pudding took a deep breath and hitched up her britches. 'He just thinks I'm a nuisance. And I have to go and talk to Tanner.'

'Pudding, no – leave it to the police!'

'But he might disappear before the police get to him – he's done that before, when something's happened around here that they might want to talk to him about. No – I need to go and catch him unawares.' Pudding swallowed, not sounding half as sure as her words, and Irene saw how nervous she was.

'I really don't think it's a good idea. Just . . . wait a bit. Wait until we find out something else . . . why don't you come with me to the mill, to look through Alistair's papers there?'

'Haven't you done that yet?'

'I haven't had the chance. And I don't want Nancy to know – she wouldn't approve one bit.'

'All right. But first let me run after Pete, and get him to take you in to see Blackman.'

Superintendent Blackman's eyes, behind his round glasses, were as dark and inscrutable as Irene remembered them. He sat her down in front of his desk with a few stiff words, offered her refreshment politely enough, then sat watching her with his hands loosely grasping the arms of his chair, all the while making her feel like a guilty schoolgirl. Perhaps it was the way he never smiled, and hardly blinked.

'I understand you have something you'd like to tell me,' he said, his eyes never leaving her face, and Irene wondered if he thought she'd come to confess to something. She cleared her throat.

'Yes. I think . . . I think Miss Cartwright might be on to something, linking my husband's murder to the earlier murder she's uncovered, in 1872,' she said, as calmly as she could.

'The investigation into your husband's death is closed, Mrs Hadleigh.'

'Well, perhaps it oughtn't to be,' she said. Superintendent Blackman continued to stare, but Irene thought she detected a subtle interest kindling in him. He didn't speak, so she hurried on, and described everything in the graveyard, just as before. When she got to the end, and could think of nothing to add, Blackman still hadn't moved or said a word. Irene waited, uncomfortably. When Blackman suddenly reached forward and picked up his pen, she jumped.

'This would be Mr Tanner of Thatch Cottage, Germain's Lane, Slaughterford?' he said.

'Well, yes. You must know him? I thought the police—' Irene cut herself off.

'It never pays to make assumptions, Mrs Hadleigh. From what I've learned, a good deal of the Tanners' reputation is based upon rumour and . . . grudge. A community needs villains – scapegoats, if you will.' He gave her that blankly piercing look again, and Irene's pulse picked up.

'I only came to relay a conversation I thought might be relevant. For no other reason than that . . . well, it might be relevant,' she said, trying not to sound rattled.

'Indeed,' said the policeman, adding something to the notes

on his jotter. 'But perhaps Donald Cartwright being cleared of suspicion would also clear suspicion from other people of his acquaintance.'

'If he didn't do it, oughtn't he to be cleared?'

'Indeed. However, I see absolutely no reason to suppose that he didn't do it, Mrs Hadleigh,' said Blackman. 'Tell me more about this doll, if you would. Where exactly was it found, and how did Mr Tanner come to know of it?' So Irene told him in as much detail as she could, and when she finished Blackman fell still, pen poised, staring into space. After a while, he looked up as though a little surprised to find her still there. 'Was there anything else, Mrs Hadleigh?' he said.

'No,' said Irene. 'Well, no.' She got up, and Blackman rose as well, though he made no move to come out from behind his desk. 'So, will you look into it? Will you talk to Tanner – Mr Tanner?' she asked, knowing that she'd face the same questions from Pudding. Superintendent Blackman seemed surprised to be asked.

'If I deem it necessary, Mrs Hadleigh,' he said.

'Oh,' she said, defeated. 'Good day, then.' She let herself out.

Pudding was as let down by the superintendent's reaction as Irene, who was getting used to seeing the girl's shoulders drop and her chest deflate as all the fight went out of her, just for that moment.

'It's like he doesn't *want* it to be anyone but Donny,' she said, heavily.

'I know.' Pudding looked in need of contact – a hug, or a reassuring squeeze of her arm, at least. Other people did such things so easily, so naturally. Irene was still wondering the best way to go about it when Pudding picked herself up yet again.

'Well. Never mind. We've done all we can do with the police, and it looks like we'll have to carry on without their help.' It was lunchtime, and they were sitting at the table at Spring Cottage as Ruth cleared away the plates. Louise Cartwright was sitting with them, but in that peculiar way of hers she was simultaneously *not* with them. She turned to watch whoever was speaking with a look of benign incomprehension, as though Pudding and Irene were children, talking of a game she knew nothing about. She smiled whenever Irene looked across at her, and Irene smiled back, having all the while the gnawing feeling that she was being horribly rude. From the sink, Ruth tutted her tongue.

'First time in history the coppers *don't* want to think some rotten deed was done by a Tanner, and sure enough they couldn't have picked a worse time,' she said, grimly.

'The superintendent said he thinks their reputation is based mostly upon sour grapes,' said Irene.

'Don't you believe it, Mrs Hadleigh. That Blackman's new 'round here – down from Hereford, I heard; he don't *know*. Maybe they ain't each last one of them bad to the bone, but most of them are. And as for Tanner himself . . .' She shook her head. 'God knows, I shouldn't like to meet him in the lane on a dark night.'

'Well,' said Pudding, to Irene. 'Shall we go down to the mill?' They looked at one another, and Irene knew that the same nightmare images as were in her own mind were in Pudding's too. Alistair, lying dead with Nancy weeping at his side; his blood on the floor; his wounds so obscene, so darkly black and red and grey. The thought of going into the old farmhouse still filled her with dread.

'I suppose we must,' she said, and Pudding nodded.

The door to the offices was open, propped with a chunk of stone. Irene caught Pudding glancing across into the generator room, and remembered that her brother was wont to wander in there, to watch the machinery. When Pudding turned away, it was with the wince of someone being forcibly reminded of a loss. A look of such intense sorrow passed over her face that it brought a lump to Irene's throat.

'Ready?' said Irene, swallowing. Pudding looked up at her with haunted eyes; it was the first time she'd returned to the mill since the murder. The bustle and thump of the machines filled the silence between them. Inside, they heard George Turner at his desk, clearing his throat. Without another word Irene knocked lightly, stepped into the comparative darkness within, and into another moment of panic almost as bad as the time before. The spectre of the Alistair-doll reared up in front of her, and she stepped backwards directly onto Pudding's toe.

'Ow!' Pudding cried, staggering slightly to get out of the way. Irene turned, and the sight of Pudding's freckled face, her clear blue eyes and stubborn hair was so familiar, and so comforting, that her panic lost its grip at once.

'Sorry,' she said. 'I just . . . I thought for a moment . . .'

'It's all right,' said Pudding. 'Nothing's broken – you weigh almost nothing. You should hear me yell when Baron stands on my toe.'

'Ladies,' said George Turner, who'd got to his feet. 'How may I be of service?'

'Hello again, Mr Turner.' Irene's nerves thinned her voice. 'How do you do?'

'Passably well, thank you, and it's kind of you to ask, Mrs Hadleigh. All our thoughts here at the mill continue to be with you.'

'Yes,' said Irene. 'Thank you. And Mrs Turner?'

'I believe we have seen an improvement of late, thank you.' George smiled kindly and then stood, waiting, his hands behind his back. Pudding gave Irene a nudge.

'I was . . . we were . . . just going up to my husband's office.

To see . . . well,' she said, floundering, but George merely nodded.

'Of course, Mrs Hadleigh. You'll find the door unlocked. Is there anything I can fetch for you?'

'No, thank you.' With a shiver, Irene walked across the place where Alistair had died, and took the stairs with Pudding at her heels. The office junior watched, bored, from behind his cramped desk at the far end of the room.

Sunlight streamed benignly onto Alistair's leather-topped desk, where there wasn't a single speck of dust. Nor was there a speck on his bookshelves, which were full of files, ledgers and books about paper-making; nor on the elm floorboards that showed around the fancy crimson rug; nor on the brass fender around the fireplace, swept clean for summer.

'Somebody must still be coming in here and cleaning,' said Irene, and Pudding nodded.

'Ready for you to come in and . . . er . . . do business, I suppose,' said Pudding. Irene blinked. 'You own all this now, don't forget.' Pudding went to the window and pointed out at the array of buildings, the stores and workings, the busy employees. 'All of this is yours. Crumbs, that must feel strange. Does it?'

'Stranger than I can tell you,' said Irene. It didn't feel at all real to her.

'Look at it all,' Pudding breathed, running her eyes along the shelved files, all neatly labelled and in order. 'We've quite a task.'

'Surely . . . you can't mean for us to look through *everything*?' said Irene, incredulously.

'Well . . . why else are we here?' said Pudding. 'We don't know what we're looking for, that's the problem.' Irene took a deep breath and let it out slowly.

'We mustn't make a mess,' she said. 'We must leave it all

just as we find it.' She didn't know why that was important, just that it was. She sat down in the captain's chair and ran her hands along the edge of the desk, worn smooth by being leant against and polished, over and over again. The leather top had been warmed by the sun, and Irene spread her hands on it, seeing how pale and frail her fingers looked against the bottle green. She felt, again, that she didn't belong where she was, so could achieve nothing, but this time she fought back against it. She could get justice for Alistair, even if she didn't belong.

'Are you all right?' Pudding asked, and Irene nodded, pulling herself together.

'Yes. Well. Best to make a start, I suppose.'

She opened the top drawer of the desk, and found bottles of ink, pens, pencils, a sharpening knife, paperclips and a paperweight fashioned from a chunk of quartz. The drawer had a familiar, schoolroom smell but no papers at all, so she moved on to the next, and so the afternoon ticked by. Now and then they heard George Turner talking to his junior, or to somebody who'd come into the farmhouse; now and then the foreman went out on some errand elsewhere in the mill. Other voices, those of workers, echoed in the yard as the shift changed, but other than that, and the constant noise of the machines, the office was a peaceful, almost drowsy place. Even Pudding, devoted to the task, sighed each time she stood, returned a file to the shelf and fetched another. At five George Turner came up to them with a tray of tea, his face registering mild concern.

'If there's anything you'd like to learn, Mrs Hadleigh, I'd be more than happy to oblige you, if it's within my capacity to do so.'

'No, thank you, Mr Turner. That is, not unless . . .' Irene considered her next question. 'I'm sure the police have already spoken to you, Mr Turner, only I'd be most interested to know if there was anyone here at the mill, or anyone my husband had dealings with, who you think might have held a grievance towards him.' Irene held her nerve, and the manager's eye, as she waited for his reply. She saw his discomfort and confusion.

'Well, now,' he said, uneasily, flicking his eyes towards Pudding, who coloured. 'Surely . . . surely there's little question as to what happened to your husband, Mrs Hadleigh?'

'But I should like to know, all the same,' said Irene.

'As I told the authorities, everyone who'd ever had business with Mr Hadleigh knew him to be an honest man, fair and straight in all his dealings. No business acquaintance of his can have had a grudge against him. Not even Mr Tanner.'

'What about the other Tanner boys working at the mill?' said Irene. 'Have they . . . been in any trouble?'

'Trouble? No, not at all. Young Elijah is a firebrand – he takes after his father, and no mistake. He sent some black looks my way when Tanner was laid off again, and now it seems he's taken himself off somewhere else. But for the most part they need the work, and they work hard. And they would be more likely to be angry with me than with Mr Hadleigh.'

'Why's that?' said Pudding.

'I counselled that Mr Tanner ought to be let go for good this time, but your husband was always very tolerant towards the family. Too generous by half, I always thought. But Mr Hadleigh said if he didn't give them a chance, what chance would they have?'

'Yes,' said Irene. 'That sounds like Alistair.'

'But might Mr Hadleigh have had an argument with any of them, and not told you?' asked Pudding.

'No.' George shook his head. 'I'd have been informed.' Irene nodded as she took this in. She trusted her instinctive fear of Tanner; the memory of him coming at her in the churchyard made her shiver, as did thoughts of her visit to

Thatch Cottage. But if he'd had cause to hurt Alistair, then the reason for it was something far older, and far darker, than an argument over a job.

Irene was suddenly completely certain that they were wasting their time looking through invoices and receipts. She felt a flare of impatience, and the maddening sensation that she *knew* the answer, but couldn't see it, and was about to suggest that they called a halt when she was cut off by the sudden sound of quick, determined footsteps on the stairs. Nancy strode into the room, glaring as though they'd all been caught in her bedroom, going through her smalls.

'I heard your voices – what on earth is going on?' she demanded, and before anyone could answer, added: 'This is Alistair's office! *Nobody* should be in here.'

'Nancy, Pudding and I were just looking for some . . . clue, I suppose. Something that might help to explain what's happened,' said Irene.

'If you'll excuse me, ladies,' said George Turner, uncomfortably. 'I've some matters to attend to.' Nancy didn't even look at the foreman. Her eyes were fixed on Irene and Pudding, and blazing.

'There is no question about what happened.' Her voice was low and trembling. 'I simply do *not* understand why you must keep on . . . muckraking in this way! You're only making things worse.'

'They can't get worse,' said Pudding, meekly, but Nancy's glare silenced her.

'Shame on you, Irene,' said Nancy. 'I thought you were starting to show some sense, on the whole. But now I find you recklessly encouraging the dratted girl in her fantasies – you're only making it worse for her in the long run, you know. Pudding's a child and doesn't know any better, but you ought.'

'Pudding isn't a child,' said Irene, her pulse racing. As she said it, she realised how true it was. However naive Pudding was in some ways, the responsibilities she'd been forced to shoulder had pushed her beyond her years. 'And I don't think she's a fantasist either.'

'Really? And what about when she pointed the finger at *you* for Alistair's death?'

'Well, never mind that. I . . . I have had an encounter with Mr Tanner myself, which has made me think that perhaps—'

'No.' Nancy cut her off, stonily. 'I don't want to hear any more. I won't hear any more. Every time you bring it up it's like you're . . . you're disturbing Alistair's grave! It's obscene! I want you out of here, the pair of you. You've no business going through my brother's things like a . . . a pair of *thieves*. Go on – I insist that you leave.'

'Sorry, Miss H,' Pudding mumbled, making for the door with her eyes down, but Irene put out a hand to stop her.

'Wait, Pudding. Nancy . . . I'm sorry, but we're not finished yet. These are my husband's things, not your brother's – or your nephew's – any more. I know this is hard for you – that seeing anyone in here must be very hard for you. I promise we will leave everything just as we found it.' As she spoke, Irene began to feel calmer, more resolved.

'You will leave,' said Nancy, and she and Irene stared at one another for a long time.

'We will, when we've finished,' said Irene. The air between them seemed to freeze, and a second later Nancy turned on her heel and left them there, and Pudding exhaled massively.

'Heavens, Irene,' she said, 'I've never seen anyone face down Miss Hadleigh like that before!'

'I'm not surprised,' said Irene. She perched on the edge of the desk for a moment, pressing her fingers to her lips. 'I hope I don't live to regret it.'

*

Clemmie slunk back into Weavern Farm like an errant cat – silently, after dark. She curled up under the blankets next to Josie and went straight to sleep, feeling that while much was still wrong, much was also right again. In the morning, Josie gave a little gasp when she opened her eyes and found her sister there, but then she smiled.

'You're back,' she said. When Mary and Liz woke up they clustered around her, peering closely, pinching her and pulling detritus from her hair.

'Have you been living under a hedge? Smells like it.'

'You gave us quite the jolt. It wasn't the same without you, Clemmie,' said Mary. 'Where on earth have you been?' But Clemmie couldn't tell them about the long hours of walking, lost, through Swindon's confusing streets, and the feeling of starting to fly as she left the city behind her; or that she'd hitched two rides – the first with a farmer in his high-wheeled gig, who'd been travelling back from burying his brother. She'd had to run away when he'd turned in at a field gate and made a grab for her. The second was with an elderly couple who spoke no more than she did, and only nodded for her to climb into the back of their small wagon, which carried a load of old furniture – a carver chair, a commode, a washstand with a cracked top, all mildewed. Clemmie had slept for hours with her head on a rat-chewed prayer stool. They'd brought her as far as Marshfield, and she'd walked the last stretch, tired and afraid but driven forwards, pulled towards home. 'Oh, why can't you talk?' said Mary, but she didn't expect an answer. 'Ma! Clemmie's back!' she shouted down from the top of the stairs, and they all heard Rose's oath from below.

She was berated and hugged in equal measure by her mother; scowled at and ignored by her father; questioned and cajoled by her sisters. Clemmie paced and gestured and even tried some sounds – anything to prompt them to start asking the right questions, but they did not. Only Josie got close, as they were milking.

'Clemmie – did you go off with your sweetheart? With the baby's father?' she asked, and Clemmie nodded eagerly, and waited for her to ask more. 'But where is he now? You've left him?' Clemmie nodded and then shook her head. 'Yes *and* no, Clem?' Josie frowned. 'But how can that be?' She thought for a moment, chewing her lip. 'Is he coming here, Clem? Is that it? Will you be wed?' Josie's face lit up, but Clemmie only frowned. She couldn't say yes, not when she knew Eli would never return to live in Slaughterford while his father remained. She *had* to make her plan to get rid of Isaac Tanner work, and she couldn't let herself think about what Eli might be thinking, or feeling. Abandoned, discarded; cheated out of his new life, his new family, his fresh start. He would be in so much pain. Such thoughts made her weak with remorse, and something else, nearly unbearable – something close to terror. She sent out thoughts to him, and longed for him to hear them, and know the contents of her heart. At times, her projected thoughts made such a loud roar in her head that she was sure he must hear them; at others, she knew he could not and never would. She wondered if he would think she planned to turn him in for what happened at the mill. She wondered if he would come to find her, and gut instinct said that he would. She wondered if he was on his way, if he was getting closer, if he was almost at her heels. And one thing that was clear, once a few days had passed, was that however much she could show them that she needed to tell them something, her family were never, ever going to ask her the right questions. She would have to say out loud what she needed to say.

Her need to speak kept her awake all night, and in the daytime made her wayward and tearful. Her mother, Rose, came to check on her frequently, appearing wherever Clemmie was with a worried expression that eased when she saw her daughter, and coming out with some excuse.

'Oh, there you are. I was just wondering if you'd . . . seen the filleting knife?' At which Clemmie would rise from whatever she was at and take her mother to where the filleting knife lay, in the drawer where it was always kept. Whenever she was alone, she began to practise. She needed as short a sentence as possible, with words as short as possible, and she needed to decide who to say them to. She thought she ought to say them directly to one of the policemen who'd been around the mill in the first days afterwards, but they'd all gone now and she didn't know how to find them. There was the police constable in Ford, and the one in Corsham, but they were both strangers, in any case, and that would only make it worse. She thought about Nancy Hadleigh, who was the kind of person who would get something done in Alistair's absence, but then she thought of Nancy's grief, and her anger, and her misunderstanding, and knew she couldn't approach her. There were her mother and father, of course, and there was Mrs Tanner, Eli's mother – but afterwards, when they went to the police, it might just seem like some scheme cooked up between them to point the finger at Isaac. Then there was the foreman at the mill with the foxy whiskers, who had always been kind and treated Clemmie as a whole person. He might be the one. But she needed the right words to say, and she needed to be able to say them.

If she could say *Isaac* then she wouldn't need to say *Tanner*, which was good, since the letter *t* was one of the worst with which to start a word; if she could say *rob* then she wouldn't have to say *attacked*; if she could say *guilty*, *revenge*, *money* and *I heard*, then she wouldn't have to say *Eli*, *innocent* or *threatened*. The phrase she came up with, though the thought of actually having to say it was exhausting before she'd even started, was: *I heard Isaac say he would rob Mr Hadleigh; he is the guilty one*. If she was believed then more questions would be asked, and she could answer yes or no; then surely the police would have to take Isaac away, and then perhaps the Tanner clan would have the courage to speak out against him, and keep him locked up for good. And word would get out, and Eli would come back, and when he knew what she had done he would understand her whole plan, and then they would wed, and she would bring him to Weavern Farm and they would not be turned away. Clemmie shut her eyes and thought through this chain of events so many times that it started to seem less unlikely, less fly-away, and began to seem like it could actually happen. Like it *would* happen – because it had to. Clemmie could think of no alternative, since she could not live where Eli was, and he could not live where she was. And there was the chance – just a slight chance, that she didn't dwell upon – that he would not let her live apart from him. She began to practise the words, and she started with *Isaac*.

❧ ❧

Superintendent Blackman was driven up to Spring Cottage in the black car by a young constable; the car's roof was folded back so that both men had a fair dusting from the lanes. Blackman was polishing the lenses of his spectacles when Pudding rushed out to find out what was new, and to invite him inside, but Blackman held up a hand to forestall her. He took off his hat and patted the dust from it as Dr Cartwright came out to stand beside his daughter.

'Thank you, Miss Cartwright, Dr Cartwright, but I'll not be stopping long enough for tea today,' he said. 'I only wanted to let you know that I have interviewed Mr Tanner again, and not only has he a firm alibi for the time of Mr Hadleigh's death, he has no reason at all to have harmed him.'

'But what about the doll, and the grave where he laid the flowers – the one with the year 1872 on it, the year of the first murder?'

'Mr Tanner denies being the one who laid those flowers; he claims not to know to whom that particular grave might belong, and he looked mystified when I mentioned the doll Mrs Hadleigh found at Manor Farm. And given that there is not a scrap of evidence—'

'He's lying!'

'And given that there is not a scrap of evidence that he was involved, please, let that be an end to it, Miss Cartwright. I understand you will be disappointed at the termination of this new line of enquiry, but I beg you not to seek a fresh one. Make no more accusations, Miss Cartwright.'

'Pudding?' said Dr Cartwright. 'What new line of enquiry is this?'

'But . . . what about all the things he said to Irene, in the churchyard?' said Pudding to Blackman, ignoring her father. 'He's lying about the grave – I just have to find out who's buried there. There has to be a connection – Tanner is old enough to have killed them both. It *has* to be him!' Pudding felt breathless with the need to be heard, to be believed. She felt it all slipping away from her – the chance that she could bring Donny home, and the strength that had come with that. Without it, she didn't know what she would do. How she would carry on. 'The Tanners are thieves and liars and killers! Everybody knows that!'

'Pudding, that's enough,' said the doctor firmly, putting his hand on her shoulder. Frustration filled her eyes with tears, but she was sick of crying.

'Casting a wide net of aspersions won't help your brother, Miss Cartwright,' said Blackman. 'I've already spent more time following up your theories than I ought to have.'

'Well, what *will* help Donny?' Pudding demanded. The superintendent looked at her gravely.

'Addressing himself to his conscience, as best he can, and remaining calm tomorrow, in front of the magistrates,' he said. 'I've come to talk to you in person, Miss Cartwright, to tell you that it's time to let things stand. The investigation is closed.' He put his hat back on and turned to climb back into the car.

'It's not closed,' Pudding murmured, staring at Blackman as his constable inched the car forwards and began, jerkily, to turn it around. At the last moment, Blackman opened his mouth as though he might say something else, but in the end he didn't. Pudding wondered if he looked as wholly convinced as his words sounded, but then, that might just have been wishful thinking, and wishful thinking had yet to get her anywhere.

The car chugged away and left a cloud of dust that the low sun turned golden. The first mad green of summer had passed, Pudding realised; it was the tenth of August and the land was drying out, ripening, going over. Pudding put up her hand to shield her eyes, squinting as the breeze swirled the dust around her and her father. They both stood where they were until the sound of the car's engine had completely disappeared, and only the tinkling of the spring into its trough remained. With no patients to see, Dr Cartwright didn't seem to know what to do with himself. And if she had no leads to chase, then Pudding didn't know what to do with *her*self, either. A black and white cat appeared from nowhere and wound around her shins, but when she reached down to stroke it, it dodged away. Laughter drifted up from the potato field behind the mill, where youngsters were picking the tubers from the turned dark furrows.

'Well,' said Dr Cartwright. 'Come along inside, Pudding, and let's think about some supper, shall we?'

'I'm not terribly hungry, Dad.'

'No. Well. Nevertheless, you must eat. We've a big day

tomorrow.' Pudding looked at her father and he gave her a sad smile. He didn't need to say it might be a terrible day; one of the worst. The day of Donny's hearing in Devizes.

'I really didn't think it would come to this, Dad,' she said. 'I really thought I'd find out who truly killed Alistair, and that tomorrow they'd let Donny come home.'

'They may yet; they may yet. I know you've done your best. We all know you've done your best.' He took his watch out of its pocket and buffed the surface against his waistcoat, peering down at it. 'Five o'clock,' he said, though Pudding hadn't asked. 'Some tea, at least,' he said, absently. 'I'm sure your mother would love a cup.' He patted her shoulder again before going inside, and Pudding realised that he had given up completely. Given up on the idea that Donny would ever be released. She stood a while in his absence, fighting against the similar death of her own hopes. Without them, the world was a bleak and empty place.

Louise Cartwright insisted on coming with them to Devizes the following day, and wouldn't be persuaded otherwise. Pudding and her father exchanged a long look. The thought of her confusion when they got to the New Bridewell and she saw Donny with his hands cuffed and his head stitched, in his prison clothes and as pale as he'd become, was awful. But in the end they couldn't refuse her.

'Tell me a good reason why I oughtn't to see my son?' she said, quite firmly, and neither of them could.

'I'll come too,' said Ruth, frowning. 'I needn't come inside, but I can wait in case you need ... any help with anything.'

'Thank you, Ruth,' said Dr Cartwright. Pudding put on her smartest clothes, with the nagging feeling that it somehow might help Donny's case. She wore a sky-blue skirt that came to the middle of her calves, and a white voile blouse embroidered with dobby spots. Her mother usually watched her like a hawk when she wore it, just waiting for her to spill something down it, or lean against something grubby. But the triumph of arriving in Devizes still pristine, after a bus ride to Chippenham and two trains, was very much muted. Louise smiled politely at the prison guards as they were led through to the sad, cold room where visits were permitted, but none of the guards smiled back. They sat themselves down on one side of a long, unadorned table, and Donny was brought in to them, looking hollow, hunched and vacant.

'Oh,' said Louise, her eyes fearful. Pudding took her hand and squeezed it tight. Pudding had seen Donny every week of his month-long incarceration, and his steady decline had been obvious each time. To Louise, seeing him for the first time since his arrest, the change was clearly shocking. He was so much thinner, and his skin had a yellowish pallor; a sore on his lip was crusted and weeping; the bruising around his head wound had deepened to an alarming crimson; but worst of all was the look of lost exhaustion in his eyes. 'Oh, my boy,' she said. 'What's happened? What's happened to him?' she demanded of her husband.

'There, there, my dear. I am sure they're looking after him. He took a bit of a knock on the head, but he was seen by a doctor. It's really only the want of a bit of sunshine and a few home comforts that ails him.' The doctor didn't sound at all convincing.

'Hello, Mum, Dad. Hello, Puddy,' said Donny, looking at each of them in turn.

'Hello, Donny,' said Pudding, reaching for his hand and smiling.

'Oh!' said Louise, and started to cry.

'I should like to come home now,' said Donny, and Pudding did her level best not to start crying too.

They were only allowed to sit with him for twenty minutes, and in that time Dr Cartwright did his best to explain to Donny what was going to happen during the hearing, even though the lawyer had already done so. Donny just nodded now and then, when prompted, and didn't seem interested. He looked like half the person he had been before, and that person had been only half of the one who'd gone off to the war. Pudding didn't like to think how much more halving her brother could survive. She felt numb, and a kind of sickness crept up on her, which thickened her throat and made it hard to talk. It felt like her heart was struggling to beat, and when she followed her parents out of the prison and over to the courthouse to wait in the public gallery, she felt as though half of her had gone missing as well. Louise Cartwright turned glassy and faint, and Ruth went with her to catch an earlier train home.

'You go too, Pudding. You look done in, and there's no need for you to stay – Donny will see that I'm here, and he'll know you—'

'I'm staying, Dad,' she said. Dr Cartwright nodded wanly, and pushed his spectacles up his nose.

'We must prepare ourselves to be stalwart in the face of . . . of fear and distress, Pudding,' he said. Pudding didn't think she could, and didn't like to lie, but she nodded, for his sake. And then Donny's case was called, and they brought him in and he confirmed his name and address, with some prompting, and a thudding in Pudding's ears meant she could hardly hear him.

Donny pleaded not guilty to wilful murder, and not guilty to manslaughter on the grounds of diminished responsibility. The prosecution lawyer spoke, and none of their witness statements were contested by the defence. The defence lawyer spoke last, and asked Donny to describe what he had seen and done on the morning of Alistair's death, but since Donny was better at answering exactly what he was asked than he was at expanding or volunteering information, he didn't say a great deal, and seemed uncooperative. More uncontested statements, mostly about Donny's good character and his head injuries, were submitted, and the magistrate, who had a face like a rook's – all beak and bright eyes – sifted through them. And then he expressed a heavy heart, given Donny's service in the war, and sent him to stand trial before the crown at the next Wiltshire assizes, for the crime of wilful murder. Due to the nature of the crime, and to continued incidences of violence whilst he had been in custody, no bail was set. And Pudding was entirely powerless to do anything about it.

Afterwards, Pudding and the doctor stood on the platform in silence, waiting for their train back to Chippenham. The breeze rolled and rustled an old news-sheet along the tracks; pink and white fleabane crowded the rails, and sparrows hopped around, picking up crumbs from people's sandwiches. One of Pudding's earliest memories was of being on a train, when she was no more than four. She didn't remember where they'd been going – the destination wasn't half as exciting as the ride there. She remembered Donny, twelve or thirteen, leaning out of the window as they rounded each bend, trying to catch a glimpse of the engine in full steam, then turning back to them with smuts in his teeth, his hair on end and a grin from ear to ear. Pudding took a sharp breath and tried to banish the image, which only seemed to make it worse. Wherever she stood, she couldn't seem to get away from a cloud of pipe smoke wafting from an elderly man along the platform. It stung her eyes and made her throat itch, and was as distracting as a cloud of midges.

'Please stop fidgeting, Pudding,' her father snapped, shooting her a harried look before returning to staring at the ground.

'What should we do next, Dad?'

'Do?' The doctor looked at her as though she wasn't speaking sense. '*Do?* There's nothing more we can do, Pudding.'

'But oughtn't we to . . . appeal against there being no bail, at least? Donny should be at home until the trial, where we can look after him. The other men might pick on him . . . or goad him into doing something. I've got until the trial to find out a way to save him, so—'

'Enough, Pudding!' Her father's sudden shout stunned Pudding to silence. She couldn't remember when she had last heard him raise his voice. The man with the pipe, and several others, glanced in their direction. 'Just . . . stop it. Please. Stop talking about "finding something out to save Donny". Stop trying to think of ways to bring him home.'

'But . . . you mustn't give up, Dad!' Pudding's throat ached as she spoke, and her voice came out strangled. 'You mustn't. Donny's innocent, and I—'

'No, Pudding! No!' Dr Cartwright shook his head, and wouldn't look at her.

'You can't mean to say . . . that you think Donny did it? You can't mean that.'

'Donald is my son.' The doctor spoke so quietly that Pudding could hardly hear him. 'He's my son, and God knows that I love him. But he . . . the war changed him. And now he has done this thing. And it can't be undone, Pudding. However much we wish it.'

'No, Dad – Donny didn't do it. I *know* he didn't – Irene knows it too!'

'Who?'

'I'm not going to give up. I'm going to find a way to bring him home, Dad, I promise.'

'No, you *won't*, Pudding! You must stop this! It . . . it does no good. It does no good at all! We have . . . we have lost your brother. However hard it is, it is the truth. And we must strive to . . . We must endeavour to . . .' The doctor trailed into silence, shaking his head. He sounded faint, and far away.

The train squealed and hissed to a halt beside them. Dr Cartwright climbed aboard without ushering Pudding ahead of him, or waiting to see if she were following. As though he'd forgotten she was even there. For a second, Pudding imagined it was true. She imagined that Donny had killed Alistair, and would now be hanged for it. It turned her cold all over, and exhausted. It felt like being lost in the middle of the night, all alone, and knowing that she could never go home. She shuddered, and refused to think it, silently reiterating her belief in Donny's innocence. But the lost feeling wouldn't go, because they were going to hang him anyway.

❧ ☙

A letter from Fin. Irene stared at it on the breakfast table and couldn't decide what to feel. After so many weeks, after so much had happened, and after he had told her to stop writing, he had written to her. Nancy cleared her throat as Irene came into the room, dabbed the corners of her mouth with her napkin and got up to go without a word.

'Nancy, please,' said Irene. 'Can't we declare peace? I'm sorry if I . . . ran roughshod over you. But it was important.'

'Was it indeed.' Nancy's face was as immovable as ever, but there were shadows under her eyes and the whites were shot pink with blood.

'It was. Won't you forgive us for going in there?'

'It's yours now, of course. All of it's yours. You may go where you wish, and do just as you please, without my blessing.'

'But I don't plan to do just as I please at all. Really, I don't. It's only fair that Pudding be allowed to . . . to try all she can to reach a peace with what's happened. And to help her brother.

Don't you agree?' As she spoke, Nancy's spine softened just a fraction. It did every time Irene reminded her that whatever Pudding did, she did for her brother.

'I suppose so,' she said, with a sigh. 'You and Pudding are certainly thick these days. But a young friend is better than none, I suppose. Aren't you going to open that?'

'Yes,' said Irene. 'Though I can't for the life of me think what he might have to say.'

'Well, if you're still in one piece afterwards, come and find me in the top skillings, if you'd like. The new curly-coat pigs are arriving.' Nancy took a final sip of her coffee before leaving the room.

Irene drank some coffee and ate some toast and marmalade, still unsure how she was feeling. Then she took a deep breath and opened Fin's letter. It wasn't long – his spidery writing barely filled one side of the paper. He had only recently heard about Alistair, and sent his condolences. They had been out of the country. He was now back in London on business, though Serena had stayed away. He asked if she was in town. He asked if she wanted to meet with him, discreetly, of course, perhaps at a location between London and the west – at a hotel, for example. Irene read it twice more until she was quite sure he was suggesting what she thought he was suggesting. The hurt of it was there, and her love for him as well – still there, beneath the surface, like a bruise. But that was it, she realised – it was like a bruise now, deeper beneath the surface and far less like an open wound or a broken bone. The pain was no longer crippling. She remembered standing beneath the station clock at King's Cross; she remembered her clothes blowing down the street after Serena had thrown her case from the steps – Finlay in the house behind her, overhearing the scene, doing nothing. She thought about replying to his letter and using the word Pudding had used – *worm*. But in the end she simply tore it into two neat halves, tucked it into the bucket of kindling by the fire, and went out after Nancy.

❧ ❧

Clemmie risked a visit to Mrs Tanner. For two hours, she waited in the shade of the Friends' chapel halfway up the hill, sitting on a mossy gravestone, watching Thatch Cottage to be sure Isaac Tanner was not inside. Only when she was certain did she pick her way down to the yard. There were raised voices from within; both were female, but since Clemmie didn't recognise one of them, she lurked beneath a window and waited.

'Well, it's good and ruined now, isn't it? By my reckoning, you owe me a new 'un!' said the voice she didn't know.

'How's it ruined, then, Dot? It'll still keep the rain off you. Working fine, by my reckoning.'

'That'll be the last and final time I lend you a thing, Annie Tanner, make no mistake!'

'Well, then, it'll be the last time I let you pay me in favours,' said Mrs Tanner, calmly. There was some more grumbling, in lower tones, then a skinny woman with brown rats' tails for hair stomped out and marched away towards the lane, carrying a black and white umbrella. Cautiously, Clemmie slipped into the open doorway.

'Clemmie! What in hell are you doing here? Come in, come in,' said Mrs Tanner, looking surprised and confused to see her. 'There's tea just brewed. Dotty didn't stay in the end.' She gave a chuckle, and Clemmie tipped her head curiously. 'Silly mare. She lent me her umbrella and now she says I've spoilt it. We gave it to the old man upstairs to hold while we whitewashed his ceiling – he can't get up, see, and he don't like to be moved. Now it's got a pattern of spots on it and she's not happy.' She gave Clemmie a quick hug then sat her down at the table, her eyes searching. 'Never mind that. What are you *doing* here? Where's Eli?'

Clemmie heaved a wobbling sigh, and since she couldn't say, and the weight of it was so great, she started to cry. She pictured Eli there with her, as he had been the last time; fetching out the special doll for his little brother, and stroking the boy's hair. The thought of him supposing she didn't want to be with him was becoming intolerable. Mrs Tanner watched her carefully for a while. 'Eli's not back with you, then? Did something happen to him?' she said, and Clemmie shook her head. 'That's a mercy – that he's well and that he's away. Isaac's been going wild over him running off – he calls it disloyalty, and he never would stand for that.' For a moment Mrs Tanner's face was heavy, and careworn. 'Best Eli stays away a goodly while yet, and lets the dust settle. The baby – you've still got it?' Clemmie nodded again, and Mrs Tanner patted her hand, relieved. 'So, what then? You've left him?' At this Clemmie's face crumpled. But she had to nod. Mrs Tanner nodded too, and thought for a while. She leaned towards Clemmie and looked her deep in the eyes. 'You love my Eli, don't you?' she said, and Clemmie nodded urgently, grasping at Mrs Tanner's hands. 'Did he raise his hand to you?' she asked, flatly. Clemmie shook her head, and Mrs Tanner thought some more. 'Then . . . you missed your home too badly?' Sorrowfully, Clemmie nodded, and Mrs Tanner sighed. 'Ar, well. I don't know what he was thinking, trying to take you off to live in the city. What with you as natural as the day you was born.' She shook her head.

They sat for a while with their tea, listening to Eli's grandmother snoring by the stove. She stirred and muttered at a sudden flurry of noise as a knot of children ran in, dodged about, arguing, then ran out again. There was an angry thumping from upstairs, and Mrs Tanner rolled her eyes. 'I shan't bother to answer him; he'll nod off again soon enough,' she said, to nobody in particular. 'Well, Clem, my girl. What's to do?' she said. Clemmie wiped her streaming nose and wet chin on the backs of her hands. 'He'll know where you are, of course, even if you didn't tell him. I hope to God he doesn't come looking for you just yet. Did he have work? Good. That might hold him there a bit. Have you thought about what you'll do?' Clemmie thought for a moment, then nodded. Mrs Tanner studied her serious expression. 'Something's afoot with you, isn't it?' she said. 'By God, if I could feed you a herb that'd bring you to speak, then believe me, I would.' She sighed again and looked away, and Clemmie felt exhausted with everything she was carrying, and all the unspoken words that had been building up; she felt like a dam about to burst; a bridge about to crack. She shut her eyes and concentrated, and as her heart began to thud she gripped the edge of the table, gouging her fingernails into it.

'I,' she said. 'I . . . I . . .' She took another breath, and her tongue stuck to the roof of her dry mouth. 'I . . . Isaac,' she said. Eli's mother stared at her, dumbstruck.

❧ ❧

When Pudding got to the stables the following day, Irene came at once to ask what had happened at the hearing, and then clearly didn't know what else to say. There was nothing *to* say, Pudding supposed. Hilarius came across from the barn, hands in his pockets, when he saw her tying up Bally Girl out on the yard. He nodded as she set about the mare with a dandy brush.

'Good girl,' he said, shortly. ''Tis the only way.'

'Is it?' said Pudding, but she had no stomach for any kind of argument. She had no stomach for anything. Hilarius watched for a long time. When Pudding glanced at him she saw his eyes following her every move, until she couldn't stand it any more. 'What is it, Hilarius?' But the old man simply looked away and worked his jaw behind his closed lips, chewing on whatever he wasn't saying. In the end he took her copy of *Murder Most Foul* from his coat pocket, and handed it back to her.

'Plenty o' truths in there,' he said. 'And all of 'em bitter.'

'Yes, well,' said Pudding, putting the book on the cobwebby window sill of Bally Girl's stable. 'It's a book about violent crime. It would be bitter.'

'You're not looking deep enough, girl,' he muttered.

'I am!' Pudding snapped. 'I did! And I know that whoever killed that girl fifty years ago killed Alistair. But it doesn't do any good because I can't prove it and Donny has been sent to trial and won't be let home . . . and none of it does any *good*!' she cried. Bally Girl turned her head and blew softly at Pudding in consternation.

'It weren't the same person. No,' said Hilarius, with a shake of his head. 'I do doubt that.'

'Well, unless you can tell me more than who it *wasn't*, please . . .' She took a steadying breath. 'Please just leave me alone.'

At lunchtime she couldn't face going into the farmhouse, or going home. At home they were walking on eggshells around one another, waiting to see who would crack first. Her father, who had been turning inwards on himself ever since Donny's arrest, now seemed all but oblivious to the rest of them. Her mother was agitated, even when she couldn't quite remember what was upsetting her. She was clumsy and tearful and Pudding didn't have the wherewithal to soothe her just then. Ruth had been left to hold the household together, which she did by scowling, berating them for moping, and cajoling them through their daily routine. Pudding flip-flopped between resenting her and being grateful to have her there.

'Not all days'll be like these days,' she'd said to Pudding at breakfast that morning.

'No. Some'll be worse,' said Pudding, thinking of the long wait until Donny's trial; the trial and how it was likely to go; Donny being moved to Cornhill Prison in Shepton Mallet, where Thomas Pierrepoint was said to be able to hang a man with such precision that death was instant and painless. Pudding knew that was a good thing, of sorts, but it felt like nothing of the kind.

'Want to just lie down and die, then, do you?' Ruth had said, thrusting out her chin belligerently. 'Then chop-chop and get on with it. Or buck up, and pass me those plates. It ain't over till it's over.'

Swallowing past the ever-present ache in her throat, Pudding wandered away from Manor Farm towards the churchyard. She missed Alistair almost as much as she missed Donny, and knew that if he'd been there he would have got everything sorted out somehow, in his calm and gentle way. Which was ridiculous since, had he been there, Donny would have been too, and there'd be nothing to sort. It had been a long time since she'd been to his grave, and though it wasn't even nearly the same as seeing him, she couldn't think where else to go. She went around to the 1872 headstone that Irene had found, but the forget-me-nots were shrivelled and spread about, their colour quite gone, and they hadn't been renewed. She ran her fingers over the weathered stone, with its pattern of silver and orange lichen, but the inscription was no clearer to her than it had been to Irene. Wearily, she remembered that she hadn't got around to finding out whose grave it was. It didn't seem to matter much, anyway. It wouldn't help Donny, and she had no curiosity left for anything else. Alistair's grave was immaculate and only too fresh in comparison. The turves that had been lain over the mound were crisping at the edges in the sun, and needed watering. Did one water a grave? She could make almost no connection between the sight of it and the memory of the man she'd loved. Alistair seemed a million miles away, somewhere else altogether. She spent a while there, and thought about telling him out loud what was going on, but it seemed every bit as pointless as everything else. She left the churchyard and went down into the village, and only realised where she was going when she was almost there.

She paused for a moment at the gateway to Thatch Cottage. She knew she wasn't welcome there, but somehow she wasn't afraid any more. She couldn't care less, in fact. She wanted them to know that their deeds and their lies had put a noose around Donny's neck, and even if they weren't sorry she could at least hope that it would gnaw at them, somewhere deep inside. Either way, she wanted them to *know*. She regretted it as soon as she stepped into the yard, though. She saw movement behind the cottage, near the outhouse, and a woman's frightened face as she turned and hurried away, and then Tanner himself, glowering blackly at her. Pudding froze in shock. Tanner came striding towards her, his arms loose at his sides, hands curled into fists.

'You,' he said, jabbing a finger at her. Pudding took a step back and thought about running, but that wouldn't do. She was there for Donny, so she stood up straighter and met the man's eye. '*You* brought the police to my door! You and that chit of a thing from up the farm.' He stood close enough for her to feel the heat of his breath, and smell the animal scent of his skin and hair and unwashed clothes.

'Yes, we did. I did,' she said. Her mouth had gone dry but she felt oddly calm.

'We don't talk to the bloody police, here. You send 'em round again and I'll—'

'You'll what? Kill me like you killed Alistair Hadleigh? Like you killed Sarah Martock fifty years ago?' Quick as a flash, Tanner dealt her a slap to the side of her face with the back of his hand; it was light, it barely hurt, and she knew he could have hit her far harder, but the shock of it left her speechless and tears flooded her eyes.

'Watch your bloody tongue, or I'll have it out,' said Tanner, but there was no weight behind the words. They sounded like a habit, and his eyes had gone wide and he had paled, and he seemed startled by something she'd said. He was silent for a moment, his eyes searching the distant trees for something. 'Watch your bloody tongue,' he repeated, quietly this time, almost absently. Pudding wondered if he were drunk again, but for once alcohol wasn't part of his smell.

'Do what you like,' she said, tremulously. 'I know you lied – I know your alibi was a lie! I *know* you killed Alistair! Why – because he was going to sack you from the mill for good? It was no better than you deserved! I saw you asleep in the coal heap, hugging an empty bottle! I saw you! And for *that*, you killed him? Or did he find out something about Sarah Martock? And now you're three times a killer, because they're going to hang my brother for it – did you know that? They've sent him to be tried for wilful murder, and the case is closed, and they'll hang him for it! So I hope you're happy with yourself! I hope you can live with yourself. No – I hope you *can't*!' she cried, and turned on her heel. Tanner caught her arm; she looked back, alarmed, and though her vision was a blur his expression was not what she'd expected. His face was twisted up in some emotion, but it wasn't anger or cruelty; it looked more like pain, and it turned his wrinkled eyes to slits so that only a sliver of blue showed through. 'Let go!' Pudding shouted. 'Let go of me!'

Tanner kept up his grip on her arm and there was no hope of breaking it. In spite of his age he was all bone and sinew; his hands were long and strong.

'I never . . .' he said. He shook his head but didn't finish the sentence, and Pudding thought she saw a glimmer in his eyes. But that couldn't be right. Tanner didn't cry. Tanner was a monster and a drunk, who terrorised his family and everyone he met. And he was a killer. 'Is that true, girl? 'Bout your brother?' he said eventually.

'Of course it's true! Why would anyone make something like that up? I'm surprised you haven't heard – everyone's gossiping about it; everyone has their opinion about it, and none of them seem to care a damn for the fact that Donny didn't *do* it!' She wrenched her arm again and this time Tanner let her go. He was scowling and silent; eyes downcast. 'Get gone,' he said, gruffly. 'And don't come round here again.'

'Why would I want to?' Pudding shouted. 'Why would I want to be *anywhere* near *you*?' And with that she walked away, more slowly than she would have liked but it was hard to see, and she couldn't get her breath for the sobs hitching in her chest. Her arm throbbed where Tanner had held it, and her cheek stung where he'd hit it, and she knew, beyond a shadow of a doubt, that he was the guilty one. *He* was the one who deserved to be punished. The thought sent a tingle right through her. Her footsteps slowed, then stopped.

❧ ❧

Irene stood at the kitchen window and looked out at the woman with the pale, unruly hair, who was waiting by the back gate to the apple orchard. The woman walked slowly away down the hill at one point, but stopped halfway to the church, put her hands on her hips, twitched her head and turned back again, seeming to be in an agony of indecision. When she noticed Irene at the window their eyes locked, and Irene found she couldn't look away. She went out onto the terrace at the back of the house.

'Hello,' she called, and gave a small wave. The woman simply stared, frozen in place, as the warm breeze pushed locks of fluffy hair into her eyes. Irene wondered whether to invite her inside, but her clothes were a mess and she looked half-wild, so she thought better of it. She was just about to go across and try to speak to her when Nancy appeared beside her.

'She's here again, I see,' said Nancy. Irene turned to her.

'You know her? I've seen her outside here before, too.'

'She lives out on one of the farms.' Nancy raised a hand to shield her eyes, and beneath it her mouth was thin and lipless.

'It looks as though she has something she wants to say,' said Irene.

'Oh, she never says anything. She just lurks.'

'What do you think she wants?'

'Who knows?' Nancy dropped her hand and folded her arms, and Irene was wondering whether to call out again when Nancy stepped down from the terrace and walked towards the woman at the gate. She'd gone only three paces, however, when the stranger stiffened, gave Irene one last glance and set off across the field towards the church. Nancy stopped and watched for a while, then returned to the terrace with a grunt. 'See? Odd creature,' she said, and went back inside. Irene waited in case the woman turned back again, but she had soon disappeared behind St Nicholas'.

The day felt odd, to Irene. It had since the moment she'd woken from a frightening dream that had vanished in an instant; as though, again, the world were holding its breath for something – had cut itself and was waiting for the pain. She paced from room to room, seeing nothing amiss, and then retreated into the cool, clammy quiet of her writing room. She'd yet to write a thing in it apart from letters; there was a film of dust on each key of her typewriter, since Florence was too worried about damaging it to clean it. Tense, Irene sat down on the edge of her chair and stared at the fireplace with its brand new marble surround. Then she looked around the room slowly, remembering the way Alistair had wanted her to make it her home. Instead, she had recreated a corner of her parents' house. Nothing looked right – all the expensive things she'd chosen, close together in this one room, looked garish and smug. The opposite of comfortable. She would ask Nancy about swapping a few of her things with others from the house. Her eyes came back to rest on the fireplace, which leaked a steady draught of air that might have been warm when it had entered the chimney pot at the top, but was cool and reeked of smuts by the bottom. Just as Nancy had warned it would. She thought back to the day it was opened – the day Verney Blunt and the young Tanner boy had broken off the boards and let the slew of soot and mess carry a lost, bedraggled doll out into the room.

On a whim, Irene went to fetch the doll from where she'd stowed it, wanting to see it, and perhaps provoke again the feeling it had given her, in case it was any clearer this time. But it had gone from the drawer. She pulled open a few more drawers, in case she'd remembered wrong, though she knew she hadn't, but the doll was not in any of them. Irene went to ask the housekeeper.

'I don't make it my business to take things out o' drawers in the family rooms, Mrs Hadleigh,' Clara told her, stiffly.

'No, I'm not accusing you of anything, Mrs Gosling. I just wondered—'

'Nor Florence, neither. She's a good girl,' said the housekeeper, folding her arms.

'Right you are,' said Irene, retreating. She found Nancy looking through invoices for sheep drench and pig pellets in the corner of the back sitting room where she had her desk. 'I'm sorry to bother you, Nancy, only I've misplaced that old doll we found in the chimney of the schoolroom. I just wondered if you'd seen it anywhere?'

'You've what?' Nancy peered up over her reading glasses, and Irene marvelled that after so many weeks under the same roof, and with the tumult of the emotions they'd survived, she still couldn't read a thing from Nancy's face.

'That doll we found in the chimney. I put it in a drawer up in our room, and now I can't find it.'

'Well,' said Nancy, and blinked. 'I expect Clara put it out with the rubbish, where it belonged.'

'She says not – quite adamantly.'

'Well, gracious, Irene, I'm afraid I haven't a clue,' Nancy said with some asperity. 'Is it terribly important?'

'I suppose not. It's just . . . strange, that's all.'

'I don't know why you wanted to keep it anyway. It was hideous.' Nancy adjusted her glasses and returned to the invoices with such immaculate unconcern that Irene's nameless unease increased.

She was halfway across the yard to see Pudding when she stopped. Old Hilarius was sweeping out the cob house, which was one of Pudding's jobs, and she realised at once that the wrongness of the morning was that Pudding wasn't there. Not even the day of Alistair's death – the day of her brother's arrest – had she not turned up for work. Irene turned and searched the yard, then stared out at the paddocks; all the horses were there, grazing, swishing their tails, not being ridden by Pudding. Anxiously, she suppressed her reluctance and went over to Hilarius, who had stopped sweeping and was watching her with his far-off eyes. The summer had put a deep crimson shine across his hawk's beak of a nose, and turned every other scrap of exposed skin the colour of saddlery.

'Hilarius, has Pudding not come up today?' Irene asked. The old man shook his head but didn't speak. Irene looked around again. 'Well, it's odd, isn't it? I don't like it. There isn't a phone anywhere in the village, is there? I shall have to go up to them. Is Dundee in?' she said.

'Out. Trouble, you reckon? Quicker to walk,' said Hilarius. 'You know the footpath to Spring Cottage, far side of the river?'

'Yes,' said Irene. 'I'll go right away.'

'I'll come along.' Hilarius leant the broom against the wall. 'She wanted to be careful,' he muttered. 'I never said, when I should o' said. She wanted to be *careful*.'

'Pudding ought to have been careful? Careful of what? What's happened?' said Irene, suspiciously, as the old man led her out of the yard, but before he could answer, the creaking of a bicycle chain and the sound of laboured breathing stopped them, and Constable Pete Dempsey pedalled up the hill towards them.

'Mrs Hadleigh,' he gasped, swallowing, fighting for breath. 'I'm looking for Pudding. Is she here?'

'No – we were just going to try to find her. Is she all right? What's happened?'

'I don't know – I don't know where she is, but we have to find her! The most *unbelievable* thing has happened!'

❧ ❧

Clemmie was awake before dawn. She slid out from under the blankets, and tucked Betsy's doll under her arm. It reminded her of Eli, in a strange way – it was the one thing, besides herself, that had been in the place where she still pictured him.

In the quiet dark she ran one hand over her middle, where there was definitely a bump now – a tautening of the skin, the flesh beneath less giving. The baby was growing: safe, well, on its way. Betsy's doll would be its first birthday present, Clemmie decided, and when she thought of that day – the day she would finally hold the piglet – she pictured a roaring fire in Weavern farmhouse; it would be winter, and her mother would be red-faced and clammy from the heat, and she herself red-faced and serene; she imagined the baby's first cries softening towards sleep; her sisters hovering about, and Eli upstairs with her father, waiting, possibly drinking; or out at work on the land, if it came in the daytime. She willed this future into being, as she hurried up the path between the fields, and along Weavern to Germain's Lane.

She had managed to say *Isaac* in front of Mrs Tanner. It might have seemed a small thing to most people, but to Clemmie it was huge. But she worried that even that one word had been too much to give away – or rather that that one particular word had been the wrong one to say to Eli's mother, who loved her son but was married to Isaac, a man who would not tolerate disloyalty. Mrs Tanner had asked many more questions after Clemmie had managed to say it, but none of them had been the right ones, and Clemmie hadn't managed to say another word. She never could when she was upset or afraid – it took focus, and as much calm dissociation as she could muster, when instead she was hounded by the feeling that time was somehow running out. Rose still watched her daily, and her sisters pestered her with their theories and ideas and all their wrong questions, and she knew she needed a peaceful place. So she was going to the mill, to Alistair Hadleigh's empty office, to find it.

The mill was quiet; the first shift hadn't yet started and there was almost nobody about. Two men crossed the yard, their footsteps echoing in the early calm, but they were used to seeing Clemmie and paid her no mind. The air was as still and smooth as deep water; softly grey, neither cold nor warm. She waited outside the old farmhouse until she was sure that the foreman, with his red whiskers, was not inside. However kind he was, she was sure she wouldn't be allowed up to Alistair's office by herself. Satisfied, she crossed from the lee of a store-house and slipped inside. Up in Mr Hadleigh's room she shut the door behind her, softly.

The office was cool, steady and still. Immediately, Clemmie felt steadier herself. She leant against the door and let the breath run out of her lungs. His desk, his books and papers, his heavy wooden chair, the brass instruments he used to check the paper – all were unchanged by his absence. It was subtly different without him – as though a piece of furniture had been moved out of its normal place and she couldn't put her finger on what had changed. Someone had brought up a bucket of coal for the scuttle, and had left it and a grubby shovel against the wall by the hearth, which would never have happened if Mr Hadleigh had been there. But it was still the room in which, under Alistair's tutelage, she had managed to say more words than anywhere else. At once, she began to remember some of the things he'd made her try – breaking a word into its separate parts and saying each part on its own – in the wrong order, even – rather than trying to run all the sounds together; starting with the second sound a word made rather than the first, if the first wouldn't come; using a rhythm, like in a clapping game, and almost turning the word into a song. She put her back to the window, closed her eyes, imagined Mr Hadleigh there, and got to work.

The sun slid higher, flooding the sky outside with colour, but Clemmie didn't notice. She hummed some sounds, and sang others, and spoke the ones she could. She went through the two phrases of her declaration in her head until she knew them back to front and inside out, and could come at them sideways, surprising her tongue with them. Some were easier than others. *Isaac*, she could say with relative ease, but *heard* refused to take any kind of shape. She could say *Mr Hadleigh* well enough, as long as she left off the H; and she could say *he is the one* almost fluently, as long as she left out *guilty*. Other parts of her statement dodged and darted out of her reach, or tied her up in long minutes of agonised silence, but she persevered, and tried not to let herself get angry, or impatient, or wound up. It was exhausting; she could feel the blood pounding hotly in her face. At one point she realised she had Betsy's doll in a chokehold, her fingers gouging holes in the fabric and disfiguring its face. When she felt despair creeping up on her, and felt it all slipping out of her grasp, she went back to the phrases she had mastered. *Mr Hadleigh. He is the one*. Over and over. Immersed in the sounds and the labour of it, she forgot where she was and didn't notice time pass. And then the office door was flung open without warning, and Clemmie gasped in fright.

Two Confessions

Pudding went through to the lock-ups at the back of Chippenham police station with a feeling she couldn't name. Her pulse was ticking in her fingertips, and it didn't feel as though her head were connected properly to her body. Just a few weeks ago – the longest weeks of her life – she'd been there to visit Donny; now she was there to visit Alistair Hadleigh's real killer. A tall man, almost elderly but not quite, was sitting hunched on the narrow bench, just as Donny had sat. He looked up as Pudding came to stand in front of the iron bars that ran from floor to ceiling, caging him, and he was at once familiar and unknowable to her. A strange expression worked across his face, like clouds crossing the sun; it was an expression his face looked ill-built for – like years without practice had left it unsuited to anything so tender. But it vanished again as he stood up, hidden by resentment and well-worn anger lines. Pudding took a step backwards as Eli Tanner came to the bars.

'Have you come to crow?' he said. His breath was stale, his grey hair dirty and his chin furred with whiskers. Pudding swallowed, and shook her head.

'To say thank you,' she said. Tanner was silent, waiting. 'They've . . . they've let my brother go,' she said, still hardly able to believe it. 'He's at home now – Superintendent Blackman brought him in the motor car. Donny thought it was the best fun ever; he had this huge grin on his face by the time they got home . . .' She trailed off, realising she was gabbling. 'Why did you do it?' she said.

'It weren't right, them hanging the lad when he never touched Hadleigh. Why'd he have to go and pick up that shovel, and carry it away? Why'd he have to go and do that, the gormless bugger? I had my alibi all sorted up at the pub . . . I had 'em convinced I was out of it, so I could slip away and back come morning, and not be seen. The coppers wouldn't 'ave known where to look, till he went in and picked up that bloody shovel. I thought I could let him swing for it, with him being dummel, and half shot-away. But I couldn't. She wouldn't have wanted me to. It was like the kit rabbit I let go for her, back when first we met – it would 'ave been a wrong thing. A wrong killing. I knew it then and I know it now.'

'No – I mean, I understand why you've confessed, and I'm . . . I'm glad you have. But I meant to ask why you killed Mr Hadleigh in the first place.' Tanner stared at her, hard and unreadable. Pudding waited a good while, but he didn't reply. 'Please, I . . . I have to know,' she continued, her throat tightening. 'I mean, he was . . . such a good man. Such a kind man. I'm sure he'd never hurt a soul in his whole life . . . Was it because you were fired from the mill? Were you . . . drunk when you did it?'

'That's what folk say, is it?' Eli grabbed the bars angrily, putting his face up close to them. 'That a Tanner'd kill for so small a slight? That *I* would – kill a man that showed me and my family more respect than anyone, because I'd had too much beer? And you believe it, do you?'

'But *why* then?'

'I'll tell you for why!' Tanner yanked at the bars but they didn't budge, so he jolted himself instead. 'He killed the one person I loved more than any other! He killed a girl as innocent as a newborn!'

'What? What girl?' Pudding shook her head. 'Alistair never killed anyone!'

'I did for him same as he did for her. In that old farmhouse, cut down with a shovel.'

'You can't mean . . .' Pudding's mind ran to catch up. 'You can't mean Sarah Martock, the "Maid of the Mill"?'

'Matlock. Her name was Matlock, not Martock. That weasel from the newspaper wrote it down wrong, then everyone copied his mistake. Sarah was her given name but she weren't ever called that,' said Eli, his voice thick with grief. 'She was called Clemmie.'

'But that was *fifty years* ago!' said Pudding. 'Alistair wasn't even born!'

'My Clemmie. We were to be wed.' Eli wasn't listening to Pudding; he was in the past, looking at a face she couldn't see. 'I only found out about her real name after she died; her mother told me it. To me she was Clemmie, for Clematis – nicknamed after that mad hair of hers; and it did look just like a winter hedgerow, snowy with the stuff. She were that lovely.' The old man shook his head. 'She were that lovely she stole your breath away. I should 'ave come straight after her from Swindon. But I wanted to keep that job, and find some way to fetch her back. If I'd come right after her, it wouldn't 'ave happened.'

Pudding touched his knuckles gingerly to get his attention. Eli's eyes jerked back to her and she flinched.

'Mr Tanner,' she said. 'She died fifty years ago – how can Alistair Hadleigh *possibly* have killed her? It's madness!'

'His father, then! The other Alistair Hadleigh! How else did Betsy's doll wind up hidden in the manor these fifty years? How else? I'd waited half a century for some clue . . . for something to prove who took her. She'd carried that doll about with her ever since Swindon, her folks said. She was even killed in his room at the mill, but that family were above suspicion. Above everything! She used to go to him to get lessons in speaking, since she was mute. She was in and out of there, all the time. I wish I'd known it then; I could have put a stop to it. But her family and me never spoke till after.' He curled his hands into fists around the bars, turning his knuckles white with the force of it.

'You . . . you killed Alistair to punish his *father*?'

'How else could I take anything from the man? When he took *everything* from me?' Eli shook himself against the bars again; his eyes sparkled, and there was rage and pain in the tears. 'She had our baby in her belly when he did it.'

'Oh, no,' Pudding breathed.

'Only the Hadleighs knew, outside of our families. Rose Matlock went and told 'em, like they'd have helped. But it weren't her fault – she never knew about me and Clem till after. We never told the police – they'd only have painted her a harlot. But it was my baby. My family.'

'Mr Tanner . . . that's so awful. It's so sad.' Tears prickled Pudding's nose, and turned her face hot, but they were for Alistair – her Alistair. 'But you shouldn't have. You shouldn't have! Our Alistair was the best of men. It wasn't his fault, if his father did . . . what you say he did.'

'He did it all right!' said Eli, vehemently. 'As soon as you and the new wife brought that doll down to the cottage, I knew it. All this time I waited . . . long years of strife, just waiting to find out who took that girl from me, then in you two walk, carrying Betsy's doll, I knew I finally had my answer. And I could finally punish the man that hurt her. When you love like that . . . when you're loved like that, it doesn't ever go.'

'But Alistair was innocent!' Pudding blew her nose and stepped back from the bars. She shook her head. 'It wasn't right. Whatever his father did, it wasn't right!' Tanner's face twisted in anger.

'Well, the law'll agree with you, I daresay, so don't you fret.

I'll swing for it soon enough. And I don't mind that so much. Not now I know I've done what I could for Clemmie.' He let go of the bars, shoulders sagging, face sagging. 'Best part of me died with her anyhow. Scant difference it'll make.'

❧ ❧

Irene knew something was wrong as soon as Pudding relayed to her everything Eli Tanner had said. The girl suffered a fresh storm of weeping when she finished speaking, but it was less bitter than it had been; less frightened, more sorrowful. They were sitting either side of a pot of tea at Manor Farm's kitchen table, and Pudding blew her nose wetly into the handkerchief Irene passed her.

'Why are you frowning like that?' she said. Irene shook her head.

'Look . . . something's not right. I think . . . I think Mr Tanner's got it wrong. Well – he must have,' said Irene. Pudding's eyes went wide.

'What? Why? He was adamant – the doll you found belonged to Sarah Martock. Matlock, I mean. Old Alistair used to try to teach her to speak in his office – she was mute, you see – and that's where she was killed . . .'

'Yes, but, Pudding – Alistair's father was in America when she was killed! He was getting married to Alistair's mother. I've seen the marriage certificate. There's no way whatsoever he could have travelled between here and there so quickly. It's impossible,' said Irene. Pudding stared ahead blankly as this sank in.

'Oh, hell and damnation,' she said. 'He *has* got it wrong, then. He's killed Alistair for no reason at all. Oh, *Irene*! It's just too bloody awful!' she cried. Irene nodded, and Pudding put her face in her hands for a moment. 'I know I should be happy because they know Donny didn't do it – and I am happy! And I know nothing could ever have brought Alistair back. But . . . but for it to have happened for *no reason* at all? How can that be fair?'

'It isn't fair,' Irene agreed. She got up and went around to Pudding's side of the table, put her arm around her and squeezed. 'Life isn't, as my mother likes to say. Sadly, it's true,' she said.

'And whoever *did* kill Sarah – Clemmie, Tanner says she was known as – has got off scot-free.'

'It seems so. But, you know, she was killed *fifty* years ago. To have found out the truth now would have been remarkable.'

'But then . . . how on earth did Clemmie's doll get into the chimney here at the farm?'

'I don't know . . .' Irene thought about it. 'Somebody who was working here, perhaps . . . or I suppose anybody could have sneaked in.' She thought of old Hilarius, and felt a thrill all along her spine. But she hunted around for positive things to say. 'At least Donny's home. Your parents must be so happy.'

'They can hardly believe it. Dad, that is,' said Pudding, blowing her nose again. 'Mum carries on as if he never went anywhere. Dad has this look of . . . astonishment on his face. He keeps checking on Donny wherever he is, as though he might just vanish again.'

'And they must all be so grateful to you,' said Irene, smiling at her. 'After all, if you hadn't kept digging at it, the truth might very well have stayed hidden forever.'

'I don't know,' Pudding demurred. 'Perhaps Mr Tanner would have confessed anyway.'

'I'm not so sure.'

'Gosh, what a turn-up,' said Nancy, when Irene told her the news. She wore a strange look, as she always did when discussing anything to do with her nephew's death – tense, distant, almost as though waiting for something. Irene wondered if some part of her were waiting to hear that it was all a mistake and he hadn't been killed at all. Nancy raised a hand to her lips for a moment then let it drop back into her lap, where her withered fingers grasped her other hand, claw-like.

'So . . . we'll have young Donny back at work, of course?' said Irene.

'What? Yes. Yes, of course,' said Nancy.

'Right. I'll let Pudding know,' said Irene. She thought about touching Nancy, since there was something abject in her posture, in the way she sat, so straight and hard that she looked as brittle as glass. But she still wasn't sure enough of herself, or of Nancy.

'Have we any idea *why* Tanner killed my boy?' Nancy asked, in a small voice, as Irene turned to go. Irene paused.

'He . . . it was revenge, it would seem. Served very cold. He's convinced that . . . your brother, Alistair's father, killed Sarah Matlock, who was his sweetheart. His betrothed, really, but it was all secret. They'd planned to wed, and she was carrying his child when she died.'

'*His* child?' said Nancy. She looked bewildered, her eyes searching for something in the corners of the room but not finding it. 'No,' she said, quietly.

'I know. It couldn't possibly have been him – you were all in New York, for the wedding,' said Irene. Nancy blinked, and nodded. She opened her mouth but didn't speak at first.

'Foolish,' she said, eventually.

'Well,' said Irene. 'Shall I get you some tea, Nancy?'

'Oh, no,' said Nancy, her eyes still so veiled that Irene couldn't tell if she was refusing the tea, or something else altogether.

She went into the kitchen to put the kettle on, more for something to do than out of any real desire for it. Something was still pestering the hindquarters of her brain, preventing her from feeling any satisfaction at all at the real killer being brought to light; at having got justice for her husband. It wasn't done yet, she knew. There were missing pieces. She was staring out of the window at the sun-drenched fields of daisies and dandelions when she saw a familiar figure at the orchard gate – the same woman she'd seen several times before, dressed like a peasant, surrounded by a long mass of frizzy hair gone white with age. Irene took the kettle off the stove and went straight out to her, and they met in the shade of an apple tree older than both of them put together.

'Hello, I'm Irene Hadleigh,' she said. The old woman nodded.

'I know that. I'm Rose Matlock,' she said, in a voice as thin as winter sun.

'Matlock?' Irene lit upon the name. Rose nodded.

'Clemmie's ma.'

'You've been trying to come and talk to me for a while, haven't you? Did you know that . . . that Eli Tanner had killed my husband?' she asked. Rose nodded. Through her hair, her scalp showed pinkly; as pink as the rims of her pouched eyes, and the gaps in her gums when she spoke.

'I don't blame Eli, mind, and I were willing to let it lie till they took that boy for it instead.'

'You'd have let Eli Tanner get away with it?' said Irene. Rose's face hardened.

''Bout time my girl had some justice. An eye for an eye.'

'But my husband didn't kill her!'

'Blood's blood,' said Rose, darkly.

'His father didn't, either. Mr Tanner got it wrong – Alistair senior was in America when it happened, getting married. All the Hadleighs were. He couldn't have killed your daughter.'

'We'll see,' said the old woman, and Irene wondered if her

wits were quite intact. 'What else was Eli supposed to do? Ever since you showed him that doll he's set about falling apart all over again.'

'It was her grave he was visiting when I saw him in the churchyard, wasn't it? I saw him crying, and he'd taken flowers.'

'He loved my Clem like breath, though I only found it out after she was killed.'

'Why was that?'

'Well, she couldn't tell us – she might not've even if she could. Thought we'd never accept him, they did – especially Clemmie's dad – what with him being a Tanner.' She shook her head sadly. 'Maybe they was right about that, but if he'd only got around to wedding her, we'd have taken them in, and the baby, all three. William would have come around in the end. But there was other trouble with the Tanners that summer – a robbery at the mill, and the office boy bludgeoned near to death when he stumbled upon it. He lay in a stupor for weeks afterwards, and the police arrested some pedlar who happened to be passing. Had to let him go again, o' course, since he weren't to blame. Isaac had bought himself an alibi but folk knew who to blame – near as good as evading the law as they are at breaking it, that family. Old Isaac was the devil himself, and he'd just been laid off from the mill again. And I suspect he'd made Eli go along with him. Eli tried taking Clem off to Swindon to start over, but she had her roots in this land and came back without him.' Rose fell silent for a moment. 'People pointed their fingers at the Tanners for murdering her, but seventeen strappers saw Isaac sleeping it off in Obby Hancock's hay barn at the time, and Eli was in Swindon. Not that he'd have harmed a hair on her head. We never did know who done it, till you found that doll Betsy gave her. She was never without it after she was back from Swindon. We guessed she'd had it with her when she died, but we never found it. Till now.'

Irene caught the old woman's scent, hanging around her. Milk and cow manure, unwashed clothes and carbolic soap. Her hands, though gnarled, were spotlessly clean.

'You live out on one of the farms, Nancy told me?' she said. Rose nodded.

'Weavern. My eldest, Mary, has it now, with her husband, Norman. My William's long dead – a seizure took him not long after Clemmie went. Her death broke what was left of his heart after our little Walter. He was killed when Rag Mill's boiler blew up,' she said. 'So many have gone on before me, but I weather on. Not many folks my age can still climb these hills, and I can still help with the milking,' she said, with a touch of grim pride. 'I've been on that farm since I was a girl of seventeen, and I'll leave it in my coffin, whenever that day may come. They left it a sad place for me, though, my Walter, and my Clemmie, and Will.'

'Why did you want to talk to me, then, if you weren't going to give Tanner away?' said Irene. Rose thought before she answered. The breeze fluttered her worn-out blouse against her ribs, and Irene saw how thin she was, how frail. 'Would you like to come inside, and sit down?' she said, but Rose shook her head at once.

'I'll not set foot in that house again,' she said. 'I mean no offence, I'm sure, ma'am. Thing was, folk used to say my Clemmie was touched. They thought she was slow, because she was silent, and some folk treated her like she was worth less because of it. And she only half belonged to us, it's true – half to us, half to the birds and bees. But she was right as rain, truly, just different to the rest – just like the doctor's boy. They were quick enough to believe he'd done it, because he's different to the rest of them. People can be as vicious as rats in a nest, eating their weakest.' She shook her head. 'My Clemmie would have burned with the injustice of it. I came up here because I wanted to say it weren't him. But I couldn't say who it weren't without sayin' who it *were*, see. So.' She shrugged. 'Eli came to see me when you found that doll. Told me what it meant, and what he would do. Since they took the doctor's boy off, I've been working on his conscience to come clean.'

'You . . . you *knew* Tanner planned to kill Alistair? And you told nobody?' Irene went cold.

'Ar. Tell that to the police and you'll find my wits quite scattered by my very great age,' said Rose, curtly. 'Blood for blood. A lot of things got broken the day she died, Eli Tanner's heart not the least of them. He'd waited long enough to make a body pay for that.'

'But the *wrong* body. The *wrong* man. A good and blameless man!' Irene cried. She found her eyes stinging with tears of outrage, and wiped them away with her fingers. 'Why come now and tell me any of this? It changes nothing, after all,' she said. Rose Matlock nodded slowly.

'I wanted you to understand. I'm sorry for your loss. It's all of it a pity, and a black stain on each of us. In some folk, grief is like a slow poison; I hope it won't be so for you. But I wanted you to see, Eli had no choice. Somebody had to pay.'

'Yes! But it ought to have been the *right* person.' Irene was suddenly angry at the skin and bones woman in front of her, with her flawed logic and her defensive stare. Alistair's death had been as entirely futile as Pudding had declared it, and the unfairness of that was staggering.

'I'm sorry for your loss,' Rose said again, nodding as if Irene had agreed with everything she'd been told. 'But the real crime happened before you were even born, ma'am. In time, you might come to see it.'

❧ ❧

Ma Tanner sat in her carver chair and flexed her hands around the armrests. Her eyes were on the old man, asleep in his truckle bed against the far wall. Pudding sat awkwardly, her hands clasped around a cup of tea she was loath to drink. It smelled of mouldy hay, and the cup had a crust of grime around its rim.

'Isaac Tanner, you're the fount of so much grief,' said Ma, at last. Pudding followed her gaze to the old man, whose face was so slack and grey in sleep he looked like a corpse. 'That man there. Do you know why I married him?' she asked. Pudding shook her head. 'Because I was *frightened* of him. What a way to start out a life together. What a way to bring a clutch of babies into the world! He fancied the looks of me, and I was too scared of him to turn him down.' She shook her head. 'We wed when I fell pregnant. I figured he might change. Ha! What a fool. Figured having littl'uns about would soften him, I did.'

'Oh,' said Pudding, uncomfortably.

'He only ever got worse. Not his fault, you understand?' Ma switched her stern eyes back to Pudding. 'His own father brutalised him, and sent him out into the world thinking that was the only way to be. Why I should be surprised that he then brutalised his own, I don't know. Why I should be surprised that Eli . . .' She paused, shutting her eyes for a moment. 'Why I should be surprised that my soft Eli should end up swinging for murder, I don't know.' She opened her eyes with a snap. 'He had a *chance*, he did! He *loved* that girl from Weavern! He'd got away from Isaac . . . They had a chance, the two of them.'

Pudding took a sip of the tea for something to do, and, sure enough, wished she hadn't. She tried to think of Eli Tanner as *soft*, but couldn't. He was a figure of evil legend, and she'd been afraid of him all her life. She wasn't sure why she'd come back to Thatch Cottage, other than because of a vague sense that she had somehow contributed to the chain of events that had led Ma Tanner to lose her son, and the agonising thought that it had been for nothing.

'Eli's . . . been very brave, in turning himself in,' she said, then cursed herself silently for reminding Ma what would soon happen to her son. The old woman sighed, and looked pained.

'Loyalty,' she muttered. 'In a family like this, if you can't count on that from each other, what can you count on? I would never have uttered a word against my boy, no matter what I knew.'

'I understand,' said Pudding, biting down her anger on Donny's behalf. But Ma Tanner saw it.

'The way you feel about your brother, child, is how I feel about my Eli,' she said, pointedly. Pudding refrained from saying that Donny hadn't killed anybody. She didn't count the war; she refused to think about the war.

'You know he's wrong about Alistair's father being the one to kill Clemmie, though, don't you?' she said, cautiously. Ma Tanner was staring at Isaac's denuded figure again.

'He done the robbery at the mill that summer, and was never fingered for it. Not long before Clem was killed. Made Eli and John go with him; made them guilty too.'

'There was a robbery?'

'He'd been fired from the mill – been on the bottle again, he had. We were that hard-up, that year . . . I thought we'd starve come winter, I did, and the bairns along with us. He took the boys and went down to rob the wages from the mill – and rob it they did – but one of the office boys was there, working late. Isaac gave him such a blow on the head he damn near killed the kid. He lay in a stupor for such a long while, and I held my breath the whole time, waiting for him to die. Waiting for Isaac to have made murderers of my boys.' Ma sighed again. 'He came to, eventually, thank God, but it was the last straw for Eli, I think. The violence of it; the shadow of the noose. That finally gave him the strength to get away from his father. That, and the chance Clemmie gave him. A chance of something better.'

'Why didn't they just get married? And move away?' said Pudding. Ma shrugged one shoulder.

'I suppose they couldn't without telling her folks. They hadn't a coin between them. And Clemmie wasn't like the rest – she needed to be here. She needed her farm, and her family. Besides, you don't know the . . . the *hold* a person can have on you, if you're scared o' them. Once you're proper scared o' them, they've a hold on you it's fiendish hard to break. But Eli was doing it . . . he might have done it for good, if Clemmie hadn't been killed. After it, he got more and more like Isaac with every day that passed. After it, he was in ruins.'

They sat in silence for a while, and Pudding raised her cup to her lips, remembering just in time not to drink. The injustice, and the pointlessness, of Alistair's death was like a dreadful ache that she couldn't ignore. She knew she shouldn't say anything else about it, but she also couldn't quite bring herself to leave until she had.

'Still,' she said. 'Poor Mr Hadleigh—'

'Poor Mr Hadleigh indeed,' Ma Tanner interrupted her. 'Lord knows, he were a good sort. But he got caught up in something bigger and older than himself.'

'But he wasn't caught up at all! It was nothing to do with him – not if his father wasn't the original killer!'

'Is that so,' said Ma, cryptically. Eli's wife, Trish, came in, carrying a heavy sack that she let thump to the floor inside the door. She straightened to stretch her back. At the noise, Isaac Tanner opened his rheumy blue eyes and glared at her. Pinch-faced, she glared right back.

'All right, Annie,' she greeted Ma, wearily. 'I got a good price on 'em.' When her eyes adjusted and she saw Pudding,

Trish Tanner stopped, and stared. Her expression was openly hostile, and Pudding shrank from it.

'Well done. Go on out and see that the sow hasn't rolled on any more of the littl'uns, will you?' Ma said. Trish folded her arms and puckered her mouth, but obeyed without a word. 'She don't like any mention of Clemmie,' Ma explained, when she'd gone. 'God help the woman, but she only went and fell in love with Eli. He married her just for the sake of it, though, and she knows it. He never stopped loving Clem, and she knows that too.'

'Ma, what did you mean by "is that so"? There's no question as to where Alistair's father was at the time.'

'No, there ain't,' Ma agreed.

'What then?' she pressed. Ma studied her calmly, as though weighing up what to say, and what not to say. Just as she always had before.

'Spoken to that old tinker, Hilarius, have you?' she said, in the end.

'Yes. Well, no – I don't know. What about?'

'He owes the Hadleighs his whole life, you know. They took him in when he was a tiddler, and his folks had died – they were tinkers, travelling folk, and they froze out in the snow one night when no one round here would take 'em in. That was a fierce winter, and no mistake. Not that the Hadleighs raised him as one of their own, but they fed him and kept him warm, and gave him work. He was about five when he came here, I think, and he never left.'

'You can't mean . . .' Pudding was astonished. 'You can't mean that he's "the snow child", from my murder book?' She felt as though she'd just seen a paper bird flap its wings, and take flight. Ma Tanner shrugged. 'In my book, *Murder Most Foul*, in the story of "The Snow Child" . . . It says the family went from door to door asking for shelter, and that everyone who turned them away was partly guilty of murder. His mother and father died on either side of him and his sister. They died trying to keep the children warm.'

'As foul a thing as any these parts have known, and the whole village has carried the guilt of it ever since. Folks has never warmed to him, have they? Expecting him to hate them, you see. Expecting him to take revenge on 'em somehow. Feeling that they deserve as much.' Ma shook her head. 'I was six, the year it happened, but I remember it. They came here, see. We turned them away, same as everyone. We had no space, no food, no wood to burn. My grandmother died that same winter, for want of hot food. We heard them knocking and we didn't even open the door – didn't want to let the cold air in. So we're as guilty as all the rest.'

'But they must have tried at Manor Farm as well. And been turned away. Did the Hadleighs feel guilty – is that why they took the boy in afterwards?'

'Who knows? But he's loyal to that family, make no mistake on it. He owes them what life he's had, and he'd not speak out willingly. Not unless you ask him the right questions. But he'll not lie – have you noticed that? He says little enough, but what he does say, he means, and it's always the truth.'

'What questions? What should I ask?' said Pudding, still befuddled by the incredible thing she'd been told. Annie Tanner settled back into her chair, staring resentfully at her bedridden husband, and Pudding thought it through. 'Irene has never warmed to him, you know. To Hilarius,' she said, in the end. 'She says she can see a darkness around him, or something like that. A shadow – something unnatural.' At this, Annie's eyes came sharply into focus. 'He read about Clemmie's death in my murder book, when I left it up in the tack room, and he asked to read it a second time, and yet he never said a word about the two murders being the same. He must have realised it though, surely? He was here in Slaughterford for both of them, after all,' she said.

'Sounds to me as that city girl has a touch o' the sight,' said Ma, and then wouldn't say another word about it.

❧ ❧

They found Hilarius applying a poultice to the hoof of one of the shires. It had pierced the sole of its foot on a sharp stone; a stinking puddle of black pus, which Hilarius had drained from the abscess, was on the cobbles, and the horse had a shiver to its skin and sweat on its shoulders. Irene blenched at the smell, and held her nose. She drew breath to speak but Pudding took her arm, and shook her head. They waited until the sticky dressing – kaolin clay, ash, certain herbs – was bandaged tight to the hoof, and Hilarius had let go of the horse's leg and straightened up. The shire rested its toe gingerly on the ground, and looked miserable.

'Will she be all right?' said Pudding, as Hilarius wiped his hands on a rag and kicked straw over the pus, on which flies were attempting to land. He shrugged with his eyebrows.

'If the fever is less by tomorrow, we'll know.'

'Could we perhaps go outside?' said Irene, still struggling with the stench. Once they were in sunshine and relative fresh air, Irene looked at Pudding, and Pudding looked at Irene, and the old man looked at both of them.

'Out with it,' he said, gruffly.

'Hilarius,' Pudding began, 'I went to see Ma Tanner.'

'Ar. And how is the hag?' he said, without rancour.

'Well enough. Upset about her son, of course,' said Pudding. 'Angry with her husband.' Hilarius nodded.

'Isaac Tanner were a scourge, back when he had the strength to be.'

'Yes. Well. She told me . . . she told me how you came to be here at Manor Farm, Hilarius. Your story is in my murder book, isn't it? Is that what you meant when you said there were plenty of truths in it?'

Hilarius fiddled with some clay on his fingers, frowning down at them, and Irene realised that the darkness she had always sensed around him had indeed been the shadow of death – the deaths of his parents and his sister, who died with their arms clamped tight around him, bodies pressing in, hardening as they froze. How could such a thing not leave a stain? And he had been inside Manor Farm – the morning afterwards, when he was found and brought into the warm. 'Do you . . . do you remember your parents?' Pudding asked, her fascination for the story getting the better of her.

'Pudding,' Irene checked her. She felt strongly that the old man's grief ought not to be touched.

'Not a lot,' said Hilarius, still not looking at them. 'My sister's name was Ilsa, and she had hair the colour of a copper pan. I remember the night they all died. The wind was a shriek, and full o' knives, but I felt warm.' He fell silent, though Pudding's face was rapt, and she would clearly have loved to hear more.

'It must be terrible to think about,' said Irene, to head Pudding off. 'Ma Tanner said something else, in fact,' she said, and Pudding nodded.

'Yes. She told me . . . how loyal to the Hadleighs you are,' she said, at which Hilarius's head came up, and unease filled his narrow eyes. 'She told me how they took you in, and that you owed them an awful lot, and wouldn't betray them willingly.' In the pause chickens hectored one another, and the mill rumbled. When it became clear that Hilarius wasn't going to elucidate, Irene took a breath.

'There's still a mystery, you see, about how the girl's doll came to be hidden here at the farm – Sarah Matlock's doll. Her family are sure she had it with her when she was killed, and Eli Tanner recognised it at once, when he saw it. *Somebody* put it up the chimney in the schoolroom, but it can't have been Alistair senior, whatever Eli thinks. The Hadleighs were all away at his wedding when it happened.' Irene waited, and Pudding fidgeted, but Hilarius still said nothing.

'Hilarius, do you know?' Pudding burst out. 'Ma said I'd have to ask you the right questions . . . Do you know who hid it in the chimney?'

'No. I don't *know*,' said the old man, and Pudding deflated.

'But you suspect?' said Irene, and got no reply. 'Was it you?' she pressed, to more silence. Pudding chewed her lip, and Irene felt the nagging threads of something, just out of her grasp.

'The day Alistair died, you said to me that he had gone a long way towards lighting the darkness here, or something like that,' said Pudding. She glanced apologetically at Irene. 'I only just remembered,' she said. 'What did you mean, Hilarius?' There was a long pause.

'You got to be certain o' what you think is fact,' said the old man, at last. He shook his head, and turned to go.

'What does that mean?' said Pudding.

'Which part have we got wrong?' said Irene, catching on. Hilarius glanced back, and gave her a shrewd nod.

'Think along them lines.'

Pudding heaved a frustrated sigh, but Irene held up a hand to forestall her. She raked back through everything they had just said, looking for a fact that might be wrong. And then she thought of the unseasonal fire she'd found, smouldering in the grate in the back sitting room, weeks ago, before Alistair had died – the overheated fug in the room, and the tantalising scraps of blue in the ashes. Blue, like the dress Clemmie's doll had worn. The empty drawer where she knew she'd stowed it. She gave Pudding a startled look, and turned at once for the house.

'What is it, Irene?' Pudding called, hurrying after her. Irene went straight to Alistair's study, where his parents' wedding photo hung on the wall, framed in ebony, overshadowed by the vast family portraits. She stared at it, then took it off its nail and over to the window for more light. 'What is it?' Pudding repeated, but Irene didn't answer her until she was sure. She handed the photograph to Pudding.

'Look. It's Alistair's parents' wedding party. Alistair and Tabitha's wedding party. The whole wedding party, in New York, in July 1872.' Pudding stared at it for a moment – the old-fashioned bouffant hairstyles, the tailcoats and hooped skirts and corsets.

'So what? What should I see?' she said.

'Where's Nancy?' said Irene. Pudding frowned and looked again. She tipped the photo to the light. The moment stretched, the air seemed to grow heavy. Then she looked up at Irene, bewildered.

'She's not there.'

'She's not there,' Irene echoed. 'Come on.'

They went back out to the yard and found Hilarius simply standing in the barn, as if he'd been waiting for them to return. His arms were loose at his sides, his face hung sadly, and he seemed awkward, as though he didn't know what to do or how to behave. He nodded as they approached.

'Hilarius ... did Nancy go to her brother's wedding, back in 1872?' asked Irene. Hilarius took a deep, slow breath and let it go, and Irene thought she saw relief in his eyes.

'Couldn't stand to,' he replied, shortly. 'Said somebody needed to stop here and oversee, but the truth of it were, she couldn't bear to watch.' Irene remembered the hints Cora

McKinley had dropped, about Nancy being all *too* close to her twin brother.

'Do you remember when the fireplace in the old schoolroom was blocked up? Was it that summer?' she asked. Hilarius gave a single nod, his unhappiness and reluctance all too plain. Pudding had gone silent and still, and Irene had to remind herself that the girl had known – and respected – Nancy Hadleigh all her life. She steeled herself, dry-mouthed and recoiling already from what she knew was coming. 'Hilarius, did Nancy ask for the fireplace to be blocked up?' she said.

'Who else?' he said.

'Did you . . . see her, the day Clemmie Matlock was killed? Did you see anything . . . untoward?' Hilarius stared at Irene for a long time, until she understood how long he had known, and how heavy the knowledge had been, and yet how loath he was to give it up now. Then he nodded.

❧ ❧

Alistair Hadleigh's office door banged against the wood panelling as it opened, and Clemmie jumped around in fright. Nancy Hadleigh's face was ashy white, and the red patches on her cheeks looked too bright in comparison; her dark hair shone in its elaborate braids. She slammed the door behind her, walked three smart paces into the room, kicking up her hem, then stopped in front of Clemmie with her fists at her sides. Clemmie stayed still, rooted by shock.

'You . . . you *thief*!' Nancy hissed at her. Clemmie shook her head, confused by the accusation. 'I heard you – I *heard* what you're trying to say! All this time he's been teaching you to talk, out of goodness, and yet you'll use your first words to defame him, will you? Is that gratitude, you wretch?' She swept her eyes over Clemmie, curling her lip in disgust as she took in the curve of her midriff, and the doll clasped in her hands. 'How dare you?' she ground out, through her teeth. 'You little trollop, how *dare* you?' Clemmie didn't understand what she was being accused of; she didn't have the words to defend herself. She tried to dodge around Nancy and get away, but Alistair's sister stepped in front of her. She was slight, but her body was hard with anger. She put her face too close to Clemmie's as she spoke. 'He's been ... he's lain with you, I know. You aren't the only one – don't go fooling yourself that he loves you!' Clemmie shook her head. 'You won't get a thing from us for that bastard you're carrying – I won't let you ruin this for him. For us. I won't *let* you, do you understand? I demand your word you won't name him. I want your word!' she snapped.

Horrified by Nancy's inexplicable rage, Clemmie whimpered, twisting on the spot. Then she took flight, barging past Nancy and sending her reeling back, making for the door. Nancy made an incoherent sound of fury. Clemmie had the door knob in her grasp. Her hands were shaking so badly that she couldn't turn it far enough; she yanked at it but the door wouldn't open. Then a fire blazed through her head, and the world turned itself upside down; she had the taste of the woollen rug on her lips, the smell of iron in her nose, and a stabbing pain inside her that made her more afraid than she had ever been. *Eli, come to get me!* she thought, wildly, desperately. Then she sank down into darkness.

❧ ❧

Irene requested a tea tray from Clara and took Pudding into her writing room – the old schoolroom – to think before they acted. She spoke a great deal, but Pudding took in very little of it. Paper birds were taking flight again – stories from books were coming to life; the ground was made of clouds and the sky of stone. She didn't know what to do, or say, or think; she didn't trust her own memories any more, or any of the things she thought she knew. It felt as though someone had picked up her brain and shaken it until nothing was in its right place. She was profoundly grateful to have Irene there, who seemed to have gone very calm – though it might have been shock. Pudding hoped she would eventually tell her what they should do, because she herself had no clue.

'Well, what do you think?' said Irene, looking right at her with those smudged, dark eyes.

'What?' said Pudding, helplessly. Irene blinked.

'Right. Pudding, I think you should go home. Go home, and I'll . . . I'll talk to Nancy myself,' she said. 'There's really no need for you to be . . . involved.'

'No,' said Pudding, stirring herself. Part of her wanted nothing more than to go home and be hugged by her father, to see her mother's vague smile, and Donny waiting patiently at the table for his tea. But in spite of that she knew she couldn't go until things were finished. 'I'll stay,' she said, after thinking for a time. 'You might . . . you might need me.'

Irene nodded.

'The footprint they found in the blood, in 1872 – the footprint in Clemmie's blood,' said Pudding, muzzily.

'What about it?'

'They discounted it as a clue. Pete said they decided it couldn't be a footprint because it was too small,' said Pudding. They both went silent for a while, picturing Nancy's tiny feet.

Nancy wasn't anywhere in the house, and without needing to think Irene led Pudding out of the farm, and down across the field to the churchyard. There they found her, sitting on the bench all dressed in black, staring at the grave plot that contained her parents, her brother and her nephew. She didn't look up as they approached, and they stood awkwardly in front of her, blocking her view. Nancy's face was closed off; her mouth was a straight line, cheeks hollow, hands clasped in her lap.

'There's really nothing you can tell me that I don't already know,' she said, stiffly. Pudding stared at her and tried to believe what she was having to – that Nancy had killed Clemmie Matlock, fifty years before. It was unreal. It was berserk.

'Berserk,' she said, then bit her tongue to keep quiet.

'Yes,' said Nancy. 'I suppose I was a bit, that summer.' Now she looked up at Pudding, her eyes crystalline. 'You of all people ought to understand, Pudding,' she said.

'Me?' said Pudding, shocked. 'Why me?'

'You'd do anything for that brother of yours. Well, so would I have.' She looked away. 'So I did,' she said, more quietly.

'But why, Nancy? Why on earth did you do such a thing?' said Irene. For a long time, Nancy didn't reply. Her eyes, her face, were blank.

'She was going to ruin everything. Tabitha was devout. Everything depended on the marriage – our whole life here depended on it. Everything!'

'You thought Clemmie's baby was your brother's? And that would jeopardise his marriage?' said Irene.

'But it wasn't!' Pudding cried. 'It was Eli Tanner's baby! They were going to get married.' Again, Nancy said nothing. Irene shook her head.

'I don't understand,' she said. 'The wedding was already going ahead – it had already gone ahead, two days before. There was no way Tabitha could have found out about any . . . indiscretion . . . beforehand, and called it off.'

'It would have made things difficult,' said Nancy, tonelessly. 'I did what I had to do to keep my family together. To keep our good name. As I have always done.'

'You can't be talking about the bloody Hadleigh standard, surely?' Irene shook her head again, thinking hard. 'No. It wasn't that, was it? What could possibly have made you angry enough with her to kill her?'

A soft breeze tugged at them, and made the flowers on Alistair's grave bob their heads prettily. Nancy gritted her teeth, working the muscles beneath the skin at the corners of her jaw. Otherwise, she didn't react. Pudding felt at a complete loss.

'No,' said Irene again, her eyes locked on Nancy, her face tense as she thought it through, and worked it out. 'It was Alistair you were angry with, wasn't it? It was *him*, not her. You were angry with your brother for getting married, and leaving you.'

'He had no choice,' said Nancy, stonily. 'Her money was the only thing that could keep us here.'

'Because *he* had gambled it all away!' said Irene. 'It was all his fault. But you couldn't take it out on him. You loved him too much. You had to move away when Tabitha came here, didn't you? Was that one of her conditions, or could you just not stand to be around them – around her?' Nancy showed no sign of having heard. Irene fell silent for a while, a frown of concentration putting a crease between her eyebrows. 'Were you . . . were you *jealous* of Clemmie? When you thought she and your brother had . . .' At this, Nancy's head turned sharply.

'Don't be *disgusting*!' she said

'Is that why you took the doll? I can't work out why you'd do that – take something so incriminating from her. But perhaps it was a symbol of . . . of . . . I don't know.' Irene thought again. 'A symbol of the child she carried? Or rather, the one you thought she was carrying? A symbol of your brother's child?' Irene was relentless, and Pudding began to feel exhausted. So tired she might be sick, or just lie down there, on the grass. But no – she didn't want to be near Nancy. She wanted to be nowhere near her.

'Let's just go, Irene,' she mumbled, but Irene didn't seem to hear her.

'That dumb wretch,' said Nancy, quietly. 'Why should she have had anything of his?' And then she shuddered, as if the warm breeze had turned suddenly chill. After it she seemed somehow smaller than before, and less alive.

Pudding took Irene's arm, and tried to tug her away.

'Let's just go,' she said again. Irene looked round at her, and nodded. They turned to leave, but Nancy's voice called them back.

'Well,' she said, her glass edges beginning to fracture, giving them a glimpse of the fear inside her. 'What will you do?'

'Hilarius saw you come back from the mill, carrying the doll and with your clothes all bloodied. He heard you telling the laundress the dogs had killed a sheep. He remembers you asking that the schoolroom chimney be boarded up, with the doll inside it,' Irene told her.

'What doll?'

'I saw it, before you burned it. Several Tanners did too; Verney Blunt, and Pudding here. And I saw the remains of it in the grate.'

'Hilarius won't testify against me. It'd be cruel of you to ask him,' said Nancy, and her voice sounded different, not like her at all. Pudding had never heard her sound uncertain before – not once. 'And nobody would believe anything a Tanner had to say.'

'I'm not so sure about that. Superintendent Blackman isn't as ready as everybody else to denounce the Tanners.'

'You can't be serious, Irene?' said Nancy. She'd tried to sound scathing, Pudding guessed, but merely sounded panicked. 'After fifty years? Don't be *absurd*.'

'You don't think you ought to be punished, Nancy? For killing an innocent girl?' said Irene. Nancy seamed her lips tight together and turned away, back to her silent study of Alistair's grave. 'But then ...' Irene went on. 'What you did back then has led *directly* to your nephew being killed now. I hope you realise that. Blood is blood, as Rose Matlock said to me. I think perhaps she guessed the truth; and Ma Tanner as well. So perhaps Eli Tanner has got his vengeance for Clemmie after all – in making you responsible for the death of the one person you loved most in all the world.' Before they turned to go, Pudding saw the realisation of this truth hit Nancy Hadleigh. She slumped bonelessly, her rigid posture failing her; her chin dropped onto her chest and her hands came up to cover her face. She looked so unlike herself that with little effort, Pudding could imagine her to be a different person altogether to the one she'd known.

II

Beginnings

In the cool of early morning, Pudding put the kettle on to boil. It *was* cool – the night air had dropped several degrees in the past few days. It was nearly September, and the long summer was finally running out of steam. The kitchen tiles beneath her bare feet were on the verge of being chilly. Pudding went to the back door of Spring Cottage and looked out across the valley, to where Manor Farm was visible through a slight mist on the opposite hill. The fields were golden now – even the pasture. Thistles had turned brown and frizzled; the dandelions were all clocks; the lambs were almost the same size as their parents, and too busy eating to gambol any more. There were crisp brown edges on the horse chestnut leaves. The kettle hissed; Dr Cartwright came out of the privy at the bottom of the garden and looked at his watch; upstairs, Pudding could hear her mother moving about, getting dressed. And Donny was weeding the vegetable patch, where the last of the beans were turning thick and stringy and the lettuces had bolted. He'd been helping Louise with it more, since coming back from the New Bridewell. He didn't like going to the mill any more, and spent more time at home.

'Pudding – how did you sleep?' said her father, putting a kiss on her cheek.

'Well, thank you,' she said. 'Cup of tea?'

'No time, I fear. I said I'd call on Mr Long first thing, and he's a very early riser.' Since Donny had been cleared and sent home, the doctor had more patients again. As though some taint had been removed from him, and people felt sheepish for having believed in Donny's guilt. He picked up his bag from its spot by the door, patted a pocket for his spectacles and gave her a smile. 'Cheerio; I'll be back for lunch.'

By the time Louise came downstairs, anxiously fingering the buttons of her cardigan, Pudding had got breakfast on the table, and she and Donny were tucking in.

'I'm awfully sorry I'm late,' said Louise.

'It doesn't matter at all, Mum,' said Pudding. Donny had muddy fingernails, and was licking marmalade off them; the dent in his head was as hideous as ever and he was having nightmares again, but he was home. Louise had more days when she was confused, to some degree, than days when she was not. The horrible notion that she was slipping further and further inside herself, out of their reach, was ever-present. But the four of them were together again, and were going to remain together. Knowing that, Pudding found, made the rest of it seem surmountable. As she set off down the hill to work, with Donny walking calmly at her side, Pudding wondered how many more times she would make the journey. Irene Hadleigh had put Nancy and Alistair's horses, Bally Girl and Baron, up for sale, and ancient Tufty was unlikely to last out another winter, which only left Dundee and Robin – hardly enough work for a full-time girl groom.

'What'll you be doing today, Donny?' she asked. Her brother frowned, trying to remember.

'Cutting the grass in the orchard,' he said at last, and Pudding smiled.

'Your favourite,' she said. Donny nodded. He liked the visible results, the neat lines he created, pushing the mower up and down in stripes. Donny had a job for life at the farm, Irene had said, but if she didn't stay on there herself, what then? And if Pudding didn't stay on either, where would she go instead? Things were very different to before. The mill looked the same; Manor Farm looked the same, as did the village and the yard and Spring Cottage. But they weren't the same. Everything had changed, and Pudding didn't know if she could carry on there, confronted at every turn by memories, and the echoes of her previous, more innocent life. She put her shoulders back and her chin up. She certainly wouldn't be going off to any secretarial college, or leaving her family, so whatever came next, she would just have to get on with it.

When the horses were done and the stables clean, Pudding hitched Dundee to the Stanhope and Irene came across from the house, pulling on leather gloves, still looking too smart in a diaphanous shirt and block-heeled shoes.

'Ready?' she said, looking decidedly uneasy.

'Yes, if you are.' Pudding nodded. They climbed aboard and Irene took up the reins, clucking her tongue at Dundee. 'That's it,' said Pudding. 'And if he's feeling lazy and doesn't budge, just say *"up"*, in a sharper tone.' Painstakingly, Irene steered the cob – who knew exactly where he should go anyway – out of the yard, and down the hill. They went sedately through Slaughterford; past the tiny shop, the bridge and the mill; past Thatch Cottage, at which neither of them looked too closely. They didn't know quite how to feel about the Tanners, after all that had happened. There was no rancour, but there could be no forgiveness either, and certainly no forgetting. The leather collar creaked as Dundee leant into it up the steep hill of Germain's Lane. Where the track curved towards Biddestone they turned right, onto Weavern Lane. They were going to see Rose Matlock and Mary Black, Clemmie's mother and sister. It had been Irene's idea, and she'd asked Pudding to go with her, as much for courage and support as she drove, Pudding suspected, as for the visit itself. But Pudding had been happy to go. She'd been to Honeybrook Farm once before, when her whole family had been invited to supper after Dr Cartwright had nursed their littlest, Daniel, through whooping cough, but she'd never been to Weavern. To Pudding, Clemmie Matlock was one more paper bird who'd taken flight; the thought of seeing her home, and meeting her mother, had the compulsive allure of a pilgrimage.

The track wove down into the wooded valley, steep and stony.

'How on earth do they manage in winter, when it's muddy?' said Irene, as the little gig squeaked and rocked along the ruts, and Dundee's hooves rattled with a hollow sound against chunks of limestone.

'On foot, I think,' said Pudding. 'Or out the other way, perhaps – I think there's a better lane southwards, up to the Bath Road.' On the far side of a small stream the track rose steeply again, through woods, and then finally crested a rise to reveal Weavern Farm, huddled at the feet of the fat green hills. The By Brook curled past it in a series of wide loops, golden in the sun, and a small dairy herd was grazing the paddock between the yard and the water; mellow farm buildings sat neatly around three sides of a square yard.

'Gosh, isn't it pretty?' said Pudding.

'It looks like a Victorian painting of the English country-side,' said Irene, and Pudding wasn't sure if that was supposed to be a good thing or not. As they approached they saw that there were tiles missing from the roof; the window frames were peeling, and some had lost their glass. The yard was cracked earth, dotted with nettles, dock and poultry mess; a butterfly bush was growing in the gutter, and another up by the chimney; dry grass whispered along the farmhouse's foundations; toadflax and pennywort had invaded the wall around the well. A solitary pig gazed at them from behind the bars of its door, but the rest of a long run of open skillings sat empty. Weavern Farm was in its declining years. The yard gate hung skewed from its hinges, and was tied shut with string. Pudding jumped down to open it, and Irene manoeuvred the Stanhope through with the frowning concentration of someone walking a tightrope.

'Where shall I park?' she called down to Pudding, who tried not to smile.

'Park? Oh, er . . . over by the barn there. Look – there's a post we can hitch Dundee to.'

A tall woman opened the door to them. Her face was ruddy and hard, drawn tight over her cheekbones and jaw; her hair was iron grey, and she stood with the stoop of a body tired out by decades of work. Pudding was slightly taken aback. She knew, of course, that Clemmie's sister would be more or less the same age as Eli Tanner – seventy or so – but somehow, since Clemmie was frozen in time, she'd pictured her sister Mary the same way. Still young, still a girl. A fresh-faced milkmaid. Mary led them into a large kitchen and sat them at the table, sweeping a chicken aside with one arm as she did so. The hen clucked in outraged tones as it made its way outside, and then Rose Matlock came through from a room at the back of the house, her thistledown hair tucked away beneath an old-fashioned cotton sun bonnet, her figure swamped by a shapeless pinafore. She sat down at the table with them and a strange silence prevailed, neither awkward nor comfortable, whilst Mary made tea and came to join them.

'First time in all the long years we've had a visitor from Manor Farm,' said Rose. 'Even when the first Alistair Hadleigh asked to try and teach our Clemmie to speak, he did it by a note.' She cleared her throat, coughed, then grunted. 'He never did manage to get her to talk, mind you. I wondered . . . I did wonder for a while, after it happened, if he was the one as had got her into trouble.' She shook her head. 'Never thought for a second he would hurt her though. Not till Eli came along last month, and told me you'd found Betsy's doll. And even then, I had doubts. Doubts I couldn't put my finger on.' She gave Irene a steady look.

'You've worked it out, haven't you?' said Irene. 'That's what you meant when you said "blood's blood" to me. Eli blamed the wrong Hadleigh.'

'Blamed the wrong one, but punished the right one.' The old woman nodded.

'If it hadn't been Alistair Hadleigh that took the doll and hid it, it had to be his sister,' said Mary. 'And Nancy always was a half-mad bitch.' Her language made Pudding flinch, and then feel oddly as though she might cry. Nancy had been one of the foundation stones of her whole life. Not as lovable as Alistair, not as easy to like, but constant; Pudding was having a hard time relinquishing the affection she still felt for her.

'I wanted to come and tell you. I wanted to make sure you knew who had really killed Clemmie, because I . . . thought you ought to. Nancy thought it was Alistair's baby too, you see,' said Irene.

'I remembered. Too late for your husband, Mrs Hadleigh . . . But I remembered that his dad was off at his wedding when it happened. Eli's pickled his brain in beer and gin over the years – I'm surprised he can fetch up his own name, some days – but I remembered in the end. Alistair was off getting wed, and his sister stayed behind. I'd tried talking to her about the baby, see. That's how she knew about it, though everyone would have seen it before much longer. That's what I say to myself, when I get to blaming myself for it.' Rose shook her head sadly, and Mary gave her a hard glare.

'Ain't no one to blame but that shrew at Manor Farm, Mum,' she said.

'She's not there any more,' said Irene, firmly. 'Nancy's gone, and she won't be coming back.'

The silence returned, and Pudding looked around at the cluttered shelves looped with cobwebs; the ancient, grimed stove, black with smuts and baked-on grease; the skin-and-bones cat asleep on the window sill. The wind nudged in through the open door and set the peeling labels on ranks of dusty jars and tins to flapping. There was something spectral and ineffably sad about the place. She knew, from things Rose had told Irene and from things they had found out from Ma Tanner, that Clemmie had had three sisters, and all had still been at home at the time of her death. She knew that their little brother, Walter, had been killed while he was still a child, in the accident at Rag Mill when the boiler had blown up. She knew that the sisters had married and moved away one by one, and that Mary and her husband Bert Black had moved back when her father, William, had died. Josie had died at the age of forty, of the flu; Liz in her late twenties, giving birth to her third child. It was no wonder the farm felt as though its heart had stopped beating.

'Have you a picture of Clemmie?' Pudding asked. 'I should love to see it. I first read about her ages ago, in a book of mine, you see. I never dreamed of her being a real person, if you see what I mean. I never dreamed I should ever sit at the table where she grew up . . . and ate her suppers . . .' Pudding stopped, wondering if she was being horribly tactless. But their pain was old, not fresh, and Mary simply shook her head.

'We never had a picture of her, nor of Walter. You didn't take photographs just like that, back then. It cost money to go into town and have one done, and that money was far better spent elsewhere. I can still see her face like I saw it yesterday, though. She was the prettiest of all of us, and we had our fair share of admirers. Who can describe that, though? She had blue eyes and mad hair the colour of cream, like Mum; cheeks, forehead, chin, same as any of us 'as got, but on her they came together that much better, somehow. And a faraway look in her eyes – like she knew more than everyone else, but nothing at all at the same time.' Mary shook her head again. 'Used to drive us potty sometimes, she did. Mooning about, not pulling her weight and getting away with it, even with Dad. None of us knew what she meant to us till she was dead. The world didn't seem right after that. Blameless as a babe, she were. I saw the world different after what happened to her.'

Rose nodded heavily, but said nothing for a while. Pudding watched Irene sip her tea and stifle a wince. It managed to be weak and stewed at the same time.

'I'd have had Eli Tanner as my son, I would,' said Rose, eventually. 'He weren't like the others. At least, not then. Now,' she gave a shrug, 'now he's a tosspot, and a killer. But what made him a killer? Not being a Tanner. Not something he was born with. *Nancy Hadleigh* made him a killer.'

'But you didn't know him before Clemmie died, did you?' said Irene.

'We got to know him after. We got to hear of his plans for them, and how he loved her. How he despised old Isaac and wanted nothing to do with the villain. All of that died with her. He stayed in the village – trying to find out who'd killed her, at first, but then simply treading in his father's footsteps. He was eaten up with anger over it, and took to the drink, and turned so black inside people came to fear him just as they feared Isaac. The lad I caught a glimpse of just after she died . . . the lad with all the plans and the desire to make a better life . . . that lad was murdered as sure as Clemmie was.' At this, Irene looked down into her cup, and said nothing. Pudding guessed she was thinking of the Eli Tanner who had killed their Alistair in such a horribly violent way. Trying to imagine him as a lad, madly in love and planning a new life with a young wife and child, was difficult. 'He'll not mind being hanged,' Rose said, flatly. 'He'll not mind it at all.'

'No,' said Pudding. 'He said as much to me when I went to see him.'

They didn't stay long. There was nothing much to say, and Pudding was sure she could see the same claustrophobic sadness creeping over Irene as was creeping over herself. She was relieved when Irene stood and thanked the two elderly women for the tea. They had no words of comfort for one another; the two wrongs that had been done would never add up to a right. Pudding felt sorry for them, and sorry for the farm, in a peculiar way. She was sure it had been a happy place, once; vibrant with life and the laughter of its youthful inhabitants. Now it felt forgotten; it was neglected, unloved by the handful of inhabitants that were left to it, and dogged by the hopeless air of all abandoned things. Pudding's grief for Alistair waited for her every morning at Manor Farm, and she knew she would keep missing him, and always think of him, but at least the *place* was still alive, and had a chance of moving on, thanks to Irene and the servants and the inexorable sense of life going on. Weavern Farm was more like the corpse of a place, steadily decaying. Pudding and Irene didn't speak as Dundee towed them back up the hill, through the trees and onto Germain's Lane. Each lost in their own thoughts, they stared straight ahead until, at the shop, Irene pulled the pony to a halt.

'Let's get some biscuits for tea from Mrs Glover,' she said, impulsively.

'*Bought* biscuits? But . . . Mrs Gosling will be outraged,' said Pudding.

'I know,' said Irene, smiling. 'Isn't it terrible?'

*

Pudding performed a self-conscious twirl in front of the mirror. They were up in Irene's dressing room, with early evening light gilding the furniture and their faces.

'Well?' said Irene. 'What do you think?' She'd let out a dress she'd found at a frock exchange in Chippenham for Pudding; the girl's height – and bust – made it hang shorter on her; it was just below the knee, which was becoming the fashion in London but would definitely raise eyebrows in Wiltshire. The dress was made of a teal-coloured fabric that draped nicely, was flattering over Pudding's more exuberant curves, and brought out the blue of her eyes.

'Are you *sure* I don't look like a ship in sail?' Pudding fretted, smoothing the fabric over her hips.

'I think you look wonderful,' Irene assured her. 'Very sophisticated. And I am *completely* sure that Constable Dempsey will agree with me.' At the mention of his name, Pudding blushed. She was still having trouble dealing with Pete Dempsey's blatant regard for her, even though the reflection in the mirror was of a tall, handsome young woman with one hell of a bosom, not a chubby little girl. Her hair was still a bushy thatch, but Irene had trimmed it, and pinned it as close to her head as it could be induced to go. Pete was taking her to see *Dick Turpin's Ride to York* at the pictures – their first official excursion together. 'Really – you look thoroughly dashing. And nobody ought to be calling you Pudding any more,' said Irene. 'What's your real name? I asked Alistair, once, but he never told me.'

'Laetitia,' said Pudding, looking dismayed. 'Laetitia Marie Cartwright. Oh dear,' she added, and Irene smiled.

'Laetitia? That's ... so grown-up. It's a lovely name,' she said, but couldn't keep her smile from widening when Pudding met her eye. 'I fear it might be difficult to make it stick, after all this time,' she said.

'Won't it just,' Pudding said, ruefully.

'How about Tish? I think I could get used to Tish. Perhaps Pete might, too.'

'Pete? Oh, there's no chance of that. He's known me since we were knee-high – I'm sure I'll always be Pudding to him.'

'Ah, well.'

Irene picked a thread off her skirt and got up, hooking a thumb under her waistband to reposition it. She might have to let out a few of her own clothes soon, if she kept on eating the way she had been. The thought caused a residual tweak of anxiety, until she remembered that she wasn't in London now, or anywhere near her mother, and didn't need to care about being so thin she hardly had the energy to stand. 'I was thinking, Pudding, about you having enough to do once we're down to two horses and Tufty,' she said, and saw from Pudding's worried expression that she had been thinking about it too. 'I have a number of ideas,' she said. 'But, obviously, it'll be entirely up to you. Could we rent out some of the stables and grazing to people who need extra, do you think?'

'Oh, yes! Livery service, that's called – it's quite common.'

'I've no idea if there's any demand for it, around here,' said Irene. 'Since there's so very much grass everywhere. But we could try. And, you know, Hilarius would probably like a little more help with the shires, come the winter. He's not getting any younger, after all.'

'Do you mean to stay on, then?' said Pudding, looking hopeful.

'I . . . I haven't completely decided. But I shan't simply sell up and leave you all in the lurch, I promise.' Irene hurried on to forestall Pudding's crestfallen expression. 'You might even get your own horse, Pudding, and keep it here if you wished.'

'Really? Oh! That would be stupendous!' Pudding cried. Then she sagged. 'I should never afford the livery and keep.'

'I dare say we could hash something out,' said Irene, smiling.

The house was very quiet after Pudding had gone – off up the lane with Pete in his dad's pony and gig. His face had blazed appropriately when Pudding had emerged in the teal dress, and he'd stumbled through the debonair *good evening* he'd clearly been rehearsing. Irene wondered about hiring more servants to fill the space, but there was hardly enough for Clara and Florence to do as it was, with only Irene in residence. She took a book and went out onto the terrace. The house felt slightly off kilter somehow, and Irene suspected it was because Nancy had gone, and none of them had yet adjusted to her absence. For the first time since the hiatus between Alistair's father marrying and then becoming a widower, Nancy Hadleigh was not in residence. And would not be, ever again.

Irene had thought it all through at least twenty times before concluding that there was nothing to be gained by reporting Nancy to the police. The doll was flimsy enough evidence, and they didn't even have it any more. Whatever Hilarius had seen, it had been fifty years ago, and his testimony alone wouldn't be proof enough if Nancy denied it all. And she was being well punished by Alistair's death, and her role in bringing it about – Irene was certain of that. She would carry the grief and the blame around with her the rest of her days. A slow poison, as Rose Matlock had termed it. As the mistress of Manor Farm, Irene had told her to go, and never to come back. Nancy had given her a steely look that hadn't quite concealed the fear and anger it was meant to, and Irene had gone along with her to Chippenham station to make sure she got on the London train. The Hadleighs still had their Mayfair apartment, but as far as Irene knew – thanks to a letter from Cora McKinley – Nancy had gone to Italy on a one-way ticket. It had been a tentative olive branch of a letter from Cora, full of apologies for absence and curiosity about the events at Manor Farm.

Irene sat a while in the sinking sun, absorbing the last of its warmth. St Nicholas' sat in the middle of the field below, doing just the same. There were fewer flowers on the Hadleigh plot since Nancy's departure, but Irene had resolved to visit once a week, and to refresh a small arrangement there whilst there were still flowers to be had from the garden. The mill steamed, down in the valley, and the brewery leaked its hoppy smell, and she noticed that the stone tile roofs of the cottages had moss in the crevices of their northern slopes. The tall trees on the valley sides were a darkening green, and dusty. She couldn't stay on at Manor Farm. She simply didn't belong there, though she had no idea where else she might belong. She would be too lonely, for starters. She had a friend in Pudding, but that was all. Somehow, she would have to find a way to make more. There was still an emptiness where Alistair should have been; it was still his house, *his* home, not hers. He had wanted her to make it hers too, but without him she didn't know if it could ever feel right. She had to admit to herself, though, that the view of the valley had come to look beautiful to her, and the smells of the farmyard were familiar rather than offensive now, and she liked the walk down the hill to the bridge across the By Brook. She even liked riding out with Pudding, though she still wasn't ready for the lead rein to be taken off, and objected to the way the smell of horse lingered for hours, even after she'd scrubbed her arms to the elbow. She took a slow breath, and tried to hear Alistair's footsteps on the terrace behind her, coming from the house with a smile and a gin and tonic. She wished she would hear it; wished to see his smile one more time, and fall into the safety net he'd offered.

Hand in hand with the loneliness she knew was coming was

the certainty of boredom, since clearly she didn't have anything to write about, just yet – unless it were some chronicle of her new life – a humorous, fish-out-of-water type of thing. The idea caused barely a flicker of interest. Or, of course, the story of Clemmie Matlock's short life – how it ended, and how that had led to the death of Alistair Hadleigh. A story of lies, secret grief and secret jealousy; a story of ruined lives and lost chances. A sudden conviction took hold of her, a sudden surety. She would write it, and it would be her final act of gratitude towards Alistair: the truth of his death. And in a way it would be an act of justice towards Eli Tanner, since his life had been ruined too, many years before. However gravely he had transgressed now, he had been gravely wronged himself. A little justice for Clemmie and Eli and Alistair. A little justice, of a different kind, for Nancy. She would wait until Eli's trial was over. The truth was bound to cause a stir; it might even cause the police to question Nancy – if they could find her. Any money the book made could go to the Tanners and the Matlocks, and however unhappy some people might be about what she would write, it would be the truth. So that was that. Not too long before, she would have shied away from causing any kind of trouble, and drawing any kind of attention to herself. But it didn't scare her as it once had. Some things were simply more important.

She would have to find a way to involve herself in the farm, and the mill, and the village – which might be even harder now, since she was sure she'd be blamed for Nancy's sudden departure. She wouldn't be able to tell people the true reason, at first, and just had to hope that Clara or Florence had been listening at doors as usual, and that word would get about. Ruth, the Cartwrights' daily, might be quite useful in that regard as well. The church fête, and dinner parties; the hunt meet and Sunday school outings. She couldn't possibly take it all on. The thought of knocking on doors and introducing herself, of sending out invitations and holding parties for people she barely knew – these things did still fill Irene with dread. But she would have to start, if she stayed. Perhaps she could begin on a small scale – making peace with Cora McKinley, for example. She might even invite some of her old school friends down from London, in due course. There were a few who might have got bored enough of the London scandal, and be curious enough about the Slaughterford scandal, to accept. She went into the pantry for a glass of lemonade, fetched paper and a pencil, then returned to the terrace and continued to make her plans. Because that was what she was doing, she realised, as the sun slunk lower towards the western hills. She was making plans to stay.

Author's Note and Acknowledgements

Whilst Slaughterford and its mills, geography and prominent buildings do exist, and have been recreated with some historical accuracy in this novel, all the people and events I describe are entirely fictitious – with the exception of the boiler explosion at Rag Mill, an accident in which three people, including ten year old Vincent Watt, were killed. This tragic event took place in November 1867.

My thanks to Michael Woodman, for talking to me about his life and work at Chapps Mill, and for lending me his books; to Angus Thompson and Karin Crawford, the present owners of Chapps Mill in Slaughterford, for showing me around; and to Janet and John Jones at Manor Farm, for sharing their memories and letting me look around their home.

A huge thank you to my brilliant editor, Laura Gerrard; to my wonderful agent, Nicola Barr; and to all the talented people at Orion Books, working so hard behind the scenes.

Find your next compelling historical drama from Katherine Webb ...

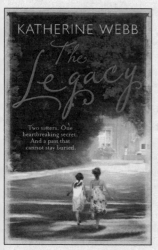

Two sisters. One heartbreaking secret. A past that cannot stay buried ...

In the depths of a harsh winter, following the death of their grandmother, Erica Calcott and her sister Beth return to Storton Manor, a grand and imposing Wiltshire house where they spent their summer holidays as children. When Erica begins to sort through her grandmother's belongings, she is flooded with memories of her childhood – and of her cousin, Henry, whose disappearance from the manor tore the family apart. Erica sets out to discover what happened to Henry, so that the past can be laid to rest, and her sister, Beth, might finally find some peace.

Gradually, as Erica begins to sift through the remnants of the past, a secret family history emerges; one that stretches all the way back to turn-of-the-century America, to a beautiful society heiress and a haunting, savage land. As past and present converge, Erica and Beth must come to terms with two terrible acts of betrayal – and the heartbreaking legacy left behind ...

A compelling tale of love, deception and illusion

England, 1911. When a free-spirited young woman arrives in a sleepy Berkshire village to work as a maid in the household of The Reverend and Mrs Canning, she sets in motion a chain of events which changes all their lives. For Cat has a past – a past her new mistress is willing to overlook, but will never understand ...

This is not all Hester Canning has to cope with. When her husband invites a young man into their home, he brings with him a dangerous obsession ...

During the long, oppressive summer, the rectory becomes charges with ambition, love and jealousy – with the most devastating consequences.

A searing novel of secrets and feuds, set in 1920s Italy

Puglia, Italy. 1921. Leandro returns home, now a rich man, with a glamorous American wife, determined to make his mark. But how did he get so wealthy – and what haunts his outwardly exuberant wife?

Boyd, a quiet English architect, is hired to build the house of Leandro's dreams. But why is he so afraid of Leandro, and what really happened between them years before, in New York?

Clare, Boyd's diffident wife, is summoned to Puglia with her stepson. At first desperate to leave, she soon finds a compelling reason to stay.

Ettore, starving, poor and grieving for his lost fiancée, is too proud to ask his Uncle Leandro for help. Until events conspire to force his hand.

Tensions are high as poverty leads veterans of the Great War to the brink of rebellion. And under the burning sky, a reckless love and a violent enmity will bring brutal truths to light . . .

In a land full of secrets, you can make your own rules

Joan Seabrook has fulfilled her lifelong dream to travel to Arabia and has arrived in the ancient city of Muscat with her fiancé, Rory. Desperate to escape the pain of a personal tragedy, she longs to explore the desert fort of Jabrin and unearth the wonders held within.

But Oman is a land lost in time, and gaining permission to explore could prove impossible. Joan's disappointment is only eased by the thrill of meeting her childhood heroine, pioneering explorer Maude Vickery, and hearing the stories that captured her imagination as a child. The friendship that forms between the two women will change everything.

Both have desires to fulfil and secrets to keep. As their bond grows, Joan is inspired by the thrill of her friend's past and finds herself swept up in a bold and dangerous adventure of Maude's making. Only too late does she begin to question her actions – actions that will spark a wild, and potentially devastating, chain of events.